OXFORD WORLD'S CLASSICS

GREEN TEA

AND OTHER WEIRD STORIES

JOSEPH THOMAS SHERIDAN LE FANU (1814–73) was born in Dublin, the elder son of a clergyman whose Huguenot forebears had married into the Sheridan family. In 1826, the Revd Le Fanu was promoted Dean of Emly and with his family went to live at Abington, County Limerick. Educated at Trinity College and the King's Inns, Dublin, Sheridan Le Fanu had already launched himself as a journalist and writer of fiction by the end of the 1830s. In 1843 he married Susanna Bennett, the daughter of a leading Irish Q.C. The 1840s proved a compromising decade for Le Fanu—a conservative by instinct and recent experience—for, in the wake of the famine of 1847, he found himself implicated on the fringes of the 1848 rebellion. After an unsuccessful attempt to get a Tory nomination in 1852, he withdrew into editorial work on the newspapers and into the tensions of a household increasingly affected by his wife's neurotic symptoms. Following her death in 1858, and his mother's death in 1861, Sheridan Le Fanu resumed fiction-writing with an Irish historical romance, *The House by the Churchyard* (1861–3); *Wylder's Hand* and *Uncle Silas* both appeared in 1864. The subsequent novels are less impressive, though *Checkmate* (1871) is an effective Victorian thriller-mystery. Throughout his writing life, Le Fanu published accomplished short stories and tales, the best of which are collected in *Chronicles of Golden Friars* (1871) and *In a Glass Darkly* (1872).

AARON WORTH is an Associate Professor of Rhetoric at Boston University. He has written essays discussing the work of such Victorian horror writers as Arthur Machen, M. R. James, and Richard Marsh. He has also edited Arthur Machen's *The Great God Pan and other Horror Stories* for Oxford World's Classics.

T0043734

OXFORD WORLD'S CLASSICS

*For over 100 years Oxford World's Classics have brought
readers closer to the world's great literature. Now with over 700
titles—from the 4,000-year-old myths of Mesopotamia to the
twentieth century's greatest novels—the series makes available
lesser-known as well as celebrated writing.*

*The pocket-sized hardbacks of the early years contained
introductions by Virginia Woolf, T.S. Eliot, Graham Greene,
and other literary figures which enriched the experience of reading.
Today the series is recognized for its fine scholarship and
reliability in texts that span world literature, drama and poetry,
religion, philosophy, and politics. Each edition includes perceptive
commentary and essential background information to meet the
changing needs of readers.*

OXFORD WORLD'S CLASSICS

SHERIDAN LE FANU

Green Tea
and Other Weird Stories

Edited with an Introduction and Notes by
AARON WORTH

OXFORD
UNIVERSITY PRESS

OXFORD

UNIVERSITY PRESS

Great Clarendon Street, Oxford, OX2 6DP,
United Kingdom

Oxford University Press is a department of the University of Oxford.
It furthers the University's objective of excellence in research, scholarship,
and education by publishing worldwide. Oxford is a registered trade mark of
Oxford University Press in the UK and in certain other countries

Editorial material © Aaron Worth 2020

The moral rights of the author have been asserted

First published as an Oxford World's Classics paperback 2020

Impression: 6

Published in the United States of America by Oxford University Press
198 Madison Avenue, New York, NY 10016, United States of America

British Library Cataloguing in Publication Data

Data available

Library of Congress Control Number: 2020009613

ISBN 978-0-19-883588-2

Printed and bound in Great Britain by
Clays Ltd, Elcograf S.p.A.

ACKNOWLEDGEMENTS

I WOULD like first to thank Luciana O'Flaherty and Kizzy Taylor-Richelieu at OUP; invaluable assistance was also provided by Dorothy McCarthy, Peter Gibbs, and Lisa Eaton. I also owe thanks to a number of experts in fields ranging from Gothic literature to dendrology, particularly Bill McCormack and Jim Rockhill, as well as Oliver Teale, Kevin Rockett, Victor Sage, James Machin, Brian Showers, Josh Jones, S. T. Joshi, Catherine Woodward, Nicki Cagle, John Storey, Jennifer Skipp, Bart Wallet, Marion Bodian, and Tom McGimsey of MESH Architects. I am grateful, as well, to staff members at the Royal Irish Academy, the British Library, the RSPCA, and the Brandeis University and Boston University libraries, particularly Rhoda Bilansky and the interlibrary loan staff at BU's Mugar Library. Michelle Worth helped to penetrate the mystery of the elusive Eumia Le Faun, and Judith Frediani provided much-needed working time; the book is dedicated to Charlotte Worth, who may (or may not) someday enjoy reading 'scary stories' as much as she now delights in discussing them in the abstract, from a safe distance.

CONTENTS

THE STORIES

INTRODUCTION

Readers who are unfamiliar with the stories may prefer to treat the Introduction as an Afterword.

HE wrote mostly in bed at night, using copy-books for his manuscript. He always had two candles by his side on a small table; one of these dimly glimmering tapers would be left burning while he took a brief sleep. Then, when he awoke about 2 a.m. amid the darkling shadows of the heavy furnishings and hangings of his old-fashioned room, he would brew himself some strong tea . . . and write for a couple of hours in that eerie period of the night when human vitality is at its lowest ebb and the Powers of Darkness rampant and terrifying. What wonder then, that, with his brain ever peopled by day and by night with mysterious and terrible beings, he became afflicted by horrible dreams, which . . . were the bases of his last stories of the supernatural.[1]

This is the myth of Joseph Sheridan Le Fanu, or a piece of it—the Gothicized biographical template which would be repeated, and embellished upon, in seemingly innumerable twentieth-century accounts of the writer who, in the judgement of M. R. James, 'succeed[ed] in inspiring a mysterious terror better than any other'.[2] The core elements of the legend were established in the years following Le Fanu's death by two men: his son, George Brinsley Le Fanu, and family friend Alfred Perceval Graves. Both were creative artists in their own right (Brinsley an illustrator, Graves a poet)—a salient fact, given that the Gothic portrait which they produced should itself be seen as a creative work, a posthumous attempt imaginatively to inscribe the dead author into the world of his own fiction. In his 'Memoir of Joseph Sheridan Le Fanu', written as an introduction to the collection *The Purcell Papers* (1880), Graves first brought onstage, as it were, the mysterious character called 'The Invisible Prince'—a widower transformed by his bereavement into an inconsolable recluse, one who seems already to belong, at least in part, to the world of spirits. This figure never appears in public, 'unless at odd hours of the evening, when he might occasionally be seen stealing, like the ghost of his former self, between his newspaper office and his home in Merrion Square; sometimes, too, he was to be

[1] S. M. Ellis, *Wilkie Collins, Le Fanu, and Others* (London, 1931), 174–5.
[2] M. R. James, 'M. R. James on J. S. Le Fanu', in *Reflections in a Glass Darkly: Essays on J. Sheridan Le Fanu*, ed. Gary William Crawford, Jim Rockhill, and Brian J. Showers (New York, 2011), 87.

encountered in an old out-of-the-way bookshop poring over some rare black letter Astrology or Demonology'.[3] Brinsley Le Fanu would later feed biographer Stewart Marsh Ellis further details, including the description, quoted above, of the 'peculiar habits of life' which, he said, helped fuel his father's 'weird tales'.[4] Here, too, one finds the first appearance of the dramatic story of Le Fanu's death—lurid and improbable enough in its original telling, and only gaining in both qualities in subsequent iterations by scholars indulging their inner penny-blood writer. The following version, for example, dates from the 1970s:

One of the most recurrent of the weird dreams that haunted him during his lonely years was of a vast and mysterious crumbling old mansion—of the type which he had often recounted in his tales—threatening imminently to fall upon and crush him. . . . On that fateful February night when the end came and the doctor wrenched open the bedroom door, he beheld the terror-stricken eyes of the dead man in the sputtering light of the candle. Le Fanu's arms were flung wide, his bearded chin tilted up at a sharp angle, his eyes fixed and staring. . . . The doctor exclaimed: 'I feared this—that house fell at last.'[5]

The story is both too good to be true and a little too on the nose: a sceptic might well suspect Brinsley of having blended, consciously or not, Poe's 'Fall of the House of Usher' with one of his father's own master story-types, the dream-narrative which ends in real death for the dreamer.[6] But then, are not such anecdotes always meant to be less descriptive than performative? Myths, after all, are part of a writer's brand, and writers of the mysterious and macabre surely deserve mysterious and macabre ones: only think, for example, of Matthew 'Monk' Lewis's coffined corpse, rising like a phantom from the waters of the Caribbean, or of Ambrose Bierce walking one day across the border into Mexico . . . and oblivion. Who could blame Le Fanu's family and friends for engaging in a similar bit of branding, to stimulate interest in his work, to help keep his memory alive?

What is somewhat more surprising, given his relative obscurity as well as—one presumes—the absence of any clandestine machinations

[3] Alfred Perceval Graves, 'Memoir of Joseph Sheridan Le Fanu', in Joseph Sheridan Le Fanu, *The Purcell Papers*, vol. 1 (London, 1880), pp. v–xxxi, xxix.

[4] Ellis, *Wilkie Collins*, 174–5.

[5] Devendra P. Varma, 'Musings on the Life and Works of Joseph Sheridan Le Fanu, a Forgotten Creator of Ghosts', in Joseph Sheridan Le Fanu, *The Watcher and Other Weird Stories* (New York, 1977), p. ii.

[6] These include 'The Drunkard's Dream', 'The Vision of Tom Chuff', and 'The Spectre Lovers'. (For a discussion of this narrative category in Le Fanu, see Ivan Melada, *Sheridan Le Fanu* (Boston, 1987), 114–16.)

on the part of his descendants, a new Le Fanu myth has arisen in the twenty-first century, one whose replication and swift dissemination have been facilitated, like a copying error, by the Internet. This myth takes the form of a twofold claim: first, that Le Fanu coined the term (and perhaps envisioned the modern conceptual category of) 'weird fiction', and second, that H. P. Lovecraft, the key figure in the theorization of 'the Weird', consciously appropriated it from him. The Wikipedia entry on 'Weird Fiction' is most likely the proximate source behind the proliferation of these claims, which are in fact entirely without foundation.[7] Ultimately, however, their origins can most likely be traced to the very same marketing efforts which gave rise, in an earlier generation of Le Fanu scholarship, to the all-but-unkillable myth of the Invisible Prince of Merrion Square and his entirely too *à propos* demise. For Le Fanu was, in fact, one of the earliest writers of supernatural fiction whose work was to appear under the aegis of the Weird, albeit not until shortly after his death. He was not, strictly speaking, *the* first: fellow Irish ghost-story writer Charlotte Riddell's *Weird Stories*, for instance, appeared in 1882, while a two-volume translation of E. T. A. Hoffmann's fiction was published by John C. Nimmo as *Weird Tales* in 1885.[8] But someone digging for early examples of the epithet in publishing might understandably have settled upon one, or both, of two Le Fanu collections as points of origin: *The Watcher and Other Weird Stories*, illustrated and introduced by Brinsley Le Fanu (1895), and *A Stable for Nightmares; or, Weird Tales* (1896).[9] 'Weird' seems indeed to have been, then as now, a sexy label somewhat indiscriminately applied by booksellers. In the context of the marketplace, indeed, one is reminded of

[7] 'H. P. Lovecraft adopted the term from Sheridan Le Fanu and popularized it in his essays', 'Weird Fiction', Wikipedia.org. (Interestingly, this line was removed from the article shortly after I began making enquiries about its veracity among scholars of weird fiction, but only a character in one of Le Fanu's more paranoiac tales would infer any connection between the two events.) The claim would be subsequently cited as fact in e.g. 'H. P. Lovecraft Gives Five Tips for Writing a Horror Story, or Any Piece of "Weird Fiction"', *Open Culture* (29 Oct. 2014); 'Weird Fiction Is Alive', *New Republic* (7 May 2018); 'Schalken the Painter: Celebrating the 200th Anniversary of Le Fanu's Birth', *Weird Fiction Review* (2014).

[8] For an informative and thoroughly documented discussion of the emergent category of 'weird' fiction in the nineteenth century, particularly as against or opposed to the 'mere' ghost story, see the Introduction to James Machin's *Weird Fiction in Britain, 1880–1939* (London, 2018).

[9] The second work, in fact, contains only a single Le Fanu story, which, along with the 'weird' label, was added to an earlier anthology for marketing purposes. But the book was prominently advertised, and has since been catalogued, as by Le Fanu, and Le Fanu alone.

Orwell's remark about the word 'democracy': 'not only is there no
agreed definition, but the attempt to make one is resisted from all
sides . . . [for] fear that they might have to stop using that word if it
were tied down to any one meaning'.[10] In critical contexts, meanwhile,
its meaning has tended, on the contrary, to become increasingly con-
stricted, and it is by no means clear whether Le Fanu, far from being
the founder of a new mode or genre, can even be counted among its
practitioners. Is there, then, any reason to call Le Fanu a 'weird' writer
today? We shall perhaps be in a better position to judge after looking
more closely at the development of his imaginative vision within the
context of his life and times.

Beginnings

The figure of the real-life nightmare from which there is no escape
recurs again and again in Le Fanu's fiction (most unforgettably, perhaps, in 'The Room in the Dragon Volant'), and while this is a trope
that admits of many interpretations, it is difficult not to feel that history,
as well as heredity (the two being, for Le Fanu and the caste to which
he belonged, inextricably intertwined), counted very much among the
things that weighed heavily upon his brain. The first Le Fanus in
Ireland had been Huguenots from Normandy, that is to say, Protestants
fleeing persecution in France.[11] But these particular refugees had
arrived with drawn swords in hand, helping a Dutch warrior-king to
impose his (and their) faith on another people—a whipsaw reversal of
roles, and an irony, captured by Yeats in his gloss to 'Parnell's Funeral':
'When Huguenot artists designed the tapestries for the Irish House of
Lords, depicting the battle of the Boyne and the siege of Derry, they
celebrated the defeat of their old enemy Louis XIV, and the establishment of a Protestant Ascendancy which was to impose upon Catholic
Ireland an oppression copied in all details from that imposed upon the
French Protestants.'[12] If so much Le Fanu criticism has centred upon
his consciousness of belonging to a minority ruling class whose uncertain position at the top of the pole was grounded in past acts of violence,
dispossession, and betrayal, it is for good reason: his fiction, much like

---

[10] 'Politics and the English Language', *A Collection of Essays* (New York, 1981), 162.

[11] Alison Milbank points to the 'double hybridity' of the Huguenot 'strand of Anglo-
Irish Protestantism' in her essay 'Joseph Sheridan Le Fanu: Gothic Grotesque and the
Huguenot Inheritance', *A Companion to Irish Literature*, ed. Julia M. Wright (Chichester
and Malden, 2010), 363.

[12] William Butler Yeats, *The Collected Works*, vol. 1 (New York, 1997), 672.

that of his American contemporary Nathaniel Hawthorne, sifts the soil of history in search of guilty acts, for which condign retribution must follow, as day follows night. Yet the Anglo-Irish legacy—like that of Hawthorne's Puritans—was a deeply ambivalent one as well, evoking feelings of pride as well as guilt or shame. Over the course of its eighteenth-century heyday, Ireland under the Ascendancy could call a roll of intellectual and literary genius—Jonathan Swift, George Berkeley, Oliver Goldsmith, Edmund Burke, Richard Brinsley Sheridan—which few nations could match; Le Fanu's blood—for he was a Sheridan as well, the two families having been joined by marriage in the 1780s—thus connected him with the glories, as well as the sins, of Ascendancy culture.

By the time Joseph Sheridan Le Fanu was born in 1814, however, there was a palpable sense that the glory, at least, had evaporated. Insurrection at the end of the eighteenth century, and legislative union with Britain—which meant the dissolution of the Dublin Parliament—at the beginning of the nineteenth, set a course of long decline for the city of Le Fanu's birth, which 'soon settled down to become for over a century a provincial town, known for eccentricity rather than genius'.[13] A similar sense of belatedness hung over many of the Anglo-Irish networks and institutions to which Le Fanu would be connected throughout his life, not least the Protestant Church of Ireland which provided the family's livelihood. Le Fanu's early years were spent in Dublin's Phoenix Park, where the Revd Thomas Le Fanu served as chaplain at the Royal Hibernian Military School. According to his younger brother William, these were idyllic times: 'Never can I forget our rambles through that lovely park, the delight we took in the military reviews, sham fights, and races held near the school.'[14] And if the family's removal to County Limerick in 1826, where Le Fanu's father had been named Dean of Emly and Rector of Abington, was not quite an expulsion from Eden, it certainly meant something like a loss of political innocence, as the oppressive character of an institution which sustained itself by feeding, as it were, upon the meagre resources of a Catholic majority was rendered painfully visible, and brought painfully close to home:

In 1831 came the tithe war, and with it our friendly relations with the priests and people ceased. The former, not unnaturally, threw themselves heart and soul into the agitation. The Protestant clergy were denounced by agitators and

[13] W. J. McCormack, *Sheridan Le Fanu and Victorian Ireland* (Oxford, 1980), 9.
[14] William Le Fanu, *Seventy Years of Irish Life* (London, 1893), 1.

priests from platform and from altar, and branded as the worst enemies of the
people, who were told to hunt them like mad dogs from the country; they were
insulted wherever they went, many were attacked, some were murdered. It is
hard now to realize the suddenness with which kindness and good-will were
changed to insult and hate . . .[15]

During these years in Abington, Le Fanu's education, ostensibly under
the direction of an entirely useless tutor, took the form of a self-guided
course of reading in his father's substantial library, supplemented by
plentiful exposure to Irish folklore and legend outside of it. In 1832, he
entered Trinity College, then still 'to all intents and purposes a semin-
ary where the sons of Anglo-Irish gentry could prepare themselves for
the professions'.[16] There he read Classics, made connections, weighed
options. After a period of legal training, he was called, in 1839, to the
Irish Bar. But he never practised; in the spare moments snatched (one
imagines) from the study of Blackstone's *Commentaries*, Le Fanu had
taken the first few steps down the path of his true vocation.

Or rather, 'vocations', as Le Fanu's headfirst plunge into the world
of periodical publication seemed to involve his donning every possible
hat at once: proprietor, editor, writer, journalist. By 1842 he owned two
publications, and had a share in three others. But of greatest consequence to his career as a fiction writer was his relationship with the
recently founded *Dublin University Magazine*, the organ of conservative
Protestant Irish opinion in which the bulk of his work would appear.
Beginning with 'The Ghost and the Bone-Setter', which appeared in
January 1838, he produced a steady stream of stories over the next two
years which would be assembled posthumously by Alfred Graves as
The Purcell Papers (London, 1880).[17] These pieces, which range in tone
and type from the farcical to the horrific, are linked by the device of
a Catholic priest of 'literary' interests (one Francis Purcell, a priest 'of
the old school, a race now nearly extinct') who has collected or recorded
the tales, sometimes in dialect, in the course of half a century of peri-
patetic duty in his (fictitious) Limerick parish of Drumcoolagh.[18] *The
Purcell Papers* is a seminal collection of stories in the true, if humbler,
sense of the word, in that it contains seeds from which better-developed,
better-known works would later sprout: the Faustian tale 'The Fortunes
of Sir Robert Ardagh' would be re-imagined, over three decades later,

[15] Ibid. 55.   [16] Nelson Browne, *Sheridan Le Fanu* (London, 1951), 19.
[17] Also included is the 1850 story 'Billy Malowney's Taste of Love and Glory'.
[18] Interestingly, Le Fanu's writing career is bookended by story collections whose
unity, such as it is, derives from such a framing device.

as the novella 'The Haunted Baronet', while two of Le Fanu's full-length novels, including the masterful *Uncle Silas* (1864), are present here in germinal form; it has been argued, too, that Emily and (more plausibly) Charlotte Brontë borrowed significantly from these early stories in writing *Wuthering Heights* and *Jane Eyre*, respectively.[19]

In keeping with the conceit of the wandering parish priest, the 'Purcell' stories had all been (the best of them, 'Schalken the Painter', excepted) not only Irish stories, but country stories. After an imaginative excursion to Renaissance Italy in the gripping if not entirely coherent Gothic novella 'Spalatro' (1843),[20] Le Fanu turned for the first time to Dublin as a fictional setting, in the Walter Scott-influenced novel *The Cock and Anchor; Being a Chronicle of Old Dublin City* (1845). Neither this nor his second attempt in the genre, *The Fortunes of Colonel Torlogh O'Brien* (1846–7), found sufficient favour with readers and critics to encourage Le Fanu to continue in this vein, but immediately after this foray into historical fiction, he produced another tale of 'old Dublin city', a haunting story of guilt and preternatural retribution whose scrupulous attention to matters of historical detail actively contributes to its potency, much of which derives from Le Fanu's trenchant, if perhaps not entirely conscious, indictment of the caste to which he belonged.

'The Watcher', later retitled 'The Familiar',[21] brings to life, albeit an uncanny kind of half-life, the city-in-process that was Dublin in the 1790s ('Somewhere about the year 1794', as Le Fanu's narrator puts it in a somewhat insouciant combination of vagueness and exactitude). Georgian Dublin represented the ultimate embodiment of the power and wealth of the Anglo-Irish in the eighteenth century—wealth largely derived from the growing global dominion of the British Empire.[22] The story depicts several architectural fruits of that power, including the new Parliament House, and a central feature of the story

[19] See especially Edna Kenton, 'A Forgotten Creator of Ghosts: Joseph Sheridan Le Fanu, Possible Inspirer of the Brontës', *Bookman* 69 (July 1929), 528–34.

[20] As Miles Stribling observes, what begins as a non-supernatural tale of mystery and suspense 'rapidly disintegrates', in the final reel, 'into a Hoffmannesque nightmare'. Introduction, *Spalatro: Two Italian Tales* (Mountain Ash, Wales, 2001), p. xi.

[21] See headnote to 'The Watcher' for a detailed discussion of all three variants of the story: the original *Dublin University Magazine* version, included here (1847), the revised version included in the 1851 collection *Ghost Stories and Tales of Mystery*, and the further revision, which in several important respects returns to the *DUM* version, retitled 'The Familiar' and included in the 1872 collection *In a Glass Darkly*.

[22] As Nicholas Allen notes, 'This city to be is built from objects of transnational trade'. 'Sheridan Le Fanu and the Spectral Empire', *The Ghost Story from the Middle Ages to the 20th Century: A Ghostly Genre*, ed. Helen Conrad-O'Briain and Julie Anne Stevens (Dublin, 2010), 115.

is the 'projected'[23] network of streets that was then radically reshaping
the face of the city, following a 1757 Act of Parliament. In returning
home (perhaps to Le Fanu's own Merrion Square, to the south of the
Liffey) from his de facto fiancée's house in the north (likely in the new
Mountjoy Square), the haunted protagonist Captain Barton's 'shortest
way . . . lay, for a considerable space, through a line of streets which had
as yet been merely laid out, and little more than the foundations of the
houses constructed' (p. 25); presumably his route takes him along
Gardiner Street, which would bring him to yet another node of British
imperial power, the just-completed Custom House.[24] The story's virtual cityscape makes an unforgettably eerie backdrop for Barton's 'nocturnal walks', but it is also freighted, from the Victorian perspective,
with considerable irony. Indeed, that irony is itself the source of much
of the eeriness: if Le Fanu here depicts a 'phantom city of the future',[25]
it is a future which will, in a very real sense, never be realized. 'The
Watcher' is set (as could only be seen, of course, in retrospect) at the
high-tide moment of Ascendancy culture, or something very near to it
(the new Parliament house will belong to the Bank of Ireland in less
than a decade).[26] These spectral streets will indeed be completed, but
the dream they were to have symbolized, of a total and permanent 'projection' of Anglo-Irish power upon city and nation, never will.

But this is not only an 'Irish' story; Le Fanu also implicates his own
class—which was strongly represented in the ranks of British colonial
administrators and military officers—in Britain's broader imperial
project as well. Barton is a captain in the Royal Navy who has recently
come from one theatre of colonial war, in the western hemisphere;
meanwhile, his prospective father-in-law, General Montague, has been
away on the other side of the world, in India, then under the rule of the
East India Company (in whose service we will also find Philip Feltram's
brother, in 'The Haunted Baronet');[27] even as the Anglo-Irish class is
new-modelling Dublin by Parliamentary fiat, its representatives are

---

[23] Meaning 'planned', but the word also suggests the projection of power.

[24] It was targeted in 1921 for its symbolic value by the IRA, who declared it 'the seat
of an alien tyranny'.

[25] Robert Tracy, Introduction, *In a Glass Darkly* (Oxford, 1993), p. xvi.

[26] 'The Watcher' takes place during the brief window between the legislative independence of the Irish Parliament (won in 1782) and its abolition with the 1800 Act of
Union.

[27] By having the General use the phrase 'cry *peccavi*' ('I have sinned') Le Fanu subtly
invokes Sir Charles Napier's (supposed) punning use of the phrase three years earlier, to
mean 'I have Sindh', thereby extending, perhaps, his critique to Indian rule in his own
time.

circulating within the global network of the larger Empire. We are not directly told anything about India or Montague's activities there, though it is interesting to reflect that, in 1794, Warren Hastings was being prosecuted in Parliament by Edmund Burke, who had long fulminated against Company corruption and brutality. With bitter irony, Le Fanu's famous great-uncle had decried 'the horrors of fire and sword . . . accomplished by the friendship, generosity, and kindness of the English nation', dramatically describing flogging and other examples of 'corporal infliction' directed by Hastings.[28] General Montague, fresh from the East, seems to be unable to repress for long the topic of 'corporal infliction', threats—or fantasies—of which bubble to his lips four times in his first, brief, appearance. He does not know that Barton has, in effect, created his own supernatural tormentor through just such 'official' exercises of discipline, having ordered the flogging of a crew member which has caused his death by tetanus. (It is possible that Le Fanu had in mind here the 'Death by Flogging', some ten years earlier, of one Thomas Ramsay, a private in the Royal Marines who had died of 'locked-jaw' after 'receiv[ing] 150 lashes, that is, 1350 lashes, in fact, each stroke inflicting nine wounds'.[29]) The dead sailor returns as a shrunken, compressed, all-but-mute version of himself, in a dream-logic literalization of the uncontrollable muscular 'contraction' caused by lockjaw.[30] Is the 'watcher' an Irishman? He is described only as '*like* a foreigner' in appearance (emphasis added), though his 'fur cap and red vest' (and, perhaps, his acquaintance with the French language) may mark him as 'a radical republican or rank-and-file United Irishman of the period'.[31] Is it, then, above all the horror of the Great Famine (still, in 1847, very much under way) that inflects this tale of guilt and vengeance? This was, after all, a colonial or quasi-colonial catastrophe which left the native Irish population a shrunken and increasingly

---

[28] '[T]hese venerable, but unfortunate men were fated to encounter every aggravation of horror and distress. It, moreover, appears that they were both cruelly flogged, though one was above seventy years of age.' Richard Brinsley Sheridan, 'Speech at the Trial of Warren Hastings', *Orations of British Orators*, vol. 1 (New York, 1899), 558.

[29] J. A. Roebuck, 'England, a Step-Mother to Her Soldiers', *Pamphlets for the People* (London, 1835), 4.

[30] Yet more networks: the 'watcher' suffers through his muscular system, Barton through his 'nervous system', as well as by the merciless 'spiritual system' he now discerns in the workings of the cosmos. Even before reading Emmanuel Swedenborg (as far as we know), Le Fanu sees 'correspondences' everywhere.

[31] Julian Moynahan, *Anglo-Irish: The Literary Imagination in a Hyphenated Culture* (Princeton, 1995), 128.

voiceless—literally 'language-less'—version of its former self.[32] If this is so, however, then the story insists that this is an imperial tragedy with global, rather than merely local, implications and resonances.

Animals and Other Machines

In his implacable pursuit of Barton, the 'watcher' hacks or hijacks a number of systems: the new streets of the city, the new penny post of the nation. But in the larger context of Le Fanu's work, it is highly significant that the vehicle or medium which he 'rides' to his final vengeance is an owl, the Montagues' Clontarf house being apparently chock-full of domestic, or domesticized, representatives of the animal kingdom: 'Young ladies', as the narrator informs the reader, 'are much given to the cultivation of pets'—a 'caprice' ultimately facilitating the story's horrifying dénouement. In fact, Le Fanu's stories are full of animals: the 'small black monkey' in 'Green Tea', the 'White Cat of Drumgunniol', and the anthropomorphic trio of birds (macaw, kite, and jay) in 'The Haunted Baronet', as well as assorted grotesque or demonic familiars: the dog in 'Borrhomeo the Astrologer', with 'its ungainly bones . . . carrying its huge head so low to the ground', for instance, and the similarly 'big-headed' cat in 'The Mysterious Lodger'. Particularly prominent is the theme of the ensouled animal, or the animal as a vehicle for souls, as in 'The Watcher', the comic tale of transmigration 'The Quare Gander', and the novella 'Squire Toby's Will', in which the Squire's spirit enters into a 'large, half-starved bull-dog'. Le Fanu and Charles Darwin were of the same generation, so while it is certainly possible for a later story like 'Green Tea' to bear traces of influence,[33] we must look elsewhere when considering the first two decades, at least, of his writing career. One place to look might be within early nineteenth-century conversations about what we would call 'animal rights', conversations concerned less with the bestiality of man than with the potential humanity of beasts. Such discourses had intriguing local and family connections: Richard Brinsley Sheridan had stood with Galway MP Richard Martin ('Humanity Dick') in support of the

---

[32] The population was reduced (by emigration as well as death) by as much as a quarter, while the Famine may have struck what would ultimately prove a death-blow to the Irish language (see e.g. David Crystal, *Language Death* (Cambridge, 2000), 71).

[33] 'Jennings's monkey may reflect Victorian anxieties after Darwin's unwelcome suggestion that man was of simian ancestry' (Tracy, *In a Glass Darkly*, p. xiv). See also e.g. Leonora Ledwon, 'Darwin's Ghosts: The Influence of Darwinism on the Nineteenth-Century Ghost Story', *Proteus* 6 (1989), 10–16.

world's first animal protection bill, the Preventing the Practice of Bull-baiting Bill of 1800; in an earlier Parliamentary dispute regarding dogs, Sheridan had accused an opponent of being 'a Pythagorean who had taken a dislike in some former existence as another animal'. Later, the *Dublin Star* would wonder if Martin had become a 'Brahmin' convert to the doctrine of metempsychosis, very nearly anticipating the premise of 'Squire Toby's Will': 'Only conceive how Mr. Martin would look if he were transformed into a huge, surly mastiff.'[34] In 1850, Le Fanu's mother wrote the prize essay for Martin's Royal Society for the Prevention of Cruelty to Animals, subsequently published by the Society,[35] while in 1831, shortly before the Le Fanu family's return to Dublin, the newly formed Zoological Society of Ireland had opened the Dublin Zoo, one of the first modern zoos, in Le Fanu's childhood home of Phoenix Park. The arguments made by the Society's founders for the importance of a zoo centred upon both the idea of a continuum linking people and animals (postmortem dissections of animals would help further the practical knowledge of human anatomy) and the animal-welfare discourses pioneered by Martin and the fledgling RSPCA.[36] By 1840, the *Dublin University Magazine* could write, in an introduction to a lecture on 'The Intellectuality of Domestic Animals', 'Beyond a doubt, a change has come over the habits and tastes of the better classes in Dublin—the third part of a century shows an alteration in their pursuits and pleasures not a little remarkable', waggishly going on to suggest that a resurrected 'lady of the eighteenth century' would be scandalized to see 'how fashionables were now flocking to an evening lecture' at Dublin's Zoological Society, 'instead of to the play-house'.[37]

However, Le Fanu's particular interest in animals must also be considered alongside his parallel fascination with, and similar treatment of, a set of other, interrelated, figures: the robot, the cyborg, the zombie, the

---

[34] See Katheryn Shevelow, *For the Love of Animals: The Rise of the Animal Protection Movement* (New York, 2008), 214, 273.

[35] *On the Ameliorating Influence of the Humane Principles Advocated by the Royal Society for the Prevention of Cruelty to Animals on Society and on Individuals: A Prize Essay* by Emma Le Fanu (London, 1850). (The Society's actual leader was Arthur Broome, though Martin's association at its founding was crucial; see e.g. Ivan Kreilkamp, 'The Ass Got a Verdict: Martin's Act and the Founding of the Society for the Prevention of Cruelty to Animals, 1822', in *BRANCH: Britain, Representation and Nineteenth-Century History*, ed. Dino Franco Felluga (published April 2012).)

[36] 'The boy who, day after day, shares his cake with the bear who runs up a pole to receive it . . . will scarcely go out of his way to see such an animal baited and torn to pieces' (quoted in Catherine de Courcy, *Dublin Zoo: An Illustrated History* (Cork, 2009), 3.

[37] Editorial Introduction, 'The Intellectuality of Domestic Animals', *DUM* (May 1840), 495.

puppet.[38] Underlying much of Le Fanu's fiction is a potent strain of what we might term Cartesian horror—a constellation of metaphysical anxieties immediately recognizable to anyone familiar with much twentieth- and twenty-first-century weird fiction, film, and television. In the *Discours de la méthode* (1637), René Descartes had first written of the 'beast-machine' (*bête machine*), arguing that animals were nothing but clockwork—automata, governed by purely materialist laws. More troublingly, he went on to say that the human body was a machine as well, even while giving assurances—not, perhaps, terribly convincing ones—that in our case there was, so to speak, a soul in the driver's seat: a ghost, in Gilbert Ryle's phrase, in every machine. But it did not take much for the *philosophes* of the next century—the 'sensationalist abominations' Diderot, d'Holbach, d'Alembert, Helvétius, and de La Mettrie—to strip away the fig leaf of Cartesian dualism, propagating in its place their 'vile and revolting theories' of full-blown Materialism and Atheism.[39] If these last were uppermost among the dreaded 'French principles' (which sometimes went about, it was true, in less Gallic garb[40]) mentioned in 'The Watcher', they were also principles which contributed to protracted and intense mental anguish within the Le Fanu household. In 1843, Le Fanu had married Susanna Bennett, the daughter of a prominent Dublin barrister, who sometime before her death in 1858[41] had begun to be tormented by that most quintessentially Victorian of anxieties, as Le Fanu recorded in one of the relatively few samples of his personal writing which we possess:

[M]y darling's mind was harrassed [*sic*] with incessant doubts about the truth of revealed religion. She was acute in detecting apparent weakness, & quick in suggesting difficulties, and I was much distressed, for she was too volatile & rapid to bear a protracted & minute argument, & although I thought I often

[38] The terminology is anachronistic but not, I think, the conceptual underpinnings involved here.

[39] 'Our Foreign Courier', *Dublin University Magazine* (Mar. 1858), 371–2. One wonders how much of the deluxe, complete set of Diderot's dangerously materialistic *Encyclopédie* in the Le Fanu family library young Joseph made it through; even just the 'A's ('*Androïde*', '*Automate*', '*Athéisme*', '*Ame des Bêtes*' ['Souls of Beasts']) would have given him a lot to chew on. I am indebted to Bill McCormack for photographing for me the contents of the sale catalogue of Thomas Le Fanu's library in the possession of the Royal Irish Academy.

[40] The narrator of 'The Mysterious Lodger' reads Hume, Paine, and Shelley in addition to Voltaire; the eponymous Lodger subsequently introduces him to an unnamed, spiritually corrosive work which considerably pre-dates the soul-transforming or -destroying tomes in Oscar Wilde's *Picture of Dorian Gray*, Robert W. Chambers's *The King in Yellow*, and H. P. Lovecraft's *Necronomicon* tales.

[41] In the passage quoted here, Le Fanu claims that this occurred around 1856, but his fiction of the period would seem to tell a different story.

had the answer to her objection, yet her attention generally failed & passed off to some other difficulty before I had completed my reply.[42]

One cannot help but wonder to what extent Le Fanu's tone of concerned condescension might have served as a defence mechanism or coping strategy, a way to corral or quiet his own metaphysical terrors. For if Le Fanu wrote 'ghost stories', these are also, and perhaps more disturbingly, 'machine stories', which collectively suggest a nightmare vision of Cartesian dualism, one in which consciousness, untethered, animates beast-machines and corpse-machines—like Vanderhausen's cadaver in 'Schalken the Painter' or Feltram's in 'The Haunted Baronet'—with equal facility. Conversely, the consciousness may be locked into the prison-house of a dead or dead-alive body, as in 'Borrhomeo the Astrologer' and 'The Room in the Dragon Volant',[43] stories demonstrating Le Fanu's obsession with the theme of catalepsis,[44] or, as we would call it today, 'locked-in syndrome', the terrifying condition featured in the 2017 British horror film *Ghost Stories* (a film with many affinities with Le Fanu's imaginative world). And if such parodies or travesties of dualism indicate a troubled relationship between mind, or soul, and body, Le Fanu's ubiquitous representations of 'prosthetic man'[45] probe disconcertingly at the boundaries—if there are any—between body and machine, insistently asking, in the transhumanist cliché, 'what it means to be human'. Bodies in Le Fanu are everywhere augmented, or burdened, with multifarious 'extensions of man', as Marshall McLuhan called them: false teeth, glass eyes, a Hoffmannesque array of optical aids; one particularly 'transhuman' figure, complete with Darth-Vader-like breathing mask and waxwork-flesh, is encountered in 'The Mysterious Lodger' (a long story not included here):

[42] Quoted in McCormack, *Sheridan Le Fanu*, 295.

[43] The trope of the conscious mind reduced entirely to the capacity for perception, sensation, and cognition, without the power to act, suggests a decidedly modern species of philosophical horror, a Gothicized thought experiment from the pages of a Descartes, Molyneux, or Berkeley.

[44] An interest shared by more than one writer for the influential *Blackwood's Magazine* (see, for instance, John Galt's harrowing 'The Buried Alive', 1821), as well as Edgar Allan Poe; the 'lockjaw' which afflicts the 'watcher' is surely a related malady, symbolically speaking at least. (A possible source for the 'Imago Mortis' drug from 'The Room in the Dragon Volant' specifically may be the 'narcotique' used to similar purpose, and with similar effect, on a protagonist with the splendidly Cartesian name 'René', in Paul Féval's novel *La Vampire*, discussed in relation to 'Carmilla' in the Explanatory Notes.)

[45] The phrase is Freud's. Interestingly, in 'Green Tea' Le Fanu's Dr Hesselius quotes, though he does not name, the founding figure of modern prosthetics, the Huguenot barber-surgeon Ambroise Paré (1510–90).

The light fell full upon him. He wore a long, ill-made, black surtout [overcoat], buttoned across, and which wrinkled and bagged about his lank figure; his hat was none of the best, and rather broad in the brim; a sort of white woolen muffler enveloped the lower part of his face; a pair of prominent green goggles, fenced round with leather, completely concealed his eyes; and nothing of the genuine man, but a little bit of yellow forehead, and a small transverse segment of equally yellow cheek and nose, encountered the curious gaze . . . on reaching his bedroom, he immediately removed his hat, showing a sinister, black scratch-wig underneath, and then began unrolling the mighty woolen wrapping of his mouth and chin . . . under his muffler was a loose cravat, which stood up in front of his chin, and upon his mouth, he wore a respirator—an instrument which I had never seen before. . . . There was something so excessively odd in the effect of this piece of unknown mechanism upon his mouth, surmounted by the huge goggles which encased his eyes . . .[46]

Then there is the puppet-like Madam Crowl ('She goes on wires, she does', warns the housekeeper of Applewale House):

So, softly, softly I draws the curtain, and there, sure enough, I sid before me, stretched out like the painted lady on the tomb-stean in Lexhoe Church, the famous Dame Crowl, of Applewale House. There she was, dressed out. You never sid the like in they days. Satin and silk, and scarlet and green, and gold and pint lace; by Jen! 'twas a sight! A big powdered wig, half as high as herself, was a-top o' her head, and, wow!—was ever such wrinkles?—and her old baggy throat all powdered white, and her cheeks rouged, and mouse-skin eyebrows, that Mrs Wyvern used to stick on, and there she lay grand and stark, wi' a pair o' clocked silk hose on, and heels to her shoon as tall as nine-pins. . . . And in an instant she opens her eyes, and up she sits, and spins herself round, and down wi' her, wi' a clack on her two tall heels on the floor, facin' me, ogglin' in my face wi' her two great glassy eyes, and a wicked simper wi' her old wrinkled lips, and lang fause teeth. . . . She had her fingers straight out pointin' at me, and her back was crooked, round again wi' age. . . . If I'd a thought an instant, I'd a turned about and run. But I couldn't take my eyes off her, and I backed from her as soon as I could; and she came clatterin' after, like a thing on wires, with her fingers pointing to my throat, and she makin' all the time a sound with her tongue like zizz-zizz-zizz. (p. 131)

Arabella Crowl will later appear in the story as both a spirit and a corpse, but it is the living person, the ensouled machine, which is, incomparably, the worst of all: 'Well, a corpse is a natural thing', the narrator is prompted to remark, in an apparent non sequitur, 'but this was the dreadfullest sight I ever sid.'

Projecting Terror

If much of Le Fanu's fiction is troubled by post-Cartesian ghosts and machines, it is also true that, in many of his ghost stories, the ghosts themselves seem to have come from machines—that, in other words, his conception of the spectral is profoundly indebted to the media technologies of his time, optical media in particular. In this, he was not alone: such technologies had influenced Gothic writers since the later eighteenth century, when the projection device known as the magic lantern (like the one carried by the itinerant mountebank in 'Carmilla') became integrated into the immersive, multimedia horror-show known as the phantasmagoria.[47] Or, to put it more accurately, these new technologies, and the Gothic itself as a mode or genre, became enmeshed in a kind of symbiosis during these years. To be sure, it is tempting to draw a facile distinction between the two Le Fanu brothers: while William the railway engineer (who became, in 1863, Commissioner of Public Works in Ireland) embraced modernity, bookish Joseph shunned it, taking gloomy refuge in a candlelit world of perukes and sedan-chairs. But, no less than the writers and filmmakers of today, Le Fanu drew heavily upon contemporary media in evolving his own distinctive art of the macabre: both 'Schalken the Painter' and 'Borrhomeo the Astrologer', for example, contain echoes of the new recording technology of photography (it is the imprinting of Borrhomeo's image upon a disc-shaped 'picture' which puts the final seal upon his soul's bondage to Satan). But it is the proto-cinematic technologies developed on the Continent near the end of the eighteenth century that most decisively inflected his conception of the horror story.[48] Sometimes his

[47] The literary uses of these technologies by such figures as Friedrich Schiller, E. T. A. Hoffmann, James Hogg, and Edgar Allan Poe are discussed in Terry Castle, *The Female Thermometer: Eighteenth-Century Culture and the Invention of the Uncanny* (New York and Oxford, 1995); Marina Warner, *Phantasmagoria: Spirit Visions, Metaphors, and Media into the Twenty-First Century* (Oxford, 2006); Friedrich Kittler, *Optical Media: Berlin Lectures 1999* (Cambridge, 2010); Stefan Andriopoulos, *Ghostly Apparitions: German Idealism, the Gothic Novel, and Optical Media* (Brooklyn, 2013), and elsewhere.

[48] James Walton notes that '[t]he *word* "phantasmagoria" . . . appears in Le Fanu's fiction at least a dozen times, referring in three cases to the impression made by real ghosts, in nine to disordered or deluded perceptions . . . he also resorts to the magic lantern, the pan- and di-orama, the kaleidoscope and . . . *camera obscura* as vehicles for conveying his sense of the uncanniness of experience' (*Vision and Vacancy: The Fictions of J. S. Le Fanu* (Dublin, 2007), 191); David Annwn suggests that Le Fanu's fiction contains 'at least 17 direct references to these media [magic lantern and phantasmagoria]…. There are at least four times as many of these references in Le Fanu's oeuvre as in the writings of other mature novelists of the period' ('Dazzling Ghostland: Sheridan Le Fanu's Phantasmagoria', *The Irish Journal of Gothic and Horror Studies* 6 (2009), 4). Both

invocation of the phantasmagoria (in particular) is explicit, and his use of it chiefly descriptive or metaphorical; in 'The Spectre Lovers', for example, a ghostly column of soldiers appears to a bewildered, and not entirely sober, young Irishman:

It was owing either to some temporary defect in Peter's vision, or to some illusion attendant upon mist and moonlight, or perhaps to some other cause, that the whole procession had a certain waving and vapoury character which perplexed and tasked his eyes not a little. It was like the pictured pageant of a phantasmagoria reflected upon smoke. It was as if every breath disturbed it; sometimes it was blurred, sometimes obliterated; now here, now there. Sometimes, while the upper part was quite distinct, the legs of the column would nearly fade away or vanish outright, and then again they would come out into clear relief, marching on with measured tread, while the cocked hats and shoulders grew, as it were, transparent, and all but disappeared.[49]

In his *Letters on Natural Magic*, a reply to Walter Scott's *Letters on Demonology and Witchcraft*, the scientist (and inventor of the kaleidoscope) Sir David Brewster described the innovations—in particular the concealment of the operator, the mounting of the projecting lantern on rail or wheels, and the development of the 'dissolving view'—which had transformed a seventeenth-century device into the spectacular entertainment which now thrilled and terrified audiences on both sides of the Channel:

The power of the magic lantern has been greatly extended. . . . An exhibition depending on these principles was brought out by M. Philipstall [*sic*] in 1802, under the name of the Phantasmagoria, and when it was shown in London and Edinburgh, it produced the most impressive effects upon the spectators. The small theatre of exhibition was lighted only by one hanging lamp, the flame of which was drawn up into an opaque chimney or shade when the performance began . . . the spectators in total darkness found themselves in the middle of thunder and lightning . . . followed by the figures of ghosts, skeletons, and known individuals, whose eyes and mouth were made to move by the shifting of combined sliders. . . . [T]he first figure . . . began to grow less and less, as if removed to a great distance, and at last vanished . . . the germ of another figure began to appear, and gradually grew larger and larger,

of these studies consider Le Fanu's treatment of the phantasmagoria (and in Walton's case, the Panorama as well) in texts including *Uncle Silas*, *The Cock and Anchor*, 'Carmilla', 'The Evil Guest', 'The Haunted Baronet', 'Spalatro', and 'The Spectre Lovers'; the topic is also discussed, in somewhat less detail, in W. J. McCormack, Introduction, *Uncle Silas* (Oxford, 1981) and Victor Sage, *Le Fanu's Gothic* (London, 2004).

[49] 'Ghost Stories of Chapelizod', *Dublin University Magazine* (Jan. 1851), 93–4.

and approached the spectators, till it attained its perfect development. In this manner the head of Dr. Franklin was transformed into a skull. . . . The exhibition of these transmutations was followed by spectres, skeletons, and terrific figures, which, instead of receding and vanishing as before, suddenly advanced upon the spectators, becoming larger as they approached them, and finally vanished by appearing to sink into the ground. . . . The spectators were not only surprised but agitated, and many of them were of opinion that they could have touched the figures.[50]

The rail-mounted lantern created an illusion of smooth motion, as well as defamiliarizing effects of size and scale; projection onto smoke, sometimes aided by the use of mirrors, produced anamorphotic and other distorting effects; and the use of 'sliders' generated surprising metamorphoses. Phantasmagoria shows, too, while to some extent parasitic upon literary texts, possessed a narrative logic, or illogic, all their own, as much of their disconcerting power derived from their very discontinuity. The phantasmagoric experience was largely a matter of atmosphere, a succession or accumulation of effects, perhaps concluding with a 'rational' accounting by the showman which did not explain away the spectator's terror and unease.

This might just as easily be a description of such stories as 'An Account of Some Strange Disturbances in an Old House in Aungier-Street', in which the 'phantasm' even appears first to the horrified spectator as a kind of poster affixed to his bedroom window, not unlike a particularly aggressive advertising campaign for one of Paul de Philipsthal's or M. Robertson's shows. Even in stories that do not (as 'Aungier Street' does) explicitly invoke the phantasmagoria, there is a sense that its characteristic effects have been liberated or decoupled from their original context and distributed, as it were, throughout Le Fanu's fiction, whether as anamorphoses and other 'optical delusions', ubiquitous 'gliding' figures (which rather anticipate the unsettling 'double-dolly' tracking shots particularly associated with filmmaker Spike Lee), images seemingly projected upon screens, columns, or 'films' of smoke, or, perhaps most strikingly, his many depictions of uncanny protraction, extension, expansion, and contraction—as when, for instance, the 'ill-favoured' fairy lord in 'Laura Silver Bell' stalks into the forest: 'Sulkily he turned away at her words, and strode slowly towards the wood from which he had come; and as he approached it, he seemed to grow taller and taller, and stalked into it as high as a tree' (p. 442); later, in the form of a black cat, he follows Laura through the wood, 'seem[ing] to her to grow bigger and bigger as the darkness deepened' (p. 447).[51]

A more sustained exploitation of this and other phantasmagoric effects is found in 'Wicked Captain Walshawe, of Wauling' (1864), the story of a fortune-hunting English rake who cynically marries a 'potato-faced' Irish girl of means. When, after years of unhappy marriage, she dies, her peasant serving-woman has her laid out in a habit of brown serge, hands clutching rosary and holy candle. Enraged at the sight of such Catholic 'trumpery', the drunken Walshawe snatches the candle from the corpse, extinguishing it. The servant—'witch', Walshawe calls her—pronounces a curse: his own 'sowl' is to be imprisoned within the wick of the candle until it is burnt out. Some forty years later Walshawe himself dies, and his heir, Watson (the narrator's uncle), happens to light the candle again. As it comes to its guttering end, he snuffs it; then, after an interval punctuated by a series of strange phenomena, Watson is forced to watch in horror as a homunculus or manikin version of his dead kinsman emerges from beneath the 'extinguisher':

Out came a little foot then and there, and a pair of wee legs, in short silk stockings and buckled shoes, then the rest of the figure; and, with the arms holding about the socket, the little legs stretched and stretched, hanging about the stem of the candlestick till the feet reached the base, and so down the satyr-like leg of the table, till they reached the floor, extending elastically, and strangely enlarging in all proportions as they approached the ground, where the feet and buckles were those of a well-shaped, full grown man, and the figure tapering upward until it dwindled to its original fairy dimensions at the top, like an object seen in some strangely curved mirror.

Standing upon the floor he expanded, my amazed uncle could not tell how, into his proper proportions . . . (p. 93)

These deformations of 'proportion' and scale continue a moment later, as the uncanny figure turns its attention to the bewildered spectator, winking at him. The keynote of the spectral performance then shifts, for its final act, from anamorphosis to metamorphosis, as the figure undergoes a series of disconcerting transformations, first ageing rapidly, then swelling to grotesque proportions. Meanwhile the military uniform of Walshawe's younger days is transmuted into grave-clothes ('with these changes, which came indefinitely but rapidly as those of a sunset cloud, the fine regimentals faded away, and a loose, gray, woollen drapery,

---

[51] Le Fanu's near-contemporary Lewis Carroll, we might note, conjured with a similar set of effects in his fiction.

somehow, was there in its stead'), alive with worms which themselves then morph (the intrusively modern verb seems all but unavoidable here) into 'little wriggling knots of sparks' (p. 94). It is, finally and appropriately, a figure of ash that flies up the chimney, into the tempestuous night and, presumably, to judgement: ashes to ashes.[52] Interestingly, Le Fanu precisely sets the story in 1822, the year that a French conjurer called M. Charles came to Dublin, bringing to the Sans Pareil theatre his 'Lectures on Apparitions and Ghosts'. This performance is notable in the history of optical media as marking the second debut, so to speak,[53] of the celebrated dissolving-view technique, by means of which '[t]he original picture fades insensibly from the sight, and another as stealthily takes its place';[54] during the same Dublin performance, we also read that, 'instead of a transparent medium he exhibited the figures in a thin film of smoke . . . the object then appeared through the smoke, which, from its undulations, gave an aërial appearance to the spectres'.[55] Did an 8-year-old Joseph Le Fanu attend this performance in the newly-built Royal Arcade, perhaps drawing upon the memory of it, years later, in his account of the wicked Captain's return? We cannot know, but by envisioning his art as, in part, a response to, or engagement with, a dynamic media ecology, an art shaped and nourished by intermedial as well as intertextual influences, we are in a better position to evaluate his contribution to the development of modern horror.

English Subjects, Modern Settings

This 1864 story is emblematic, too, of several important transitions which characterized the final phase of Le Fanu's creative life. The death of the

---

[52] Both chimney and tempest also recall components of the phantasmagoric *mise-en-scène*, as described by Brewster and others.

[53] The first, according to an 1842 article in the London weekly paper *The Mirror of Literature, Amusement, and Instruction*, had also taken place in Ireland, and in connection with the same Dublin optician, Edward Clarke.

[54] *The Mirror of Literature, Amusement, and Instruction*, vol. 1, no. 7 (12 Feb. 1842), 98, reproduced in Laurent Mannoni, *Light and Movement: Incunabula of the Motion Picture, 1420–1896* (Gemona, 1995), 137. For the history of the phantasmagoria, and of optical entertainments in early nineteenth-century Ireland, I have drawn upon Mervyn Heard, *Phantasmagoria: The Secret Life of the Magic Lantern* (Hastings, 2006) and Kevin Rockett and Emer Rockett, *Magic Lantern, Panorama and Moving Picture Shows in Ireland, 1786–1909* (Dublin, 2011), as well as the titles noted above.

[55] *The Mirror of Literature*, 98, reproduced in Mannoni, *Light and Movement*, 137. Le Fanu writes of 'the horrid ripples and deflections which were constantly disturbing the proportions of the figure, as if it were seen through some unequal and perverting medium' (p. 94).

doubt-tormented, 'hysterical' Susanna Le Fanu in 1858, under circumstances which remain far from clear, had inaugurated the gloomy reign of
Dublin's 'Invisible Prince'. Yet the widowed author's famed 'invisibility'
operated, so to speak, only in the social realm; on the printed page, Le
Fanu became more visible than ever, as the last dozen or so years remaining to him were, in stark contrast to the previous decade of married life,
remarkably productive ones. Between 1861 and 1873, the year of his own
death, Le Fanu published over a dozen novels and some twenty stories, at
least a third of which deserve to be called novellas, as well as the Byronic
verse-drama *Beatrice* and some other poems. To some extent, then, this
tale of the death of an ill-used wife, and her cruel husband's come-uppance,
may constitute an exercise in symbolic self-punishment, an expression of
the guilt Le Fanu felt over a traumatic loss which seems nevertheless to
have liberated his creative energies, perhaps by allowing him to explore
certain subjects with greater freedom. Also telling is the fact that
'Walshawe' shifts ground during the narrative from Ireland to England—a
trajectory mirroring the course of Le Fanu's own career at this time, with
respect to both his choice of fictional settings and the new markets which
he was beginning to pursue across the Irish Sea. In 1861, Le Fanu had
purchased the *Dublin University Magazine*, taking personal control of the
outlet in which all of his fiction, excepting the two early historical novels,
had appeared to date. Over the next eight years, no fewer than nine of his
novels would be serialized in its pages, but only the first was set in Ireland.
This was *The House by the Churchyard* (1861–3), a tale of the eighteenth
century set in the fondly remembered Dublin outskirts of Le Fanu's
childhood, with one of his ancestors, the Huguenot Charles de Cresserons,
imaginatively resurrected in the role of narrator. Further Irish novels—and
historical novels—might very well have followed, had Le Fanu not come
to an agreement with London publisher Richard Bentley, who gave him
a simple formula for future work: English subjects, modern settings. Le
Fanu delivered, with a string of sensational novels beginning with *Wylder's
Hand* (1863–4), the first of his English novels to make an Irish debut
before winging their way over the water to London binderies (some of
these, including the outstanding *Uncle Silas*, were in fact earlier Irish tales
re-mapped in place and time and elaborated to three-volume length).[56]

---

[56] The three full-length novels, *Uncle Silas*, *The Wyvern Mystery* (1869), and *A Lost
Name* (1867–8), derive ultimately (I omit mention here of further, intermediate iterations) from 'Passage in the Secret History of an Irish Countess' (1838), 'A Chapter in
the History of the Tyrone Family' (1839), and 'Some Account of the Latter Days of
Richard Marston, of Dunoran' (1848), respectively. Other post-Bentley stories which
constitute, to a greater or lesser extent, reworkings of earlier Irish material include 'The

Meanwhile, he began to turn his eye to major English periodicals, including Bentley's *Temple Bar, Belgravia, All the Year Round, Cassell's Magazine,* and *Once a Week,* as an outlet for his shorter fiction ('Walshawe' was his last story in the *Dublin University Magazine*). This placed Le Fanu in the company, and in some cases under the editorial eye, of such bestselling Victorian authors as Charles Dickens, Wilkie Collins, Mary Elizabeth Braddon, and Charles Reade.

It was in the pages of these London magazines that many of Le Fanu's most famous and enduring stories first appeared, including the Swedenborgian tale of simian-demonic haunting 'Green Tea', the compelling suspense novella 'The Room in the Dragon Volant', and the potently mythopoeic vampire story 'Carmilla'. ('Carmilla', long noted as an influence on such writers and filmmakers as Bram Stoker, Carl Theodor Dreyer, and Anne Rice, continues to live in such unmistakably twenty-first-century productions as the episodic Canadian web series *Carmilla* and Netflix's animated series *Castlevania.*) These three stories formed the core of Le Fanu's third collection of shorter fiction, and the last to be published before his death, *In a Glass Darkly* (Bentley, 1872). Two additional stories—one new, one a quarter-century old—rounded out the book: 'Mr. Justice Harbottle', which had appeared earlier that year in Braddon's *Belgravia* magazine as 'The Haunted House in Westminster', and 'The Watcher', now recast as 'The Familiar'. Certainly, as *Uncle Silas,* at least, proves, Le Fanu was capable of producing powerful effects upon the expansive canvas of the Victorian three-decker, as he also was within the limited compass of the short story form proper, particularly in such *Kunstmärchen*-like tales, redolent of Irish folklore, as 'The Child that Went with the Fairies' and 'Laura Silver Bell' (though the latter has a Cumbrian, rather than an Irish, setting). But what the fictions of *In a Glass Darkly,* to which one should add 'The Haunted Baronet' (included in his 1871 Bentley collection, *Chronicles of Golden Friars*), clearly demonstrate is that, in the generic borderland between the long tale and the short novel, Le Fanu had found his true métier. Scale, indeed, is a crucial element of Le Fanu's style, if one may put it that way, and the 'amphibious' forms (to use the adjective applied by Van Helsing prototype Baron Vordenburg to Carmilla herself) in which he particularly excelled would prove to be especially well suited to exploring other liminal spaces, conceptual and ontological—the spaces, above all, between natural and supernatural, subjective and objective, and realistic and fantastic.

Haunted Baronet' (1870), 'The Vision of Tom Chuff' (1870), and 'Mr. Justice Harbottle' (1872).

Le Fanu was not the first to traffic in these ambiguities; the example of E. T. A. Hoffmann—a possible influence—comes readily to mind. But it is noteworthy that in the decades following Le Fanu's death (which, contrary to his dark hagiography, appears to have been perfectly peaceful), so much of the most ambitious and enduring macabre fiction in English—by Vernon Lee, Arthur Machen, Henry James, Algernon Blackwood, and others—would be cast in the same mould of formal and metaphysical indeterminacy as his best work.

The Alien God

In Robert Browning's dramatic monologue 'Fra Lippo Lippi', the sanguine quattrocento painter says, 'The world's no blot for us, | Nor blank; it means intensely, and means good'. With the exception of that optimistic last word, this exactly describes the fictional reality of Le Fanu's stories. *Everything* has meaning. The natural world, no less than the human world of texts and artifacts, is shot through with innate significance (it becomes, indeed, increasingly difficult to distinguish between the two). This is particularly the case with Le Fanu's later tales, written after he had discovered the writings of Emmanuel Swedenborg, who saw the universe as a divinely ordered 'habitation of symbols', though the Swedenborgian influence represented, in this respect, less a revelation than an intensification or crystallization of an existing tendency in Le Fanu's thought.[57] The worlds of stories like 'The Haunted Baronet' and 'The Room in the Dragon Volant', while very different in many respects, are everywhere suffused or charged with emblematic significance, even if what is signified may be, at times, only the fact of hermetic or cabalistic signification itself.[58] There is, of course, a state of mind which corresponds to such an absolute insistence on the significance of everything—the belief that everything has meaning, that everything is connected: paranoia. And it is no accident that Le Fanu's fiction so often hinges upon tropes of conspiracy and persecution, scenarios in which malign agents are watching, plotting, or perhaps—like the hidden operator of the phantasmagoria, or Descartes's premised deceiver-god—projecting illusions from an unseen place. In place

---

[57] One author represented in Thomas Le Fanu's library (among many others who might be mentioned in this connection) was the emblematic poet Francis Quarles (1592–1644), specifically his books *Emblematike* and *Hieroglyphikes*.

[58] In 'The Haunted Baronet', Feltram—or whatever now wears his shape—can read this world of signs in a way that Sir Bale cannot.

of an indifferent cosmos, we find a malignant, exquisitely 'humanocentric'[59] Other, who is perhaps the God of the Old Testament, the God of Job, who lamented, in a passage Le Fanu would use in his fiction: 'What is man, that thou shouldest magnify him? and that thou shouldest set thine heart upon him? And that thou shouldest visit him every morning, and try him every moment? How long wilt thou not depart from me, nor let me alone till I swallow down my spittle?' (There was a man, surely, who would have appreciated a little cosmic indifference.)

There is also a structure of belief corresponding to this mind-set, one embodied in the kindred strains of heretical Christianity which in modern times have borne the shared label of 'Gnosticism'. Of course, Le Fanu was not 'really' a Gnostic, or for that matter a paranoiac, any more than he was 'really' a Swedenborgian. As a matter of fact, these are not at all far from being the same thing—Gnostic and Swedenborgian, that is (though the Freud family doctor Eduard Hitschmann, among many others, thought that Swedenborg, like that other 'ghost-seer' Daniel Paul Schreber, was clinically paranoid).[60] But even beyond, and prior to, the influence of Swedenborg, Le Fanu was likely to have been well acquainted with Gnostic history and mythology, the theologically-oriented library of his youthful self-education having contained the works of such authorities on the subject as seventeenth-century philosopher Henry More (who coined the term 'Gnosticism') and church historians Johann Lorenz Mosheim, Isaac de Beausobre, and Henry Hart Milman, among others, as well as the substantial entries to be found in Pierre Bayle's *Dictionnaire historique et critique*, Diderot's *Encyclopédie*, and John Robinson's *Theological, Biblical, and Ecclesiastical Dictionary*. More broadly, the nineteenth century saw a marked resurgence of interest in the ancient heresies of Basilides, Valentinus, et al., particularly in the wake of Swedenborg biographer Jacques Matter's *Histoire critique du Gnosticisme* (1828); in Britain, this revival, punctuated by Charles William King's book *The Gnostics and their Remains* (1864) and the influential philosopher Henry Longueville Mansel's Oxford lectures on the subject in 1868, would reach a climax in the

---

[59] The term used, rather contemptuously, by H. P. Lovecraft, to describe fiction antithetical to his own philosophy of 'cosmic indifferentism'.

[60] On the similarities between Gnosticism and Swedenborg's thought see e.g. Louis Dupré, *The Enlightenment and the Intellectual Foundations of Modern Culture* (New Haven and London, 2004), 331–2. More generally, my thinking here about Gnosticism in relation to modern literature has been helpfully informed by Victoria Nelson, *The Secret Life of Puppets* (Cambridge, Mass., 2001) and John Gray, *The Soul of the Marionette: A Short Inquiry into Human Freedom* (New York, 2015).

fin-de-siècle pursuits of the Theosophists and other occultists. The theology which such accounts resurrected for the Victorian reading public was a radically dualistic one, with the soul—humanity's fragmentary spark of the divine—contingently trapped in the prison of the material body (and subject to metempsychosis).[61] To the Gnostic, the material world was itself a kind of prison of appearances, a simulation or artifact fashioned by an impostor-god. This mad or malevolent deity (the 'Demiurge') was identified with 'the Jehovah of the Jews';[62] the true God, by contrast, was an alien, a stranger, inaccessibly remote, with the soul's path from one realm to another blocked by hostile, vigilant 'Archons' (also called 'Watchers') in the service of the great Artificer. This is, it seems safe to say, an essentially paranoid vision, with humanity cast as the dupes of a grand deception, a cosmic conspiracy of which only a small, elect group, who seek salvation through esoteric or cabalistic knowledge, have any awareness.

It is also, perhaps, the worldview which most economically ties together many of the seemingly disparate thematic threads in Le Fanu's fiction discussed here. One might conclude, then, by characterizing the author of such tales as 'The Watcher', 'Green Tea', and 'The Haunted Baronet' as a pioneer of 'gnostic horror', a form or mode fundamentally, and diametrically, opposed to cosmic indifferentism, the philosophy so often associated, if not conflated, with the category of 'weird fiction' as theorized in the twenty-first century. Presumably, then, Le Fanu is not, in the final analysis, truly 'weird'? It is worth pointing out that 'weird' is a word, like 'cleave' (as discussed by Freud in his essay 'The Antithetical Meaning of Primal Words'), which has come to denote something like its own opposite, its original meaning having signalled a connection (as with Shakespeare's Weird Sisters) to fate, which is to say to a coherent, ordered cosmic system: terrible and inexorable, perhaps, but ultimately scaled to human understanding, to human being itself. One modern response to this ostensibly outdated belief—the more familiar one—is to create an ontological frisson by revealing, or

---

[61] The 'ethereal spirit was to be emancipated from its impure companionship; and Egypt, or rather the whole East, lent the doctrine of the transmigration of souls, in order to carry this stranger upon earth through the gradations of successive purification'. Henry Hart Milman, *The History of Christianity: From the Birth of Christ to the Abolition of Paganism in the Roman Empire*, vol. 2 (London, 1840), 118.

[62] 'The Creator of the material world . . . was a secondary being . . . [the Gnostic sects identified] the God of the Jewish covenant with the inferior and malignant author of the material creation . . . the whole of the Old Testament was abandoned to the inspiration of an inferior and evil dæmon.' Ibid. 106–10.

revelling in, cosmic meaninglessness. But another is precisely to affirm the existence of a grand system, while 'making it strange'—to depict the divine order as a malignant, oppressive dispensation which, one senses, *should not be here any longer*: 'weird', that is, in something like the sense which Mark Fisher has recently elaborated.[63] If the power of Philip K. Dick's paranoid fantasies, Thomas Ligotti's puppet-haunted fictions, and films like *The Matrix* and *Ghost Stories* to unsettle us is any indication, Le Fanu's own brand of *horror metaphysicus* is, in its own way, equally 'modern'—and not likely to leave us any time soon. If anything, it may very well be in the ascendant today.

[63] *The Weird and the Eerie* (London, 2016).

NOTE ON THE TEXT

THE texts of all stories have been taken from their original publication in the following periodicals: the *Dublin University Magazine*, *All the Year Round*, *Belgravia*, *The Dark Blue*, and *London Society*. For subsequent book publication (as in *Ghost Stories and Tales of Mystery* (Dublin: James McGlashan, 1851) and *In a Glass Darkly* (London: Richard Bentley, 1872)), Le Fanu revised, and sometimes retitled, stories: for instance, the text of 'The Haunted House in Westminster' (*Belgravia*, 1872) was altered only slightly for inclusion in *In a Glass Darkly*, but the story was given a new title, so that it is as 'Mr Justice Harbottle' that it is better known. On the other hand, 'The Watcher' (*DUM*, 1847) was significantly revised for *Ghost Stories and Tales of Mystery*; then, for *In a Glass Darkly*, it was retitled 'The Familiar', with further revisions which *restored* many aspects of the original *DUM* text. In the Explanatory Notes, such variants are discussed further; also included there are the 'Dr Hesselius' prologues added to 'The Watcher' (as 'The Familiar'), 'The Haunted House in Westminster' (as 'Mr Justice Harbottle'), 'Carmilla', and 'The Room in the Dragon Volant' for *In a Glass Darkly* (the prologue to 'Green Tea' is part of the story as it originally appeared in *All the Year Round*).

SELECT BIBLIOGRAPHY

Biographies

Begnal, Michael H., *Joseph Sheridan Le Fanu* (Lewisburg, 1971).

Browne, Nelson, *Sheridan Le Fanu* (London, 1951).

McCormack, W. J., *Sheridan Le Fanu and Victorian Ireland* (Oxford, 1980). Far and away the fullest, and best, biography.

Bibliography

Crawford, Gary William, *J. Sheridan Le Fanu: A Bio-Bibliography* (Greenwood, Conn., 1995).

Critical Studies

Allen, Nicholas, 'Sheridan Le Fanu and the Spectral Empire', in *The Ghost Story from the Middle Ages to the 20th Century: A Ghostly Genre*, ed. Helen Conrad-O'Briain and Julie Anne Stevens (Dublin, 2010), 112–23.

Annwn, David, 'Dazzling Ghostland: Sheridan Le Fanu's Phantasmagoria', *The Irish Journal of Gothic and Horror Studies* 6 (2009), 2–16.

Briggs, Julia, *Night Visitors: The Rise and Fall of the English Ghost Story* (London, 1977).

Crawford, Gary William, Jim Rockhill, and Brian J. Showers, eds, *Reflections in a Glass Darkly: Essays on J. Sheridan Le Fanu* (New York, 2011).

McCormack, W. J., *Dissolute Characters: Irish Literary History through Balzac, Sheridan Le Fanu, Yeats and Bowen* (Manchester and New York, 1993).

McCormack, W. J., Introduction, *Uncle Silas* (Oxford, 1981).

Melada, Ivan, *Sheridan Le Fanu* (Boston, 1987).

Milbank, Alison, 'Joseph Sheridan Le Fanu: Gothic Grotesque and the Huguenot Inheritance', in *A Companion to Irish Literature*, ed. Julia M. Wright (Malden, 2010), 362–76.

Moynahan, Julian, *Anglo-Irish: The Literary Imagination in a Hyphenated Culture* (Princeton, 1995).

Ridenhour, Jamieson, Introduction, *Carmilla* (Kansas City, 2009).

Rockhill, Jim, Introductions to *Schalken the Painter and Others*, *The Haunted Baronet and Others*, and *Mr Justice Harbottle and Others* (Ashcroft, British Columbia, 2002–5).

Sage, Victor, *Le Fanu's Gothic: The Rhetoric of Darkness* (Basingstoke, 2004).

Sullivan, Jack, *Elegant Nightmares: The English Ghost Story from Le Fanu to Blackwood* (Athens, Ohio, 1978).

Swafford, James, 'Tradition and Guilt in Le Fanu's "Schalken the Painter"', *The Canadian Journal of Irish Studies* vol. 14, no. 2 (Jan. 1989), 48–59.

Tracy, Robert, Introduction, *In a Glass Darkly* (Oxford, 1993).

Walton, James, *Vision and Vacancy: The Fictions of J. S. Le Fanu* (Dublin, 2007).

Further Reading in Oxford World's Classics

Horror Stories from Hoffmann to Hodgson, ed. Darryl Jones.

James, M. R., *Collected Stories*, ed. Darryl Jones.

Le Fanu, Sheridan, *Uncle Silas*, ed. W. J. McCormack.

Lovecraft, H. P., *The Classic Horror Stories*, ed. Roger Luckhurst.

Machen, Arthur, *The Great God Pan and Other Horror Stories*, ed. Aaron Worth.

Poe, Edgar Allan, *The Pit and the Pendulum and Other Tales*, ed. David Van Leer.

Polidori, John, *The Vampyre and Other Tales of the Macabre*, ed. Robert Morrison and Chris Baldick.

Stoker, Bram, *Dracula*, ed. Roger Luckhurst.

A CHRONOLOGY OF SHERIDAN LE FANU

1814 Joseph Thomas Sheridan Le Fanu born on 28 August in Lower Dominick Street, Dublin; early childhood spent in the suburb of Phoenix Park, where his father, the Revd Thomas Le Fanu, served as chaplain at the Royal Hibernian Military School.

1826 Thomas Le Fanu appointed Rector of Abington and Dean of Emly; the Le Fanu family moves to County Limerick.

1831 Beginning of the Tithe Wars; Le Fanu's brother William attacked by hostile villagers.

1832 Le Fanu enters Trinity College Dublin; reads Classics.

1832–3 Irish cholera epidemic.

1838 Publication of Le Fanu's first story, 'The Ghost and the Bone-Setter', in the *Dublin University Magazine*; it is the first of his stories ostensibly retold by Francis Purcell, parish priest of a fictitious Limerick parish.

1839 Called to the Irish Bar, but does not practise.

1841 Death of sister Catherine Le Fanu.

1843 Le Fanu marries Susanna Bennett, the daughter of a prominent Dublin attorney.

1845 Le Fanu's first novel, *The Cock and Anchor*, published by William Curry Jr and Company in Dublin; death of Thomas Le Fanu.

1845–9 Great Famine in Ireland.

1851 Publication of Le Fanu's early story collection, *Ghost Stories and Tales of Mystery*; Le Fanu and his family move to Merrion Square, Dublin.

1858 Death of Susanna Le Fanu.

1861 Le Fanu assumes control of the *Dublin University Magazine*, serializing a succession of novels in its pages during the 1860s, beginning with what would be his last Irish novel, *The House by the Churchyard*. Death of mother Emma Le Fanu.

1863 Le Fanu begins association with London publisher Richard Bentley.

1864 First novel published by Bentley, the sensational *Wylder's Hand*; it is, as Bentley demanded, 'the story of an English subject and in modern times'.

1865 Publication by Bentley of Gothic novel *Uncle Silas*, which had appeared the previous year as 'Maud Ruthyn' in the *Dublin University Magazine*.

1869   'Green Tea' serialized in Charles Dickens's *All the Year Round*.

1871   Publication by Bentley of the three-volume *Chronicles of Golden Friars*, including the novellas 'A Strange Adventure in the Life of Miss Laura Mildmay' (which incorporates 'Madam Crowl's Ghost') and 'The Haunted Baronet'.

1871–2 'Carmilla' serialized in *The Dark Blue*.

1872   'The Room in the Dragon Volant' serialized in *London Society*; publication of landmark collection *In a Glass Darkly* by Bentley, comprising four recently serialized novellas and a revision of the 1847 story 'The Watcher', retitled 'The Familiar'.

1873   Death of Le Fanu in Merrion Square.

1880   Posthumous publication by Bentley of *The Purcell Papers*, which collects stories originally appearing in the *Dublin University Magazine* from 1838 to 1850, with a Memoir by Alfred Perceval Graves.

1895   Publication of *The Watcher and Other Weird Stories*, with illustrations by Le Fanu's son Brinsley Sheridan.

1896   Publication of *The Poems of Joseph Sheridan Le Fanu*, edited and introduced by Alfred Perceval Graves, as well as *A Stable for Nightmares; or, Weird Tales*, as by Le Fanu. The latter is in fact a resurrection of an earlier anthology of stories by various authors, with Le Fanu's 'Dickon the Devil' added (this collection will contribute to confusion in the future).

1923   M. R. James collects a number of unattributed Le Fanu stories from the *Dublin University Magazine*, including 'Some Strange Disturbances in an Old House in Aungier-Street' and 'Wicked Captain Walshawe, of Wauling'; publishes them with prologue and biographical epilogue as *Madam Crowl's Ghost, and Other Tales of Mystery*.

1980   W. J. McCormack identifies further Le Fanu stories 'Spalatro' and 'Borrhomeo the Astrologer' in his important biography *Sheridan Le Fanu and Victorian Ireland* (Oxford University Press, 1980).

GREEN TEA

and Other Weird Stories

STRANGE EVENT IN THE LIFE
OF SCHALKEN THE PAINTER

*Being a Seventh Extract from the Legacy of the late
Francis Purcell, * p.p. of Drumcoolagh*

You will, no doubt, be surprised, my dear friend, at the subject of the
following narrative. What had I to do with Schalken,* or Schalken with
me? He had returned to his native land, and was probably dead and
buried before I was born; I never visited Holland nor spoke with
a native of that country. So much I believe you already know. I must,
then, give you my authority, and state to you frankly the ground upon
which rests the credibility of the strange story which I am about to lay
before you. I was acquainted, in my early days, with a Captain Vandael,
whose father had served King William in the Low Countries, and also
in my own unhappy land during the Irish campaigns.* I know not how
it happened that I liked this man's society spite of his politics and religion: but so it was; and it was by means of the free intercourse to which
our intimacy gave rise that I became possessed of the curious tale which
you are about to hear. I had often been struck, while visiting Vandael, by
a remarkable picture, in which, though no *connoisseur* myself, I could not
fail to discern some very strong peculiarities, particularly in the distribution of light and shade,* as also a certain oddity in the design itself,
which interested my curiosity. It represented the interior of what might
be a chamber in some antique religious building—the foreground was
occupied by a female figure, arrayed in a species of white robe, part of
which is arranged so as to form a veil. The dress, however, is not strictly
that of any religious order. In its hand the figure bears a lamp, by whose
light alone the form and face are illuminated; the features are marked by
an arch smile, such as pretty women wear when engaged in successfully
practising some roguish trick; in the background, and, excepting where
the dim red light of an expiring fire serves to define the form, totally in
the shade, stands the figure of a man equipped in the old fashion,* with
doublet and so forth, in an attitude of alarm, his hand being placed
upon the hilt of his sword, which he appears to be in the act of drawing.

'There are some pictures,' said I to my friend, 'which impress one,
I know not how, with a conviction that they represent not the mere ideal

shapes and combinations which have floated through the imagination of the artist, but scenes, faces, and situations which have actually existed. When I look upon that picture, something assures me that I behold the representation of a reality.'

Vandael smiled, and, fixing his eyes upon the painting musingly, he said—

'Your fancy has not deceived you, my good friend, for that picture is the record, and I believe a faithful one, of a remarkable and mysterious occurrence. It was painted by Schalken, and contains, in the face of the female figure, which occupies the most prominent place in the design, an accurate portrait of Rose Velderkaust, the niece of Gerard Douw, the first, and, I believe, the only love of Godfrey Schalken. My father knew the painter well, and from Schalken himself he learned the story of the mysterious drama, one scene of which the picture has embodied. This painting, which is accounted a fine specimen of Schalken's style, was bequeathed to my father by the artist's will, and, as you have observed, is a very striking and interesting production.'

I had only to request Vandael to tell the story of the painting in order to be gratified; and thus it is that I am enabled to submit to you a faithful recital of what I heard myself, leaving you to reject or to allow the evidence upon which the truth of the tradition depends, with this one assurance, that Schalken was an honest, blunt Dutchman, and, I believe, wholly incapable of committing a flight of imagination; and further, that Vandael, from whom I heard the story, appeared firmly convinced of its truth.

There are few forms upon which the mantle of mystery and romance could seem to hang more ungracefully than upon that of the uncouth and clownish Schalken—the Dutch boor—the rude and dogged, but most cunning worker of oils, whose pieces delight the initiated of the present day almost as much as his manners disgusted the refined of his own; and yet this man, so rude, so dogged, so slovenly, I had almost said so savage, in mien and manner, during his after successes, had been selected by the capricious goddess, in his early life, to figure as the hero of a romance by no means devoid of interest or of mystery. Who can tell how meet he may have been in his young days to play the part of the lover or of the hero—who can say that in early life he had been the same harsh, *unlicked*,* and rugged boor which, in his maturer age, he proved—or how far the neglected rudeness which afterwards marked his air, and garb, and manners, may not have been the growth of that reckless apathy not unfrequently produced by bitter misfortunes and disappointments in early life? These questions can never now be answered. We must content ourselves, then, with a plain statement of facts, or what have been received and transmitted as such, leaving matters of speculation to those who like them.

When Schalken studied under the immortal Gerard Douw, he was a young man; and in spite of the phlegmatic constitution and unexcitable manner which he shared (we believe) with his countrymen, he was not incapable of deep and vivid impressions, for it is an established fact that the young painter looked with considerable interest upon the beautiful niece of his wealthy master. Rose Velderkaust was very young, having, at the period of which we speak, not yet attained her seventeenth year, and, if tradition speaks truth, possessed all the soft dimpling charms of the fair, light-haired Flemish maidens. Schalken had not studied long in the school of Gerard Douw, when he felt this interest deepening into something of a keener and intenser feeling than was quite consistent with the tranquillity of his honest Dutch heart; and at the same time he perceived, or thought he perceived, flattering symptoms of a reciprocity of liking, and this was quite sufficient to determine whatever indecision he might have heretofore experienced, and to lead him to devote exclusively to her every hope and feeling of his heart. In short, he was as much in love as a Dutchman could be. He was not long in making his passion known to the pretty maiden herself, and his declaration was followed by a corresponding confession upon her part. Schalken, however, was a poor man, and he possessed no counterbalancing advantages of birth or otherwise to induce the old man to consent to a union which must involve his niece and ward in the strugglings and difficulties of a young and nearly friendless artist. He was, therefore, to wait until time had furnished him with opportunity and accident with success; and then, if his labours were found sufficiently lucrative, it was to be hoped that his proposals might at least be listened to by her jealous guardian. Months passed away, and, cheered by the smiles of the little Rose, Schalken's labours were redoubled, and with such effect and improvement as reasonably to promise the realization of his hopes, and no contemptible eminence in his art, before many years should have elapsed.

The even course of this cheering prosperity was, however, destined to experience a sudden and formidable interruption, and that, too, in a manner so strange and mysterious as to baffle all investigation, and throw upon the events themselves a shadow of almost supernatural horror.

Schalken had one evening remained in the master's *studio* considerably longer than his more volatile companions, who had gladly availed

themselves of the excuse which the dusk of evening afforded, to withdraw from their several tasks, in order to finish a day of labour in the
jollity and conviviality of the tavern. But Schalken worked for improvement, or rather for love. Besides, he was now engaged merely in sketch-
ing a design, an operation which, unlike that of colouring, might be
continued as long as there was light sufficient to distinguish between
canvas and charcoal. He had not then, nor, indeed, until long after,
discovered the peculiar powers of his pencil, and he was engaged in
composing a group of extremely roguish-looking and grotesque imps
and demons, who were inflicting various ingenious torments upon
a perspiring and pot-bellied St Anthony,* who reclined in the midst of
them, apparently in the last stage of drunkenness. The young artist,
however, though incapable of executing, or even of appreciating, any
thing of true sublimity, had, nevertheless, discernment enough to prevent his being by any means satisfied with his work; and many were the
patient erasures and corrections which the limbs and features of saint
and devil underwent, yet all without producing in their new arrangement
any thing of improvement or increased effect: The large, old-fashioned
room was silent, and, with the exception of himself, quite deserted
by its usual inmates. An hour had passed—nearly two—without any
improved result. Daylight had already declined, and twilight was fast
giving way to the darkness of night. The patience of the young man was
exhausted, and he stood before his unfinished production, absorbed in
no very pleasing ruminations, one hand buried in the folds of his long
dark hair, and the other holding the piece of charcoal which had so ill
executed its office, and which he now rubbed, without much regard
to the sable streaks which it produced, with irritable pressure upon
his ample Flemish inexpressibles.*—'Pshaw!' said the young man
aloud, 'would that picture, devils, saint, and all, were where they should
be—in hell!' A short, sudden laugh, uttered startlingly close to his ear,
instantly responded to the ejaculation. The artist turned sharply round,
and now for the first time became aware that his labours had been overlooked by a stranger. Within about a yard and half, and rather behind
him, there stood what was, or appeared to be, the figure of an elderly
man: he wore a short cloak, and broad-brimmed hat, with a conical crown,
and in his hand, which was protected with a heavy, gauntlet-shaped
glove, he carried a long ebony walking-stick, surmounted with what
appeared, as it glittered dimly in the twilight, to be a massive head of
gold, and upon the breast, through the folds of the cloak, there shone
what appeared to be the links of a rich chain of the same metal. The
room was so obscure that nothing further of the appearance of the

figure could be ascertained, and the face was altogether overshadowed by the heavy flap of the beaver* which overhung it, so that not a feature could be discerned. A quantity of dark hair escaped from beneath this sombre hat, a circumstance which, connected with the firm, upright carriage of the intruder, proved that his years could not yet exceed three-score or thereabouts. There was an air of gravity and importance about the garb of this person, and something indescribably odd, I might, say awful, in the perfect, stone-like movelessness of the figure, that effectually checked the testy comment which had at once risen to the lips of the irritated artist. He, therefore, as soon as he had sufficiently recovered the surprise, asked the stranger, civilly, to be seated, and desired to know if he had any message to leave for his master.

'Tell Gerard Douw,' said the unknown, without altering his attitude in the smallest degree, 'that Minheer Vanderhausen, of Rotterdam,* desires to speak with him on to-morrow evening at this hour, and, if he please, in this room, upon matters of weight—that is all—good night.'

The stranger, having finished this message, turned abruptly, and, with a quick but silent step quitted the room, before Schalken had time to say a word in reply. The young man felt a curiosity to see in what direction the burgher of Rotterdam would turn on quitting the *studio*, and for that purpose he went directly to the window which commanded the door. A lobby of considerable extent intervened between the inner door of the painter's room and the street entrance, so that Schalken occupied the post of observation before the old man could possibly have reached the street. He watched in vain, however. There was no other mode of exit. Had the old man vanished, or was he lurking about the recesses of the lobby for some bad purpose? This last suggestion filled the mind of Schalken with a vague horror, which was so unaccountably intense as to make him alike afraid to remain in the room alone and reluctant to pass through the lobby. However, with an effort which appeared very disproportioned to the occasion, he summoned resolution to leave the room, and, having double-locked the door and thrust the key in his pocket, without looking to the right or left, he traversed the passage which had so recently, perhaps still, contained the person of his mysterious visitant, scarcely venturing to breathe till he had arrived in the open street.

'Minheer Vanderhausen,' said Gerard Douw within himself, as the appointed hour approached, 'Minheer Vanderhausen of Rotterdam! I never heard of the man till yesterday. What can he want of me? A portrait, perhaps, to be painted; or a younger son or a poor relation to be apprenticed; or a collection to be valued; or—pshaw, there's no one in

Rotterdam to leave me a legacy. Well, whatever the business may be, we shall soon know it all.'

It was now the close of day, and every easel, except that of Schalken, was deserted. Gerard Douw was pacing the apartment with the restless step of impatient expectation, every now and then humming a passage from a piece of music which he was himself composing; for, though no great proficient, he admired the art; sometimes pausing to glance over the work of one of his absent pupils, but more frequently placing himself at the window, from whence he might observe the passengers who threaded the obscure by-street in which his studio was placed.

'Said you not, Godfrey,' exclaimed Douw, after a long and fruitless gaze from his post of observation, and turning to Schalken—'said you not the hour of appointment was at about seven by the clock of the Stadhouse?'*

'It had just told seven when I first saw him, sir,' answered the student.

'The hour is close at hand, then,' said the master, consulting a horologe* as large and as round as a full-grown orange. 'Minheer Vanderhausen from Rotterdam—is it not so?'

'Such was the name.'

'And an elderly man, richly clad?' continued Douw.

'As well as I might see,' replied his pupil; 'he could not be young, nor yet very old neither, and his dress was rich and grave, as might become a citizen of wealth and consideration.'

At this moment the sonorous boom of the Stadhouse clock told, stroke after stroke, the hour of seven; the eyes of both master and student were directed to the door; and it was not until the last peal of the old bell had ceased to vibrate, that Douw exclaimed—

'So, so; we shall have his worship presently—that is, if he means to keep his hour; if not, thou may'st wait for him, Godfrey, if you court the acquaintance of a capricious burgomaster; as for me, I think our old Leyden contains a sufficiency of such commodities, without an importation from Rotterdam.'

Schalken laughed, as in duty bound; and after a pause of some minutes, Douw suddenly exclaimed—

'What if it should all prove a jest, a piece of mummery got up by Vankarp, or some such worthy. I wish you had run all risks, and cudgelled the old burgomaster, stadholder, or whatever else he may be, soundly. I would wager a dozen of Rhenish, his worship would have pleaded old acquaintance before the third application.'

'Here he comes, sir,' said Schalken, in a low admonitory tone; and instantly upon turning towards the door, Gerard Douw observed the same figure which had, on the day before, so unexpectedly greeted the vision of his pupil Schalken.

There was something in the air and mien of the figure which at once satisfied the painter that there was no *mummery* in the case, and that he really stood in the presence of a man of worship; and so, without hesitation, he doffed his cap, and, courteously saluting the stranger, requested him to be seated. The visitor waved his hand slightly, as if in acknowledgment of the courtesy, but remained standing.

'I have the honour to see Minheer Vanderhausen of Rotterdam?' said Gerard Douw.

'The same,' was the laconic reply of his visitant.

'I understand your worship desires to speak with me,' continued Douw, 'and I am here by appointment to wait your commands.'

'Is that a man of trust?' said Vanderhausen, turning towards Schalken, who stood at a little distance behind his master.

'Certainly,' replied Gerard.

'Then let him take this box and get the nearest jeweller or goldsmith to value its contents, and let him return hither with a certificate of the valuation.'

At the same time, he placed a small case about nine inches square in the hands of Gerard Douw, who was as much amazed at its weight as at the strange abruptness with which it was handed to him. In accordance with the wishes of the stranger, he delivered it into the hands of Schalken, and repeating *his* directions, despatched him upon the mission.

Schalken disposed his precious charge securely beneath the folds of his cloak, and rapidly traversing two or three narrow streets, he stopped at a corner house, the lower part of which was then occupied by the shop of a Jewish goldsmith.* Schalken entered the shop, and calling the little Hebrew into the obscurity of its back recesses, he proceeded to lay before him Vanderhausen's packet. On being examined by the light of a lamp, it appeared entirely cased with lead, the outer surface of which was much scraped and soiled, and nearly white with age. This was with difficulty partially removed, and disclosed beneath a box of some dark and singularly hard wood; this too was forced, and after the removal of two or three folds of linen, its contents proved to be a mass of golden ingots, closely packed, and, as the Jew declared, of the most perfect quality. Every ingot underwent the scrutiny of the little Jew, who seemed to feel an epicurean delight in touching and testing these morsels of the glorious metal; and each one of them was replaced in its birth with the exclamation; '*Mein Gott*, how very perfect! not one grain of alloy—beautiful, beautiful.' The task was at length finished, and the Jew certified under his hand the value of the ingots submitted to his examination, to amount to many thousand rix-dollars.* With the desired document in his bosom, and the rich box of gold carefully pressed under his arm, and concealed by his cloak, he retraced his way, and entering the studio, found his master and the stranger in close confer- ence. Schalken had no sooner left the room, in order to execute the commission he had taken in charge, than Vanderhausen addressed Gerard Douw in the following terms—

'I may not tarry with you to-night more than a few minutes, and so I shall briefly tell you the matter upon which I come. You visited the town of Rotterdam some four months ago, and then I saw in the church of St Lawrence* your niece, Rose Velderkaust. I desire to marry her, and if I satisfy you as to the fact that I am very wealthy, more wealthy than any husband you could dream of for her, I expect that you will forward my views to the utmost of your authority. If you approve my proposal, you must close with it at once, for I cannot command time enough to wait for calculations and delays.'

Gerard Douw was, perhaps, as much astonished as any one could be, by the very unexpected nature of Minheer Vanderhausen's communi- cation, but he did not give vent to any unseemly expression of surprise, for besides the motives supplied by prudence and politeness, the painter experienced a kind of chill and oppressive sensation, something like that which is supposed to affect a man who is placed unconsciously in immediate contact with something to which he has a natural antipathy— an undefined horror and dread while standing in the presence of the eccentric stranger, which made him very unwilling to say any thing which might reasonably prove offensive.

'I have no doubt,' said Gerard, after two or three prefatory hems, 'that the connection which you propose would prove alike advantageous and honourable to my niece; but you must be aware that she has a will of her own, and may not acquiesce in what *we* may design for her advantage.'

'Do not seek to deceive me, sir painter,' said Vanderhausen; 'you are her guardian—she is your ward—she is mine if *you* like to make her so.'

The man of Rotterdam moved forward a little as he spoke, and Gerard Douw, he scarce knew why, inwardly prayed for the speedy return of Schalken.

'I desire,' said the mysterious gentleman, 'to place in your hands at once an evidence of my wealth, and a security for my liberal dealing with your niece. The lad will return in a minute or two with a sum in value five times the fortune which she has a right to expect from a husband. This shall lie in your hands, together with her dowry, and you may apply the united sum as suits her interest best; it shall be all exclusively hers while she lives—is that liberal?'

Douw assented, and inwardly thought that fortune had been extraordinarily kind to his niece; the stranger, he thought, must be both wealthy and generous, and such an offer was not to be despised, though made by a humourist, and one of no very prepossessing presence. Rose had no very high pretensions, for she was almost without dowry; indeed altogether so, excepting so far as the deficiency had been supplied by the generosity of her uncle; neither had she any right to raise any scruples against the match on the score of birth, for her own origin was by no means elevated, and as to other objections, Gerard resolved, and, indeed, by the usages of the time, was warranted in resolving not to listen to them for a moment.

'Sir,' said he, addressing the stranger, 'your offer is most liberal, and whatever hesitation I may feel in closing with it immediately, arises solely from my not having the honour of knowing any thing of your family or station. Upon these points you can, of course, satisfy me without difficulty?'

'As to my respectability,' said the stranger, drily, 'you must take that for granted at present; pester me with no inquiries; you can discover nothing more about me than I choose to make known. You shall have sufficient security for my respectability—my word, if you are honourable: if you are sordid, my gold.'

'A testy old gentleman,' thought Douw, 'he must have his own way; but, all things considered, I am justified in giving my niece to him; were she my own daughter, I would do the like by her. I will not pledge myself unnecessarily however.'

'You will not pledge yourself unnecessarily,' said Vanderhausen, strangely uttering the very words which had just floated through the mind of his companion; 'but you will do so if it *is* necessary, I presume; and I will show you that I consider it indispensable. If the gold I mean to leave in your hands satisfy you, and if you desire that my proposal shall not be at once withdrawn, you must, before I leave this room, write your name to this engagement.'

Having thus spoken, he placed a paper in the hands of Gerard, the contents of which expressed an engagement entered into by Gerard Douw, to give to Wilken Vanderhausen of Rotterdam, in marriage, Rose Velderkaust, and so forth, within one week of the date hereof. While the painter was employed in reading this covenant, Schalken, as we have stated, entered the studio, and having delivered the box and the valuation of the Jew, into the hands of the stranger, he was about to retire, when Vanderhausen called to him to wait; and, presenting the case and the certificate to Gerard Douw, he waited in silence until he had satisfied himself by an inspection of both as to the value of the pledge left in his hands. At length he said—

'Are you content?'

The painter said he would fain have another day to consider.

'Not an hour,' said the suitor coolly.

'Well then,' said Douw, 'I am content—it is a bargain.'

'Then sign at once,' said Vanderhausen, 'I am weary.'

At the same time he produced a small case of writing materials, and Gerard signed the important document.

'Let this youth witness the covenant,' said the old man; and Godfrey Schalken unconsciously signed the instrument which bestowed upon another that hand which he had so long regarded as the object and reward of all his labours. The compact being thus completed, the strange visitor folded up the paper, and stowed it safely in an inner pocket.

'I will visit you to-morrow night at nine of the clock, at your house, Gerard Douw, and will see the subject of our contract—farewell'; and so saying, Wilken Vanderhausen moved stiffly, but rapidly out of the room.

Schalken, eager to resolve his doubts, had placed himself by the window, in order to watch the street entrance; but the experiment served only to support his suspicions, for the old man did not issue from the door. This was very strange, very odd, very fearful; he and his master returned together, and talked but little on the way, for each had his own subjects of reflection, of anxiety, and of hope. Schalken, however, did not know the ruin which threatened his cherished schemes.

Gerard Douw knew nothing of the attachment which had sprung up between his pupil and his niece; and even if he had, it is doubtful whether he would have regarded its existence as any serious obstruction to the wishes of Minheer Vanderhausen. Marriages were then and there matters of traffic and calculation; and it would have appeared as absurd in the eyes of the guardian to make a mutual attachment an essential element in a contract of marriage, as it would have been to draw up his bonds and receipts in the language of chivalrous romance. The painter, however, did not communicate to his niece the important step which he had taken in her behalf, and his resolution arose not from any anticipation of opposition on her part, but solely from a ludicrous consciousness that if his ward were, as she very naturally might do, to ask him to describe the appearance of the bridegroom whom he destined for her, he would be forced to confess that he had not seen his face, and if called upon, would find it impossible to identify him. Upon the next day, Gerard Douw having dined, called his niece to him, and having scanned her person with an air of satisfaction, he took her hand, and looking upon her pretty, innocent face with a smile of kindness, he said—

'Rose, my girl, that face of yours will make your fortune.' Rose blushed and smiled. 'Such faces and such tempers seldom go together, and when they do, the compound is a love potion, which few heads or hearts can resist; trust me, thou wilt soon be a bride, girl; but this is trifling, and I am pressed for time, so make ready the large room by eight o'clock to-night, and give directions for supper at nine. I expect a friend to-night; and observe me, child, do thou trick thyself out handsomely. I would not have him think us poor or sluttish.'

With these words he left the chamber, and took his way to the room to which we have already had occasion to introduce our readers—that in which his pupils worked.

When the evening closed in, Gerard called Schalken, who was about to take his departure to his obscure and comfortless lodgings, and asked him to come home and sup with Rose and Vanderhausen. The invitation was, of course, accepted, and Gerard Douw and his pupil soon found themselves in the handsome and somewhat antique-looking room which had been prepared for the reception of the stranger. A cheerful wood fire blazed in the capacious hearth; a little at one side an old-fashioned table, with richly carved legs, was placed—destined, no doubt, to receive the supper, for which preparations were going forward; and ranged with exact regularity, stood the tall-backed chairs, whose ungracefulness was more than counterbalanced by their comfort. The little party, consisting of Rose, her uncle, and the artist, awaited the arrival of the expected visitor with considerable impatience. Nine o'clock at length came, and with it a summons at the street door, which being speedily answered, was followed by a slow and emphatic tread upon the staircase; the steps moved heavily across the lobby, the door of the room in which the party which we have described were assembled slowly opened, and there entered a figure which startled, almost appalled, the phlegmatic Dutchmen, and nearly made Rose scream with affright; it was the form, and arrayed in the garb of Minheer Vanderhausen; the air, the gait, the height was the same, but the features had never been seen by any of the party before. The stranger stopped at the door of the room, and displayed his form and face completely. He wore a dark-coloured cloth cloak, which was short and full, not falling quite to the knees; his legs were cased in dark purple silk stockings, and his shoes were adorned with roses of the same colour. The opening of the cloak in front showed the under-suit to consist of some very dark, perhaps sable material, and his hands were enclosed in a pair of heavy leather gloves, which ran up considerably above the wrist, in the manner of a gauntlet. In one hand he carried his walking-stick and his hat, which he had removed, and the other hung heavily by his side. A quantity of grizzled hair descended in long tresses from his head, and its folds rested upon the plaits of a stiff ruff, which effectually concealed his neck. So far all was well; but the face!—all the flesh of the face was coloured with the bluish leaden hue, which is sometimes produced by the operation of metallic medicines,* administered in excessive quantities; the eyes were enormous, and the white appeared both above and below the iris, which gave to them an expression of insanity, which was heightened by their glassy fixedness; the nose was well enough, but the mouth was writhed considerably to one side, where it opened in order to give egress to two long, discoloured fangs, which projected from the upper jaw, far below the lower lip—the hue of the lips themselves bore the usual relation to that of the face, and was, consequently, nearly black; the character of the face was malignant, even satanic, to the last degree; and, indeed, such a combination of horror could hardly be accounted for, except by supposing the corpse of some atrocious malefactor which had long hung blackening upon the gibbet to have at length become the habitation of a demon—the frightful sport of satanic possession. It was remarkable that the worshipful stranger suffered as little as possible of his flesh to appear, and that during his visit he did not once remove his gloves. Having stood for some moments at the door, Gerard Douw at length found breath and collectedness to bid him welcome, and with a mute inclination of the head, the stranger stepped forward into the room. There was something indescribably odd, even horrible, about all his motions, something undefinable, that was unnatural, unhuman—it was as if the limbs were guided and directed by a spirit unused to the management of bodily machinery. The stranger said hardly any thing during his visit, which did not exceed half an hour; and the host himself could scarcely muster courage enough to utter the few necessary salutations and courtesies; and, indeed, such was the nervous terror which the presence of Vanderhausen inspired, that very little would have made all his entertainers fly bellowing from the room. They had not so far lost all self-possession, however, as to fail to observe two strange peculiarities of their visitor. During his stay he did not once suffer his eyelids to close, nor even to move in the slightest degree; and farther, there was a death-like stillness in his whole person, owing to the total absence of the heaving motion of the chest, caused by the process of respiration. These two peculiarities, though when told they may appear trifling, produced a very striking and unpleasant effect when seen and observed. Vanderhausen at length relieved the painter of Leyden of his inauspicious presence; and with no small gratification the little party heard the street door close after him.

'Dear uncle,' said Rose, 'what a frightful man! I would not see him again for the wealth of the States.'*

'Tush, foolish girl,' said Douw, whose sensations were any thing but comfortable. 'A man may be as ugly as the devil, and yet if his heart and actions are good, he is worth all the pretty-faced, perfumed puppies that walk the Mall. Rose, my girl, it is very true he has not thy pretty face, but I know him to be wealthy and liberal; and were he ten times more ugly'—('which is inconceivable,' observed Rose)—'these two virtues would be sufficient,' continued her uncle, 'to counterbalance all his deformity, and if not of power sufficient actually to alter the shape of the features, at least of efficacy enough to prevent one thinking them amiss.'

'Do you know, uncle,' said Rose, 'when I saw him standing at the door, I could not get it out of my head that I saw the old, painted, wooden figure that used to frighten me so much in the church of St Laurence of Rotterdam.'

Gerard laughed, though he could not help inwardly acknowledging the justness of the comparison. He was resolved, however, as far as he could, to check his niece's inclination to ridicule the ugliness of her intended bridegroom, although he was not a little pleased to observe that she appeared totally exempt from that mysterious dread of the stranger, which he could not disguise it from himself, considerably affected him, as also his pupil Godfrey Schalken.

Early on the next day there arrived from various quarters of the town, rich presents of silks, velvets, jewellery, and so forth, for Rose; and also a packet directed to Gerard Douw, which, on being opened, was found to contain a contract of marriage, formally drawn up, between Wilken Vanderhausen of the *Boom-quay*,* in Rotterdam, and Rose Velderkaust of Leyden, niece to Gerard Douw, master in the art of painting, also of the same city; and containing engagements on the part of Vanderhausen to make settlements upon his bride, far more splendid than he had before led her guardian to believe likely, and which were to be secured to her use in the most unexceptionable manner possible—the money being placed in the hands of Gerard Douw himself.

I have no sentimental scenes to describe, no cruelty of guardians, or magnanimity of wards, or agonies of lovers. The record I have to make is one of sordidness, levity, and interest. In less than a week after the first interview which we have just described, the contract of marriage was fulfilled, and Schalken saw the prize which he would have risked any thing to secure, carried off triumphantly by his attractive rival. For two or three days he absented himself from the school; he then returned and worked, if with less cheerfulness, with far more dogged resolution than before—the slumbers of love had given place to that of ambition. Months passed away, and, contrary to his expectation, and, indeed, to the direct promise of the parties, Gerard Douw heard nothing of his niece or her worshipful spouse. The interest of the money which was to have been demanded in quarterly sums, lay unclaimed in his hands. He began to grow extremely uneasy. Minheer Vanderhausen's direction in Rotterdam he was fully possessed of; after some irresolution he finally determined to journey thither—a trifling undertaking, and easily accomplished—and thus to satisfy himself of the safety and comfort of his ward, for whom he entertained an honest and strong affection. His search was in vain, however; no one in Rotterdam had ever heard of Minheer Vanderhausen. Gerard Douw left not a house in the Boom-quay untried; but all in vain—no one could give him any information whatever touching the object of his inquiry; and he was obliged to return to Leyden nothing wiser than when he had left it. On his arrival he hastened to the establishment from which Vanderhausen had hired the lumbering, though, considering the times, most luxurious vehicle, which the bridal party had employed to convey them to Rotterdam. From the driver of this machine he learned, that having proceeded by slow stages, they had late in the evening approached Rotterdam; but that before they entered the city, and while yet nearly a mile from it, a small party of men, soberly clad, and after the old fashion, with peaked beards and mustaches, standing in the centre of the road,* obstructed the further progress of the carriage. The driver reined in his horses, much fearing, from the obscurity of the hour, and the loneliness of the road, that some mischief was intended. His fears were, however, some-what allayed by his observing that these strange men carried a large litter, of an antique shape, and which they immediately set down upon the pavement, whereupon the bridegroom, having opened the coach-door from within, descended, and having assisted his bride to do likewise, led her, weeping bitterly and wringing her hands, to the litter, which they both entered. It was then raised by the men who surrounded it, and speedily carried towards the city, and before it had proceeded many yards, the darkness concealed it from the view of the Dutch charioteer. In the inside of the vehicle he found a purse, whose contents more than thrice paid the hire of the carriage and man. He saw and could tell nothing more of Minheer Vanderhausen and his beautiful lady. This mystery was a source of deep anxiety and almost of grief to Gerard Douw. There was evidently fraud in the dealing of Vanderhausen with him, though for what purpose committed he could not imagine. He greatly doubted how far it was possible for a man possessing in his countenance so strong an evidence of the presence of the most demoniac feelings, to be in reality any thing but a villain, and every day that passed without his hearing from or of his niece, instead of inducing him to forget his fears, on the contrary tended more and more to exasperate them. The loss of his niece's cheerful society tended also to depress his spirits; and in order to dispel this despondency, which often crept upon his mind after his daily employment was over, he was wont frequently to prevail upon Schalken to accompany him home, and by his presence to dispel, in some degree, the gloom of his otherwise solitary supper. One evening, the painter and his pupil were sitting by the fire, having accomplished a comfortable supper, and had yielded to that silent pensiveness some-times induced by the process of digestion, when their reflections were disturbed by a loud sound at the street door, as if occasioned by some person rushing forcibly and repeatedly against it. A domestic had run without delay to ascertain the cause of the disturbance, and they heard him twice or thrice interrogate the applicant for admission, but without producing an answer or any cessation of the sounds. They heard him then open the hall-door, and immediately there followed a light and rapid tread upon the staircase, Schalken laid his hand on his sword, and advanced towards the door. It opened before he reached it, and Rose rushed into the room. She looked wild and haggard, and pale with exhaustion and terror, but her dress surprised them as much even as her unexpected appearance. It consisted of a kind of white woollen wrap-per, made close about the neck, and descending to the very ground. It was much deranged and travel-soiled. The poor creature had hardly entered the chamber when she fell senseless on the floor. With some difficulty they succeeded in reviving her, and on recovering her senses, she instantly exclaimed, in a tone of eager, terrified impatience—

'Wine, wine, quickly, or I'm lost.'

Much alarmed at the strange agitation in which the call was made, they at once administered to her wishes, and she drank some wine with a haste and eagerness which surprised them. She had hardly swallowed it, when she exclaimed, with the same urgency,

'Food, food, at once, or I perish.'

A considerable fragment of a roast joint was upon the table, and Schalken immediately proceeded to cut some, but he was anticipated, for no sooner had she become aware of its presence, than she darted at it with the rapacity of a vulture, and, seizing it in her hands, she tore off the flesh with her teeth, and swallowed it. When the paroxysm of hunger had been a little appeased, she appeared suddenly to become aware how strange her conduct had been, or it may have been that other more agitating thoughts recurred to her mind, for she began to weep bitterly and to wring her hands.

'Oh, send for a minister of God,' said she; 'I am not safe till he comes; send for him speedily.'

Gerard Douw despatched a messenger instantly, and prevailed on his niece to allow him to surrender his bedchamber to her use; he also persuaded her to retire to it at once and to rest; her consent was extorted upon the condition that they would not leave her for a moment.

'Oh, that the holy man were here,' she said; 'he can deliver me—the dead and the living can never be one—God has forbidden it.'

With these mysterious words she surrendered herself to their guidance, and they proceeded to the chamber which Gerard Douw had assigned to her use.

'Do not, do not leave me for a moment,' said she; 'I am lost for ever if you do.'

Gerard Douw's chamber was approached through a spacious apartment, which they were now about to enter. Gerard Douw and Schalken each carried a wax candle, so that a sufficient degree of light was cast upon all surrounding objects. They were now entering the large chamber, which, as I have said, communicated with Douw's apartment, when Rose suddenly stopped, and, in a whisper which seemed to thrill with horror, she said—

'Oh, God! he is here, he is here; see, see, there he goes.'

She pointed towards the door of the inner room, and Schalken thought he saw a shadowy and ill-defined form gliding into that apartment. He drew his sword, and, raising the candle so as to throw its light with increased distinctness upon the objects in the room, he entered the chamber into which the shadow had glided. No figure was there—nothing but the furniture which belonged to the room, and yet he could not be deceived as to the fact that something had moved before them into the chamber. A sickening dread came upon him, and the cold perspiration broke out in heavy drops upon his forehead; nor was he more composed, when he heard the increased urgency, the agony of entreaty, with which Rose implored them not to leave her for a moment.

'I saw him,' said she; 'he's here. I cannot be deceived—I know him—he's by me—he is with me—he's in the room; then, for God's sake, as you would save me, do not stir from beside me.'

They at length prevailed upon her to lie down upon the bed, where she continued to urge them to stay by her. She frequently uttered incoherent sentences, repeating, again and again, 'the dead and the living cannot be one*—God has forbidden it'; and then again, 'rest to the wakeful—sleep to the sleep-walkers.' These and such mysterious and broken sentences, she continued to utter until the clergyman arrived. Gerard Douw began to fear, naturally enough, that the poor girl, owing to terror or ill-treatment, had become deranged, and he half suspected, by the suddenness of her appearance, and the unseasonableness of the hour, and, above all, from the wildness and terror of her manner, that she had made her escape from some place of confinement for lunatics, and was in immediate fear of pursuit. He resolved to summon medical advice, as soon as the mind of his niece had been in some measure set at rest by the offices of the clergyman whose attendance she had so earnestly desired; and until this object had been attained, he did not venture to put any questions to her, which might possibly, by reviving painful or horrible recollections, increase her agitation. The clergyman soon arrived—a man of ascetic countenance and venerable age—one whom Gerard Douw respected much, forasmuch as he was a veteran polemic,* though one, perhaps, more dreaded as a combatant than beloved as a Christian—of pure morality, subtle brain, and frozen heart. He entered the chamber which communicated with that in which Rose reclined, and immediately on his arrival, she requested him to pray for her, as for one who lay in the hands of Satan, and who could hope for deliverance—only from heaven.

That our readers may distinctly understand all the circumstances of the event which we are about imperfectly to describe, it is necessary to state the relative position of the parties who were engaged in it. The old clergyman and Schalken were in the ante-room of which we have already spoken; Rose lay in the inner chamber, the door of which was open; and by the side of the bed, at her urgent desire, stood her guardian; a candle burned in the bedchamber, and three were lighted in the outer apartment. The old man now cleared his voice, as if about to commence, but before he had time to begin, a sudden gust of air blew out the candle which served to illuminate the room in which the poor girl lay, and she, with hurried alarm, exclaimed—

'Godfrey, bring in another candle; the darkness is unsafe.'

Gerard Douw, forgetting for the moment her repeated injunctions, in the immediate impulse, stepped from the bedchamber into the other, in order to supply what she desired.

'Oh God! do not go, dear uncle,' shrieked the unhappy girl—and at the same time she sprung from the bed, and darted after him, in order, by her grasp, to detain him. But the warning came too late, for scarcely had he passed the threshold, and hardly had his niece had time to utter the startling exclamation, when the door which divided the two rooms closed violently after him, as if swung to by a strong blast of wind. Schalken and he both rushed to the door, but their united and desperate efforts could not avail so much as to shake it. Shriek after shriek burst from the inner chamber, with all the piercing loudness of despairing terror. Schalken and Douw applied every energy and strained every nerve to force open the door; but all in vain. There was no sound of struggling from within, but the screams seemed to increase in loudness, and at the same time they heard the bolts of the latticed window withdrawn, and the window itself grated upon the sill as if thrown open. One *last* shriek, so long and piercing and agonized as to be scarcely human, swelled from the room, and suddenly there followed a deathlike silence. A light step was heard crossing the floor, as if from the bed to the window; and almost at the same instant the door gave way, and, yielding to the pressure of the external applicants, they were nearly precipitated into the room. It was empty. The window was open, and Schalken sprung to a chair and gazed out upon the street and canal below. He saw no form, but he beheld, or thought he beheld, the waters of the broad canal beneath settling ring after ring in heavy circular ripples, as if a moment before disturbed by the immersion of some large and heavy mass.

No trace of Rose was ever after discovered, nor was any thing certain respecting her mysterious wooer detected or even suspected—no clue whereby to trace the intricacies of the labyrinth and to arrive at a distinct conclusion was to be found. But an incident occurred, which, though it will not be received by our rational leaders as at all approaching to evidence upon the matter, nevertheless produced a strong and a lasting impression upon the mind of Schalken. Many years after the events which we have detailed, Schalken, then remotely situated, received an intimation of his father's death, and of his intended burial upon a fixed day in the church of Rotterdam. It was necessary that a very considerable journey should be performed by the funeral procession, which, as it will readily be believed, was not very numerously attended. Schalken with difficulty arrived in Rotterdam late in the day upon which the funeral was appointed to take place. It had not then arrived. Evening closed in, and still it did not appear.

Schalken strolled down to the church—he found it open—notice of the arrival of the funeral had been given, and the vault in which the body was to be laid had been opened. The officer, who is analogous to our sexton, on seeing a well-dressed gentleman, whose object was to attend the expected funeral, pacing the aisle of the church, hospitably invited him to share with him the comforts of a blazing wood fire, which, as was his custom in winter time upon such occasions, he had kindled in the hearth of a chamber which communicated, by a flight of steps, with the vault below. In this chamber Schalken and his entertainer seated themselves, and the sexton, after some fruitless attempts to engage his guest in conversation, was obliged to apply himself to his tobacco-pipe and can, to solace his solitude. In spite of his grief and cares, the fatigues of a rapid journey of nearly forty hours gradually overcame the mind and body of Godfrey Schalken, and he sank into a deep sleep, from which he was awakened by some one's shaking him gently by the shoulder. He first thought that the old sexton had called him, but *he* was no longer in the room. He roused himself, and as soon as he could clearly see what was around him, he perceived a female form, clothed in a kind of light robe of muslin, part of which was so disposed as to act as a veil, and in her hand she carried a lamp. She was moving rather away from him, and towards the flight of steps which conducted towards the vaults. Schalken felt a vague alarm at the sight of this figure, and at the same time an irresistible impulse to follow its guidance. He followed it towards the vaults, but when it reached the head of the stairs, he paused—the figure paused also, and, turning gently round, displayed, by the light of the lamp it carried, the face and features of his first love, Rose Velderkaust. There was nothing horrible, or even sad, in the countenance. On the contrary, it wore the same arch smile which used to enchant the artist long before in his happy days. A feeling of awe and of interest, too intense to be resisted, prompted him to follow the spectre, if spectre it were. She descended the stairs—he followed—and, turning to the left, through a narrow passage, she led him, to his infinite surprise, into what appeared to be an old-fashioned Dutch apartment, such as the pictures of Gerard Douw have served to immortalize. Abundance of costly antique furniture was disposed about the room, and in one corner stood a four-post bed, with heavy black cloth curtains around it; the figure frequently turned towards him with the same arch smile; and when she came to the side of the bed, she drew the curtains, and, by the light of the lamp, which she held towards its contents, she disclosed to the horror-stricken painter, sitting bolt upright in the bed, the livid and demoniac form of Vanderhausen. Schalken had hardly seen him, when he fell senseless upon the floor, where he lay until discovered, on the next morning, by persons employed in closing the passages into the vaults. He was lying in a cell of considerable size, which had not been disturbed for a long time, and he had fallen beside a large coffin, which was supported upon small stone pillars, a security against the attacks of vermin.

To his dying day Schalken was satisfied of the reality of the vision which he had witnessed, and he has left behind him a curious evidence of the impression which it wrought upon his fancy, in a painting executed shortly after the event we have narrated, and which is valuable as exhibiting not only the peculiarities which have made Schalken's pictures sought after, but even more so as presenting a portrait as close and faithful as one taken from memory can be, of his early love, Rose Velderkaust, whose mysterious fate must ever remain matter of speculation. The picture represents a chamber of antique masonry, such as might be found in most old cathedrals, and is lighted faintly by a lamp carried in the hand of a female figure, such as we have above attempted to describe; and in the background, and to the left of him who examines the painting, there stands the form of a man apparently aroused from sleep, and by his attitude, his hand being laid upon his sword, exhibiting considerable alarm: this last figure is illuminated only by the expiring glare of a wood or charcoal fire. The whole production exhibits a beautiful specimen of that artful and singular distribution of light and shade which has rendered the name of Schalken immortal among the artists of his country. This tale is traditionary, and the reader will easily perceive, by our studiously omitting to heighten many points of the narrative, when a little additional colouring might have added effect to the recital, that we have desired to lay before him, not a figment of the brain, but a curious tradition connected with, and belonging to, the biography of a famous artist.

THE WATCHER

From the Reminiscences of a Bachelor

It is now more than fifty years since the occurrences which I am about to relate caused a strange sensation in the gay society of Dublin. The fashionable world, however, is no recorder of traditions—the memory of selfishness seldom reaches far—and the events which occasionally disturb the polite monotony of its pleasant and heartless progress, however stamped with the characters of misery and horror, scarcely ever outlive the gossip of a season; and, except perhaps in the remembrance of a few more directly interested in the consequences of the catastrophe, are in a little time lost to the recollection of all. The appetite for scandal, or for horror, has been sated—the incident can yield no more of interest or of novelty—curiosity, frustrated by impenetrable mystery, gives over the pursuit in despair—the tale has ceased to be new, grows stale and flat—and so, in a few years, inquiry subsides into indifference, and all is forgotten.

I was a young man at the time, and intimately acquainted with some of the actors in this strange tale; the impression which its incidents made upon me, therefore, were deep and lasting. I shall now endeavour, with fulness and precision, to relate them all, combining, of course, in the narrative, whatever I have learned from various sources, tending, however imperfectly, to illuminate the darkness which involves its progress and termination.

Somewhere about the year 1794, the younger brother of a certain baronet, whom I shall call Sir James Barton, returned to Dublin. He had served in the navy with some distinction, having commanded one of his majesty's frigates during the greater part of the American war.* Captain Barton was now apparently some two or three-and-forty years of age. He was an intelligent and agreeable companion, when he pleased it, though generally reserved, and occasionally even moody. In society, however, he deported himself as a man of the world, and a gentleman. He had not contracted any of the noisy brusqueness sometimes acquired at sea; on the contrary, his manners were remarkably easy, quiet, and even polished. He was in person about the middle size, and somewhat strongly formed—his countenance was marked with the lines of thought, and on the whole wore an expression of gravity and even of melancholy; being however, as we have said, a man of perfect breeding, as well as of affluent circumstances and good family, he had, of course, ready access to the best society of the metropolis, without the necessity of any other credentials. In his personal habits Mr Barton was un-expensive. He occupied lodgings in one of the *then* fashionable streets in the south side of the town*—kept but one horse and one servant—and though a reputed free-thinker,* yet lived an orderly and moral life—indulging neither in gaming, drinking, nor any other vicious pursuit—living very much to himself, without forming any intimacies, or choosing any companions, and appearing to mix in gay society rather for the sake of its bustle and distraction, than for any opportunities which it offered of interchanging either thoughts or feelings with its votaries. Barton was therefore pronounced a saving, prudent, unsocial sort of a fellow, who bid fair to maintain his celibacy alike against stratagem and assault, and was likely to live to a good old age, die rich, and leave his money to an hospital.

It was soon apparent, however, that the nature of Mr Barton's plans had been totally misconceived. A young lady, whom we shall call Miss Montague, was at this time introduced into the gay world of Dublin, by her aunt, the Dowager Lady L——.* Miss Montague was decidedly pretty and accomplished, and having some natural cleverness, and a great deal of gaiety, became for a while a reigning toast.* Her popularity, however, gained her, for a time, nothing more than that unsubstantial admiration which, however pleasant as an incense to vanity, is by no means necessarily antecedent to matrimony—for, unhappily for the young lady in question, it was an understood thing, that beyond her personal attractions, she had no kind of earthly provision. Such being the state of affairs, it will readily be believed that no little surprise was consequent upon the appearance of Captain Barton as the avowed lover of the penniless Miss Montague.

His suit prospered, as might have been expected, and in a short time it was confidentially communicated by old Lady L—— to each of her hundred-and-fifty particular friends in succession, that Captain Barton had actually tendered proposals of marriage, with her approbation, to her niece, Miss Montague, who had, moreover, accepted the offer of his hand, conditionally upon the consent of her father, who was then upon his homeward voyage from India, and expected in two or three months at furthest. About this consent there could be no doubt—the delay, therefore, was one merely of form—they were looked upon as absolutely engaged, and Lady L——, with a rigour of old-fashioned decorum with which her niece would, no doubt, gladly have dispensed, withdrew her thenceforward from all further participation in the gaieties of the town. Captain Barton was a constant visitor, as well as a frequent guest at the house, and was permitted all the privileges of intimacy which a betrothed suitor is usually accorded. Such was the relation of parties, when the mysterious circumstances which darken this narrative with inexplicable melancholy, first begun to unfold themselves.

Lady L—— resided in a handsome mansion at the north side of Dublin,* and Captain Barton's lodgings, as we have already said, were situated at the south. The distance intervening was considerable, and it was Captain Barton's habit generally to walk home without an attendant, as often as he passed the evening with the old lady and her fair charge. His shortest way in such nocturnal walks, lay, for a considerable space, through a line of street which had as yet been merely laid out,* and little more than the foundations of the houses constructed. One night, shortly after his engagement with Miss Montague had commenced, he happened to remain unusually late, in company only with her and Lady L——. The conversation had turned upon the evidences of revelation,* which he had disputed with the callous scepticism of a confirmed infidel. What were called 'French principles',* had in those days found their way a good deal into fashionable society, especially that portion of it which professed allegiance to Whiggism, and neither the old lady nor her charge were so perfectly free from the taint, as to look upon Mr Barton's views as any serious objection to the proposed union. The discussion had degenerated into one upon the supernatural and the marvellous, in which he had pursued precisely the same line of argument and ridicule. In all this, it is but truth to state, Captain Barton was guilty of no affectation—the doctrines upon which he insisted, were, in reality, but too truly the basis of his own fixed belief, if so it might be called; and perhaps not the least strange of the many strange circumstances connected with this narrative, was the fact, that the subject of the fearful influences we are about to describe, was himself, from the deliberate conviction of years, an utter disbeliever in what are usually termed preternatural agencies.

It was considerably past midnight when Mr Barton took his leave, and set out upon his solitary walk homeward. He had now reached the lonely road, with its unfinished dwarf walls tracing the foundations of the projected rows of houses on either side—the moon was shining mistily, and its imperfect light made the road he trod but additionally dreary—that utter silence which has in it something indefinably exciting, reigned there, and made the sound of his steps, which alone broke it, unnaturally loud and distinct. He had proceeded thus some way, when he on a sudden heard other footfalls, pattering at a measured pace, and, as it seemed, about two score steps behind him. The suspicion of being dogged is at all times unpleasant; it is, however, especially so in a spot so desolate and lonely; and this suspicion became so strong in the mind of Captain Barton, that he abruptly turned about to confront his pursuers, but, though there was quite sufficient moonlight to disclose any object upon the road he had traversed, no form of any kind was visible there. The steps he had heard could not have been the reverberation of his own, for he stamped his foot upon the ground, and walked briskly up and down, in the vain attempt to awake an echo; though by no means a fanciful person, therefore he was at last fain to charge the sounds upon his imagination, and treat them as an illusion. Thus satisfying himself, he resumed his walk, and before he had proceeded a dozen paces, the mysterious footfalls were again audible from behind, and this time, as if with the special design of showing that the sounds were not the responses of an echo—the steps sometimes slackened nearly to a halt, and sometimes hurried for six or eight strides to a run, and again abated to a walk. Captain Barton, as before, turned suddenly round, and with the same result—no object was visible above the deserted level of the road. He walked back over the same ground, determined that, whatever might have been the cause of the sounds which had so disconcerted him, it should not escape his search—the endeavour, however, was unrewarded. In spite of all his scepticism, he felt something like a superstitious fear stealing fast upon him, and with these unwonted and uncomfortable sensations, he once more turned and pursued his way. There was no repetition of these haunting sounds, until he had reached the point where he had last stopped to retrace his steps—here they were resumed—and with sudden starts of running, which threatened to bring the unseen pursuer close up to the alarmed pedestrian. Captain Barton arrested his course as formerly—the unaccountable nature of the occurrence filled him with vague and horrible sensations—and yielding to the excitement he felt gaining upon him, he shouted sternly, 'Who goes there?' The sound of one's own voice, thus exerted, in utter solitude, and followed by total silence, has in it something unpleasantly exciting, and he felt a degree of nervousness which, perhaps, from no cause had he ever known before. To the very end of this solitary street the steps pursued him—and it required a strong effort of stubborn pride on his part, to resist the impulse that prompted him every moment to run for safety at the top of his speed. It was not until he had reached his lodging, and sate by his own fire-side, that he felt sufficiently reassured to rearrange and reconsider in his own mind the occurrences which had so discomposed him. So little a matter, after all, is sufficient to upset the pride of scepticism and vindicate the old simple laws of nature within us.

Mr Barton was next morning sitting at a late breakfast, reflecting upon the incidents of the previous night, with more of inquisitiveness than awe, so speedily do gloomy impressions upon the fancy disappear under the cheerful influences of day, when a letter just delivered by the postman* was placed upon the table before him. There was nothing remarkable in the address of this missive, except that it was written in a hand which he did not know—perhaps it was disguised—for the tall narrow characters were sloped backward; and with the self-inflicted suspense which we so often see practised in such cases, he puzzled over the inscription for a full minute before he broke the seal. When he did so, he read the following words, written in the same hand:—

Mr Barton, late captain of the 'Dolphin', is warned of DANGER. He will do wisely to avoid —— street—[here the locality of his last night's adventure was named]—if he walks there as usual he will meet with something bad—let him take warning, once for all, for he has good reason to dread

'THE WATCHER.'

Captain Barton read and re-read this strange effusion; in every light and in every direction he turned it over and over; he examined the paper on which it was written, and scrutinized the hand-writing even more. Defeated here, he turned to the seal; it was nothing but a patch of wax, upon which the accidental impression of a coarse thumb was imperfectly visible. There was not the slightest mark, no clue or indication of any kind, to lead him to even a guess as to its possible origin. The writer's object seemed a friendly one, and yet he subscribed himself as one whom he had 'good reason to dread.' Altogether the letter, its author, and its real purpose, were to him an inexplicable puzzle, and one, moreover, unpleasantly suggestive, in his mind, of associations connected with his last night's adventure.

In obedience to some feeling—perhaps of pride—Mr Barton did not communicate, even to his intended bride, the occurrences which we have just detailed. Trifling as they might appear, they had in reality most disagreeably affected his imagination, and he cared not to disclose, even to the young lady in question, what she might possibly look upon as evidences of weakness. The letter might very well be but a hoax, and the mysterious footfall but a delusion of his fancy. But although he affected to treat the whole affair as unworthy of a thought, it yet haunted him pertinaciously, tormenting him with perplexing doubts, and depressing him with undefined apprehensions. Certain it is, that for a considerable time afterwards he carefully avoided the street indicated in the letter as the scene of danger.

It was not until about a week after the receipt of the letter which I have transcribed, that anything further occurred to remind Captain Barton of its contents, or to counteract the gradual disappearance from his mind of the disagreeable impressions which he had then received. He was returning one night, after the interval I have stated, from the theatre, which was then situated in Crow-street,* and having there handed Miss Montague and Lady L—— into their carriage, he loitered for some time with two or three acquaintances. With these, however, he parted close to the college,* and pursued his way alone. It was now fully one o'clock, and the streets quite deserted. During the whole of his walk with the companions from whom he had just parted, he had been at times painfully aware of the sound of steps, as it seemed, dogging them on their way. Once or twice he had looked back, in the uneasy anticipation that he was again about to experience the same mysterious annoyances which had so much disconcerted him a week before, and earnestly hoping that he might *see* some form from whom the sounds might naturally proceed. But the street was deserted—no form was visible. Proceeding now quite alone upon his homeward way, he grew really nervous and uncomfortable, as he became sensible, with increased distinctness, of the well-known and now absolutely dreaded sounds.

By the side of the dead wall* which bounded the college park, the sounds followed, re-commencing almost simultaneously with his own steps. The same unequal pace—sometimes slow, sometimes for a score yards or so, quickened to a run—was audible from behind him. Again and again he turned; quickly and stealthily he glanced over his shoulder—almost at every half-dozen steps; but no one was visible. The horrors of this intangible and unseen persecution became gradually all but intolerable; and when at last he reached his home, his nerves were strung to such a pitch of excitement that he could not rest, and did not attempt even to lie down until after the day-light had broken.

He was awakened by a knock at his chamber-door, and his servant entering, handed him several letters which had just been received by the penny post. One among them instantly arrested his attention—a single glance at the direction aroused him thoroughly. He at once recognized its character, and read as follows:—

You may as well think, Captain Barton, to escape from your own shadow as from me; do what you may, I will see you as often as I please, and you shall see me, for I do not want to hide myself, as you fancy. Do not let it trouble

your rest, Captain Barton; for, with a *good conscience*, what need you fear
from the eye of

'THE WATCHER.'

It is scarcely necessary to dwell upon the feelings elicited by
a perusal of this strange communication. Captain Barton was observed
to be unusually absent and out of spirits for several days afterwards;
but no one divined the cause. Whatever he might think as to the
phantom steps which followed him, there could be no possible illusion about the letters he had received; and, to say the least of it, their
immediate sequence upon the mysterious sounds which had haunted
him, was an odd coincidence. The whole circumstance was, in his own
mind, vaguely and instinctively connected with certain passages in
his past life, which, of all others, he hated to remember. It happened,
however, that in addition to his own approaching nuptials, Captain
Barton had just then—fortunately, perhaps, for himself—some business of an engrossing kind connected with the adjustment of a large
and long-litigated claim upon certain properties. The hurry and
excitement of business had its natural effect in gradually dispelling
the marked gloom which had for a time occasionally oppressed
him, and in a little while his spirits had entirely resumed their accustomed tone.

During all this time, however, he was occasionally dismayed by
indistinct and half-heard repetitions of the same annoyance, and that
in lonely places, in the day-time as well as after nightfall. These
renewals of the strange impressions from which he had suffered so
much, were, however, desultory and faint, insomuch that often he
really could not, to his own satisfaction, distinguish between them
and the mere suggestions of an excited imagination. One evening he
walked down to the House of Commons* with a member,* an
acquaintance of his and mine. This was one of the few occasions upon
which I have been in company with Captain Barton. As we walked
down together, I observed that he became absent and silent, and to
a degree so marked as scarcely to consist with good breeding, and
which, in one who was obviously, in all his habits, perfectly a gentleman, seemed to argue the pressure of some urgent and absorbing
anxiety. I afterwards learned that, during the whole of our walk, he
had heard the well-known footsteps dogging him as we proceeded.
This, however, was the last time he suffered from this phase of the
persecution, of which he was already the anxious victim. A new and
a very different one was about to be presented.

Of the new series of impressions which were afterwards gradually to
work out his destiny, I that evening witnessed the first; and but for its
relation to the train of events which followed, the incident would scarcely
have been now remembered by me. As we were walking in at the passage,*
a man, of whom I remember only that he was short in stature, looked like
a foreigner, and wore a kind of travelling-cap, walked very rapidly, and as
if under some fierce excitement, directly toward us, muttering to himself,
fast and vehemently the while. This odd-looking person walked straight
toward Barton, who was fore-most of the three, and halted, regarding
him for a moment or two with a look of menace and fury almost maniacal;
and then turning about as abruptly, he walked before us at the same agitated pace, and disappeared at a side passage. I do distinctly remember
being a good deal shocked at the countenance and bearing of this man,
which indeed irresistibly impressed me with an undefined sense of danger, such as I have never felt before or since from the presence of anything human; but these sensations were, on my part, far from amounting
to anything so disconcerting as to flurry or excite me—I had seen only
a singularly evil countenance, agitated, as it seemed, with the excitement
of madness. I was absolutely astonished, however, at the effect of this
apparition upon Captain Barton. I knew him to be a man of proud courage and coolness in real danger—a circumstance which made his conduct upon this occasion the more conspicuously odd. He recoiled a step
or two as the stranger advanced, and clutched my arm in silence, with
what seemed to me to be a spasm of agony or terror; and then, as the
figure disappeared, shoving me roughly back, he followed it for a few
paces, stopped in great disorder, and sat down upon a form.* I never
beheld a countenance more ghastly and haggard.

'For God's sake, Barton, what is the matter?' said ——, our companion, really alarmed at his appearance. 'You're not hurt, are you?—or
unwell? What is it?'

'What did he say?—I did not hear it—what was it?' asked Barton,
wholly disregarding the question.

'Tut, tut—nonsense,' said ——, greatly surprised; 'who cares what
the fellow said. You are unwell, Barton—decidedly unwell; let me call
a coach.'

'Unwell! Yes—no—not exactly unwell,' he said, evidently making
an effort to recover his self-possession; 'but, to say the truth, I am
fatigued—a little over-worked—and perhaps over anxious. You know
I have been in chancery,* and the winding up of a suit is always a nervous affair. I have felt uncomfortable all this evening; but I am better
now. Come, come—shall we go on?'

'No, no. Take my advice, Barton, and go home; you really do need rest; you are looking absolutely ill. I really do insist on your allowing me to see you home,' replied his friend.

I seconded ——'s advice, the more readily as it was obvious that Barton was not himself disinclined to be persuaded. He left us, politely declining our offered escort. I was not sufficiently intimate with —— to discuss the scene which we had both just witnessed, and in which his friend had appeared in so strange a light. I was, however, convinced, from his manner in the few common-place comments and regrets which we exchanged, that he was just as little satisfied as I with the extempore plea of illness with which he had accounted for the strange exhibition, and that we were both agreed in suspecting some lurking mystery in the matter.

I called next day at Barton's lodgings, to inquire for him, and learned from the servant that he had not left his room since his return the night before; but that he was not seriously indisposed, and hoped to be out again in a few days. That evening he sent for Doctor R——* then in large and fashionable practice in Dublin, and their interview was, it is said, an odd one.

He entered into a detail of his own symptoms in an abstracted and desultory kind of way, which seemed to argue a strange want of interest in his own cure, and, at all events, made it manifest that there was some topic engaging his mind of more engrossing importance than his present ailment. He complained of occasional palpitations, and head-ache. Doctor R—— asked him, among other questions, whether there was any irritating circumstance or anxiety then occupying his thoughts. This he denied quickly and almost peevishly; and the physician thereupon declared it his opinion, that there was nothing amiss except some slight derangement of the digestion, for which he accordingly wrote a prescription, and was about to withdraw, when Mr Barton, with the air of a man who suddenly recollects a topic which had nearly escaped him, recalled him.

'I beg your pardon, doctor, but I had really almost forgot; will you permit me to ask you two or three medical questions—rather odd ones, perhaps, but as a wager depends upon their solution, you will, I hope, excuse my unreasonableness.'

The physician readily undertook to satisfy the inquirer.

Barton seemed to have some difficulty about opening the proposed interrogatories, for he was silent for a minute, then walked to his book case, and returned as he had gone; at last he sat down, and said—

'You'll think them very childish questions, but I can't recover my wager without a decision; so I must put them. I want to know first about lock-jaw.* If a man actually has had that complaint, and appears to have died of it—so much so, that a physician of average skill pronounces him actually dead—may he, after all, recover?'

The physician smiled, and shook his head.

'But—but a blunder may be made,' resumed Barton. 'Suppose an ignorant pretender to medical skill; may *he* be so deceived by any stage of the complaint, as to mistake what is only a part of the progress of the disease, for death itself?'

'No one who had ever seen death,' answered he, 'could mistake it in a case of lock-jaw.'

Barton mused for a few minutes. 'I am going to ask you a question, perhaps, still more childish; but first, tell me, are not the regulations of foreign hospitals,* such as that of, let us say, ——, very lax and bungling. May not all kinds of blunders and slips occur in their entries of names, and so forth?'

Doctor R—— professed his incompetence to answer that query.

'Well, then, doctor, here is the last of my questions. You will, probably, laugh at it; but it must out, nevertheless. Is there any disease, in all the range of human maladies, which would have the effect of perceptibly contracting the stature, and the whole frame—causing the man to shrink in all his proportions, and yet to preserve his exact resemblance to himself in every particular—with the one exception, his height and bulk; *any* disease, mark—no matter how rare—how little believed in, generally—which could possibly result in producing such an effect?'

The physician replied with a smile, and a very decided negative.

'Tell me, then,' said Barton, abruptly, 'if a man be in reasonable fear of assault from a lunatic who is at large, can he not procure a warrant for his arrest and detention?'

'Really, that is more a lawyer's question than one in my way,' replied Doctor R——; 'but I believe, on applying to a magistrate, such a course would be directed.'

The physician then took his leave; but, just as he reached the hall-door, remembered that he had left his cane up stairs, and returned. His reappearance was awkward, for a piece of paper, which he recognized as his own prescription, was slowly burning upon the fire, and Barton sitting close by with an expression of settled gloom and dismay. Doctor R—— had too much tact to appear to observe what presented itself; but he had seen quite enough to assure him that the mind, and not the body, of Captain Barton was in reality the seat of suffering.

A few days afterwards, the following advertisement appeared in the Dublin newspapers:—

If Sylvester Yelland, formerly a foremast-man* on board his Majesty's frigate Dolphin, or his nearest of kin, will apply to Mr Robert Smith, solicitor, at his office, Dame-street, he or they may hear of something greatly to his or their advantage. Admission may be had at any hour up to twelve o'clock at night, for the next fortnight, should parties desire to avoid observation; and the strictest secrecy, as to all communications intended to be confidential, shall be honourably observed.

The Dolphin, as I have mentioned, was the vessel which Captain Barton had commanded; and this circumstance, connected with the extraordinary exertions made by the circulation of hand-bills, etc., as well as by repeated advertisements, to secure for this strange notice the utmost possible publicity, suggested to Doctor R—— the idea that Captain Barton's extreme uneasiness was somehow connected with the individual to whom the advertisement was addressed, and he himself the author of it. This, however, it is needless to add, was no more than a conjecture. No information whatsoever, as to the real purpose of the advertisement itself, was divulged by the agent, nor yet any hint as to who his employer might be.

Mr Barton, although he had latterly begun to earn for himself the character of a hypochondriac, was yet very far from deserving it. Though by no means lively, he had yet, naturally, what are termed 'even spirits', and was not subject to undue depressions. He soon, therefore, began to return to his former habits; and one of the earliest symptoms of this healthier tone of spirits was, his appearing at a grand dinner of the Freemasons,* of which worthy fraternity he was himself a brother. Barton, who had been at first gloomy and abstracted, drank much more freely than was his wont—possibly with the purpose of dispelling his own secret anxieties—and under the influence of good wine, and pleasant company, became gradually (unlike his usual *self*) talkative, and even noisy. It was under this unwonted excitement that he left his company at about half-past ten o'clock; and, as conviviality is a strong incentive to gallantry, it occurred to him to proceed forthwith to Lady L——'s, and pass the remainder of the evening with her and his destined bride.

Accordingly, he was soon at —— street, and chatting gaily with the ladies. It is not to be supposed that Capt. Barton had exceeded the limits which propriety prescribes to good fellowship—he had merely taken enough wine to raise his spirits, without, however, in the least degree unsteadying his mind, or affecting his manners. With this undue elevation of spirits had supervened an entire oblivion or contempt of those undefined apprehensions which had for so long weighed upon his mind, and to a certain extent estranged him from society; but as the night wore away, and his artificial gaiety began to flag, these painful feelings gradually intruded themselves again, and he grew abstracted and anxious as heretofore. He took his leave at length, with an unpleasant foreboding of some coming mischief, and with a mind haunted with a thousand mysterious apprehensions, such as, even while he acutely felt their pressure, he, nevertheless, inwardly strove, or affected to contemn.

It was this proud defiance of what he considered as his own weakness, which prompted him upon the present occasion to that course which brought about the adventure which we are now about to relate. Mr Barton might have easily called a coach, but he was conscious that his strong inclination to do so proceeded from no cause other than what he desperately persisted in representing to himself to be his own superstitious tremors. He might also have returned home by a *route* different from that against which he had been warned by his mysterious correspondent; but for the same reason he dismissed this idea also, and with a dogged and half desperate resolution to force matters to a crisis of some kind, if there were any reality in the causes of his former suffering, and if not, satisfactorily to bring their delusiveness to the proof, he determined to follow precisely the course which he had trodden upon the night so painfully memorable in his own mind as that on which his strange persecution had commenced. Though, sooth to say, the pilot who for the first time steers his vessel under the muzzles of a hostile battery, never felt his resolution more severely tasked than did Captain Barton as he breathlessly pursued this solitary path—a path which, spite of every effort of scepticism and reason, he felt to be infested by some (as respected *him*) malignant influence.

He pursued his way steadily and rapidly, scarcely breathing from intensity of suspense; he, however, was troubled by no renewal of the dreaded footsteps, and was beginning to feel a return of confidence, as more than three-fourths of the way being accomplished with impunity, he approached the long line of twinkling oil lamps* which indicated the frequented streets. This feeling of self-gratulation was, however, but momentary. The report of a musket at some two hundred yards behind him, and the whistle of a bullet close to his head, disagreeably and startlingly dispelled it. His first impulse was to retrace his steps in pursuit of the assassin; but the road on either side was, as we have said, embarrassed by the foundations of a street, beyond which extended waste fields, full of rubbish and neglected lime and brick kilns, and all now as utterly silent as though no sound had ever disturbed their dark and unsightly solitude. The futility of, single-handed, attempting, under such circumstances, a search for the murderer, was apparent, especially as no sound, either of retreating steps or otherwise, was audible to direct his pursuit.

With the tumultuous sensations of one whose life has just been exposed to a murderous attempt, and whose escape has been the narrowest possible, Captain Barton turned, and without, however, quickening his pace actually to a run, hurriedly pursued his way. He had turned, as we have said, after a pause of a few seconds, and had just commenced his rapid retreat, when on a sudden he met the well-remembered little man in the fur cap. The encounter was but momentary. The figure was walking at the same exaggerated pace, and with the same strange air of menace as before; and as it passed him, he thought he heard it say, in a furious whisper, 'Still alive—still alive!'

The state of Mr Barton's spirits began now to work a corresponding alteration in his health and looks, and to such a degree that it was impossible that the change should escape general remark. For some reasons, known but to himself, he took no step whatsoever to bring the attempt upon his life, which he had so narrowly escaped, under the notice of the authorities; on the contrary, he kept it jealously to himself; and it was not for many weeks after the occurrence that he mentioned it, and then in strict confidence, to a gentleman, whom the torments of his mind at last compelled him to consult.

Spite of his blue devils, however, poor Barton, having no satisfactory reason to render to the public for any undue remissness in the attentions which the relation subsisting between him and Miss Montague required, was obliged to exert himself, and present to the world a confident and cheerful bearing. The true source of his sufferings, and every circumstance connected with them, he guarded with a reserve so jealous, that it seemed dictated by at least a suspicion that the origin of his strange persecution was known to himself, and that it was of a nature which, upon his own account, he could not or dared not disclose.

The mind thus turned in upon itself, and constantly occupied with a haunting anxiety which it dared not reveal or confide to any human breast, became daily more excited, and, of course, more vividly impressible, by a system of attack which operated through the nervous system; and in this state he was destined to sustain, with increasing frequency, the stealthy visitations of that apparition which from the first had seemed to possess so unearthly and terrible a hold upon his imagination.

It was about this time that Captain Barton called upon the then celebrated preacher, Dr ——,* with whom he had a slight acquaintance, and an extraordinary conversation ensued. The divine was seated in his chambers in college, surrounded with works upon his favourite pursuit, and deep in theology, when Barton was announced. There was something at once embarrassed and excited in his manner, which, along with his wan and haggard countenance, impressed the student with the unpleasant consciousness that his visitor must have recently suffered terribly indeed, to account for an alteration so striking—almost shocking.

After the usual interchange of polite greeting, and a few common-place remarks, Captain Barton, who obviously perceived the surprise which his visit had excited, and which Doctor —— was unable wholly to conceal, interrupted a brief pause by remarking—

'This is a strange call, Doctor ——, perhaps scarcely warranted by an acquaintance so slight as mine with you. I should not under ordinary circumstances have ventured to disturb you; but my visit is neither an idle nor impertinent intrusion. I am sure you will not so account it, when——'

Doctor —— interrupted him with assurances such as good breeding suggested, and Barton resumed—

'I am come to task your patience by asking your advice. When I say your patience, I might, indeed, say more; I might have said your humanity—your compassion; for I have been and am a great sufferer.'

'My dear sir, replied the churchman, 'it will, indeed, afford me infinite gratification if I can give you comfort in any distress of mind; but—but—'

'I know what you would say,' resumed Barton, quickly; 'I am an unbeliever, and, therefore, incapable of deriving help from religion; but don't take that for granted. At least you must not assume that, however unsettled my convictions may be, I do not feel a deep—a very deep—interest in the subject. Circumstances have lately forced it upon my attention, in such a way as to compel me to review the whole question in a more candid and teachable spirit, I believe, than I ever studied it in before.'

'Your difficulties, I take it for granted, refer to the evidences of revelation,' suggested the clergyman.

'Why—no—yes; in fact I am ashamed to say I have not considered even my objections sufficiently to state them connectedly; but—but there is one subject on which I feel a peculiar interest.'

He paused again, and Doctor —— pressed him to proceed.

'The fact is,' said Barton, 'whatever may be my uncertainty as to the authenticity of what we are taught to call revelation, of one fact I am deeply and horribly convinced, that there does exist beyond this a spiritual world—a system whose workings are generally in mercy hidden from us—a system which may be, and which is sometimes, partially and terribly revealed. I am sure—I *know*,' continued Barton, with increasing excitement, 'that there is a God—a dreadful God—and that retribution follows guilt. In ways the most mysterious and stupendous—by agencies the most inexplicable and terrific—there is a spiritual system—great God, how frightfully I have been convinced!—a system malignant, and implacable, and omnipotent, under whose persecutions I am, and have been, suffering the torments of the damned!—yes, sir—yes—the fires and frenzy of hell!'

As Barton spoke, his agitation became so vehement that the divine was shocked, and even alarmed. The wild and excited rapidity with which he spoke, and, above all, the indefinable horror which stamped his features, afforded a contrast to his ordinary cool and unimpassioned self-possession striking and painful in the last degree.

'My dear sir,' said Doctor ——, after a brief pause, 'I fear you have been suffering much, indeed; but I venture to predict that the depression under which you labour will be found to originate in purely physical causes, and that with a change of air, and the aid of a few tonics, your spirits will return, and the tone of your mind be once more cheerful and tranquil as heretofore. There was, after all, more truth than we are quite willing to admit in the classic theories which assigned the undue predominance of any one affection of the mind, to the undue action or torpidity of one or other of our bodily organs. Believe me, that a little attention to diet, exercise, and the other essentials of health, under competent direction, will make you as much yourself as you can wish.'

'Doctor ——,' said Barton, with something like a shudder, 'I *cannot* delude myself with such a hope. I have no hope to cling to but one, and that is, that by some other spiritual agency more potent than that which tortures me, *it* may be combated, and I delivered. If this may not be, I am lost—now and for ever lost.'

'But, Mr Barton, you must remember,' urged his companion, 'that others have suffered as you have done, and——'

'No, no, no,' interrupted he, with irritability—'no, sir, I am not a credulous—far from a superstitious man. I have been, perhaps, too much the reverse—too sceptical, too slow of belief; but unless I were one whom no amount of evidence could convince, unless I were to contemn the repeated, the *perpetual* evidence of my own senses, I am now—now at last constrained to believe—I have no escape from the conviction—the overwhelming certainty—that I am haunted and dogged, go where I may, by—by a DEMON!'

There was an almost preternatural energy of horror in Barton's face, as, with its damp and deathlike lineaments turned towards his companion, he thus delivered himself.

'God help you, my poor friend,' said Doctor ——, much shocked— 'God help you; for, indeed, you *are* a sufferer, however your sufferings may have been caused.'

'Ay, ay, God help me,' echoed Barton, sternly; 'but *will* he help me—will he help me.'

'Pray to him—pray in an humble and trusting spirit,' said he.

'Pray, pray,' echoed he again; 'I can't pray—I could as easily move a mountain by an effort of my will. I have not belief enough to pray; there is something within me that will not pray. You prescribe impossibilities—literal impossibilities.'

'You will not find it so, if you will but try,' said Doctor ——.

'Try!—I *have* tried, and the attempt only fills me with confusion and terror; I have tried in vain, and more than in vain. The awful, unutterable idea of eternity and infinity oppresses and maddens my brain whenever my mind approaches the contemplation of the Creator; I recoil from the effort scared, confounded, terrified. I tell you, Doctor ——, if I am to be saved, it must be by other means. The idea of the Creator is to me intolerable—my mind cannot support it.'

'Say, then, my dear sir,' urged he—'say how you would have me serve you—what you would learn of me—what I can do or say to relieve you?'

'Listen to me first,' replied Captain Barton, with a subdued air, and an evident effort to suppress his excitement—'listen to me while I detail the circumstances of the terrible persecution under which my life has become all but intolerable—a persecution which has made me fear *death* and the world beyond the grave as much as I have grown to hate existence.'

Barton then proceeded to relate the circumstances which we have already detailed, and then continued—

'This has now become habitual—an accustomed thing. I do not mean the actual seeing him in the flesh—thank God, *that* at least is not permitted daily. Thank God, from the unutterable horrors of that visitation I have been mercifully allowed intervals of repose, though none of security; but from the consciousness that a malignant spirit is following and watching me wherever I go, I have never, for a single instant, a temporary respite. I am pursued with blasphemies, cries of despair and appalling hatred. I hear those dreadful sounds called after me as I turn the corners of streets; they come in the night-time, while I sit in my chamber alone; they haunt me everywhere, charging me with hideous crimes, and—great God!—threatening me with coming vengeance and eternal misery. Hush!—do you hear *that*!' he cried with a horrible smile of triumph; 'there—there, will that convince you?'

The clergyman felt the chillness of horror irresistibly steal over him, while, during the wail of a sudden gust of wind, he heard, or fancied he heard, the half articulate sounds of rage and derision mingling in the sough.

'Well, what do you think of *that*?' at length Barton cried, drawing a long breath through his teeth.

'I heard the wind,' said Doctor ———. 'What should I think of it—what is there remarkable about it?'

'The prince of the powers of the air,'* muttered Barton, with a shudder.

'Tut, tut! my dear sir,' said the student, with an effort to reassure himself; for though it was broad daylight, there was nevertheless something disagreeably contagious in the nervous excitement under which his visitor so obviously suffered. 'You must not give way to those wild fancies; you must resist these impulses of the imagination.'

'Ay, ay; "resist the devil and he will flee from thee",'* said Barton, in the same tone; 'but *how* resist him? ay, there it is—there is the rub. What—*what* am I to do? what *can* I do?'

'My dear sir, this is fancy,' said the man of folios; 'you are your own tormentor.'

'No, no, sir—fancy has no part in it,' answered Barton, somewhat sternly. 'Fancy, forsooth! Was it that made *you*, as well as me, hear, but this moment, those appalling accents of hell? Fancy, indeed! No, no.'

'But you have seen this person frequently,' said the ecclesiastic;— 'why have you not accosted or secured him? Is it not somewhat precipitate, to say no more, to assume, as you have done, the existence of preternatural agency, when, after all, everything may be easily accountable, if only proper means were taken to sift the matter.'

'There are circumstances connected with this—this *appearance*,' said Barton, 'which it were needless to disclose, but which to *me* are proof of its horrible and unearthly nature. I know that the being who haunts me is not *man*—I say I *know* this; I could prove it to your own conviction.' He paused for a minute, and then added, 'And as to accosting it, I dare not, I could not; when I see it I am powerless; I stand in the gaze of death, in the triumphant presence of preter-human power and malignity. My strength, and faculties, and memory all forsake me. O God, I fear, sir, you know not what you speak of. Mercy, mercy; heaven have pity on me!'

He leaned his elbow on the table, and passed his hand across his eyes, as if to exclude some image of horror, muttering the last words of the sentence he had just concluded, again and again.

'Doctor ——, he said, abruptly raising himself, and looking full upon the clergyman with an imploring eye, 'I know you will do for me whatever may be done. You know now fully the circumstances and the nature of the mysterious agency of which I am the victim. I tell you I cannot help myself; I cannot hope to escape; I am utterly passive. I conjure you, then, to weigh my case well, and if anything may be done for me by vicarious supplication—by the intercession of the good—or by any aid or influence whatsoever, I implore of you, I adjure you in the name of the Most High, give me the benefit of that influence—deliver me from the body of this death. Strive for me, pity me; I know you will; you cannot refuse this; it is the purpose and object of my visit. Send me away with some hope, however little, some faint hope of ultimate deliverance, and I will nerve myself to endure, from hour to hour, the hideous dream into which my existence has been transformed.'

Doctor —— assured him that all he could do was to pray earnestly for him, and that so much he would not fail to do. They parted with a hurried and melancholy valediction. Barton hastened to the carriage, which awaited him at the door, drew the blinds, and drove away, while Doctor —— returned to his chamber, to ruminate at leisure upon the strange interview which had just interrupted his studies.

It was not to be expected that Captain Barton's changed and eccentric habits should long escape remark and discussion. Various were the theories suggested to account for it. Some attributed the alteration to the pressure of secret pecuniary embarrassments; others to a repugnance to fulfil an engagement into which he was presumed to have too precipitately entered; and others, again, to the supposed incipiency of mental disease, which latter, indeed, was the most plausible, as well as the most generally received, of the hypotheses circulated in the gossip of the day.

From the very commencement of this change, at first so gradual in its advances, Miss Montague had of course been aware of it. The intimacy involved in their peculiar relation, as well as the near interest which it inspired, afforded, in her case, a like opportunity and motive for the successful exercise of that keen and penetrating observation peculiar to the sex. His visits became, at length, so interrupted, and his manner, while they lasted, so abstracted, strange, and agitated, that Lady L——, after hinting her anxiety and her suspicions more than once, at length distinctly stated her anxiety, and pressed for an explanation. The explanation was given, and although its nature at first relieved the worst solicitudes of the old lady and her niece, yet the circumstances which attended it, and the really dreadful consequences which it obviously indicated, as regarded the spirits, and indeed the reason of the now wretched man, who made the strange declaration, were enough, upon a little reflection, to fill their minds with perturbation and alarm.

General Montague, the young lady's father, at length arrived. He had himself slightly known Barton, some ten or twelve years previously, and being aware of his fortune and connexions, was disposed to regard him as an unexceptionable and indeed a most desirable match for his daughter. He laughed at the story of Barton's supernatural visitations, and lost not a moment in calling upon his intended son-in-law.

'My dear Barton,' he continued, gaily, after a little conversation, 'my sister tells me that you are a victim to blue devils, in quite a new and original shape.'

Barton changed countenance, and sighed profoundly.

'Come, come; I protest this will never do,' continued the general; 'you are more like a man on his way to the gallows than to the altar. These devils have made quite a saint of you.'

Barton made an effort to change the conversation.

'No, no, it won't do,' said his visitor, laughing; 'I am resolved to say out what I have to say upon this magnificent mock mystery of yours. Come, you must not be angry, but really it is too bad to see you, at your time of life, absolutely frightened into good behaviour, like a naughty child, by a bugaboo, and as far as I can learn, a very particularly contemptible one. Seriously, though, my dear Barton, I have been a good deal annoyed at what they tell me; but, at the same time, thoroughly convinced that there is nothing in the matter that may not be cleared up, with just a little attention and management, within a week at furthest.'

'Ah, general, you do not know——' he began.

'Yes, but I do know quite enough to warrant my confidence,' interrupted the soldier; 'don't I know that all your annoyance proceeds from the occasional appearance of a certain little man in a cap and great-coat, with a red vest and a bad face, who follows you about, and pops upon you at the corners of lanes, and throws you into ague* fits. Now, my dear fellow, I'll make it my business to *catch* this mischievous little mountebank, and either beat him into a jelly with my own hands, or have him whipped through the town, at the cart's-tail,* before a month passes.'

'If *you* knew what *I* know,' said Barton, with gloomy agitation, 'you would speak very differently. Don't imagine that I am so weak and foolish as to assume, without proof the most overwhelming, the conclusion to which I have been forced—the proofs are here, locked up here.'

As he spoke he tapped upon his breast, and with an anxious sigh continued to walk up and down the room.

'Well, well, Barton,' said his visitor, 'I'll wager a rump and dozen* I collar the ghost, and convince yourself before many days are over.'

He was running on in the same strain when he was suddenly arrested, and not a little shocked, by observing Barton, who had approached the window, stagger slowly back, like one who had received a stunning blow; his arm extended toward the street—his face and his very lips white as ashes—while he muttered, 'There—there—there!'

General Montague started mechanically to his feet, and, from the window of the drawing-room, saw a figure corresponding, as well as his hurry would permit him to discern, with the description of the person, whose appearance so constantly and dreadfully disturbed the repose of his friend. The figure was just turning from the rails of the area upon which it had been leaning, and, without waiting to see more, the old gentleman snatched his cane and hat, and rushed down the stairs and into the street, in the furious hope of securing the person, and punishing the audacity of the mysterious stranger. He looked around him, but, in vain, for any trace of the form he had himself distinctly beheld. He ran breathlessly to the nearest corner, expecting to see from thence the retreating figure, but no such form was visible. Back and forward, from crossing to crossing, he ran, at fault, and it was not until the curious gaze and laughing countenances of the passers-by reminded him of the absurdity of his pursuit, that he checked his hurried pace, lowered his walking-cane from the menacing altitude which he had mechanically given it, adjusted his hat, and walked composedly back again, inwardly vexed and flurried. He found Barton pale and trembling in every joint; they both remained silent, though under emotions very different. At last Barton whispered, 'You saw it?'

'*It!—him*—some one—you mean—to be sure I did,' replied Montague, testily. 'But where is the good or the harm of seeing him? The fellow runs like a lamp-lighter.* I wanted to *catch* him, but he had stolen away before I could reach the hall-door. However, it is no great matter; next time, I dare say, I'll do better; and egad, if I once come within reach of him, I'll introduce his shoulders to the weight of my cane, in a way to make him cry *peccavi*.'*

Notwithstanding General Montague's undertakings and exhortations, however, Barton continued to suffer from the self-same unexplained cause; go how, when, or where he would, he was still constantly dogged or confronted by the hateful being who had established over him so dreadful and mysterious an influence; nowhere and at no time was he secure against the odious appearance which haunted him with such diabolic perseverance. His depression, misery, and excitement became more settled and alarming every day, and the mental agonies that ceaselessly preyed upon him, began at last so sensibly to affect his health, that Lady L—— and General Montague succeeded, without, indeed, much difficulty, in persuading him to try a short tour on the Continent, in the hope that an entire change of scene would, at all events, have the effect of breaking through the influences of local association, which the more sceptical of his friends assumed to be by no means inoperative in suggesting and perpetuating what they conceived to be a mere form of nervous illusion. General Montague indeed was persuaded that the figure which haunted his intended son-in-law was by no means the creation of his own imagination, but, on the contrary, a substantial form of flesh and blood, animated by a spiteful and obstinate resolution, perhaps with some murderous object in perspective, to watch and follow the unfortunate gentleman. Even this hypothesis was not a very pleasant one; yet it was plain that if Barton could ever be convinced that there was nothing preternatural in the phenomenon which he had hitherto regarded in that light, the affair would lose all its terrors in his eyes, and wholly cease to exercise upon his health and spirits the baleful influence which it had hitherto done. He therefore reasoned, that if the annoyance were actually escaped by mere locomotion and change of scene, it obviously could not have originated in any supernatural agency.

Yielding to their persuasions, Barton left Dublin for England, accompanied by General Montague. They posted rapidly to London, and thence to Dover, whence they took the packet with a fair wind for Calais.* The general's confidence in the result of the expedition on Barton's spirits had risen day by day, since their departure from the shores of Ireland; for, to the inexpressible relief and delight of the latter, he had not, since then, so much as even once fancied a repetition of those impressions which had, when at home, drawn him gradually down to the very depths of horror and despair. This exemption from what he had begun to regard as the inevitable condition of his existence, and the sense of security which began to pervade his mind, were inexpressibly delightful; and in the exultation of what he considered his deliverance, he indulged in a thousand happy anticipations for a future into which so lately he had hardly dared to look; and in short, both he and his companion secretly congratulated themselves upon the termination of that persecution which had been to its immediate victim a source of such unspeakable agony.

It, was a beautiful day, and a crowd of idlers stood upon the jetty to receive the packet, and enjoy the bustle of the new arrivals. Montague walked a few paces in advance of his friend, and as he made his way through the crowd, a little man touched his arm, and said to him, in a broad provincial *patois**—

'Monsieur is walking too fast; he will lose his sick comrade in the throng, for, by my faith, the poor gentleman seems to be fainting.' Montague turned quickly, and observed that Barton did indeed look deadly pale. He hastened to his side.

'My dear fellow, are you ill?' he asked anxiously.

The question was unheeded and twice repeated, ere Barton stammered—

I saw him—by—, I saw him!'

'*Him!*—the—the wretch—who—where—when did you see him—where is he?' cried Montague, looking around him.'

'I saw him—but he is gone,' repeated Barton, faintly.

'But where—where? For God's sake, speak,' urged Montague, vehemently.

'It is but this moment—*here*,' said he.

'But what did he look like—what had he on—what did he wear—quick, quick,' urged his excited companion, ready to dart among the crowd, and collar the delinquent on the spot.

'He touched your arm—he spoke to you—he pointed to me. God be merciful to me, there is no escape,' said Barton, in the low, subdued tones of intense despair.

Montague had already bustled away in all the flurry of mingled hope and indignation; but though the singular *personnel** of the stranger who had accosted him was vividly and perfectly impressed upon his recollection, he failed to discover among the crowd even the slightest resemblance to him. After a fruitless search, in which he enlisted the services of several of the bystanders, who aided all the more zealously, as they believed he had been robbed, he at length, out of breath and baffled, gave over the attempt.

'Ah, my friend, it won't do,' said Barton, with the faint voice and bewildered, ghastly look of one who has been stunned by some mortal shock; 'there is no use in contending with it; whatever it is, the dreadful association between me and it is now established—I shall never escape—never, never!'

'Nonsense, nonsense, my dear fellow; don't talk so,' said Montague, with something at once of irritation and dismay; 'you must not, I say; we'll jockey* the scoundrel yet; never mind, I say—never mind.'

It was, however, but lost labour to endeavour henceforward to inspire Barton with one ray of hope; he became utterly desponding. This intangible, and, as it seemed, utterly inadequate influence was fast destroying his energies of intellect, character, and health. His first object was now to return to Ireland, there, as he believed, and now almost hoped, speedily to die.

To Ireland accordingly he came, and one of the first faces he saw upon the shore, was again that of his implacable and dreaded persecutor. Barton seemed at last to have lost not only all enjoyment and every hope in existence, but all independence of will besides. He now submitted himself passively to the management of the friends most nearly interested in his welfare. With the apathy of entire despair, he implicitly assented to whatever measures they suggested and advised; and as a last resource, it was determined to remove him to a house of Lady L———'s, in the neighbourhood of Clontarf,* where, with the advice of his medical attendant, who persisted in his opinion that the whole train of consequences resulted merely from some nervous derangement, it was resolved that he was to confine himself strictly to the house, and to make use only of those apartments which commanded a view of an enclosed yard, the gates of which were to be kept jealously locked. Those precautions would certainly secure him against the casual appearance of any living form, which his excited imagination might possibly confound with the spectre which, as it was contended, his fancy recognized in every figure which bore even a distant or general resemblance to the traits with which he had at first invested it. A month or six weeks' absolute seclusion under these conditions, it was hoped might, by interrupting the series of these terrible impressions, gradually dispel the predisposing apprehensions, and effectually break up the associations which had confirmed the supposed disease, and rendered recovery hopeless. Cheerful society and that of his friends was to be constantly supplied, and on the whole, very sanguine expectations were indulged in, to the effect that under the treatment thus detailed, the obstinate hypochondria of the patient might at length give way.

Accompanied, therefore, by Lady L———, General Montague and his daughter—his own affianced bride—poor Barton—himself never daring to cherish a hope of his ultimate emancipation from the strange horrors under which his life was literally wasting away—took possession of the apartments, whose situation protected him against the dreadful intrusions, from which he shrunk with such unutterable terror.

After a little time, a steady persistence in this system began to manifest its results, in a very marked though gradual improvement, alike in the health and spirits of the invalid. Not, indeed, that anything at all approaching to complete recovery was yet discernible. On the contrary, to those who had not seen him since the commencement of his strange sufferings, such an alteration would have been apparent as might well have shocked them. The improvement, however, such as it was, was welcomed with gratitude and delight, especially by the poor young lady, whom her attachment to him, as well as her now singularly painful position, consequent on his mysterious and protracted illness, rendered an object of pity scarcely one degree less to be commiserated than himself.

A week passed—a fortnight—a month—and yet no recurrence of the hated visitation had agitated and terrified him as usual. The treatment had, so far forth, been followed by complete success. The chain of associations* had been broken. The constant pressure upon the overtasked spirits had been removed, and, under these comparatively favourable circumstances, the sense of social community with the world about him, and something of human interest, if not of enjoyment, began to reanimate his mind.

It was about this time that Lady L——, who, like most old ladies of the day, was deep in family receipts, and a great pretender to medical science, being engaged in the concoction of certain unpalatable mixtures, of marvellous virtue, dispatched her own maid to the kitchen garden, with a list of herbs, which were there to be carefully culled, and brought back to her for the purpose stated. The handmaiden, however, returned with her task scarce half completed, and a good deal flurried and alarmed. Her mode of accounting for her precipitate retreat and evident agitation was odd, and, to the old lady, unpleasantly startling.

It appeared that she had repaired to the kitchen garden, pursuant to her mistress's directions, and had there begun to make the specified selection among the rank and neglected herbs which crowded one corner of the enclosure, and while engaged in this pleasant labour, she carelessly sang a fragment of an old song, as she said, 'to keep herself company'. She was, however, interrupted by an ill-natured laugh; and, looking up, she saw through the old thorn hedge, which surrounded the garden, a singularly ill-looking little man, whose countenance wore the stamp of menace and malignity, standing close to her, at the other side of the hawthorn screen. She described herself as utterly unable to move or speak, while he charged her with a message for Captain Barton; the substance of which she distinctly remembered to have been to the effect, that he, Captain Barton, must come abroad as usual, and show himself to his friends, out of doors, or else prepare for a visit in his own chamber. On concluding this brief message, the stranger had, with a threatening air, got down into the outer ditch, and, seizing the hawthorn stems in his hands, seemed on the point of climbing through the fence—a feat which might have been accomplished without much difficulty. Without, of course, awaiting this result, the girl—throwing down her treasures of thyme and rosemary—had turned and ran, with the swiftness of terror, to the house. Lady L—— commanded her, on pain of instant dismissal, to observe an absolute silence respecting all that passed of the incident which related to Captain Barton; and, at the same time, directed instant search to be made by her men, in the garden and the fields adjacent. This measure, however, was attended with the usual unsuccess, and, filled with fearful and undefinable misgivings, Lady L—— communicated the incident to her brother. The story, however, until long afterwards, went no further, and, of course, it was jealously guarded from Barton, who continued to amend, though slowly and imperfectly.

Barton now began to walk occasionally in the court-yard which we have mentioned, and which being surrounded by a high wall, commanded no view beyond its own extent. Here he, therefore, considered himself perfectly secure; and, but for a careless violation of orders by one of the grooms, he might have enjoyed, at least for some time longer, his much prized immunity. Opening upon the public road, this yard was entered by a wooden gate, with a wicket in it, and which was further defended by an iron gate upon the outside. Strict orders had been given to keep them carefully locked; but, spite of these, it had happened that one day, as Barton was slowly pacing this narrow enclosure, in his accustomed walk, and reaching the further extremity, was turning to retrace his steps, he saw the boarded wicket ajar, and the face of his tormentor immovably looking at him through the iron bars. For a few seconds he stood riveted to the earth—breathless and bloodless—in the fascination of that dreaded gaze, and then fell helplessly and insensibly upon the pavement.

There he was found a few minutes afterwards, and conveyed to his room—the apartment which he was never afterwards to leave alive. Henceforward a marked and unaccountable change was observable in the tone of his mind. Captain Barton was now no longer the excited and despairing man he had been before; a strange alteration had passed upon him—an unearthly tranquillity reigned in his mind—it was the anticipated stillness of the grave.

'Montague, my friend, this struggle is nearly ended now,' he said, tranquilly, but with a look of fixed and fearful awe. 'I have, at last, some comfort from that world of spirits, from which my punishment has come. I now know that my sufferings will soon be over.'

Montague pressed him to speak on.

'Yes,' said he, in a softened voice, 'my punishment is nearly ended. From sorrow, perhaps, I shall never, in time or eternity, escape; but my *agony* is almost over. Comfort has been revealed to me, and what remains of my allotted struggle I will bear with submission—even with hope.'

'I am glad to hear you speak so tranquilly, my dear fellow,' said Montague; 'peace and cheer of mind are all you need to make you what you were.'

'No, no—I never can be that,' said he, mournfully. 'I am no longer fit for life. I am soon to die: I do not shrink from death as I did. I am to see *him* but once again, and then all is ended.'

'He said so, then?' suggested Montague.

'*He?*—No, no: good tidings could scarcely come through him; and these were good and welcome; and they came so solemnly and sweetly—with unutterable love and melancholy, such as I could not—without saying more than is needful, or fitting, of other long-past scenes and persons—fully explain to you.' As Barton said this he shed tears.

'Come, come,' said Montague, mistaking the source of his emotions, 'you must not give way. What is it, after all, but a pack of dreams and nonsense; or, at worst, the practices of a scheming rascal that enjoys his power of playing upon your nerves, and loves to exert it—a sneaking vagabond that owes you a grudge, and pays it off this way, not daring to try a more manly one.'

'A grudge, indeed, he owes me—you say rightly,' said Barton, with a sudden shudder; 'a grudge, as you call it. Oh, my God ! when the justice of heaven permits the Evil one to carry out a scheme of vengeance—when its execution is committed to the lost and terrible victim of sin, who owes his own ruin to the man, the very man, whom he is commissioned to pursue—then, indeed, the torments and terrors of hell are anticipated on earth. But heaven has dealt mercifully with me—hope has opened to me at last; and if death could come without the dreadful sight I am doomed to see, I would gladly close my eyes this moment upon the world. But though death is welcome, I shrink with an agony you cannot understand—a maddening agony, an actual frenzy of terror—from the last encounter with that—that DEMON, who has drawn me thus to the verge of the chasm, and who is himself to plunge me down. I am to see him again—once more—but under circumstances unutterably more terrific than ever.'

As Barton thus spoke, he trembled so violently that Montague was really alarmed at the extremity of his sudden agitation, and hastened to lead him back to the topic which had before seemed to exert so tranquillizing an effect upon his mind.

'It was not a dream,' he said, after a time; 'I was in a different state— I felt differently and strangely; and yet it was all as real, as clear, and vivid, as what I now see and hear—it was a reality.'

'And what *did* you see and hear?' urged his companion.

'When I awakened from the swoon I fell into on seeing *him*,' said Barton, continuing as if he had not heard the question, 'it was slowly, very slowly—I was reclining by the margin of a broad lake, with misty hills all round, and a soft, melancholy, rose-coloured light illuminated it all. It was unusually sad and lonely, and yet more beautiful than any earthly scene. My head was leaning on the lap of a girl, and she was singing a strange and wondrous song, that told, I know not how— whether by words or harmonies—of all my life—all that is past, and all that is still to come; and with the song the old feelings that I thought had perished within me came back, and tears flowed from my eyes— partly for the song and its mysterious beauty, and partly for the unearthly sweetness of her voice; and yet I knew the voice—oh! how well; and I was spellbound as I listened and looked at the strange and solitary scene, without stirring, almost without breathing—and, alas! alas! without turning my eyes toward the face that I knew was near me, so sweetly powerful was the enchantment that held me. And so, slowly and softly, the song and scene grew fainter, and ever fainter, to my senses, till all was dark and still again. And then I wakened to this world, as you saw, comforted, for I knew that I was forgiven much.' Barton wept again long and bitterly.

From this time, as we have said, the prevailing tone of his mind was one of profound and tranquil melancholy. This, however, was not without its interruptions. He was thoroughly impressed with the conviction that he was to experience another and a final visitation, illimitably transcending in horror all he had before experienced. From this anticipated and unknown agony, he often shrunk in such paroxysms of abject terror and distraction, as filled the whole household with dismay and superstitious panic. Even those among them who affected to discredit the supposition of preternatural agency in the matter, were often in their secret souls visited during the darkness and solitude of night with qualms and apprehensions, which they would not have readily confessed; and none of them attempted to dissuade Barton from the resolution on which he now systematically acted, of shutting himself up in his own apartment. The window-blinds of this room were kept jealously down; and his own man was seldom out of his presence, day or night, his bed being placed in the same chamber.

This man was an attached and respectable servant; and his duties, in addition to those ordinarily imposed upon *valets*, but which Barton's independent habits generally dispensed with, were to attend carefully to the simple precautions by means of which his master hoped to exclude the dreaded recurrence of the 'watcher', as the strange letter he had at first received had designated his persecutor. And, in addition to attending to these arrangements, which consisted merely in anticipating the possibility of his master's being, through any unscreened window or open door, exposed to the dreaded influence, the valet was never to suffer him to be for one moment alone—total solitude, even for a minute, had become to him now almost as intolerable as the idea of going abroad into the public ways—it was like some instinctive anticipation of what was coming.

It is needless to say, that under these mysterious and horrible circumstances, no steps were taken toward the fulfilment of that engagement into which he had entered. There was quite disparity enough in point of years, and indeed of habits, between the young lady and Captain Barton, to have precluded anything like very vehement or romantic attachment on her part. Though grieved and anxious, therefore, she was very far from being heart-broken; a circumstance which, for the sentimental purposes of our tale, is much to be deplored. But truth must be told, especially in a narration, whose chief, if not only, pretensions to interest consist in a rigid adherence to facts, or what are so reported to have been.

Miss Montague, however, devoted much of her time to a patient but fruitless attempt to cheer the unhappy invalid. She read for him, and conversed with him; but it was apparent that whatever exertions he made, the endeavour to escape from the one constant and ever present fear that preyed upon him, was utterly and miserably unavailing.

Young ladies are much given to the cultivation of pets; and among those who shared the favour of Miss Montague was a fine old owl, which the gardener, who caught him napping among the ivy of a ruined stable, had dutifully presented to that young lady.

The caprice which regulates such preferences was manifested in the extravagant favour with which this grim and ill-favoured bird was at once distinguished by his mistress; and, trifling as this whimsical circumstance may seem, I am forced to mention it, inasmuch as it is connected, oddly enough, with the concluding scene of the story. Barton, so far from sharing in this liking for the new favourite, regarded it from the first with an antipathy as violent as it was utterly unaccountable. Its very vicinity was unsupportable to him. He seemed to hate and dread it with a vehemence absolutely laughable, and which, to those who have never witnessed the exhibition of antipathies of this kind, would seem all but incredible.

With these few words of preliminary explanation, I shall proceed to state the particulars of the last scene in this strange series of incidents. It was almost two o'clock one winter's night, and Barton was, as usual at that hour, in his bed; the servant we have mentioned occupied a smaller bed in the same room, and a light was burning. The man was on a sudden aroused by his master, who said—

'I can't get it out of my head that that accursed bird has got out somehow, and is lurking in some corner of the room. I have been dreaming of him. Get up, Smith, and look about; search for him. Such hateful dreams!'

The servant rose, and examined the chamber, and while engaged in so doing, he heard the well-known sound, more like a long-drawn gasp than a hiss, with which these birds from their secret haunts affright the quiet of the night. This ghostly indication of its proximity—for the sound proceeded from the passage upon which Barton's chamber-door opened—determined the search of the servant, who, opening the door, proceeded a step or two forward for the purpose of driving the bird away. He had, however, hardly entered the lobby, when the door behind him slowly swung to under the impulse, as it seemed, of some gentle current of air; but as immediately over the door there was a kind of window, intended in the day-time to aid in lighting the passage, and through which at present the rays of the candle were issuing, the valet could see quite enough for his purpose. As he advanced he heard his master—who, lying in a well-curtained bed, had not, as it seemed, per-ceived his exit from the room—call him by name, and direct him to place the candle on the table by his bed. The servant, who was now some way in the long passage, and not liking to raise his voice for the purpose of replying, lest he should startle the sleeping inmates of the house, began to walk hurriedly and softly back again, when, to his amazement, he heard a voice in the interior of the chamber answering calmly, and actually saw, through the window which overtopped the door, that the light was slowly shifting, as if carried across the chamber in answer to his master's call. Palsied by a feeling akin to terror, yet not unmingled with a horrible curiosity, he stood breathless and listening at the threshold, unable to summon resolution to push open the door and enter. Then came a rustling of the curtains, and a sound like that of one who in a low voice hushes a child to rest, in the midst of which he heard Barton say, in a tone of stifled horror—'Oh, God—oh, my God!' and repeat the same exclamation several times. Then ensued a silence, which again was broken by the same strange soothing sound; and at last there burst forth, in one swelling peal, a yell of agony so appalling and hideous, that, under some impulse of ungovernable horror, the man rushed to the door, and with his whole strength strove to force it open. Whether it was that, in his agitation, he had himself but imperfectly turned the handle, or that the door was really secured upon the inside, he failed to effect an entrance; and as he tugged and pushed, yell after yell rang louder and wilder through the chamber, accompanied all the while by the same hushed sounds. Actually freezing with terror, and scarce knowing what he did, the man turned and ran down the passage, wringing his hands in the extremity of horror and irresolution. At the stair-head he was encountered by General Montague, scared and eager, and just as they met the fearful sounds had ceased.

'What is it?—who—where is your master?' said Montague with the incoherence of extreme agitation. 'Has anything—for God's sake, is anything wrong?'

'Lord have mercy on us, it's all over,' said the man, staring wildly toward his master's chamber. 'He's dead, sir—I'm sure he's dead.'

Without waiting for inquiry or explanation, Montague, closely followed by the servant, hurried to the chamber-door, turned the handle, and pushed it open. As the door yielded to his pressure, the ill-omened bird of which the servant had been in search, uttering its spectral warning, started suddenly from the far side of the bed, and flying through the door-way close over their heads, and extinguishing, in his passage, the candle which Montague carried, crashed through the skylight that overlooked the lobby, and sailed away into the darkness of the outer space.

'There it is, God bless us,' whispered the man, after a breathless pause.

'Curse that bird,' muttered the general, startled by the suddenness of the apparition, and unable to conceal his discomposure.

'The candle is moved,' said the man, after another breathless pause; 'see, they put it by the bed.'

'Draw the curtains, fellow, and don't stand gaping there,' whispered Montague, sternly.

The man hesitated.

'Hold this, then,' said Montague, impatiently thrusting the candle-stick into the servant's hand, and himself advancing to the bed-side, he drew the curtains apart. The light of the candle, which was still burning at the bedside, fell upon a figure huddled together, and half upright, at the head of the bed. It seemed as though it had slunk back as far as the solid panelling would allow, and the hands were still clutched in the bed clothes.

'Barton, Barton, Barton!' cried the general, with a strange mixture of awe and vehemence. He took the candle, and held it so that it shone full upon the face. The features were fixed, stern, and white; the jaw was fallen; and the sightless eyes, still open, gazed vacantly forward toward the front of the bed. 'God Almighty, he's dead,' muttered the general, as he looked upon this fearful spectacle. They both continued to gaze upon it in silence for a minute or more. 'And cold, too,' whispered Montague, withdrawing his hand from that of the dead man.

'And see, see—may I never have life, sir,' added the man, after another pause, with a shudder, 'but there was something else on the bed with him. Look there—look there—see that, sir.'

As the man thus spoke, he pointed to a deep indenture, as if caused by a heavy pressure, near the foot of the bed.

Montague was silent.

'Come, sir, come away, for God's sake,' whispered the man, drawing close up to him, and holding fast by his arm, while he glanced fearfully round; 'what good can be done here now—come away, for God's sake!'

At this moment they heard the steps of more than one approaching, and Montague, hastily desiring the servant to arrest their progress, endeavoured to loose the rigid gripe with which the fingers of the dead man were clutched in the bed-clothes, and drew, as well as he was able, the awful figure into a reclining posture; then closing the curtains carefully upon it, he hastened himself to meet those persons that were approaching.

It is needless to follow the personages so slightly connected with this narrative, into the events of their after life; it is enough for us to remark, that no clue to the solution of these mysterious occurrences was ever after discovered; and so long an interval having now passed since the event which we have just described concluded this strange history, it is scarcely to be expected that time can throw any new lights upon its dark and inexplicable outline. Until the secrets of the earth shall be no longer hidden, therefore, these transactions must remain shrouded in their original impenetrable obscurity.

The only occurrence in Captain Barton's former life to which reference was ever made, as having any possible connexion with the sufferings with which his existence closed, and which he himself seemed to regard as working out a retribution for some grievous sin of his past life, was a circumstance which not for several years after his death was brought to light. The nature of this disclosure was painful to his relatives, and discreditable to his memory. As, however, we have exercised the caution of employing fictitious names; and as there are now very few living who will be able to refer to the actors in this drama, their *real* names and places in society, there is nothing to prevent our stating, in two or three lines, the substance of this discovery.

It appeared, then, that some six years before Captain Barton's final return to Dublin, he had formed, in the town of Plymouth,* a guilty attachment, the object of which was the daughter of one of the ship's crew under his command. The father had visited the frailty of his unhappy child with extreme harshness, and even brutality, and it was said that she had died heart-broken. Presuming upon Barton's implication in her guilt, this man had conducted himself toward him with marked insolence, and Barton retaliated this, and what he resented with still more exasperated bitterness—his treatment of the unfortunate girl—by a systematic exercise of those terrible and arbitrary severities* which the regulations of the navy placed at the command of those who are responsible for its discipline. The man had at length made his escape, while the vessel was in port at Lisbon, but died, as it was said, in an hospital in that town, of the wounds inflicted in one of his recent and sanguinary punishments.

Whether these circumstances in reality bear, or not, upon the occurrences of Barton's after-life, it is, of course, impossible to say. It seems, however, more than probable that they were, at least in his own mind, closely associated with them. But however the truth may be, as to the origin and motives of this mysterious persecution, there can be no doubt that, with respect to the agencies by which it was accomplished, absolute and impenetrable mystery is like to prevail until the day of doom.

AN ACCOUNT OF SOME STRANGE DISTURBANCES IN AN OLD HOUSE IN AUNGIER-STREET

IT is not worth telling, this story of mine—at least, not worth writing. Told, indeed, as I have sometimes been called upon to tell it, to a circle of intelligent and eager faces, lighted up by a good after-dinner fire on a winter's evening, with a cold wind rising and wailing outside, and all snug and cosy within, it has gone off—though I say it, who should not—indifferent well. But it is a venture to do as you would have me. Pen, ink, and paper are cold vehicles for the marvellous, and a 'reader' decidedly a more critical animal than a 'listener'. If, however, you can induce your friends to read it after nightfall, and when the fireside talk has run for a while on thrilling tales of shapeless terror; in short, if you will secure me the '*mollia tempora fandi*',* I will go to my work, and say my say, with better heart. Well, then, these conditions pre-supposed, I shall waste no more words, but tell you simply how it all happened.

My cousin (Tom Ludlow) and I studied medicine together. I think he would have succeeded, had he stuck to the profession; but he pre-ferred the Church, poor fellow, and died early, a sacrifice to contagion,* contracted in the noble discharge of his duties. For my present pur-pose, I say enough of his character when I mention, that he was of a sedate but frank and cheerful nature; very exact in his observance of truth, and not by any means like myself—of an excitable or nervous temperament.

My uncle Ludlow—Tom's father—while we were attending lec-tures, purchased three or four old houses in Aungier-street, one of which was unoccupied. *He* resided in the country, and Tom proposed that we should take up our abode in the untenanted house, so long as it should continue unlet; a move which would accomplish the double end of settling us nearer alike to our lecture-rooms and to our amuse-ments, and of relieving us from the weekly charge of rent for our lodgings.

Our furniture was very scant—our whole equipage remarkably modest and primitive; and, in short, our arrangements pretty nearly as simple as those of a bivouac. Our new plan was, therefore, executed almost as soon as conceived. The front drawing-room was our sitting-room.

I had the bedroom over it, and Tom the back bedroom on the same floor, which nothing could have induced me to occupy.

The house, to begin with, was a very old one. It had been, I believe, newly fronted about fifty years before; but, with this exception, it had nothing modern about it. The agent who bought it and looked into the titles for my uncle, told me that it was sold, along with much other forfeited property, at Chichester-House,* I think, in 1702; and had belonged to Sir Thomas Hacket, who was Lord Mayor of Dublin in James II's time.* How old it was *then*, I can't say; but, at all events, it had seen years and changes enough to have contracted all that mysterious and saddened air, at once exciting and depressing, which belongs to most old mansions.

There had been very little done in the way of modernizing details; and, perhaps, it was better so; for there was something queer and by-gone in the very walls and ceilings—in the shape of doors and windows—in the odd diagonal site of the chimneypieces—in the beams and ponderous cornices—not to mention the singular solidity of all the wood-work, from the banisters to the window-frames, which hopelessly defied disguise, and would have emphatically proclaimed their antiquity through any conceivable amount of modern finery and varnish.

An effort had, indeed, been made to the extent of papering the drawing-rooms; but somehow, the paper looked raw and out of keeping; and the old woman, who kept a little dirt-pie of a shop in the lane, and whose daughter—a girl of two and fifty—was our solitary handmaid, coming in at sunrise, and chastely receding again so soon as she had made all ready for tea in our state apartment;—this woman, I say, remembered it, when old Judge Horrocks* (who, having earned the reputation of a particularly 'hanging judge', ended by hanging himself, as the coroner's jury found, under an impulse of 'temporary insanity', with a child's skipping-rope, over the massive old banisters) resided there, entertaining good company, with fine venison and rare old port. In those halcyon days, the drawing-rooms were hung with gilded leather, and, I dare say, cut a good figure, for they were really spacious rooms.

The bedrooms were wainscotted, but the front one was not gloomy; and in it the cosiness of antiquity quite overcame its sombre associations. But the back bedroom, with its two queerly-placed melancholy windows, staring vacantly at the foot of the bed, and with the shadowy recess to be found in most old houses in Dublin, like a large ghostly closet, which, from congeniality of temperament, had amalgamated with the bedchamber, and dissolved the partition. At night-time, this 'alcove'—as our 'maid' was wont to call it—had, in my eyes, a specially sinister and suggestive character. Tom's distant and solitary candle glimmered vainly into its darkness. *There* it was always overlooking him—always itself impenetrable. But this was only part of the effect. The whole room was, I can't tell how, repulsive to me. There was, I suppose, in its proportions and features, a latent discord—a certain mysterious and indescribable relation, which jarred indistinctly upon some secret sense of the fitting and the safe, and raised indefinable suspicions and apprehensions of the imagination. On the whole, as I began by saying, nothing could have induced me to pass a night alone in it.

I had never pretended to conceal from poor Tom my superstitious weakness; and he, on the other hand, most unaffectedly ridiculed my tremors. The sceptic was, however, destined to receive a lesson, as you shall hear.

We had not been very long in occupation of our respective dormitories, when I began to complain of uneasy nights and disturbed sleep. I was, I suppose, the more impatient under this annoyance, as I was usually a sound sleeper, and by no means prone to nightmares. It was now, however, my destiny, instead of enjoying my customary repose, every night to 'sup full of horrors'.* After a preliminary course of disagreeable and frightful dreams, my troubles took a definite form, and the same vision, without an appreciable variation in a single detail, visited me at least (on an average) every second night in the week.

Now, this dream, nightmare, or infernal illusion—which you please— of which I was the miserable sport, was on this wise:—I saw, or thought I saw, with the most abominable distinctness, although at the time in profound darkness, every article of furniture and accidental arrangement of the chamber in which I lay. This, as you know, is incidental to ordinary nightmare. Well, while in this clairvoyant condition, which seemed but the lighting up of the theatre in which was to be exhibited the monotonous tableau of horror, which made my nights insupportable, my attention invariably became, I know not why, fixed upon the windows opposite the foot of my bed; and, uniformly with the same effect. A sense of dreadful anticipation always took slow but sure possession of me. I became somehow conscious of a sort of horrid but undefined preparation going forward in some unknown quarter, and by some unknown agency, for my torment; and, after an interval, which always seemed to me of the same length, a picture suddenly flew up to the window, where it remained fixed, as if by an electrical attraction, and my discipline of horror then commenced, to last perhaps for hours. The picture thus mysteriously glued to the window-panes, was the portrait of an old man, in a crimson flowered silk dressing-gown, the folds of which I could now describe, with a countenance embodying a strange mixture of intellect, sensuality, and power, but withal sinister and full of malignant omen. His nose was hooked, like the beak of a vulture; his eyes large, grey, and prominent, and lighted up with a more than mortal cruelty and coldness. These features were surmounted by a crimson velvet cap, the hair that peeped from under which was white with age,* while the eyebrows retained their original blackness. Well I remember every line, hue, and shadow of that stony countenance, and well I may! The gaze of this hellish visage was fixed upon me, and mine returned it with the inexplicable fascination of nightmare, for what appeared to me to be hours of agony. At last—

'The cock he crew, away then flew'*

the fiend who had enslaved me through the awful watches of the night; and, harassed and nervous, I rose to the duties of the day.

I had—I can't say exactly why, but it may have been from the exquisite anguish and profound impressions of unearthly horror, with which this strange phantasmagoria* was associated—an insurmountable antipathy to describing the exact nature of my nightly troubles to my friend and comrade. Generally, however, I told him that I was haunted by abominable dreams; and, true to the imputed materialism of medicine, we put our heads together to dispel my horrors, not by an exorcism, but by a tonic.

I will do this tonic justice, and frankly admit that the accursed portrait began to intermit its visits under its influence. What of that? Was this singular apparition—as full of character as of terror—therefore the creation of my fancy, or the invention of my poor stomach?* Was it, in short, *subjective* (to borrow the technical slang of the day), and not the palpable aggression and intrusion of an external agent? That, good friend, as we will both admit, by no means follows. The evil spirit, who enthralled my senses in the shape of that portrait, may have been just as near me, just as energetic, just as malignant, though I saw him not. What means the whole moral code of revealed religion regarding the due keeping of our own bodies, soberness, temperance, etc.? Here is an obvious connexion between the material and the invisible; the healthy tone of the system, and its unimpaired energy, may, for aught we can tell, guard us against influences which would otherwise render life itself terrific. The mesmerist and the electro-biologist will fail upon an average with nine patients out of ten—so may the evil spirit. Special conditions of the corporeal system are indispensable to the production of certain spiritual phenomena. The operation succeeds sometimes— sometimes fails—that is all.

I found afterwards that my would-be sceptical companion had his troubles too. But of these I knew nothing yet. One night, for a wonder, I was sleeping soundly, when I was roused by a step on the lobby outside my room, followed by the loud clang of what turned out to be a large brass candlestick, flung with all his force by poor Tom Ludlow over the banisters, and rattling with a rebound down the second flight of stairs; and almost concurrently with this, Tom burst open my door, and bounced into my room backwards, in a state of extraordinary agitation.

I had jumped out of bed and clutched him by the arm before I had any distinct idea of my own whereabouts. There we were—in our shirts—standing before the open door—staring through the great old banister opposite, at the lobby window, through which the sickly light of a clouded moon was gleaming.

'What's the matter, Tom? What's the matter with you? What the devil's the matter with you, Tom?' I demanded, shaking him with nervous impatience.

He took a long breath before he answered me, and then it was not very coherently.

'It's nothing, nothing at all—did I speak?—what did I say?—where's the candle, Richard? It's dark; I—I had a candle!'

'Yes, dark enough,' I said; 'but what's the matter?—what *is* it?—why don't you speak, Tom?—have you lost your wits?—what is the matter?'

'The matter?—oh, it is all over. It must have been a dream—nothing at all but a dream—don't you think so? It could not be anything more than a dream.'

'Of *course*,' said I, feeling uncommonly nervous, 'it *was* a dream.'

'I thought,' he said, 'there was a man in my room, and—and I jumped out of bed; and—and—where's the candle?'

'In your room, most likely,' I said; 'shall I go and bring it?'

'No; stay here—don't go; it's no matter—don't, I tell you; it was all a dream. Bolt the door, Dick; I'll stay here with you—I feel nervous. So, Dick, like a good fellow, light your candle and open the window—I am in a *shocking state*.'

I did as he asked me, and robing himself like Granuaile in one of my blankets,* he seated himself close beside my bed.

Every body knows how contagious is fear of all sorts, but more especially that particular kind of fear under which poor Tom was at that moment labouring. I would not have heard, nor I believe would he have recapitulated, just at that moment, for half the world, the details of the hideous vision which had so unmanned him.

'Don't mind telling me anything about your nonsensical dream, Tom,' said I, affecting contempt, really in a panic; 'let us talk about something else; but it is quite plain that this dirty old house disagrees with us both, and hang me if I stay here any longer, to be pestered with indigestion and—and—bad nights, so we may as well look out for lodgings—don't you think so?—at once.'

Tom agreed, and, after an interval, said—

'I have been thinking, Richard, that it is a long time since I saw my father, and I have made up my mind to go down to-morrow and return in a day or two, and you can take rooms for us in the meantime.'

I fancied that this resolution, obviously the result of the vision which had so profoundly scared him, would probably vanish next morning with the damps and shadows of night. But I was mistaken. Off went Tom at peep of day to the country, having agreed that so soon as I had secured suitable lodgings, I was to recall him by letter from his visit to my Uncle Ludlow.

Now, anxious as I was to change my quarters, it so happened, owing to a series of petty procrastinations and accidents, that nearly a week elapsed before my bargain was made and my letter of recall on the wing to Tom; and, in the meantime, a trifling adventure or two had occurred to your humble servant, which, absurd as they now appear, diminished by distance, did certainly at the time serve to whet my appetite for change considerably.

A night or two after the departure of my comrade, I was sitting by my bedroom fire, the door locked, and the ingredients of a tumbler of hot whisky-punch upon the crazy spider-table; for, as the best mode of keeping the

'Black spirits and white,
Blue spirits and grey',*

with which I was environed, at bay, I had adopted the practice recommended by the wisdom of my ancestors, and 'kept my spirits up by pouring spirits down'.* I had thrown aside my volume of 'Anatomy',* and was treating myself by way of a tonic, preparatory to my punch and bed, to half-a-dozen pages of the 'Spectator',* when I heard a step on the flight of stairs descending from the attics. It was two o'clock, and the streets were as silent as a churchyard—the sounds were, therefore, perfectly distinct. There was a slow, heavy tread, characterized by the emphasis and deliberation of age, descending by the narrow staircase from above; and, what made the sound more singular, it was plain that the feet which produced it were perfectly bare, measuring the descent with something between a pound and a flop, very ugly to hear.

I knew quite well that my attendant had gone away many hours before, and that nobody but myself had any business in the house. It was quite plain also that the person who was coming down stairs had no intention whatever of concealing his movements; but, on the contrary, appeared disposed to make even more noise, and proceed more deliberately, than was at all necessary. When the step reached the foot of the stairs outside my room, it seemed to stop; and I expected every moment to see my door open spontaneously, and give admission to the original of my detested portrait. I was, however, relieved in a few seconds by hearing the descent renewed, just in the same manner, upon the staircase leading down to the drawing-rooms, and thence, after another pause, down the next flight, and so on to the hall, whence I heard no more.

Now, by the time the sound had ceased, I was wound up, as they say, to a very unpleasant pitch of excitement. I listened, but there was not a stir. I screwed up my courage to a decisive experiment—opened my door, and in a Stentorian voice bawled over the banisters, 'Who's there?' There was no answer, but the ringing of my own voice through the empty old house—no renewal of the movement; nothing, in short, to give my unpleasant sensations a definite direction. There is, I think, something most disagreeably disenchanting in the sound of one's own voice under such circumstances, exerted in solitude, and in vain. It redoubled my sense of isolation, and my misgivings increased on perceiving that the door, which I certainly thought I had left open, was closed behind me; in a vague alarm, lest my retreat should be cut off, I got again into my room as quickly as I could, where I remained in a state of imaginary blockade, and very uncomfortable indeed, till morning.

Next night brought no return of my barefooted fellow-lodger; but the night following, being in my bed, and in the dark—somewhere, I suppose, about the same hour as before, I distinctly heard the old fellow again descending from the garrets.

This time I had had my punch, and the *morale* of the garrison was consequently excellent. I jumped out of bed, clutched the poker as I passed the expiring fire, and in a moment was upon the lobby. The sound had ceased by this time—the dark and chill were discouraging; and, guess my horror, when I saw, or thought I saw, a black monster, whether in the shape of a man or a bear I could not say, standing, with its back to the wall, on the lobby, facing me, with a pair of great greenish eyes shining dimly out. Now, I must be frank, and confess that the cupboard which displayed our plates and cups stood just there, though at the moment I did not recollect it. At the same time I must honestly say, that making every allowance for an excited imagination, I never could satisfy myself that I was made the dupe of my own fancy in this matter; for this apparition, after one or two shiftings of shape, as if in the act of incipient transformation, began, as it seemed on second thoughts, to advance upon me in its original form. From an instinct of terror rather than of courage, I hurled the poker, with all my force, at its head; and to the music of a horrid crash made my way into my room, and double-locked the door. Then, in a minute more, I heard the horrid bare feet walk down the stairs, till the sound ceased in the hall, as on the former occasion.

If the apparition of the night before was an ocular delusion of my fancy sporting with the dark outlines of our cupboard, and if its horrid eyes were nothing but a pair of inverted teacups, I had, at all events, the satisfaction of having launched the poker with admirable effect, and in true 'fancy' phrase,* 'knocked its two daylights into one', as the com-mingled fragments of my tea-service testified. I did my best to gather comfort and courage from these evidences; but it would not do. And then what could I say of those horrid bare feet, and the regular tramp, tramp, tramp, which measured the distance of the entire staircase through the solitude of my haunted dwelling, and at an hour when no good influence was stirring? Confound it!—the whole affair was abom-inable. I was out of spirits, and dreaded the approach of night.

It came, ushered ominously in with a thunder-storm and dull torrents of depressing rain. Earlier than usual the streets grew silent; and by twelve o'clock nothing but the comfortless pattering of the rain was to be heard.

I made myself as snug as I could. I lighted *two* candles, instead of one. I forswore bed, and held myself in readiness for a sally, candle in hand; for, *coute qui coute,** I was resolved to *see* the being, if visible at all, who troubled the nightly stillness of my mansion. I was fidgetty and nervous, and tried in vain to interest myself with my books. I walked up and down my room, whistling in turn martial and hilarious music, and listening ever and anon for the dreaded noise. I sate down and stared at the square label on the solemn and reserved-looking black bottle, until 'FLANAGAN AND CO.'S BEST OLD MALT WHISKY' grew into a sort of subdued accompaniment to all the fantastic and horrible speculations which chased one another through my brain.

Silence, meanwhile, grew more silent, and darkness darker. I listened in vain for the rumble of a vehicle, or the mellowed clamor of a distant row. There was nothing but the sound of a rising wind, which had

succeeded the thunder-storm that had travelled over the Dublin mountains quite out of hearing. In the middle of this great city I began to feel
myself alone with nature, and Heaven knows what beside. My courage
was ebbing. Punch, however, which makes beasts of so many, made
a man of me again—just in time to hear with tolerable nerve and firmness
the lumpy, flabby, naked feet deliberately descending the stairs again.

I took a candle, not without a tremor. As I crossed the floor I tried to
extemporize a prayer, but stopped short to listen, and never finished it.
The steps continued. I confess I hesitated for some seconds at the door
before I took heart of grace and opened it. When I peeped out the lobby
was perfectly empty—there was no monster standing on the staircase;
and, as the detested sound ceased, I was reassured enough to venture
forward nearly to the banisters. Horror of horrors! within a stair or two
beneath the spot where I stood the unearthly tread smote the floor. My eye
caught something in motion; it was about the size of Goliath's* foot—it
was grey, heavy, and flapped with a dead weight from one step to another.
As I am alive, it was the most monstrous grey rat I ever beheld or imagined.

Shakspeare says*—'Some men there are cannot abide a gaping pig,
and some that are mad if they behold a cat.' I went well-nigh out of my
wits when I beheld this *rat*; for, laugh at me as you may, it fixed upon
me, I thought, a perfectly human expression of malice; and, as it shuffled about and looked up into my face almost from between my feet,
I saw, I could swear it—I felt it then, and know it now, the infernal gaze
and the accursed countenance of my old friend in the portrait, trans-
fused into the visage of the bloated vermin before me.

I bounced into my room again with a feeling of loathing and horror
I cannot describe, and locked and bolted my door as if a lion had been
at the other side. D—n him or *it*; curse the portrait and its original!
I felt in my soul that the rat—yes, the *rat*, the RAT I had just seen, was
that evil being in masquerade, and rambling through the house upon
some infernal night lark.

Next morning I was early trudging through the miry streets; and,
among other transactions, posted a peremptory note recalling Tom. On
my return, however, I found a letter from my absent 'chum',* announcing his intended return next day. I was doubly rejoiced at this, because
I had succeeded in getting rooms; and because the change of scene and
return of my comrade were rendered specially pleasant by the last
night's half ridiculous half horrible adventure.

I slept extemporaneously in my new quarters in Digges'-street* that
night, and next morning returned for breakfast to the haunted mansion, where I was certain Tom would call immediately on his arrival.

I was quite right—he came; and almost his first question referred to the primary object of our change of residence.

'Thank God,' he said with genuine fervor, on hearing that all was arranged. 'On *your* account I am delighted. As to myself, I assure you that no earthly consideration could have induced me ever again to pass a night in this disastrous old house.'

'Confound the house!' I ejaculated, with a genuine mixture of fear and detestation, 'we have not had a pleasant hour since we came to live here'; and so I went on, and related incidentally my adventure with the plethoric* old rat.

'Well, if that were *all*,' said my cousin, affecting to make light of the matter, 'I don't think I should have minded it very much.'

'Ay, but its eye—its countenance, my dear Tom,' urged I; 'if you had seen *that*, you would have felt it might be *any*thing but what it seemed.'

'I incline to think the best conjurer in such a case would be an able-bodied cat,' he said, with a provoking chuckle.

'But let us hear your own adventure,' I said, tartly.

At this challenge he looked uneasily round him. I had poked up a very unpleasant recollection.

'You shall hear it, Dick; I'll tell it to you,' he said. 'Begad, sir, I should feel quite queer, though, in telling it *here*, though we are too strong a body for ghosts to meddle with just now.'

Though he spoke this like a joke, I think it was a serious calculation. Our Hebe* was in a corner of the room, unpacking our cracked delf* tea and dinner-services in a basket. She soon suspended operations, and with mouth and eyes wide open became an absorbed listener. Tom's experiences were told nearly in these words:—

'I saw it three times, Dick—three distinct times; and I am perfectly certain it meant me some infernal harm. I was, I say, in danger—in *extreme* danger; for, if nothing else had happened, my reason would most certainly have failed me, unless I had escaped so soon. Thank God, I *did* escape.

'The first night of this hateful disturbance, I was lying in the attitude of sleep, in that lumbering old bed. I hate to think of it. I was really wide awake, though I had put out my candle, and was lying as quietly as if I had been asleep; and although accidentally restless, my thoughts were running in a cheerful and agreeable channel.

'I think it must have been two o'clock at least when I thought I heard a sound in that—that odious dark recess at the far end of the bedroom. It was as if some one was drawing a piece of cord slowly along the floor, lifting it up, and dropping it softly down again in coils. I sate up once or twice in my bed, but could see nothing, so I concluded it must be mice in the wainscot. I felt no emotion graver than curiosity, and after a few minutes ceased to observe it.

While lying in this state, strange to say, without at first a suspicion of anything supernatural, on a sudden I saw an old man, rather stout and square, in a sort of roan-red dressing-gown, and with a black cap* on his head, moving stiffly and slowly in a diagonal direction, from the recess, across the floor of the bedroom, passing my bed at the foot, and entering the lumber-closet at the left. He had something under his arm; his head hung a little at one side; and, merciful God! when I saw his face.'

Tom stopped for a while, and then said—

'That awful countenance, which living or dying I never can forget, disclosed what he was. Without turning to the right or left, he passed beside me, and entered the closet by the bed's head.

'While this fearful and indescribable type of death and guilt was passing, I felt that I had no more power to speak or stir than if I had been myself a corpse. For hours after it had disappeared I was too terrified and weak to move. As soon as daylight came, I took courage, and examined the room, and especially the course which the frightful intruder had seemed to take, but there was not a vestige to indicate anybody's having passed there; no sign of any disturbing agency visible among the lumber that strewed the floor of the closet.

'I now began to recover a little. I was fagged and exhausted, and at last, overpowered by a feverish sleep. I came down late; and finding you out of spirits, on account of your dreams about the portrait, whose *original* I am now certain disclosed himself to me, I did not care to talk about the infernal vision. In fact, I was trying to persuade myself that the whole thing was an illusion, and I did not like to revive in their intensity the hated impressions of the past night—or, to risk the constancy of my scepticism, by recounting the tale of my sufferings.

'It required some nerve, I can tell you, to go to my haunted chamber next night, and lie down quietly in the same bed,' continued Tom. 'I did so with a degree of trepidation, which, I am not ashamed to say, a very little matter would have sufficed to stimulate to downright panic. This night, however, passed off quietly enough, as also the next; and so too did two or three more. I grew more confident, and began to fancy that I believed in the theories of spectral illusions, with which I had at first vainly tried to impose upon my convictions.

'The apparition had been, indeed, altogether anomalous. It had crossed the room without any recognition of my presence: I had not disturbed *it*, and *it* had no mission to *me*. What, then, was the imaginable use of its crossing the room in a visible shape at all? Of course it might have *been* in the closet instead of *going* there, as easily as it introduced itself into the recess without entering the chamber in a shape discernible by the senses. Besides, how the deuce *had* I seen it? It was a dark night; I had no candle; there was no fire; and yet I saw it as distinctly, in colouring and outline, as ever I beheld human form! A cataleptic dream would explain it all; and I was determined that a dream it should be.

'One of the most remarkable phenomena connected with the practice of mendacity is the vast number of deliberate lies we tell to ourselves, whom, of all persons, we can least expect to deceive. In all this, I need hardly tell you, Dick, I was simply lying to myself, and did not believe one word of the wretched humbug. Yet I went on, as men will do, like persevering charlatans and impostors, who tire people into credulity by the mere force of reiteration; so I hoped to win myself over at last to a comfortable scepticism about the ghost.

'He had not appeared a second time—that certainly was a comfort; and what, after all, did I care for him, and his queer old toggery and strange looks? Not a fig! I was nothing the worse for having seen him, and a good story the better. So I tumbled into bed, put out my candle, and, cheered by a loud drunken quarrel in the back lane, went fast asleep.

'From this deep slumber I awoke with a start. I knew I had had a horrible dream; but what it was I could not remember. My heart was thumping furiously; I felt bewildered and feverish; I sate up in the bed, and looked about the room. A broad flood of moonlight came in through the curtainless window; everything was as I had last seen it; and though the domestic squabble in the back lane was, unhappily for me, allayed, I yet could hear a pleasant fellow singing, on his way home, the then popular comic ditty* called, "Murphy Delany". Taking advantage of this diversion I lay down again, with my face towards the fire-place, and closing my eyes, did my best to think of nothing else but the song, which was every moment growing fainter in the distance:—

> ' " 'Twas Murphy Delany, so funny and frisky,
>   Stept into a shebeen shop to get his skin full;
> He reeled out again pretty well lined with whiskey,
>   As fresh as a shamrock, as blind as a bull."

'The singer, whose condition I dare say resembled that of his hero, was soon too far off to regale my ears any more; and as his music died away, I myself sank into a doze, neither sound nor refreshing. Somehow the song had got into my head, and I went meandering on through the adventures of my respectable fellow-countryman, who, on emerging from the "shebeen shop", fell into a river, from which he was fished up to be "sat upon" by a coroner's jury, who having learned from "a horse-doctor" that he was "dead as a door-nail, so there was an end", returned their verdict accordingly, just as he returned to his senses; when an angry altercation and a pitched battle between the body and the coroner winds up the lay with due spirit and pleasantry.

'Through this ballad I continued with a weary monotony to plod, down to the very last line, and then *da capo*, and so on, in my uncomfortable half-sleep, for how long, I can't conjecture. I found myself at last, however, muttering "*dead* as a door-nail, so there was an end"; and something like another voice within me, seemed to say, very faintly, but sharply, "dead! dead! *dead!* and may the Lord have mercy on your soul!" and instantaneously I was wide awake, and staring right before me from the pillow.

'Now—will you believe it, Dick?—I saw the same accursed figure standing full front, and gazing at me with its stony and fiendish countenance, not two yards from the bedside.'

Tom stopped here, and wiped the perspiration from his face. I felt very queer. The girl was as pale as Tom; and, assembled as we were in the very scene of these adventures, we were all, I dare say, equally grateful for the clear daylight and the resuming bustle out of doors.

'For about three seconds only I saw it plainly; then it grew indistinct; but, for a long time, there was something like a column of dark vapour where it had been standing, between me and the wall; and I felt sure that he still was there. After a good while, this appearance went too. I took my clothes down stairs to the hall, and dressed there, with the door half open; then went out into the street, and walked about the town till morning, when I came back, in a miserable state of nervousness and exhaustion. I was such a fool, Dick, as to be ashamed to tell you how I came to be so upset. I thought you would laugh at me; especially as I had always talked philosophy, and treated *your* ghosts with contempt. I concluded you would give me no quarter; and so kept my tale of horror to myself.

'Now, Dick, you will hardly believe me, when I assure you, that for many nights after this last experience, I did not go to my room at all. I used to sit up for a while in the drawing-room after you had gone up to your bed; and then steal down softly to the hall-door, let myself out, and sit in the "Robin Hood" tavern* until the last guest went off; and then I got through the night like a sentry, pacing the streets till morning.

'For more than a week I never slept in a bed. I sometimes had a snooze on a form in the "Robin Hood", and sometimes a nap in a chair during the day; but regular sleep I had absolutely none.

'I was quite resolved that we should get into another house; but I could not bring myself to tell you the reason, and I somehow put it off from day to day, although my life was, during every hour of this procrastination, rendered as miserable as that of a felon with the constables on his track. I was growing absolutely ill from this wretched mode of life.

'One afternoon I determined to enjoy an hour's sleep upon your bed. I hated mine; so that I had never, except in a stealthy visit every day to unmake it, lest Martha should discover the secret of my nightly absence, entered the ill-omened chamber.

'As ill-luck would have it, you had locked your bedroom, and taken away the key. I went into my own to unsettle the bedclothes, as usual, and give the bed the appearance of having been slept in. Now, a variety of circumstances concurred to bring about the dreadful scene through which I was that night to pass. In the first place, I was literally overpowered with fatigue, and longing for sleep; in the next place, the effect of this extreme exhaustion upon my nerves resembled that of a narcotic, and rendered me less susceptible than, perhaps, I should in any other condition have been, of the exciting fears which had become habitual to me. Then again, a little bit of the window was open, a pleasant freshness pervaded the room, and, to crown all, the cheerful sun of day was making the room quite pleasant. What was to prevent my enjoying an hour's nap *here?* The whole air was resonant with the cheerful hum of life, and the broad matter-of-fact light of day filled every corner of the room.

'I yielded—stifling my qualms—to the almost overpowering temptation; and merely throwing off my coat, and loosening my cravat, I lay down, limiting myself to *half*-an-hour's doze in the unwonted enjoyment of a feather bed, a coverlet, and bolster.

'It was horribly insidious; and the demon, no doubt, marked my infatuated preparations. Dolt that I was, I fancied, with mind and body worn out for want of sleep, and an arrear of a full week's rest to my credit, that such a measure as *half*-an-hour's sleep, in such a situation, was possible. My sleep was death-like, long, and dreamless.

'Without a start or fearful sensation of any kind, I waked gently, but completely. It was, as you have good reason to remember, long past mid-night—I believe, about two o'clock. When sleep has been deep and long enough to satisfy nature thoroughly, one often wakens in this way, suddenly, tranquilly, and completely.

'There was a figure seated in that lumbering, old sofa-chair, near the fire-place. Its back was rather towards me, but I could not be mistaken; it turned slowly round, and, merciful heavens! there was the stony face, with its infernal lineaments of malignity and despair, gloating on me. There was now no doubt as to its consciousness of my presence, and the hellish malice with which it was animated, for it arose, and drew close to the bedside. There was a rope about its neck, and the other end, coiled up, it held stiffly in its hand.

'My good angel nerved me for this horrible crisis. I remained for some seconds transfixed by the gaze of this tremendous phantom. He came close to the bed, and appeared on the point of mounting upon it. The next instant I was upon the floor at the far side, and in a moment more was, I don't know how, upon the lobby.

'But the spell was not yet broken; the valley of the shadow of death was not yet traversed. The abhorred phantom was before me there; it was standing near the banisters, stooping a little, and with one end of the rope round its own neck, was poising a noose at the other, as if to throw over mine; and while engaged in this baleful pantomime, it wore a smile so sensual, so unspeakably dreadful, that my senses were nearly overpowered. I saw and remember nothing more, until I found myself in your room.

'I had a wonderful escape, Dick—there is no disputing *that*—an escape for which, while I live, I shall bless the mercy of heaven. No one can conceive or imagine what it is for flesh and blood to stand in the presence of such a thing, but one who has had the terrific experience. Dick, Dick, a shadow has passed over me—a chill has crossed my blood and marrow, and I will never be the same again—never, Dick—never!'

Our handmaid, a mature girl of five-and-forty,* as I have said, stayed her hand, as Tom's story proceeded, and by little and little drew near to us, with open mouth, and her brows contracted over her little, beady black eyes, till stealing a glance over her shoulder now and then, she established herself close behind us. During the relation, she had made various earnest comments, in an undertone; but these and her ejaculations, for the sake of brevity and simplicity, I have omitted in my narration.

'It's often I heard tell of it,' she now said, 'but I never believed it rightly till now—though, indeed, why should not I? Does not my mother, down there in the lane, know quare stories, God bless us, beyant telling about it? But you ought not to have slept in the back bedroom. She was loath to let me be going in and out of that room even in the day time, let alone for any Christian to spend the night in it; for sure she says it was his own bedroom.'

'*Whose* own bedroom?' we asked, in a breath.

'Why, *his*—the ould Judge's—Judge Horrock's, to be sure, God rest his sowl'; and she looked fearfully round.

'Amen!' I muttered. 'But did he die there?'

'Die there! No, not quite *there*,' she said. 'Shure, was not it over the banisters he hung himself, the ould sinner, God be merciful to us all? and was not it in the alcove they found the handles of the skipping-rope cut off, and the knife where he was settling the cord, God bless us, to hang himself with? It was his housekeeper's daughter owned the rope, my mother often told me, and the child never throve after, and used to be starting up out of her sleep, and screeching in the night time, wid dhrames and frights that cum an her; and they said how it was the sperrit of the ould Judge that was tormentin' her; and she used to be roaring and yelling out to hould back the big ould fellow with the crooked neck; and then she'd screech "Oh, the master! the master! he's stampin' at me, and beckoning to me! Mother, darling, don't let me go!" And so the poor crathure died at last, and the docthers said it was wather on the brain, for it was all they could say.'

'How long ago was all this?' I asked.

'Oh, then, how would I know?' she answered. 'But it must be a wond-herful long time ago, for the house-keeper was an ould woman, with a pipe in her mouth, and not a tooth left, and betther nor eighty years ould when my mother was first married; and they said she was a rale buxom, fine-dressed woman when the ould Judge come to his end; an', indeed, my mother's not far from eighty years ould herself this day; and what made it worse for the unnatural ould villain, God rest his soul, to frighten the little girl out of the world the way he did, was what was mostly thought and believed by every one. My mother says how the poor little crathure was his own child; for he was by all accounts an ould villain every way, an' the hangin'est judge that ever was known in Ireland's ground.'

'From what you said about the danger of sleeping in that bedroom,' said I, 'I suppose there were stories about the ghost having appeared there to others.'

'Well, there *was* things said—quare things, surely,' she answered, as it seemed, with some reluctance. 'And why would not there? Sure was it not up in that same room he slept for more than twenty years? and was it not in the *alcove* he got the rope ready that done his own business at last, the way he done many a betther man's in his lifetime?—and was not the body lying in the same bed afther death, and put in the coffin there, too, and carried out to his grave from it in Pether's churchyard,*

afther the coroner was done? But there was quare stories—my mother
has them all—about how one Nicholas Spaight got into trouble on the
head of it.'

'And what did they say of this Nicholas Spaight?' I asked.

'Oh, for that matther, it's soon told,' she answered.

And she certainly did relate a very strange story, which so piqued my
curiosity, that I took occasion to visit the ancient lady, her mother, from
whom I learned many very curious particulars. Indeed, I am tempted to
tell the tale, but my fingers are weary, and I must defer it. But if you
wish to hear it another time, I shall do my best.

When we had heard the strange tale I have *not* told you, we put one
or two further questions to her about the alleged spectral visitations, to
which the house had, ever since the death of the wicked old Judge, been
subjected.

'No one ever had luck in it,' she told us. 'There was always cross
accidents, sudden deaths, and short times in it. The first that tuck it was
a family—I forget their name—but at any rate there was two young
ladies and their papa. He was about sixty, and a stout healthy gentleman
as you'd wish to see at that age. Well, he slept in that unlucky back bedroom; and, God between us an' harm! sure enough he was found dead
one morning, half out of the bed, with his head as black as a sloe, and
swelled like a puddin', hanging down near the floor. It was a fit, they
said. He was as dead as a mackerel, and so *he* could not say what it was;
but the ould people was all sure that it was nothing at all but the ould
Judge, God bless us! that frightened him out of his senses and his life
together.

'Some time after there was a rich old maiden lady took the house.
I don't know which room *she* slept in, but she lived alone; and at any
rate, one morning, the servants going down early to their work, found
her sitting on the passage-stairs, shivering and talkin' to herself, quite
mad; and never a word more could any of *them* or her friends get from
her ever afterwards but, "Don't ask me to go, for I promised to wait for
him." They never made out from her who it was she meant by *him*, but
of course those that knew all about the ould house were at no loss for
the meaning of all that happened to her.

'Then afterwards, when the house was let out in lodgings, there was
Micky Byrne that took the same room, with his wife and three little
children; and sure I heard Mrs Byrne myself telling how the children
used to be lifted up in the bed at night, she could not see by what mains;
and how they were starting and screeching every hour, just all as one as
the housekeeper's little girl that died, till at last one night poor Micky

had a dhrop in him, the way he used now and again; and what do you think, in the middle of the night he thought he heard a noise on the stairs, and being in liquor, nothing less id do him but out he must go himself to see what was wrong. Well, after that, all she ever heard of him was himself sayin' "Oh, God!" and a tumble that shook the very house; and there, sure enough, he was lying on the lower stairs, under the lobby, with his neck smashed double undher him, where he was flung over the banisters.'

Then the handmaiden added—

'I'll go down to the lane, and send up Joe Gavvey to pack up the rest of the taythings,* and bring all the things across to your new lodgings.'

And so we all sallied out together, each of us breathing more freely, I have no doubt, as we crossed that ill-omened threshold for the last time.

Now, I may add thus much, in compliance with the immemorial usage of the realm of fiction, which sees the hero not only through his adventures, but fairly out of the world. You must have perceived that what the flesh, blood, and bone hero of romance proper is to the regular compounder of fiction, this old house of brick, wood, and mortar is to the humble recorder of this true tale. I, therefore, relate, as in duty bound, the catastrophe which ultimately befell it, which was simply this—that about two years subsequently to my story it was taken by a quack doctor, who called himself Baron Duhlstoerf, and filled the parlour windows with bottles of indescribable horrors preserved in brandy, and the newspapers with the usual grandiloquent and mendacious advertisements. This gentleman among his virtues did not reckon sobriety, and one night, being overcome with much wine, he set fire to his bed curtains, partially burned himself, and totally consumed the house. It was afterwards rebuilt, and for a time an undertaker established himself in the premises.

I have now told you my own and Tom's adventures, together with some valuable collateral particulars; and having acquitted myself of my engagement, I wish you a very good night, and pleasant dreams.

BORRHOMEO THE ASTROLOGER

A Monkish Tale

At the period of the famous plague of Milan* in 1630, a frenzy of superstition seized upon the population high and low. Old prophecies of a diabolical visitation reserved for their city, in that particular year of grace, prepared the way for this wild panic of the imagination. When the plague broke out terror seems to have acted to a degree scarcely paralleled upon the fancy or the credulity of the people. Excitement in very many cases produced absolutely the hallucinations of madness. Persons deposed, in the most solemn and consistent terms, to having themselves witnessed diabolical processions, spoken with an awful impersonation of Satan, and been solicited amidst scenes and personages altogether supernatural, to lend their human agency to the nefarious designs of the fiend, by consenting to disseminate by certain prescribed means, the virus* of the pestilence.

Some of the stories related of persons possessed by these awful fancies are in print; and by no means destitute of a certain original and romantic horror. That which I am about to tell, however, has I believe, never been printed. At all events I saw it only in MSS., sewed up in vellum, with a psaltery and half-a-dozen lives of saints, in the library of the old Dominican monastery which stands about two leagues to the north-east of the city. With your permission I am about to give you the best translation I was able to make of this short but odd story, of the truth of which, judging from the company in which I found it, the honest monks entertained no sort of doubt. You are to remember that all sorts of tales of wonder were at that time flying about and believed in Milan, and that many of these were authenticated in such a way as to leave no doubt as to the *bona fides* of those who believed themselves to have been eye-witnesses of what they told. Monks and country padres of course believed; but so did men who stood highest in the church, and who, unless fame belied them, believed little else.

In the year of our Lord, 1630, when Satan, by divine permission, appearing among us in person, afflicted our beautiful city of Milan with a pestilence unheard of in its severity, there lived in the *Strada Piana*, which has lately been pulled down, an astrologer calling himself Borrhomeo. Some say he came from Perrugia, others from Venice; I know not. He it was who first predicted, in the year of our Lord, 1628, by means of his art, that the pale comet which then appeared would speedily be followed, not by war or by famine, but by pestilence; which accordingly came to pass. Beside his skill in astrology, which was wonderful, he was profoundly versed in alchymy.* He was a man great in stature, and strong, though old in years, and with a most reverent beard. But though seemingly austere in his life, it is said that he was given up, in secret, to enormous wickedness.

Having shut himself up in his house for more than a month, with his furnace and crucibles (truly he had made repeated and near approaches to the grand arcanum*) he had arrived, as he supposed, at the moment of projection.*

He collects the powder and tries it on molten lead; it was a failure.* He was too wise to be angry; the long pursuit of his art had taught him patience. But while he is pondering in a profound and gloomy reverie, a retort, which he had forgotten in the furnace, explodes.

He sees in the smoke a pale young man, dressed in mourning, with black hair, and viewing him with a sad and reproachful countenance.

Borrhomeo who lived among chimaeras, is not utterly overcome, as another man might be, and confronts him, amazed, indeed, but not terrified.

The stranger shook his head like a holy young confessor, who hears an evil shrift; and says he, rather sternly—'Borrhomeo! Beware of covetousness which is idolatry. On this sordid pursuit which you call a science, have you wasted your days on earth and your peace hereafter.'

'Young man,' says the alchymist, too much struck by the manner and reproof of the stranger to ask himself how he came there—'Wealth is power to do good as well as evil. To seek it is, therefore, an ambition as honourable as any other.'

'We both know why you seek it, and how you would employ it,' answers the young man gravely.

The old man's face flushed with anger at this rebuke, and he looked down frowningly to the table whereon lay the book of his spells. But he bethought him this must be a good spirit, and he was abashed. Nevertheless, he roused his courage, and shook his white mane back, and was on the point of answering sternly, when the young man said with a melancholy smile—

'Besides, you will never discover the grand arcanum—the elixir vitae, or the philosopher's stone.'

His words, which were as soft as snow flakes, fell like an iron mace upon the heart of the seer.

'Perhaps not,' said the astrologer frigidly.

'Not perhaps,' said the stranger.

'At all events, young man—for as such you appear—and I know what spirits seek who take that shape, the science has its charms for me; and when the pleasures of the young are as harmless as the amusements of the aged I'll hear you question mine.'

'You know not what spirit you are of. As for me, I am contrite and humble—well I may,' says the stranger faintly with a sigh. 'Besides, what you have pursued in vain, and will never by your own researches find, I have discovered.'

'What! the——'

'Yes, the tincture that can prolong life to virtual immortality, and the dust that can change that lead into gold; but I care for neither.'

'Why, young man, if this be true,' says Borrhomeo in a rapture of wonder, 'you stand before me an angel of wisdom, in power and immortality like a god!'*

'No,' says the stranger, 'a long-lived fellow, with a long purse—that's all.'

'All?—every thing?' cries the old man. 'Will you—*will* you——'

'Yes, sir, you shall see,' says the young man in black. 'Give me that crucible. It is all a matter of proportions. Water, clay, and air are the material of all the vegetable world—the flowers and forests, the wines and the fruits—the seed is both the laboratory and the chemist, and knows how, with the sun's help, to apportion and combine.'

While he said this with the abstracted manner of one whose mind is mazed in a double reverie, while his hands work out some familiar problem, he tumbled over the alchymist's papers, and unstopped and stopped his bottles of crystals, precipitates, and elixirs—taking a little from this and a little from that, and throwing all into a small gold cup that stood on the table; but like a juggler, he moved those bottles so deftly, that the quick eyes and retentive soul of the old man vainly sought to catch or keep the order of the process. When he had done there was hardly a thimble-full.

'Is that it?' whispered the old man, twinkling with greedy eyes.

'No,' said the stranger, with a sly smile, 'there is one very simple ingredient which you have forgotten.'

He took a large, flat, oval gold box, with some hair set under a crystal in the lid of it, and looking at it for a moment, he seemed to sigh. He tapped it like a snuff-box—there was within it a powder like vermilion, and on the inside of the lid, in the centre, was the small enamel portrait of a beautiful but sinister female face. The features were so very beautiful, and the expression so strangely blended with horror, that it fixed the gaze of the old man for a moment; and—was it illusion?—he thought he saw the face steadily dilating as if it would gradually fill the lid of the box, and even expand to human dimensions.

'Yes,' said the stranger, as having taken some of the red powder, he shut the cover down again with a snap, 'she was beautiful, and her lineaments are still clear and bright—nothing like darkness to keep them from fading, and so the poor little miniature is again in prison'; and he dropped the box back into his pocket.

Then he took two iron ladles, and heating in the one his powder to a white heat, and bidding the alchymist melt a pellet of lead in the other, and pour it into the ladle which held the powder, there arose a beautiful purple fire in the bottom of it, with an intense fringe of green and yellow; and when it subsided there was a little nut of gold there of the bigness of the leaden pellet.

The fiery eyes of the alchymist almost leaped from their sockets into the iron cup, and he could have clasped his marvellous visitor round the knees and worshipped him.

'And now,' says the stranger very gently and earnestly, 'in return for satisfying your curiosity, I ask only your solemn promise to prosecute this dread science no more. Ha! you'll not give it. Take, then, my warning, and remember the wages of this knowledge is sorrow.'

'But won't you tell me how to commute*—and—and—you have not produced the elixir,' the old man cried.

''Tis folly—and, as I've told you, worse—a snare,' answered the young man, sighing heavily. 'I came not to satisfy but to rebuke your dangerous though fruitless frenzy. Besides, I hear my friend still pacing the street. Hark! he taps at the window.'

Then came a sharp rattle as of a cane tapping angrily on the window.

The young man bowed, smiling sadly, and somehow got himself away, though without hurry, yet so quickly that the old man could not reach the door till after it had closed and he was gone.

'Oaf that I am!' cried the astrologer, losing patience and stamping on the ground, 'how have I let him go? He hesitated—he would have yielded—his scruples, benevolent perhaps, I could have quieted—and yet in the very crisis I was tongue-tied and motionless, and let him go!'

He pushed open the little window, from which he observed the street, and thought he saw the stranger walking round the corner, conversing with a little hunchback in a red cloak, and followed by an ugly dog.

At sight of the great white head and beard, and the fierce features of the alchymist, bleared and tanned in the smoke of his furnace, people stopped and looked. So he withdrew, and in haste got him ready for the street, waiting for no refreshment, though he had fasted long; for he had the strength as well as the stature of a giant, and forth he went.

By this time the twilight had passed into night. He had his mantle about him, and his rapier and dagger—for the streets were danger-ous, and a feather in his cap, and his white beard hidden behind the fold of his cloak. So he might have passed for a tall soldier of the guard.

The pestilence kept people much within doors, and the streets more solitary than was customary. He had walked through the town two hours and more, before he met with any thing to speak of. Then—lo!—on a sudden, near the Fountain of the Lion—it being then moonlight—he discovers, in a solitude, the figure of his visiter, standing with the hunchback and the dog, which he knew by its ungainly bones, and its carrying its huge head so near the ground.

So he shouts along the silent street, 'Stay a moment, signor', and he mends his pace.

But they were parting company there, it seemed, and away went the deformed, with his unsightly beast at his heels, and this way came the youth in black.

So standing full in his way, and doffing his cap, and throwing back his cloak, that his snowy beard and head might appear, and the stranger recognize him when he drew nigh. He cried—

'Borrhomeo implores thee to take pity on his ignorance.'

'What! still mad?' said the young man. 'This man will waste the small remnant of his years in godless search after gold and immortality; better he should know all, and feel their vanity.'

'Better a thousand times!' cried the old man, in ecstacy.

'There is in this city, signor, at this time, in great secrecy, the master who taught me,' says the youth, 'the master of all alchymists. Many centuries since he found out the elixir vitae. From him I've learned the few secrets that I know, and without his leave I dare not impart them. If you desire it, I will bring you before him; but, once in his presence, you cannot recede, and his conditions you must accept.'

'All, all, with my whole heart. But some reasonable pleasures——'

'With your pleasures he will not interfere; he cannot change your heart,' said the young man, with one of his heavy sighs; 'but you know what gold is, and what the elixir is, and power and immortality are not to be had for nothing.'

'Lead on, signor, I'm ready,' cries the old man, whose face flushed, and his eyes burned with the fires of an evil rapture.

'Take my hand,' said the young man, more stern and pale than he had yet appeared. So he did, and his conductor seized it with a cold gripe, and they walked swiftly on.

Now he led him through several streets, and on their way Borrhomeo passes his notary, and, lingering a moment, asks him whether he has a bond, signed by a certain merchant, with whom he had contracted for a loan. The notary, who was talking to another, says, suddenly, to that other—

'Per Baccho!* I've just called to mind a matter that must be looked after for Signor Borrhomeo'; and he called him a nick-name, which incensed the astrologer, who struck him a lusty box upon the ear.

'There's a humming in my ear tonight,' said the notary, going into his house; 'I hope it is no sign of the plague.'

So on they walked, side by side, till they reached the shop of a vintner of no good repute. It was well known to Borrhomeo—a house of evil resort, where the philosopher sometimes stole, disguised, by night, to be no longer a necromancer, but a man, and, so, from a man to become a beast.

They passed through the shop. The host, with a fat pale face, and a villanous smile, was drawing wine, which a handsome damsel was waiting to take away with her. He kissed her as she paid, and she gave him a cuff on his fat white chops, and laughed.

'What's become of Signor Borrhomeo,' said the girl, 'that he never comes here now.'

'Why, here he is!' cries Borrhomeo, with a saturnine smile, and he slaps his broad palm on her shoulder.

But the girl only shrugged, with a little shiver, and said, 'What a chill down my back—they're walking over my grave now.'

[The Italian phrase here is very nearly equivalent.]

'Why they neither hear nor see me!' said the astrologer, amazed.

They went into the inner room, where guests used to sit and drink. But the plague had stopped all that, and the room was empty.

'He's in there,' said the young man; 'you'll see him presently.'

Borrhomeo was filled with an awful curiosity. He knew the room, he thought, well; and there never had been, he thought, a door where the young man had pointed; but there was now a drapery there like what covers a doorway, and it swelled and swayed slowly in the wind.

'Some centuries?' said the astrologer, looking on the dark drapery. 'Geber, perhaps, or Alfarabi*——'

'It matters not a pin's point what his name; you'll call him "my lord", simply; and—observe—we alchymists are a potent order, and it behoves you to keep your word with us.'

'I will be true,' said Borrhomeo.

'And use the powers you gain, beneficently,' repeated his guide.

'I'm but a sinner. I will strive, with only an exception, in favour of such things as make wealth and life worth having,' answered the philosopher.

'See, take this, and do as I bid you,' said the youth, giving him a thin round film of human skin.*

[How the honest monk who wrote the tale, or even Borrhomeo himself, knew this and many other matters he describes, 'tis for him to say.]

'Breathe on it,' said he.

And when he did so he made him stretch it to the size of a sheet of paper, which he did quite easily.

'Now cover your face with it as with a napkin.'

So he did.

''Twill do; give it to me. It is but a picture. See.'

And it slowly shrunk until its disc was just the same as that of the lady's miniature in the lid of the box, over which he fixed it.

Borrhomeo beheld his own picture.

'Every adept has his portrait here,' said the young man. 'So good a likeness is always pleasant; but these have a power beside, and establish a sympathy between their originals and their possessor which secures discipline and silence.'

'How does it work?' asked Borrhomeo.

'Have I not been your good angel?' said the young man, sitting before him. He extends his legs—pushing out his feet, and letting his chin sink on his chest—he fixes his eyes upon him with a horrible and sarcastic glare, and one of his feet contracts and divides into a goatish stump.

Borrhomeo would have burst into a yell, but he could not.

'It is a nightmare, is it not?' said the stranger, who seemed delighted to hold him, minute after minute, in that spell. At last the shoe and hose that seemed to have shrunk apart like burning parchment, closed over the goatish shin and hoof; and rising, he shook him by the shoulder. With a gasp, the astrologer started to his feet.

'There, I told you it was a nightmare, or—or what you please. I could not have done it but through the picture. You see how fast we have you. You must for once resemble a Christian, Borrhomeo, and with us deal truly and honestly.'

'You've promised me the elixir vitae,' the old man said, fearful lest the secret should escape him.

'And you shall have it. Go, bring a cup of wine. He'll not see you, nor the wine, nor the cup.'

So he brought a cup of Falernian,* which he loved the best.

'There's fifty years of life for every drop,' said the youth.

'Let me live a thousand years, to begin with,' cries Borrhomeo.

'Beware. You'll tire of it——'

'Nay. Give me the twenty drops.'

So he took the cup, and measured the drops; and as they fell, the wine was agitated with a gentle simmer all over, and threw out ring after ring of purple, green, and gold. And Borrhomeo drank it, and sucked in the last drop in ecstacy, and cried out, blaspheming, with joy and sensual delight—

'And I'm to have this secret, too.'

'This and all others, when you claim them,' said the young man.

'See, 'tis time,' he added.

And Borrhomeo saw that the great misshapen dog he had seen in the street, was sniffing by the stranger's feet.

When they went into the inner room there was a large table, and many men at either side; and at the head a gigantic man, with a face like the face of a beast, but the flesh was as of a man. Borrhomeo quaked in his presence.

'I am aware of what hath passed, Borrhomeo,' he said. 'The condition is this:—You take this vial, and with the fluid it contains and the sponge trace the letter S on every door of every church and religious house within the walls of Milan. The dog will go with you.'

It was a fiend in dog's shape, says the monkish writer; and had he failed in his task would have torn him in pieces.

So Borrhomeo, that old arch-villain, undertook this office cheerfully, well knowing what its purpose was. For it was a thing notorious, that Satan was himself in a bodily, though phantasmal, shape seen before in Milan, and that he had tempted others to a like fascinorous* action; but, happily for their souls, in vain. The Stygian* satellites of the fiend had power to smear the door of every unconsecrated house in Milan with that pestilential virus, as, indeed, the citizens with their own eyes, when first the plague broke out, beheld upon their own doors. But they could not defile the church gates, nor the doors of the monasteries; and according to the conditions under which their infernal malice is bound, they could in nowise effect it save by the hand of one who was baptized, which, to the baleful abuse of that holy sacrament, the wretch, Borrhomeo, had been.

He did his accursed and murderous office well and fearlessly. His reward mammon and indefinite long life. The hell-dog by his side compelling him, and the belief in his invisibility making him confident withal. But therein was shown forth to all the world the craft of the fiend, and the just judgment of heaven; for he was plainly seen in the very act by the Sexton of the Church of Saint Mary of the Passion, and by the Pastor of the convent of Saint Justina of Padua, and the same officer of the Olivetans of Saint Victor. So, finding in the morning the only too plain and fatal traces of what he had been doing, with a mob at their heels, who would have had his life but for the guard, they arrested him in his house next morning, and the mob breaking in, smashed all the instruments of his infernal art, and would have burnt the house had they been allowed.

He being duly arraigned was, according to law, put to the torture, and forthwith confessed all the particulars I have related. So he was cast into a dungeon to await execution, which secretly he dreaded not, being confident in the efficacy of the elixir he had swallowed.

He was not to be put to death by decapitation. It was justly thought too honourable for so sordid a miscreant. He was sentenced to be hanged, and after hanging a day and a night he was to be laid in an open grave outside the gate on the Roman road, and there impaled, and after three days' exposure to be covered in, and so committed to the keeping of the earth, no more to groan under his living enormities.

The night before his execution, thinking deeply on the virtue of the elixir, and having assured himself, by many notable instances, which he easily brought to remembrance, that they could not deprive him, even by this severity, of his life, he lifted up his eyes and beheld the young man, in mourning suit, whose visit had been his ruin, standing near him in the cell.

This slave of Satan affected a sad countenance at first; and said he, 'We are cast down, Borrhomeo, by reason of thy sentence.'

'But we've cheated them,' answers he, pretending, maybe, more confidence than he had; 'they can't kill me.'

'That's certain,' rejoins the fiend.

'I shall live for a thousand years,' says he.

'Ay, you must continue to live for full one thousand years; 'tis a fair term—is it not?'

'A great deal may be done in that time,' says the old man, while beads of perspiration covered his puckered forehead, and he thought that, perhaps, he might cheat *him* too, and make his peace with heaven.

'They can't hang me,' says Borrhomeo.

'Oh! yes, they will certainly hang you; but, then, you'll live through it.'

'Ay, the elixir,' cried the prisoner.

'Thus stands the case: when an ordinary man is hanged he dies outright; but you can't die.'

'No—ha, ha!—I can't die!'

'Therefore, when you are hanged, you feel, think, hear, and so forth during the process.'

'St Anthony! But then 'tis only an hour—one hour of agony—and it ends.'

'You are to hang for a whole day and night,' continued the fiend; 'but that don't signify. Then when they take you down, you continue to feel, hear, think, and, if they leave your eyes open, to see, just as usual.'

'Why, yes, certainly, I'm alive,' cries Borrhomeo.

'Yes, alive, quite alive, although you appear to be dead,' says the daemon with a smile.

'Ay; but what's the best moment to make my escape?' says Borrhomeo.

'Escape! why, you *have* escaped. They can't kill you. No one can kill you, until your time is out. Then you know they lay you in an open grave and impale you.'

'What! ah, ha!' roared the old sinner, 'you are jesting.'

'Hush! depend upon it they will go through with it.'

The old man shook in every joint.

'Then, after three days and nights, they bury you,' said his visitor.

'I'll lose my life, or I'll break from them!' shouts the gigantic astrologer.

'But you can't lose your life, and you can't break from them,' says the fiend, softly.

'Why not? Oh! blessed saints! I'm stronger than you think.'

'Ay, muscle, bones—you are an old giant!'

'Surely,' cries the old man, 'and the terror of a dead man rising; ha! don't you see? They fly before me, and so I escape.'

'But you can't rise.'

'Say—say in heaven's name what you mean,' thundered old Borrhomeo.

'Do you remember, signor, that nightmare, as we jocularly called it, at the sign of the "Red Hat"?'

'Yes.'

'Well, a man who having swallowed the elixir vitae, suffers that sort of shock which in other mortals is a violent death, is afflicted during the remainder of his period of life, whether he be decapitated, or dismembered, or is laid unmutilated in the grave, with that sort of catalepsy, which you experienced for a minute—a catalepsy that does not relax or intermit. For that reason you ought to have carefully avoided this predicament.'

''Tis a lie,' roared the old man, and he ground his teeth, '*that's* not living.'

'You'll find, upon my honour, that it *is* living,' answered the fiend, with a gentle smile, and withdrawing from the cell.

Borrhomeo told all this to a priest, not under seal of confession, but to induce him to plead for his life. But the good man seeing he had already made himself the liegeman and accomplice of Satan, refused. Nor would his intercession have prevailed in any wise.

So Borrhomeo was hanged, impaled, and buried, according to his sentence; and it came to pass that fourteen years afterwards, that grave was opened in making a great drain from the group of houses thereby, and Borrhomeo was found just as he was laid therein, in no wise decayed, but fresh and sound,* which, indeed, showed that there did remain in him that sort of life which was supposed to ward off the common consequences of death.

So he was thrown into a great pit, and with many curses, covered in with stones and earth, where his stupendous punishment proceeds.

Get thee hence, Satan.*

WICKED CAPTAIN WALSHAWE, OF WAULING

CHAPTER I

PEG O'NEILL PAYS THE CAPTAIN'S DEBTS

A VERY odd thing happened to my uncle, Mr Watson, of Haddlestone; and to enable you to understand it, I must begin at the beginning.

In the year 1822, Mr James Walshawe, more commonly known as Captain Walshawe, died at the age of eighty-one years. The Captain in his early days, and so long as health and strength permitted, was a scamp of the active, intriguing sort; and spent his days and nights in sowing his wild oats, of which he seemed to have an inexhaustible stock. The harvest of this tillage was plentifully interspersed with thorns, nettles, and thistles, which stung the husbandman unpleasantly, and did not enrich him.

Captain Walshawe was very well known in the neighbourhood of Wauling, and very generally avoided there. A 'captain' by courtesy, for he had never reached that rank in the army list. He had quitted the service in 1766, at the age of twenty-five; immediately previous to which period his debts had grown so troublesome, that he was induced to extricate himself by running away with and marrying an heiress.

Though not so wealthy quite as he had imagined, she proved a very comfortable investment for what remained of his shattered affections; and he lived and enjoyed himself very much in his old way, upon her income, getting into no end of scrapes and scandals, and a good deal of debt and money trouble.

When he married his wife, he was quartered in Ireland, at Clonmel, where was a nunnery, in which, as pensioner, resided Miss O'Neill, or as she was called in the country, Peg O'Neill—the heiress of whom I have spoken.

Her situation was the only ingredient of romance in the affair, for the young lady was decidedly plain, though good-humoured looking, with that style of features which is termed *potato*; and in figure she was a little too plump, and rather short. But she was impressible; and the handsome young English Lieutenant was too much for her monastic tendencies, and she eloped.

In England there are traditions of Irish fortune-hunters, and in Ireland of English. The fact is, it was the vagrant class of each country that chiefly visited the other in old times; and a handsome vagabond, whether at home or abroad, I suppose, made the most of his face, which was also his fortune.

At all events, he carried off the fair one from the sanctuary; and for some sufficient reason, I suppose, they took up their abode at Wauling, in Lancashire.

Here the gallant captain amused himself after his fashion, sometimes running up, of course on business, to London. I believe few wives have ever cried more in a given time than did that poor, dumpy, potato-faced heiress, who got over the nunnery garden wall, and jumped into the handsome Captain's arms, for love.

He spent her income, frightened her out of her wits with oaths and threats, and broke her heart.

Latterly she shut herself up pretty nearly altogether in her room. She had an old, rather grim, Irish servant-woman in attendance upon her. This domestic was tall, lean, and religious, and the Captain knew instinctively she hated him; and he hated her in return, and often threatened to put her out of the house, and sometimes even to kick her out of the window. And whenever a wet day confined him to the house, or the stable, and he grew tired of smoking, he would begin to swear and curse at her for a *diddled* old mischief-maker, that could never be easy, and was always troubling the house with her cursed stories, and so forth.

But years passed away, and old Molly Doyle remained still in her original position. Perhaps he thought that there must be somebody there, and that he was not, after all, very likely to change for the better.

CHAPTER II

THE BLESSED CANDLE

HE tolerated another intrusion, too, and thought himself a paragon of patience and easy good-nature for so doing. A Roman Catholic clergyman, in a long black frock, with a low standing collar, and a little white muslin fillet round his neck—tall, sallow, with blue chin, and dark steady eyes—used to glide up and down the stairs, and through the passages; and the Captain sometimes met him in one place and sometimes in another. But by a caprice incident to such tempers he treated this cleric exceptionally, and even with a surly sort of courtesy, though he grumbled about his visits behind his back.

I do not know that he had a great deal of moral courage, and the ecclesiastic looked severe and self-possessed; and somehow he thought he had no good opinion of him, and if a natural occasion were offered, might say extremely unpleasant things, and hard to be answered.

Well the time came at last, when poor Peg O'Neill—in an evil hour Mrs James Walshawe—must cry, and quake, and pray her last. The doctor came from Penlynden, and was just as vague as usual, but more gloomy, and for about a week came and went oftener. The cleric in the long black frock was also daily there. And at last came that last sacrament in the gates of death, when the sinner is traversing those dread steps that never can be retraced; when the face is turned for ever from life, and we see a receding shape, and hear a voice already irrevocably in the land of spirits.

So the poor lady died; and some people said the Captain 'felt it very much'. I don't think he did. But he was not very well just then, and looked the part of mourner and penitent to admiration—being seedy and sick. He drank a great deal of brandy and water that night, and called in Farmer Dobbs, for want of better company, to drink with him; and told him all his grievances, and how happy he and 'the poor lady upstairs' might have been, had it not been for liars, and pick-thanks, and tale-bearers, and the like, who came between them—meaning Molly Doyle—whom, as he waxed eloquent over his liquor, he came at last to curse and rail at by name, with more than his accustomed freedom. And he described his own natural character and amiability in such moving terms, that he wept maudlin tears of sensibility over his theme; and when Dobbs was gone, drank some more grog, and took to railing and cursing again by himself; and then mounted the stairs unsteadily, to see 'what the devil Doyle and the other——old witches were about in poor Peg's room.'

When he pushed open the door, he found some half-dozen crones, chiefly Irish, from the neighbouring town of Hackleton, sitting over tea and snuff, etc., with candles lighted round the corpse, which was arrayed in a strangely cut robe of brown serge. She had secretly belonged to some order—I think the Carmelite, but I am not certain—and wore the habit in her coffin.

'What the d—— are you doing with my wife?' cried the Captain, rather thickly. 'How dare you dress her up in this——trumpery, you—you cheating old witch; and what's that candle doing in her hand?'

I think he was a little startled, for the spectacle was grisly enough. The dead lady was arrayed in this strange brown robe, and in her rigid fingers, as in a socket, with the large wooden beads and cross wound round it, burned a wax candle,* shedding its white light over the sharp features of the corpse. Moll Doyle was not to be put down by the Captain, whom she hated, and accordingly, in her phrase, 'he got as good as he gave'. And the Captain's wrath waxed fiercer, and he chucked the wax taper from the dead hand, and was on the point of flinging it at the old serving-woman's head.

'The holy candle, you sinner!' cried she.

'I've a mind to make you eat it, you beast,' cried the Captain.

But I think he had not known before what it was, for he subsided a little sulkily, and he stuffed his hand with the candle (quite extinct by this time) into his pocket, and said he—

'You know devilish well you had no business going on with y-y-your d—— *witch*-craft about my poor wife, without my leave—you do—and you'll please to take off that d—— brown pinafore, and get her decently into her coffin, and I'll pitch your devil's waxlight into the sink.'

And the Captain stalked out of the room.

'An' now her poor sowl's in prison, you wretch, be the mains o' ye; an' may yer own be shut into the wick o' that same candle, till it's burned out, ye savage.'

'I'd have you ducked for a witch, for two-pence,' roared the Captain up the staircase, with his hand on the banisters, standing on the lobby. But the door of the chamber of death clapped angrily, and he went down to the parlour, where he examined the holy candle for a while, with a tipsy gravity, and then with something of that reverential feeling for the symbolic, which is not uncommon in rakes and scamps, he thoughtfully locked it up in a press,* where were accumulated all sorts of obsolete rubbish—soiled packs of cards, disused tobacco-pipes, broken powder-flasks, his military sword, and a dusky bundle of the 'Flash Songster',* and other questionable literature.

He did not trouble the dead lady's room any more. Being a volatile man it is probable that more cheerful plans and occupations began to entertain his fancy.

CHAPTER III

MY UNCLE WATSON VISITS WAULING

So the poor lady was buried decently, and Captain Walshawe reigned alone for many years at Wauling. He was too shrewd and too experienced by this time to run violently down the steep hill that leads to ruin. So there was a method in his madness; and after a widowed career of more than forty years, he, too, died at last with some guineas in his purse.

Forty years and upwards is a great *edax rerum*,* and a wonderful chemical power. It acted forcibly upon the gay Captain Walshawe. Gout supervened, and was no more conducive to temper than to enjoyment, and made his elegant hands lumpy at all the small joints, and turned them slowly into crippled claws. He grew stout when his exercise was interfered with, and ultimately almost corpulent, he suffered from what Mr Holloway* calls 'bad legs', and was wheeled about in a great leathern-backed chair, and his infirmities went on accumulating with his years.

I am sorry to say, I never heard that he repented, or turned his thoughts seriously to the future. On the contrary, his talk grew fouler, and his fun ran upon his favourite sins, and his temper waxed more truculent. But he did not sink into dotage. Considering his bodily infirmities, his energies and his malignities, which were many and active, were marvellously little abated by time. So he went on to the close. When his temper was stirred, he cursed and swore in a way that made decent people tremble. It was a word and a blow with him; the latter, luckily, not very sure now. But he would seize his crutch and make a swoop or a pound at the offender, or shy his medicine-bottle, or his tumbler, at his head.

It was a peculiarity of Captain Walshawe that he, by this time, hated nearly everybody. My uncle, Mr Watson, of Haddlestone, was cousin to the Captain, and his heir-at-law. But my uncle had lent him money on mortgage of his estates, and there had been a treaty to sell, and terms and a price were agreed upon, in 'articles' which the lawyers said were still in force.

I think the ill-conditioned Captain bore him a grudge for being richer than he, and would have liked to do him an ill turn. But it did not lie in his way; at least while he was living.

My Uncle Watson was a Methodist, and what they call a 'class-leader';* and, on the whole, a very good man. He was now near fifty—grave, as beseemed his profession—somewhat dry—and a little severe, perhaps—but a just man.

A letter from the Penlynden doctor reached him at Haddlestone, announcing the death of the wicked old Captain; and suggesting his attendance at the funeral, and the expediency of his being on the spot to look after things at Wauling. The reasonableness of this striking my good uncle, he made his journey to the old house in Lancashire incontinently, and reached in time for the funeral.

My Uncle, whose traditions of the Captain were derived from his mother, who remembered him in his slim, handsome youth—in shorts, cocked-hat and lace, was amazed at the bulk of the coffin which contained his mortal remains; but the lid being already screwed down, he did not see the face of the bloated old sinner.

CHAPTER IV

IN THE PARLOUR

WHAT I relate, I had from the lips of my Uncle, who was a truthful man, and not prone to fancies.

The day turning out awfully rainy and tempestuous, he persuaded the doctor and the attorney to remain for the night at Wauling.

There was no will—the attorney was sure of that; for the Captain's enmities were perpetually shifting, and he could never quite make up his mind, as to how best to give effect to a malignity whose direction was being constantly modified. He had had instructions for drawing a will a dozen times over. But the process had always been arrested by the intending testator.

Search being made, no will was found. The papers, indeed were all right, with one important exception, the leases were nowhere to be seen. There were special circumstances connected with several of the principal tenancies on the estate—unnecessary here to detail—which rendered the loss of these documents one of very serious moment, and even of very obvious danger.

My Uncle, therefore, searched strenuously. The attorney was at his elbow, and the doctor helped with a suggestion now and then. The old serving-man seemed an honest deaf creature, and really knew nothing.

My Uncle Watson was very much perturbed. He fancied—but this possibly was only fancy—that he had detected for a moment a queer look in the attorney's face; and from that instant it became fixed in his mind that he knew all about the leases. Mr Watson expounded that evening in the parlour to the doctor, the attorney, and the deaf servant. Ananias and Sapphira* figured in the foreground; and the awful nature of fraud and theft, or tampering in anywise with the plain rule of honesty in matters pertaining to estates, etc., were pointedly dwelt upon; and then came a long and strenuous prayer, in which he entreated with fervour and aplomb that the hard heart of the sinner who had abstracted the leases might be softened or broken in such a way as to lead to their restitution: or that, if he continued reserved and contumacious, it might at least be the will of Heaven to bring him to public justice and the documents to light. The fact is, that he was praying all this time at the attorney.

When these religious exercises were over, the visiters retired to their rooms, and my Uncle Watson wrote two or three pressing letters by the fire. When his task was done, it had grown late: the candles were flaring in their sockets, and all in bed, and, I suppose, asleep, but he.

The fire was nearly out, he chilly, and the flame of the candles throbbing strangely in their sockets shed alternate glare and shadow round the old wainscoted room and its quaint furniture. Outside were the wild thunder and piping of the storm; and the rattling of distant windows sounded through the passages, and down the stairs, like angry people astir in the house.

My Uncle Watson belonged to a sect who by no means reject the supernatural, and whose founder, on the contrary, has sanctioned ghosts* in the most emphatic way. He was glad therefore to remember, that in prosecuting his search that day, he had seen some six inches of wax candle in the press in the parlour; for he had no fancy to be overtaken by darkness in his present situation. He had no time to lose; and taking the bunch of keys—of which he was now master—he soon fitted the lock, and secured the candle—a treasure in his circumstances; and lighting it, he stuffed it into the socket of one of the expiring candles, and extinguishing the other, he looked round the room in the steady light reassured. At the same moment, an unusually violent gust of the storm blew a handful of gravel against the parlour window, with a sharp rattle that startled him in the midst of the roar and hubbub; and the flame of the candle itself was agitated by the air.

CHAPTER V

THE BED-CHAMBER

MY Uncle walked up to bed, guarding his candle with his hand, for the lobby windows were rattling furiously, and he disliked the idea of being left in the dark more than ever.

His bedroom was comfortable, though old-fashioned. He shut and bolted the door. There was a tall looking-glass opposite the foot of his four-poster, on the dressing-table between the windows. He tried to make the curtains meet, but they would not draw; and like many a gentleman in a like perplexity, he did not possess a pin, nor was there one in the huge pincushion beneath the glass.

He turned the face of the mirror away therefore, so that its back was presented to the bed, pulled the curtains together, and placed a chair against them, to prevent their falling open again. There was a good fire, and a reinforcement of round coal and wood inside the fender. So he piled it up to ensure a cheerful blaze through the night, and placing a little black mahogany table, with the legs of a Satyr,* beside the bed, and his candle upon it, he got between the sheets, and laid his red night-capped head upon his pillow, and disposed himself to sleep.

The first thing that made him uncomfortable was a sound at the foot of his bed, quite distinct in a momentary lull of the storm. It was only the gentle rustle and rush of the curtains, which fell open again; and as his eyes opened, he saw them resuming their perpendicular dependence, and sat up in his bed almost expecting to see something uncanny in the aperture.

There was nothing, however, but the dressing-table, and other dark furniture, and the window-curtains faintly undulating in the violence of the storm. He did not care to get up, therefore—the fire being bright and cheery—to replace the curtains by a chair, in the position in which he had left them, anticipating possibly a new recurrence of the relapse which had startled him from his incipient doze.

So he got to sleep in a little while again, but he was disturbed by a sound, as he fancied, at the table on which stood the candle. He could not say what it was, only that he wakened with a start, and lying so in some amaze, he did distinctly hear a sound which startled him a good deal, though there was nothing necessarily supernatural in it. He described it as resembling what would occur if you fancied a thinnish table-leaf, with a convex warp in it, depressed the reverse way, and suddenly with a spring recovering its natural convexity. It was a loud, sudden thump, which made the heavy candlestick jump, and there was an end, except that my uncle did not get again into a doze for ten minutes at least

The next time he awoke, it was in that odd, serene way that some-times occurs. We open our eyes, we know not why, quite placidly, and are on the instant wide awake. He had had a nap of some duration this time, for his candle-flame was fluttering and flaring, *in articulo,** in the silver socket. But the fire was still bright and cheery; so he popped the extinguisher on the socket, and almost at the same time there came a tap at his door, and a sort of crescendo 'hush-sh-sh!' Once more my Uncle was sitting up, scared and perturbed, in his bed. He recollected, however, that he had bolted his door; and such inveterate materialists are we in the midst of our spiritualism, that this reassured him, and he breathed a deep sigh, and began to grow tranquil. But after a rest of a minute or two, there came a louder and sharper knock at his door; so that instinctively he called out, 'Who's there?' in a loud, stern key. There was no sort of response, however. The nervous effect of the start subsided; and I think my uncle must have remembered how constantly, especially on a stormy night, these creaks or cracks which simulate all manner of goblin noises, make themselves naturally audible.

CHAPTER VI

THE EXTINGUISHER IS LIFTED

AFTER a while, then, he lay down with his back turned toward that side of the bed at which was the door, and his face toward the table on which stood the massive old candlestick capped with its extinguisher, and in that position he closed his eyes. But sleep would not revisit them. All kinds of queer fancies began to trouble him—some of them I remember.

He felt the point of a finger, he averred, pressed most distinctly on the tip of his great toe, as if a living hand were between his sheets, and making a sort of signal of attention or silence. Then again he felt something as large as a rat make a sudden bounce in the middle of his bolster, just under his head. Then a voice said 'oh!' very gently, close at the back of his head. All these things he felt certain of, and yet investigation led to nothing. He felt odd little cramps stealing now and then about him; and then, on a sudden, the middle finger of his right hand was plucked backwards, with a light playful jerk that frightened him awfully.

Meanwhile the storm kept singing, and howling, and ha-ha-hooing hoarsely among the limbs of the old trees and the chimney-pots; and my Uncle Watson, although he prayed and meditated as was his wont when he lay awake, felt his heart throb excitedly, and sometimes thought he was beset with evil spirits, and at others that he was in the early stage of a fever.

He resolutely kept his eyes closed, however, and, like St Paul's shipwrecked companions,* wished for the day. At last another little doze seems to have stolen upon his senses, for he awoke quietly and completely as before—opening his eyes all at once, and seeing everything as if he had not slept for a moment.

The fire was still blazing redly—nothing uncertain in the light—the massive silver candlestick, topped with its tall extinguisher, stood on the centre of the black mahogany table as before; and, looking by what seemed a sort of accident to the apex of this, he beheld something which made him quite misdoubt the evidence of his eyes.

He saw the extinguisher lifted by a tiny hand, from beneath, and a small human face, no bigger than a thumb-nail, with nicely proportioned features peep from beneath it. In this Lilliputian* countenance was such a ghastly consternation as horrified my Uncle unspeakably. Out came a little foot then and there, and a pair of wee legs, in short silk stockings and buckled shoes, then the rest of the figure; and, with the arms holding about the socket, the little legs stretched and stretched, hanging about the stem of the candlestick till the feet reached the base, and so down the Satyr-like leg of the table, till they reached the floor, extending elastically, and strangely enlarging in all proportions as they approached the ground, where the feet and buckles were those of a well-shaped, full-grown man, and the figure tapering upward until it dwindled to its original fairy dimensions at the top, like an object seen in some strangely curved mirror.

Standing upon the floor he expanded, my amazed uncle could not tell how, into his proper proportions; and stood pretty nearly in profile at the bed side, a handsome and elegantly shaped young man, in a by-gone military costume, with a small laced three-cocked hat and plume on his head, but looking like a man going to be hanged—in unspeakable despair.

He stepped lightly to the hearth, and turned for a few seconds very dejectedly with his back toward the bed and the mantel piece, and he saw the hilt of his rapier glittering in the fire-light; and then walking across the room he placed himself at the dressing-table, visible through the divided curtains at the foot of the bed. The fire was blazing still so brightly that my uncle saw him as distinctly as if half-a-dozen candles were burning.

CHAPTER VII

THE VISITATION CULMINATES

THE looking-glass was an old-fashioned piece of furniture, and had a drawer beneath it. My Uncle had searched it carefully for the papers in the day-time; but the silent figure pulled the drawer quite out, pressed a spring at the side, disclosing a false receptacle behind it, and from this he drew a parcel of papers tied together with pink tape.

All this time my uncle was staring at him in a horrified state, neither winking nor breathing, and the apparition had not once given the smallest intimation of consciousness that a living person was in the same room. But now, for the first time, it turned its livid stare full upon my uncle with a hateful smile of significance, lifting up the little parcel of papers between his slender finger and thumb. Then he made a long, cunning wink at him, and seemed to blow out one of his cheeks in a burlesque grimace, which, but for the horrific circumstances, would have been ludicrous. My Uncle could not tell whether this was really an intentional distortion or only one of those horrid ripples and deflections which were constantly disturbing the proportions of the figure, as if it were seen through some unequal and perverting medium.

The figure now approached the bed, seeming to grow exhausted and malignant as it did so. My Uncle's terror nearly culminated at this point, for he believed it was drawing near him with an evil purpose. But it was not so; for the soldier, over whom twenty years seemed to have passed in his brief transit to the dressing-table and back again, threw himself into a great high-backed arm-chair of stuffed leather at the far side of the fire, and placed his heels on the fender. His feet and legs seemed indistinctly to swell, and swathings showed themselves round them, and they grew into something enormous, and the upper figure swayed and shaped itself into corresponding proportions, a great mass of corpulence, with a cadaverous and malignant face, and the furrows of a great old age, and colourless glassy eyes; and with these changes, which came indefinitely but rapidly as those of a sunset cloud, the fine regimentals faded away, and a loose, gray, woollen drapery, somehow, was there in its stead; and all seemed to be stained and rotten, for swarms of worms seemed creeping in and out, while the figure grew paler and paler, till my Uncle, who liked his pipe, and employed the simile naturally, said the whole effigy grew to the colour of tobacco ashes, and the clusters of worms into little wriggling knots of sparks such as we see running over the residuum of a burnt sheet of paper. And so with the strong draught caused by the fire, and the current of air from the window, which was rattling in the storm, the feet seemed to be drawn into the fire-place, and the whole figure, light as ashes, floated away with them, and disappeared with a whisk up the capacious old chimney.

It seemed to my Uncle that the fire suddenly darkened and the air grew icy cold, and there came an awful roar and riot of tempest, which shook the old house from top to base, and sounded like the yelling of a bloodthirsty mob on receiving a new and long-expected victim.

Good Uncle Watson used to say, 'I have been in many situations of fear and danger in the course of my life, but never did I pray with so much agony before or since; for then, as now, it was clear beyond a cavil that I had actually beheld the phantom of an evil spirit.'

CONCLUSION

Now there are two curious circumstances to be observed in this relation of my Uncle's, who was, as I have said, a perfectly veracious man.

First—The wax candle which he took from the press in the parlour and burnt at his bedside on that horrible night was unquestionably, according to the testimony of the old deaf servant, who had been fifty years at Wauling, that identical piece of 'holy candle' which had stood in the fingers of the poor lady's corpse, and concerning which the old Irish crone, long since dead, had delivered the curious curse I have mentioned against the Captain.

Secondly—Behind the drawer under the looking-glass, he did actually discover a second but secret drawer, in which were concealed the identical papers which he had suspected the attorney of having made away with. There were circumstances, too, afterwards disclosed which convinced my Uncle that the old man had deposited them there preparatory to burning them, which he had nearly made up his mind to do.

Now, a very remarkable ingredient in this tale of my Uncle Watson was this, that so far as my father, who had never seen Captain Walshawe in the course of his life, could gather, the phantom had exhibited a horrible and grotesque, but unmistakable resemblance to that defunct scamp in the various stages of his long life.

Wauling was sold in the year 1837, and the old house shortly after pulled down, and a new one built nearer to the river. I often wonder whether it was rumoured to be haunted, and if so what stories were current about it. It was a commodious and stanch* old house, and withal rather handsome; and its demolition was certainly suspicious.

GREEN TEA

A Case Reported by Martin Hesselius, the
German Physician

PREFACE*

THOUGH carefully educated in medicine and surgery, I have never practised either. The study of each continues, nevertheless, to interest me profoundly. Neither idleness nor caprice caused my secession from the honourable profession which I had just entered. The cause was a very trifling scratch inflicted by a dissecting-knife. This trifle cost me the loss of two fingers, amputated promptly, and the more painful loss of my health, for I have never been quite well since, and have seldom been twelve months together in the same place.

In my wanderings I became acquainted with Dr Martin Hesselius,* a wanderer like myself, like me a physician, and like me an enthusiast in his profession. Unlike me in this, that his wanderings were voluntary, and he a man, if not of fortune, as we estimate fortune in England, at least in what our forefathers used to term 'easy circumstances'.

In Dr Martin Hesselius I found my master. His knowledge was immense, his grasp of a case was an intuition. He was the very man to inspire a young enthusiast, like me, with awe and delight. My admiration has stood the test of time and survived the separation of death. I am sure it was well-founded.

For nearly twenty years I acted as his medical secretary. His immense collection of papers he has left in my care, to be arranged, indexed, and bound. His treatment of some of these cases is curious. He writes in two distinct characters. He describes what he saw and heard as an intelligent layman might, and when in this style of narrative he has seen the patient either through his own hall-door, to the light of day, or through the gates of darkness to the caverns of the dead, he returns upon the narrative, and in the terms of his art, and with all the force and originality of genius, proceeds to the work of analysis, diagnosis, and illustration.

Here and there a case strikes me as of a kind to amuse or horrify a lay reader with an interest quite different from the peculiar one which it may possess for an expert. With slight modifications, chiefly of language, and of course a change of names, I copy the following. The narrator is

Dr Martin Hesselius. I find it among the voluminous notes of cases which he made during a tour in England about fifty-four years ago.

It is related in a series of letters to his friend Professor Van Loo of Leyden. The professor was not a physician, but a chemist, and a man who read history and metaphysics and medicine, and had, in his day, written a play.

The narrative is therefore, if somewhat less valuable as a medical record, necessarily written in a manner more likely to interest an unlearned reader.

These letters, from a memorandum attached, appear to have been returned on the death of the professor, in 1819, to Dr Hesselius. They are written, some in English, some in French, but the greater part in German. I am a faithful, though I am conscious, by no means a graceful, translator, and although, here and there, I omit some passages, and shorten others, and disguise names, I have interpolated nothing.

CHAPTER I

DR HESSELIUS RELATES HOW HE MET
THE REV. MR JENNINGS

THE Rev. Mr Jennings is tall and thin. He is middle-aged, and dresses with a natty, old-fashioned, high-church* precision. He is naturally a little stately, but not at all stiff. His features, without being handsome, are well formed, and their expression extremely kind, but also shy.

I met him one evening at Lady Mary Heyduke's. The modesty and benevolence of his countenance are extremely prepossessing.

We were but a small party, and he joined agreeably enough in the conversation. He seems to enjoy listening very much more than contributing to the talk; but what he says is always to the purpose and well said. He is a great favourite of Lady Mary's, who, it seems, consults him upon many things, and thinks him the most happy and blessed person on earth. Little knows she about him.

The Rev. Mr Jennings is a bachelor, and has, they say, sixty thousand pounds in the funds.* He is a charitable man. He is most anxious to be actively employed in his sacred profession, and yet, though always tolerably well elsewhere, when he goes down to his vicarage in Warwickshire, to engage in the active duties of his sacred calling, his health soon fails him, and in a very strange way. So says Lady Mary.

There is no doubt that Mr Jennings's health does break down in, generally, a sudden and mysterious way, sometimes in the very act of officiating in his old and pretty church at Kenlis.* It may be his heart, it may be his brain. But so it has happened three or four times, or oftener, that after proceeding a certain way in the service, he has on a sudden stopped short, and after a silence, apparently quite unable to resume, he has fallen into solitary, inaudible prayer, his hands and eyes uplifted, and then pale as death, and in the agitation of a strange shame and horror, descended trembling, got into the vestry-room, and left his congregation, without explanation, to themselves. This occurred when his curate was absent. When he goes down to Kenlis, now, he always takes care to provide a clergyman to share his duty, and to supply his place on the instant, should he become thus suddenly incapacitated.

When Mr Jennings breaks down quite, and beats a retreat from the vicarage, and returns to London, where, in a dark street off Piccadilly, he inhabits a very narrow house, Lady Mary says that he is always perfectly well. I have my own opinion about that. There are degrees of course. We shall see.

Mr Jennings is a perfectly gentleman-like man. People, however, remark something odd. There is an impression a little ambiguous. One thing which certainly contributes to it, people, I think, don't remember—perhaps, distinctly remark. But I did, almost immediately. Mr Jennings has a way of looking sidelong upon the carpet, as if his eye followed the movements of something there. This, of course, is not always. It occurs only now and then. But often enough to give a certain oddity as I have said to his manner, and in this glance travelling along the floor, there is something both shy and anxious.

A medical philosopher, as you are good enough to call me, elaborating theories by the aid of cases sought out by himself, and by him watched and scrutinized with more time at command, and consequently infinitely more minuteness than the ordinary practitioner can afford, falls insensibly into habits of observation which accompany him everywhere, and are exercised, as some people would say, impertinently, upon every subject that presents itself with the least likelihood of rewarding inquiry.

There was a promise of this kind in this slight, timid, kindly, but reserved gentleman, whom I met for the first time at this agreeable little evening gathering. I observed, of course, more than I here set down; but I reserve all that borders on the technical for a strictly scientific paper.

I may remark, that when I here speak of medical science, I do so as I hope some day to see it more generally understood, in a much more comprehensive sense than its generally material treatment would warrant. I believe that the entire natural world is but the ultimate expression of that spiritual world from which, and in which alone, it has its life. I believe that the essential man is a spirit, that the spirit is an organized substance, but as different in point of material from what we ordinarily understand by matter, as light or electricity is; that the material body is, in the most literal sense, a vesture, and death consequently no interruption of the living man's existence, but simply his extrication from the natural body—a process which commences at the moment of what we term death, and the completion of which, at furthest, a few days later, is the resurrection 'in power'.*

The person who weighs the consequences of these positions will probably see their practical bearing upon medical science. This is, however, by no means the proper place for displaying the proofs and discussing the consequences of this too generally unrecognized state of facts.

In pursuance of my habit, I was covertly observing Mr Jennings, with all my caution—I think he perceived it—and I saw plainly that he was as cautiously observing me. Lady Mary happening to address me by my name, as Dr Hesselius, I saw that he glanced at me more sharply, and then became thoughtful for a few minutes.

After this, as I conversed with a gentleman at the other end of the room, I saw him look at me more steadily, and with an interest which I thought I understood. I then saw him take an opportunity of chatting with Lady Mary, and was, as one always is, perfectly aware of being the subject of a distant inquiry and answer.

This tall clergyman approached me by-and-by: and in a little time we had got into conversation. When two people, who like reading, and know books and places, having travelled, wish to converse, it is very strange if they can't find topics. It was not accident that brought him near me, and led him into conversation. He knew German, and had read my Essays on Metaphysical Medicine, which suggest more than they actually say.

This courteous man, gentle, shy, plainly a man of thought and reading, who moving and talking among us, was not altogether of us, and whom I already suspected of leading a life whose transactions and alarms were carefully concealed, with an impenetrable reserve from, not only the world, but his best beloved friends—was cautiously weighing in his own mind the idea of taking a certain step with regard to me.

I penetrated his thoughts without his being aware of it, and was careful to say nothing which could betray to his sensitive vigilance my suspicions respecting his position, or my surmises about his plans respecting myself.

We chatted upon indifferent subjects for a time; but at last he said:

'I was very much interested by some papers of yours, Dr Hesselius, upon what you term Metaphysical Medicine—I read them in German, ten or twelve years ago—have they been translated?'

'No, I'm sure they have not—I should have heard. They would have asked my leave, I think.'

'I asked the publishers here, a few months ago, to get the book for me in the original German; but they tell me it is out of print.'

'So it is, and has been for some years; but it flatters me as an author to find that you have not forgotten my little book, although,' I added, laughing, 'ten or twelve years is a considerable time to have managed without it; but I suppose you have been turning the subject over again in your mind, or something has happened lately to revive your interest in it.'

At this remark, accompanied by a glance of inquiry, a sudden embarrassment disturbed Mr Jennings, analogous to that which makes a young lady blush and look foolish. He dropped his eyes, and folded his hands together uneasily, and looked oddly, and you would have said, guilty for a moment.

I helped him out of his awkwardness in the best way, by appearing not to observe it, and going straight on, I said: 'Those revivals of interest in a subject happen to me often; one book suggests another, and often sends me back a wild-goose chase over an interval of twenty years. But if you still care to possess a copy, I shall be only too happy to provide you; I have still got two or three by me—and if you allow me to present one I shall be very much honoured.'

'You are very good indeed,' he said, quite at his ease again, in a moment: 'I almost despaired—I don't know how to thank you.'

'Pray don't say a word; the thing is really so little worth that I am only ashamed of having offered it, and if you thank me any more I shall throw it into the fire in a fit of modesty.'

Mr Jennings laughed. He inquired where I was staying in London, and after a little more conversation on a variety of subjects, he took his departure.

CHAPTER II

THE DOCTOR QUESTIONS LADY MARY, AND SHE ANSWERS

'I LIKE your vicar so much, Lady Mary,' said I, so soon as he was gone. 'He has read, travelled, and thought, and having also suffered, he ought to be an accomplished companion.'

'So he is, and, better still, he is a really good man,' said she. 'His advice is invaluable about my schools, and all my little undertakings at Dawlbridge, and he's so painstaking, he takes so much trouble—you have no idea—wherever he thinks he can be of use: he's so good-natured and so sensible.'

'It is pleasant to hear so good an account of his neighbourly virtues. I can only testify to his being an agreeable and gentle companion, and in addition to what you have told me, I think I can tell you two or three things about him,' said I.

'Really!'

'Yes, to begin with, he's unmarried.'

'Yes, that's right,—go on.'

'He has been writing, that is he *was*, but for two or three years, perhaps, he has not gone on with his work, and the book was upon some rather abstract subject—perhaps theology.'

'Well, he was writing a book, as you say; I'm not quite sure what it was about, but only that it was nothing that I cared for, very likely you are right, and he certainly did stop—yes.'

'And although he only drank a little coffee here to-night, he likes tea, at least, did like it, extravagantly.'

'Yes; that's *quite* true.'

'He drank green tea, a good deal, didn't he?' I pursued.

'Well, that's very odd! Green tea was a subject on which we used almost to quarrel.'

'But he has quite given that up,' I continued.

'So he has.'

'And, now, one more fact. His mother, or his father, did you know them?'

'Yes, both; his father is only ten years dead, and their place is near Dawlbridge. We knew them very well,' she answered.

'Well, either his mother or his father—I should rather think his father—saw a ghost,' said I.

'Well, you really are a conjurer, Doctor Hesselius.'

'Conjurer or no, haven't I said right?' I answered, merrily.

'You certainly have, and it *was* his father: he was a silent, whimsical man, and he used to bore my father about his dreams, and at last he told him a story about a ghost he had seen and talked with, and a very odd story it was. I remember it particularly because I was so afraid of him. This story was long before he died—when I was quite a child—and his ways were so silent and moping, and he used to drop in, sometimes, in the dusk, when I was alone in the drawing-room, and I used to fancy there were ghosts about him.'

I smiled and nodded.

'And now having established my character as a conjurer I think I must say good-night,' said I.

'But how *did* you find it out?'

'By the planets of course, as the gipsies do,' I answered, and so, gaily, we said good-night.

Next morning I sent the little book he had been inquiring after, and a note to Mr Jennings, and on returning late that evening, I found that he had called and left his card. He asked whether I was at home, and asked at what hour he would be most likely to find me.

Does he intend opening his case, and consulting me 'professionally', as they say? I hope so. I have already conceived a theory about him. It is supported by Lady Mary's answers to my parting questions. I should like much to ascertain from his own lips. But what can I do consistently with good breeding to invite a confession? Nothing. I rather think he meditates one. At all events, my dear Van L., I shan't make myself difficult of access; I mean to return his visit tomorrow. It will be only civil in return for his politeness, to ask to see him. Perhaps something may come of it. Whether much, little, or nothing, my dear Van L., you shall hear.

CHAPTER III

DR HESSELIUS PICKS UP SOMETHING IN LATIN BOOKS

WELL, I have called at Blank-street.

On inquiring at the door, the servant told me that Mr Jennings was engaged very particularly with a gentleman, a clergyman from Kenlis, his parish in the country. Intending to reserve my privilege and to call again, I merely intimated that I should try another time, and had turned to go, when the servant begged my pardon, and asked me, looking at me a little more attentively than well-bred persons of his order usually do, whether I was Dr Hesselius, and, on learning that I was, he said, 'Perhaps then, sir, you would allow me to mention it to Mr Jennings, for I am sure he wishes to see you.'

The servant returned in a moment, with a message from Mr Jennings, asking me to go into his study, which was in effect his back drawing-room, promising to be with me in a very few minutes.

This was really a study—almost a library. The room was lofty, with two tall slender windows, and rich dark curtains. It was much larger than I had expected, and stored with books on every side, from the floor to the ceiling. The upper carpet—for to my tread it felt that there were two or three—was a Turkey* carpet. My steps fell noiselessly. The book-cases standing out, placed the windows, particularly narrow ones, in deep recesses. The effect of the room was, although extremely comfortable, and even luxurious, decidedly gloomy, and aided by the silence, almost oppressive. Perhaps, however, I ought to have allowed something for association. My mind had connected peculiar ideas with Mr Jennings. I stepped into this perfectly silent room, of a very silent house, with a peculiar foreboding; and its darkness, and solemn cloth-ing of books, for except where two narrow looking-glasses were set in the wall, they were everywhere, helped this sombre feeling.

While awaiting Mr Jennings's arrival, I amused myself by looking into some of the books with which his shelves were laden. Not among these, but immediately under them, with their backs upward, on the floor, I lighted upon a complete set of Swedenborg's Arcana Caelestia, in the original Latin,* a very fine folio set, bound in the natty livery which theology affects, pure vellum, namely, gold letters, and carmine edges. There were paper markers in several of these volumes. I raised and placed them, one after the other, upon the table, and opening where these papers were placed, I read in the solemn Latin phraseology, a series of sentences indicated by a pencilled line at the margin. Of these I copy here a few, translating them into English.

'When man's interior sight is opened, which is that of his spirit, then there appear the things of another life, which cannot possibly be made visible to the bodily sight.' . . .

'By the internal sight it has been granted me to see the things that are in the other life, more clearly than I see those that are in the world. From these considerations, it is evident that external vision exists from interior vision, and this from a vision still more interior, and so on.' . . .

'There are with every man at least two evil spirits.'* . . .

'With wicked genii there is also a fluent speech, but harsh and grat-ing. There is also among them, a speech which is not fluent, wherein the dissent of the thoughts is perceived as something secretly creeping along within it.' . . .

'The evil spirits associated with man are, indeed, from the hells, but when with man they are not then in hell, but are taken out thence. The place where they then are is in the midst between heaven and hell, and is called the world of spirits—when the evil spirits who are with man, are in that world, they are not in any infernal torment, but in every thought and affection of the man, and so, in all that the man himself enjoys. But when they are remitted into their hell, they return to their former state.' . . .

'If evil spirits could perceive that they were associated with man, and yet that they were spirits separate from him, and if they could flow in into the things of his body, they would attempt by a thousand means to destroy him; for they hate man with a deadly hatred.' . . .

'Knowing, therefore, that I was a man in the body, they were continually striving to destroy me, not as to the body only, but especially as to the soul; for to destroy any man or spirit is the very delight of the life of all who are in hell; but I have been continually protected by the Lord. Hence it appears how dangerous it is for man to be in a living consort with spirits, unless he be in the good of faith.' . . .

'Nothing is more carefully guarded from the knowledge of associate spirits than their being thus conjoint with a man, for if they knew it they would speak to him, with the intention to destroy him.' . . .

'The delight of hell is to do evil to man, and to hasten his eternal ruin.'

A long note, written with a very sharp and fine pencil, in Mr Jennings's neat hand, at the foot of the page, caught my eye. Expecting his criticism upon the text, I read a word or two, and stopped, for it was something quite different, and began with these words, Deus misereatur mei—'May God compassionate me.' Thus warned of its private nature, I averted my eyes, and shut the book, replacing all the volumes as I had found them, except one which interested me, and in which, as men studious and solitary in their habits will do, I grew so absorbed as to take no cognizance of the outer world, nor to remember where I was.

I was reading some pages which refer to 'representatives' and 'correspondents', in the technical language of Swedenborg, and had arrived at a passage, the substance of which is, that evil spirits, when seen by other eyes than those of their infernal associates, present themselves, by 'correspondence', in the shape of the beast (fera) which represents their particular lust and life in aspect direful and atrocious. This is a long passage, and particularizes a number of those bestial forms.

CHAPTER IV

FOUR EYES WERE READING THE PASSAGE

I was running the head of my pencil-case along the line as I read it, and something caused me to raise my eyes.

Directly before me was one of the mirrors I have mentioned, in which I saw reflected the tall shape of my friend Mr Jennings leaning over my shoulder, and reading the page at which I was busy, and with a face so dark and wild that I should hardly have known him.

I turned and rose. He stood erect also, and with an effort laughed a little, saying:

'I came in and asked you how you did, but without succeeding in awaking you from your book; so I could not restrain my curiosity, and very impertinently, I'm afraid, peeped over your shoulder. This is not your first time of looking into those pages. You have looked into Swedenborg, no doubt, long ago?'

'Oh dear, yes! I owe Swedenborg a great deal; you will discover traces of him in the little book on Metaphysical Medicine, which you were so good as to remember.'

Although my friend affected a gaiety of manner, there was a slight flush in his face, and I could perceive that he was inwardly much perturbed.

'I'm scarcely yet qualified, I know so little of Swedenborg. I've only had them a fortnight,' he answered, 'and I think they are rather likely to make a solitary man nervous—that is, judging from the very little I have read—I don't say that they have made me so,' he laughed; 'and I'm so very much obliged for the book. I hope you got my note?'

I made all proper acknowledgments and modest disclaimers.

'I never read a book that I go with so entirely as that of yours,' he continued. 'I saw at once there is more in it than is quite unfolded. Do you know Dr Harley?'* he asked, rather abruptly.

In passing, the editor remarks that the physician here named was one of the most eminent who ever practised in England.

I did, having had letters to him, and had experienced from him great courtesy and considerable assistance during my visit to England.

'I think that man one of the very greatest fools I ever met in my life,' said Mr Jennings.

This was the first time I had ever heard him say a sharp thing of anybody, and such a term applied to so high a name a little startled me.

'Really! and in what way?' I asked.

'In his profession,' he answered.

I smiled.

'I mean this,' he said: 'he seems to me, one half, blind—I mean one half of all he looks at is dark—preternaturally bright and vivid all the rest; and the worst of it is, it seems *wilful*. I can't get him—I mean he won't—I've had some experience of him as a physician, but I look on him as, in that sense, no better than a paralytic mind, an intellect half dead. I'll tell you—I know I shall some time—all about it,' he said, with a little agitation. 'You stay some months longer in England. If I should be out of town during your stay for a little time, would you allow me to trouble you with a letter?'

'I should be only too happy,' I assured him.

'Very good of you. I am so utterly dissatisfied with Harley.'

'A little leaning to the materialistic school,' I said.

'A *mere* materialist,' he corrected me; 'you can't think how that sort of thing worries one who knows better. You won't tell any one—any of my friends you know—that I am hippish;* now, for instance, no one knows—not even Lady Mary—that I have seen Dr Harley, or any other doctor. So pray don't mention it; and, if I should have any threatening of an attack, you'll kindly let me write, or, should I be in town, have a little talk with you.'

I was full of conjecture, and unconsciously I found I had fixed my eyes gravely on him, for he lowered his for a moment, and he said:

'I see you think I might as well tell you now, or else you are forming a conjecture; but you may as well give it up. If you were guessing all the rest of your life, you will never hit on it.'

He shook his head smiling, and over that wintry sunshine a black cloud suddenly came down, and he drew his breath in, through his teeth, as men do in pain.

'Sorry, of course, to learn that you apprehend occasion to consult any of us; but, command me when and how you like, and I need not assure you that your confidence is sacred.'

He then talked of quite other things, and in a comparatively cheerful way; and, after a little time, I took my leave.

CHAPTER V

DOCTOR HESSELIUS IS SUMMONED TO RICHMOND

WE parted cheerfully, but he was not cheerful, nor was I. There are certain expressions of that powerful organ of spirit—the human face—which, although I have seen them often, and possess a doctor's nerve, yet disturb me profoundly. One look of Mr Jennings haunted me. It had seized my imagination with so dismal a power that I changed my plans for the evening, and went to the opera, feeling that I wanted a change of ideas.

I heard nothing of or from him for two or three days, when a note in his hand reached me. It was cheerful, and full of hope. He said that he had been for some little time so much better—quite well, in fact—that he was going to make a little experiment, and run down for a month or so to his parish, to try whether a little work might not quite set him up. There was in it a fervent religious expression of gratitude for his restoration, as he now almost hoped he might call it.

A day or two later I saw Lady Mary, who repeated what his note had announced, and told me that he was actually in Warwickshire, having resumed his clerical duties at Kenlis; and she added, 'I begin to think that he is really perfectly well, and that there never was anything the matter, more than nerves and fancy; we are all nervous, but I fancy there is nothing like a little hard work for that kind of weakness, and he has made up his mind to try it. I should not be surprised if he did not come back for a year.'

Notwithstanding all this confidence, only two days later I had this note, dated from his house off Piccadilly:

'Dear sir. I have returned disappointed. If I should feel at all able to see you, I shall write to ask you kindly to call. At present I am too low, and, in fact, simply unable to say all I wish to say. Pray don't mention my name to my friends. I can see no one. By-and-by, please God, you shall hear from me. I mean to take a run into Shropshire, where some of my people are. God bless you! May we, on my return, meet more happily than I can now write.'

About a week after this I saw Lady Mary at her own house, the last person, she said, left in town, and just on the wing for Brighton, for the London season was quite over. She told me that she had heard from Mr Jennings's niece, Martha, in Shropshire. There was nothing to be gathered from her letter, more than that he was low and nervous. In those words, of which healthy people think so lightly, what a world of suffering is sometimes hidden!

Nearly five weeks passed without any further news of Mr Jennings. At the end of that time I received a note from him. He wrote:

I have been in the country, and have had change of air, change of scene, change of faces, change of everything and in everything—but *myself*. I have made up my mind, so far as the most irresolute creature on earth can do it, to tell my case fully to you. If your engagements will permit, pray come to me to-day, to-morrow, or the next day; but, pray defer as little as possible. You know not how much I need help. I have a quiet house at Richmond, where I now am. Perhaps you can manage to come to dinner, or to luncheon, or even to tea. You shall have no trouble in finding me out. The servant at Blank-street, who takes this note, will have a carriage at your door at any hour you please; and I am always to be found. You will say that I ought not to be alone. I have tried everything. Come and see.

I called up the servant, and decided on going out the same evening, which accordingly I did.

He would have been much better in a lodging-house, or a hotel, I thought, as I drove up through a short double row of sombre elms to a very old-fashioned brick house, darkened by the foliage of these trees, which over-topped, and nearly surrounded it. It was a perverse choice, for nothing could be imagined more triste and silent. The house, I found, belonged to him. He had stayed for a day or two in town, and, finding it for some cause insupportable, had come out here, probably because being furnished and his own, he was relieved of the thought and delay of selection, by coming here.

The sun had already set, and the red reflected light of the western sky illuminated the scene with the peculiar effect with which we are all familiar. The hall seemed very dark, but, getting to the back drawing-room, whose windows command the west, I was again in the same dusky light. I sat down, looking out upon the richly-wooded landscape that glowed in the grand and melancholy light which was every moment fading. The corners of the room were already dark; all was growing dim, and the gloom was insensibly toning my mind, already prepared for what was sinister. I was waiting alone for his arrival, which soon took place. The door communicating with the front room opened, and the tall figure of Mr Jennings, faintly seen in the ruddy twilight, came, with quiet stealthy steps, into the room.

We shook hands, and, taking a chair to the window, where there was still light enough to enable us to see each other's faces, he sat down beside me, and, placing his hand upon my arm, with scarcely a word of preface, began his narrative.

CHAPTER VI

HOW MR JENNINGS MET HIS COMPANION

THE faint glow of the west, the pomp of the then lonely woods of Richmond, were before us, behind and about us the darkening room, and on the stony face of the sufferer—for the character of his face, though still gentle and secret, was changed—rested that dim, odd glow which seems to descend and produce, where it touches, lights, sudden though faint, which are lost, almost without gradation, in darkness. The silence, too, was utter; not a distant wheel, or bark, or whistle from without; and within the depressing stillness of an invalid bachelor's house.

I guessed well the nature, though not even vaguely the particulars, of the revelations I was about to receive, from that fixed face of suffering that, so oddly flushed, stood out, like a portrait of Schalken's,* before its background of darkness.

'It began,' he said, 'on the 15th of October, three years and eleven weeks ago, and two days—I keep very accurate count, for every day is torment. If I leave anywhere a chasm in my narrative tell me.

'About four years ago I began a work, which had cost me very much thought and reading. It was upon the religious metaphysics of the ancients.'

'I know,' said I; 'the actual religion of educated and thinking paganism, quite apart from symbolic worship? A wide and very interesting field.'

'Yes; but not good for the mind—the Christian mind, I mean. Paganism is all bound together in essential unity, and, with evil sympathy, their religion involves their art, and both their manners, and the subject is a degrading fascination and the nemesis* sure. God forgive me!

'I wrote a great deal; I wrote late at night. I was always thinking on the subject, walking about, wherever I was, everywhere. It thoroughly infected me. You are to remember that all the material ideas connected with it were more or less of the beautiful, the subject itself delightfully interesting, and I, then, without a care.'

He sighed heavily.

'I believe that every one who sets about writing in earnest does his work, as a friend of mine phrased it, *on* something—tea, or coffee, or tobacco.* I suppose there is a material waste that must be hourly supplied in such occupations, or that we should grow too abstracted, and the mind, as it were, pass out of the body, unless it were reminded often of the connexion by actual sensation. At all events, I felt the want, and I supplied it. Tea was my companion—at first the ordinary black tea, made in the usual way, not too strong; but I drank a great deal, and increased its strength as I went on. I never experienced an uncomfortable symptom from it. I began to take a little green tea. I found the effect pleasanter, it cleared and intensified the power of thought so. I had come to take it frequently, but not stronger than one might take it for pleasure. I wrote a great deal out here, it was so quiet, and in this room. I used to sit up very late, and it became a habit with me to sip my tea—green tea—every now and then as my work proceeded. I had a little kettle on my table, that swung over a lamp, and made tea two or three times between eleven o'clock and two or three in the morning, my hours of going to bed. I used to go into town every day. I was not a monk, and, although I often spent an hour or two in a library, hunting up authorities and looking out lights upon my theme, I was in no morbid state, so far as I can judge. I met my friends pretty much as usual, and enjoyed their society, and, on the whole, existence had never been, I think, so pleasant before.

'I had met with a man who had some odd old books, German editions in mediaeval Latin, and I was only too happy to be permitted access to them. This obliging person's books were in the City,* a very out-of-the-way part of it. I had rather out-stayed my intended hour, and, on coming out, seeing no cab near, I was tempted to get into the omnibus* which used to drive past this house. It was darker than this by the time the 'bus had reached an old house, you may have remarked, with four poplars at each side of the door, and there the last passenger but myself got out. We drove along rather faster. It was twilight now. I leaned back in my corner next the door ruminating pleasantly.

'The interior of the omnibus was nearly dark. I had observed in the corner opposite to me at the other side, and at the end next the horses, two small circular reflections, as it seemed to me, of a reddish light. They were about two inches apart, and about the size of those small brass buttons that yachting men used to put upon their jackets. I began to speculate, as listless men will, upon this trifle, as it seemed. From what centre did that faint but deep red light come, and from what—glass beads, buttons, toy decorations—was it reflected? We were lumbering along gently, having nearly a mile still to go. I had not solved the puzzle, and it became in another minute more odd, for these two luminous points, with a sudden jerk, descended nearer the floor, keeping still their relative distance and horizontal position, and then, as suddenly, they rose to the level of the seat on which I was sitting, and I saw them no more.

'My curiosity was now really excited, and, before I had time to think, I saw again these two dull lamps, again together near the floor; again they disappeared, and again in their old corner I saw them.

'So, keeping my eyes upon them, I edged quietly up my own side, towards the end at which I still saw these tiny discs of red.

'There was very little light in the 'bus. It was nearly dark. I leaned forward to aid my endeavour to discover what these little circles really were. They shifted their position a little as I did so. I began now to perceive an outline of something black, and I soon saw with tolerable distinctness the outline of a small black monkey,* pushing its face forward in mimicry to meet mine; those were its eyes, and I now dimly saw its teeth grinning at me.

'I drew back, not knowing whether it might not meditate a spring. I fancied that one of the passengers had forgot this ugly pet, and wishing to ascertain something of its temper, though not caring to trust my fingers to it, I poked my umbrella softly towards it. It remained immovable—up to it—*through* it! For through it, and back and forward, it passed, without the slightest resistance.

'I can't, in the least, convey to you the kind of horror that I felt. When I had ascertained that the thing was an illusion, as I then supposed, there came a misgiving about myself and a terror that fascinated me in impotence to remove my gaze from the eyes of the brute for some moments. As I looked, it made a little skip back, quite into the corner, and I, in a panic, found myself at the door, having put my head out, drawing deep breaths of the outer air, and staring at the lights and trees we were passing, too glad to reassure myself of reality.

'I stopped the 'bus, and got out. I perceived the man look oddly at me as I paid him. I dare say there was something unusual in my looks and manner, for I had never felt so strangely before.'

CHAPTER VII

THE JOURNEY: FIRST STAGE

'WHEN the omnibus drove on, and I was alone upon the road, I looked carefully round to ascertain whether the monkey had followed me. To my indescribable relief I saw it nowhere. I can't describe easily what a shock I had received, and my sense of genuine gratitude on finding myself, as I supposed, quite rid of it.

'I had got out a little before we reached this house, two or three hundred steps away. A brick wall runs along the footpath, and inside the wall is a hedge of yew or some dark evergreen of that kind, and within that again the row of fine trees which you may have remarked as you came.

'This brick wall is about as high as my shoulder, and happening to raise my eyes I saw the monkey, with that stooping gait, on all fours, walking or creeping, close beside me on top of the wall. I stopped looking at it with a feeling of loathing and horror. As I stopped so did it. It sat up on the wall with its long hands on its knees looking at me. There was not light enough to see it much more than in outline, nor was it dark enough to bring the peculiar light of its eyes into strong relief. I still saw, however, that red foggy light plainly enough. It did not show its teeth, nor exhibit any sign of irritation, but seemed jaded and sulky, and was observing me steadily.

'I drew back into the middle of the road. It was an unconscious recoil, and there I stood, still looking at it. It did not move.

'With an instinctive determination to try something—anything, I turned about and walked briskly towards town with a scaunce* look, all the time watching the movements of the beast. It crept swiftly along the wall, at exactly my pace.

'Where the wall ends, near the turn of the road, it came down and with a wiry spring or two brought itself close to my feet, and continued to keep up to me, as I quickened my pace. It was at my left side, so close to my leg that I felt every moment as if I should tread upon it.

'The road was quite deserted and silent, and it was darker every moment. I stopped dismayed and bewildered, turning as I did so, the other way—I mean, towards this house, away from which I had been walking. When I stood still, the monkey drew back to a distance of, I suppose, about five or six yards, and remained stationary, watching me.

'I had been more agitated than I have said. I had read, of course, as every one has, something about "spectral illusions",* as you physicians term the phenomena of such cases. I considered my situation and looked my misfortune in the face.

'These affections, I had read, are sometimes transitory and sometimes obstinate. I had read of cases in which the appearance, at first harmless, had, step by step, degenerated into something direful and insupportable, and ended by wearing its victim out. Still as I stood there, but for my bestial companion, quite alone, I tried to comfort myself by repeating again and again the assurance, "the thing is purely disease, a well-known physical affection, as distinctly as small-pox or neuralgia. Doctors are all agreed on that, philosophy demonstrates it. I must not be a fool. I've been sitting up too late, and I dare say my digestion is quite wrong, and with God's help, I shall be all right, and this is but a symptom of nervous dyspepsia." Did I believe all this? Not one word of it, no more than any other miserable being ever did who is once seized and riveted in this satanic captivity. Against my convictions, I might say my knowledge, I was simply bullying myself into a false courage.

'I now walked homeward. I had only a few hundred yards to go. I had forced myself into a sort of resignation, but I had not got over the sickening shock and the flurry of the first certainty of my misfortune.

'I made up my mind to pass the night at home. The brute moved close beside me, and I fancied there was the sort of anxious drawing toward the house, which one sees in tired horses or dogs, sometimes as they come toward home.

'I was afraid to go into town—I was afraid of any one's seeing and recognizing me. I was conscious of an irrepressible agitation in my manner. Also, I was afraid of any violent change in my habits, such as going to a place of amusement, or walking from home in order to fatigue myself. At the hall-door it waited till I mounted the steps, and when the door was opened entered with me.

'I drank no tea that night. I got cigars and some brandy-and-water. My idea was that I should act upon my material system, and by living for a while in sensation apart from thought, send myself forcibly, as it were, into a new groove. I came up here to this drawing-room. I sat just here. The monkey got upon a small table that then stood *there*. It looked dazed and languid. An irrepressible uneasiness as to its movements kept my eyes always upon it. Its eyes were half-closed, but I could see them glow. It was looking steadily at me. In all situations, at all hours, it is awake and looking at me. That never changes.

'I shall not continue in detail my narrative of this particular night. I shall describe, rather, the phenomena of the first year, which never varied, collectively. I shall describe the monkey as it appeared in daylight. In the dark, as you shall presently hear, there are peculiarities. It is a small monkey, perfectly black. It had only one peculiarity—a character of malignity—unfathomable malignity. During the first year it looked sullen and sick. But this character of intense malice and vigilance was always underlying that surly languor. During all that time it acted as if on a plan of giving me as little trouble as was consistent with watching me. Its eyes were never off me. I have never lost sight of it, except in my sleep, light or dark, day or night, since it came here, excepting when it withdraws for some weeks at a time, unaccountably.

'In total dark it is visible as in daylight. I do not mean merely its eyes. It is *all* visible distinctly in a halo that resembles a glow of red embers, and which accompanies it in all its movements.

'When it leaves me for a time, it is always at night, in the dark, and in the same way. It grows at first uneasy, and then furious, and then advances towards me, grinning and shaking its paws clenched, and, at the same time, there comes the appearance of fire in the grate. I never have any fire. I can't sleep in the room where there is any, and it draws nearer and nearer to the chimney, quivering, it seems, with rage, and when its fury rises to the highest pitch, it springs into the grate, and up the chimney, and I see it no more.

'When first this happened I thought I was released. I was a new man. A day passed—a night—and no return, and a blessed week—a week—another week. I was always on my knees, Dr Hesselius, always, thanking God and praying. A whole month passed of liberty, but on a sudden, it was with me again.'

CHAPTER VIII
THE SECOND STAGE

'It was with me, and the malice which before was torpid under a sullen exterior, was now active. It was perfectly unchanged in every other respect. This new energy was apparent in its activity and its looks, and soon in other ways.

'For a time, you will understand, the change was shown only in an increased vivacity, and an air of menace, as if it was always brooding over some atrocious plan. Its eyes, as before, were never off me.'

'Is it here now?' I asked.

'No,' he replied, 'it has been absent exactly a fortnight and a day— fifteen days. It has sometimes been away so long as nearly two months, once for three. Its absence always exceeds a fortnight, although it may be but by a single day. Fifteen days having past since I saw it last, it may return now at any moment.'

'Is its return,' I asked, 'accompanied by any peculiar manifestation?'

'Nothing—no,' he said. 'It is simply with me again. On lifting my eyes from a book, or turning my head, I see it, as usual, looking at me, and then it remains, as before, for its appointed time. I have never told so much and so minutely before to any one.'

I perceived that he was agitated, and looking like death, and he repeatedly applied his handkerchief to his forehead, and I suggested that he might be tired, and told him that I would call, with pleasure, in the morning, but he said:

'No, if you don't mind hearing it all now. I have got so far, and I should prefer making one effort of it. When I spoke to Dr Harley, I had nothing like so much to tell. You are a philosophic physician. You give spirit its proper rank. If this thing is real——'

He paused, looking at me with agitated inquiry.

'We can discuss it by-and-by, and very fully. I will give you all I think,' I answered, after an interval.

'Well—very well. If it is anything real, I say, it is prevailing, little by little; and drawing me more interiorly into hell. Optic nerves, he talked of. Ah! well—there are other nerves of communication. May God Almighty help me! You shall hear.

'Its power of action, I tell you, had increased. Its malice became, in a way, aggressive. About two years ago, some questions that were pending between me and the bishop, having been settled, I went down to my parish in Warwickshire, anxious to find occupation in my profession. I was not prepared for what happened, although I have since thought I might have apprehended something like it. The reason of my saying so, is this——'

He was beginning to speak with a great deal more effort and reluctance, and sighed often, and seemed at times nearly overcome. But at this time his manner was not agitated. It was more like that of a sinking patient, who has given himself up.

'Yes, but I will first tell you about Kenlis, my parish.

'It was with me when I left this for Dawlbridge. It was my silent travelling companion, and it remained with me at the vicarage. When I entered on the discharge of my duties, another change took place. The thing exhibited an atrocious determination to thwart me. It was with me in the church—in the reading-desk—in the pulpit—within the communion-rails. At last, it reached this extremity, that while I was reading to the congregation, it would spring upon the open book and squat there, so that I was unable to see the page. This happened more than once.

'I left Dawlbridge for a time. I placed myself in Dr Harley's hands. I did everything he told me. He gave my case a great deal of thought. It interested him, I think. He seemed successful. For nearly three months I was perfectly free from a return. I began to think I was safe. With his full assent I returned to Dawlbridge.

'I travelled in a chaise. I was in good spirits. I was more—I was happy and grateful. I was returning, as I thought, delivered from a dreadful hallucination, to the scene of duties which I longed to enter upon. It was a beautiful sunny evening, everything looked serene and cheerful, and I was delighted. I remember looking out of the window to see the spire of my church at Kenlis among the trees, at the point where one has the earliest view of it. It is exactly where the little stream that bounds the parish, passes under the road by a culvert, and where it emerges at the road-side, a stone with an old inscription is placed. As we passed this point, I drew my head in and sat down, and in the corner of the chaise was the monkey.

'For a moment I felt faint, and then quite wild with despair and horror. I called to the driver, and got out, and sat down at the road-side, and prayed to God silently for mercy. A despairing resignation supervened. My companion was with me as I re-entered the vicarage. The same persecution followed. After a short struggle I submitted, and soon I left the place.

'I told you,' he said 'that the beast has before this become in certain ways aggressive. I will explain a little. It seemed to be actuated by intense and increasing fury, whenever I said my prayers, or even meditated prayer. It amounted at last to a dreadful interruption. You will ask, how could a silent immaterial phantom effect that? It was thus, whenever I meditated praying; it was always before me, and nearer and nearer.

'It used to spring on a table, on the back of a chair, on the chimney-piece, and slowly to swing itself from side to side, looking at me all the time. There is in its motion an indefinable power to dissipate thought,* and to contract one's attention to that monotony, till the ideas shrink, as it were, to a point, and at last to nothing—and unless I had started up, and shook off the catalepsy I have felt as if my mind were on the point of losing itself. There are other ways,' he sighed heavily; 'thus, for instance, while I pray with my eyes closed, it comes closer and closer, and I see it. I know it is not to be accounted for physically, but I do actually see it, though my lids are closed, and so it rocks my mind, as it were, and overpowers me, and I am obliged to rise from my knees. If you had ever yourself known this, you would be acquainted with desperation.'

CHAPTER IX

THE THIRD STAGE

'I SEE, Dr Hesselius, that you don't lose one word of my statement. I need not ask you to listen specially to what I am now going to tell you. They talk of the optic nerves,* and of spectral illusions, as if the organ of sight was the only point assailable by the influences that have fastened upon me—I know better. For two years in my direful case that limitation prevailed. But as food is taken in softly at the lips, and then brought under the teeth, as the tip of the little finger caught in a mill-crank will draw in the hand, and the arm, and the whole body, so the miserable mortal who has been once caught firmly by the end of the finest fibre of his nerve, is drawn in and in, by the enormous machinery of hell, until he is as I am. Yes, doctor, as *I* am, for while I talk to you, and implore relief, I feel that my prayer is for the impossible, and my pleading with the inexorable.'

I endeavoured to calm his visibly increasing agitation, and told him that he must not despair.

While we talked the night had overtaken us. The filmy moonlight was wide over the scene which the window commanded, and I said:

'Perhaps you would prefer having candles. This light, you know, is odd. I should wish you, as much as possible, under your usual conditions while I make my diagnosis, shall I call it—otherwise I don't care.'

'All lights are the same to me,' he said: 'except when I read or write, I care not if night were perpetual. I am going to tell you what happened about a year ago. The thing began to speak to me.'

'Speak! How do you mean—speak as a man does, do you mean?'

'Yes; speak in words and consecutive sentences, with perfect coherence and articulation; but there is a peculiarity. It is not like the tone of a human voice. It is not by my ears it reaches me—it comes like a singing through my head.

'This faculty, the power of speaking to me, will be my undoing. It won't let me pray, it interrupts me with dreadful blasphemies. I dare not go on, I could not. Oh! doctor, can the skill, and thought, and prayers of man avail me nothing!'

'You must promise me, my dear sir, not to trouble yourself with unnecessarily exciting thoughts; confine yourself strictly to the narrative of *facts*; and recollect, above all, that even if the thing that infests you be as you seem to suppose, a reality with an actual independent life and will, yet it can have no power to hurt you, unless it be given from above: its access to your senses depends mainly upon your physical condition—this is, under God, your comfort and reliance: we are all alike environed. It is only that in your case, the "paries",* the veil of the flesh, the screen, is a little out of repair, and sights and sounds are transmitted. We must enter on a new course, sir—be encouraged. I'll give to-night to the careful consideration of the whole case.'

'You are very good, sir; you think it worth trying, you don't give me quite up; but, sir, you don't know, it is gaining such an influence over me: it orders me about, it is such a tyrant, and I'm growing so helpless. May God deliver me!'

'It orders you about—of course you mean by speech?'

'Yes, yes; it is always urging me to crimes, to injure others, or myself. You see, doctor, the situation is urgent, it is indeed. When I was in Shropshire, a few weeks ago' (Mr Jennings was speaking rapidly and trembling now, holding my arm with one hand, and looking in my face), 'I went out one day with a party of friends for a walk: my persecutor, I tell you, was with me at the time. I lagged behind the rest: the country near the Dee,* you know, is beautiful. Our path happened to lie near a coal mine, and at the verge of the wood is a perpendicular shaft, they say, a hundred and fifty feet deep. My niece had remained behind with me—she knows, of course, nothing of the nature of my sufferings. She knew, however, that I had been ill, and was low, and she remained to prevent my being quite alone. As we loitered slowly on together the brute that accompanied me was urging me to throw myself down the shaft. I tell you now—oh, sir, think of it!—the one consideration that saved me from that hideous death was the fear lest the shock of witnessing the occurrence should be too much for the poor girl. I asked her to go on and take her walk with her friends, saying that I could go no further. She made excuses, and the more I urged her the firmer she became. She looked doubtful and frightened. I suppose there was something in my looks or manner that alarmed her; but she would not go, and that literally saved me. You had no idea, sir, that a living man could be made so abject a slave of Satan,' he said, with a ghastly groan and a shudder.

There was a pause here, and I said, 'You *were* preserved nevertheless. It was the act of God. You are in his hands and in the power of no other being: be therefore confident for the future.'

CHAPTER X

HOME

I MADE him have candles lighted, and saw the room looking cheery and inhabited before I left him. I told him that he must regard his illness strictly as one dependent on physical, though *subtle* physical, causes. I told him that he had evidence of God's care and love in the deliverance which he had just described, and that I had perceived with pain that he seemed to regard its peculiar features as indicating that he had been delivered over to spiritual reprobation. Than such a conclusion nothing could be, I insisted, less warranted; and not only so, but more contrary to facts, as disclosed in his mysterious deliverance from that murderous influence during his Shropshire excursion. First, his niece had been retained by his side without his intending to keep her near him; and, secondly, there had been infused into his mind an irresistible repugnance to execute the dreadful suggestion in her presence.

As I reasoned this point with him, Mr Jennings wept. He seemed comforted. One promise I exacted, which was that should the monkey at any time return, I should be sent for immediately; and, repeating my assurance that I would give neither time nor thought to any other subject until I had thoroughly investigated his case, and that to-morrow he should hear the result, I took my leave.

Before getting into the carriage I told the servant that his master was far from well, and that he should make a point of frequently looking into his room.

My own arrangements I made with a view to being quite secure from interruption.

I merely called at my lodgings, and, with a travelling-desk and carpet-bag, set off in a hackney-carriage for an inn about two miles out of town, called The Horns, a very quiet and comfortable house, with good thick walls. And there I resolved, without the possibility of intrusion or distraction, to devote some hours of the night, in my comfortable sitting-room, to Mr Jennings's case, and so much of the morning as it might require.

(There occurs here a careful note of Dr Hesselius's opinion upon the case, and of the habits, dietary, and medicines which he prescribed. It is curious—some people would say mystical. But on the whole I doubt whether it would sufficiently interest a reader of the kind I am likely to meet with to warrant its being here reprinted. This whole letter was plainly written at the inn in which he had hid himself for the occasion. The next letter is dated from his town lodgings.)

I left town for the inn where I slept last night at half-past nine, and did not arrive at my room in town until one o'clock this afternoon. I found a letter in Mr Jennings's hand upon my table. It had not come by post, and on inquiry, I learned that Mr Jennings's servant had brought it, and on learning that I was not to return until to-day, and that no one could tell him my address, he seemed very uncomfortable, and said that his orders from his master were that he was not to return without an answer.

I opened the letter, and read:

Dear Dr Hesselius. It is here. You had not been an hour gone when it returned. It is speaking. It knows all that has happened. It knows everything—it knows you, and is frantic and atrocious. It reviles. I send you this. It knows every word I have written—I write. This I promised, and I therefore write, but I fear very confused, very incoherently. I am so interrupted, disturbed.

Ever yours, sincerely yours,
ROBERT LYNDER JENNINGS

'When did this come?' I asked.

'About eleven last night; the man was here again, and has been here three times to-day. The last time is about an hour since.'

Thus answered, and with the notes I had made upon his case in my pocket, I was, in a few minutes, driving out to Richmond, to see Mr Jennings.

I by no means, as you perceive, despaired of Mr Jennings's case. He had himself remembered and applied, though quite in a mistaken way, the principle which I lay down in my Metaphysical Medicine, and which governs all such cases. I was about to apply it in earnest. I was profoundly interested, and very anxious to see and examine him while the 'enemy' was actually present.

I drove up to the sombre house, and ran up the steps, and knocked. The door, in a little time, was opened by a tall woman in black silk. She looked ill, and as if she had been crying. She curtseyed, and heard my question, but she did not answer. She turned her face away, extending her hand hurriedly towards two men who were coming down-stairs; and thus having, as it were, tacitly made me over to them, she passed through a side-door hastily and shut it.

The man who was nearest the hall, I at once accosted, but being now close to him, I was shocked to see that both his hands were covered with blood.

I drew back a little, and the man passing down-stairs merely said in a low tone, 'Here's the servant, sir.'

The servant had stopped on the stairs, confounded and dumb at seeing me. He was rubbing his hands in a handkerchief, and it was steeped in blood.

'Jones, what is it, what has happened?' I asked, while a sickening suspicion overpowered me.

The man asked me to come up to the lobby. I was beside him in a moment, and frowning and pallid, with contracted eyes, he told me the horror which I already half guessed.

His master had made away with himself.

I went up-stairs with him to the room—what I saw there I won't tell you. He had cut his throat with his razor. It was a frightful gash. The two men had laid him upon the bed and composed his limbs. It had happened, as the immense pool of blood on the floor declared, at some distance between the bed and the window. There was carpet round his bed, and a carpet under his dressing-table, but none on the rest of the floor, for the man said he did not like carpet on his bedroom. In this sombre, and now terrible room, one of the great elms that darkened the house was slowly moving the shadow of one of its great boughs upon this dreadful floor.

I beckoned to the servant and we went down-stairs together. I turned, off the hall, into an old-fashioned panelled room, and there standing, I heard all the servant had to tell. It was not a great deal.

'I concluded, sir, from your words, and looks, sir, as you left last night, that you thought my master seriously ill. I thought it might be that you were afraid of a fit, or something. So I attended very close to your directions. He sat up late, till past three o'clock. He was not writing or reading. He was talking a great deal to himself, but that was nothing unusual. At about that hour I assisted him to undress, and left him in his slippers and dressing-gown. I went back softly in about half an hour. He was in his bed, quite undressed, and a pair of candles lighted on the table beside his bed. He was leaning on his elbow and looking out at the other side of the bed when I came in. I asked him if he wanted anything, and he said no.

'I don't know whether it was what you said to me, sir, or something a little unusual about him, but I was uneasy, uncommon uneasy, about him last night.

'In another half hour, or it might be a little more, I went up again. I did not hear him talking as before. I opened the door a little. The candles were both out, which was not usual. I had a bedroom candle, and I let the light in, a little bit, looking softly round. I saw him sitting in that chair beside the dressing-table with his clothes on again. He turned round and looked at me. I thought it strange he should get up and dress, and put out the candles to sit in the dark, that way. But I only asked him again if I could do anything for him. He said, no, rather sharp, I thought. I asked if I might light the candles, and he said, "Do as you like, Jones." So I lighted them, and I lingered a little about the room, and he said, "Tell me truth, Jones, why did you come again—you did not hear any one cursing?" "No, sir," I said, wondering what he could mean.

'"No," said he, after me, "of course, no"; and I said to him, "Wouldn't it be well, sir, you went to bed? It's just five o'clock"; and he said nothing but, "Very likely: good-night, Jones." So I went, sir, but in less than an hour I came again. The door was fast, and he heard me, and called as

I thought from the bed to know what I wanted, and he desired me not to disturb him again. I lay down and slept for a little. It must have been between six and seven when I went up again. The door was still fast, and he made no answer, so I did not like to disturb him, and thinking he was asleep, I left him till nine. It was his custom to ring when he wished me to come, and I had no particular hour for calling him. I tapped very gently, and getting no answer, I stayed away a good while, supposing he was getting some rest then. It was not till eleven o'clock I grew really uncomfortable about him—for at the latest he was never, that I could remember, later than half-past ten. I got no answer. I knocked and called, and still no answer. So not being able to force the door, I called Thomas from the stables, and together we forced it, and found him in the shocking way you saw.'

Jones had no more to tell. Poor Mr Jennings was very gentle, and very kind. All his people were fond of him. I could see that the servant was very much moved.

So, dejected and agitated, I passed from that terrible house, and its dark canopy of elms, and I hope I shall never see it more. While I write to you I feel like a man who has but half waked from a frightful and monotonous dream. My memory rejects the picture with incredulity and horror. Yet I know it is true. It is the story of the process of a poison, a poison which excites the reciprocal action of spirit and nerve, and paralyses the tissue that separates those cognate functions of the senses, the external and the interior. Thus we find strange bed-fellows, and the mortal and immortal prematurely make acquaintance.

CONCLUSION

A WORD FOR THOSE WHO SUFFER

MY dear Van L., you have suffered from an affection similar to that which I have just described. You twice complained of a return of it.

Who, under God, cured you? Your humble servant, Martin Hesselius. Let me rather adopt the more emphasized piety of a certain good old French surgeon* of three hundred years ago: 'I treated, and God cured you.'

Come, my friend, you are not to be hippish. Let me tell you a fact.

I have met with, and treated, as my book shows, fifty-seven cases of this kind of vision, which I term indifferently 'sublimated', 'precocious', and 'interior'.

There is another class of affections which are truly termed—though commonly confounded with those which I describe—spectral illusions. These latter I look upon as being no less simply curable than a cold in the head or a trifling dyspepsia.

It is those which rank in the first category that test our promptitude of thought. Fifty-seven such cases have I encountered, neither more nor less. And in how many of these have I failed? In no one single instance.

There is no one affliction of mortality more easily and certainly reducible, with a little patience, and a rational confidence in the physician. With these simple conditions, I look upon the cure as absolutely certain.

You are to remember that I had not even commenced to treat Mr Jennings's case. I have not any doubt that I should have cured him perfectly in eighteen months, or possibly it might have extended to two years. Some cases are very rapidly curable, others extremely tedious. Every intelligent physician who will give thought and diligence to the task, will effect a cure.

You know my tract on The Cardinal Functions of the Brain. I there, by the evidence of innumerable facts, prove, as I think, the high probability of a circulation arterial and venous in its mechanism, through the nerves. Of this system, thus considered, the brain is the heart. The fluid, which is propagated hence through one class of nerves, returns in an altered state through another, and the nature of that fluid is spiritual, though not immaterial, any more than, as I before remarked, light or electricity are so.

By various abuses, among which the habitual use of such agents as green tea is one, this fluid may be affected as to its quality, but it is more frequently disturbed as to equilibrium. This fluid being that which we have in common with spirits, a congestion found upon the masses of brain or nerve, connected with the interior sense, forms a surface unduly exposed, on which disembodied spirits may operate: communication is thus more or less effectually established. Between this brain circulation and the heart circulation there is an intimate sympathy. The seat, or rather the instrument of exterior vision, is the eye. The seat of interior vision is the nervous tissue and brain, immediately about and above the eyebrow. You remember how effectually I dissipated your pictures by the simple application of iced eau-de-cologne. Few cases, however, can be treated exactly alike with anything like rapid success. Cold acts powerfully as a repellant of the nervous fluid. Long enough continued it will even produce that permanent insensibility which we call numbness, and a little longer, muscular as well as sensational paralysis.

I have not, I repeat, the slightest doubt that I should have first dimmed and ultimately sealed that inner eye which Mr Jennings had inadvertently opened. The same senses are opened in delirium tremens, and entirely shut up again when the over-action of the cerebral heart, and the prodigious nervous congestions that attend it, are terminated by a decided change in the state of the body. It is by acting steadily upon the body, by a simple process, that this result is produced—and inevitably produced—I have never yet failed.

Poor Mr Jennings made away with himself. But that catastrophe was the result of a totally different malady, which, as it were, projected itself upon that disease which was established. His case was in the distinctive manner a complication, and the complaint under which he really succumbed, was hereditary suicidal mania. Poor Mr Jennings I cannot call a patient of mine, for I had not even begun to treat his case, and he had not yet given me, I am convinced, his full and unreserved confidence. If the patient do not array himself on the side of the disease, his cure is certain.

MADAM CROWL'S GHOST

I'M an ald woman now; and I was but thirteen, my last birthday, the night I came to Applewale House. My aunt was the housekeeper there, and a sort o' one-horse carriage was down at Lexhoe* to take me and my box up to Applewale.

I was a bit frightened by the time I got to Lexhoe, and when I saw the carriage and horse, I wished myself back again with my mother at Hazelden. I was crying when I got into the 'shay'—that's what we used to call it—and old John Mulbery that drove it, and was a good-natured fellow, bought me a handful of apples at the Golden Lion, to cheer me up a bit; and he told me that there was a currant-cake, and tea, and pork-chops, waiting for me, all hot, in my aunt's room at the great house. It was a fine moonlight night, and I eat the apples, lookin' out o' the shay winda.

It is a shame for gentlemen to frighten a poor foolish child like I was. I sometimes think it might be tricks. There was two on 'em on the tap o' the coach beside me. And they began to question me after nightfall, when the moon rose, where I was going to. Well, I told them it was to wait on Dame Arabella Crowl, of Applewale House, near by Lexhoe.

'Ho, then,' says one of them, 'you'll not be long there!'

And I looked at him, as much as to say, 'Why not?' for I had spoke out when I told them where I was goin', as if 'twas something clever I hed to say.

'Because,' says he—'and don't you for your life tell no one, only watch her and see—she's possessed by the devil, and more an half a ghost. Have you got a Bible?'

'Yes, sir,' says I. For my mother put my little Bible in my box, and I knew it was there: and by the same token, though the print's too small for my ald eyes, I have it in my press to this hour.

As I looked up at him, saying 'Yes, sir,' I thought I saw him winkin' at his friend; but I could not be sure.

'Well,' says he, 'be sure you put it under your bolster every night, it will keep the ald girl's claws aff ye.'

And I got such a fright when he said that, you wouldn't fancy! And I'd a liked to ask him a lot about the ald lady, but I was too shy, and he and his friend began talkin' together about their own consarns, and dowly* enough I got down, as I told ye, at Lexhoe. My heart sank as

I drove into the dark avenue. The trees stands very thick and big, as ald as the ald house almost, and four people, with their arms out and finger-tips touchin', barely girds round some of them.

Well, my neck was stretched out o' the winda, looking for the first view o' the great house; and, all at once we pulled up in front of it.

A great white-and-black house it is, wi' great black beams across and right up it, and gables lookin' out, as white as a sheet, to the moon, and the shadows o' the trees, two or three up and down upon the front, you could count the leaves on them, and all the little diamond-shaped winda-panes, glimmering on the great hall winda, and great shutters, in the old fashion, hinged on the wall outside, boulted across all the rest o' the windas in front, for there was but three or four servants, and the old lady in the house, and most o' t'rooms was locked up.

My heart was in my mouth when I sid the journey was over, and this, the great house afoore me, and I sa near my aunt that I never sid till noo, and Dame Crowl, that I was come to wait upon, and was afeard on already.

My aunt kissed me in the hall, and brought me to her room. She was tall and thin, wi' a pale face and black eyes, and long thin hands wi' black mittins on. She was past fifty, and her word was short; but her word was law. I hev no complaints to make of her; but she was a hard woman, and I think she would hev bin kinder to me if I had bin her sister's child in place of her brother's. But all that's o' no consequence noo.

The squire—his name was Mr Chevenix Crowl, he was Dame Crowl's grandson—came down there, by way of seeing that the old lady was well treated, about twice or thrice in the year. I sid him but twice all the time I was at Applewale House.

I can't say but she was well taken care of, notwithstanding; but that was because my aunt and Meg Wyvern, that was her maid, had a conscience, and did their duty by her.

Mrs Wyvern—Meg Wyvern my aunt called her to herself, and Mrs Wyvern to me—was a fat, jolly lass of fifty, a good height and a good breadth, always good-humoured, and walked slow. She had fine wages, but she was a bit stingy, and kept all her fine clothes under lock and key, and wore, mostly, a twilled chocolate cotton, wi' red, and yellow, and green sprigs and balls on it, and it lasted wonderful.

She never gave me nout, not the vally o' a brass thimble, all the time I was there; but she was good-humoured, and always laughin', and she talked no end o' proas* over her tea; and, seeing me sa sackless* and dowly, she roused me up wi' her laughin' and stories; and I think I liked her better than my aunt—children is so taken wi' a bit o' fun or a story—though my aunt was very good to me, but a hard woman about some things, and silent always.

My aunt took me into her bed-chamber, that I might rest myself a bit while she was settin' the tea in her room. But first she patted me on the shouther, and said I was a tall lass o' my years, and had spired* up well, and asked me if I could do plain work and stitchin'; and she looked in my face, and said I was like my father, her brother, that was dead and gone, and she hoped I was a better Christian, and wad na du a' that lids.*

It was a hard sayin' the first time I set my foot in her room, I thought.

When I went into the next room, the housekeeper's room—very comfortable, yak* all round—there was a fine fire blazin' away, wi' coal, and peat, and wood, all in a low together, and tea on the table, and hot cake, and smokin' meat; and there was Mrs Wyvern, fat, jolly, and talkin' away, more in an hour than my aunt would in a year.

While I was still at my tea my aunt went up-stairs to see Madam Crowl.

'She's agone up to see that old Judith Squailes is awake,' says Mrs Wyvern. 'Judith sits with Madam Crowl when me and Mrs Shutters'—that was my aunt's name—'is away. She's a troublesome old lady. Ye'll hev to be sharp wi' her, or she'll be into the fire, or out o' t' winda. She goes on wires, she does, old though she be.'

'How old, ma'am?' says I.

'Ninety-three her last birthday, and that's eight months gone,' says she; and she laughed. 'And don't be askin' questions about her before your aunt—mind, I tell ye; just take her as you find her, and that's all.'

'And what's to be my business about her, please ma'am?' says I.

'About the old lady? Well,' says she, 'your aunt, Mrs Shutters, will tell you that; but I suppose you'll hev to sit in the room with your work, and see she's at no mischief, and let her amuse herself with her things on the table, and get her her food or drink as she calls for it, and keep her out o' mischief, and ring the bell hard if she's troublesome.'

'Is she deaf, ma'am?'

'No, nor blind,' says she; 'as sharp as a needle, but she's gone quite aupy,* and can't remember nout rightly; and Jack the Giant Killer, or Goody Twoshoes* will please her as well as the king's court, or the affairs of the nation.'

'And what did the little girl go away for, ma'am, that went on Friday last? My aunt wrote to my mother she was to go.'

'Yes; she's gone.'

'What for?' says I again.

'She didn't answer Mrs Shutters, I do suppose,' says she. 'I don't know. Don't be talkin'; your aunt can't abide a talkin' child.'

'And please, ma'am, is the old lady well in health?' says I.

'It ain't no harm to ask that,' says she. 'She's torflin'* a bit lately, but better this week past, and I dare say she'll last out her hundred years yet. Hish! Here's your aunt coming down the passage.'

In comes my aunt, and begins talkin' to Mrs Wyvern, and I, beginnin' to feel more comfortable and at home like, was walkin' about the room lookin' at this thing and at that. There was pretty old china things on the cupboard, and pictures again the wall; and there was a door open in the wainscot, and I sees a queer old leathern jacket, wi' straps and buckles to it, and sleeves as long as the bed-post hangin' up inside.

'What's that you're at, child?' says my aunt, sharp enough, turning about when I thought she least minded. 'What's that in your hand?'

'This, ma'am?' says I, turning about with the leathern jacket. 'I don't know what it is, ma'am.'

Pale as she was, the red came up in her cheeks, and her eyes flashed wi' anger, and I think only she had half a dozen steps to take, between her and me, she'd a gev me a sizzup.* But she did give me a shake by the shouther, and she plucked the thing out o' my hand, and says she, 'While ever you stay here, don't ye meddle wi' nout that don't belong to ye', and she hung it up on the pin that was there, and shut the door wi' a bang and locked it fast.

Mrs Wyvern was liftin' up her hands and laughin' all this time, quietly, in her chair, rolling herself a bit in it, as she used when she was kinkin'.*

The tears was in my eyes, and she winked at my aunt, and says she, dryin' her own eyes that was wet wi' the laughin', 'Tut, the child meant no harm—come here to me, child. It's only a pair o' crutches for lame ducks, and ask us no questions mind, and we'll tell ye no lies; and come here and sit down, and drink a mug o' beer before ye go to your bed.'

My room, mind ye, was up-stairs, next to the old lady's, and Mrs Wyvern's bed was near hers in her room, and I was to be ready at call, if need should be.

The old lady was in one of her tantrums that night and part of the day before. She used to take fits o' the sulks. Sometimes she would not let them dress her, and other times she would not let them take her clothes off. She was a great beauty, they said, in her day. But there was no one about Applewale that remembered her in her prime. And she was dreadful fond o' dress, and had thick silks, and stiff satins, and velvets, and laces, and all sorts, enough to set up seven shops at the least. All her dresses was old-fashioned and queer, but worth a fortune.

Well, I went to my bed. I lay for a while awake; for a' things was new to me; and I think the tea was in my nerves, too, for I wasn't used to it, except now and then on a holiday, or the like. And I heard Mrs Wyvern talkin', and I listened with my hand to my ear; but I could not hear Mrs Crowl, and I don't think she said a word.

There was great care took of her. The people at Applewale knew that when she died they would every one get the sack; and their situations was well paid and easy.

The doctor come twice a week to see the old lady, and you may be sure they all did as he bid them. One thing was the same every time; they were never to cross or frump* her, any way, but to humour and please her in everything.

So she lay in her clothes all that night, and next day, not a word she said, and I was at my needlework all that day, in my own room, except when I went down to my dinner.

I would a liked to see the ald lady, and even to hear her speak. But she might as well a' bin in Lunnon a' the time for me.

When I had my dinner my aunt sent me out for a walk for an hour. I was glad when I came back, the trees was so big, and the place so dark and lonesome, and 'twas a cloudy day, and I cried a deal, thinkin' of home, while I was walkin' alone there. That evening, the candles bein' alight, I was sittin' in my room, and the door was open into Madam Crowl's chamber, where my aunt was. It was, then, for the first time I heard what I suppose was the ald lady talking.

It was a queer noise like, I couldn't well say which, a bird, or a beast, only it had a bleatin' sound in it, and was very small.

I pricked my ears to hear all I could. But I could not make out one word she said. And my aunt answered:

'The evil one can't hurt no one, ma'am, bout the Lord permits.'

Then the same queer voice from the bed says something more that I couldn't make head nor tail on.

And my aunt med answer again: 'Let them pull faces, ma'am, and say what they will; if the Lord be for us, who can be against us?'

I kept listenin' with my ear turned to the door, holdin' my breath, but not another word or sound came in from the room. In about twenty minutes, as I was sittin' by the table, lookin' at the pictures in the old Aesop's Fables,* I was aware o' something moving at the door, and lookin' up I sid my aunt's face lookin' in at the door, and her hand raised.

'Hish!' says she, very soft, and comes over to me on tiptoe, and she says in a whisper: 'Thank God, she's asleep at last, and don't ye make no noise till I come back, for I'm goin' down to take my cup o' tea, and I'll be back i' noo*—me and Mrs Wyvern, and she'll be sleepin' in the room, and you can run down when we come up, and Judith will gie ye yaur supper in my room.'

And with that away she goes.

I kep' looking at the picture-book, as before, listenin' every noo and then, but there was no sound, not a breath, that I could hear; an' I began whisperin' to the pictures and talkin' to myself to keep my heart up, for I was growin' feared in that big room.

And at last up I got, and began walkin' about the room, lookin' at this and peepin' at that, to amuse my mind, ye'll understand. And at last what sud I do but peeps into Madame Crowl's bed-chamber.

A grand chamber it was, wi' a great four-poster, wi' flowered silk curtains as tall as the ceilin', and foldin' down on the floor, and drawn close all round. There was a lookin'-glass, the biggest I ever sid before, and the room was a blaze o' light. I counted twenty-two wax-candles, all alight. Such was her fancy, and no one dared say her nay.

I listened at the door, and gaped and wondered all round. When I heard there was not a breath, and did not see so much as a stir in the curtains, I took heart, and I walked into the room on tiptoe, and looked round again. Then I takes a keek at myself in the big glass; and at last it came in my head, 'Why couldn't I ha' a keek at the ald lady herself in the bed?'

Ye'd think me a fule if ye knew half how I longed to see Dame Crowl, and I thought to myself if I didn't peep now I might wait many a day before I got so gude a chance again.

Well, my dear, I came to the side o' the bed, the curtains bein' close, and my heart a'most failed me. But I took courage, and I slips my finger in between the thick curtains, and then my hand. So I waits a bit, but all was still as death. So, softly, softly I draws the curtain, and there, sure enough, I sid before me, stretched out like the painted lady on the tomb-stean in Lexhoe Church, the famous Dame Crowl, of Applewale House. There she was, dressed out. You never sid the like in they days. Satin and silk, and scarlet and green, and gold and pint lace; by Jen!* 'twas a sight! A big powdered wig, half as high as herself, was a-top o' her head, and, wow!—was ever such wrinkles?—and her old baggy throat all powdered white, and her cheeks rouged, and mouse-skin eyebrows, that Mrs Wyvern used to stick on, and there she lay grand and stark, wi' a pair o' clocked silk hose on, and heels to her shoon as tall as nine-pins. Lawk! But her nose was crooked and thin, and half the whites o' her eyes was open. She used to stand, dressed as she was, gigglin' and dribblin' before the lookin'-glass, wi' a fan in her hand, and a big nosegay in her bodice. Her wrinkled little hands was stretched down by her sides, and such long nails, all cut into points, I never sid in my days. Could it ever a bin the fashion for grit fowk to wear their fingertips-nails so?

Well, I think ye'd a-bin frightened yourself if ye'd a sid such a sight. I couldn't let go the curtain, nor move an inch, nor take my eyes off her; my very heart stood still. And in an instant she opens her eyes, and up she sits, and spins herself round, and down wi' her, wi' a clack on her two tall heels on the floor, facin' me, ogglin'* in my face wi' her two great glassy eyes, and a wicked simper wi' her old wrinkled lips, and lang fause teeth.

Well, a corpse is a natural thing; but this was the dreadfullest sight I ever sid. She had her fingers straight out pointin' at me, and her back was crooked, round again wi' age. Says she:

'Ye little limb! what for did ye say I killed the boy? I'll tickle ye till ye're stiff!'

If I'd a thought an instant, I'd a turned about and run. But I couldn't take my eyes off her, and I backed from her as soon as I could; and she came clatterin' after, like a thing on wires, with her fingers pointing to my throat, and she makin' all the time a sound with her tongue like zizz-zizz-zizz.

I kept backin' and backin' as quick as I could, and her fingers was only a few inches away from my throat, and I felt I'd lose my wits if she touched me.

I went back this way, right into the corner, and I gev a yellock, ye'd think saul and body was partin', and that minute my aunt, from the door, calls out wi' a blare, and the ald lady turns round on her, and I turns about, and ran through my room, and down the back stairs, as hard as my legs could carry me.

I cried hearty, I can tell you, when I got down to the housekeeper's room. Mrs Wyvern laughed a deal when I told her what happened. But she changed her key when she heard the ald lady's words.

'Say them again,' says she.

So I told her.

'Ye little limb! What for did ye say I killed the boy? I'll tickle ye till ye're stiff.'

'And did ye say she killed a boy?' says she.

'Not I, ma'am,' says I.

Judith was always up with me, after that, when the two elder women was away from her. I would a jumped out at winda, rather than stay alone in the same room wi' her.

It was about a week after, as well as I can remember, Mrs Wyvern, one day when me and her was alone, told me a thing about Madam Crowl that I did not know before.

She being young, and a great beauty, full seventy year before, hed married Squire Crowl, of Applewale. But he was a widower, and had a son about nine year old.

There never was tale or tidings of this boy after one mornin'. No one could say where he went to. He was allowed too much liberty, and used to be off in the morning, one day, to the keeper's cottage, and breakfast wi' him, and away to the warren, and not home, mayhap, till evening, and another time down to the lake, and bathe there, and spend the day fishin' there, or paddlin' about in the boat. Well, no one could say what was gone wi' him; only this, that his hat was found by the lake, under a haathorn that grows thar to this day, and 'twas thought he was drowned bathin'. And the squire's son, by his second marriage, by this Madam Crowl that lived sa dreadful lang, came in for the estates. It was his son, the ald lady's grandson, Squire Chevenix Crowl, that owned the estates at the time I came to Applewale.

There was a deal o' talk lang before my aunt's time about it; and 'twas said the step-mother knew more than she was like to let out. And she managed her husband, the ald squire, wi' her whiteheft* and flatteries. And as the boy was never seen more, in course of time the thing died out of fowks' minds.

I'm goin' to tell ye noo about what I sid wi' my own een.

I was not there six months, and it was winter time, when the ald lady took her last sickness.

The doctor was afeard she might a took a fit o' madness, as she did fifteen years befoore, and was buckled up, many a time, in a strait-waistcoat, which was the very leathern jerkin I sid in the closet, off my aunt's room.

Well, she didn't. She pined, and windered, and went off, torflin', torflin', quiet enough, till a day or two before her flittin',* and then she took to rabblin', and sometimes skirlin' in the bed, ye'd think a robber had a knife to her throat, and she used to work out o' the bed, and not being strong enough, then, to walk or stand, she'd fall on the flure, wi' her ald wizened hands stretched before her face, and skirlin' still for mercy.

Ye may guess I didn't go into the room, and I used to be shiverin' in my bed wi' fear, at her skirlin' and scrafflin'* on the flure, and blarin' out words that id make your skin turn blue.

My aunt, and Mrs Wyvern, and Judith Squailes, and a woman from Lexhoe, was always about her. At last she took fits, and they wore her out.

T' sir was there, and prayed for her; but she was past praying with. I suppose it was right, but none could think there was much good in it, and sa at lang last she made her flittin', and a' was over, and old Dame Crowl was shrouded and coffined, and Squire Chevenix was wrote for. But he was away in France, and the delay was sa lang, that t' sir and doctor both agreed it would not du to keep her langer out o' her place, and no one cared but just them two, and my aunt and the rest o' us, from Applewale, to go to the buryin'. So the old lady of Applewale was laid in the vault under Lexhoe Church; and we lived up at the great house till such time as the squire should come to tell his will about us, and pay off such as he chose to discharge.

I was put into another room, two doors away from what was Dame Crowl's chamber, after her death, and this thing happened the night before Squire Chevenix came to Applewale.

The room I was in now was a large square chamber, covered wi' yak pannels, but unfurnished except for my bed, which had no curtains to it, and a chair and a table, or so, that looked nothing at all in such a big room. And the big looking-glass, that the old lady used to keek into and admire herself from head to heel, now that there was na mair o' that wark, was put out of the way, and stood against the wall in my room, for there was shiftin' o' many things in her chambers ye may suppose, when she came to be coffined.

The news had come that day that the squire was to be down next morning at Applewale; and not sorry was I, for I thought I was sure to be sent home again to my mother. And right glad was I, and I was thinkin' of a' at hame, and my sister Janet, and the kitten and the pymag,* and Trimmer the tike,* and all the rest, and I got sa fidgetty, I couldn't sleep, and the clock struck twelve, and me wide awake, and the room as dark as pick. My back was turned to the door, and my eyes toward the wall opposite.

Well, it could na be a full quarter past twelve, when I sees a lightin' on the wall befoore me, as if something took fire behind, and the shadas o' the bed, and the chair, and my gown, that was hangin' from the wall, was dancin' up and down on the ceilin' beams and the yak pannels; and I turns my head ower my shouther quick, thinkin' something must a gone a' fire.

And what sud I see, by Jen! but the likeness o' the ald beldame, bedizened out in her satins and velvets, on her dead body, simperin', wi' her eyes as wide as saucers, and her face like the fiend himself. 'Twas a red light that rose about her in a fuffin low,* as if her dress round her feet was blazin'. She was drivin' on right for me, wi' her ald shrivelled hands crooked as if she was goin' to claw me. I could not stir, but she passed me straight by, wi' a blast o' cald air, and I sid her, at the wall, in the alcove as my aunt used to call it, which was a recess where the state bed used to stand in ald times, wi' a door open wide, and her hands gropin' in at somethin' was there. I never sid that door befoore. And she turned round to me, like a thing on a pivot, flyrin', and all at once the room was dark, and I standin' at the far side o' the bed; I don't know how I got there, and I found my tongue at last, and if I did na blare a yellock, rennin' down the gallery and almost pulled Mrs Wyvern's door off t' hooks, and frighted her half out o' her wits.

Ye may guess I did na sleep that night; and wi' the first light, down wi' me to my aunt, as fast as my two legs cud carry me.

Well, my aunt did na frump or flite me, as I thought she would, but she held me by the hand, and looked hard in my face all the time. And she telt me not to be feared; and says she:

'Hed the appearance a key in its hand?'

'Yes,' says I, bringin' it to mind, 'a big key in a queer brass handle.'

'Stop a bit,' says she, lettin' go ma hand, and openin' the cupboard-door. 'Was it like this?' says she, takin' one out in her fingers, and showing it to me, with a dark look in my face.

'That was it,' says I, quick enough.

'Are ye sure?' she says, turnin' it round.

'Sart,'* says I, and I felt like I was gain' to faint when I sid it.

'Well, that will do, child,' says she, saftly thinkin', and she locked it up again.

'The squire himself will be here to-day, before twelve o'clock, and ye must tell him all about it,' says she, thinkin', 'and I suppose I'll be leavin' soon, and so the best thing for the present is, that ye should go home this afternoon, and I'll look out another place for you when I can.'

Fain was I, ye may guess, at that word.

My aunt packed up my things for me, and the three pounds that was due to me, to bring home, and Squire Crowl himself came down to Applewale that day, a handsome man, about thirty years ald. It was the second time I sid him. But this was the first time he spoke to me.

My aunt talked wi' him in the house-keeper's room, and I don't know what they said. I was a bit feared on the squire, he bein' a great gentleman down in Lexhoe, and I darn't go near till I was called. And says he, smilin':

'What's a' this ye a sen, child? it mun be a dream, for ye know there na sic a thing as a bo or a freet* in a' the world. But whatever it was, ma little maid, sit ye down and tell us all about it from first to last.'

Well, so soon as I med an end, he thought a bit, and says he to my aunt:

'I mind the place well. In old Sir Olivur's time lame Wyndel told me there was a door in that recess, to the left, where the lassie dreamed she saw my grandmother open it. He was past eighty when he telt me that, and I but a boy. It's twenty year sen. The plate and jewels used to be kept there, long ago, before the iron closet was made in the arras chamber, and he told me the key had a brass handle, and this ye say was found in the bottom o' the kist* where she kept her old fans. Now, would not it be a queer thing if we found some spoons or diamonds forgot there? Ye mun come up wi' us, lassie, and point to the very spot.'

Loth was I, and my heart in my mouth, and fast I held by my aunt's hand as I stept into that awsome room, and showed them both how she came and passed me by, and the spot where she stood, and where the door seemed to open.

There was an ald empty press against the wall then, and shoving it aside, sure enough there was the tracing of a door in the wainscot, and a keyhole stopped with wood, and planed across as smooth as the rest, and the joining of the door all stopped wi' putty the colour o' yak, and, but for the hinges that showed a bit when the press was shoved aside, ye would not consayt* there was a door there at all.

'Ha!' says he, wi' a queer smile, 'this looks like it.'

It took some minutes wi' a small chisel and hammer to pick the bit o' wood out o' the keyhole. The key fitted, sure enough, and, wi' a strang twist and a lang skreeak, the boult went back and he pulled the door open.

There was another door inside, stranger than the first, but the lacks was gone, and it opened easy. Inside was a narrow floor and walls and vault o' brick; we could not see what was in it, for 'twas dark as pick.*

When my aunt had lighted the candle the squire held it up and stept in.

My aunt stood on tiptoe tryin' to look over his shouther, and I did na see nout.

'Ha! ha!' says the squire, steppin' backward. 'What's that? Gi' ma the poker—quick!' says he to my aunt. And as she went to the hearth I peeps beside his arm, and I sid squat down in the far corner a monkey or a flayin'* on the chest, or else the maist shrivelled up, wizzened ald wife that ever was sen on yearth.

'By Jen!' says my aunt, as, puttin' the poker in his hand, she kecked by his shouther, and sid the ill-favoured thing, 'hae a care, sir, what ye're doin'. Back wi' ye, and shut to the door!'

But in place o' that he steps in saftly, wi' the poker pointed like a swoord, and he gies it a poke, and down it a' tumbles together, head and a', in a heap o' bayans* and dust, little meyar an' a hatful.

'Twas the bayans o' a child; a' the rest went to dust at a touch. They said nout for a while, but he turns round the skull as it lay on the floor.

Young as I was I consayted I knew well enough what they was thinkin' on.

'A dead cat!' says he, pushin' back and blowin' out the can'le, and shuttin' to the door. 'We'll come back, you and me, Mrs Shutters, and look on the shelves by-and-bye. I've other matters first to speak to ye about; and this little girl's goin' hame, ye say. She has her wages, and I mun mak' her a present,' says he, pattin' my shouther wi' his hand.

And he did gimma a goud pound, and I went aff to Lexhoe about an hour after, and sa hame by the stage-coach, and fain was I to be at hame again; and I niver saa ald Dame Crowl o' Applewale, God be thanked, either in appearance or in dream, at-efter.* But when I was grown to be a woman my aunt spent a day and night wi' me at Littleham, and she telt me there was na doubt it was the poor little boy that was missing sa lang sen that was shut up to die thar in the dark by that wicked beldame, whar his skirls, or his prayers, or his thumpin' cud na be heard, and his hat was left by the water's edge, whoever did it, to mak' belief he was drowned. The clothes, at the first touch, a' ran into a snuff o' dust in the cell whar the bayans was found. But there was a handful o' jet buttons, and a knife with a green handle, together wi' a couple o' pennies the poor little fella had in his pocket, I suppose, when he was decoyed in thar, and sid his last o' the light. And there was, amang the squire's papers, a copy o' the notice that was prented after he was lost, when the ald squire thought he might 'a run away, or bin took by gipsies, and it said he had a green-hefted knife wi' him, and that his buttons were o' cut jet. Sa that is a' I hev to say consarnin' ald Dame Crowl, o' Applewale House.

THE HAUNTED BARONET

CHAPTER I

THE GEORGE AND DRAGON

THE pretty little town of Golden Friars—standing by the margin of the lake, hemmed round by an amphitheatre of purple mountain, rich in tint and furrowed by ravines, high in air, when the tall gables and narrow windows of its ancient graystone houses, and the tower of the old church, from which every evening the curfew still lings, show silvery-white in the moonbeams, and the black elms that stand round throw moveless shadows upon the short level grass—is one of the most singular and beautiful sights I have ever seen.

There it rises, 'as from the stroke of the enchanter's wand',* looking so light and filmy, that you could scarcely believe it more than a picture reflected on the thin mist of night.

On such a still summer night the moon shone splendidly upon the front of the George and Dragon, the comfortable graystone inn of Golden Friars, with the grandest specimen of the old inn-sign, perhaps, left in England. It looks right across the lake; the road that skirts its margin running by the steps of the hall-door, opposite to which, at the other side of the road, between two great posts, and framed in a fanciful wrought-iron border splendid with gilding, swings the famous picture of St George and the Dragon, gorgeous with colour and gold.

In the great room of the George and Dragon, three or four of the old *habitués* of that cozy lounge were refreshing a little after the fatigues of the day.

This is a comfortable chamber, with an oak wainscot; and whenever in summer months the air is sharp enough, as on the present occasion, a fire helped to light it up; which fire, being chiefly wood, made a pleasant broad flicker on panel and ceiling, and yet did not make the room too hot.

On one side sat Doctor Torvey, the doctor of Golden Friars, who knew the weak point of every man in the town, and what medicine agreed with each inhabitant—a fat gentleman, with a jolly laugh and an appetite for all sorts of news, big and little, and who liked a pipe, and made a tumbler of punch at about this hour, with a bit of lemon-peel in it. Beside him sat William Peers, a thin old gentleman, who had lived for more than thirty years in India, and was quiet and benevolent, and

the last man in Golden Friars who wore a pigtail. Old Jack Amerald, an
ex-captain of the navy, with his short stout leg on a chair, and its wooden
companion beside it, sipped his grog, and bawled in the old-fashioned
navy way, and called his friends his 'hearties'. In the middle, opposite
the hearth, sat deaf Tom Hollar, always placid, and smoked his pipe,
looking serenely at the fire. And the landlord of the George and Dragon
every now and then strutted in, and sat down in the high-backed wooden
arm-chair, according to the old-fashioned republican ways of the place,
and took his share in the talk gravely, and was heartily welcome.

'And so Sir Bale is coming home at last,' said the Doctor. 'Tell us any
more you heard since.'

'Nothing,' answered Richard Turnbull, the host of the George.
'Nothing to speak of; only 'tis certain sure, and so best; the old house
won't look so dowly now.'

'Twyne says the estate owes a good capful o' money by this time,
hey?' said the Doctor, lowering his voice and winking.

'Weel, they do say he's been nout at dow.* I don't mind saying so to *you*,
mind, sir, where all's friends together; but he'll get that right in time.'

'More like to save here than where he is,' said the Doctor with
another grave nod.

'He does very wisely,' said Mr Peers, having blown out a thin stream
of smoke, 'and creditably, to pull-up in time. He's coming here to save
a little, and perhaps he'll marry; and it is the more creditable, if, as they
say, he dislikes the place, and would prefer staying where he is.'

And having spoken thus gently, Mr Peers resumed his pipe cheerfully.

'No, he don't like the place; that is, I'm told he *didn't*,' said the
innkeeper.

'He *hates* it,' said the Doctor with another dark nod.

'And no wonder, if all's true I've heard,' cried old Jack Amerald.
'Didn't he drown a woman and her child in the lake?'

'Hollo! my dear boy, don't let them hear you say that; you're all in the
clouds.'

'By Jen!' exclaimed the landlord after an alarmed silence, with his
mouth and eyes open, and his pipe in his hand, 'why, sir, I pay rent for
the house up there. I'm thankful—dear knows, I *am* thankful—we're
all to ourselves!'

Jack Amerald put his foot on the floor, leaving his wooden leg in its
horizontal position, and looked round a little curiously.

'Well, if it wasn't him, it was some one else. I'm sure it happened up
at Mardykes. I took the bearings on the water myself from Glads Scaur
to Mardykes Jetty, and from the George and Dragon sign down

here—down to the white house under Forrick Fells. I could fix a buoy over the very spot. Some one here told me the bearings, I'd take my oath, where the body was seen; and yet no boat could ever come up with it; and that was queer, you know, so I clapt it down in my log.'

'Ay, sir, there *was* some flummery like that, Captain,' said Turnbull; 'for folk will be gabbin'. But 'twas his grandsire was talked o', not him; and 'twould play the hangmen* wi' me doun here, if 'twas thought there was stories like that passin' in the George and Dragon.'

'Well, his grandfather; 'twas all one to the woman, I take it.'

'There never was no proof, Captain, no more than smoke; and the family up at Mardykes wouldn't allow the king to talk o' them like that, sir; for though they be lang deod* that had most right to be angered in the matter, there's none o' the name but would be half daft to think 'twas still believed, and he full out as mich as any. Not that I need care more than another, though they do say he's a bit frowsy and short-waisted;* for he can't shouther* me out o' the George while I pay my rent, till nine hundred and ninety-nine year be rin oot; and a man, be he ne'er sa het, has time to cool before then. But there's no good quarrellin' wi' teathy* folk; and it may lie in his way to do the George mony an ill turn, and mony a gude one; an' it's only fair to say it happened a long way before he was born, and there's no good in vexin' him; and I lay ye a pound, Captain, the Doctor hods wi' me.'

The Doctor, whose business was also sensitive, nodded; and then he said, 'But for all that, the story's old, Dick Turnbull—older than you or I, my jolly good friend.'

'And best forgotten,' interposed the host of the George.

'Ay, best forgotten; but that it's not like to be,' said the Doctor, plucking up courage. 'Here's our friend the Captain has heard it; and the mistake he has made shows there's one thing worse than its being quite remembered, and that is, its being *half* remembered. We can't stop people talking; and a story like that will see us all off the hooks, and be in folks' mouths as strong as ever.'

'Ay; and now I think on it, 'twas Dick Harman that has the boat down there—an old tar like myself—that told me that yarn. I was trying for pike, and he pulled me over the place, and that's how I came to hear it.—I say, Tom, my hearty, serve us out another glass of brandy, will you?' shouted the Captain's voice as the waiter crossed the room; and that florid and grizzled naval hero clapped his leg again on the chair by its wooden companion, which he was wont to call his jury-mast.

'Well, I do believe it will be spoke of longer than we are like to hear; and I don't much matter the story, if it baint told o' the wrong man.'

Here he touched his tumbler with the spoon, indicating by that little ring that Tom, who had returned with the Captain's grog, was to replenish it with punch. 'And Sir Bale is like to be a friend to this house. I don't see no reason why he shouldn't. The George and Dragon has bin in our family ever since the reign of King Charles the Second. It was William Turnbull in that time, which they called it the Restoration, he taking the lease from Sir Tony Mardykes that was then. They was but knights then. They was made baronets first in the reign of King George the Second; you may see it in the list of the baronets and the nobility. The lease was made to William Turnbull, which came from London; and he built the stables, which they was out o' repair, as you may read to this day in the lease; and the house has never had but one sign since—the George and Dragon, it is pretty well known in England—and one name to its master. It has been owned by a Turnbull from that day to this, and they have not been counted bad men.' A murmur of applause testified the assent of his guests. 'They has been steady church-goin' folk, and brewed good drink, and maintained the best o' characters, hereaways and farther off too, though 'tis I, Richard Turnbull, that says it; and while they pay their rent, no man has power to put them out; for their title's as good to the George and Dragon, and the two fields, and the croft, and the grazing o' their kye* on the green, as Sir Bale Mardykes to the Hall up there and estate. So 'tis nout to me, except in the way o' friendliness, what the family may think o' me; only the George and they has always been kind and friendly, and I don't want to break the old custom.'

'Well said, Dick!' exclaimed Doctor Torvey; 'I hold to your conclusion; but there ain't a soul here but ourselves—and we're all friends, and you are your own master—and, hang it, you'll tell us that story about the drowned woman, as you heard it from your father long ago.'

'Ay, do, and keep us to our liquor, my hearty!' cried the Captain.

Mr Peers looked his entreaty; and deaf Mr Hollar, having no interest in the petition, was at least a safe witness, and, with his pipe in his lips, a cozy piece of furniture.

Richard Turnbull had his punch beside him; he looked over his shoulder. The door was closed, the fire was cheery, and the punch was fragrant, and all friendly faces about him. So said he:

'Gentlemen, as you're pleased to wish it, I don't see no great harm in it; and at any rate, 'twill prevent mistakes. It is more than ninety years since. My father was but a boy then; and many a time I heard him tell it in this very room.'

And looking into his glass he mused, and stirred his punch slowly.

CHAPTER II

THE DROWNED WOMAN

'IT ain't much of a homminy,' said the host of the George. 'I'll not keep you long over it, gentlemen. There was a handsome young lady, Miss Mary Feltram o' Cloostedd by name. She was the last o' that family; they had gone very poor. There's but the walls o' the house left now: grass growing in the hall, and ivy over the gables; there's no one livin' has ever hard tell o' smoke out o' they chimblies. It stands on t'other side o' the lake, on the level, wi' a deal o' a'ad trees behint and aside it, at the gap o' the clough, under the pike o' Maiden Fells. Ye may see it wi' a spyin'-glass from the boat-bield at Mardykes Hall.'

'I've been there fifty times,' said the Doctor.

'Well, there was dealin's betwixt the two families; and there's good and bad in every family; but the Mardykes, in them days, was a wild lot. And when old Feltram o' Cloostedd died, and the young lady his daughter was left a ward o' Sir Jasper Mardykes—an ill day for her, poor lass!—twenty year older than her he was, an' more; and nothin' about him, they say, to make any one like or love him, ill-faur'd and little and dow.'

'Dow—that's gloomy,' Doctor Torvey instructed the Captain, aside.

'But, they do say, they has an old blud-stean* ring in the family that has a charm in't; and happen how it might, the poor lass fell in love wi' him. Some said they was married. Some said it hang'd i' the bell-ropes, and never had the priest's blessing; but anyhow, married or no, there was talk enough amang the folk, and out o' doors she would na budge. And there was two wee barns; and she prayed him hard to confess the marriage, poor thing! But 'twas a bootless bene,* and he would not allow they should bear his name, but their mother's; he was a hard man, and hed the bit in his teeth, and went his ain gait. And having tired of her, he took in his head to many a lady of the Barnets, and it behoved him to be shut o' her and her children; and so she nor them was seen no more at Mardykes Hall. And the eldest, a boy, was left in care of my grandfather's father here in the George.'

'That queer Philip Feltram that's travelling with Sir Bale so long is a descendant of his?' said the Doctor.

'Grandson,' observed Mr Peers, removing his pipe for a moment; 'and he is the last of that stock.'

'Well, no one could tell where she was gone to. Some said to distant parts, some said to the madhouse, some one thing, some another; but

neither she nor the barn was ever seen or spoke to by the folk at
Mardykes in life again. There was one Mr Wigram that lived in them
times down at Moultry, and had sarved, like the Captain here, in the
king's navy in his day; and early of a morning down he comes to the
town here for a boat, sayin' he was looking toward Snakes Island
through his spyin'-glass, and he seen a woman about a hundred and
fifty yards outside of it; the Captain here has heard the bearings right
enough. From her hips upward she was stark and straight out o' the
water, and a baby in her arms. Well, no one else could see it, nor he
neither, when they went down to the boat. But next morning he saw the
same thing, and the boatman saw it too; and they rowed for it, both
pulling might and main; but after a mile or so they could see it no more,
and gave over. The next that saw it was the vicar, I forget his name
now—but he was up the lake to a funeral at Mortlock Church; and
coming back by moonlight with a bit of a sail up, just passin' Snakes
Island, what should they hear on a sudden but a wowl like a death-cry,
shrill and bleak, as made the very blood hoot in their veins; and looking
along the water not a hundred yards away, they saw the same grizzled
sight in the moonlight; so they turned the tiller, and came near enough
to see her face—blea* it was, and drenched wi' water—and she was
above the lake to her middle, stiff as a post, holdin' the weeny barn out
to them, and flyrin' [smiling scornfully] on them as they drew nigh her.
They were half-frighted, not knowing what to make of it; but passing as
close as the boatman could bring her side, the vicar stretched over the
gunwale to catch her, and she bent forward, pushing the dead bab forward; and as she did, on a sudden she gave another yell that scared
them, and they saw her no more. 'Twas no livin' woman, for she
couldn't rise that height above the water, as they well knew when they
came to think; and they knew it was a dobby* they saw; and ye may be
sure they didn't spare prayer and blessin', and went on their course
straight before the wind; for neither would a-took the worth o' all
Mardykes to look sich a freetin' i' the face again. 'Twas seen another
time by market-folk crossin' fra Gyllenston in the self-same place;
and Snakes Island got a bad neam, and none cared to go nar it after
nightfall.'

'Do you know anything of that Feltram that has been with him
abroad?' asked the Doctor.

'They say he's no good at anything—a harmless mafflin; he was
a lang gaumless gawky* when he went awa,' said Richard Turnbull.
'The Feltrams and the Mardykes was sib,* ye know; and that made what
passed in the misfortune o' that young lady spoken of all the harder;

and this poor young man ye speak of is grandson o' the lad that was put here in care o' my grandfather.'

'*Great*-grandson. His father was grandson,' said Mr Peers; 'he held a commission in the army, and died in the West Indies. This Philip Feltram is the last of that line—illegitimate, you know, it is held—and the little that remained of the Feltram property went nearly fourscore years ago to the Mardykes, and this Philip is maintained by Sir Bale; it is pleasant, notwithstanding all the stories one hears, gentlemen, that the only thing we know of him for certain should be so creditable to his kindness.'

'To be sure,' acquiesced Mr Turnbull.

While they talked, the horn sounded, and the mail-coach drew up at the door of the George and Dragon to set down a passenger and his luggage.

Dick Turnbull rose and went out to the hall with careful bustle, and Doctor Torvey followed as far as the door, which commanded a view of it, and saw several trunks cased in canvas pitched into the hall, and by careful Tom and a boy lifted one on top of the other, behind the corner of the banister. It would have been below the dignity of his cloth to go out and read the labels on these, or the Doctor would have done otherwise, so great was his curiosity.

CHAPTER III
PHILIP FELTRAM

THE new guest was now in the hall of the George, and Doctor Torvey could hear him talking with Mr Turnbull. Being himself one of the dignitaries of Golden Friars, the Doctor, having regard to first impressions, did not care to be seen in his post of observation; and closing the door gently, returned to his chair by the fire, and in an under-tone informed his cronies that there was a new arrival in the George, and he could not hear, but would not wonder if he were taking a private room; and he seemed to have trunks enough to build a church with.

'Don't be too sure we haven't Sir Bale on board,' said Amerald, who would have followed his crony the Doctor to the door—for never was retired naval hero of a village more curious than he—were it not that his wooden leg made a distinct pounding on the floor that was inimical, as experience had taught him, to mystery.

'That can't be,' answered the Doctor; 'Charley Twyne knows everything about it, and has a letter every second day; and there's no chance of Sir Bale before the tenth; this is a tourist, you'll find. I don't know what the d—l keeps Turnbull; he knows well enough we are all naturally anxious to hear who it is.'

'Well, he won't trouble us here, I bet ye;' and catching deaf Mr Hollar's eye, the Captain nodded, and pointed to the little table beside him, and made a gesture imitative of the rattling of a dice-box; at which that quiet old gentleman nodded also sunnily; and up got the Captain and conveyed the backgammon-box to the table, near Hollar's elbow, and the two worthies were soon sincducing and catre-acing,* with the pleasant clatter that accompanies that ancient game. Hollar had thrown sixes and made his double point, and the honest Captain, who could stand many things better than Hollar's throwing such throws so early in the evening, cursed his opponent's luck and sneered at his play, and called the company to witness, with a distinctness which a stranger to smiling Hollar's deafness would have thought hardly civil; and just at this moment the door opened, and Richard Turnbull showed his new guest into the room, and ushered him to a vacant seat near the other corner of the table before the fire.

The stranger advanced slowly and shyly, with something a little deprecatory in his air, to which a lathy figure, a slight stoop, and a very gentle and even heart-broken look in his long pale face, gave a more marked character of shrinking and timidity.

He thanked the landlord aside, as it were, and took his seat with a furtive glance round, as if he had no right to come in and intrude upon the happiness of these honest gentlemen.

He saw the Captain scanning him from under his shaggy gray eyebrows while he was pretending to look only at his game; and the Doctor was able to recount to Mrs Torvey when he went home every article of the stranger's dress.

It was odd and melancholy as his peaked face.

He had come into the room with a short black cloak on, and a rather tall foreign felt hat, and a pair of shiny leather gaiters or leggings on his thin legs; and altogether presented a general resemblance to the conventional figure of Guy Fawkes.*

Not one of the company assembled there knew the appearance of the Baronet. The Doctor and old Mr Peers remembered something of his looks; and certainly they had no likeness, but the reverse, to those presented by the new-comer. The Baronet, as now described by people who had chanced to see him, was a dark man, not above the middle size, and with a certain decision in his air and talk; whereas this person was tall, pale, and in air and manner feeble. So this broken trader in the world's commerce, with whom all seemed to have gone wrong, could not possibly be he.

Presently, in one of his stealthy glances, the Doctor's eye encountered that of the stranger, who was by this time drinking his tea—a thin and feminine liquor little used in that room.

The stranger did not seem put out; and the Doctor, interpreting his look as a permission to converse, cleared his voice, and said urbanely,

'We have had a little frost by night down here, sir, and a little fire is no great harm—it is rather pleasant, don't you think?'

The stranger bowed acquiescence with a transient wintry smile, and looked gratefully on the fire.

'This place is a good deal admired, sir, and people come a good way to see it; you have been here perhaps before?'

'Many years ago.'

Here was another pause.

'Places change imperceptibly—in detail, at least—a good deal,' said the Doctor, making an effort to keep up a conversation that plainly would not go on of itself; 'and people too; population shifts—there's an old fellow, sir, they call *Death*.'

'And an old fellow they call the *Doctor*, that helps him,'* threw in the Captain humorously, allowing his attention to get entangled in the conversation, and treating them to one of his tempestuous ha-ha-ha's.

'We are expecting the return of a gentleman who would be a very leading member of our little society down here,' said the Doctor, without noticing the Captain's joke. 'I mean Sir Bale Mardykes. Mardykes Hall is a pretty object from the water, sir, and a very fine old place.'

The melancholy stranger bowed slightly, but rather in courtesy to the relator, it seemed, than that the Doctor's lore interested him much.

'And on the opposite side of the lake,' continued Doctor Torvey, 'there is a building that contrasts very well with it—the old house of the Feltrams—quite a ruin now, at the mouth of the glen—Cloostedd House, a very picturesque object.'

'Exactly opposite,' said the stranger dreamily, but whether in the tone of acquiescence or of interrogatory, the Doctor could not be quite sure.

'That was one of our great families down here that has disappeared. It has dwindled down to nothing.'

'Duce ace,' remarked Mr Hollar, who was attending to his game.

'While others have mounted more suddenly and amazingly still,' observed gentle Mr Peers, who was great upon county genealogies.

'Sizes!' thundered the Captain, thumping the table with an oath of disgust.

'And Snakes Island is a very pretty object; they say there used to be snakes there,' said the Doctor, enlightening the visitor.

'Ah! that's a mistake,' said the dejected guest, making his first original observation. 'It should be spelt *Snaiks*. In the old papers it is called Sen-aiks Island, from the seven oaks that grew in a clump there.'

'Hey? that's very curious, egad! I daresay,' said the Doctor, set right thus by the stranger, and eyeing him curiously.

'Very true, sir,' observed Mr Peers; 'three of those oaks, though, two of them little better than stumps, are there still; and Clewson of Heckleston has an old document—'

Here, unhappily, the landlord entered the room in a fuss, and walking up to the stranger, said, 'The chaise is at the door, Mr Feltram, and the trunks up, sir.'

Mr Feltram rose quietly and took out his purse, and said,

'I suppose I had better pay at the bar?'

'As you like best, sir,' said Richard Turnbull.

Mr Feltram bowed all round to the gentlemen, who smiled, ducked, or waved their hands; and the Doctor fussily followed him to the hall-door, and welcomed him back to Golden Friars—there was real kindness in this welcome—and proffered his broad brown hand, which Mr Feltram took; and then he plunged into his chaise, and the door being shut, away he glided, chaise, horses, and driver, like shadows, by the margin of the moonlighted lake, towards Mardykes Hall.

And after a minute's stand upon the steps, looking along the shadowy track of the chaise, they returned to the glow of the room, in which a pleasant perfume of punch still prevailed; and beside Mr Philip Feltram's deserted tea-things, the host of the George enlightened his guests by communicating freely the little he had picked up. The principal fact he had to tell was, that Sir Bale adhered strictly to his original plan, and was to arrive on the tenth. A few days would bring them to that, and the nine-days wonder run its course and lose its interest. But in the mean time, all Golden Friars was anxious to see what Sir Bale Mardykes was like.

CHAPTER IV
THE BARONET APPEARS

As the candles burn blue and the air smells of brimstone at the approach of the Evil One,* so, in the quiet and healthy air of Golden Friars, a depressing and agitating influence announced the coming of the long-absent Baronet.

From abroad, no good whatever had been at any time heard of him, and a great deal that was, in the ears of simple folk living in that unsophisticated part of the world, vaguely awful.

Stories that travel so far, however, lose something of their authority, as well as definiteness, on the way; there was always room for charity to suggest a mistake or exaggeration; and if good men turned up their hands and eyes after a new story, and ladies of experience, who knew mankind, held their heads high and looked grim and mysterious at mention of his name, nevertheless an interval of silence softened matters a little, and the sulphureous perfume dissipated itself in time.

Now that Sir Bale Mardykes had arrived at the Hall, there were hurried consultations held in many households. And though he was tried and sentenced by drum-head* over some austere hearths, as a rule the law of gravitation prevailed, and the greater house drew the lesser about it, and country people within the visiting radius paid their respects at the Hall.

The Reverend Martin Bedel, the then vicar of Golden Friars, a stout short man, with a mulberry-coloured nose and small gray eyes, and taciturn habits, called and entered the drawing-room at Mardykes Hall, with his fat and garrulous wife on his arm.

The drawing-room had a great projecting Tudor window looking out on the lake, with its magnificent background of furrowed and purple mountains.

Sir Bale was not there, and Mrs Bedel examined the pictures, and ornaments, and the books, making such remarks as she saw fit; and then she looked out of the window, and admired the prospect. She wished to stand well with the Baronet, and was in a mood to praise everything.

You may suppose she was curious to see him, having heard for years such strange tales of his doings.

She expected the hero of a brilliant and wicked romance; and listened for the step of the truant Lovelace who was to fulfil her idea of manly beauty and fascination.

She sustained a slight shock when he did appear.

Sir Bale Mardykes was, as she might easily have remembered, a middle-aged man—and he looked it. He was not even an imposing-looking man for his time of life: he was of about the middle height, slightly made, and dark featured. She had expected something of the gaiety and animation of Versailles, and an evident cultivation of the art of pleasing. What she did see was a remarkable gravity, not to say gloom, of countenance—the only feature of which that struck her being a pair of large dark-gray eyes, that were cold and earnest. His manners had the ease of perfect confidence; and his talk and air were those of a person who might have known how to please, if it were worth the trouble, but who did not care two-pence whether he pleased or not.

He made them each a bow, courtly enough, but there was no smile—not even an affectation of cordiality. Sir Bale, however, was chatty, and did not seem to care much what he said, or what people thought of him; and there was a suspicion of sarcasm in what he said that the rustic literality of good Mrs Bedel did not always detect.

'I believe I have not a clergyman but *you*, sir, within any reasonable distance?'

'Golden Friars *is* the nearest,' said Mrs Bedel, answering, as was her pleasure on all practicable occasions, for her husband. 'And southwards, the nearest is Wyllarden—and by a bird's flight that is thirteen miles and a half, and by the road more than nineteen—twenty, I may say, by the road. Ha, ha, ha! it is a long way to look for a clergyman.'

'Twenty miles of road to carry you thirteen miles across, hey? The road-makers lead you a pretty dance here; those gentlemen know how to make money, and like to show people the scenery from a variety of points. No one likes a straight road but the man who pays for it, and who, when he travels, is brute enough to wish to get to his journey's end.'

'That is so true, Sir Bale; one never cares if one is not in a hurry. That's what Martin thinks—don't we, Martin?—And then, you know, coming home is the time you *are* in a hurry—when you are thinking of your cup of tea and the children; and *then*, you know, you have the fall of the ground all in your favour.'

'It's well to have anything in your favour in this place. And so there are children?'

'A good many,' said Mrs Bedel, with a proud and mysterious smile, and a nod; 'you wouldn't guess how many.'

'Not I; I only wonder you did not bring them all.'

'That's very good-natured of you, Sir Bale, but all could not come at *one* bout; there are—tell him, Martin—ha, ha, ha! there are eleven.'

'It must be very cheerful down at the vicarage,' said Sir Bale graciously; and turning to the vicar he added, 'But how unequally blessings are divided! you have eleven, and I not one—that I'm aware of.'

'And then, in that direction straight before you, you have the lake, and then the fells; and five miles from the foot of the mountain at the other side, before you reach Fottrell—and that is twenty-five miles by the road—'

'Dear me! how far apart they are set! My gardener told me this morning that asparagus grows very thinly in this part of the world. How thinly clergymen grow also down here—in one sense,' he added politely, for the vicar was stout.

'We were looking out of the window—we amused ourselves that way before you came—and your view is certainly the very best, anywhere round this side; your view of the lake and the fells—what mountains they are, Sir Bale!'

''Pon my soul, they are! I wish I could blow them asunder with a charge of duck-shot, and I shouldn't he stifled by them long. But I suppose, as we can't get rid of them, the next best thing is to admire them. We are pretty well married to them, and there is no use in quarrelling.'

'I know you don't think so, Sir Bale, ha, ha, ha! You wouldn't take a good deal and spoil Mardykes Hall.'

'You can't get a mouthful of air, or see the sun of a morning, for those frightful mountains,' he said with a peevish frown at them.

'Well, the lake at all events—that you *must* admire, Sir Bale?'

'No, ma'am, I don't admire the lake. I'd drain the lake if I could—I hate the lake. There's nothing so gloomy as a lake pent up among barren mountains. I can't conceive what possessed my people to build our house down here, at the edge of a lake; unless it was the fish, and precious fish it is—pike! I don't know how people digest it—*I* can't. I'd as soon think of eating a watchman's pike.'

'I thought that having travelled so much abroad, you would have acquired a great liking for that kind of scenery, Sir Bale; there is a great deal of it on the Continent, ain't there?' said Mrs Bedel. 'And the boating.'

'Boating, my dear Mrs Bedel, is the dullest of all things; don't you think so? Because a boat looks very pretty from the shore, we fancy the shore must look very pretty from a boat; and when we try it, we find we have only got down into a pit and can see nothing rightly. For my part I hate boating, and I hate the water; and I'd rather have my house, like Haworth,* at the edge of a moss, with good wholesome peat to look at, and an open horizon—savage and stupid and bleak as all that is—than be suffocated among impassable mountains, or upset in a black lake and drowned like a kitten. O, there's luncheon in the next room; won't you take some?'

CHAPTER V

MRS JULAPER'S ROOM

SIR BALE MARDYKES being now established in his ancestral house, people had time to form conclusions respecting him. It must be allowed he was not popular. There was, perhaps, in his conduct something of the caprice of contempt. At all events his temper and conduct were uncertain, and his moods sometimes violent and insulting.

With respect to but one person was his conduct uniform, and that was Philip Feltram. He was a sort of aide-de-camp near Sir Bale's person, and chargeable with all commissions and offices which could not be suitably intrusted to a mere servant. But in many respects he was treated worse than any servant of the Baronet's. Sir Bale swore at him, and cursed him; laid the blame of everything that went wrong in house, stable, or field upon his shoulders; railed at him, and used him, as people said, worse than a dog.

Why did Feltram endure this contumelious life?* What could he do but endure it? was the answer. What was the power that induced strong soldiers to put off their jackets and shirts, and present their hands to be tied up, and tortured for hours, it might be, under the scourge, with an air of ready volition? The moral coercion of despair; the result of an unconscious calculation of chances which satisfies them that it is ultimately better to do all that, bad as it is, than try the alternative. These unconscious calculations are going on every day with each of us, and the results embody themselves in our lives; and no one knows that there has been a process and a balance struck, and that what they see, and very likely blame, is by the fiat of an invisible but quite irresistible power.

A man of spirit would rather break stones on the highway than eat that bitter bread, was the burden of every man's song on Feltram's bondage. But he was not so sure that even the stone-breaker's employment was open to him, or that he could break stones well enough to retain it on a fair trial. And he had other ideas of providing for himself, and a different alternative in his mind.

Good-natured Mrs Julaper, the old housekeeper at Mardykes Hall, was kind to Feltram, as to all others who lay in her way and were in affliction.

She was one of those good women whom Nature provides to receive the burden of other people's secrets, as the reeds did long ago, only that no chance wind could steal them away, and send them singing into strange ears.

You may still see her snuggery* in Mardykes Hall, though the housekeeper's room is now in a different part of the house.

Mrs Julaper's room was in the oldest quarter of that old house. It was wainscoted, in black panels, up to the ceiling, which was stuccoed over in the fanciful diagrams of James the First's time. Several dingy portraits, banished from time to time from other statelier rooms, found a temporary abode in this quiet spot, where they had come finally to settle and drop out of remembrance. There is a lady in white satin and a ruff; a gentleman whose legs have faded out of view, with a peaked beard, and a hawk on his wrist. There is another in a black periwig lost in the dark background, and with a steel cuirass, the gleam of which out of the darkness strikes the eye, and a scarf is dimly discoverable across it. This is that foolish Sir Guy Mardykes, who crossed the Border and joined Dundee, and was shot through the temple at Killiecrankie,* and whom more prudent and whiggish scions of the Mardykes family removed forthwith from his place in the Hall, and found him a retirement here, from which he has not since emerged.

At the far end of this snug room is a second door, on opening which you find yourself looking down upon the great kitchen, with a little balcony before you, from which the housekeeper used to issue her commands to the cook, and exercise a sovereign supervision.

There is a shelf here on which Mrs Julaper had her Bible, her *Whole Duty of Man*, and her *Pilgrim's Progress*;* and, in a file beside them, her books of housewifery, and among them volumes of MS. recipes, cookery-books, and some too on surgery and medicine, as practised by the Ladies Bountiful* of the Elizabethan age, for which an antiquarian would nowadays give an eye or a hand.

Gentle half-foolish Philip Feltram would tell the story of his wrongs, and weep and wish he was dead; and kind Mrs Julaper, who remembered him a child, would comfort him with cold pie and cherry-brandy, or a cup of coffee, or some little dainty.

'O, ma'am, I'm tired of my life. What's the good of living, if a poor devil is never let alone, and called worse names than a dog? Would not it be better, Mrs Julaper, to be dead? Wouldn't it be better, ma'am? I think so; I think it night and day. I'm always thinking the same thing. I don't care, I'll just tell him what I think, and have it off my mind. I'll tell him I can't live and bear it longer.'

'There now, don't you be frettin'; but just sip this, and remember you're not to judge a friend by a wry word. He does not mean it, not he. They all had a rough side to their tongue now and again; but no one minded that. I don't, nor you needn't, no more than other folk; for the tongue, be it never so bitin', it can't draw blood, mind ye, and hard words break no bones; and I'll make a cup o' tea—ye like a cup o' tea—and we'll take a cup together, and ye'll chirp up a bit, and see how pleasant and ruddy the sun shines in the lake this evening.'

She was patting him gently on the shoulder, as she stood slim and stiff in her dark silk by his chair, and her rosy little face smiled down on him. She was, for an old woman, wonderfully pretty still. What a delicate skin she must have had! The wrinkles were etched upon it with so fine a needle, you scarcely could see them a little way off; and as she smiled her cheeks looked fresh and smooth as two ruddy little apples.

'Look out, I say,' and she nodded towards the window, deep set in the thick wall. 'See how bright and soft everything looks in that pleasant light; *that's* better, child, than the finest picture man's hand ever painted yet, and God gives it us for nothing; and how pretty Snakes Island glows up in that light!'

The dejected man, hardly raising his head, followed with his eyes the glance of the old woman, and looked mournfully through the window.

'That island troubles me, Mrs Julaper.'

'Everything troubles you, my poor goose-cap. I'll pull your lug for ye, child, if ye be so dowly'; and with a mimic pluck the good-natured old housekeeper pinched his ear and laughed.

'I'll go to the still-room now, where the water's boiling, and I'll make a cup of tea; and if I find ye so dow when I come back, I'll throw it all out o' the window, mind.'

It was indeed a beautiful picture that Feltram saw in its deep frame of old masonry. The near part of the lake was flushed all over with the low western light; the more distant waters lay dark in the shadow of the mountains; and against this shadow of purple the rocks on Snakes Island, illuminated by the setting sun, started into sharp clear light.

But this beautiful view had no charm—at least, none powerful enough to master the latent horror associated with its prettiest feature—for the weak and dismal man who was looking at it; and being now alone, he rose and leant on the window, and looked out, and then with a kind of shudder clutching his hands together, and walking distractedly about the room.

Without his perceiving, while his back was turned, the housekeeper came back; and seeing him walking in this distracted way, she thought to herself, as he leant again upon the window:

'Well, it *is* a burning shame to worrit any poor soul into that state. Sir Bale was always down on someone or something, man or beast; there always was something he hated, and could never let alone. It was not pretty; it was his nature. Happen, poor fellow, he could not help it; but so it was.'

A maid came in and set the tea-things down; and Mrs Julaper drew her sad guest over by the arm, and made him sit down, and she said: 'What has a man to do, frettin' in that way? By Jen, I'm ashamed o' ye, Master Philip! Ye like three lumps o' sugar, I think, and—look cheerful, ye must!—a good deal o' cream?'

'You're so kind, Mrs Julaper, you're so cheery. I feel quite comfortable after awhile when I'm with you; I feel quite happy,' and he began to cry.

She understood him very well by this time, and took no notice, but went on chatting gaily, and made his tea as he liked it; and he dried up his tears hastily, thinking she had not observed.

So the clouds began to clear. This innocent fellow liked nothing better than a cup of tea and a chat with gentle and cheery old Mrs Julaper, and a talk in which the shadowy old times which he remembered as a child emerged into sunlight and lived again.

When he began to feel better, drawn into the kindly old times by the tinkle of that harmless old woman's tongue, he said:

'I sometimes think I would not so much mind—I should not care so much—if my spirits were not so much depressed, and I so agitated. I suppose I am not quite well.'

'Well, tell me what's wrong, child, and it's odd but I have a recipe on the shelf there that will do you good.'

'It is not a matter of that sort I mean; though I'd rather have you than any doctor, if I needed medicine, to prescribe for me.'

Mrs Julaper smiled in spite of herself, well pleased; for her skill in pharmacy was a point on which the good lady prided herself, and was open to flattery, which, without intending it, the simple fellow administered.

'No, I'm well enough; I can't say I ever was better. It is only, ma'am, that I have such dreams—you have no idea.'

'There are dreams and dreams, my dear: there's some signifies no more than the babble of the lake down there on the pebbles, and there's others that has a meaning; there's dreams that is but vanity, and there's dreams that is good, and dreams that is bad. Lady Mardykes—heavens be her bed this day! that's his grandmother I mean—was very sharp for reading dreams. Take another cup of tea. Dear me! what a noise the crows keep aboon our heads, going home! and how high they wing it!—that's a sure sign of fine weather. An' what do you dream about? tell me your dream, and I may show you it's a good one, after all. For many a dream is ugly to see and ugly to tell, and a good dream, with a happy meaning, for all that.'

CHAPTER VI

THE INTRUDER

'WELL, Mrs Julaper, dreams I've dreamed like other people, old and young; but this, ma'am, has taken a fast hold of me,' said Mr Feltram dejectedly, leaning back in his chair and looking down with his hands in his pockets. 'I think, Mrs Julaper, it is getting into me. I think it's like possession.'

'Possession, child! what do you mean?'

'I think there is something trying to influence me. Perhaps it is the way fellows go mad; but it won't let me alone. I've seen it three times, think of that!'

'Well, dear, and what *have* ye seen?' she asked with an uneasy cheerfulness, smiling, with eyes fixed steadily upon him; for the idea of a madman—even gentle Philip in that state—was not quieting.

'Do you remember the picture, full-length, that had no frame—the lady in the white-satin saque*—she was beautiful, *funeste*,'* he added, talking more to himself; and then more distinctly to Mrs Julaper again—'in the white-satin saque; and with the little mob-cap* and blue ribbons to it, and a bouquet in her fingers; that was—that—you know who she was?'

'That was your great-grandmother, my dear,' said Mrs Julaper, lowering her eyes. 'It was a dreadful pity it was spoiled. The boys in the pantry had it for a year there on the table for a tray, to wash the glasses on and the like. It was a shame; that was the prettiest picture in the house, with the gentlest, rosiest face.'

'It ain't so gentle or rosy now, I can tell you,' said Philip. 'As fixed as marble; with thin lips, and a curve at the nostril. Do you remember the woman that was found dead in the clough, when I was a boy, that the gipsies murdered, it was thought,—a cruel-looking woman?'

'Agoy! Master Philip dear! ye would not name that terrible-looking creature with the pretty, fresh, kindly face!'

'Faces change, you see; no matter what she's like; it's her talk that frightens me. She wants to make use of me; and, you see, it is like getting a share in my mind, and a voice in my thoughts, and a command over me gradually; and it is just one idea, as straight as a line of light across the lake—see what she's come to. O Lord, help me!'

'Well, now, don't you be talkin' like that. It is just a little bit dowly and troubled, because the master says a wry word now and then; and so ye let your spirits go down, don't ye see, and all sorts o' fancies comes into your head.'

'There's no fancy in my head,' he said with a quick look of suspicion; 'only you asked me what I dreamed. I don't care if all the world knew. I dreamed I went down steps into the lake, and got a message. There are no steps near Snakes Island, we all know that,' and he laughed chillily. 'I'm out of spirits, as you say; and—and—O dear! I wish—Mrs Julaper—I wish I was in my coffin, and quiet.'

'Now that's very wrong of you, Master Philip; you should think of all the blessings you have, and not be makin' mountains o' molehills; and those little bits o' temper Sir Bale shows, why, no one minds 'em—that is, to take 'em to heart like you do, don't ye see?'

'I daresay; I suppose, Mrs Julaper, you are right. I'm unreasonable often, I know,' said gentle Philip Feltram. 'I daresay I make too much of it; I'll try. I'm his secretary, and I know I'm not so bright as he is, and it is natural he should sometimes be a little impatient; I ought to be more reasonable, I'm sure. It is all that thing that has been disturbing me—I mean fretting; and, I think, I'm not quite well; and—and letting myself think too much of vexations. It's my own fault, I'm sure, Mrs Julaper; and I know I'm to blame.'

'That's quite right, that's spoken like a wise lad; only I don't say you're to blame, nor no one; for folk can't help frettin' sometimes, no more than they can help a headache—none but a mafflin would say that—and I'll not deny but he has dowly ways when the fit's on him, and he frumps us all round, if such be his humour. But who is there hasn't his faults? We must bear and forbear, and take what we get and be cheerful. So chirp up, my lad; Philip, didn't I often ring the a'ad rhyme in your ear long ago?

> Be always as merry as ever yon can,
> For no one delights in a sorrowful man.*

So don't ye be gettin' up off your chair like that, and tramping about the room wi' your hands in your pockets, looking out o' this window and staring out o' that, and sighing and crying, and looking so black-ox-trodden,* 'twould break a body's heart to see you. Ye must be cheery; and happen you're hungry, and don't know it. I'll tell the cook to grill a hot bit for ye.'

'But I'm not hungry, Mrs Julaper. How kind you are! dear me, Mrs Julaper, I'm not worthy of it; I don't deserve half your kindness. I'd have been heart-broken long ago, but for you.'

'And I'll make a sup of something hot for you; you'll take a rummer-glass of punch—you must.'

'But I like the tea better; I do indeed, Mrs Julaper.'

'Tea is no drink for a man when his heart's down. It should be something with a leg in it, lad; something hot that will warm your courage up for ye, and set your blood a-dancing, and make ye talk brave and merry; and will you have a bit of a broil first? No? Well then, you'll have a drop o' punch?—ye sha'n't say no.'

And so, all resistance overpowered, the consolation of Philip Feltram proceeded.

A gentler spirit than poor Feltram, a more good-natured soul than the old housekeeper, were nowhere among the children of earth.

Philip Feltram, who was reserved enough elsewhere, used to come into her room and cry, and take her by both hands piteously, standing before her and looking down in her face, while tears ran deviously down his cheeks.

'Did you ever know such a case? was there ever a fellow like *me*? did you ever *know* such a thing? You know what I am, Mrs Julaper, and who I am. They call me Feltram; but Sir Bale knows as well as I that my true name is not that. I'm Philip Mardykes; and another fellow would make a row about it, and claim his name and his rights, as she is always croaking in my ear I ought. But you know that is not reasonable. My grandmother was married; she was the true Lady Mardykes; *think* what it was to see a woman like that turned out of doors, and her children robbed of their very name. O, ma'am, you *can't* think it; unless you were me, you couldn't—you couldn't—you couldn't!'

'Come, come, Master Philip, don't you be taking on so; and ye mustn't be talking like that, d'ye mind? You know he wouldn't stand that; and it's an old story now, and there's naught can be proved concerning it; and what I think is this—I wouldn't wonder the poor lady was beguiled. But anyhow she surely thought she was his lawful wife; and though the law may hev found a flaw somewhere—and I take it 'twas so—yet sure I am she was an honourable lady. But where's the use of stirring that old sorrow? or how can ye prove aught? and the dead hold their peace, you know; dead mice, they say, feels no cold; and dead folks are past fooling. So don't you talk like that; for stone walls have ears, and ye might say that ye couldn't *unsay*; and death's day is doom's day. So leave all in the keeping of God; and, above all, never lift hand when ye can't strike.'

'Lift my hand! O, Mrs Julaper, you couldn't think that; you little know me; I did not mean that; I never dreamed of hurting Sir Bale. Good heavens! Mrs Julaper, you couldn't think *that*! It all comes of my poor impatient temper, and complaining as I do, and my misery; but O, Mrs Julaper, you could not think I ever meant to trouble him by law, or any other annoyance! I'd like to see a stain removed from my family, and my name restored; but to touch his property, O, no!—O, no! that never entered my mind; by heaven! that never entered my mind, Mrs Julaper. I'm not cruel; I'm not rapacious; I don't care for money; don't you know that, Mrs Julaper? O, surely you won't think me capable of attacking the man whose bread I have been eating so long! I never dreamed of it; I should hate myself. Tell me you don't believe it; O, Mrs Julaper, say you don't!'

And the gentle feeble creature burst into tears, and good Mrs Julaper comforted him with kind words; and he said,

'Thank you, ma'am; thank you. God knows I would not hurt Bale, nor give him one uneasy hour. It is only this: that I'm—I'm so miserable; and I'm only casting in my mind where to turn to, and what to do. So little a thing would be enough, and then I shall leave Mardykes. I'll go; not in any anger, Mrs Julaper—don't think that; but I can't stay, I must be gone.'

'Well, now, there's nothing yet, Master Philip, to fret you like that. You should not be talking so wild-like. Master Bale has his sharp word and his short temper now and again; but I'm sure he likes you. If he didn't, he'd a-said so to me long ago. I'm sure he likes you well.'

'Hollo! I say, who's there? Where the devil's Mr Feltram?' screamed the voice of the Baronet, at a fierce pitch, along the passage.

'La! Mr Feltram, it's him! Ye'd better run to him,' whispered Mrs Julaper.

'D—n me! does nobody hear? Mrs Julaper! Hollo! ho! house, there! ho! D—n me, will nobody answer?'

And Sir Bale began to slap the wainscot fast and furiously with his walking-cane with a clatter like a harlequin's lath in a pantomime.

Mrs Julaper, a little paler than usual, opened her door, and stood with the handle in hand, making a little curtsey, enframed in the doorcase; and Sir Bale, being in a fume, when he saw her, ceased whacking the panels of the corridor, and stamped on the floor, crying,

'Upon my soul, ma'am, I'm glad to see you! Perhaps you can tell me where Feltram is?'

'He's in my room, Sir Bale. Shall I tell him you want him, please?'

'Never mind; thanks,' said the Baronet. 'I've a tongue in my head'; marching down the passage to the housekeeper's room, with his cane clutched hard, glaring savagely, and with his teeth fast set, like a fellow advancing to beat a vicious horse that has chafed his temper.

CHAPTER VII

THE BANK-NOTE

Sir Bale brushed by the housekeeper as he strode into her sanctuary, and there found Philip Feltram awaiting him dejectedly, but with no signs of agitation.

If one were to judge by the appearance the master of Mardykes presented, very grave surmises as to impending violence would have suggested themselves; but though he clutched his cane so hard that it quivered in his grasp, he had no notion of committing the outrage of a blow. The Baronet was unusually angry notwithstanding, and stopping short about three steps away, addressed Feltram with a pale face and gleaming eyes. It was quite plain that there was something very exciting upon his mind.

'I've been looking for you, Mr Feltram; I want a word or two, if you have done your—your—whatever it is.' He whisked the point of his stick towards the modest tea-tray. 'I should like five minutes in the library.'

The Baronet was all this time eyeing Feltram with a hard suspicious gaze, as if he expected to read in his face the shrinkings and trepidations of guilt; and then turning suddenly on his heel he led the way to his library—a good long march, with a good many turnings. He walked very fast, and was not long in getting there. And as Sir Bale reached the hearth, on which was smouldering a great log of wood, and turned about suddenly, facing the door, Philip Feltram entered.

The Baronet looked oddly and stern—so oddly, it seemed to Feltram, that he could not take his eyes off him, and returned his grim and somewhat embarrassed gaze with a stare of alarm and speculation.

And so doing, his step was shortened, and grew slow and slower, and came quite to a stop before he had got far from the door—a wide stretch of that wide floor still intervening between him and Sir Bale, who stood upon the hearthrug, with his heels together and his back to the fire, cane in hand, like a drill-sergeant, facing him.

'Shut that door, please; that will do; come nearer now. I don't want to bawl what I have to say. Now listen.'

The Baronet cleared his voice and paused, with his eyes upon Feltram.

'It is only two or three days ago,' said he, 'that you said you wished you had a hundred pounds. Am I right?'

'Yes; I think so.'

'*Think?* you know it, sir, devilish well. You said that you wished to get away. I have nothing particular to say against that, more especially now. Do you understand what I say?'

'Understand, Sir Bale? I do, sir—quite.'

'I daresay *quite*,' he repeated with an angry sneer. 'Here, sir, is an odd coincidence: you want a hundred pounds, and you can't earn it, and you can't borrow it—there's another way, it seems—but I have got it—a Bank-of-England note of 100*l*.—locked up in that desk'; and he poked the end of his cane against the brass lock of it viciously. 'There it is, and there are the papers you work at; and there are two keys—I've got one and you have the other—and devil another key in or out of the house has any one living. Well, do you begin to see? Don't mind. I don't want any d—d lying about it.'

Feltram was indeed beginning to see that he was suspected of something very bad, but exactly what, he was not yet sure; and being a man of that unhappy temperament which shrinks from suspicion, as others do from detection, he looked very much put out indeed.

'Ha, ha! I think we do begin to see,' said Sir Bale savagely. 'It's a bore, I know, troubling a fellow with a story that he knows before; but I'll make mine short. When I take my key, intending to send the note to pay the crown and quit-rents that you know—you—you—no matter—you know well enough must he paid, I open it so—and so—and look *there*, where I left it, for my note; and the note's gone—you understand, the note's *gone*!'

Here was a pause, during which, under the Baronet's hard insulting eye, poor Feltram winced, and cleared his voice, and essayed to speak, but said nothing.

'It's gone, and we know where. Now, Mr Feltram, *I* did not steal that note, and no one but you and I has access to this desk. You wish to go away, and I have no objection to that—but d—n me if you take away that note with you; and you may as well produce it now and here, as hereafter in a worse place.'

'O, my good heaven!' exclaimed poor Feltram at last. 'I'm very ill.'

'So you are, of course. It takes a stiff emetic to get all that money off a fellow's stomach; and it's like parting with a tooth to give up a banknote. Of course you're ill, but that's no sign of innocence, and I'm no fool. You had better give the thing up quietly.'

'May my Maker strike me—'

'So He will, you d—d rascal, if there's justice in heaven, unless you produce the money. I don't want to hang you. I'm willing to let you off if you'll let me, but I'm cursed if I let my note off along with you; and unless you give it up forthwith, I'll get a warrant and have you searched, pockets, bag, and baggage.'

'Lord! am I awake?' exclaimed Philip Feltram.

'Wide awake, and so am I,' replied Sir Bale. 'You don't happen to have got it about you?'

'God forbid, sir! O, Sir—O, Sir Bale—why, Bale, *Bale*, it's impossible! You *can't* believe it. When did I ever wrong you? You knew me since I was not higher than the table, and—and—'

He burst into tears.

'Stop your snivelling, sir, and give-up the note. You know devilish well I can't spare it; and I won't spare you if you put me to it. I've said my say.'

Sir Bale signed towards the door; and like a somnambulist, with dilated gaze and pale as death, Philip Feltram, at his wit's end, went out of the room. It was not till he had again reached the housekeeper's door that he recollected in what direction he was going. His shut hand was pressed with all his force to his heart, and the first breath he was conscious of was a deep wild sob or two that quivered from his heart as he looked from the lobby-window upon a landscape which he did not see.

All he had ever suffered before was mild in comparison with this dire paroxysm. Now, for the first time, was he made acquainted with his real capacity for pain, and how near he might be to madness and yet retain intellect enough to weigh every scruple, and calculate every chance and consequence, in his torture.

Sir Bale, in the mean time, had walked out a little more excited than he would have allowed. He was still convinced that Feltram had stolen the note, but not quite so certain as he had been. There were things in his manner that confirmed, and others that perplexed, Sir Bale.

The Baronet stood upon the margin of the lake, almost under the evening shadow of the house, looking towards Snakes Island. There were two things about Mardykes he specially disliked.

One was Philip Feltram, who, right or wrong, he fancied knew more than was pleasant of his past life.

The other was the lake. It was a beautiful piece of water, his eye, educated at least in the excellences of landscape-painting, acknowledged. But although he could pull a good oar, and liked other lakes, to this particular sheet of water there lurked within him an insurmountable antipathy. It was engendered by a variety of associations.

There is a faculty in man that will acknowledge the unseen. He may scout and scare religion from him; but if he does, superstition perches near. His boding was made-up of omens, dreams, and such stuff as he most affected to despise, and there fluttered at his heart a presentiment and disgust.

His foot was on the gunwale of the boat, that was chained to its ring at the margin; but he would not have crossed that water in it for any reason that man could urge.

What was the mischief that sooner or later was to befall him from that lake, he could not define; but that some fatal danger lurked there, was the one idea concerning it that had possession of his fancy.

He was now looking along its still waters, towards the copse and rocks of Snakes Island, thinking of Philip Feltram; and the yellow level sunbeams touched his dark features, that bore a saturnine resemblance to those of Charles II,* and marked sharply their firm glim lines, and left his deep-set eyes in shadow.

Who has the happy gift to seize the present, as a child does, and live in it? Who is not often looking far off for his happiness, as Sidney Smith* says, like a man looking for his hat when it is upon his head? Sir Bale was brooding over his double hatred, of Feltram and of the lake. It would have been better had he struck down the raven that croaked upon his shoulder, and listened to the harmless birds that were whistling all round among the branches in the golden sunset.

CHAPTER VIII
FELTRAM'S PLAN

THIS horror of the beautiful lake, which other people thought so lovely, was, in that mind which affected to scoff at the unseen, a distinct creation of downright superstition.

The nursery tales which had scared him in his childhood were founded on the tragedy of Snakes Island, and haunted him with an unavowed persistence still. Strange dreams untold had visited him, and a German conjurer,* who had made some strangely successful vaticinations, had told him that his worst enemy would come to him from a lake. He had heard very nearly the same thing from a fortune-teller in France; and once at Lucerne, when he was waiting alone in his room for the hour at which he had appointed to go upon the lake, all being quiet, there came to the window, which was open, a sunburnt, lean, wicked face. Its ragged owner leaned his arm on the window-frame, and with his head in the room, said in his patois, 'Ho! waiting are you? You'll have enough of the lake one day. Don't you mind watching; they'll send for you, my friend, when you're wanted'; and twisting his yellow face into a malicious distortion, he went on.

This thing had occurred so suddenly, and chimed-in so oddly with his thoughts, which were at that moment at distant Mardykes and the haunted lake, that it disconcerted him. He laughed, he looked out of the window. He would have given that fellow money to tell him why he said that. But there was no good in looking for the scamp; he was gone.

A memory not preoccupied with that lake and its omens, and a presentiment about himself, would not have noted such things. But *his* mind they touched indelibly; and he was ashamed of his childish slavery, but could not help it.

The foundation of all this had been laid in the nursery, in the winter's tales told by its fireside, and which seized upon his fancy and his fears with a strange congeniality.

There is a large bedroom at Mardykes Hall, which tradition assigns to the lady who had perished tragically in the lake. Mrs Julaper was sure of it; for her aunt, who died a very old woman twenty years before, remembered the time of the lady's death, and when she grew to woman's estate had opportunity in abundance; for the old people who surrounded her could remember forty years farther back, and tell everything connected with the old house in beautiful Miss Feltram's time.

This large old-fashioned room, commanding a view of Snakes Island, the fells, and the lake—somewhat vast and gloomy, and furnished in a stately old fashion—was said to be haunted, especially when the wind blew from the direction of Golden Friars, the point from which it blew on the night of her death in the lake; or when the sky was overcast, and thunder rolled among the lofty fells, and lightning gleamed blue on the wide sheet of water.

It was on a night like this that a lady visitor, who long after that event occupied, in entire ignorance of its supernatural character, that large room; and being herself a lady of a picturesque turn, and loving the grander melodrama of Nature, bid her maid leave the shutters open, and watched the splendid effects from her bed, until, the storm being still distant, she fell asleep.

It was travelling slowly across the lake, and it was the deep-mouthed clangor of its near approach that startled her, at dead of night, from her slumber, to witness the same phenomena in the tremendous loudness and brilliancy of their near approach.

At this magnificent spectacle she was looking with the awful ecstasy of an observer in whom the sense of danger is subordinated to that of the sublime, when there came suddenly to the window a woman dishevelled, loosely clothed, and whose long hair and dress seemed drenched with water. She was gazing into the room with great eyes that seemed distended and wild with terror, and was shaking the sash of the window with an imploring vehemence that seemed to supplicate shelter. Having stood there for a few seconds, and before the lady who beheld all this from her bed could make up her mind what to do, the storm-beaten woman, wringing her hands, went swiftly away.

Possessed with the idea that she had seen some poor woman overtaken in the storm, who, failing to procure admission there, had gone round to some of the many doors of the mansion, and obtained an entry there, she again fell asleep.

It was not till the morning, when she went to her window to look out upon the now tranquil scene, that she discovered what, being a stranger to the house, she had quite forgotten, that this room was at a great height—some thirty feet—from the ground.

Another story was that of good old Mr Randal Rymer, who was often a visitor at the house in the late Lady Mardykes' day. In his youth he had been a campaigner; and now that he was a preacher he maintained his hardy habits, and always slept, summer and winter, with a bit of his window up. Being in that room in his bed, and after a short sleep lying awake, the moon shining softly through the window, there passed by that aperture into the room a figure dressed, it seemed to him, in gray that was nearly white. It passed straight to the hearth, where was an expiring wood fire; and cowering over it with outstretched hands, it appeared to be cold and shivering, and gathering what little heat was to be had. Mr Rymer, amazed and awestruck, made a movement in his bed; and the figure gave one look round, with large eyes that in the moonlight looked like melting snow, and stretching its long arms up the chimney, they and the figure itself seemed to blend with the smoke, and so pass up and away.

Sir Bale, I have said, did not like Feltram. His father, Sir William, had left a letter creating a trust, it was said, in favour of Philip Feltram. The document had been found with the will, addressed to Sir Bale in the form of a letter.

'That is mine,' said the Baronet, when it dropped out of the will; and he slipped it into his pocket, and no one ever saw it after.

But Mr Charles Twyne, the attorney of Golden Friars, whenever he got drunk, which was pretty often, used to tell his friends with a grave wink that he knew a thing or two about that letter. It gave Philip Feltram two hundred a-year, charged on Harfax. It was only a direction. It made Sir Bale a trustee, however; and having made away with the 'letter', the Baronet had been robbing Philip Feltram ever since.

Old Twyne was cautious, even in his cups, in his choice of an audience, and was a little enigmatical in his revelations. For he was afraid of Sir Bale, though he hated him for employing a lawyer who lived seven miles away, and was a rival of old Twyne's. So people were not quite sure whether Mr Twyne was telling lies or truth, and the principal fact that corroborated his story was Sir Bale's manifest hatred of his secretary. In fact, Sir Bale's retaining him in his house, detesting him as he seemed to do, was not easily to be accounted for, except on the principle of a tacit compromise—a miserable compensation for having robbed him of his rights.

The battle about the bank-note proceeded. Sir Bale certainly had doubts, and vacillated; for moral evidence made powerfully in favour of poor Feltram, though the evidence of circumstance made as powerfully against him. But Sir Bale admitted suspicion easily, and in weighing probabilities would count a virtue very lightly against temptation and opportunity; and whatever his doubts might sometimes be, he resisted and quenched them, and never let that ungrateful scoundrel Philip Feltram so much as suspect their existence.

For two days Sir Bale had not spoken to Feltram. He passed him by on stair and passage, carrying his head high, and with a thundrous countenance, rolling conclusions and revenges in his soul.

Poor Feltram all this time existed in one long agony. He would have left Mardykes, were it not that he looked vaguely to some just power—to chance itself—against this hideous imputation. To go with this indictment ringing in his ears, would amount to a confession and flight.

Mrs Julaper consoled him with might and main. She was a sympathetic and trusting spirit, and knew poor Philip Feltram, in her simplicity, better than the shrewdest profligate on earth could have known him. She cried with him in his misery. She was fired with indignation by these suspicions, and still more at what followed.

Sir Bale showed no signs of relenting. It might have been that he was not very sorry that so unexceptionable an opportunity of getting rid of Feltram, who, people thought, knew something about him which it galled the Baronet's pride that he should know.

The Baronet had another shorter and sterner interview with Feltram in his study. The result was, that unless he restored the missing note before ten o'clock next morning, he should leave Mardykes.

To leave Mardykes was no more than Philip Feltram, feeble as he was of will, had already resolved. But what was to become of him? He did not very much care, if he could find any calling, however humble, that would just give him bread.

There was an old fellow and his wife (an ancient dame), who lived at the other side of the lake, on the old territories of the Feltrams, and who, from some tradition of loyalty, perhaps, were fond of poor Philip Feltram. They lived somewhat high up on the fells—about as high as trees would grow—and those which were clumped about their rude dwelling were nearly the last you passed in your ascent of the mountain. These people had a multitude of sheep and goats, and lived in their airy solitude a pastoral and simple life, and were childless. Philip Feltram was hardy and active, having passed his early days among that arduous scenery. Cold and rain did not trouble him; and these people being wealthy in their way, and loving him, would be glad to find him employment of that desultory pastoral kind which would best suit him.

This vague idea was the only thing resembling a plan in his mind.

When Philip Feltram came to Mrs Julaper's room, and told her that he had made up his mind to leave the house forthwith—to cross the lake to the Cloostedd side in Tom Marlin's boat, and then to make his way up the hill alone to Trebeck's lonely farmstead, Mrs Julaper was overwhelmed.

'Ye'll do no such thing to-night, anyhow. You're not to go like that. Ye'll come into the small room here, where he can't follow; and we'll sit down and talk it over a bit, and ye'll find 'twill all come straight; and this will be no night, anyhow, for such a march. Why, man, 'twould take an hour and more to cross the lake, and then a long uphill walk before ye could reach Trebeck's place; and if the night should fall while you were still on the mountain, ye might lose your life among the rocks. It can't be 'tis come to that yet; and the call was in the air, I'm told, all yesterday, and distant thunder to-day, travelling this way over Blarwyn Fells; and 'twill be a night no one will be out, much less on the mountain side.'

CHAPTER IX

THE CRAZY PARSON

MRS JULAPER had grown weather-wise, living for so long among this noble and solitary scenery, where people must observe Nature or else nothing—where signs of coming storm or change are almost local, and record themselves on particular headlands and mountain-peaks, or in the mists, or in mirrored tints of the familiar lake, and are easily learned or remembered. At all events, her presage proved true too.

The sun had set an hour and more. It was dark; and an awful thunder-storm, whose march, like the distant reverberations of an invading army, had been faintly heard beyond the barriers of Blarwyn Fells throughout the afternoon, was near them now, and had burst in deep-mouthed battle among the ravines at the other side, and over the broad lake, that glared like a sheet of burnished steel under its flashes of dazzling blue. Wild and fitful blasts sweeping down the hollows and cloughs of the fells of Golden Friars agitated the lake, and bent the trees low, and whirled away their sere leaves in melancholy drift in their tremendous gusts. And from the window, looking on a scene enveloped in more than the darkness of night, you saw in the pulsations of the lightning, 'before the speedy gleams the darkness swallowed',* the tossing trees and the flying foam and eddies on the lake.

In the midst of the hurlyburly, a loud and long knocking came at the hall-door of Mardykes. How long it had lasted before a chance lull made it audible I do not know.

There was nothing picturesquely poor, any more than there were evidences of wealth, anywhere in Sir Bale Mardykes' household. He had no lack of servants, but they were of an inexpensive and homely sort; and the hall-door being opened by the son of an old tenant on the estate—the tempest beating on the other side of the house, and comparative shelter under the gables at the front—he saw standing before him, in the agitated air, a thin old man, who muttering, it might be, a benediction, stepped into the hall, and displayed long silver tresses, just as the storm had blown them, ascetic and eager features, and a pair of large light eyes that wandered wildly. He was dressed thinly, in threadbare black; a pair of long leather gaiters, buckled high above his knee, protected his thin shanks through moss and pool; and the singularity of his appearance was heightened by a wide-leafed* felt hat, over which he had tied his handkerchief, so as to bring the leaf of it over his ears, and to secure it from being whirled from his head by the storm.

This odd and storm-beaten figure—tall, and a little stooping, as well as thin—was not unknown to the servant, who saluted him with something of fear as well as of respect as he bid him reverently welcome, and asked him to come in and sit by the fire.

'Get you to your master, and tell him I have a message to him from one he has not seen for two-and-forty years.'

As the old man, with his harsh old voice, thus spoke, he unknotted his handkerchief and beat the dust and rain-drops from his hat upon his knee.

The servant knocked at the library-door, where he found Sir Bale.

'Well, what's the matter?' cried Sir Bale sharply, from his chair before the fire, with angry eyes looking over his shoulder.

'Here's 't sir cumman, Sir Bale,' he answered.

'Sir', or 'the Sir', is still used as the clergyman's title in the Northumbrian counties.

'What sir?'

'Sir Hugh Creswell, if you please, Sir Bale.'

'Ho!—mad Creswell?—O, the crazy parson. Well, tell Mrs Julaper to let him have some supper—and—and to let him have a bed in some suitable place. That's what he wants. These mad fellows know what they are about.'

'No, Sir Bale Mardykes, that is not what he wants,' said the loud wild voice of the daft sir over the servant's shoulder. 'Often has Mardykes Hall given me share of its cheer and its shelter and the warmth of its fire; and I bless the house that has been an inn to the wayfarer of the Lord. But to-night I go up the lake to Pindar's Bield, three miles on; and there I rest and refresh—not here.'

'And why not *here*, Mr Creswell?' asked the Baronet; for about this crazy old man, who preached in the fields, and appeared and disappeared so suddenly in the orbit of his wide and unknown perambulations of those northern and border counties, there was that sort of superstitious feeling which attaches to the mysterious and the good—an idea that it was lucky to harbour and dangerous to offend him. No one knew whence he came or whither he went. Once in a year, perhaps, he might appear at a lonely farmstead door among the fells, salute the house, enter, and be gone in the morning. His life was austere; his piety enthusiastic, severe, and tinged with the craze which inspired among the rustic population a sort of awe.

'I'll not sleep at Mardykes to-night; neither will I eat, nor drink, nor sit me down—no, nor so much as stretch my hands to the fire. As the man of God came out of Judah to king Jeroboam,* so come I to you, sent by a vision, to bear a warning; and as he said, "If thou wilt give me half thy house, I will not go in with thee, neither will I eat bread nor drink water in this place", so also say I.'

'Do as you please,' said Sir Bale, a little sulkily. 'Say your say; and you are welcome to stay or go, if go you will on so mad a night as this.'

'Leave us,' said Creswell, beckoning the servant back with his thin hands; 'what I have to say is to your master.'

The servant went, in obedience to a gesture from Sir Bale, and shut the door.

The old man drew nearer to the Baronet, and lowering his loud stern voice a little, and interrupting his discourse from time to time, to allow the near thunder-peals to subside, he said,

'Answer me, Sir Bale—what is this that has chanced between you and Philip Feltram?'

The Baronet, under the influence of that blunt and peremptory demand, told him shortly and sternly enough.

'And of all these facts you are sure, else ye would not blast your early companion and kinsman with the name of thief?'

'I *am* sure,' said Sir Bale grimly.

'Unlock that cabinet,' said the old man with the long white locks.

'I've no objection,' said Sir Bale; and he did unlock an old oak cabinet that stood, carved in high relief with strange figures and gothic grotesques, against the wall, opposite the fireplace. On opening it there were displayed a system of little drawers and pigeonholes such as we see in more modern escritoires.

'Open that drawer with the red mark of a seal upon it,' continued Hugh Creswell, pointing to it with his lank finger.

Sir Bale did so; and to his momentary amazement, and even consternation, there lay the missing note, which now, with one of those sudden caprices of memory which depend on the laws of suggestion and association, he remembered having placed there with his own hand.

'That is it,' said old Creswell with a pallid smile, and fixing his wild eyes on the Baronet. The smile subsided into a frown, and said he: 'Last night I slept near Haworth Moss; and your father came to me in a dream, and said: "My son Bale accuses Philip of having stolen a bank-note from his desk. He forgets that he himself placed it in his cabinet. Come with me." I was, in the spirit, in this room; and he led me to this cabinet, which he opened; and in that drawer he showed me that note. "Go," said he, "and tell him to ask Philip Feltram's pardon, else he will but go in weakness to return in power";* and he said that which it is not lawful to repeat. My message is told. Now, a word from myself,' he added sternly. 'The dead, through my lips, has spoken, and under God's thunder and lightning his words have found ye. Why so uppish wi' Philip Feltram? See how ye threaped, and yet were wrong. He's no tazzle—he's no taggelt. *Mind* ye ask his pardon. Ye must change, or he will change. Go in weakness, come in power: mark ye the words. 'Twill make a peal that will be heard in toon and desert, in the swirls o' the mountain, through pikes and valleys, and mak' a waaly* man o' thee.'

The old man with these words, uttered in the broad northern dialect of his common speech, strode from the room and shut the door. In another minute he was forth into the storm, pursuing what remained of his long march to Pindar's Bield.

'Upon my soul!' said Sir Bale, recovering from the sort of stun which the sudden and strange visit had left, 'that's a cool old fellow! Come to rate me and teach me my own business in my own house!' and he rapped out a fierce oath. 'Change his mind or no, here he sha'n't stay to-night—not an hour.'

Sir Bale was in the lobby in a moment, and thundered to his servants:

'I say, put that impudent fool out of the door—put him out by the shoulder, and never let him get his foot inside it more!'

But the old man's yea was yea, and his nay nay. He had quite meant what he said; and, as I related, was beyond the reach of the indignity of extrusion.

Sir Bale on his return shut his door as violently as if it were in the face of the old prophet.

'Ask Feltram's pardon indeed! For what? Why, any jury on earth would have hanged him on half the evidence; and I, like a fool, was going to let him off with his liberty and my hundred pounds! Ask his pardon indeed!'

Still there were misgivings in his mind; a consciousness that he did owe explanation and apology to Feltram, and an insurmountable reluctance to undertake either. The old dislike—a contempt mingled with fear—not any fear of his malevolence, a fear only of his carelessness and folly; for, as I have said, Feltram knew many things, it was believed, of the Baronet's continental and Asiatic life, and had even gently remonstrated with him upon the dangers into which he was running. A simple fellow like Philip Feltram is a dangerous depositary of a secret. This Baronet was proud, too; and the mere possession of his secrets by Feltram was an involuntary insult, which Sir Bale could not forgive. He wished him far away; and except for the recovery of his bank-note, which he could ill spare, he was sorry that this suspicion was cleared up.

The thunder and storm were unabated; it seemed indeed that they were growing wilder and more awful.

He opened the window-shutter and looked out upon that sublimest of scenes; and so intense and magnificent were its phenomena, that Sir Bale was for a while absorbed in this contemplation.

When he turned about, the sight of his 100*l.* note, still between his finger and thumb, made him smile grimly.

The more he thought of it, the clearer it was that he could not leave matters as they were. Well, what should he do? He would send for Mrs Julaper, and tell her vaguely that he had changed his mind about

Feltram, and that he might continue to stay at Mardykes Hall as usual. That would suffice. She could speak to Feltram.

He sent for her; and soon, in the lulls of the great uproar without, he could hear the jingle of Mrs Julaper's keys and her light tread upon the lobby.

'Mrs Julaper,' said the Baronet in his dry careless way, 'Feltram may remain; your eloquence has prevailed. What have you been crying about?' he asked, observing that his housekeeper's usually cheerful face was, in her own phrase, 'all cried'.

'It is too late, sir; he's gone.'

'And when did he go?' asked Sir Bale, a little put out. 'He chose an odd evening, didn't he? So like him!'

'He went about half an hour ago; and I'm very sorry, sir; it's a sore sight to see the poor lad going from the place he was reared in, and a hard thing, sir; and on such a night, above all.'

'No one asked him to go to-night. Where is he gone to?'

'I don't know, I'm sure; he left my room, sir, when I was upstairs; and Janet saw him pass the window not ten minutes after Mr Creswell left the house.'

'Well, then, there's no good, Mrs Julaper, in thinking more about it; he has settled the matter his own way; and as he so ordains it—amen, say I. Good-night.'

CHAPTER X

ADVENTURE IN TOM MARLIN'S BOAT

PHILIP FELTRAM was liked very well—a gentle, kindly, and very timid creature, and, before he became so heart-broken, a fellow who liked a joke or a pleasant story, and could laugh heartily. Where will Sir Bale find so unresisting and respectful a butt and retainer? and whom will he bully now?

Something like remorse was troubling Sir Bale's heart a little; and the more he thought on the strange visit of Hugh Creswell that night, with its unexplained menace, the more uneasy he became.

The storm continued; and even to him there seemed something exaggerated and inhuman in the severity of his expulsion on such a night. It was his own doing, it was true; but would people believe that? and would he have thought of leaving Mardykes at all if it had not been for his kinsman's cruelty? Nay, was it not certain that if Sir Bale had done as Hugh Creswell had urged him, and sent for Feltram forthwith, and told him how all had been cleared up, and been a little friendly with him, he would have found him still in the house?—for he had not yet gone for ten minutes after Creswell's departure, and thus all that was to follow might have been averted. But it was now too late, and Sir Bale would let the affair take its own course.

Below him, outside the window at which he stood ruminating, he heard voices mingling with the storm. He could with tolerable certainty perceive, looking into the obscurity, that there were three men passing close under it, carrying some very heavy burden among them.

He did not know what these three black figures in the obscurity were about. He saw them pass round the corner of the building toward the front, and in the lulls of the storm could hear their gruff voices talking.

We have all experienced what a presentiment is, and we all know with what an intuition the faculty of observation is sometimes heightened. It was such an apprehension as sometimes gives its peculiar horror to a dream—a sort of knowledge that what those people were about was in a dreadful way connected with his own fate.

He watched for a time, thinking that they might return; but they did not. He was very uncomfortable, and in a state of suspense.

'If they want me, they won't have much trouble in finding me, nor any scruple in plaguing me; they never have.'

Sir Bale returned to his letters, a score of which he was that night getting off his conscience—an arrear which would not have troubled him had he not ceased, for two or three days, altogether to employ Philip Feltram, who had been accustomed to take all that sort of drudgery off his hands.

All the time he was writing now he had a feeling that the shadows he had seen pass under his window were machinating some trouble for him, and an uncomfortable suspense made him lift his eyes now and then to the door, fancying sounds and footsteps; and after a resultless wait he would say to himself, 'If any one is coming, why the devil don't they come?' and apply himself again to his letters.

But on a sudden he heard good Mrs Julaper's step trotting along the lobby, and the tiny ringing of her keys.

Here was news coming; and the Baronet stood up looking at the door, on which presently came a hurried rapping; and before he had answered, in the midst of an awful thunder-clap that suddenly broke, rattling over the house, the good woman opened the door in great agitation, and cried with a tremulous uplifting of her hands,

'O, Sir Bale! O, la, sir! here's poor dear Philip Feltram come home drowned!'

Sir Bale stared at her sternly for some seconds.

'Come, now, do be distinct,' said Sir Bale; 'what has happened?'

'He's lying on the sofer in the old still-room. You never saw—my God!—O, sir—what is life?'

'D——n it, can't you cry by and by, and tell me what's the matter *now?*'

'A bit o' fire there, as luck would have it; but what is hot or cold now? La, sir, they're all doin' what they can, and Tom Warren is on the gallop down to Golden Friars for Doctor Torvey.'

'*Is* he drowned, or is it only a ducking? Come, bring me to the place. Dead men don't usually want a fire, or consult doctors. I'll see for myself.'

So Sir Bale Mardykes, pale and grim, accompanied by the light-footed Mrs Julaper, strode along the passages, and was led by her into the old still-room, which had ceased to be used for its original purpose. All the servants in the house were now collected there, and three men also who lived by the margin of the lake; one of them thoroughly drenched, with rivulets of water still trickling from his sleeves, water down the wrinkles and pockets of his waistcoat and from the feet of his trousers, and pumping and oozing from his shoes, and streaming from his hair down the channels of his cheeks like a continuous rain of tears.

The people drew back a little as Sir Bale entered with a quick step and a sharp pallid frown on his face. There was a silence as he stooped over Philip Feltram, who lay on a low bed next the wall, dimly lighted by two or three candles here and there about the room.

He laid his hand, for a moment, on his cold wet breast.

Sir Bale knew what should be done in order to give a man in such a case his last chance for life. Everybody was speedily put in motion. Philip's drenched clothes were removed, hot blankets enveloped him, warming-pans and hot bricks lent their aid; he was placed at the pre-scribed angle, so that water flowed freely from his mouth. The old expedient for inducing artificial breathing was employed, and a lusty pair of kitchen bellows did duty for his lungs.

But these helps to life, and suggestions to nature, availed not. Forlorn and peaceful lay the features of poor Philip Feltram; cold and dull to the touch; no breath through the blue lips; no sight in the fish-like eyes; pulseless and cold in the midst of all the hot bricks and warming-pans about him.

At length, everything having been tried, Sir Bale, who had been directing, placed his hand within the clothes, and laid it silently on Philip's shoulder and over his heart; and after a little wait, he shook his head, and looking down on his sunken face, he said,

'I'm afraid he's gone. Yes, he's gone, poor fellow! And bear you this in mind, all of you; Mrs Julaper there can tell you more about it. She knows that it was certainly in no compliance with my wish that he left the house to-night: it was his own obstinate perversity, and perhaps—I forgive him for it—a wish in his unreasonable resentment to throw some odium upon this house, as having refused him shelter on such a night, than which imputation nothing can be more utterly false. Mrs Julaper there knows how welcome he was to stay the night; but he would not; he had made up his mind, it seems, without telling any person. Had he told you, Mrs Julaper?'

'No, sir,' sobbed Mrs Julaper from the centre of a pocket-handkerchief in which her face was buried.

'Not a human being: an angry whim of his own. Poor Feltram! and here's the result,' said the Baronet. 'We have done our best—done everything. I don't think the doctor, when he comes, will say that any-thing has been omitted; but all won't do. Does any one here know how it happened?'

Two men knew very well—the man who had been ducked, and his companion, a younger man, who was also in the still-room, and had lent a hand in carrying Feltram up to the house.

Tom Marlin had a queer old stone tenement by the edge of the lake just under Mardykes Hall. Some people said it was the stump of an old tower that had once belonged to Mardykes Castle, of which in the mod-ern building scarcely a relic was discoverable.

This Tom Marlin had an ancient right of fishing in the lake, where he caught pike enough for all Golden Friars; and keeping a couple of boats, he made money beside by ferrying passengers over now and then. This fellow, with a furrowed face and shaggy eyebrows, bald at top, but with long grizzled locks falling upon his shoulders, said,

'He wer wi' me this mornin', sayin' he'd want t' boat to cross the lake in, but he didn't say what hour; and when it came on to thunder and blow like this, ye may guess I did not look to see him to-night. Well, my wife was just lightin' a pig-tail—tho' light enough and to spare there was in the lift already—when who should come clatterin' at the latch-pin in the blow o' wind and thunder but Philip, poor lad, himself; and an ill hour for him it was. He's been some time in ill fettle, though he was never frowsy, not he, but always kind and dooce, and canty once, like anither; and he asked me to take the boat across the lake at once to the Clough o' Cloostedd at t'other side. The woman took the pet and wodn't hear o't; and, "Dall me, if I go to-night," quoth I. But he would not be put off so, not he; and ding-drive he went to it, cryin' and putrein', ye'd a-said, poor fellow, he was wrang i' his garrets a'most. So at long last I bethought me, there's nout o' a sea to the north o' Snakes Island, so I'll pull him by that side—for the storm is blowin' right up by Golden Friars, ye mind—and when we get near the point, thinks I, he'll see wi' his een how the lake is, and gie it up. For I liked him, poor lad; and seein' he'd set his heart on't, I wouldn't vex him, nor frump him wi' a no. So down we three—myself, and Bill there, and Philip Feltram—come to the boat; and we pulled out, keeping Snakes Island atwixt us and the wind. 'Twas smooth water wi'us, for 'twas a scug* there, but white enough was all beyont the point; and passing the finger-stone, not forty fathom from the shore o' the island, Bill and me pullin' and he sittin' in the stern, poor lad, up he rises, a bit rabblin' to himself, wi' his hands lifted so.

'"Look a-head!" says I, thinkin' something was comin' atort us.

'But 'twasn't that. The boat was quiet, for while we looked oo'er our shouthers oo'er her bows, we didn't pull, so she lay still; and lookin' back again on Philip, he was rabblin' on all the same.

'"It's nobbut a prass wi' himsel',* poor lad," thinks I.

'But that wasn't it neither; for I sid something white come out o' t'water, by the gunwale, like a hand.* By Jen! and he leans oo'er and tuk it; and he sagged like, and so it drew him in, under the mere, before I cud du nout. There was nout to thraa tu him, and no time; down he went, and I followed; and thrice I dived before I found him, and brought him up by the hair at last; and there he is, poor lad! and all one if he lay at the bottom o' t' mere.'

As Tom Marlin ended his narrative—often interrupted by the noise of the tempest without, and the peals of thunder that echoed awfully above, like the chorus of a melancholy ballad—the sudden clang of the hall-door bell, and a more faintly-heard knocking, announced a new arrival.

CHAPTER XI

SIR BALE'S DREAM

IT was Doctor Torvey who entered the old still-room now, buttoned-up to the chin in his greatcoat, and with a muffler of many colours wrapped partly over that feature.

'Well!—hey? So poor Feltram's had an accident?'

The Doctor was addressing Sir Bale, and getting to the bedside as he pulled off his gloves.

'I see you've been keeping him warm—that's right; and a considerable flow of water from the mouth; turn him a little that way. Hey? O, ho!' said the Doctor, as he placed his hand upon Philip, and gently stirred his limbs. 'It's more than an hour since this happened. I'm afraid there's very little to be done now'; and in a lower tone, with his hand on poor Philip Feltram's arm, and so down to his fingers, he said in Sir Bale Mardyke's ear, with a shake of his head,

'Here, you see, poor fellow, here's the cadaveric stiffness; it's very melancholy, but it's all over, he's gone; there's no good trying any more.—Come here, Mrs Julaper. Did you ever see any one dead? Look at his eyes, look at his mouth. You ought to have known that, with half an eye.—And you know,' he added again confidentially in Sir Bale's ear, 'trying anything more *now* is all my eye.'*

Then after a few more words with the Baronet, and having heard his narrative, he said from time to time, 'Quite right; nothing could be better; capital practice, sir', and so forth. And at the close of all this, amid the sobs of kind Mrs Julaper and the general whimpering of the humbler handmaids, the Doctor standing by the bed, with his knuckles on the coverlet, and a glance now and then, on the dead face beside him, said—by way of 'quieting men's minds', as the old tract-writers used to say—a few words to the following effect:

'Everything has been done here that the most experienced physician could have wished. Everything has been done in the best way. I don't know anything that has not been done, in fact. If I had been here myself, I don't know—hot bricks—salt isn't a bad thing. I don't know, I say, that anything of any consequence has been omitted.' And looking at the body, 'You see', and he drew the fingers a little this way and that, letting them return, as they stiffly did, to their former attitude, 'you may be sure that the poor gentleman was quite dead by the time he arrived here. So, since he was laid there, nothing has been lost by delay.—And, Sir Bale, if you have any directions to send to Golden Friars, sir, I shall be most happy to undertake your message.'

'Nothing, thanks; it is a melancholy ending, poor fellow! You must come to the study with me, Doctor Torvey, and talk a little bit more; and—very sad, doctor—and you must have a glass of sherry, or some port—the port used not to be had here; I don't take it—but very melancholy it is—bring port and sherry; and, Mrs Julaper, you'll be good enough to see that everything that should be done here is looked to; and let Marlin and the men have supper and something to drink. You have been too long in your wet clothes, Marlin.'

So, with gracious words all round, he led the Doctor to the library where he had been sitting, and was affable and hospitable, and told him his own version of all that had passed between him and Philip Feltram, and presented himself in an amiable point of view, and pleased the Doctor with his port and flatteries—for he could not afford to lose any one's good word just now; and the Doctor was a bit of a gossip, and in most houses in that region, in one character or another, every three months in the year.

So in due time the Doctor drove back to Golden Friars, with a high opinion of Sir Bale, and higher still of his port, and highest of all of himself: in the best possible humour with the world, not minding the storm that blew in his face, and which he defied in good-humoured mock-heroics* spoken in somewhat thick accents, and regarding the thunder and lightning as a lively gala of fireworks; and if there had been a chance of finding his cronies still in the George and Dragon, he would have been among them forthwith, to relate the tragedy of the night, and tell what a good fellow, after all, Sir Bale was; and what a fool, at best, poor Philip Feltram.

But the George was quiet for that night. The thunder rolled over voiceless chambers; and the lights had been put out within the windows, on whose multitudinous small panes the lightning glared. So the Doctor went home to Mrs Torvey, whom he charmed into good-humoured curiosity by the tale of wonder he had to relate.

Sir Bale's qualms were symptomatic of something a little less sublime and more selfish than conscience. He was not sorry that Philip Feltram was out of the way. His lips might begin to babble inconveniently at any time, and why should not his mouth be stopped? and what stopper so effectual as that plug of clay which fate had introduced? But he did not want to be charged with the odium of the catastrophe. Every man cares something for the opinion of his fellows. And seeing that Feltram had been well liked, and that his death had excited a vehement commiseration, Sir Bale did not wish it to be said that he had made the house too hot to hold him, and had so driven him to extremity.

Sir Bale's first agitation had subsided. It was now late, he had written many letters, and he was tired. It was not wonderful, then, that having turned his lounging-chair to the fire, he should have fallen asleep in it, as at last he did.

The storm was passing gradually away by this time. The thunder was now echoing among the distant glens and gorges of Daulness Fells, and the angry roar and gusts of the tempest were subsiding into the melancholy soughing and piping that soothe like a lullaby.

Sir Bale therefore had his unpremeditated sleep very comfortably, except that his head was hanging a little uneasily; which, perhaps, helped him to this dream.

It was one of those dreams in which the continuity of the waking state that immediately preceded it seems unbroken; for he thought that he was sitting in the chair which he occupied, and in the room where he actually was. It seemed to him that he got up, took a candle in his hand, and went through the passages to the old still-room where Philip Feltram lay. The house seemed perfectly still. He could hear the chirp of the crickets faintly from the distant kitchen, and the tick of the clock sounded loud and hollow along the passage. In the old still-room, as he opened the door, was no light, except what was admitted from the candle he carried. He found the body of poor Philip Feltram just as he had left it—his gentle face, saddened by the touch of death, was turned upwards, with white lips; with traces of suffering fixed in its outlines, such as caused Sir Bale, standing by the bed, to draw the coverlet over the dead man's features, which seemed silently to upbraid him. 'Gone in weakness!' said Sir Bale, repeating the words of the 'daft sir', Hugh Creswell; and as he did so, a voice whispered near him, with a great sigh, 'Come in power!' He looked round, in his dream, but there was no one; the light seemed to fail, and a horror slowly overcame him, especially as he thought he saw the figure under the coverlet stealthily beginning to move. Backing towards the door, for he could not take his eyes off it, he saw something like a huge black ape creep out at the foot of the bed; and springing at him, it griped him by the throat, so that he could not breathe; and a thousand voices were instantly round him, holloaing, cursing, laughing in his ears; and in this direful plight he waked.

Was it the ring of those voices still in his ears, or a real shriek, and another, and a long peal, shriek after shriek, swelling madly through the distant passages, that held him still, freezing in the horror of his dream?

I will tell you what this noise was.

CHAPTER XII

MARCELLA BLIGH AND JUDITH WALE KEEP WATCH

AFTER his bottle of port with Sir Bale, the Doctor had gone down again to the room where poor Philip Feltram lay.

Mrs Julaper had dried her eyes, and was busy by this time; and two old women were making all their arrangements for a night-watch by the body, which they had washed, and, as their phrase goes, 'laid out' in the humble bed where it had lain while there was still a hope that a spark sufficient to rekindle the fire of life might remain. These old women had points of resemblance: they were lean, sallow, and wonderfully wrinkled, and looked each malign and ugly enough for a witch.

Marcella Bligh's thin hooked nose was now like the beak of a bird of prey over the face of the drowned man, upon whose eyelids she was placing penny-pieces, to keep them from opening; and her one eye was fixed on her work, its sightless companion showing white in its socket, with an ugly leer.

Judith Wale was lifting the pail of hot-water with which they had just washed the body. She had long lean arms, a hunched back, a great sharp chin sunk on her hollow breast, and small eyes restless as a ferret's; and she clattered about in great bowls of shoes, old and clouted, that were made for a foot as big as two of hers.

The Doctor knew these two old women, who were often employed in such dismal offices.

'How does Mrs Bligh? See me with half an eye? Hey—that's rhyme, isn't it?—And, Judy lass—why, I thought you lived nearer the town—here making poor Mr Feltram's last toilet. You have helped to dress many a poor fellow for his last journey. Not a bad notion of drill either—they stand at attention stiff and straight enough in the sentry-box. Your recruits do you credit, Mrs Wale.'

The Doctor stood at the foot of the bed to inspect, breathing forth a vapour of very fine old port, his hands in his pockets, speaking with a lazy thickness, and looking so comfortable and facetious, that Mrs Julaper would have liked to turn him out of the room.

But the Doctor was not unkind, only extremely comfortable. He was a good-natured fellow, and had thought and care for the living, but not a great deal of sentiment for the dead, whom he had looked in the face too often to be much disturbed by the spectacle.

'You'll have to keep that bandage on. You should be sharp; you should know all about it, girl, by this time, and not let those muscles stiffen. I need not tell you the mouth shuts as easily as this snuff-box, if you only take it in time.—I suppose, Mrs Julaper, you'll send to Jos Fringer for the poor fellow's outfit. Fringer is a very proper man—there ain't a properer und-aker in England. I always re-mmend Fringer—in Church-street in Golden Friars. You know Fringer, I daresay.'

'I can't say, sir, I'm sure. That will be as Sir Bale may please to direct,' answered Mrs Julaper.

'You've got him very straight, straighter than I thought you could; but the large joints were not so stiff. A very little longer wait, and you'd hardly have got him into his coffin. He'll want a vr-r-ry long one, poor lad. Short cake is life, ma'am. Sad thing this. They'll open their eyes, I promise you, down in the town. 'Twill be cool enough, I'd shay, afire all th-thunr-thunnle, you know. I think I'll take a nip, Mrs Jool-fr, if you wouldn't mine makin' me out a thimmle-ful bran-band-bran-rand-andy, eh, Mishs Joolfr?'

And the Doctor took a chair by the fire; and Mrs Julaper, with a dubious conscience and dry hospitality, procured the brandy-flask and wine-glass, and helped the physician in a thin hesitating stream, which left him ample opportunity to cry 'Hold—enough!' had he been so minded. But that able physician had no confidence, it would seem, in any dose under a bumper, which he sipped with commendation, and then fell asleep with the firelight on his face—to tender-hearted Mrs Julaper's disgust—and snored with a sensual disregard of the solemnity of his situation; until with a profound nod, or rather dive, toward the fire, he awoke, got up and shook his ears with a kind of start, and standing with his back to the fire, asked for his muffler and horse; and so took his leave of the weird sisters, who were still pottering about the body, with croak and whisper, and nod and ogle. He took his leave also of good Mrs Julaper, who was completing arrangements with teapot and kettle, spiced elderberry wine, and other comforts, to support them through their proposed vigil. And finally, in a sort of way, he took his leave of the body, with a long business-like stare, from the foot of the bed, with his short hands stuffed into his pockets. And so, to Mrs Julaper's relief, this unseemly doctor, speaking thickly, departed.

And now, the Doctor being gone, and all things prepared for the 'wake' to be observed by withered Mrs Bligh of the one eye, and yellow Mrs Wale of the crooked back, the house grew gradually still. The thunder had by this time died into the solemn boom of distant battle, and the fury of the gale had subsided to the long sobbing wail that is charged with so eerie a melancholy. Within all was stirless, and the two old women, each a 'Mrs' by courtesy, who had not much to thank Nature or the world for, sad and cynical, and in a sort outcasts told off by fortune to these sad and grizzly services, sat themselves down by the fire, each perhaps feeling unusually at home in the other's society; and in this soured and forlorn comfort, trimming their fire, quickening the song of the kettle to a boil, and waxing polite and chatty; each treating the other with that deprecatory and formal courtesy which invites a return in kind, and both growing strangely happy in this little world of their own, in the unusual and momentary sense of an importance and consideration which were delightful.

The old still-room of Mardykes Hall is an oblong room wainscoted. From the door you look its full length to the wide stone-shafted Tudor window at the other end. At your left is the ponderous mantelpiece, supported by two spiral stone pillars; and close to the door at the right was the bed in which the two crones had just stretched poor Philip Feltram, who lay as still as an uncoloured wax-work, with a heavy penny-piece on each eye, and a bandage under his jaw, making his mouth look stern. And the two old ladies over their tea by the fire conversed agreeably, compared their rheumatisms and other ailments wordily, and talked of old times, and early recollections, and of sick-beds they had attended, and corpses that 'you would not know, so pined and windered' were they; and others so fresh and canny, you'd say the dead had never looked so bonny in life.

Then they began to talk of people who grew tall in their coffins, of others who had been buried alive, and of others who walked after death. Stories as true as holy writ.

'Were you ever down by Hawarth, Mrs Bligh—hard by Dalworth Moss?' asked crook-backed Mrs Wale, holding her spoon suspended over her cup.

'Neea whaar sooa far south, Mrs Wale, ma'am; but ma father was ofttimes down thar cuttin' peat.'

'Ah, then ye'll not a kenned farmer Dykes that lived by the Lin-tree Scaur. 'Tweer I that laid him out, poor aad fellow, and a dow man he was when aught went cross wi' him; and he cursed and sweared, twad gar ye dodder to hear him. They said he was a hard man wi' some folk; but he kep a good house, and liked to see plenty, and many a time when I was swai-mous about my food, he'd clap t' meat on ma plate, and mak' me eat ma fill. Na, na—there was good as well as bad in farmer Dykes. It was a year after he deed, and Tom Ettles was walkin' down by the Birken Stoop one night, and not a soul nigh, when he sees a big ball, as high as his knee, whirlin' and spangin' away before him on the road. What it wer he could not think; but he never consayted there was a freet or a bo thereaway; so he kep near it, watchin' every spang and turn it took, till it ran into the gripe by the roadside. There was a gravel-pit just there, and Tom Ettles wished to take another gliff at it before he went on. But when he keeked into the pit, what should he see but a man attoppa a horse that could not get up or on; and says he, "I think ye be at a dead-lift there, gaffer." And wi' the word, up looks the man, and who sud it be but farmer Dykes him-sel; and Tom Ettles saw him plain eneugh, and kenned the horse too for Black Jack, the farmer's aad beast, that broke his leg and was shot two years and more befor the farmer died. "Ay," says farmer Dykes, lookin' very bad; "forsett-and-backsett, ye'll tak' me oot, Tom Ettles, and clap ye doun behint me quick, or I'll claw ho'd o' thee." Tom felt his hair risin' stiff on his heed, and his tongue so fast to the roof o' his mouth he could scarce get oot a word; but says he, "If Black Jack can't do it o' noo, he'll ne'er do't and carry double." "I ken my ain business best," says Dykes. " If ye gar me gie ye a look, 'twill gie ye the creepin's while ye live; so git ye doun, Tom"; and with that the dobby lifts its neaf; and Tom saw there was a red light round horse and man, like the glow of a peat fire. And says Tom, "In the name o' God, ye'll let me pass"; and with the word the gooast draws itsel' doun, all a-creaked, like a man wi' a sudden pain; and Tom Ettles took to his heels more deed than alive.'

They had approached their heads, and the story had sunk to that mysterious murmur that thrills the listener, when in the brief silence that followed they heard a low odd laugh near the door.

In that direction each lady looked aghast, and saw Feltram sitting straight up in the bed, with the white bandage in his hand, and as it seemed, for one foot was below the coverlet, near the floor, about to glide forth.

Mrs Bligh, uttering a hideous shriek, clutched Mrs Wale, and Mrs Wale, with a scream as dreadful, gripped Mrs Bligh; and quite forgetting their somewhat formal politeness, they reeled and tugged, wrestling towards the window, each struggling to place her companion between her and the 'dobby', and both uniting in a direful peal of yells.

This was the uproar which had startled Sir Bale from his dream, and was now startling the servants from theirs.

CHAPTER XIII

THE MIST ON THE MOUNTAIN

DOCTOR TORVEY was sent for early next morning, and came full of wonder, learning, and scepticism. Seeing is believing, however; and there was Philip Feltram living, and soon to be, in all bodily functions, just as usual.

'Upon my soul, Sir Bale, I couldn't have believed it, if I had not seen it with my eyes,' said the Doctor impressively, while sipping a glass of sherry in the 'breakfast-parlour', as the great panelled and pictured room next the dining-room was called. 'I don't think there is any similar case on record—no pulse, no more than the poker; no respiration, by Jove, no more than the chimney-piece; as cold as a lead image in the garden there. Well, you'll say all that might possibly be fallacious; but what will you say to the cadaveric stiffness? Old Judy Wale can tell you; and my friend Marcella—Monocula would be nearer the mark—Mrs Bligh, she knows all those common, and I may say up to this, infallible, signs of death, as well as I do. There is no mystery about them; they'll depose to the literality of the symptoms. You heard how they gave tongue. Upon my honour, I'll send the whole case up to my old chief, Sir Hervey Hansard, to London. You'll hear what a noise it will make among the profession. There never was—and it ain't too much to say there never *will* be—another case like it.'

During this lecture, and a great deal more, Sir Bale leaned hack in his chair, with his legs extended, his heels on the ground, and his arms folded, looking sourly up in the face of a tall lady in white satin, in a ruff, and with a bird on her hand, who smiled down superciliously from her frame upon the Baronet. Sir Bale seemed a little bit high and dry with the Doctor.

'You physicians are unquestionably,' he said, 'a very learned profession.'

The Doctor bowed.

'But there's just one thing you know nothing about—'

'Eh? What's that?' inquired Doctor Torvey.

'Medicine,' answered Sir Bale. 'I was aware you never knew what was the matter with a sick man; but I didn't know, till now, that you couldn't tell when he was dead.'

'Ha, ha!—well—ha, ha!—*yes*—well, you see, you—ha, ha!—you certainly have me there. But it's a case without a parallel—it is, upon my honour. You'll find it will not only be talked about, but written about; and, whatever papers appear upon it, will come to me; and I'll take care, Sir Bale, you shall have an opportunity of reading them.'

'Of which I sha'n't avail myself,' answered Sir Bale. 'Take another glass of sherry, Doctor.'

The Doctor made his acknowledgments and filled his glass, and looked through the wine between him and the window.

'Ha, ha!—see there, your port, Sir Bale, gives a fellow such habits—looking for the beeswing,* by Jove. It isn't easy, in one sense at least, to get your port out of a fellow's head when once he has tasted it.'

But if the honest Doctor meant a hint for a glass of that admirable bin, it fell pointless; and Sir Bale had no notion of making another libation of that precious liquor in honour of Doctor Torvey.

'And I take it for granted,' said Sir Bale, 'that Feltram will do very well; and, should anything go wrong, I can send for you—unless he should die again; and in that case I think I shall take my own opinion.'

So he and the Doctor parted.

Sir Bale, although he did not consult the Doctor on his own case, was not particularly well. 'That lonely place, those frightful mountains, and that damp black lake'—which features in the landscape he cursed all round—'are enough to give any man blue devils; and when a fellow's spirits go, he's all gone. That's why I'm dyspeptic—that and those d—d debts—and the post, with its flight of croaking and screaming letters from London. I wish there was no post here.* I wish it was like Sir Amerald's time, when they shot the York mercer that came to dun him, and no one ever took him to task about it; and now they can pelt you at any distance they please through the post; and fellows lose their spirits and their appetite and any sort of miserable comfort that is possible in this odious abyss.'

Was there gout in Sir Bale's case, or 'vapours'? I know not what the faculty* would have called it; but Sir Bale's mode of treatment was simply to work off the attack by long and laborious walking.

This evening his walk was upon the Fells of Golden Friars—long after the landscape below was in the eclipse of twilight, the broad bare sides and angles of these gigantic uplands still lighted by the misty western sun.

There is no such sense of solitude as that which we experience upon the silent and vast elevations of great mountains. Lifted high above the level of human sounds and habitations, among the wild expanses and colossal features of Nature, we are thrilled in our loneliness with a strange fear and elation—an ascent above the reach of life's vexations or companionship, and the tremblings of a wild and undefined misgiving. The filmy disc of the moon had risen in the east, and was already faintly silvering the shadowy scenery below, while yet Sir Bale stood in the mellow light of the western sun, which still touched also the summits of the opposite peaks of Morvyn Fells.

Sir Bale Mardykes did not, as a stranger might, in prudence, hasten his descent from the heights at which he stood while yet a gleam of daylight remained to him. For he was, from his boyhood, familiar with those solitary regions; and, beside this, the thin circle of the moon, hung in the eastern sky, would brighten as the sunlight sank, and hang like a lamp above his steps.

There was in the bronzed and resolute face of the Baronet, lighted now in the parting beams of sunset, a resemblance to that of Charles the Second—not our 'merry' ideal, but the more energetic and saturnine face which the portraits have preserved to us.

He stood with folded arms on the side of the slope, admiring, in spite of his prejudice, the unusual effects of a view so strangely lighted—the sunset tints on the opposite peaks, lost in the misty twilight, now deepening lower down into a darker shade, through which the outlines of the stone gables and tower of Golden Friars and the light of fire or candle in their windows were dimly visible.

As he stood and looked, his more distant sunset went down, and sudden twilight was upon him, and he began to remember the beautiful Homeric picture of a landscape coming out, rock and headland, in the moonlight.

There had hung upon the higher summits, at his right, a heavy fold of white cloud, which on a sudden broke, and, like the smoke of artillery, came rolling down the slopes towards him. Its principal volume, however, unfolded itself in a mighty flood down the side of the mountain towards the lake; and that which spread towards and soon enveloped the ground on which he stood was by no means so dense a fog. A thick mist enough it was; but still, to a distance of twenty or thirty yards, he could discern the outline of a rock or scaur,* but not beyond it.

There are few sensations more intimidating than that of being thus enveloped on a lonely mountain-side, which, like this one, here and there breaks into precipice.

There is another sensation, too, which affects the imagination. Overtaken thus on the solitary expanse, there comes a new chill and tremour as this treacherous medium surrounds us, through which unperceived those shapes which fancy conjures up might approach so near and bar our path.

From the risk of being reduced to an actual standstill he knew he was exempt. The point from which the wind blew, light as it was, assured him of that. Still the mist was thick enough seriously to embarrass him. It had overtaken him as he was looking down upon the lake; and he now looked to his left, to try whether in that direction it was too thick to permit a view of the nearest landmarks. Through this white film he saw a figure standing only about five-and-twenty steps away, looking down, as it seemed, in precisely the same direction as he, quite motionless, and standing like a shadow projected upon the smoky vapour. It was the figure of a slight tall man, with his arm extended, as if pointing to a remote object, which no mortal eye certainly could discern through the mist. Sir Bale gazed at this figure, doubtful whether he were in a waking dream, unable to conjecture whence it had come; and as he looked, it moved, and was almost instantly out of sight.

He descended the mountain cautiously. The mist was now thinner, and through the haze he was beginning to see objects more distinctly, and, without danger, to proceed at a quicker pace. He had still a long walk by the uplands towards Mardykes Hall, before he descended to the level of the lake.

The mist was still quite thick enough to circumscribe his view and to hide the general features of the landscape; and well was it, perhaps, for Sir Bale that his boyhood had familiarized him with the landmarks on the mountain-side.

He had made nearly four miles on his solitary homeward way, when, passing under a ledge of rock which bears the name of the Cat's Skaitch, he saw the same figure in the short cloak standing within some thirty or forty yards of him—the thin curtain of mist, through which the moon-light touched it, giving to it an airy and unsubstantial character.

Sir Bale came to a standstill. The man in the short cloak nodded and drew back, and was concealed by the angle of the rock.

Sir Bale was now irritated, as men are after a start, and shouting to the stranger to halt, he 'slapped' after him, as the northern phrase goes, at his best pace. But again he was gone, and nowhere could he see him, the mist favouring his evasion.

Looking down the fells that overhang Mardykes Hall, the mountain-side dips gradually into a glen, which, as it descends, becomes precipitous and wooded. A footpath through this ravine conducts the wayfarer to the level ground that borders the lake; and by this dark pass Sir Bale Mardykes strode, in comparatively clear air, along the rocky path dappled with moonlight.

As he emerged upon the lower ground he again encountered the same figure. It approached. It was Philip Feltram.

CHAPTER XIV

A NEW PHILIP FELTRAM

THE Baronet had not seen Feltram since his strange escape from death. His last interview with him had been stern and threatening; Sir Bale dealing with appearances in the spirit of an incensed judge, Philip Feltram lamenting in the submission of a helpless despair.

Feltram was full in the moonlight now, standing erect, and smiling cynically on the Baronet.

There was that in the hearing and countenance of Feltram that disconcerted him more than the surprise of the sudden meeting.

He had determined to meet Feltram in a friendly way, whenever that not very comfortable interview became inevitable. But he was confused by the suddenness of Feltram's appearance; and the tone, cold and stern, in which he had last spoken to him came first, and he spoke in it after a brief silence.

'I fancied, Mr Feltram, you were in your bed; I little expected to find you here. I think the Doctor gave very particular directions, and said that you were to remain perfectly quiet.'

'But I know more than the Doctor,' replied Feltram, still smiling unpleasantly.

'I think, sir, you would have been better in your bed,' said Sir Bale loftily.

'Come, come, come, come!' exclaimed Philip Feltram contemptuously.

'It seems to me, sir,' said Sir Bale, a good deal astonished, 'you rather forget yourself.'

'Easier to forget oneself than to forgive others, at times, Sir Bale,' replied Philip Feltram in his unparalleled mood.

'That's the way fools knock themselves up,' continued Sir Bale. 'You've been walking ever so far—away to the Fells of Golden Friars. It was you whom I saw there. What d—d folly! What brought you there?'

'To observe you,' he replied.

'And have you walked the whole way there and back again? How did you get there?'

'Pooh! how did I come—how did you come—how did the fog come? From the lake, I suppose. We all come up, and then down.' So spoke Philip Feltram, with serene insolence.

'You are pleased to talk nonsense,' said Sir Bale.

'Because I like it—with a *meaning*.'

Sir Bale looked at him, not knowing whether to believe his eyes and ears. He did not know what to make of him.

'I had intended speaking to you in a conciliatory way; you seem to wish to make that impossible'—Philip Feltram's face wore its repulsive smile;—'and in fact I don't know what to make of you, unless you are ill; and ill you well may be. You can't have walked much less than twelve miles.'

'Wonderful effort for me!' said Feltram with the same sneer.

'Rather surprising for a man so nearly drowned,' answered Sir Bale Mardykes.

'A dip: you don't like the lake, sir; but I do. And so it is: as Antaeus* touched the earth, so I the water, and rise refreshed.'

'I think you'd better get in and refresh there. I meant to tell you that all the unpleasantness about that bank-note is over.'

'Is it?'

'Yes. It has been recovered by Mr Creswell, who came here last night. I've got it, and you're not to blame,' said Sir Bale.

'But some one *is* to blame,' observed Mr Feltram, smiling still.

'Well, *you* are not, and that ends it,' said the Baronet peremptorily.

'Ends it? Really, how good! how very good!'

Sir Bale looked at him, for there was something ambiguous and even derisive in the tone of Feltram's voice.

But before he could quite make up his mind, Feltram spoke again.

'Everything is settled about you and me?'

'There is nothing to prevent your staying at Mardykes now,' said Sir Bale graciously.

'I shall be with you for two years, and then I go on my travels,' answered Feltram, with a saturnine and somewhat wild look around him.

'Is he going mad?' thought the Baronet.

'But before I go, I'm to put you in a way of paying off your mortgages. That is my business here.'

Sir Bale looked at him sharply. But now there was not the unpleasant smile, but the darkened look of a man in secret pain.

'You shall know it by and by.'

And without more ceremony, and with a darkening face, Philip Feltram made his way under the boughs of the thick oaks that grew there, leaving on Sir Bale's mind an impression that he had been watching some one at a distance, and had gone in consequence of a signal.

In a few seconds he followed in the same direction, halloaing after Feltram; for he did not like the idea of his wandering about the country by moonlight, or possibly losing his life among the precipices, and bringing a new discredit upon his house. But no answer came; nor could he in that thick copse gain sight of him again.

When Sir Bale reached Mardykes Hall he summoned Mrs Julaper, and had a long talk with her. But she could not say that there appeared anything amiss with Philip Feltram; only he seemed more reserved, and as if he was brooding over something he did not intend to tell.

'But, you know, Sir Bale, what happened might well make a thoughtful man of him. If he's ever to think of Death, it should be after looking him so hard in the face; and I'm not ashamed to say, I'm glad to see he has grace to take the lesson, and I hope his experiences may be sanctified to him, poor fellow! Amen.'

'Very good song, and very well sung,' said Sir Bale; 'but it doesn't seem to me that he has been improved, Mrs Julaper. He seems, on the contrary, in a queer temper and anything but a heavenly frame of mind; and I thought I'd ask you, because if he is ill—I mean feverish—it might account for his eccentricities, as well as make it necessary to send after him, and bring him home, and put him to bed. But I suppose it is as you say,—his adventure has upset him a little, and he'll sober in a day or two, and return to his old ways.'

But this did not happen. A change, more comprehensive than at first appeared, had taken place, and a singular alteration was gradually established.

He grew thin, his eyes hollow, his face gradually forbidding.

His ways and temper were changed: he was a new man with Sir Bale; and the Baronet after a time, people said, began to grow afraid of him. And certainly Feltram had acquired an extraordinary influence over the Baronet, who a little while ago had regarded and treated him with so much contempt.

CHAPTER XV

THE PURSE OF GOLD

THE Baronet was very slightly known in his county. He had led a reserved and inhospitable life. He was pressed upon by heavy debts; and being a proud man, held aloof from society and its doings. He wished people to understand that he was nursing his estate; but somehow the estate did not thrive at nurse. In the country other people's business is admirably well known; and the lord of Mardykes was conscious, perhaps, that his neighbours knew as well as he did that the utmost he could do was to pay the interest charged upon it, and to live in a frugal way enough.

The lake measures some four or five miles across, from the little jetty under the walls of Mardykes Hall to Cloostedd.

Philip Feltram, changed and morose, loved a solitary row upon the lake; and sometimes, with no one to aid him in its management, would take the little sail-boat and pass the whole day upon those lonely waters.

Frequently he crossed to Cloostedd; and mooring the boat under the solemn trees that stand reflected in that dark mirror, he would disembark and wander among the lonely woodlands, as people thought, cherishing in those ancestral scenes the memory of ineffaceable injuries, and the wrath and revenge that seemed of late to darken his countenance, and to hold him always in a moody silence.

One autumnal evening Sir Bale Mardykes was sourly ruminating after his solitary meal. A very red sun was pouring its last beams through the valley at the western extremity of the lake, across its elsewhere sombre waters, and touching with a sudden and blood-red tint the sail of the skiff in which Feltram was returning from his lonely cruise.

'Here comes my domestic water-fiend,' sneered Sir Bale, as he lay back in his cumbrous arm-chair. 'Cheerful place, pleasant people, delicious fate! The place alone has been enough to set that fool out of his little senses, d—n him!'

Sir Bale averted his eyes, and another subject not pleasanter entered his mind. He was thinking of the races that were coming off next week at Heckleston Downs, and what sums of money might be made there, and how hard it was that he should be excluded by fortune from that brilliant lottery.

'Ah, Mrs Julaper, is that you?'

Mrs Julaper, who was still at the door, curtsied, and said, 'I came, Sir Bale, to see whether you'd please to like a jug of mulled claret, sir.'

'Not I, my dear. I'll take a mug of beer and my pipe; that homely solace better befits a ruined gentleman.'

'H'm, sir; you're not that, Sir Bale; you're no worse than half the lords and great men that are going. I would not hear another say that of you, sir.'

'That's very kind of you, Mrs Julaper; but you won't call *me* out for backbiting myself, especially as it is true, d—d true, Mrs Julaper! Look ye; there never was a Mardykes here before but he could lay his hundred or his thousand pounds on the winner of the Heckleston Cup; and what could I bet? Little more than that mug of beer I spoke of. It was my great-grandfather who opened the course on the Downs of Heckleston, and now *I* can't show there! Well, what must I do? Grin and bear it, that's all. If you please, Mrs Julaper, I will have that jug of claret you offered. I want spice and hot wine to keep me alive; but I'll smoke my pipe first, and in an hour's time it will do.'

When Mrs Julaper was gone, he lighted his pipe, and drew near the window, through which he looked upon the now fading sky and the twilight landscape.

He smoked his pipe out, and by that time it had grown nearly dark. He was still looking out upon the faint outlines of the view, and thinking angrily what a little bit of luck at the races would do for many a man who probably did not want it half so much as he. Vague and sombre as his thoughts were, they had, like the darkening landscape outside, shape enough to define their general character. Bitter and impious they were—as those of egotistic men naturally are in suffering. And after brooding, and muttering by fits and starts, he said:

'How many tens and hundreds of thousands of pounds will change hands at Heckleston next week; and not a shilling in all the change and shuffle will stick to me! How many a fellow would sell himself, like Dr Faustus,* just for the knowledge of who was to be the winner! But he's no fool, and does not buy his own.'

Something caught his eye; something moving on the wall. The fire was lighted, and cast a flickering and gigantic shadow upward; the figure of a man standing behind Sir Bale Mardykes, on whose shoulder he placed a lean hand. Sir Bale turned suddenly about, and saw Philip Feltram. He was looking dark and stern, and did not remove his hand from his shoulder as he peered into the Baronet's face with his deep-set mad eyes.

'Ha, Philip, upon my soul!' exclaimed Sir Bale, surprised. 'How time flies! It seems only this minute since I saw the boat a mile and a half away from the shore. Well—yes; there has been time; it is dark now. Ha, ha! I assure you, you startled me. Won't you take something? Do. Shall I touch the bell?'

'You have been troubled about those mortgages. I told you I should pay them off, I thought.'

Here there was a pause, and Sir Bale looked hard in Feltram's face. If he had been in his ordinary spirits, or perhaps in some of his haunts less solitary than Mardykes, he would have laughed; but here he had grown unlike himself, gloomy and credulous, and was, in fact, a nervous man.

Sir Bale smiled, and shook his head dismally.

'It is very kind of you, Feltram; the idea shows a kindly disposition. I know you would do me a kindness if you could.'

As Sir Bale, each looking in the other's eyes, repeated in this sentence the words 'kind', 'kindly', 'kindness', a smile lighted Feltram's face with at each word an intenser light; and Sir Bale grew sombre in its glare; and when he had done speaking, Feltram's face also on a sudden darkened.

'I have found a fortune-teller in Cloostedd Wood. Look here.'

And he drew from his pocket a leathern purse, which he placed on the table in his hand; and Sir Bale heard the pleasant clank of coin in it.

'A fortune-teller! You don't mean to say she gave you that?' said Sir Bale.

Feltram smiled again, and nodded.

'It *was* the custom to give the fortune-teller a trifle. It is a great improvement making *her* fee you,' observed Sir Bale, with an approach to his old manner.

'He put that in my hand, with a message,' said Feltram.

'He? O, then it was a male fortune-teller!'

'Gipsies go in gangs, men and women. *He* might lend, though *she* told fortunes,' said Feltram.

'It's the first time I ever heard of gipsies lending money'; and he eyed the purse with a whimsical smile.

With his lean fingers still holding it, Feltram sat down at the table. His face darkened as if in cunning thought, and his chin sank upon his breast as he leaned back.

'I think,' continued Sir Bale, 'ever since they were spoiled, the Egyptians* have been a little shy of lending, and leave that branch of business to the Hebrews.'

'What would you give to know, now, the winner at Heckleston races?' said Feltram suddenly, raising his eyes.

'Yes; that would be worth something,' answered Sir Bale, looking at him with more interest than the incredulity he affected would quite warrant.

'And this money I have power to lend you, to make your game.'

'Do you mean that really?' said Sir Bale, with a new energy in tone, manner, and features.

'That's heavy; there are some guineas there,' said Feltram with a dark smile, raising the purse in his hand a little, and letting it drop upon the table with a clang.

'There is *something* there, at all events,' said Sir Bale.

Feltram took the purse by the bottom, and poured out on the table a handsome pile of guineas.

'And do you mean to say, you got all that from a gipsy in Cloostedd Wood?'

'A friend, who is—*my self*,' answered Philip Feltram.

'Yourself! Then it is yours—*you* lend it?' said the Baronet, amazed; for there was no getting over the heap of guineas, and the wonder was pretty equal whence they had come.

'Myself, and not myself,' said Feltram oracularly; 'as like as voice and echo, man and shadow.'

Had Feltram in some of his solitary wanderings and potterings lighted upon hidden treasure? There was a story of two Feltrams of Cloostedd, brothers, who had joined the king's army and fought at Marston Moor,* having buried in Cloostedd Wood a great deal of gold and plate and jewels. They had, it was said, intrusted one tried servant with the secret; and that servant remained at home. But by a perverse fatality the three witnesses had perished within a month: the two brothers at Marston Moor; and the confidant, of fever, at Cloostedd. From that day forth treasure-seekers had from time to time explored the woods of Cloostedd; and many a tree of mark was dug beside, and the earth beneath many a stone and scar and other landmark in that solitary forest was opened by night, until hope gradually died out, and the tradition had long ceased to prompt to action, and had become a story and nothing more.

The image of the nursery-tale had now recurred to Sir Bale after so long a reach of years; and the only imaginable way, in his mind, of accounting for penniless Philip Feltram having all that gold in his possession was that, in some of his lonely wanderings, chance had led him to the undiscovered hoard of the two Feltrams who had died in the great civil wars.

'Perhaps those gipsies you speak of found the money where you found them; and in that case, as Cloostedd Forest, and all that is in it, is my property, their sending it to me is more like my servant's handing me my hat and stick when I'm going out, than making me a present.'

'You will not be wise to rely upon the law, Sir Bale, and to refuse the help that comes unasked. But if you like your mortgages as they are, keep them; and if you like my terms as they are, take them; and when you have made up your mind, let me know.'

Philip Feltram dropped the heavy purse into his capacious coat-pocket, and walked, muttering, out of the room.

CHAPTER XVI

THE MESSAGE FROM CLOOSTEDD

'COME back, Feltram; come back, Philip!' cried Sir Bale hastily. 'Let us talk, can't we? Come and talk this odd business over a little; you must have mistaken what I meant; I should like to hear all about it.'

'All is not much, sir,' said Philip Feltram, re-entering the room, whose door he had half closed after him. 'In the forest of Cloostedd I met to-day some people, one of whom can foretell events, and told me the names of the winners of the first three races at Heckleston, and gave me this purse, with leave to lend you so much money as you care to stake upon the races. I take no security; you sha'n't be troubled; and you'll never see the lender, unless you seek him out.'

'Well, those are not bad terms,' said Sir Bale, smiling wistfully at the purse, which Feltram had again placed upon the table.

'No, not bad,' repeated Feltram, in the harsh low tone in which he now habitually spoke.

'You'll tell me what the prophet said about the winners; I should like to hear the names.'

'The names I shall tell you, if you walk out with me,' said Feltram.

'Why not here?' asked Sir Bale.

'My memory does not serve me here so well. Some people, in some places, though they be silent, obstruct thought. Come, let us speak,' said Philip Feltram, leading the way.

Sir Bale, with a shrug, followed him.

By this time it was dark. Feltram was walking slowly towards the margin of the lake; and Sir Bale, more curious as the delay increased, followed him, and smiled faintly as he looked after his tall gaunt figure, as if, even in the dark, expressing a ridicule which he did not honestly feel, and the expression of which, even if there had been light, there was no one near enough to see.

When he reached the edge of the lake, Feltram stooped, and Sir Bale thought that his attitude was that of one who whispers to and caresses a reclining person. What he fancied was a dark figure lying horizontally in the shallow water, near the edge, turned out to be, as he drew near, no more than a shadow on the elsewhere lighter water; and with his change of position it had shifted and was gone, and Philip Feltram was but dabbling his hand this way and that in the water, and muttering faintly to himself. He rose as the Baronet drew near, and standing upright, said,

'I like to listen to the ripple of the water among the grass and pebbles; the tongue and lips of the lake are lapping and whispering all along. It is the merest poetry; but you are so romantic, you excuse me.'

There was an angry curve in Feltram's eyebrows, and a cynical smile, and something in the tone which to the satirical Baronet was almost insulting. But even had he been less curious, I don't think he would have betrayed his mortification; for an odd and unavowed influence which he hated was gradually establishing in Feltram an ascendency* which sometimes vexed and sometimes cowed him.

'You are not to tell,' said Feltram, drawing near him in the dusk. 'The secret is yours when you promise.'

'Of course I promise,' said Sir Bale. 'If I believed it, you don't think I could be such an ass as to tell it; and if I didn't believe it, I'd hardly take the trouble.'

Feltram stooped, and dipping the hollow of his hand in the water, he raised it full, and said he, 'Hold out your hand—the hollow of your hand—like this. I divide the water for a sign—share to me and share to you.' And he turned his hand, so as to pour half the water into the hollow palm of Sir Bale, who was smiling, with some uneasiness mixed in his mockery.

'Now, you promise to keep all secrets respecting the teller and the finder, be that who it may?'

'Yes, I promise,' said Sir Bale.

'Now do as I do,' said Feltram. And he shed the water on the ground, and with his wet fingers touched his forehead and his breast; and then he joined his hand with Sir Bale's, and said, 'Now you are my safe man.'

Sir Bale laughed. 'That's the game they call "grand mufti",'* said he.

'Exactly; and means nothing,' said Feltram, 'except that some day it will serve you to remember by. And now the names. Don't speak; listen—you may break the thought else. The winner of the first is *Beeswing*; of the second, *Falcon*; and of the third, *Lightning*.'

He had stood for some seconds in silence before he spoke; his eyes were closed; he seemed to bring up thought and speech with difficulty, and spoke faintly and drowsily, both his hands a little raised, and the fingers extended, with the groping air of a man who moves in the dark. In this odd way, slowly, faintly, with many a sigh and scarcely audible groan, he gradually delivered his message and was silent. He stood, it seemed, scarcely half awake, muttering indistinctly and sighing to himself. You would have said that he was exhausted and suffering, like a man at his last hour resigning himself to death.

At length he opened his eyes, looked round a little wildly and languidly, and with another great sigh sat down on a large rock that lies by the margin of the lake, and sighed heavily again and again. You might have fancied that he was a second time recovering from drowning.

Then he got up, and looked drowsily round again, and sighed like a man worn out with fatigue, and was silent.

Sir Bale did not care to speak until he seemed a little more likely to obtain an answer. When that time came, he said, 'I wish, for the sake of my believing, that your list was a little less incredible. Not one of the horses you name is the least likely; not one of them has a chance.'

'So much the better for you; you'll get what odds you please. You had better seize your luck; on Tuesday Beeswing runs,' said Feltram. 'When you want money for the purpose, I'm your banker—here is your bank.'

He touched his breast, where he had placed the purse, and then he turned and walked swiftly away.

Sir Bale looked after him till he disappeared in the dark. He fluctuated among many surmises about Feltram. Was he insane, or was he practising an imposture? or was he fool enough to believe the predictions of some real gipsies? and had he borrowed this money, which in Sir Bale's eyes seemed the greatest miracle in the matter, from those thriving shepherd mountaineers, the old Trebecks, who, he believed, were attached to him? Feltram had, he thought, borrowed it as if for himself; and having, as Sir Bale in his egotism supposed, 'a sneaking regard' for him, had meant the loan for his patron, and conceived the idea of his using his revelations for the purpose of making his fortune. So, seeing no risk, and the temptation being strong, Sir Bale resolved to avail himself of the purse, and use his own judgment as to what horse to back.

About eleven o'clock Feltram, unannounced, walked, with his hat still on, into Sir Bale's library, and sat down at the opposite side of his table, looking darkly into the Baronet's face for a time.

'Shall you want the purse?' he asked at last.

'Certainly; I always want a purse,' said Sir Bale energetically.

'The condition is, that you shall back each of the three horses I have named. But you may back them for much or little, as you like, only the sum must not be less than five pounds in each hundred which this purse contains. That is the condition, and if you violate it, you will make some powerful people very angry, and you will feel it. Do you agree?'

'Of course; five pounds in the hundred—certainly; and how many hundreds are there?'

'Three.'

'Well, a fellow with luck may win something with three hundred pounds, but it ain't very much.'

'Quite enough, if you use it aright.'

'Three hundred pounds,' repeated the Baronet, as he emptied the purse, which Feltram had just placed in his hand, upon the table; and contemplating them with grave interest, he began telling them off in little heaps of five-and-twenty each. He might have thanked Feltram, but he was thinking more of the guineas than of the grizzly donor.

'Ay,' said he, after a second counting, 'I think there *are* exactly three hundred. Well, so you say I must apply three times five—fifteen of these. It is an awful pity backing those queer horses you have named; but if I must make the sacrifice, I must, I suppose?' he added, with a hesitating inquiry in the tone.

'If you don't, you'll rue it,' said Feltram coldly, and so left the room.

'Penny in pocket's a merry companion,' says the old English proverb, and Sir Bale felt in better spirits and temper than he had for many a day as he replaced the guineas in the purse.

It was long since he had visited either the race-course or any other place of amusement. Now he might face his kind without fear that his pride should be mortified, and dabble in the fascinating agitations of the turf once more.

'Who knows how this little venture may turn out?' he thought. 'It's time the luck should turn. My last summer in Germany, my last winter in Paris—d—n me, I'm owed something. It's time I should win a bit.'

Sir Bale had suffered the indolence of a solitary and discontented life imperceptibly to steal upon him. It would not do to appear for the first time on Heckleston Lea with any of those signs of negligence which, in his case, might easily be taken for poverty. All his appointments, therefore, were carefully looked after; and on the Monday following, he, followed by his groom, rode away for the Saracen's Head at Heckleston, where he was to put up, for the races that were to begin on the day following, and presented as handsome an appearance as a peer in those days need have cared to show.

CHAPTER XVII

ON THE COURSE — BEESWING, FALCON, AND LIGHTNING

As he rode towards Golden Friars, through which his route lay, in the early morning light, in which the mists of night were clearing, he looked back towards Mardykes with a hope of speedy deliverance from that hated imprisonment, and of a return to the continental life in which he took delight. He saw the summits and angles of the old building touched with the cheerful beams, and the grand old trees, and at the opposite side the fells dark, with their backs towards the east; and down the side of the wooded and precipitous clough of Feltram, the light, with a pleasant contrast against the beetling purple of the fells, was breaking in the faint distance. On the lake he saw the white speck that indicated the sail of Philip Feltram's boat, now midway between Mardykes and the wooded shores of Cloostedd.

'Going on the same errand,' thought Sir Bale, 'I should not wonder. I wish him the same luck. Yes, he's going to Cloostedd Forest. I hope he may meet his gipsies there—the Trebecks, or whoever they are.'

And as a momentary sense of degradation in being thus beholden to such people smote him, 'Well,' thought he, 'who knows? Many a fellow will make a handsome sum of a poorer purse than this at Heckleston. It will be a light matter paying them then.'

Through Golden Friars he rode. Some of the spectators who did not like him, wondered audibly at the gallant show, hoped it was paid for, and conjectured that he had ridden out in search of a wife. On the whole, however, the appearance of their Baronet in a smarter style than usual was popular, and accepted as a change to the advantage of the town.

Next morning he was on the race-course of Heckleston, renewing old acquaintance and making himself as agreeable as he could—an object, among some people, of curiosity and even interest. Leaving the carriage-sides, the hoods and bonnets, Sir Bale was soon among the betting men, deep in more serious business.

How did he make his book? He did not break his word. He backed Beeswing, Falcon, and Lightning. But it must be owned not for a shilling more than the five guineas each, to which he stood pledged. The odds were forty-five to one against Beeswing, sixty to one against Lightning, and fifty to one against Falcon.

'A pretty lot to choose!' exclaimed Sir Bale, with vexation. 'As if I had money so often, that I should throw it away!'

The Baronet was testy in thinking over all this, and looked on Feltram's message as an impertinence and the money as his own.

Let us now see how Sir Bale Mardyke's pocket fared.

Sulkily enough at the close of the week he turned his back on Heckleston race-course, and took the road to Golden Friars.

He was in a rage with his luck, and by no means satisfied with himself; and yet he had won something. The result of the racing had been curious. In the three principal races the favourites had been beaten: one by an accident, another on a technical point, and the third by fair running. And what horses had won? The names were precisely those which the 'fortune-teller' had predicted.

Well, then, how was Sir Bale in pocket as he rode up to his ancestral house of Mardykes, where a few thousand pounds would have been very welcome? He had won exactly 775 guineas; and had he staked a hundred instead of five on each of the names communicated by Feltram, he would have won 15,500 guineas.

He dismounted before his hall-door, therefore, with the discontent of a man who had lost nearly 15,000 pounds. Feltram was upon the steps, and laughed dryly.

'What do you laugh at?' asked Sir Bale tartly.

'You've won, haven't you?'

'Yes, I've won; I've won a trifle.'

'On the horses I named?'

'Well, yes; it so turned out, by the merest accident.'

Feltram laughed again dryly, and turned away.

Sir Bale entered Mardykes Hall, and was surly. He was in a much worse mood than before he had ridden to Heckleston. But after a week or so ruminating upon the occurrence, he wondered that Feltram spoke no more of it. It was undoubtedly wonderful. There had been no hint of repayment yet, and he had made some hundreds by the loan; and, contrary to all likelihood, the three horses named by the unknown soothsayer had won. Who was this gipsy? It would be worth bringing the soothsayer to Mardykes, and giving his people a camp on the warren, and all the poultry they could catch, and a pig or a sheep every now and then. Why, that seer was worth the philosopher's stone, and could make Sir Bale's fortune in a season. Some one else would be sure to pick him up if *he* did not.

So, tired of waiting for Feltram to begin, he opened the subject one day himself. He had not seen him for two or three days; and in the wood of Mardykes he saw his lank figure standing among the thick trees, upon a little knoll, leaning on a staff which he sometimes carried with him in his excursions up the mountains.

'Feltram!' shouted Sir Bale.

Feltram turned and beckoned. Sir Bale Mardykes muttered, but obeyed the signal.

'I brought you here, because you can from this point with unusual clearness to-day see the opening of the Clough of Feltram at the other side, and the clump of trees, where you will find the way to reach the person about whom you are always thinking.'

'Who said I am always thinking about him?' said the Baronet angrily; for he felt like a man detected in a weakness, and resented it.

'*I* say it, because I *know* it; and *you* know it also. See that clump of trees standing solitary in the hollow? Among them, to the left, grows an ancient oak. Cut in its bark are two enormous letters H–F; so large and bold, that the rugged furrows of the oak bark fail to obscure them, although they are ancient and spread by time. Standing against the trunk of this great tree, with your back to these letters, you are looking up the Glen or Clough of Feltram, that opens northward, where stands Cloostedd Forest spreading far and thick. Now, how do you find our fortune-teller?'

'That is exactly what I wish to know,' answered Sir Bale; 'because, although I can't, of course, believe that he's a witch, yet he has either made the most marvellous fluke I've heard of, or else he has got extraordinary sources of information; or perhaps he acts partly on chance, partly on facts. Be it which you please, I say he's a marvellous fellow; and I should like to see him, and have a talk with him; and perhaps he could arrange with me. I should be very glad to make an arrangement with him to give me the benefit of his advice about any matter of the same kind again.'

'I think he's willing to see you; but he's a fellow with a queer fancy and a pig-head. He'll not come here; you must go to him; and approach him his own way too, or you may fail to find him. On these terms he invites you.'

Sir Bale laughed.

'He knows his value, and means to make his own terms.'

'Well, there's nothing unfair in that; and I don't see that I should dispute it. How is one to find him?'

'Stand, as I told you, with your back to those letters cut in the oak. Right before you lies an old Druidic altar-stone.* Cast your eye over its surface, and on some part of it you are sure to see a black stain about the size of a man's hand. Standing, as I suppose you, against the oak, that stain, which changes its place from day to day, will give you the line you must follow through the forest in order to light upon him. Take carefully from it such trees or objects as will guide you; and when the forest thickens, do the best you can to keep to the same line. You are sure to find him.'

'You'll come, Feltram. I should lose myself in that wilderness, and probably fail to discover him,' said Sir Bale; 'and I really wish to see him.'

'When two people wish to meet, it is hard if they don't. I can go with you a bit of the way; I can walk a little through the forest by your side, until I see the small flower that grows peeping here and there, that always springs where those people walk; and when I begin to see that sign, I must leave you. And, first, I'll take you across the lake.'

'By Jove, you'll do no such thing!' said Sir Bale hastily.

'But that is the way he chooses to be approached,' said Philip Feltram.

'I have a sort of feeling about that lake; it's the one childish spot that is left in my imagination. The nursery is to blame for it—old stories and warnings; and I can't think of that. I should feel that I had invoked an evil omen if I did. I know it is all nonsense; but we are queer creatures, Feltram. I must only ride there.'

'Why, it is five-and-twenty miles round the lake to that; and after all were done, he would not see you. He knows what he's worth, and he'll have his own way,' answered Feltram. 'The sun will soon set. See that withered spray, near Snakes Island, that looks like fingers rising from the water? When its points grow tipped with red, the sun has but three minutes more to live.'

'That is a wonder which I can't see; it is too far away.'

'Yes; the lake has many signs; but it needs sight to see them,' said Feltram.

'So it does,' said the Baronet; 'more than most men have got. I'll ride round, I say; and I make my visit, for this time, my own way.'

'You'll not find him, then; and he wants his money. It would be a pity to vex him.'

'It was to you he lent the money,' said Sir Bale.

'Yes.'

'Well, you are the proper person to find him out and pay him,' urged Sir Bale.

'Perhaps so; but he invites you; and if you don't go, he may be offended, and you may hear no more from him.'

'We'll try. When can you go? There are races to come off next week, for once and away, at Langton. I should not mind trying my luck there. What do you say?'

'I know nothing about it. What can I say?'

'You can go there and pay him, and ask the same question—what horses, I mean, are to win. All the county are to be there; and plenty of money will change hands.'

'I'll try,' said Feltram.

'When will you go?'

'To-morrow,' he answered.

'I have an odd idea, Feltram, that you are really going to pay off those cursed mortgages.'

He laid his hand with at least a gesture of kindness on the thin arm of Feltram, who coldly answered,

'So have I'; and walked down the side of the little knoll and away, without another word or look.

CHAPTER XVIII

ON THE LAKE, AT LAST

NEXT day Philip Feltram crossed the lake; and Sir Bale, seeing the boat on the water, guessed its destination, and watched its progress with no little interest, until he saw it moored and its sail drop at the rude pier that affords a landing at the Clough of Feltram. He was now satisfied that Philip had actually gone to seek out the 'cunning man',* and gather hints for the next race.

When that evening Feltram returned, and, later still, entered Sir

Bale's library, the master of Mardykes was gladder to see him and more interested about his news than he would have cared to confess.

Philip Feltram did not affect unconsciousness of that anxiety, but, with great directness, proceeded to satisfy it.

'I was in Cloostedd Forest to-day, nearly all day—and found the old gentleman in a wax.* He did not ask me to drink, nor show me any kindness. He was huffed* because you would not take the trouble to cross the lake to speak to him yourself. He took the money you sent him, and counted it over, and dropped it into his pocket; and he called you hard names enough and to spare; but I brought him round, and at last he did talk.'

'And what did he say?'

'He said that the estate of Mardykes would belong to a Feltram.'

'He might have said something more likely,' said Sir Bale sourly. 'Did he say anything more?'

'Yes. He said the winner at Langton Lea would be Silver Bell.'

'Any other name?'

'No.'

'Silver Bell? Well, that's not so odd as the last. Silver Bell stands high in the list. He has a good many backers—long odds in his favour against most of the field. I should not mind backing Silver Bell.'

The fact is, that he had no idea of backing any other horse from the moment he heard the soothsayer's prediction. He made up his mind to no half measures this time. He would go in to win something handsome.

He was in great force and full of confidence on the race-course. He had no fears for the result. He bet heavily. There was a good margin still untouched of the Mardykes estate; and Sir Bale was a good old name in the county. He found a ready market for his offers, and had soon staked—such is the growing frenzy of that excitement—about twenty thousand pounds on his favourite, and stood to win seven.

He did not win, however. He lost his twenty thousand pounds.

And now the Mardykes estate was in imminent danger. Sir Bale returned, having distributed I O Us and promissory notes in all directions about him—quite at his wit's end.

Feltram was standing—as on the occasion of his former happier return—on the steps of Mardykes Hall, in the evening sun, throwing eastward a long shadow that was lost in the lake. He received him, as before, with a laugh.

Sir Bale was too much broken to resent this laugh as furiously as he might, had he been a degree less desperate.

He looked at Feltram savagely, and dismounted.

'Last time you would not trust him, and this time he would not trust you. He's huffed, and played you false.'

'It was not he. I should have backed that d——d horse in any case,' said Sir Bale, grinding his teeth. 'What a witch you have discovered! One thing is true, perhaps. If there was a Feltram rich enough, he might have the estate now; but there ain't. They are all beggars. So much for your conjurer.'

'He may make amends to you, if you make amends to him.'

'He! Why, what can that wretched impostor do? D——n me, I'm past helping now.'

'Don't you talk so,' said Feltram. 'Be civil. You must please the old gentleman. He'll make it up. He's placable when it suits him. Why not go to him his own way? I hear you are nearly ruined. You must go and make it up.'

'Make it up! With whom? With a fellow who can't make even a guess at what's coming? Why should I trouble my head about him more?'

'No man, young or old, likes to be frumped.* Why did you cross his fancy? He won't see you unless you go to him as he chooses.'

'If he waits for that, he may wait till doomsday. I don't choose to go on that water—and cross it I won't,' said Sir Bale.

But when his distracting reminders began to pour in upon him, and the idea of dismembering what remained of his property came home to him, his resolution faltered.

'I say, Feltram, what difference can it possibly make to him if I choose to ride round to Cloostedd Forest instead of crossing the lake in a boat?'

Feltram smiled darkly, and answered,

'I can't tell. Can you?'

'Of course I can't—I say I can't; besides, what audacity of a fellow like that presuming to prescribe to me! Utterly ludicrous! And he can't predict—do you really think or believe, Feltram, that he can?'

'I know he can. I know he misled you on purpose. He likes to punish those who don't respect his will; and there is a reason in it, often quite clear—not ill-natured. Now you see he compels you to seek him out, and when you do, I think he'll help you through your trouble. He said he would.'

'Then you have seen him since?'

'Yesterday. He has put a pressure on you; but he means to help you.'

'If he means to help me, let him remember I want a banker more than a seer. Let him give me a lift, as he did before. He must lend me money.'

'He'll not stick at that. When he takes up a man, he carries him through.'

'The races of Byermere—I might retrieve at them. But they don't come off for a month nearly; and what is a man like me to do in the mean time?'

'Every man should know his own business best. I'm not like you,' said Feltram grimly.

Now Sir Bale's trouble increased, for some people were pressing. Something like panic supervened; for it happened that land was bringing just then a bad price, and more must be sold in consequence.

'All I can tell them is, I am selling land. It can't be done in an hour. I'm selling enough to pay them all twice over. Gentlemen used to be able to wait till a man sold his acres for payment. D—n them! do they want my body, that they can't let me alone for five minutes?'

The end of it was, that before a week Sir Bale told Feltram that he would go by boat, since that fellow insisted on it; and he did not very much care if he were drowned.

It was a beautiful autumnal day. Everything was bright in that mellowed sun, and the deep blue of the lake was tremulous with golden ripples; and crag and peak and scattered wood, faint in the distance, came out with a filmy distinctness on the fells in that pleasant light.

Sir Bale had been ill, and sent down the night before for Doctor Torvey. He was away with a patient. Now, in the morning, he had arrived inopportunely. He met Sir Bale as he issued from the house, and had a word with him in the court, for he would not turn back.

'Well,' said the Doctor, after his brief inspection, 'you ought to be in your bed; that's all I can say. You are perfectly mad to think of knocking about like this. Your pulse is at a hundred and ten; and, if you go across the lake and walk about Cloostedd, you'll be raving before you come back.'

Sir Bale told him, apologetically, as if his life were more to his doctor than to himself, that he would take care not to fatigue himself, and that the air would do him good, and that in any case he could not avoid going; and so they parted.

Sir Bale took his seat beside Feltram in the boat, the sail was spread, and, bending to the light breeze that blew from Golden Friars, she glided from the jetty under Mardykes Hall, and the eventful voyage had begun.

CHAPTER XIX

MYSTAGOGUS*

THE sail was loosed, the boat touched the stone step, and Feltram sprang out and made her fast to the old iron ring. The Baronet followed.

So! he had ventured upon that water without being drowned. He looked round him as if in a dream. He had not been there since his boyhood. There were no regrets, no sentiment, no remorse; only an odd return of the associations and fresh feelings of boyhood, and a long reach of time suddenly annihilated.

The little hollow in which he stood; the three hawthorn trees at his right; every crease and undulation of the sward, every angle and crack in the lichen-covered rock at his feet, recurred with a sharp and instant-aneous recognition to his memory.

'Many a time your brother and I fished for hours together from that bank there, just where the bramble grows. That bramble has not grown an inch ever since, not a leaf altered; we used to pick blackberries off it, with our rods stuck in the bank—it was later in the year than now—till we stript it quite bare after a day or two. The steward used to come over—they were marking timber for cutting—and we used to stay here while they rambled through the wood there, with an axe marking the trees that were to come down. I wonder whether the big old boat is still anywhere. I suppose she was broken up, or left to rot; I have not seen her since we came home. It was in the wood that lies at the right—the other wood is called the forest; they say in old times it was eight miles long, northward up the shore of the lake, and full of deer; with a for-ester, and a reeve, and a verderer, and all that. Your brother was older than you; he went to India, or the Colonies;* is he living still?'

'I care not.'

'That's good-natured, at all events; but do you know?'

'Not I; and what matter? If he's living, I warrant he has his share of the curse, the sweat of his brow and his bitter crust;* and if he is dead, he's dust or worse, he's rotten, and smells accordingly.'

Sir Bale looked at him; for this was the brother over whom, only a year or two ago, Philip used to cry tears of pathetic longing. Feltram looked darkly in his face, and sneered with a cold laugh.

'I suppose you mean to jest?' said Sir Bale.

'Not I; it is the truth. It is what you'd say, if you were honest. If he's alive, let him keep where he is; and if he's dead, I'll have none of him, body or soul. Do you hear that sound?'

'Like the wind moaning in the forest?' said Sir Bale.

'Yes.'

'But I feel no wind. There's hardly a leaf stirring.'

'I think so,' said Feltram. 'Come along.'

And he began striding up the gentle slope of the glen, with many a rock peeping through its sward, and tufted ferns and furze, giving a wild and neglected character to the scene; the background of which, where the glen loses itself in a distant turn, is formed by its craggy and wooded side.

Up they marched, side by side, in silence, towards that irregular clump of trees, to which Feltram had pointed from the Mardykes side.

As they approached, it showed more scattered, and two or three of the trees were of grander dimensions than in the distance they had appeared; and as they walked, the broad valley of Cloostedd Forest opened grandly on their left, studding the sides of the valley with solitary trees or groups, which thickened as it descended to the broad level, in parts nearly three miles wide, on which stands the noble forest of Cloostedd, now majestically reposing in the stirless air, gilded and flushed with the melancholy tints of autumn.

I am now going to relate wonderful things; but they rest on the report, strangely consistent, it is true, of Sir Bale Mardykes. That all his senses, however, were sick and feverish, and his brain by no means to be relied on at that moment, is a fact of which sceptics have a right to make all they please and can.

Startled at their approach, a bird like a huge mackaw started from the boughs of the trees, and sped away toward the shelter of the forest, fluttering and hopping close by the side of the little brook which, emerging from the forest, winds into the glen, and beside the course of which Sir Bale and Philip Feltram had ascended from the margin of the lake.

It fluttered on, as if one of its wings were hurt, and kept hopping and bobbing and flying along the ground at its swiftest, screaming all the time discordantly.

'That must be old Mrs Amerald's bird, that got away a week ago,' said Sir Bale, stopping and looking after it. 'Was not it a mackaw?'

'No,' said Feltram; 'that was a gray parrot; but there are strange birds in Cloostedd Forest, for my ancestors collected all that would live in our climate, and were at pains to find them the food and shelter they were accustomed to, until they grew hardy—that is how it happens.'

'By Jove, that's a secret worth knowing,' said Sir Bale. 'That would make quite a feature. What a fat brute that bird was! and green and dusky-crimson and yellow; but its head is white—age, I suspect; and what a broken beak—hideous bird! splendid plumage; something between a mackaw and a vulture.'

Sir Bale spoke jocularly, but with the interest of a bird-fancier; a taste which, when young, he had indulged; and for the moment forgot his cares and the object of his unwonted excursion.

A moment after, a lank slim bird, perfectly white, started from the same boughs, and winged its way to the forest.

'A kite, I think; but its body is a little too long, isn't it?' said Sir Bale again, stopping and looking after its flight also.

'A foreign kite, I daresay,' said Feltram.

All this time there was hopping near them a jay, with the tameness of a bird accustomed to these solitudes. It peered over its slender wing curiously at the visitors, pecking here and nodding there; and thus hopping, it made a circle round them more than once. Then it fluttered up, and perched on a bough of the old oak, from the deep labyrinth of whose branches the other birds had emerged; and from thence it flew down and lighted on the old druidic stone, that stood like a cyclopean table on its sunken stone props, before the snakelike roots of the oak.

Across this it hopped conceitedly, as over a stage on which it figured becomingly; and after a momentary hesitation, with a little spring, it rose and winged its way in the same direction which the other birds had taken, and was quickly lost in the thick of the forest to the left.

'Here,' said Feltram, 'this is the tree.'

'I remember it well! A gigantic trunk; and, yes, those marks; but I never before read them as letters. Yes, H. F., so they are—very odd I should not have remarked them. They are so large, and so strangely drawn-out in some places, and filled-in in others, and distorted, and the moss has grown about them; I don't wonder I took them for natural cracks and chasms in the bark,' said Sir Bale.

'Very like,' said Feltram.

Sir Bale had remarked, ever since they had begun their walk from the shore, that Feltram seemed to undergo a gloomy change. Sharper, grimmer, wilder grew his features, and shadow after shadow darkened his face.

The solitude and grandeur of the forest, and the repulsive gloom of his companion's countenance and demeanour, communicated a tone of anxiety to Sir Bale; and they stood still, side by side, in total silence for a time, looking toward the forest glades; between themselves and which, on the level sward of the valley, stood many a noble tree and fantastic group of forked birch and thorn, in the irregular formations into which Nature had thrown them.

'Now you stand between the letters. Cast your eyes on the stone,' said Feltram suddenly, and his low stern tones almost startled the Baronet.

Looking round, he perceived that he had so placed himself that his point of vision was exactly from between the two great letters, now half-obliterated, which he had been scrutinizing just as he turned about to look toward the forest of Cloostedd.

'Yes, so I am,' said Sir Bale.

There was within him an excitement and misgiving, akin to the sensation of a man going into battle, and which corresponded with the sombre frown which Feltram wore, and the manifest change which had come upon him.

'Look on the stone steadily for a time, and tell me if you see a black mark, about the size of your hand, anywhere upon its surface,' said Feltram.

Sir Bale affected no airs of scepticism now; his imagination was stirred, and a sense of some unknown reality at the bottom of that which he had affected to treat before as illusion, inspired a strange interest in the experiment.

'Do you see it?' asked Feltram.

Sir Bale was watching patiently, but he had observed nothing of the kind.

Sharper, darker, more eager grew the face of Philip Feltram, as his eyes traversed the surface of that huge horizontal block.

'Now?' asked Feltram again.

No, he had seen nothing.

Feltram was growing manifestly uneasy, angry almost; he walked away a little, and back again, and then two or three times round the tree, with his hands shut, and treading the ground like a man trying to warm his feet, and so impatiently he returned, and looked again on the stone.

Sir Bale was still looking, and very soon said, drawing his brows together and looking hard,

'Ha!—yes—hush. There it is, by Jove!—wait—yes—there; it is growing quite plain.'

It seemed not as if a shadow fell upon the stone, but rather as if the stone became semi-transparent, and just under its surface was something dark—a hand, he thought it—and darker and darker it grew, and after some little wavering, it fixed itself movelessly, pointing, as he thought, toward the forest.

'It looks like a hand,' said he. 'By Jove, it *is* a hand—pointing towards the forest with a finger.'

'Don't mind the finger; look only on that black blurred mark, and from the point where you stand, taking that point for your direction, look to the forest. Take some tree or other landmark for an object, enter the forest there, and pursue the same line, as well as you can, until you find little flowers with leaves like wood-sorrel, and with tall stems and a red blossom, such as you have not seen before, growing among the trees, and follow where they seem to grow thickest, and there you will find him.'

All the time that Feltram was making this little address, Sir Bale was endeavouring to fix his route by such indications as Feltram described; and when he had succeeded in quite establishing the form of a peculiar tree—a melancholy ash, one huge limb of which had been blasted by lightning, and its partly stricken arm stood high and barkless, stretching its white fingers, as it were, into the forest, and signing the way for him—

'I have it now,' said he. 'Come, Feltram, you'll come a bit of the way with me.'

Feltram made no answer, but slowly shook his head, and turned and walked away, leaving Sir Bale to undertake his adventure alone.

The strange sound they had heard from the midst of the forest, like the rumble of a storm or the distant roar of a furnace, had quite ceased. Not a bird was hopping on the grass, or visible on bough or in the sky. Not a living creature was in sight—never was stillness more complete, or silence more oppressive.

It would have been ridiculous to give way to the odd reluctance which struggled within him. Feltram had strode down the slope, and was concealed by a screen of bushes from his view. So quite alone, and full of an interest quite new to him, he set out in quest of his adventures.

CHAPTER XX

THE HAUNTED FOREST

SIR BALE MARDYKES walked in a straight line, by bush and scaur, over the undulating ground, to the blighted ash-tree; and as he approached it, its withered bough stretched more gigantically into the air, and the forest seemed to open where it pointed.

He passed it by, and in a few minutes had lost sight of it again, and was striding onward under the shadow of the forest, which already enclosed him. He was directing his march with all the care he could, in exactly that line which, according to Feltram's rule, had been laid down for him. Now and then, having, as soldiers say, taken an object, and fixed it well in his memory, he would pause and look about him.

As a boy he had never entered the wood so far; for he was under a prohibition, lest he should lose himself in its intricacies, and be benighted there. He had often heard that the wood was haunted, and that too would, when a boy, have deterred him. It was on this account that the scene was so new to him, and that he cared so often to stop and look about him. Here and there a vista opened, exhibiting the same utter desertion, and opening farther perspectives through the tall stems of the trees faintly seen in the solemn shadow. No flowers could he see, but once or twice a wood anemone, and now and then a tiny grove of wood-sorrel.

Huge oak-trees now began to mingle and show themselves more and more frequently among the other timber; and gradually the forest became a great oak wood unintruded upon by any less noble tree. Vast trunks curving outwards to the roots, and expanding again at the branches, stood like enormous columns, striking out their groining boughs, with the dark vaulting of a crypt.

As he walked under the shadow of these noble trees, suddenly his eye was struck by a strange little flower, nodding quite alone by the knotted root of one of those huge trees.

He stooped and picked it up, and as he plucked it, with a harsh scream just over his head, a large bird with heavy beating wings broke away from the midst of the branches. He could not see it, but he fancied the scream was like that of the huge mackaw whose ill-poised flight he had watched. This conjecture was but founded on the odd cry he had heard.

The flower was a curious one—a stem fine as a hair supported a little bell, that looked like a drop of blood, and never ceased trembling. He walked on, holding this in his fingers; and soon he saw another of the same odd type, then another at a shorter distance, then one a little to the right and another to the left, and farther on a little group, and at last the dark slope was all over trembling with these little bells, thicker and thicker as he descended a gentle declivity to the bank of the little brook, which flowing through the forest loses itself in the lake. The low murmur of this forest stream was almost the first sound, except the shriek of the bird that startled him a little time ago, which had disturbed the profound silence of the wood since he entered it. Mingling with the faint sound of the brook, he now heard a harsh human voice calling words at intervals, the purport of which he could not yet catch; and walking on, he saw, seated upon the grass, a strange figure, corpulent, with a great hanging nose, the whole face glowing like copper. He was dressed in a bottle-green cut-velvet coat, of the style of Queen Anne's reign,* with a dusky crimson waistcoat, both overlaid with broad and tarnished gold lace, and his silk stockings on thick swollen legs, with great buckled shoes, straddling on the grass, were rolled up over his knees to his short breeches. This ill-favoured old fellow, with a powdered wig that came down to his shoulders, had a dice-box in each hand, and was apparently playing his left against his right, and calling the throws with a hoarse cawing voice.

Raising his black piggish eyes, he roared to Sir Bale, by name, to come and sit down, raising one of his dice-boxes, and then indicating a place on the grass opposite to him.

Now Sir Bale instantly guessed that this was the man, gipsy, warlock, call him what he might, of whom he had come in search. With a strange feeling of curiosity, disgust, and awe, he drew near. He was resolved to do whatever this old man required of him, and to keep him, this time, in good humour.

Sir Bale did as he bid him, and sat down; and taking the box he presented, they began throwing turn about, with three dice, the copper-faced old man teaching him the value of the throws, as he proceeded, with many a curse and oath; and when he did not like a throw, grinning with a look of such real fury, that the master of Mardykes almost expected him to whip out his sword and prick him through as he sat before him.

After some time spent at this play, in which guineas passed now this way, now that, chucked across the intervening patch of grass, or rather moss, that served them for a green cloth, the old man roared over his shoulder,

'Drink'; and picking up a long-stemmed conical glass which Sir Bale had not observed before, he handed it over to the Baronet; and taking another in his fingers, he held it up, while a very tall slim old man, dressed in a white livery, with powdered hair and cadaverous face, which seemed to run nearly all into a long thin hooked nose, advanced with a flask in each hand. Looking at the unwieldly old man, with his heavy nose, powdered head, and all the bottle-green, crimson, and gold about him, and the long slim serving-man, with sharp beak, and white from head to heel, standing by him, Sir Bale was forcibly reminded of the great old mackaw and the long slender kite, whose colours they, after their fashion, reproduced, with something, also indescribable, of the air and character of the birds. Not standing on ceremony, the old fellow held up his own glass first, which the white lackey filled from the flask, and then he filled Sir Bale's glass.

It was a large glass, and might have held about half a pint; and the liquor with which the servant filled it was something of the colour of an opal, and circles of purple and gold seemed to be spreading continually

outward from the centre, and running inward from the rim, and crossing one another, so as to form a beautiful rippling net-work.

'I drink to your better luck next time,' said the old man, lifting his
glass high, and winking with one eye, and leering knowingly with the
other; 'and you know what I mean.'

Sir Bale put the liquor to his lips. Wine? Whatever it was, never had
he tasted so delicious a flavour. He drained it to the bottom, and placing
it on the grass beside him, and looking again at the old dicer, who was
also setting down his glass, he saw, for the first time, the graceful figure
of a young woman seated on the grass. She was dressed in deep mourning, had a black hood carelessly over her head, and, strangely, wore
a black mask, such as are used at masquerades. So much of her throat
and chin as he could see were beautifully white; and there was a prettiness in her air and figure which made him think what a beautiful creature she in all likelihood was. She was reclining slightly against the
burly man in bottle-green and gold, and her arm was round his neck,
and her slender white hand showed itself over his shoulders.

'Ho! my little Geaiette,' cried the old fellow hoarsely; 'it will be time
that you and I should get home.—So, Bale Mardykes, I have nothing to
object to you this time; you've crossed the lake, and you've played with
me and won and lost, and drank your glass like a jolly devil, and now we
know one another; and an acquaintance is made that will last. I'll let you
go, and you'll come when I want you. And now you'll want to know what
horse will win next month at Rindermere races.—Whisper me, lass,
and I'll tell him.'

So her lips, under the black curtain, crept close to his ear, and she
whispered.

'It will be Rainbow,' said the old man harshly. 'And now make your
best speed out of the forest, or I'll set my black dogs at your heels, ho,
ho, ho! and we may chance to pull you down. Away!'

He cried this last order with a look so black and so savage a shake of
his huge fist, that Sir Bale, merely making his general bow to the group,
clapped his hat on his head, and hastily began his retreat; but the same
discordant voice yelled after him:

'You'll want that, you fool; pick it up.' And there came hurtling after
him a great leather bag, stained, and stuffed with a heavy burden, and
bounding by him it stopped with a little wheel that brought it exactly
before his feet.

He picked it up, and found it heavy.

Turning about to make his acknowledgments, he saw the two persons
in full retreat; the profane old scoundrel in the bottle-green limping

and stumbling, yet bowling along at a wonderful rate, with many a jerk and reel, and the slender lady in black gliding away by his side into the inner depths of the forest.

So Sir Bale, with a strange chill, and again in utter solitude, pursued his retreat, with his burden, at a swifter pace, and after an hour or so had recovered the point where he had entered the forest, and passing by the druidic stone and the mighty oak, saw down the glen at his right, standing by the edge of the lake, Philip Feltram, close to the bow of the boat.

CHAPTER XXI

RINDERMERE

FELTRAM looked grim and agitated when Sir Bale came up to him, as he stood on the flat stone by which the boat was moored.

'You found him?' said he.

'Yes.'

'And the lady in black was there?'

'She was.'

'And you played with him?'

'Yes.'

'And what is that in your hand?'

'A bag of something, I fancy money; it is heavy; he threw it after me. We shall see just now; let us get away.'

'He gave you some of his wine to drink?' said Feltram, looking darkly in his face; but there was a laugh in his eyes.

'Yes; of course I drank it; my object was to please him.'

'To be sure.'

The faint wind that carried them across the lake had quite subsided by the time they had reached the side where they now were.

There was now not wind enough to fill the sail, and it was already evening.

'Give me an oar; we can pull her over in little more than an hour,' said Sir Bale; 'only let us get away.'

He got into the boat, sat down, and placed the leather bag with its heavy freightage at his feet, and took an oar. Feltram loosed the rope and shoved the boat off; and taking his seat also, they began to pull together, without another word, until, in about ten minutes, they had got a considerable way off the Cloostedd shore.

The leather bag was too clumsy a burden to conceal; besides, Feltram knew all about the transaction, and Sir Bale had no need to make a secret. The bag was old and soiled, and tied about the 'neck' with a long leather thong, and it seemed to have been sealed with red wax, fragments of which were still sticking to it.

He got it open, and found it full of guineas.

'Halt!' cried Sir Bale, delighted, for he had half apprehended a trick upon his hopes; 'gold it is, and a lot of it, by Jove!'

Feltram did not seem to take the slightest interest in the matter. Sulkily and drowsily he was leaning with his elbow on his knee, and it seemed thinking of something far away. Sir Bale could not wait to count them any longer. He reckoned them on the bench, and found two thousand.

It took some time; and when he had got them back into the leather bag, and tied them up again, Feltram, with a sudden start, said sharply,

'Come, take your oar—unless you like the lake by night; and see, there will soon be a wind up from Golden Friars!'

He cast a wild look towards Mardykes Hall and Snakes Island, and applying himself to his oar, told Sir Bale to take his also; and nothing loath, the Baronet did so.

It was slow work, for the boat was not built for speed; and by the time they had got about midway, the sun went down, and twilight and the melancholy flush of the sunset tints were upon the lake and fells.

'Ho! here comes the breeze—up from Golden Friars,' said Feltram; 'we shall have enough to fill the sails now. If you don't fear spirits and Snakes Island, it is all the better for us it should blow from that point. If it blew from Mardykes now, it would be a stiff pull for you and me to get this tub home.'

Talking as if to himself, and laughing low, he adjusted the sail and took the tiller, and so, yielding to the rising breeze, the boat glided slowly toward still distant Mardykes Hall.

The moon came out, and the shore grew misty, and the towering fells rose like sheeted giants; and leaning on the gunwale of the boat, Sir Bale, with the rush and gurgle of the water on the boat's side sounding faintly in his ear, thought of his day's adventure, which seemed to him like a dream—incredible but for the heavy bag that lay between his feet.

As they passed Snakes Island, a little mist, like a fragment of a fog, seemed to drift with them, and Sir Bale fancied that whenever it came near the boat's side she made a dip, as if strained toward the water; and Feltram always put out his hand, as if waving it from him, and the mist seemed to obey the gesture; but returned again and again, and the same thing always happened.

It was three weeks after, that Sir Bale, sitting up in his bed, very pale and wan, with his silk night-cap nodding on one side, and his thin hand extended on the coverlet, where the doctor had been feeling his pulse, in his darkened room, related all the wonders of this day to Doctor Torvey. The doctor had attended him through a fever which followed immediately upon his visit to Cloostedd.

'And, my dear sir, by Jupiter, can you really believe all that delirium to be sober fact?' said the doctor, sitting by the bedside, and actually laughing.

'I can't help believing it, because I can't distinguish in any way between all that and everything else that happened, and which I must believe. And, except that this is more wonderful, I can find no reason to reject it, that does not as well apply to all the rest.'

'Come, come, my dear sir, this will never do—nothing is more common. These illusions accompanying fever frequently antedate the attack, and the man is actually raving before he knows he is ill.'

'But what do you make of that bag of gold?'

'Some one has lent it. You had better ask all about it of Feltram when you can see him; for in speaking to me he seemed to know all about it, and certainly did not seem to think the matter at all out of the commonplace. It is just like that fisherman's story, about the hand that drew Feltram into the water on the night he was nearly drowned. Every one can see what that was. Why of course it was simply the reflection of his own hand in the water, in that vivid lightning. When you have been out a little and have gained strength you will shake off these dreams.'

'I should not wonder,' said Sir Bale.

It is not to be supposed that Sir Bale reported all that was in his memory respecting his strange vision, if such it was, at Cloostedd. He made a selection of the incidents, and threw over the whole adventure an entirely accidental character, and described the money which the old man had thrown to him as amounting to a purse of five guineas, and mentioned nothing of the passages which bore on the coming race.

Good Doctor Torvey, therefore, reported only that Sir Bale's delirium had left two or three illusions sticking in his memory.

But if they were illusions, they survived the event of his recovery, and remained impressed on his memory with the sharpness of very recent and accurately observed fact.

He was resolved on going to the races of Rindermere, where, having in his possession so weighty a guarantee as the leather purse, he was determined to stake it all boldly on Rainbow—against which horse he was glad to hear there were very heavy odds.

The race came off. One horse was scratched, another bolted, the rider of a third turned out to have lost a buckle and three half-pence, and so was an ounce and a half under weight, a fourth knocked down the post near Rinderness churchyard, and was held to have done it with his left instead of his right knee, and so had run at the wrong side. The result was that Rainbow came in first, and I should be afraid to say how much Sir Bale won. It was a sum that paid off a heavy debt, and left his affairs in a much more manageable state.

From this time Sir Bale prospered. He visited Cloostedd no more; but Feltram often crossed to that lonely shore as heretofore, and it is believed conveyed to him messages which guided his betting. One thing is certain, his luck never deserted him. His debts disappeared; and his love of Continental life seemed to have departed. He became content with Mardykes Hall, laid out money on it, and although he never again cared to cross the lake, he seemed to like the scenery.

In some respects, however, he lived exactly the same odd and unpopular life. He saw no one at Mardykes Hall. He practised a very strict reserve. The neighbours laughed at and disliked him, and he was voted, whenever any accidental contact arose, a very disagreeable man; and he had a shrewd and ready sarcasm that made them afraid of him, and himself more disliked.

Odd rumours prevailed also about his household. It was said that his old relations with Philip Feltram had become reversed; and that he was as meek as a mouse, and Feltram the bully now. It was also said that Mrs Julaper had, one Sunday evening when she drank tea at the Vicar's, told his good lady very mysteriously, and with many charges of secrecy, that Sir Bale was none the better of his late-found wealth; that he had a load upon his spirits, that he was afraid of Feltram, and so was every one else, more or less, in the house; that he was either mad or worse; and that it was an eerie dwelling, and strange company, and she should be glad herself of a change.

Good Mrs Bedel told her friend Mrs Torvey; and all Golden Friars heard all this, and a good deal more, in an incredibly short time.

All kinds of rumours now prevailed in Golden Friars, connecting Sir Bale's successes on the turf with some mysterious doings in Cloostedd Forest. Philip Feltram laughed when he heard these stories—especially when he heard the story that a supernatural personage had lent the Baronet a purse full of money.

'You should not talk to Doctor Torvey so, sir,' said he grimly; 'he's the greatest tattler in the town. It was old Farmer Trebeck, who could buy and sell us all down here, who lent that money. Partly from good-will, but not without acknowledgment. He has my hand for the first, not worth much, and yours to a bond for the two thousand guineas you brought home with you. It seems strange you should not remember that venerable and kind old farmer whom you talked with so long that day. His grandson, who expects to stand well in his will, being a trainer in Lord Varney's stables, has sometimes a wrinkle to give, and he is the source of your information.'

'By Jove, I must be a bit mad, then, that's all,' said Sir Bale, with a smile and a shrug.

Philip Feltram moped about the house, and did precisely what he pleased. The change which had taken place in him became more and more pronounced. Dark and stern he always looked, and often malignant. He was like a man possessed of one evil thought which never left him.

There was, besides, the good old Gothic superstition of a bargain or sale of the Baronet's soul to the arch-fiend. This was, of course, very cautiously whispered in a place where he had influence. It was only a coarser and directer version of a suspicion, that in a more credulous generation penetrated a level of society quite exempt from such follies in our day.

One evening at dusk, Sir Bale, sitting after his dinner in his window, saw the tall figure of Feltram, like a dark streak, standing movelessly by the lake. An unpleasant feeling thrilled him, and then an impatience. He got up, and having primed himself with two glasses of brandy, walked down to the edge of the lake, and placed himself beside Feltram.

'Looking down from the window,' said he, nerved with his Dutch courage, 'and seeing you standing like a post, do you know what I began to think of?'

Feltram looked at him, but answered nothing.

'I began to think of taking a wife—*marrying*.'

Feltram nodded. The announcement had not produced the least effect.

'Why the devil will you make me so uncomfortable! can't you be like yourself—what you *were*, I mean? I won't go on living here alone with you. I'll take a wife, I tell you. I'll choose a good church-going woman, that will have every man, woman, and child in the house on their marrowbones twice a day, morning and evening, and three times on Sundays. How will you like that?'

'Yes, you will be married,' said Feltram, with a quiet decision which chilled Sir Bale, for he had by no means made up his mind to that desperate step.

Feltram slowly walked away, and that conversation ended.

Now an odd thing happened about this time. There was a family of Feltram—county genealogists could show how related to the vanished family of Cloostedd—living at that time on their estate not far from Carlisle. Three co-heiresses now represented it. They were great beauties—the belles of their county in their day.

One was married to Sir Oliver Haworth of Haworth, a great family in those times. He was a knight of the shire, and had refused a baronet-age, and, it was said, had his eye on a peerage. The other sister was married to Sir William Walsingham, a wealthy baronet; and the third and youngest, Miss Janet, was still unmarried, and at home at Cloudesly Hall, where her aunt, Lady Harbottle, lived with her, and made a dig-nified chaperon.

Now it so fell out that Sir Bale, having business at Carlisle, and knowing old Lady Harbottle, paid his respects at Cloudesly Hall; and being no less than five-and-forty years of age, was, for the first time in his life, seriously in love.

Miss Janet was extremely pretty—a fair beauty with brilliant red lips and large blue eyes, and ever so many pretty dimples when she talked and smiled. It was odd, but not perhaps against the course of nature, that a man, though so old as he, and quite *blasé*, should fall at last under that fascination.

But what are we to say of the strange infatuation of the young lady? No one could tell why she liked him. It was a craze. Her family were against it, her intimates, her old nurse—all would not do; and the odd-est thing was, that he seemed to take no pains to please her. The end of this strange courtship was that he married her; and she came home to Mardykes Hall, determined to please everybody, and to be the happiest woman in England.

With her came a female cousin, a good deal her senior, past thirty,—Gertrude Mainyard, pale and sad, but very gentle, and with all the prettiness that can belong to her years.

This young lady has a romance. Her hero is far away in India; and she, content to await his uncertain return with means to accomplish the hope of their lives, in that frail chance has long embarked all the pur-pose and love of her life.

When Lady Mardykes came home, a new leaf was, as the phrase is, turned over. The neighbours and all the country people were willing to give the Hall a new trial. There was visiting and returning of visits; and young Lady Mardykes was liked and admired. It could not indeed have been otherwise. But here the improvement in the relations of Mardykes Hall with other homes ceased. On one excuse or another Sir Bale postponed or evaded the hospitalities which establish intimacies. Some people said he was jealous of his young and beautiful wife. But for the most part his reserve was set down to the old inhospitable cause, some ungenial defect in his character; and in a little time the tramp of horses and roll of carriage-wheels were seldom heard up or down the broad avenue of Mardykes Hall.

Sir Bale liked this seclusion; and his wife, 'so infatuated with her idolatry of that graceless old man', as surrounding young ladies said, that she was well content to forego the society of the county people for a less interrupted enjoyment of that of her husband. 'What she could see in him' to interest or amuse her so, that for his sake she was willing to be 'buried alive in that lonely place', the same critics were perpetually wondering.

A year and more passed thus; for the young wife, happily—*very* happily indeed, had it not been for one topic on which she and her husband could not agree. This was Philip Feltram; and an odd quarrel it was.

CHAPTER XXII
SIR BALE IS FRIGHTENED

To Feltram she had conceived, at first sight, a horror. It was not a mere antipathy; fear mingled largely in it. Although she did not see him often, this restless dread grew upon her so, that she urged his dismissal upon Sir Bale, offering to provide herself for him a handsome annuity, charged on that part of her property which, by her marriage-settlement, had remained in her power. There was a time when Sir Bale was only too anxious to get rid of him. But that was changed now. Nothing could now induce the Baronet to part with him. He at first evaded and resisted quietly. But, urged with a perseverance to which he was unused, he at last broke into fury that appalled her, and swore that if he was worried more upon the subject, he would leave her and the country, and see neither again. This exhibition of violence affrighted her all the more by reason of the contrast; for up to this he had been an uxorious husband. Lady Mardykes was in hysterics, and thoroughly frightened, and remained in her room for two or three days. Sir Bale went up to London about business, and was not home for more than a week. This was the first little squall that disturbed the serenity of their sky.

This point, therefore, was settled; but soon there came other things to sadden Lady Mardykes. There occurred a little incident, soon after

Sir Bale's return from London, which recalled the topic on which they had so nearly quarrelled.

Sir Bale had a dressing-room, remote from the bedrooms, in which he sat and read and sometimes smoked. One night, after the house was all quiet, the Baronet being still up, the bell of this dressing-room rang long and furiously. It was such a peal as a person in extreme terror might ring. Lady Mardykes, with her maid in her room, heard it; and in great alarm she ran in her dressing-gown down the gallery to Sir Bale's room. Mallard the butler had already arrived, and was striving to force the door, which was secured. It gave way just as she reached it, and she rushed through.

Sir Bale was standing with the bell-rope in his hand, in the extremest agitation, looking like a ghost; and Philip Feltram was sitting in his chair, with a dark smile fixed upon him. For a minute she thought he had attempted to assassinate his master. She could not otherwise account for the scene.

There had been nothing of the kind, however; as her husband assured her again and again, as she lay sobbing on his breast, with her arms about his neck.

'To her dying hour,' she afterwards said to her cousin, 'she never could forget the dreadful look in Feltram's face.'

No explanation of that scene did she ever obtain from Sir Bale, nor any clue to the cause of the agony that was so powerfully expressed in his countenance. Thus much only she learned from him, that Feltram had sought that interview for the purpose of announcing his departure, which was to take place within the year.

'You are not sorry to hear that. But if you knew all, you might. Let the curse fly where it may, it will come back to roost. So, darling, let us discuss him no more. Your wish is granted, *dis iratis.*'*

Some crisis, in this interview, seemed to have occurred in the relations between Sir Bale and Feltram. Henceforward they seldom exchanged a word; and when they did speak, it was coldly and shortly, like men who were nearly strangers.

One day in the courtyard, Sir Bale, seeing Feltram leaning upon the parapet that overlooks the lake, approached him, and said in a low tone,

'I've been thinking, if we—that is, *I*—do owe that money to old Trebeck, it is high time I should pay it. I was ill, and had lost my head at the time; but it turned out luckily, and it ought to be paid. I don't like the idea of a bond turning up, and a lot of interest.'

'The old fellow meant it for a present. He is richer than you are; he wished to give the family a lift. He has destroyed the bond, I believe, and in no case will he take payment.'

'No fellow has a right to force his money on another,' answered Sir Bale. 'I never asked him. Besides, as you know, I was not really myself, and the whole thing seems to me quite different from what you say it was; and, so far as my brain is concerned, it was all a phantasmagoria;* but, as you say, it was he.'

'Every man is accountable for what he intends and for what he *thinks* he does,' said Feltram cynically.

'Well, I'm accountable for dealing with that wicked old dicer I *thought* I saw—isn't that it? But I must pay old Trebeck all the same, since the money was his. Can you manage a meeting?'

'Look down there. Old Trebeck has just landed; he will sleep to-night at the George and Dragon, to meet his cattle in the morning at Golden Friars fair. You can speak to him yourself.'

So saying, Feltram glided away, leaving to Sir Bale the task of opening the matter to the wealthy farmer of Cloostedd Fells.

A broad flight of steps leads down from the courtyard to the level of the jetty at the lake; and Sir Bale descended, and accosted the venerable farmer, who was bluff, honest, and as frank as a man can be who speaks a *patois* which hardly a living man but himself can understand.

Sir Bale asked him to come to the Hall and take luncheon; but Trebeck was in haste. Cattle had arrived which he wanted to look at, and a pony awaited him on the road hard by to Golden Friars; and the old fellow must mount and away.

Then Sir Bale, laying his hand upon his arm in a manner that was at once lofty and affectionate, told in his ears the subject on which he wished to be understood.

The old farmer looked hard at him, and shook his head and laughed in a way that would have been insupportable in a house, and told him, 'I hev narra bond o' thoine, mon.'

'I know how that is; so does Philip Feltram.'

'Well?'

'Well, I must replace the money.'

The old man laughed again, and in his outlandish dialect told him to wait till he asked him.

Sir Bale pressed it, but the old fellow put it off with outlandish banter; and as the Baronet grew testy, the farmer only waxed more and more hilarious, and at last, mounting his shaggy pony, rode off, still laughing, at a canter to Golden Friars; and when he reached Golden Friars, and got into the hall of the George and Dragon, he asked Richard Turnbull with a chuckle if he ever knew a man refuse an offer of money, or a man want to pay who did not owe; and inquired whether the Squire down at Mardykes Hall mightn't be a bit 'wrang in t' garrets'. All this, however, other people said, was intended merely to conceal the fact that he really had, through sheer loyalty, lent the money, or rather bestowed it, thinking the old family in jeopardy, and meaning a gift, was determined to hear no more about it. I can't say; I only know people held, some by one interpretation, some by another.

As the caterpillar sickens and changes its hue when it is about to undergo its transmutation, so an odd change took place in Feltram. He grew even more silent and morose; he seemed always in an agitation and a secret rage. He used to walk through the woodlands on the slopes of the fells above Mardykes, muttering to himself, picking up the rotten sticks with which the ground was strewn, breaking them in his hands, and hurling them from him, and stamping on the earth as he paced up and down.

One night a thunder-storm came on, the wind blowing gently up from Golden Friars. It was a night black as pitch, illuminated only by the intermittent glare of the lightning. At the foot of the stairs Sir Bale met Feltram, whom he had not seen for some days. He had his cloak and hat on.

'I am going to Cloostedd to-night,' he said; 'and if all is as I expect, I sha'n't return. We remember all, you and I.' And he nodded and walked down the passage.

Sir Bale knew that a crisis had happened in his own life. He felt faint and ill, and returned to the room where he had been sitting. Throughout that melancholy night he did not go to his bed.

In the morning he learned that Marlyn, who had been out late, saw Feltram get the boat off, and sail towards the other side. The night was so dark that he could only see him start; but the wind was light and coming up the lake, so that without a tack he could easily make the other side.

Feltram did not return. The boat was found fast to the ring at Cloostedd landing-place.

Lady Mardykes was relieved, and for a time was happier than ever. It was different with Sir Bale; and afterwards her sky grew dark also.

CHAPTER XXIII

A LADY IN BLACK

SHORTLY after this, there arrived at the George and Dragon a stranger. He was a man somewhat past forty, embrowned by distant travel, and, his years considered, wonderfully good-looking. He had good eyes; his dark-brown hair had no sprinkling of gray in it; and his kindly smile showed very white and even teeth. He made many inquiries about neighbours, especially respecting Mardykes Hall; and the answers seemed to interest him profoundly. He inquired after Philip Feltram, and shed tears when he heard that he was no longer at Mardykes Hall, and that Trebeck or other friends could give him no tidings of him.

And then he asked Richard Turnbull to show him to a quiet room; and then, taking the honest fellow by the hand, he said,

'Mr Turnbull, don't you know me?'

'No, sir,' said the host of the George and Dragon, after a puzzled stare, 'I can't say I do, sir.'

The stranger smiled a little sadly, and shook his head; and with a little laugh, still holding his hand in a very friendly way, he said,

'I should have known you anywhere, Mr Turnbull—anywhere on earth or water. Had you turned up on the Himalayas, or in a junk on the Canton river, or as a dervish in the mosque of St Sophia, I should have recognized my old friend, and asked what news from Golden Friars. But of course I'm changed. You were a little my senior; and one advantage among many you have over your juniors is that you don't change as we do. I have played many a game of hand-ball in the inn-yard of the George, Mr Turnbull. You often wagered a pot of ale on my play; you used to say I'd make the best player of fives, and the best singer of a song, within ten miles round the meer. You used to have me behind the bar when I was a boy, with more of an appetite than I have now. I was then at Mardykes Hall, and used to go back in old Marlyn's boat. Is old Marlyn still alive?'

'Ay, that—he—is,' said Turnbull slowly, as he eyed the stranger again very carefully. 'I don't know who you can be, sir, unless you are—the boy—William Feltram. La! he was seven or eight years younger than Philip. But, lawk!—Well—By Jen, and *be* you Willie Feltram? But no, you can't!'

'Ay, Mr Turnbull, that very boy—Willie Feltram—even he, and no other; and now you'll shake hands with me, not so formally, but like an old friend.'

'Ay, that I will,' said honest Richard Turnbull, with a great smile, and a hearty grasp of his guest's hand; and they both laughed together, and the younger man's eyes, for he was an affectionate fool, filled up with tears.

'And I want you to tell me this,' said William, after they had talked a little quietly, 'now that there is no one to interrupt us, what has become of my brother Philip? I heard from a friend an account of his health that has caused me unspeakable anxiety.'

'His health was not bad; no, he was a hardy lad, and liked a walk over the fells, or a pull on the lake; but he was a bit daft, every one said, and a changed man; and, in troth, they say the air o' Mardykes don't agree with every one, no more than him. But that's a tale that's neither here nor there.'

'Yes,' said William, 'that was what they told me—his mind affected. God help and guard us! I have been unhappy ever since; and if I only knew it was well with poor Philip, I think I should be too happy. And where is Philip now?'

'He crossed the lake one night, having took leave of Sir Bale. They thought he was going to old Trebeck's up the Fells. He likes the Feltrams, and likes the folk at Mardykes Hall—though those two familiars was not always o'er kind to one another. But Trebeck seed nowt o' him, nor no one else; and what has gone wi' him none can tell.'

'I heard that also,' said William with a deep sigh. 'But I hoped it had been cleared up by now, and something happier been known of the poor fellow by this time. I'd give a great deal to know—I don't know what I *would* not give to know—I'm so unhappy about him. And now, my good old friend, tell your people to get me a chaise, for I must go to Mardykes Hall; and, first, let me have a room to dress in.'

At Mardykes Hall a pale and pretty lady was looking out, alone, from the stone-shafted drawing-room window across the courtyard and the balustrade, on which stood many a great stone chalice with flowers, whose leaves were half shed and gone with the winds—emblem of her hopes. The solemn melancholy of the towering fells, the ripple of the lonely lake, deepened her sadness.

The unwonted sound of carriage-wheels awoke her from her reverie.

Before the chaise reached the steps, a hand from its window had seized the handle, the door was thrown open, and William Feltram jumped out.

She was in the hall, she knew not how; and, with a wild scream and a sob, she threw herself into his arms.

Here at last was an end of the long waiting, the dejection which had reached almost the point of despair. And like two rescued from shipwreck, they clung together in an agony of happiness.

William had come back with no very splendid fortune. It was enough, and only enough, to enable them to marry. Prudent people would have thought it, very likely, too little. But he was now home in England, with health unimpaired by his long sojourn in the East, and with intelligence and energies improved by the discipline of his arduous struggle with fortune. He reckoned, therefore, upon one way or other adding something to their income; and he knew that a few hundreds a year would make them happier than hundreds of thousands could other people.

It was five years since they had parted in France, where a journey of importance to the Indian firm, whose right hand he was, had brought him.

The refined tastes that are supposed to accompany gentle blood, his love of art, his talent for music and drawing, had accidentally attracted the attention of the little travelling-party which old Lady Harbottle chaperoned. Miss Janet, now Lady Mardykes, learning that his name was Feltram, made inquiry through a common friend, and learned what interested her still more about him. It ended in an acquaintance, which his manly and gentle nature and his entertaining qualities soon improved into an intimacy.

Feltram had chosen to work his own way, being proud, and also prosperous enough to prevent his pride, in this respect, from being placed under too severe a pressure of temptation. He heard not from but of his brother, through a friend in London, and more lately from Gertrude, whose account of him was sad and even alarming.

When Lady Mardykes came in, her delight knew no bounds. She had already formed a plan for their future, and was not to be put off—William Feltram was to take the great grazing farm that belonged to the Mardykes estate; or, if he preferred it, to farm it for her, sharing the profits. She wanted something to interest her, and this was just the thing. It was hardly half-a-mile away, up the lake, and there was such a comfortable house and garden, and she and Gertrude could be as much together as ever almost; and, in fact, Gertrude and her husband could be nearly always at Mardykes Hall.

So eager and entreating was she, that there was no escape. The plan was adopted immediately on their marriage, and no happier neighbours for a time were ever known.

But was Lady Mardykes content? was she even exempt from that heartache which each mortal thinks he has all to himself? The longing of her life was for children; and again and again had her hopes been disappointed.

One tiny pretty little baby indeed was born, and lived for two years, and then died; and none had come to supply its place and break the childless silence of the great old nursery. That was her sorrow; a greater one than men can understand.

Another source of grief was this: that Sir Bale Mardykes conceived a dislike to William Feltram that was unaccountable. At first suppressed, it betrayed itself negatively only; but with time it increased; and in the end the Baronet made little secret of his wish to get rid of him. Many and ingenious were the annoyances he contrived; and at last he told his wife plainly that he wished William Feltram to find some other abode for himself.

Lady Mardykes pleaded earnestly, and even with tears; for if Gertrude were to leave the neighbourhood, she well knew how utterly solitary her own life would become.

Sir Bale at last vouchsafed some little light as to his motives. There was an old story, he told her, that his estate would go to a Feltram. He had an instinctive distrust of that family. It was a feeling not given him for nothing; it might be the means of defeating their plotting and strategy. Old Trebeck, he fancied, had a finger in it. Philip Feltram had told him that Mardykes was to pass away to a Feltram. Well, they might conspire; but he would take what care he could that the estate should not be stolen from his family. He did not want his wife stript of her jointure, or his children, if he had any, left without bread.

All this sounded very like madness; but the idea was first propounded by Philip Feltram. His own jealousy was at bottom founded on a superstition which he would not avow and could hardly define. He bitterly blamed himself for having permitted William Feltram to place himself where he was.

In the midst of these annoyances William Feltram was seriously thinking of throwing up the farm, and seeking similar occupation somewhere else.

One day, walking alone in the thick wood that skirts the lake near his farm, he was discussing this problem with himself; and every now and then he repeated his question, 'Shall I throw it up, and give him the lease back if he likes?' On a sudden he heard a voice near him say:

'Hold it, you fool!—hold hard, you fool!—hold it, you fool!'

The situation being lonely, he was utterly puzzled to account for the interruption, until on a sudden a huge parrot, green, crimson, and yellow, plunged from among the boughs over his head to the ground, and partly flying, and partly hopping and tumbling along, got lamely, but swiftly, out of sight among the thick underwood; and he could neither start it nor hear it any more. The interruption reminded him of that which befell Robinson Crusoe.* It was more singular, however; for he owned no such bird; and its strangeness impressed the omen all the more.

He related it when he got home to his wife; and as people when living a solitary life, and also suffering, are prone to superstition, she did not laugh at the adventure, as in a healthier state of spirits, I suppose, she would.

They continued, however, to discuss the question together; and all the more industriously as a farm of the same kind, only some fifteen miles away, was now offered to all bidders, under another landlord. Gertrude, who felt Sir Bale's unkindness all the more that she was a distant cousin of his, as it had proved on comparing notes, was very strong in favour of the change, and had been urging it with true feminine ingenuity and persistence upon her husband. A very singular dream rather damped her ardour, however, and it appeared thus:

She had gone to her bed full of this subject; and she thought, although she could not remember having done so, had fallen asleep. She was still thinking, as she had been all the day, about leaving the farm. It seemed to her that she was quite awake, and a candle burning all the time in the room, awaiting the return of her husband, who was away at the fair near Haworth; she saw the interior of the room distinctly. It was a sultry night, and a little bit of the window was raised. A very slight sound in that direction attracted her attention; and to her surprise she saw a jay hop upon the window-sill, and into the room.

Up sat Gertrude, surprised and a little startled at the visit of so large a bird, without presence of mind for the moment even to frighten it away, and staring at it, as they say, with all her eyes. A sofa stood at the foot of the bed; and under this the bird swiftly hopped. She extended her hand now to take the bell-rope at the left side of the bed, and in doing so displaced the curtains, which were open only at the foot. She was amazed there to see a lady dressed entirely in black, and with the old-fashioned hood over her head. She was young and pretty, and looked kindly at her, but with now and then the slight contraction of lips and eyebrows that indicates pain. This little twitching was momentary, and recurred, it seemed, about once or twice in a minute.

How it was that she was not frightened on seeing this lady, standing like an old friend at her bedside, she could not afterwards understand. Some influence besides the kindness of her look prevented any sensation of terror at the time. With a very white hand the young lady held a white handkerchief pressed to her bosom at the top of her bodice.

'Who are you?' asked Gertrude.

'I am a kinswoman, although you don't know me; and I have come to tell you that you must not leave Faxwell' (the name of the place) 'or Janet. Abide your fortune here. If you go, I will go with you; and I can make you fear me.'

Her voice was very distinct, but also very faint, with something undulatory in it,* that seemed to enter Gertrude's head rather than her ear.

Saying this she smiled horribly, and, lifting her handkerchief, disclosed for a moment a great wound in her breast, in which Gertrude saw the head of a snake writhing.

Hereupon she uttered a wild scream of terror, and, diving under the bed-clothes, remained more dead than alive there, until her maid, alarmed by her cry, came in, and having searched the room, and shut the window at her desire, did all in her power to comfort her.

If this was a nightmare, and embodied only by a form of expression which in some states belongs to the imagination, a leading idea in the controversy in which her mind had long been employed, it had at least the effect of deciding her against leaving Faxwell. And so that point was settled; and unpleasant relations continued between the tenants of the farm and the master of Mardykes Hall.

To Lady Mardykes all this was very painful, although Sir Bale did not insist upon making a separation between his wife and her cousin. But to Mardykes Hall that cousin came no more. Even Lady Mardykes thought it better to see her at Faxwell than to risk a meeting in the temper in which Sir Bale then was. And thus several years passed.

No tidings of Philip Feltram were heard; and, in fact, none ever reached that part of the world; and if it had not been highly improbable that he could have drowned himself in the lake without his body sooner or later having risen to the surface, it would have been concluded that he had either accidentally or by design made away with himself in its waters.

Over Mardykes Hall there was a gloom—no sound of children's voices was heard there, and even the hope of that merry advent had died out.

This disappointment had no doubt helped to fix in Sir Bale's mind the idea of the insecurity of his property, and the morbid fancy that William Feltram and old Trebeck were conspiring to seize it; than which, I need hardly say, no imagination more insane could have fixed itself in his mind.

In other things, however, Sir Bale was shrewd and sharp, a clear and rapid man of business, and although this was a strange whim, it was not so unnatural in a man who was by nature so prone to suspicion as Sir Bale Mardykes.

During the years, now seven, that had elapsed since the marriage of Sir Bale and Miss Janet Feltram, there had happened but one event, except the death of their only child, to place them in mourning. That was the decease of Sir William Walsingham, the husband of Lady

Mardykes' sister. She now lived in a handsome old dower-house at Islington, and being wealthy made, now and then, an excursion to Mardykes Hall, in which she was sometimes accompanied by her sister Lady Haworth. Sir Oliver being a Parliament man was much in London and deep in politics and intrigue, and subject, as convivial rogues are, to occasional hard hits from the gout.

But change and separation had made no alteration in these ladies' mutual affections, and no three sisters were ever more attached.

Was Lady Mardykes happy with her lord? A woman so gentle and loving as she, is a happy wife with any husband who is not an absolute brute. There must have been, I suppose, some good about Sir Bale. His wife was certainly deeply attached to him. She admired his wisdom, and feared his inflexible will, and altogether made of him a domestic idol. To acquire this enviable position, I suspect there must be something not essentially disagreeable about a man. At all events, what her neighbours good-naturedly termed her infatuation continued, and indeed rather improved by time.

CHAPTER XXIV

AN OLD PORTRAIT

SIR BALE—whom some people remembered a gay and convivial man, not to say a profligate one—had grown to be a very gloomy man indeed. There was something weighing upon his mind; and I daresay some of the good gossips of Golden Friars, had there been any materials for such a case, would have believed that Sir Bale had murdered Philip Feltram, and was now the victim of the worm and fire of remorse.*

The gloom of the master of the house made his very servants gloomy, and the house itself looked sombre, as if it had been startled with strange and dismal sights.

Lady Mardykes was something of an artist. She had lighted lately, in an out-of-the-way room, upon a dozen or more old portraits. Several of these were full-lengths; and she was—with the help of her maid, both in long aprons, amid sponges and basins, soft handkerchiefs and varnish-pots and brushes—busy in removing the dust and smoke-stains, and in laying-on the varnish, which brought out the colouring, and made the transparent shadows yield up their long-buried treasures of finished detail.

Against the wall stood a full-length portrait as Sir Bale entered the room; having, for a wonder, a word to say to his wife.

'O,' said the pretty lady, turning to him in her apron, and with her brush in her hand, 'we are in such a pickle, Munnings and I, we have been cleaning these old pictures. Mrs Julaper says they are the pictures that came from Cloostedd Hall long ago. They were buried in dust in the dark room in the clock-tower. Here is such a characteristic one. It has a long powdered wig—George the First or Second,* I don't know which—and such a combination of colours, and such a face. It seems starting out of the canvas, and all but speaks. Do look; that is, I mean, Bale, if you can spare time.'

Sir Bale abstractedly drew near, and looked over his wife's shoulder on the full-length portrait that stood before him; and as he did so a strange expression for a moment passed over his face.

The picture represented a man of swarthy countenance, with signs of the bottle glowing through the dark skin; small fierce pig eyes, a rather flat pendulous nose, and a grim forbidding mouth, with a large mole a little above it. On the head hung one of those full-bottomed powdered wigs that look like a cloud of cotton-wadding; a lace cravat was about his neck; he wore short black-velvet breeches with stockings rolled over them, a bottle-green coat of cut velvet, and a crimson waist-coat with long flaps; coat and waistcoat both heavily laced with gold. He wore a sword, and leaned upon a crutch-handled cane, and his figure and aspect indicated a swollen and gouty state. He could not be far from sixty. There was uncommon force in this fierce and forbidding-looking portrait. Lady Mardykes said,

'What wonderful dresses they wore! How like a fine magic-lantern figure he looks! What gorgeous colouring! it is like the plumage of a mackaw; and what a claw his hand is! and that huge broken beak of a nose! Isn't he like a wicked old mackaw?'

'Where did you find that?' said Sir Bale.

Surprised at his tone, she looked round, and was still more surprised at his looks.

'I told you, dear Bale, I found them in the clock-tower. I hope I did right; it was not wrong bringing them here? I ought to have asked. Are you vexed, Bale?'

'Vexed! not I. I only wish it was in the fire. I must have seen that picture when I was a child. I hate to look at it. I raved about it once, when I was ill. I don't know who it is; I don't remember when I saw it. I wish you'd tell them to burn it.'

'It is one of the Feltrams,' she answered. '"Sir Hugh Feltram" is on the frame at the foot; and old Mrs Julaper says he was the father of the unhappy lady who was said to have been drowned near Snakes Island.'

'Well, suppose he is; there's nothing interesting in that. It is a disgusting picture. I connect it with my illness; and I think it is the kind of thing that would make any one half mad, if they only looked at it often enough. Tell them to burn it; and come away, come to the next room; I can't say what I want here.'

Sir Bale seemed to grow more and more agitated the longer he remained in the room. He seemed to her both frightened and furious; and taking her a little roughly by the wrist, he led her through the door.

When they were in another apartment alone, he again asked the affrighted lady who had told her that picture was there, and who told her to clean it.

She had only the truth to plead. It was, from beginning to end, the merest accident.

'If I thought, Janet, that you were taking counsel of others, talking me over, and trying clever experiments—' he stopped short with his eyes fixed on hers with black suspicion.

His wife's answer was one pleading look, and to burst into tears.

Sir Bale let-go her wrist, which he had held up to this; and placing his hand gently on her shoulder, he said,

'You must not cry, Janet; I have given you no excuse for tears. I only wished an answer to a very harmless question; and I am sure you would tell me, if by any chance you have lately seen Philip Feltram; he is capable of arranging all that. No one knows him as I do. There, you must not cry any more; but tell me truly, has he turned up? is he at Faxwell?'

She denied all this with perfect truth; and after a hesitation of some time, the matter ended. And so soon as she and he were more themselves, he had something quite different to tell her.

'Sit down, Janet; sit down, and forget that vile picture and all I have been saying. What I came to tell you, I think you will like; I am sure it will please you.'

And with this little preface he placed his arm about her neck, and kissed her tenderly. She certainly was pleased; and when his little speech was over, she, smiling, with her tears still wet upon her cheeks, put her arms round her husband's neck, and in turn kissed him with the ardour of gratitude, kissed him affectionately; again and again thanking him all the time.

It was no great matter, but from Sir Bale Mardykes it was something quite unusual.

Was it a sudden whim? what was it? Something had prompted Sir Bale, early in that dark shrewd month of December, to tell his wife that he wished to call together some of his county acquaintances, and to fill his house for a week or so, as near Christmas as she could get them to come. He wished her sisters—Lady Haworth (with her husband) and the Dowager Lady Walsingham—to be invited for an early day, before the coming of the other guests, so that she might enjoy their society for a little time quietly to herself before the less intimate guests should assemble.

Glad was Lady Mardykes to hear the resolve of her husband, and prompt to obey. She wrote to her sisters to beg of them to arrange to come together by the tenth or twelfth of the month, which they accordingly arranged to do. Sir Oliver, it is true, could not be of the party. A minister of state was drinking the waters at Bath;* and Sir Oliver thought it would do him no harm to sip a little also, and his fashionable doctor politely agreed, and 'ordered' to those therapeutic springs the knight of the shire, who was 'consumedly vexed' to lose the Christmas with that jolly dog, Bale, down at Mardykes Hall. But a fellow must have a stomach for his Christmas pudding, and politics takes it out of a fellow deucedly; and health's the first thing, egad!

So Sir Oliver went down to Bath, and I don't know that he tippled much of the waters, but he did drink the burgundy of that haunt of the ailing; and he had the honour of making a fourth not unfrequently in the secretary of state's whist-parties.

It was about the 8th of December when, in Lady Walsingham's carriage, intending to post all the way, that lady, still young, and Lady Haworth, with all the servants that were usual in such expeditions in those days, started from the great Dower House at Islington in high spirits.

Lady Haworth had not been very well—low and nervous; but the clear frosty sun, and the pleasant nature of the excursion, raised her spirits to the point of enjoyment; and expecting nothing but happiness and gaiety—for, after all, Sir Bale was but one of a large party, and even he could make an effort and be agreeable as well as hospitable on occasion—they set out on their northward expedition. The journey, which is a long one, they had resolved to break into a four days' progress; and the inns had been written to, bespeaking a comfortable reception.

CHAPTER XXV
THROUGH THE WALL

ON the third night they put-up at the comfortable old inn called the Three Nuns. With an effort they might easily have pushed on to

Mardykes Hall that night, for the distance is not more than five-and-thirty miles. But, considering her sister's health, Lady Walsingham in planning their route had resolved against anything like a forced march.

Here the ladies took possession of the best sitting-room; and, notwithstanding the fatigue of the journey, Lady Haworth sat up with her sister till near ten o'clock, chatting gaily about a thousand things.

Of the three sisters, Lady Walsingham was the eldest. She had been in the habit of taking the command at home; and now, for advice and decision, her younger sisters, less prompt and courageous than she, were wont, whenever in her neighbourhood, to throw upon her all the cares and agitations of determining what was best to be done in small things and great. It is only fair to say, in addition, that this submission was not by any means exacted; it was the deference of early habit and feebler will, for she was neither officious nor imperious.

It was now time that Lady Haworth, a good deal more fatigued than her sister, should take leave of her for the night.

Accordingly they kissed and bid each other good-night; and Lady Walsingham, not yet disposed to sleep, sat for some time longer in the comfortable room where they had taken their tea, amusing the time with the book that had, when conversation flagged, beguiled the weariness of the journey. Her sister had been in her room nearly an hour, when she became herself a little sleepy. She had lighted her candle, and was going to ring for her maid, when, to her surprise, the door opened, and her sister Lady Haworth entered in a dressing-gown, looking frightened.

'My darling Mary!' exclaimed Lady Walsingham, 'what is the matter? are you well?'

'Yes, darling,' she answered, 'quite well; that is, I don't know what is the matter—I'm frightened.' She paused, listening, with her eyes turned towards the wall. 'O, darling Maud, I am so frightened! I don't know what it can be.'

'You must not be agitated, darling; there's nothing. You have been asleep, and I suppose you have had a dream. Were you asleep?'

Lady Haworth had caught her sister fast by the arm with both her hands, and was looking wildly in her face.

'Have *you* heard nothing?' she asked, again looking towards the wall of the room, as if she expected to hear a voice through it.

'Nonsense, darling; you are dreaming still. Nothing; there has been nothing to hear. I have been awake ever since; if there had been anything to hear, I could not have missed it. Come, sit down. Sip a little of this water; you are nervous, and over-tired; and tell me plainly, like a good little soul, what is the matter; for nothing has happened here;

and you ought to know that the Three Nuns is the quietest house in England; and I'm no witch, and if you won't tell me what's the matter, I can't divine it.'

'Yes, of course,' said Mary, sitting down, and glancing round her wildly. 'I don't hear it now; *you* don't?'

'Do, my dear Mary, tell me what you mean,' said Lady Walsingham kindly but firmly.

Lady Haworth was holding the still untasted glass of water in her hand.

'Yes, I'll tell you; I have been so frightened! You are right; I had a dream, but I can scarcely remember anything of it, except the very end of it, when I wakened. But it was not the dream; only it was connected with what terrified me so. I was so tired when I went to bed, I thought I should have slept very soundly; and indeed I fell asleep immediately, and I must have slept quietly for a good while. How long is it since I left you?'

'More than an hour.'

'Yes, I must have slept a good while; for I don't think I have been ten minutes awake. How my dream began I don't know. I remember only that gradually it came to this: I was standing in a recess in a panelled gallery; it was lofty, and, I thought, belonged to a handsome but old-fashioned house. I was looking straight towards the head of a wide staircase, with a great oak banister. At the top of the stairs, as near to me, about, as that window there, was a thick short column of oak, on top of which was a candlestick. There was no other light but from that one candle; and there was a lady standing beside it, looking down the stairs, with her back turned towards me; and from her gestures I should have thought speaking to people on a lower lobby, but whom from my place I could not see. I soon perceived that this lady was in great agony of mind; for she beat her breast and wrung her hands every now and then, and wagged her head slightly from side to side, like a person in great distraction. But one word she said I could not hear. Nor when she struck her hand on the banister, or stamped, as she seemed to do in her pain, upon the floor, could I hear any sound. I found myself somehow waiting upon this lady, and was watching her with awe and sympathy. But who she was I knew not, until turning towards me I plainly saw Janet's face, pale and covered with tears, and with such a look of agony as—O God!—I can never forget.'

'Pshaw! Mary darling, what is it but a dream! I have had a thousand more startling; it is only that you are so nervous just now.'

'But that is not all—nothing; what followed is so dreadful; for either there is something very horrible going on at Mardykes, or else I am losing my reason,' said Lady Haworth in increasing agitation. 'I wakened instantly in great alarm, but I suppose no more than I have felt a hundred times on awakening from a frightful dream. I sat up in my bed; I was thinking of ringing for Winnefred, my heart was beating so, but feeling better soon I changed my mind. All this time I heard a faint sound of a voice, as if coming through a thick wall. It came from the wall at the left side of my bed, and I fancied was that of some woman lamenting in a room separated from me by that thick partition. I could only perceive that it was a sound of crying mingled with ejaculations of misery, or fear, or entreaty. I listened with a painful curiosity, wondering who it could be, and what could have happened in the neighbouring rooms of the house; and as I looked and listened, I could distinguish my own name, but at first nothing more. That, of course, might have been an accident; and I knew there were many Marys in the world besides myself. But it made me more curious; and a strange thing struck me, for I was now looking at that very wall through which the sounds were coming. I saw that there was a window in it. Thinking that the rest of the wall might nevertheless be covered by another room, I drew the curtain of it and looked out. But there is no such thing. It is the outer wall the entire way along. And it is equally impossible of the other wall, for it is to the front of the house, and has two windows in it; and the wall that the head of my bed stands against has the gallery outside it all the way; for I remarked that as I came to you.'

'Tut, tut, Mary darling, nothing on earth is so deceptive as sound; this and fancy account for everything.'

'But hear me out, darling; I have not told you all. I began to hear the voice more clearly, and at last quite distinctly. It was Janet's, and she was conjuring you by name, as well as me, to come to her to Mardykes, without delay, in her extremity; yes, *you*, just as vehemently as me. It was Janet's voice. It still seemed separated by the wall, but I heard every syllable now; and I never heard voice or words of such anguish. She was imploring of us to come on, without a moment's delay, to Mardykes; and crying that, if we were not with her, she should go mad.'

'Well, darling,' said Lady Walsingham, 'you see I'm included in this invitation as well as you, and should hate to disappoint Janet just as much; and I do assure you, in the morning you will laugh over this fancy with me; or rather, she will laugh over it with us, when we get to Mardykes. What you do want is rest, and a little sal-volatile.'

So saying she rang the bell for Lady Haworth's maid. Having comforted her sister, and made her take the nervous specific she recommended, she went with her to her room; and taking possession of the arm-chair by the fire, she told her that she would keep her company until she was fast asleep, and remain long enough to be sure that the sleep was not likely to be interrupted. Lady Haworth had not been ten minutes in her bed, when she raised herself with a start to her elbow, listening with parted lips and wild eyes, her trembling fingers behind her ears. With an exclamation of horror, she cried,

'There it is again, upbraiding us! I can't stay longer.'

She sprang from the bed, and rang the bell violently.

'Maud,' she cried in an ecstasy of horror, 'nothing shall keep me here, whether you go or not. I will set out the moment the horses are put to. If you refuse to come, Maud, mind the responsibility is yours—listen!' and with white face and starting eyes she pointed to the wall. 'Have you ears? don't you hear?'

The sight of a person in extremity of terror so mysterious, might have unnerved a ruder system than Lady Walsingham's. She was pale as she replied; for under certain circumstances those terrors which deal with the supernatural are more contagious than any others. Lady Walsingham still, in terms, held to her opinion; but the panic had touched her, and although she tried to smile, her face showed it.

'Well, dear Mary,' she said, 'as you will have it so, I see no good in resisting you longer. Here, it is plain, your nerves will not suffer you to rest. Let us go then, in heaven's name; and when you get to Mardykes Hall you will be relieved.'

All this time Lady Haworth was getting on her things, with the careless hurry of a person about to fly for her life; and Lady Walsingham issued her orders for horses, and the general preparations for resuming the journey.

It was now between ten and eleven; but the servant who rode armed with them, according to the not unnecessary usage of the times, thought that with a little judicious bribing of postboys they might easily reach Mardykes Hall before three o'clock in the morning.

When the party set forward again, Lady Haworth was comparatively tranquil. She no longer heard the unearthly mimickry of her sister's voice; there remained only the fear and suspense which that illusion or visitation had produced.

Her sister, Lady Walsingham, after a brief effort to induce something like conversation, became silent. A thin sheet of snow had covered the darkened landscape, and some light flakes were still dropping. Lady Walsingham struck her repeater* often in the dark, and inquired the distances frequently. She was anxious to get over the ground, though by no means fatigued. Something of the anxiety that lay heavy at her sister's heart had touched her own.

CHAPTER XXVI

PERPLEXED

THE roads even then were good, and very good horses the posting-houses turned out; so that by dint of extra pay the rapid rate of travelling undertaken by the servant was fully accomplished in the first two or three stages.

While Lady Walsingham was continually striking her repeater in her ear, and as they neared their destination, growing in spite of herself more anxious, her sister's uneasiness showed itself in a less reserved way; for, cold as it was, with snowflakes actually dropping, Lady Haworth's head was perpetually out at the window, and when she drew it up, sitting again in her place, she would audibly express her alarms, and apply to her sister for consolation and confidence in her suspense.

Under its thin carpet of snow, the pretty village of Golden Friars looked strangely to their eyes. It had long been fast asleep, and both ladies were excited as they drew up at the steps of the George and Dragon, and with bell and knocker roused the slumbering household.

What tidings awaited them here? In a very few minutes the door was opened, and the porter staggered down, after a word with the driver, to the carriage-window, not half awake.

'Is Lady Mardykes well?' demanded Lady Walsingham.

'Is Sir Bale well?'

'Are all the people at Mardykes Hall quite well?'

With clasped hands Lady Haworth listened to the successive answers of these questions which her sister hastily put. The answers were all satisfactory. With a great sigh and a little laugh, Lady Walsingham placed her hand affectionately on that of her sister; who, saying, 'God be thanked!' began to weep.

'When had you last news from Mardykes?' asked Lady Walsingham.

'A servant was down here about four o'clock.'

'O! no one since?' said she in a disappointed tone.

No one had been from the great house since, but all were well then.

'They are early people, you know, dear; and it is dark at four, and that is as late as they could well have heard, and nothing could have happened since—very unlikely. We have come very fast; it is only a few minutes past two, darling.'

But each felt the chill and load of their returning anxiety.

While the people at the George were rapidly getting a team of horses to, Lady Walsingham contrived a moment for an order from the other window to her servant, who knew Golden Friars perfectly, to knock-up the people at Doctor Torvey's, and to inquire whether all were well at Mardykes Hall.

There he learned that a messenger had come for Doctor Torvey at ten o'clock, and that the Doctor had not returned since. There was no news, however, of any one's being ill; and the Doctor himself did not know what he was wanted about. While Lady Haworth was talking to her maid from the window next the steps, Lady Walsingham was, unobserved, receiving this information at the other.

It made her very uncomfortable.

In a few minutes more, however, with a team of fresh horses, they were again rapidly passing the distance between them and Mardykes Hall.

About two miles on, their drivers pulled-up, and they heard a voice talking with them from the roadside. A servant from the Hall had been sent with a note for Lady Walsingham, and had been ordered, if necessary, to ride the whole way to the Three Nuns to deliver it. The note was already in Lady Walsingham's hand; her sister sat beside her, and with the corner of the open note in her fingers, she read it breathlessly at the same time by the light of a carriage-lamp which the man held to the window. It said:

My dearest love—my darling sister—dear sisters both!—in God's name, lose not a moment. I am so overpowered and *terrified*. I cannot explain; I can only implore of you to come with all the haste you can make. Waste no time, darlings. I hardly understand what I write. Only this, dear sisters; I feel that my reason will desert me, unless you come soon. You will not fail me now. Your poor distracted   JANET.

The sisters exchanged a pale glance, and Lady Haworth grasped her sister's hand.

'Where is the messenger?' asked Lady Walsingham.

A mounted servant came to the window.

'Is any one ill at home?' she asked.

'No, all were well—my lady, and Sir Bale—no one sick.'

'But the Doctor was sent for; what was that for?'

'I can't say, my lady.'

'You are quite certain that no one—think—*no* one is ill?'

'There is no one ill at the Hall, my lady, that I have heard of.'

'Is Lady Mardykes, my sister, still up?'

'Yes, my lady; and has her maid with her.'

'And Sir Bale, are you certain he is quite well?'

'Sir Bale is quite well, my lady; he has been busy settling papers to-night, and was as well as usual.'

'That will do, thanks,' said the perplexed lady; and to her own servant she added,

'On to Mardykes Hall with all the speed they can make. I'll pay them well, tell them.'

And in another minute they were gliding along the road at a pace which the muffled beating of the horses' hoofs on the thin sheet of snow that covered the road showed to have broken out of the conventional trot, and to resemble something more like a gallop.

And now they were under the huge trees, that looked black as hearse-plumes in contrast with the snow. The cold gleam of the lake in the moon which had begun to shine out now met their gaze; and the familiar outline of Snakes Island, its solemn timber bleak and leafless, standing in a group, seemed to watch Mardykes Hall with a dismal observation across the water. Through the gate and between the huge files of trees the carriage seemed to fly; and at last the steaming horses stood panting, nodding and snorting, before the steps in the courtyard.

There was a light in an upper window, and a faint light in the hall, the door of which was opened; and an old servant came down and ushered the ladies into the house.

CHAPTER XXVII
THE HOUR

LIGHTLY they stepped over the snow that lay upon the broad steps, and entering the door saw the dim figure of their sister, already in the large and faintly-lighted hall. One candle in the hand of her scared maid, and one burning on the table, leaving the distant parts of that great apartment in total darkness, touched the figures with the odd sharp lights in which Schalken delighted;* and a streak of chilly moonlight, through the open door, fell upon the floor, and was stretched like a white sheet at her feet. Lady Mardykes, with an exclamation of agitated relief, threw her arms, in turn, round the necks of her sisters, and hugging them, kissed them again and again, murmuring her thanks, calling them her 'blessed sisters', and praising God for his mercy in having sent them to her in time, and altogether in a rapture of agitation and gratitude.

Taking them each by a hand, she led them into a large room, on whose panels they could see the faint twinkle of the tall gilded frames, and the darker indication of the old portraits, in which that interesting house abounds. The moonbeams, entering obliquely through the Tudor stone-shafts of the window and thrown upon the floor, reflected an imperfect light; and the candle which the maid who followed her mistress held in her hand shone dimly from the sideboard, where she placed it. Lady Mardykes told her that she need not wait.

'They don't know; they know only that we are in some great confusion; but—God have mercy on me!—nothing of the reality. Sit down, darlings; you are tired.'

She sat down between them on a sofa, holding a hand of each. They sat opposite the window, through which appeared the magnificent view commanded from the front of the house: in the foreground the solemn trees of Snakes Island, one great branch stretching upward, bare and moveless, from the side, like an arm raised to heaven in wonder or in menace towards the house; the lake, in part swept by the icy splendour of the moon, trembling with a dazzling glimmer, and farther off lost in blackness; the Fells rising from a base of gloom, into ribs and peaks white with snow, and looking against the pale sky, thin and transparent as a haze. Right across to the storied woods of Cloostedd, and the old domains of the Feltrams, this view extended.

Thus alone, their mufflers still on, their hands clasped in hers, they breathlessly listened to her strange tale.

Connectedly told it amounted to this:

Sir Bale seemed to have been relieved of some great anxiety about the time when, ten days before, he had told her to invite her friends to Mardykes Hall. This morning he had gone out for a walk with Trevor, his under-steward, to talk over some plans about thinning the woods at this side; and also to discuss practically a proposal, lately made by a wealthy merchant, to take a very long lease, on advantageous terms to Sir Bale as he thought, of the old park and chase of Cloostedd, with the intention of building there, and making it once more a handsome residence.

In the improved state of his spirits, Sir Bale had taken a shrewd interest in this negotiation; and was actually persuaded to cross the lake that morning with his adviser, and to walk over the grounds with him.

Sir Bale had seemed unusually well, and talked with great animation. He was more like a young man who had just attained his majority, and for the first time grasped his estates, than the grim elderly Baronet who had been moping about Mardykes, and as much afraid as a cat of the water, for so many years.

As they returned to the boat, at the roots of that same scathed elm whose barkless bough had seemed, in his former visit to this old wood, to beckon him from a distance, like a skeleton arm, to enter the forest, he and his companion on a sudden missed an old map of the grounds which they had been consulting.

'We must have left it in the corner tower of Cloostedd House, which commands that view of the grounds, you remember; it would not do to lose it. It is the most accurate thing we have. I'll sit down here and rest a little till you come back.'

The man was absent little more than twenty minutes. When he returned he found that Sir Bale had changed his position, and was now walking to and fro, around and about, in what at a distance he fancied was mere impatience, on the open space a couple of hundred paces nearer to the turn in the valley towards the boat. It was not impatience. He was very much agitated. He looked very pale, and he took his companion's arm—a thing he had never thought of doing before—and said,

'Let us get away quickly. I've something to tell at home, and— I forgot it.'

Not another word did Sir Bale exchange with his companion. He sat in the stern of the boat, gloomy as a man about to glide under traitor's-gate. He entered his house in the same sombre and agitated state. He entered his library, and sat for a long time as if stunned.

At last he seemed to have made-up his mind to something; and applied himself quietly and diligently to arranging papers, docketing some and burning others. Dinner-time arrived. He sent to tell Lady Mardykes that he should not join her at dinner, but would see her afterwards.

'It was between eight and nine, I forget the exact time, when he came to the tower drawing-room where I was. I did not hear his approach. There is a stone stair, with a thick carpet on it. He told me he wished to speak to me there. It is an out-of-the-way place—a small old room with very thick walls, and there is a double door, the inner one of oak—I suppose he wished to guard against being overheard.

'There was a look in his face that frightened me; I saw he had something dreadful to tell. He looked like a man on whom a lot had fallen to put some one to death,' said Lady Mardykes. 'O, my poor Bale! my husband, my husband! My God! he knew what it would be to me.'

Here she broke into the wildest weeping, and it was some time before she resumed.

'He seemed very kind and very calm,' she said at last; 'he said but little; and, I think, these were his words: "I find, Janet, I have made a great miscalculation—I thought my hour of danger had passed. We have been many years together, but a parting must sooner or later be, and my time has come."

'I don't know what I said. I would not have so much minded—for I could not have believed, if I had not seen him—but there was that in his look and tone which no one could doubt.

'"I shall die before to-morrow morning," he said. "You must command yourself, Janet; it can't be altered now."

'"O, Bale," I cried, nearly distracted, "you would not kill yourself!"

'"Kill myself! poor child! no, indeed," he said; "it is simply that I must die. No violent death—nothing but the common subsidence of life—I have made up my mind; what happens to everybody can't be so very bad; and millions of worse men than I die every year. You must not follow me to my room, darling; I shall see you by and by."

'His language was collected and even cold; but his face looked as if it was cut in stone; you never saw, in a dream, a face like it.'

Lady Walsingham here said,

'I am certain he is ill; he's in a fever. You must not distract and torture yourself about his predictions. You sent for Doctor Torvey; what did he say?'

'I could not tell him all.'

'O, no; I don't mean that; they'd only say he was mad, and we little better for minding what he says. But did the Doctor see him? and what did he say of his health?'

'Yes; he says there is nothing wrong—no fever—nothing whatever. Poor Bale has been so kind; he saw him to please me,' she sobbed again wildly. 'I wrote to implore of him. It was my last hope, strange as it seems; and O, would to God I could think it! But there is nothing of that kind. Wait till you have seen him. There is a frightful calmness about all he says and does; and his directions are all so clear, and his mind so perfectly collected, it is quite impossible.'

And poor Lady Mardykes again burst into a frantic agony of tears.

CHAPTER XXVIII

SIR BALE IN THE GALLERY

'Now, Janet darling, you are yourself low and nervous, and you treat this fancy of Bale's as seriously as he does himself. The truth is, he is a hypochondriac, as the doctors say; and you will find that I am right; he will be quite well in the morning, and I daresay a little ashamed of himself for having frightened his poor little wife as he has. I will sit up with you. But our poor Mary is not, you know, very strong; and she ought to lie down and rest a little. Suppose you give me a cup of tea in the drawing-room. I will run up to my room and get these things off, and meet you in the drawing-room; or, if you like it better, you can sit with me in my own room; and for goodness' sake let us have candles enough, and a bright fire; and I promise you, if you will only exert your own good sense, you shall be a great deal more cheerful in a very little time.'

Lady Walsingham's address was kind and cheery, and her air confident. For a moment a ray of hope returned, and her sister Janet acknowledged at least the possibility of her theory. But if confidence is contagious, so also is panic; and Lady Walsingham experienced a sinking of the heart which she dared not confess to her sister, and vainly strove to combat.

Lady Walsingham went up with her sister Mary, and having seen her in her room, and spoken again to her in the same cheery tone in which she had lectured her sister Lady Mardykes, she went on; and having taken possession of her own room, and put off her cloaks and shawls, she was going downstairs again, when she heard Sir Bale's voice, as he approached along the gallery, issuing orders to a servant, as it seemed, exactly in his usual tone.

She turned, with a strange throb at her heart, and met him.

A little sterner, a little paler than usual he looked; she could perceive no other change. He took her hand kindly and held it, as with dilated eyes he looked with a dark inquiry for a moment in her face. He signed to the servant to go on, and said, 'I'm glad you have come, Maud. You have heard what is to happen; and I don't know how Janet could have borne it without your support. You did right to come; and you'll stay with her for a day or two, and take her away from this place as soon as you can.'

She looked at him with the embarrassment of fear. He was speaking to her with the calmness of a leave-taking in the press-room—the serenity that overlies the greatest awe and agony of which human nature is capable.

'I am glad to see you, Bale,' she began, hardly knowing what she said, and she stopped short.

'You are come, it turns out, on a sad mission,' he resumed; 'you find all in confusion. Poor Janet! it is a blow to her. I shall not live to see to-morrow's sunshine.'

'Come,' she said, startled, 'you must not talk so. No, Bale, you have no right to speak so; you can have no reason to justify it. It is cruel and wicked to trifle with your wife's feelings. If you are under a delusion, you must make an effort and shake it off, or, at least, cease to talk of it. You are not well; I know by your looks you are ill; but I am very certain we shall see you much better tomorrow, and still better the day following.'

'No, I'm not ill, sister. Feel that pulse, if you doubt me; there is no fever in it. I never was more perfectly in health; and yet I know that before the clock, that has just struck three, shall have struck five, I, who am talking to you, shall be dead.'

Lady Walsingham was frightened, and her fear irritated her.

'I have told you what I think and believe,' she said vehemently. 'I think it wrong and cowardly to torture my poor sister with your whimsical predictions. Look into your own mind, and you will see you have absolutely no reason to support what you say. How *can* you inflict all this agony upon a poor creature foolish enough to love you as she does, and weak enough to believe in your idle dreams?'

'Stay, sister; it is not a matter to be debated so. If to-morrow I can hear you, it will be time enough to upbraid me. Pray return now to your sister; she needs all you can do for her. She is much to be pitied; her sufferings afflict me. I shall see you and her again before my death. It would have been more cruel to leave her unprepared. Do all in your power to nerve and tranquillize her. What is past cannot now be helped.'

He paused, looking hard at her, as if he had half made up his mind to say something more. But if there was a question of the kind, it was determined in favour of silence.

He dropped her hand, turned quickly, and left her.

CHAPTER XXIX
DR TORVEY'S OPINION

WHEN Lady Walsingham reached the head of the stairs, she met her maid, and from her learned that her sister, Lady Mardykes, was down-stairs in the same room. On approaching she heard her sister Mary's voice talking with her, and found them together. Mary, finding that she could not sleep, had put on her clothes again, and come down to keep her sister company. The room looked more comfortable now. There were candles lighted, and a good fire burned in the grate; tea-things stood on a little table near the fire, and the two sisters were talking; Lady Mardykes appearing more collected, and only they two in the room.

'Have you seen him, Maud?' cried Lady Mardykes, rising and hastily approaching her the moment she entered.

'Yes, dear; and talked with him, and—'

'Well?'

'And I think very much as I did before. I think he is nervous; he says he is not ill; but he is nervous and whimsical, and as men always are when they happen to be out of sorts, very positive; and of course the only thing that can quite undeceive him is the lapse of the time he has fixed for his prediction, as it is sure to pass without any tragic result of any sort. We shall then all see alike the nature of his delusion.'

'O, Maud, if I were only sure you thought so! if I were sure you really had hopes! Tell me, Maud, for God's sake, what you really think.'

Lady Walsingham was a little disconcerted by the unexpected earnestness of this direct appeal.

'Come, darling, you must not be foolish,' she said; 'we can only talk of impressions, and we are imposed upon by the solemnity of his manner, and the fact that he evidently believes in his own delusion; every one does believe in his own delusion—there is nothing strange in that.'

'O, Maud darling, I see you are not convinced; you are only trying to comfort me. You have no hope—none, none, none'; and she covered her face with her hands, and wept again convulsively.

Lady Walsingham was silent for a moment, and then with an effort said, as she placed her hand on her sister's arm,

'You see, dear Janet, there is no use in my saying the same thing over and over again; an hour or two will show who is right. Sit down again, darling, and be like yourself. My maid told me that you had sent to the parlour for Doctor Torvey; he must not find you so. What would he think? Unless you mean to tell him of Bale's strange fancy; and a pretty story that would be to set afloat in Golden Friars. I think I hear him coming.'

So, in effect, he was. Doctor Torvey—with the florid gravity of a man who, having just swallowed a bottle of port, besides some glasses of sherry, is admitted to the presence of ladies whom he respects—entered the room, made what he called his 'leg and his compliments', and awaited the ladies' commands.

'Sit down, Doctor Torvey,' said Lady Walsingham, who in the incapacity of her sister undertook the doing of the honours. 'My sister, Lady Mardykes, has got it into her head somehow that Sir Bale is ill. I have been speaking to him; he certainly does not look very well, but he says he is quite well. Do you think him well?—that is, we know you don't think there is anything of importance amiss—but she wishes to know whether you think him *perfectly* well.'

The Doctor cleared his voice and delivered his lecture, a little thickly at some words, upon Sir Bale's case; the result of which was that it was no case at all; and that if he would only live something more of a country gentleman's life, he would be as well as any man could desire—as well as any man, gentle or simple, in the country.

'The utmost I should think of doing for him would be, perhaps, a little quinine,* nothing mo'—shurely—he is really and toory a very shoun' shtay of health.'

Lady Walsingham looked encouragingly at her sister and nodded.

'I've been shen' for, La'y Walsh—Walse—Walsing—*ham*; old Jack Amerald—he likshe his glass o' port,' he said roguishly, 'and shuv-versh accord'n'ly,' he continued, with a compassionating paddle of his right hand; 'one of thoshe aw—odd feels in his stomach; and as I have pretty well done all zhat I can man-n-'ge down here, I must be off, ye shee. Wind up from Golden Friars, and a little flutter ovv zhnow, thazh all'; and with some remarks about the extreme cold of the weather, and the severity of their night journey, and many respectful and polite parting speeches, the Doctor took his leave; and they soon heard the wheels of his gig and the tread of his horse, faint and muffled from the snow in the court-yard, and the Doctor, who had connected that melancholy and agitated household with the outer circle of humanity, was gone.

There was very little snow falling, half-a-dozen flakes now and again, and their flight across the window showed, as the Doctor had in a manner boasted, that the wind was in his face as he returned to Golden Friars. Even these desultory snow-flakes ceased, at times, altogether; and returning, as they say, 'by fits and starts', left for long intervals the landscape, under the brilliant light of the moon, in its wide white shroud. The curtain of the great window had not been drawn. It seemed to Lady Walsingham that the moonbeams had grown more dazzling, that Snakes Island was nearer and more distinct, and the outstretched arm of the old tree looked wilder and ghastlier, like the uplifted arm of the spectator of a tragedy, who draws silently nearer as the catastrophe approaches.

Cold, dazzling, almost repulsive in this intense moonlight and white sheeting, the familiar landscape looked in the eyes of Lady Walsingham. The sisters gradually grew more and more silent, an unearthly suspense overhung them all, and Lady Mardykes rose every now and then and listened at the open door for step or voice in vain. They all were overpowered by the intenser horror that seemed gathering around them. And thus an hour or more passed.

CHAPTER XXX

HUSH!

PALE and silent those three beautiful sisters sat. The horrible quietude of a suspense that had grown all but insupportable oppressed the guests of Lady Mardykes, and something like the numbness of despair had reduced her to the silence of a seeming apathy, the dreadful counterfeit of peace.

Sir Bale Mardykes on a sudden softly entered the room. Reflected from the floor near the window the white moonlight somehow gave to his fixed features the character of a smile. With a warning gesture, as he came in, he placed his finger to his lips, as if to enjoin silence; and then, having successively pressed the hands of his two sisters-in-law, he stooped over the almost fainting form of his wife, and twice pressed her cold forehead with his lips; and so, without a word, he passed softly from the room.

Some seconds elapsed before Lady Walsingham, recovering her presence of mind, with one of the candlesticks from the table in her hand, opened the door and followed.

She saw Sir Bale mount the last stair of the broad flight visible from the hall, and candle in hand turn the corner of the massive banister, and as the light thrown from his candle showed, he continued, without hurry, to ascend the second flight.

With the irrepressible curiosity of horror she continued to follow him at a distance.

She saw him enter his own private room, and close the door, and in a moment after she thought she heard him lock it within.

Continuing to follow she placed herself noiselessly at the door of the apartment, and in breathless silence, with a throbbing heart, listened for what should pass within.

She distinctly heard Sir Bale pace the floor up and down for some time, and then, after a pause, a sound as if some one had thrown himself heavily on the bed. A silence followed, during which her sisters, who had followed more timidly, joined her. She warned them with a look and gesture to be silent.

Lady Haworth stood a little behind, her white lips moving, and her hands clasped as if in a silent agony of prayer. Lady Mardykes leaned against the massive oak door-case.

With her hand raised to her ear, and her lips parted, Lady Walsingham listened for some seconds—for a minute, two minutes, three. At last, losing heart, she seized the handle in her panic, and turned it sharply. The door was locked on the inside, but some one close to it said from within, 'Hush, hush!'

Much alarmed now, the same lady knocked violently at the door. No answer was returned.

She knocked again more violently, and shook the door with all her fragile force. It was something of horror in her countenance as she did so, that, no doubt, terrified Lady Mardykes, who with a loud and long scream sank in a swoon upon the floor.

The servants, alarmed by these sounds, were speedily in the gallery. Lady Mardykes was carried to her room, and laid upon her bed; her sister, Lady Haworth, accompanying her. In the mean time the door was forced. Sir Bale Mardykes was found stretched upon his bed.

Those who have once seen it, will not mistake the aspect of death. Here, in Sir Bale Mardykes' room, in his bed, in his clothes, is a stranger, grim and awful; in a few days to be insupportable, and to pass alone into the prison-house, and to be seen no more.

Where is Sir Bale Mardykes now, whose roof-tree and whose place at board and bed will know him no more? Here lies a chapfallen, fish-eyed image, chilling already into clay, and stiffening in every joint.

There is a marble monument in the pretty church of Golden Friars. It stands at the left side of what antiquarians call 'the high altar'. Two pillars at each end support an arch with several armorial bearings* on as many shields sculptured above. Beneath, on a marble flooring raised some six feet, with a cornice round, lies Sir Bale Mardykes, of Mardykes Hall, ninth Baronet of that ancient family, chiseled in marble with knee-breeches and buckled-shoes, and *ailles de pigeon*,* and single-breasted coat and long waistcoat, ruffles and sword, such as gentlemen wore about the year 1770, and bearing a strong resemblance to the features of the second Charles. On the broad marble which forms the background is inscribed an epitaph, which has perpetuated to our times the estimate formed by his 'inconsolable widow', the Dowager Lady Mardykes, of the virtues and accomplishments of her deceased lord.

Lady Walsingham would have qualified two or three of the more highly-coloured hyperboles, at which the Golden Friars of those days sniffed and tittered. They don't signify now; there is no contemporary left to laugh or whisper. And if there be not much that is true in the letter of that inscription, it at least perpetuates something that is true—that wonderful glorification of partisanship, the affection of an idolizing wife.

Lady Mardykes, a few days after the funeral, left Mardykes Hall for ever. She lived a great deal with her sister, Lady Walsingham; and died, as a line cut at the foot of Sir Bale Mardykes' epitaph records, in the year 1790; her remains being laid beside those of her beloved husband in Golden Friars.

The estates had come to Sir Bale Mardykes free of entail. He had been pottering over a will, but it was never completed, nor even quite planned; and after much doubt and scrutiny, it was at last ascertained that, in default of a will and of issue, a clause in the marriage-settlement gave the entire estates to the Dowager Lady Mardykes.

By her will she bequeathed the estates to 'her cousin, also a kinsman of the late Sir Bale Mardykes her husband', William Feltram, on condition of his assuming the name and arms of Mardykes, the arms of Feltram being quartered in the shield.

Thus was oddly fulfilled the prediction which Philip Feltram had repeated, that the estates of Mardykes were to pass into the hands of a Feltram.

About the year 1795 the baronetage was revived, and William Feltram enjoyed the title for fifteen years, as Sir William Mardykes.

THE HAUNTED HOUSE
IN WESTMINSTER

THIRTY years ago, an elderly man, to whom I paid quarterly a small annuity charged on some property of mine, came on the quarter-day* to receive it. He was a dry, sad, quiet man, who had known better days, and had always maintained an unexceptionable character. No better authority could be imagined for a ghost-story.

He told me one, though with a manifest reluctance; he was drawn into the narration by his choosing to explain what I should not have remarked, that he had called two days earlier than that week after the strict day of payment, which he had usually allowed to elapse. His reason was a sudden determination to change his lodgings, and the consequent necessity of paying his rent a little before it was due.

He lodged in a dark street in Westminster,* in a spacious old house, very warm, being wainscoted from top to bottom, and furnished with no undue abundance of windows, and those fitted with thick sashes and small panes.

This house was, as the bills upon the windows testified, offered to be sold or let. But no one seemed to care to look at it.

A thin matron, in rusty black silk, very taciturn, with large, steady, alarmed eyes, that seemed to look in your face, to read what you might have seen in the dark rooms and passages through which you had passed, was in charge of it, with a solitary 'maid-of-all-work' under her command. My poor friend had taken lodgings in this house, on account of their extraordinary cheapness. He had occupied them for nearly a year without the slightest disturbance, and was the only tenant, under rent, in the house. He had two rooms; a sitting-room, and a bedroom with a closet* opening from it, in which he kept his books and papers locked up. He had gone to his bed, having also locked the outer door. Unable to sleep, he had lighted a candle, and after having read for a time, had laid the book beside him. He heard the old clock at the stair-head strike one; and very shortly after, to his alarm, he saw the closet-door, which he thought he had locked, open stealthily, and a slight dark man, particularly sinister, and somewhat about fifty, dressed in mourning of a very antique fashion, such a suit as we see in Hogarth,* enter the room on tip-toe. He was followed by an elder man, stout, and blotched with scurvy,* and whose features, fixed as a corpse's, were stamped with dreadful force with a character of sensuality and villany.

This old man wore a flowered-silk dressing-gown and ruffles, and he remarked a gold ring on his finger, and on his head a cap of velvet, such as, in the days of perukes,* gentlemen wore in undress.

This direful old man carried in his ringed and ruffled hand a coil of rope; and these two figures crossed the floor diagonally, passing the foot of his bed, from the closet-door at the farther end of the room, at the left, near the window, to the door opening upon the lobby, close to the bed's head, at his right.

He did not attempt to describe his sensations as these figures passed so near him. He merely said, that so far from sleeping in that room again, no consideration the world could offer* would induce him so much as to enter it again alone, even in the daylight. He found both doors, that of the closet, and that of the room opening upon the lobby, in the morning fast locked, as he had left them before going to bed.

In answer to a question of mine, he said that neither appeared the least conscious of his presence. They did not seem to glide, but walked as living men do and he felt a vibration of the floor as they crossed it. He so obviously suffered from speaking about the apparitions, that I asked him no more questions.

There were in his description, however, certain coincidences so very singular, as to induce me, by that very post, to write to a friend very much my senior, then living in a remote part of England, for the information which I knew he could give me. He had himself more than once pointed out that old house to my attention, and had told me, though very briefly, the strange story which I now asked him to give me in greater detail.

His answer satisfied me; and the following pages convey its substance.

Your letter (he wrote) tells me you desire some particulars about the closing years of the life of Mr Justice Harbottle, one of the judges of the Court of Common Pleas.* You refer, of course, to the extraordinary occurrences that made that period of his life long after a theme for 'winter's tales'* and metaphysical speculation. I happen to know perhaps more than any other man living of these mysterious particulars.

The old family mansion, when I revisited London, more than thirty years ago, I examined for the last time. During the years that have passed since then, I hear that improvement, with its preliminary demolitions,* has been doing wonders for the quarter of Westminster in which it stood. If I were quite certain that the house had been taken down, I should have no difficulty about naming the street in which it stood. As what I have to tell, however, is not likely to improve its letting value, and as I should not care to get into trouble, I prefer being silent on that particular point.

How old the house was, I can't tell. People said it was built by Roger Harbottle, a Turkey merchant, in the reign of King James I.* I am not a good opinion upon such questions; but having been in it, though in its forlorn and deserted state, I can tell you in a general way what it was like. It was built of dark-red brick, and the door and windows were faced with stone that had turned yellow by time. It receded some feet from the line of the other houses in the street; and it had a florid and fanciful rail of iron about the broad steps that invited your ascent to the hall-door, in which were fixed, under a file of lamps, among scrolls and twisted leaves, two immense 'extinguishers', like the conical caps of fairies, into which, in old times, the footmen used to thrust their flambeaux when their chairs* or coaches had set down their great people, in the hall or at the steps, as the case might be. That hall is square and panelled up to the ceiling, and has a large fire-place. Two or three stately old rooms open from it at each side. The windows of these are tall, with many small panes. Passing through the arch at the back of the hall, you come upon the wide and heavy well-staircase. There is a back staircase also. The mansion is large, and has not as much light, by any means, in proportion to its extent, as modern houses enjoy. When I saw it, it had long been untenanted, and had the gloomy reputation beside of a haunted house. Cobwebs floated from the ceilings or spanned the corners of the cornices, and dust lay thick over everything. The windows were stained with the dust and rain of fifty years, and darkness had thus grown darker.

When I made it my first visit, it was in company with my father, when I was still a boy, in the year 1808. I was about twelve years old, and my imagination impressible, as it always is at that age. I looked about me with great awe. I was here in the very centre and scene of those occurrences which I had heard recounted at the fireside at home, with so delightful a horror.

My father was an old bachelor of nearly sixty when he married. He had, when a child, seen Judge Harbottle* on the bench in his robes and wig a dozen times at least before his death, which took place in 1748, and his appearance made a powerful and unpleasant impression, not only on his imagination, but upon his nerves.

The Judge was at that time a man of some sixty-seven years. He had a great mulberry-coloured face, a pendulous nose, small fierce eyes, and a grim and brutal mouth. My father, who was young at the time, thought it the most formidable face he had ever seen; for there were evidences of intellectual power in the formation and lines of the forehead. His voice was loud and harsh, and gave effect to the sarcasm which was his habitual weapon on the bench.

This old gentleman had the reputation of being about the wickedest man in England. Even on the bench he now and then showed his scorn of opinion. He had carried cases his own way, it was said, in spite of counsel, authorities, and even of juries, by a sort of cajolery, violence, and bamboozling, that somehow confused and overpowered resistance. He had never actually committed himself; he was too cunning to do that. He had the character of being, however, a dangerous and unscrupulous judge; but his character did not trouble him. The associates he chose for his hours of relaxation cared as little as he did about it.

One night during the session of 1746 this old Judge went down in his chair to wait in one of the rooms of the House of Lords for the result of a division in which he and his order were interested.

This over, he was about to return to his house close by, in his chair; but the night had become so soft and fine that he changed his mind, sent it home empty, and with two footmen, each with a flambeau, set out on foot in preference. Gout had made him rather a slow pedestrian. It took him some time to get through the two or three streets he had to pass before reaching his house.

In one of these narrow streets of tall houses, perfectly silent at that hour, he overtook, slowly as he was walking, a very singular-looking old gentleman.

He had a bottle-green coat on, with a cape to it, and large stone buttons, a broad-leafed low-crowned hat, from under which a big powdered wig escaped; he stooped very much, and supported his bending knees with the aid of a crutch-handled cane, and so shuffled and tottered along painfully.

'I ask your pardon, sir,' said this old man in a very quavering voice, as the burly Judge came up with him, and he extended his hand feebly towards his arm.

Mr Justice Harbottle saw that the man was by no means poorly dressed, and his manner that of a gentleman.

The Judge stopped short, and said, in his harsh peremptory tones, 'Well, sir, how can I serve you?'

'Can you direct me to Judge Harbottle's house? I have some intelligence of the very last importance to communicate to him.'

'Can you tell it before witnesses?' asked the Judge.

'By no means; it must reach *his* ear only,' quavered the old man earnestly.

'If that be so, sir, you have only to accompany me a few steps farther to reach my house, and obtain a private audience; for I am Judge Harbottle.'

With this invitation the infirm gentleman in the white wig complied very readily; and in another minute the stranger stood in what was then termed the front parlour of the Judge's house, *tête-à-tête* with that shrewd and dangerous functionary.

He had to sit down, being very much exhausted, and unable for a little time to speak; and then he had a fit of coughing, and after that a fit of gasping; and thus two or three minutes passed, during which the Judge dropped his roquelaure on an arm-chair, and threw his cocked-hat* over that.

The venerable pedestrian in the white wig quickly recovered his voice. With closed doors they remained together for some time.

There were guests waiting in the drawing-rooms, and the sound of men's voices laughing, and then of a female voice singing to a harpsichord, were heard distinctly in the hall over the stairs; for old Judge Harbottle had arranged one of his dubious jollifications, such as might well make the hair of godly men's heads stand upright, for that night.

This old gentleman in the powdered white wig, that rested on his stooped shoulders, must have had something to say that interested the Judge very much; for he would not have parted on easy terms with the ten minutes and upwards which that conference filched from the sort of revelry in which he most delighted, and in which he was the roaring king, and in some sort the tyrant also, of his company.

The footman who showed the aged gentleman out observed that the Judge's mulberry-coloured face, pimples and all, were bleached to a dingy yellow, and there was the abstraction of agitated thought in his manner, as he bid the stranger good-night. The servant saw that the conversation had been of serious import, and that the Judge was frightened.

Instead of stumping upstairs forthwith to his scandalous hilarities, his profane company, and his great china bowl of punch—the identical bowl from which a bygone Bishop of London, good easy man, had baptized this Judge's grandfather, now clinking round the rim with silver ladles, and hung with scrolls of lemon-peel—instead, I say, of stumping and clambering up the great staircase to the cavern of his Circean enchantment,* he stood with his big nose flattened against the window-pane, watching the progress of the feeble old man, who clung stiffly to the iron rail as he got down, step by step, to the pavement.

The hall-door had hardly closed, when the old Judge was in the hall bawling hasty orders, with such stimulating expletives as old colonels under excitement sometimes indulge in nowadays,* with a stamp or two of his big foot, and a waving of his clenched fist in the air. He commanded the footman to overtake the old gentleman in the white wig, to offer him his protection on his way home, and in no case to show his face again without having ascertained where he lodged, and who he was, and all about him.

'By ——, sirrah! if you fail me in this, you doff my livery tonight!'

Forth bounced the stalwart footman, with his heavy cane under his arm, and skipped down the steps, and looked up and down the street after the singular figure, so easy to recognize.

What were his adventures I shall not tell you just now.

The old man, in the conference to which he had been admitted in that stately panelled room, had just told the Judge a very strange story. He might be himself a conspirator; he might possibly he crazed; or possibly his whole story was straight and true.

The aged gentleman in the bottle-green coat, on finding himself alone with Mr Justice Harbottle, had become agitated. He said,

'There is, perhaps you are not aware, my lord, a prisoner in Shrewsbury jail, charged with having forged a bill of exchange for a hundred and twenty pounds, and his name is Lewis Pyneweck, a grocer of that town.'

'Is there?' says the Judge, who knew well that there was.

'Yes, my lord,' says the old man.

'Then you had better say nothing to affect his case. If you do, by—I'll commit you; for I'm to try it,' says the Judge, with his terrible look and tone.

'I am not going to do anything of the kind, my lord; of him or his case I know nothing, and care nothing. But a fact has come to my knowledge which it behoves you to well consider.'

'And what may that fact be?' inquired the Judge; 'I'm in haste, sir, and beg you will use dispatch.'

'It has come to my knowledge, my lord, that a secret tribunal is in process of formation, the object of which is to take cognizance of the conduct of the judges; and first, of *your* conduct, my lord: it is a wicked conspiracy.'

'Who are of it?' demands the Judge.

'I know not a single name as yet. I know but the fact, my lord; it is most certainly true.'

'I'll have you before the Privy Council, sir,' says the Judge.

'That is what I most desire; but not for a day or two, my lord.'

'And why so?'

'I have not as yet a single name, as I told your lordship; but I expect to have a list of the most forward men in it, and some other papers connected with the plot, in two or three days.'

'You said one or two just now.'

'About that time, my lord.'

'Is this a Jacobite plot?'*

'In the main I think it is, my lord.'

'Why, then, it is political. I have tried no State prisoners, nor am like to try any such. How, then, doth it concern me?'

'From what I can gather, my lord, there are those in it who desire private revenges upon certain judges.'

'What do they call their cabal?'

'The High Court of Appeal, my lord.'

'Who are you, sir? What is your name?'

'Hugh Peters, my lord.'

'That should be a Whig name.'

'It is, my lord.'

'Where do you lodge, Mr Peters?'

'In Thames-street, my lord, over against the sign of the Three Kings.'

'Three Kings? Take care one be not too many for you, Mr Peters! How come you, being an honest Whig, as you say, to be privy to a Jacobite plot? Answer me that.'

'My lord, a person in whom I take an interest has been seduced to take a part in it; and being frightened at the unexpected wickedness of their plans, he is resolved to become an informer for the Crown.'

'He resolves like a wise man, sir. What does he say of the persons? Who are in the plot? Doth he know them?'

'Only two, my lord; but he will be introduced to the club in a few days, and he will then have a list, and more exact information of their plans, and above all of their oaths, and their hours and places of meeting, with which he wishes to be acquainted before they can have any suspicions of his intentions. And being so informed, to whom, think you, my lord, had he best go then?'

'To the king's attorney-general straight. But you say this concerns me, sir, in particular? How about this prisoner, Lewis Pyneweck? Is he one of them?'

'I can't tell, my lord; but for some reason, it is thought your lordship will be well advised if you try him not. For if you do, it is feared 'twill shorten your days.'

'So far as I can learn, Mr Peters, this business smells pretty strong of treason. The king's attorney-general will know how to deal with it. When shall I see you again, sir?'

'If you give me leave, my lord, either before your lordship's court sits, or after it rises, to-morrow. I should like to come and tell your lordship what has passed.'

'Do so, Mr Peters, at nine o'clock to-morrow morning. And see you play me no trick, sir, in this matter; if you do, by ——, sir, I'll lay you by the heels!'

'You need fear no trick from me, my lord; had I not wished to serve you, and acquit my own conscience, I never would have come all this way to talk with your lordship.'

'I'm willing to believe you, Mr Peters; I'm willing to believe you, sir.'

And upon this they parted.

'He has either painted his face, or he is consumedly sick,' thought the old Judge.

The light had shone more effectually upon his features as he turned to leave the room with a low bow, and they looked, he fancied, unnaturally chalky.

'D—— him!' said the Judge ungraciously, as he began to scale the stairs; 'he has half-spoiled my supper.'

But if he had, no one but the Judge himself perceived it, and the evidence was all, as any one might perceive, the other way.

In the mean time, the footman dispatched in pursuit of Mr Peters speedily overtook that feeble gentleman. The old man stopped when he heard the sound of pursuing steps, but any alarms that may have crossed his mind seemed to disappear on his recognizing the livery. He very gratefully accepted the proffered assistance, and placed his tremulous arm within the servant's for support. They had not gone far, however, when the old man stopped suddenly, saying,

'Dear me! as I live, I have dropped it. You heard it fall. My eyes, I fear, won't serve me, and I'm unable to stoop low enough; but if *you* will look, you shall have half the find. It is a guinea;* I carried it in my glove.'

The street was silent and deserted. The footman had hardly descended to what he termed his 'hunkers',* and begun to search the pavement about the spot which the old man indicated, when Mr Peters, who seemed very much exhausted, and breathed with difficulty, struck him a violent blow, from above, over the back of the head with a heavy instrument, and then another; and leaving him bleeding and senseless in the gutter, ran like a lamplighter* down a lane to the right, and was gone.

When, an hour later, the watchman brought the man in livery home, still stupid and covered with blood, Judge Harbottle cursed his servant roundly, swore he was drunk, threatened him with an indictment for taking bribes to betray his master, and cheered him with a perspective of the broad street leading from the Old Bailey to Tyburn, the cart's tail, and the hangman's lash.*

Notwithstanding this demonstration, the Judge was pleased. It was a disguised 'affidavit man',* or footpad, no doubt, who had been employed to frighten him. That trick had fallen through.

A 'court of appeal', such as the false Hugh Peters had indicated, with assassination for its sanction, would be an uncomfortable institution for a 'hanging judge' like the Honourable Justice Harbottle. That sarcastic and ferocious administrator of the criminal code of England, at that time a rather pharisaical,* bloody, and heinous system of justice, had reasons of his own for choosing to try that very Lewis Pyneweck, on whose behalf this audacious trick was devised. Try him he would. No man living should take that morsel out of his mouth.

Of Lewis Pyneweck of course, so far as the outer world could see, he knew nothing. He would try him after his fashion, without fear, favour, or affection.

But did he not remember a certain thin man, dressed in mourning, in whose house, in Shrewsbury, the Judge's lodgings used to be, until a scandal of his ill-treating his wife came suddenly to light? A grocer with a demure look, a soft step, and a lean face as dark as mahogany, with a nose sharp and long, standing ever so little awry, and a pair of dark steady brown eyes under thinly-traced black brows—a man whose thin lips wore always a faint unpleasant smile.

Had not that scoundrel an account to settle with the Judge? had he not been troublesome lately? and was not his name Lewis Pyneweck, some time grocer in Shrewsbury, and now prisoner in the jail of that town?

The reader may take it, if he pleases, as a sign that Judge Harbottle was a good Christian, that he suffered nothing ever from remorse. That was undoubtedly true. He had nevertheless done this grocer, forger, what you will, some five or six years before, a grievous wrong; but it was not that, but a possible scandal, and possible complications, that troubled the learned Judge now.

Did he not, as a lawyer, know, that to bring a man from his shop to the dock, the chances must be at least ninety-nine out of a hundred that he is guilty?

A weak man like his learned brother Withershins* was not a judge to keep the high-roads safe, and make crime tremble. Old Judge Harbottle

was the man to make the evil-disposed quiver, and to refresh the world
with showers of wicked blood, and thus save the innocent, to the refrain
of the ancient saw he loved to quote:

> Foolish pity
> Ruins a city.*

In hanging that fellow he could not be wrong. The eye of a man
accustomed to look upon the dock could not fail to read 'villain' written
sharp and clear in his plotting face. Of course he would try him, and no
one else should.

A saucy-looking woman, still handsome, in a mob-cap gay with blue
ribbons, in a saque* of flowered silk, with lace and rings on, much too
fine for the Judge's housekeeper, which nevertheless she was, peeped
into his study next morning, and, seeing the Judge alone, stepped in.

'Here's another letter from him, come by the post this morning.
Can't you do nothing for him?' she said wheedlingly, with her arm over
his neck, and her delicate finger and thumb fiddling with the lobe of his
purple ear.

'I'll try,' said Judge Harbottle, not raising his eyes from the paper he
was reading.

'I knew you'd do what I asked you,' she said.

The Judge clapt his gouty claw over his heart, and made her an iron-
ical bow.

'What,' she asked, 'will you do?'

'Hang him,' said the Judge with a chuckle.

'You don't mean to; no, you don't, my little man,' said she, surveying
herself in a mirror on the wall.

'I'm d—d but I think you're falling in love with your husband at
last!' said Judge Harbottle.

'I'm blest but I think you're growing jealous of him,' replied the lady
with a laugh. 'But no; he was always a bad one to me; I've done with
him long ago.'

'And he with you, by George! When he took your fortune and your
spoons and your ear-rings, he had all he wanted of you. He drove you
from his house; and when he discovered you had made yourself comfortable, and found a good situation, he'd have taken your guineas and
your silver and your ear-rings over again, and then allowed you half-a-
dozen years more to make a new harvest for his mill. You don't wish
him good; if you say you do, you lie.'

She laughed a wicked saucy laugh, and gave the terrible
Rhadamanthus* a playful tap on the chops.

'He wants me to send him money to fee a counsellor,' she said, while her eyes wandered over the pictures on the wall, and back again to the looking-glass; and certainly she did not look as if his jeopardy troubled her very much.

'Confound his impudence, the *scoundrel*!' thundered the old Judge, throwing himself back in his chair, as he used to do *in furore** on the bench, and the lines of his mouth looked brutal, and his eyes ready to leap from their sockets. 'If you answer his letter from my house to please yourself, you'll write your next from somebody else's to please me. You understand, my pretty witch, I'll not be pestered. Come, no pouting; whimpering won't do. You don't care a brass farthing for the villain, body or soul. You came here but to make a row. You are one of Mother Carey's chickens;* and where you come, the storm is up. Get you gone, baggage! get you *gone*!' he repeated with a stamp; for a knock at the hall-door made her instantaneous disappearance indispensable.

I need hardly say that the venerable Hugh Peters did not appear again. The Judge never mentioned him. But oddly enough, considering how he laughed to scorn the weak invention which had blown into dust at the very first puff, his white-wigged visitor and the conference in the dark front parlour was often in his memory.

His shrewd eye told him that, allowing for change of tints and such disguises as the playhouse affords every night, the features of this false old man, who had turned out too hard for his tall footman, were identical with those of Lewis Pyneweck.

Judge Harbottle made his registrar call upon the crown solicitor,* and tell him that there was a man in town who bore a wonderful resemblance to a prisoner in Shrewsbury jail named Lewis Pyneweck, and to make inquiry through the post forthwith whether any one was personating Pyneweck in prison, and whether he had thus or otherwise made his escape.

The prisoner was safe, however, and no question as to his identity.

In due time Judge Harbottle went circuit.* In due time the judges were in Shrewsbury. News travelled slowly in those days, and newspapers, like the wagons and stage-coaches, took matters easy. Mrs Pyneweck, in the Judge's house, with a diminished household—for the greater part of the Judge's servants had gone with him; for he had given up riding circuit, and travelled in his coach in state—kept house rather solitarily at home.

In spite of quarrels, in spite of mutual injuries—some of them, inflicted by herself, enormous—in spite of a married life of spited bickerings—a life in which there seemed no love or liking or forbearance—for years, now that Pyneweck stood in near danger of death something like remorse came suddenly upon her. She knew that in Shrewsbury were transacting the scenes which were to determine his fate. She knew she did not love him; but she could not have supposed, even a fortnight before, that the hour of suspense could have affected her so powerfully.

She knew the day on which the trial was expected to take place. She could not get it out of her head for a minute; she felt faint as it drew towards evening.

Two or three days passed; and then she knew that the trial must be over by this time. There were floods between London and Shrewsbury, and news was long delayed. She wished the floods would last for ever. It was dreadful waiting to hear; dreadful to know that the event was over, and that she could not hear till self-willed rivers subsided; dreadful to know that they must subside and the news come at last.

She had some vague trust in the Judge's good-nature, and much in the resources of chance and accident. She had contrived to send the money he wanted. He would not be without legal advice and energetic and skilled support.

At last the news did come—a long arrear, all in a gush: a letter from a female friend in Shrewsbury; a return of the sentences, sent up for the Judge; and most important, because most easily got at, being told with great aplomb and brevity, the long-deferred intelligence of the Shrewsbury Assizes in the *Morning Advertiser.** Like an impatient reader of a novel, who reads the last page first, she read with dizzy eyes the list of the executions.

Two were respited, seven were hanged; and in that capital catalogue was this line:

'Lewis Pyneweck—forgery.'

She had to read it half-a-dozen times over before she was sure she understood it. Here was the paragraph:

> *'Sentence, Death*—7.
> 'Executed accordingly, on Friday the 13th instant, to wit:
> 'Thomas Primer, *alias* Duck—highway robbery.
> 'Flora Guy—stealing to the value of 11s. 6d.
> 'Arthur Pounden—burglary.
> 'Matilda Mummery—riot.
> 'Lewis Pyneweck—forgery, bill of exchange.'

And when she reached this, she read it over and over, feeling very cold and sick.

This buxom housekeeper was known in the house as Mrs Carwell—Carwell being her maiden name, which she had resumed.

No one in the house except its master knew her history. Her introduction had been managed craftily. No one suspected that it had been concerted between her and the old reprobate in scarlet and ermine.

Flora Carwell ran up the stairs now, and took her little girl, hardly seven years of age, whom she met on the lobby, by the arm, and led her into her bedroom, without well knowing what she was doing, and sat down, placing the child before her. She was not able to speak. She held the child before her, and looked in the little girl's wondering face, and burst into tears of horror.

She thought the Judge could have saved him. I daresay he could. For a time she was furious with him; and hugged and kissed her bewildered little girl, who returned her gaze with large round eyes.

That little girl had lost her father, and knew nothing of the matter. She had been always told that her father was dead long ago.

A woman, coarse, uneducated, vain, and violent, does not reason, or even feel, very distinctly; but in these tears of consternation were mingling a self-upbraiding. She felt afraid of that little child.

But Mrs Carwell was a person who lived not upon sentiment, but upon beef and pudding; she consoled herself with punch; she did not trouble herself long even with resentments; she was a gross and material person, and could not mourn over the irrevocable for more than a limited number of hours, even if she would.

Judge Harbottle was soon in London again. Except the gout, this savage old epicurean never knew a day's sickness. He laughed and coaxed and bullied away the young woman's faint upbraidings, and in a little time Lewis Pyneweck troubled her no more; and the Judge secretly chuckled over the perfectly fair removal of a bore, who might have grown little by little into something very like a tyrant.

It was the lot of the Judge whose adventures I am now recounting to try criminal cases at the Old Bailey shortly after his return. He had commenced his charge to the jury in a case of forgery, and was, after his wont, thundering dead against the prisoner, with many a hard aggravation and cynical gibe, when suddenly all died away in silence, and, instead of looking at the jury, the eloquent Judge was gaping at some person in the body of the court.

Among the persons of small importance who stand and listen at the sides was one tall enough to show with a little prominence; a slight mean figure, dressed in seedy black, lean and dark of visage. He had* just handed a letter to the crier, before he caught the Judge's eye.

That Judge descried, to his amazement, the features of Lewis Pyneweck. He has the usual faint thin-lipped smile; and with his blue

chin raised in air, and as it seemed quite unconscious of the distinguished notice he has attracted, he was stretching his low cravat with
his crooked fingers, while he slowly turned his head from side to side—
a process which enabled the Judge to see distinctly a stripe of swollen
blue round his neck, which indicated, he thought, the grip of the rope.

This man, with a few others, had got a footing on a step, from which
he could better see the court. He now stepped down, and the Judge lost
sight of him.

His lordship signed energetically with his hand in the direction in
which this man had vanished. He turned to the tipstaff.* His first effort
to speak ended in a gasp. He cleared his throat, and told the astounded
official to arrest that man who had interrupted the court.

'He's but this moment gone down *there*. Bring him in custody before
me, within ten minutes' time, or I'll strip your gown from your shoulders, and fine the sheriff!' he thundered, while his eyes flashed round
the court in search of that functionary.

Attorneys, counsellors, idle spectators, gazed in the direction in
which Mr Justice Harbottle had shaken his gnarled old hand. They
compared notes. Not one had seen any one making a disturbance. They
asked one another if the Judge was losing his head.

Nothing came of the search. His lordship concluded his charge
a great deal more tamely; and when the jury retired, he stared round the
court with a wandering mind, and looked as if he would not have given
sixpence to have the prisoner hanged.

The Judge had received the letter; had he known from whom it came,
he would no doubt have read it instantaneously. As it was, he simply
read the direction:

> To the Honourable
> The Lord Justice
> Elijah Harbottle,
> One of his Majesty's Justices of
> the Honourable Court of Common Pleas.

It remained forgotten in his pocket till he reached home.

When he pulled out that and others from the capacious pocket of his
coat, it had its turn, as he sat in his library in his thick silk dressing-gown;
and then he found its contents to be a closely-written letter, in a clerk's
hand, and an enclosure in 'secretary hand', as I believe the angular
scrivinary* of law-writings in those days was termed, engrossed on a hit
of parchment about the size of this page. The letter said:

Mr Justice Harbottle,—My Lord,

I am ordered by the High Court of Appeal to acquaint your lordship, in order to your better preparing yourself for your trial, that a true bill* hath been sent down, and the indictment lieth against your lordship for the murder of one Lewis Pyneweck of Shrewsbury, citizen, wrongfully executed for the forgery of a bill of exchange, on the —th day of —— last, by reason of the wilful perversion of the evidence, and the undue pressure put upon the jury, together with the illegal admission of evidence by your lordship, well knowing the same to be illegal, by all which the promoter of the prosecution of the said indictment, before the High Court of Appeal, hath lost his life.

And the trial of the said indictment, I am farther ordered to acquaint your lordship, is fixed for the 10th day of —— next ensuing, by the right honourable the Lord Chief-Justice Twofold, of the court aforesaid, to wit, the High Court of Appeal, on which day it will most certainly take place. And I am farther to acquaint your lordship, to prevent any surprise or miscarriage, that your case stands first for the said day, and that the said High Court of Appeal sits day and night, and never rises; and herewith, by order of the said court, I furnish your lordship with a copy (extract) of the record in this case, except of the indictment, whereof, notwithstanding, the substance and effect is supplied to your lordship in this Notice. And farther I am to inform you, that in case the jury then to try your lordship should find you guilty, the right honourable the Lord Chief-Justice will, in passing sentence of death upon you, fix the day of execution for the 10th day of ——, being one calendar month after the day of your trial.

It was signed by

CALEB SEARCHER,
Officer of the Crown Solicitor in the
'Kingdom of Life and Death'.

The Judge glanced through the parchment.

"'Sblood!* Do they think a man like me is to be bamboozled by their buffoonery?'

The Judge's coarse features were wrung into one of his sneers; but he was pale. Possibly, after all, there was a conspiracy on foot. It was queer. Did they mean to pistol him in his carriage? or did they only aim at frightening him?

Judge Harbottle had more than enough of animal courage. He was not afraid of highwaymen, and he had fought more than his share of duels, being a foul-mouthed advocate while he held briefs at the bar. No one questioned his fighting qualities. But with respect to this particular case of Pyneweck, he lived in a house of glass. Was there not his pretty, dark-eyed, over-dressed housekeeper, Mrs Flora Carwell? Very easy for people who knew Shrewsbury to identify Mrs Pyneweck, if once put upon the scent; and had he not stormed and worked hard in that case? Had he not made it hard sailing for the prisoner? Did he not know very well what the bar thought of it? It would be the worst scandal that ever blasted judge.

So much there was intimidating in the matter, but nothing more. The Judge was a little bit gloomy for a day or two after, and more testy with every one than usual.

He locked up the papers; and about a week after he asked his housekeeper, one day, in the library:

'Had your husband never a brother?'

Mrs Carwell squalled on this sudden introduction of the funereal topic, and cried exemplary 'piggins* full', as the Judge used pleasantly to say. But he was in no mood for trifling now, and he said sternly:

'Come, madam! this wearies me. Do it another time; and give me an answer to my question.'

So she did.

Pyneweck had no brother living. He once had one; but he died in Jamaica.

'How do you know he is dead?' asked the Judge.

'Because he told me so.'

'Not the dead man?'

'Pyneweck told me so.'

'Is that all?' sneered the Judge.

He pondered this matter; and time went on.

The Judge was growing a little morose, and less enjoying.* The subject struck nearer to his thoughts than he fancied it could have done. But so it is with most undivulged vexations, and there was no one to whom he could tell this one.

It was now the ninth; and Mr Justice Harbottle was glad. He knew nothing would come of it. Still it bothered him; and to-morrow would see it well over.

Judge Harbottle went this night to the play at Drury-lane.* He was one of those old fellows who care nothing for late hours, and occasional knocking about in pursuit of pleasure. He had appointed with two cronies of Lincoln's-inn* to come home in his coach with him to sup after the play.

They were not in his box, but were to meet him near the entrance, and to get into his carriage there; and Mr Justice Harbottle, who hated waiting, was looking a little impatiently from the window.

The Judge yawned.

He told the footman to watch for Counsellor Thavies* and Counsellor Beller, who were coming; and, with another yawn, he laid his cocked-hat on his knees, closed his eyes, leaned back in his corner, wrapped his mantle closer about him, and began to think of pretty Mrs Abington.*

And being a man who could sleep like a sailor, at a moment's notice, he was thinking of taking a nap. Those fellows had no business keeping a judge waiting.

He heard their voices now. Those rake-hell counsellors were laughing, and bantering, and sparring, after their wont. The carriage swayed and jerked, as one got in, and then again as the other followed. The door clapped, and the coach was now jogging and rumbling over the pavement. The Judge was a little bit sulky. He did not care to sit up and open his eyes. Let them suppose he was asleep. He heard them laugh with more malice than good-humour, he thought, as they observed it. He would give them a d——d hard knock or two when they got to his door, and till then he would counterfeit his nap.

The clocks were chiming twelve. Beller and Thavies were silent as tombstones. They were generally loquacious and merry rascals.

The Judge suddenly felt himself roughly seized and thrust from his corner into the middle of the seat, and opening his eyes, instantly he found himself between his two companions.

Before he could blurt out the oath that was at his lips, he saw that they were two strangers—evil-looking fellows, each with a pistol in his hand, and dressed like Bow-street officers.*

The Judge clutched at the check-string.* The coach pulled up. He stared about him. They were not among houses; but through the windows, under a broad moonlight, he saw a black moor stretching lifelessly from right to left, with rotting trees, pointing fantastic branches in the air, standing here and there in groups, as if they held up their arms in horrible welcome at the Judge's coming.

A footman came to the window. He knew his long face and sunken eyes. He knew it was Dingly Chuff, fifteen years ago a footman in his service, whom he had turned off at a moment's notice, in a burst of jealousy, and indicted for a missing spoon. The man had died in an hospital;* and yet this was *he*!

The Judge drew back in utter amazement. His armed companions signed mutely; and they were again gliding over this unknown moor.

The bloated and gouty old man, in this horror, considered the question of resistance. But his athletic days were long over. This moor was a desert. There was no help to be had. He was in the hands of strange servants, even if his recognition turned out to be a delusion, and they were under the command of his captors. There was nothing for it but submission, for the present.

Suddenly the coach was brought nearly to a standstill, so that the prisoner saw an ominous sight from the window.

It was a gigantic gallows beside the road; it stood three-sided and from each of its three broad beams at top depended in chains some eight or ten bodies, from several of which the cere-clothes* had dropped away, leaving the skeletons swinging lightly by their chains. A tall ladder reached to the summit of the structure, and on the peat beneath lay bones.

On top of the dark transverse beam facing the road, from which, as from the other two completing the triangle of death, dangled a row of these unfortunates in chains, a hangman, with a pipe in his mouth, much as we see him in the famous print of the 'Idle Apprentice',* though here his perch was ever so much higher, was reclining at his ease and listlessly shying bones, from a little heap at his elbow, at the skeletons that hung round, bringing down now a rib or two, now a hand, now half a leg. A long-sighted man could have discerned that he was a dark fellow, lean; and from continually looking down on the earth from the elevation over which, in another sense, he always hung, his nose, his lips, his chin were pendulous and loose, and drawn down into a monstrous grotesque.

This fellow took his pipe from his mouth on seeing the coach, stood up, and cut some solemn capers high on his beam, and shook a new rope in the air, crying with a voice high and distant as the caw of a raven hovering over a gibbet, 'A rope for Judge Harbottle!'

The coach was now driving on at its old swift pace.

So high a gallows as that, the Judge had never, even in his most hilarious moments, dreamed of. He thought he must be raving. And the dead footman! He shook his ears and strained his eyelids; but if he was dreaming, he was not able to awake himself.

There was no good in threatening these scoundrels. A *brutum fulmen** might bring a real one on his head.

Any submission to get out of their hands; and then heaven and earth he would move to unearth and hunt them down.

Suddenly they drove round the corner of a vast white building, and under a *porte-cochère*.*

The Judge found himself in a corridor lighted with lamps, the walls of bare stone; it looked like a passage in a prison. His guards placed him in the hands of other people. Here and there he saw gigantically tall soldiers pacing to and fro, with muskets over their shoulders. He saw these by glimpses, round corners, and at the ends of passages, but he did not actually pass them by.

And now, passing through a narrow door, he found himself in the dock, confronting a judge in his scarlet robes, in a large courthouse.

There was nothing to elevate this temple of Themis* above its vulgar kind elsewhere. Dingy enough it looked, in spite of candles lighted in decent abundance. A case had just closed, and the last juror's hack was seen escaping through the door in the wall of the jury-box. There were some dozen barristers, some fiddling with pen and ink, others buried in briefs, some beckoning to their attorneys, of whom there were no lack; there were clerks to-ing and fro-ing, and the officers of the court, and the registrar, who was handing up a paper to the judge; and the tipstaff, who was presenting a note at the end of his wand to a king's counsel over the heads of the crowd between. If this was the High Court of Appeal, which never rose night or day, it might account for the pale and jaded aspect of everybody in it. An air of indescribable fatigue hung upon the pallid features of everybody here; no one ever smiled: all looked more or less secretly suffering.

'The King against Elijah Harbottle!' shouted the officer.

'Is the appellant Lewis Pyneweck in court?' asked Chief-Justice Twofold, in a voice of thunder.

Up stood Pyneweck from his place at the table.

'Arraign the prisoner!' he roared; and Judge Harbottle felt the wood-work of the dock round him, and the floor, and the rails tremble in the vibrations of that tremendous voice.

The prisoner *in limine** objected to this pretended court, as being a sham, and non-existent in point of law; and then that, even if it were a court, constituted by law (the Judge was growing dazed), it had not and could not have any jurisdiction to try him for his conduct on the bench.

Whereupon the chief-justice laughed suddenly, and every one in court, turning round upon the prisoner, laughed also, till the laugh grew and roared all round like a deafening peal of thunder; but though all the voices laughed, not a single face of all those that concentrated their gaze upon him looked like a laughing face. They all gaped dismally. The mirth subsided as suddenly as it began.

The indictment was read. Judge Harbottle actually pleaded! He pleaded 'Not guilty'. A jury were sworn. The trial proceeded. Judge Harbottle was bewildered. This could not be real. He must be either mad, or *going* mad, he thought.

One thing could not fail to strike even him. This Chief-Justice Twofold, who was knocking him about at every turn with sneer and gibe, and roaring him down with his tremendous voice, was a dilated effigy of himself; an image of Mr Justice Harbottle, at least double his size, and with all his fierce colouring, and his ferocity of eye and visage, enhanced awfully in power.*

Nothing the prisoner could argue, cite, or state was permitted to retard for a moment the march of the case toward its catastrophe.

The chief-justice seemed to feel his power over the jury, and to exult and riot in the display of it. He glared at them, he nodded to them; he seemed to have established an understanding with them. The lights were faint in that part of the court. The jurors were mere shadows, sitting in rows; the prisoner could see a dozen pair of white eyes shining, as it were phosphorically, out of the darkness; and whenever the judge in his charge, which was contemptuously brief, nodded and grinned and gibed, the prisoner could see, in the obscurity, by the dip of all these rows of eyes together, that the jury nodded in acquiescence.

And now the charge was over, the huge chief-justice leaned back panting and gloating on the prisoner. Every one in the court turned about, and gazed with steadfast hatred on the man in the dock. From the jury-box, where the twelve sworn brethren were whispering together, a sound in the general stillness like a prolonged 'hiss-s-s!' was heard; and then, in answer to the challenge of the officer, 'How say you, gentlemen of the jury, guilty or not guilty?' came in a melancholy voice the finding, 'Guilty'.

The place seemed to the eyes of the prisoner to grow gradually darker and darker, till he could discern nothing distinctly but the lumen of the strange eyes that were turned upon him from every bench and side and corner and gallery of the building. The prisoner doubtless thought he had quite enough to say, and conclusive, why sentence of death should not be pronounced upon him; but the lord chief-justice puffed it contemptuously away, like so much smoke, and proceeded to pass sentence of death upon the prisoner, having named the 10th of the ensuing month for his execution.

Before he had recovered the stun of this ominous farce, in obedience to the mandate, 'Remove the prisoner', he was led from the dock. The lamps seemed all to have gone out, and there were stoves and charcoal-fires here and there, that threw a faint crimson light on the walls of the corridors through which he passed. The stones that composed them looked now enormous, cracked, and unhewn.

He came into a vaulted smithy, where two men, naked to the waist, with heads like bulls, round shoulders, and the arms of giants, were welding red-hot chains together with hammers that pelted like thunderbolts.

They looked on the prisoner with fierce red eyes, and rested on their hammers for a minute; and said the elder to his companion, 'Take out

Elijah Harbottle's gyves';* and with pincers he plucked the end which lay dazzling in the fire from the furnace.

'One end locks,' said he, taking the cool end of the iron in one hand, while with the grip of a vice he seized the leg of the Judge, and locked the ring round his ankle. 'The other,' he said with a grin, 'is welded.'

The iron band that was to form the ring for the other leg lay still red-hot upon the stone floor, with brilliant sparks sporting up and down its surface.

His companion in his gigantic hands seized the old Judge's other leg, and pressed his foot immovably to the stone floor; while his senior in a twinkling, with a masterly application of pincers and hammer, sped the glowing bar round his ankle so tight that the skin and sinews smoked and bubbled again, and old Judge Harbottle uttered a yell that seemed to chill the very stones, and make the iron chains quiver on the wall.

Chains, vaults, smiths, and smithy all vanished in a moment; but the pain continued. Mr Justice Harbottle was suffering torture all round the ankle on which the infernal smiths had just been operating.

His friends Thavies and Beller were startled by the Judge's roar in the midst of their elegant trifling about a marriage *à-la-mode** case which was going on. The Judge was in panic as well as pain. The street-lamps and the light of his own hall-door restored him.

'I'm very bad,' growled he between his set teeth; 'my foot's blazing. Who was he that hurt my foot? 'Tis the gout—'tis the gout!' he said, awaking completely. 'How many hours have we been coming from the playhouse? 'Sblood, what has happened on the way? I've slept half the night!'

There had been no hitch or delay, and they had driven home at a good pace.

The Judge, however, was in gout; he was feverish too; and the attack, though very short, was sharp; and when, in about a fortnight, it sub-sided, his ferocious joviality did not return. He could not get this dream, as he chose to call it, out of his head.

People remarked that the Judge was in the vapours.* His doctor said he should go for a fortnight to Buxton.*

Whenever the Judge fell into a brown study, he was always conning over the terms of the sentence pronounced upon him in his vision—'in one calendar month from the date of this day'; and then the usual form, 'and you shall be hanged by the neck till you are dead', etc. 'That will be the 10th—not much in the way of being hanged. I know what stuff dreams are,* and I laugh at them; but this is continually in my thoughts, as if it forecast misfortune of some sort. I wish the day my dream gave

me were passed and over. I wish I were well purged of my gout. I wish I were as I used to be. 'Tis nothing but vapours, nothing but a maggot.'*
The parchment and letter which had announced his trial with many a snort and sneer he would read over and over again, and the scenery and people of his dream would rise about him in places the most unlikely, and steal him in a moment from all that surrounded him into a world of shadows.

The Judge had lost his iron energy and banter. He was growing taciturn and morose. The Bar remarked the change, as well they might. His friends thought him ill. The doctor said he was troubled with hypochondria, and that his gout was still lurking in his system, and ordered him to that ancient haunt of crutches and chalk-stones, Buxton.

The Judge's spirits were very low; he was frightened about himself; and he described to his housekeeper, having sent for her to his study to drink a dish of tea, his strange dream in his drive home from Drury-lane playhouse. He was sinking into the state of nervous dejection in which men lose their faith in orthodox advice, and in despair consult quacks, astrologers, and nursery story-tellers. Could such a dream mean that he was to have a fit, and so die on the 10th? She did not think so. On the contrary, it was certain some good luck must happen on that day.

The Judge kindled; and for the first time these many days he looked for a minute or two like himself, and he tapped her on the cheek with the hand that was not in flannel.

'Odsbud! odsheart!* you dear rogue! I had forgot. There is young Tom—yellow Tom, my nephew, you know, lies sick at Harrogate; why shouldn't he go that day as well as another, and if he does, I get an estate by it? Why, lookee, I asked Doctor Hedstone yesterday if I was like to take a fit any time, and he laughed, and swore I was the last man in town to go off that way.'

The Judge sent most of his servants down to Buxton to make his lodgings and all things comfortable for him. He was to follow in a day or two.

It was now the 9th; and the next day well over, he might laugh at his visions and auguries.

On the evening of the 9th, Doctor Hedstone's footman knocked at the Judge's door. The doctor ran up the dusky stairs to the drawing-room. It was a March evening, near the hour of sunset, with an east wind whistling sharply through the chimney-stacks. A wood fire blazed cheerily on the hearth. And Judge Harbottle, in what was then called a brigadier-wig, with his red roquelaure on, helped the glowing effect of the darkened chamber, which looked red all over like a room on fire.

The Judge had his feet on a stool, and his huge grim purple face confronted the fire, and seemed to pant and swell, as the blaze alternately spread upward and collapsed. He had fallen again among his blue devils,* and was thinking of retiring from the Bench, and of fifty other gloomy things.

But the doctor, who was an energetic son of Aesculapius,* would listen to no croaking, told the Judge he was full of gout, and in his present condition no judge even of his own case, but promised him leave to pronounce on all those melancholy questions a fortnight later.

In the mean time the Judge must be very careful. He was overcharged with gout, and he must not provoke an attack, till the waters of Buxton should do that office for him.

The doctor did not think him perhaps quite so well as he pretended, for he told him he wanted rest, and would be better if he went forthwith to his bed.

Mr Gerningham, his valet, assisted him, and gave him his drops; and the Judge told him to wait in his bedroom till he should go to sleep.

Three persons that night had specially odd stories to tell.

The housekeeper had got rid of the trouble of amusing her little girl at this anxious time by giving her leave to run about the sitting-rooms and look at the pictures and china, on the usual condition of touching nothing. It was not until the last gleam of sunset had for some time faded, and the twilight had so deepened that she could no longer discern the colours on the china figures on the chimneypiece or in the cabinets, that the child returned to the housekeeper's room to find her mother.

To her she related, after some prattle about the china, and the pictures, and the Judge's two grand wigs in the dressing-room off the library, an adventure of an extraordinary kind.

In the hall was placed, as was customary in those times, the sedan-chair which the master of the house occasionally used, covered with stamped leather, and studded with gilt nails, and with its red silk blinds down. In this case, the doors of this old-fashioned conveyance were locked, the windows up, and, as I said, the blinds down, but not so closely that the curious child could not peep underneath one of them, and see into the interior.

A parting beam from the setting sun, admitted through the window of a back room, shot obliquely through the open door, and lighting on the chair, shone with a dull transparency through the crimson blind.

To her surprise, the child saw in the shadow a thin man dressed in black seated in it; he had sharp dark features; his nose, she fancied, a little awry, and his brown eyes were looking straight before him; his hand was on his thigh, and he stirred no more than the waxen figure she had seen at Southwark fair.*

A child is so often lectured for asking questions and on the propriety of silence, and the superior wisdom of its elders, that it accepts most things at last in good faith; and the little girl acquiesced respectfully in the occupation of the chair by this mahogany-faced person as being all right and proper.

It was not until she asked her mother who this man was, and observed her scared face as she questioned her more minutely upon the appearance of the stranger, that she began to understand that she had seen something unaccountable.

Mrs Carwell took the key of the chair from its nail over the footman's shelf, and led the child by the hand up to the hall, having a lighted candle in her other hand.

'Peep in, Margery, again, and try if there's anything there,' she whispered, holding the candle near the blind so as to throw its light through that transparent curtain.

The child peeped, this time with a very solemn face, and intimated at once that he was gone.

'Look again, and be sure,' urged her mother.

The little girl was quite certain; and Mrs Carwell, with her mob-cap of lace and cherry-coloured ribbons, and her dark-brown hair, not yet powdered, over a very pale face, unlocked the door, looked in, and beheld emptiness.

'All a mistake, child, you see.'

'*There*, ma'am! see there! He's gone round the corner,' said the child.

'Where?' said Mrs Carwell, stepping backward a step.

'Into that room.'

'Tut, child! 'twas the shadow,' cried Mrs Carwell angrily, because she was frightened. 'I moved the candle.' But she clutched one of the poles of the chair, which leant against the wall in the corner, and pounded the floor furiously with one end of it, being afraid to pass the open door the child had pointed to.

The cook and two kitchen-maids came running up-stairs, not knowing what to make of this unwonted alarm.

They all searched the room; but it was still and empty, and no sign of any one's having been there.

Some people may suppose that the direction given to her thoughts by this odd little incident will account for a very strange illusion which Mrs Carwell herself experienced about two hours later.

She was going up the great staircase with a posset* for the Judge in a china bowl, on a little silver tray.

Across the top of the well-staircase there runs a massive oak rail; and, raising her eyes accidentally, she saw an extremely odd-looking stranger, slim and long, leaning carelessly over with a pipe between his finger and thumb. Nose, lips, and chin seemed all to droop downward into extraordinary length, as he leant his odd peering face over the banister. In his other hand he held a coil of rope, one end of which escaped from under his elbow and hung over the rail.

Mrs Carwell, who had no suspicion at the moment that he was not a real person, and fancied that he was some one employed in cording the luggage, called to know what he was doing there.

Instead of answering, he turned about, and walked across the lobby at about the same leisurely pace that she walked at, and entered a room, into which she followed him. It was an uncarpeted and unfurnished room. An open trunk lay upon the floor empty, and beside it the coil of rope; but except herself there was no one in the room.

Mrs Carwell was very much frightened, and now concluded that the child must have seen the same ghost that had just appeared to her. Perhaps, when she was able to think it over, it was a relief to believe so; for the face, figure, and dress described by the child were awfully like Pyneweck; and this certainly was not he.

Very much scared and very hysterical, Mrs Carwell ran down to her room, afraid to look over her shoulder, and got some companions about her, and wept, and talked, and drank more than one cordial, and talked and wept again, and so on, until, in those early days, it was ten o'clock, and time to go to bed.

A scullery-maid* remained up finishing some of her scouring and 'scalding' for some time after the rest of the servants—who, as I said, were few in number—that night had got to their beds. This was a low-browed, broad-faced, intrepid wench with black hair, who did not 'vally* a ghost not a button', and treated the housekeeper's hysterics with measureless scorn.

But this sceptical heroine, at near twelve o'clock, being the only person awake and about, and the house within quite still, except for the uncertain wailing of the wintry winds, audible from outside, piping high among the roofs and chimneys, or rumbling at intervals, in under gusts, through the narrow channels of the streets, was herself destined to be more terrified than even was the housekeeper.

There was a back-kitchen in this house, and from this she heard a sound like the strokes of a hammer on metal. Sometimes a dozen in sequence, at regular intervals; sometimes fewer. She was surprised to see a dusky glow issuing from this room, as if from a charcoal fire.

Looking in, she beheld a monstrous figure, black as soot, over a furnace, beating with a mighty hammer the rings and rivets of a long iron chain, which he shifted on the huge stone of a disused jack that served him for an anvil.

The strokes, swift and heavy as they looked, sounded faint and distant. The man fixed his red eyes on her, and pointed to a coarse cloth which lay upon the flags, spread like a coverlet, with a great bulk like a huge bale stretched under it.

She said something in her panic to the unknown smith, who seemed to await only that to speak. What he said she did not tell; but he drew the cloth down from the feet, slowly disclosing the bloated features and body of the old Judge, lying flat on his back, with his eyes open, and quite dead. She remarked no more; but the servants in the room close by, startled from their sleep by a hideous scream, found her in a swoon on the flags where she had just witnessed this ghastly vision.*

Startled by the girl's incoherent asseverations that she had seen the Judge's corpse on the floor, two servants went rather frightened up-stairs to ascertain whether their master was well. He had a table with candles burning by his bed, and was getting on his clothes again; and he swore and cursed at them roundly in his old style, telling them that he had business, and that he would discharge on the spot any scoundrel among them who should dare to disturb him again.

So the invalid was left to his quietude.

In the morning it was rumoured here and there in the street that the Judge was dead. A servant was sent from the house, three doors away, by Counsellor Traverse, to inquire at Judge Harbottle's hall-door.

The servant who opened it was pale and reserved, and would only say that the Judge was ill. He had had a dangerous accident; Doctor Hedstone had been with him at seven o'clock in the morning.

There were averted looks, short answers, pale and frowning faces, and all the usual signs that there was a secret that sat heavily upon their minds, and the time for disclosing which had not yet come. That time would arrive when the coroner had arrived, and the mortal scandal that had befallen the house could be no longer hidden. For that morning Mr Justice Harbottle had been found hanging by the neck from the banister at the top of the great staircase, and quite dead.

There was not the smallest sign of any struggle or resistance. There had not been heard a cry or any other noise in the slightest degree indicative of violence. There was medical evidence to show that, in his atrabilious* state, it was quite on the cards that he might have made away with himself. The jury found accordingly that it was a case of suicide. But to those who were acquainted with the strange story which Judge Harbottle had related to at least two persons, the fact that the catastrophe occurred on the morning of the 10th March seemed a startling coincidence.

A few days after, the pomp of a great funeral attended him to the grave; and so, in the language of Scripture, 'the rich man died, and was buried'.*

THE ROOM IN THE
DRAGON VOLANT

CHAPTER I

ON THE ROAD

IN the eventful year, 1815,* I was exactly three-and-twenty, and had just succeeded to a very large sum in consols, and other securities. The first fall of Napoleon had thrown the continent open to English excursionists, anxious, let us suppose, to improve their minds by foreign travel; and I—the slight check of the 'hundred days' removed, by the genius of Wellington, on the field of Waterloo—was now added to the philosophic throng.

I was posting up to Paris from Bruxelles, following, I presume, the route that the allied army had pursued but a few weeks before—more carriages than you could believe, were pursuing the same line. You could not look back or forward, without seeing into far perspective the clouds of dust which marked the line of the long series of vehicles. We were, perpetually, passing relays of return-horses, on their way, jaded and dusty, to the inns from which they had been taken. They were arduous times for those patient public servants. The whole world seemed posting up to Paris.

I ought to have noted it more particularly, but my head was so full of Paris and the future, that I passed the intervening scenery with little patience, and less attention; I think, however, that it was about four miles to the frontier side of a rather picturesque little town, the name of which, as of many more important places through which I posted in my hurried journey, I forget, and about two hours before sunset, that we came up with a carriage in distress.

It was not quite an upset. But the two leaders* were lying flat. The booted postillions had got down, and two servants who seemed very much at sea in such matters, were by way of assisting them. A pretty little bonnet and head were popped out of the window of the carriage in distress. Its *tournure*,* and that of the shoulders that also appeared for a moment, was captivating: I resolved to play the part of a good Samaritan; stopped my chaise, jumped out, and with my servant lent a very willing hand in the emergency. Alas! the lady with the pretty bonnet, wore a very thick, black veil. I could see nothing but the pattern of the Bruxelles lace,* as she drew back.

A lean old gentleman, almost at the same time, stuck his head out of the window. An invalid he seemed, for although the day was hot, he wore a black muffler which came up to his ears and nose, quite covering the lower part of his face; an arrangement which he disturbed by pulling it down for a moment, and poured forth a torrent of French thanks, as he uncovered his black wig, and gesticulated with grateful animation.

One of my very few accomplishments besides boxing, which was cultivated by all Englishmen at that time, was French; and I replied, I hope and believe, grammatically. Many bows being exchanged, the old gentleman's head went in again, and the demure, pretty little bonnet once more appeared.

The lady must have heard me speak to my servant, for she framed her little speech in such pretty, broken English, and in a voice so sweet, that I more than ever cursed the black veil that baulked my romantic curiosity.

The arms that were emblazoned on the panel were peculiar; I remember especially, one device, it was the figure of a stork, painted in carmine, upon what the heralds call a 'field or'.* The bird was standing upon one leg, and in the other claw held a stone. This is, I believe, the emblem of vigilance. Its oddity struck me, and remained impressed upon my memory. There were supporters besides, but I forget what they were.

The courtly manners of these people, the style of their servants, the elegance of their travelling carriage, and the supporters to their arms, satisfied me that they were noble.

The lady, you may be sure, was not the less interesting on that account. What a fascination a title exercises upon the imagination! I do not mean on that of snobs or moral flunkies. Superiority of rank is a powerful and genuine influence in love. The idea of superior refinement is associated with it. The careless notice of the squire tells more upon the heart of the pretty milkmaid, than years of honest Dobbin's manly devotion,* and so on and up. It is an unjust world!

But in this case there was something more. I was conscious of being good-looking. I really believe I was; and there could be no mistake about my being nearly six feet high. Why need this lady have thanked me? Had not her husband, for such I assumed him to be, thanked me quite enough, and for both? I was instinctively aware that the lady was looking on me with no unwilling eyes; and, through her veil, I felt the power of her gaze.

She was now rolling away, with a train of dust behind her wheels, in the golden sunlight, and a wise young gentleman followed her with ardent eyes, and sighed profoundly as the distance increased.

I told the postillions on no account to pass the carriage, but to keep it steadily in view, and to pull up at whatever posting-house it should stop at. We were soon in the little town, and the carriage we followed drew up at the Belle Etoile, a comfortable old inn. They got out of the carriage and entered the house.

At a leisurely pace we followed. I got down, and mounted the steps, listlessly, like a man quite apathetic and careless.

Audacious as I was, I did not care to inquire in what room I should find them. I peeped into the apartment to my right, and then into that on my left. *My* people were not there.

I ascended the stairs. A drawing-room door stood open. I entered with the most innocent air in the world. It was a spacious room, and, beside myself, contained but one living figure—a very pretty and lady-like one. There was the very bonnet with which I had fallen in love. The lady stood with her back toward me. I could not tell whether the envious veil was raised; she was reading a letter.

I stood for a minute in fixed attention, gazing upon her, in the vague hope that she might turn about, and give me an opportunity of seeing her features. She did not; but with a step or two she placed herself before a little cabriole-table, which stood against the wall, from which rose a tall mirror, in a tarnished frame.

I might, indeed, have mistaken it for a picture; for it now reflected a half-length portrait of a singularly beautiful woman.

She was looking down upon a letter which she held in her slender fingers, and in which she seemed absorbed.

The face was oval, melancholy, sweet. It had in it, nevertheless, a faint and undefinably sensual quality also. Nothing could exceed the delicacy of its features, or the brilliancy of its tints. The eyes, indeed, were lowered, so that I could not see their colour; nothing but their long lashes, and delicate eyebrows. She continued reading. She must have been deeply interested; I never saw a living form so motionless—I gazed on a tinted statue.

Being at that time blessed with long and keen vision, I saw this beautiful face with perfect distinctness. I saw even the blue veins that traced their wanderings on the whiteness of her full throat.

I ought to have retreated as noiselessly as I came in, before my presence was detected. But I was too much interested to move from the spot, for a few moments longer; and while they were passing, she raised her eyes. Those eyes were large, and of that hue which modern poets term 'violet'.

These splendid melancholy eyes were turned upon me from the glass, with a haughty stare, and hastily the lady lowered her black veil, and turned about.

I fancied that she hoped I had not seen her. I was watching every look and movement, the minutest, with an attention as intense as if an ordeal involving my life depended on them.

CHAPTER II

THE INN-YARD OF THE BELLE ETOILE

THE face was, indeed, one to fall in love with at first sight. Those sentiments that take such sudden possession of young men, were now dominating my curiosity. My audacity faltered before her; and I felt that my presence in this room was probably an impertinence. This point she quickly settled, for the same very sweet voice I had heard before, now said coldly, and this time in French, 'Monsieur cannot be aware that this apartment is not public.'

I bowed very low, faltered some apologies, and backed to the door.

I suppose I looked penitent and embarrassed. I certainly felt so; for the lady said, by way it seemed of softening matters, 'I am happy, however, to have an opportunity of again thanking monsieur for the assistance, so prompt and effectual, which he had the goodness to render us to-day.'

It was more the altered tone in which it was spoken, than the speech itself that encouraged me. It was also true that she need not have recognized me; and even if she had, she certainly was not obliged to thank me over again.

All this was indescribably flattering, and all the more so that it followed so quickly on her slight reproof.

The tone in which she spoke had become low and timid, and I observed that she turned her head quickly towards a second door of the room, I fancied that the gentleman in the black wig, a jealous husband, perhaps, might reappear through it. Almost at the same moment, a voice at once reedy and nasal, was heard snarling some directions to a servant, and evidently approaching. It was the voice that had thanked me so profusely, from the carriage windows, about an hour before.

'Monsieur will have the goodness to retire,' said the lady, in a tone that resembled entreaty, at the same time gently waving her hand toward the door through which I had entered. Bowing again very low, I stepped back, and closed the door.

I ran down the stairs, very much elated. I saw the host of the Belle Etoile which, as I said, was the sign and designation of my inn.

I described the apartment I had just quitted, said I liked it, and asked whether I could have it.

He was extremely troubled, but that apartment and two adjoining rooms were engaged—

'By whom?'

'People of distinction.'

'But who are they? They must have names, or titles.'

'Undoubtedly, monsieur, but such a stream is rolling into Paris, that we have ceased to inquire into the names or titles of our guests—we designate them simply by the rooms they occupy.'

'What stay do they make?'

'Even that, monsieur, I cannot answer. It does not interest us. Our rooms, while this continues, can never be, for a moment, disengaged.'

'I should have liked those rooms so much! Is one of them a sleeping apartment?'

'Yes, sir, and monsieur will observe that people do not usually engage bed-rooms, unless they mean to stay the night.'

'Well, I can, I suppose, have some rooms, any, I don't care in what part of the house?'

'Certainly, monsieur can have two apartments. They are the last at present disengaged.'

I took them instantly.

It was plain these people meant to make a stay here; at least they would not go till morning. I began to feel that I was all but engaged in an adventure.

I took possession of my rooms, and looked out of the window, which I found commanded the inn-yard. Many horses were being liberated from the traces, hot and weary, and others fresh from the stables, being put to. A great many vehicles—some private carriages, others, like mine, of that public class, which is equivalent to our old English post-chaise, were standing on the pavement, waiting their turn for relays. Fussy servants were to-ing and fro-ing, and idle ones lounging or laughing, and the scene, on the whole, was animated and amusing.

Among these objects, I thought I recognized the travelling carriage, and one of the servants of the 'persons of distinction' about whom I was, just then, so profoundly interested.

I therefore ran down the stairs, made my way to the back door; and so, behold me, in a moment, upon the uneven pavement, among all these sights and sounds which in such a place attend upon a period of extraordinary crush and traffic.

By this time the sun was near its setting, and threw its golden beams on the red brick chimneys of the offices, and made the two barrels, that figured as pigeon-houses, on the tops of poles, look as if they were on fire. Everything in this light becomes picturesque; and things interest us which, in the sober grey of morning, are dull enough.

After a little search, I lighted upon the very carriage, of which I was in quest. A servant was locking one of the doors, for it was made with the security of lock and key. I paused near, looking at the panel of the door.

'A very pretty device that red stork!' I observed, pointing to the shield on the door, 'and no doubt indicates a distinguished family?'

The servant looked at me, for a moment, as he placed the little key in his pocket, and said with a slightly sarcastic bow and smile, 'Monsieur is at liberty to conjecture.'

Nothing daunted, I forthwith administered that laxative which, on occasion, acts so happily upon the tongue—I mean a 'tip'.

The servant looked at the napoleon in his hand, and then, in my face, with a sincere expression of surprise.

'Monsieur is very generous!'

'Not worth mentioning—who are the lady and gentleman who came here, in this carriage, and whom, you may remember, I and my servant assisted to-day in an emergency, when their horses had come to the ground?'

'They are the Count, and the young lady we call the Countess—but I know not, she may be his daughter.'

'Can you tell me where they live?'

'Upon my honour, monsieur, I am unable—I know not.'

'Not know where your master lives! Surely you know something more about him than his name?'

'Nothing worth relating, monsieur; in fact, I was hired in Bruxelles, on the very day they started. Monsieur Picard, my fellow servant, monsieur the comte's gentleman, he has been years in his service and knows everything; but he never speaks except to communicate an order. From him I have learned nothing. We are going to Paris, however, and there I shall speedily pick up all about them. At present I am as ignorant of all that as monsieur himself.'

'And where is Monsieur Picard?'

'He has gone to the cutler's to get his razors set. But I do not think he will tell anything.'

This was a poor harvest for my golden sowing. The man, I think, spoke truth, and would honestly have betrayed the secrets of the family, if he had possessed any. I took my leave politely; and mounting the stairs, again I found myself once more in my room.

Forthwith I summoned my servant. Though I had brought him with me from England, he was a native of France—a useful fellow, sharp, bustling, and, of course, quite familiar with the ways and tricks of his countrymen.

'St Clair, shut the door; come here. I can't rest till I have made out something about those people of rank who have got the apartments under mine. Here are fifteen francs; make out the servants we assisted to-day; have them to a *petit souper*,* and come back and tell me their entire history. I have, this moment, seen one of them who knows nothing, and has communicated it. The other, whose name I forget, is the unknown nobleman's valet, and knows everything. Him you must pump. It is, of course, the venerable peer, and not the young lady who accompanies him, that interests me—you understand? Begone! fly! and return with all the details I sigh for, and every circumstance that can possibly interest me.'

It was a commission which admirably suited the tastes and spirits of my worthy St Clair, to whom, you will have observed, I had accustomed myself to talk with the peculiar familiarity which the old French comedy establishes between master and valet.

I am sure he laughed at me in secret; but nothing could be more polite and deferential.

With several wise looks, nods and shrugs, he withdrew; and looking down from my window, I saw him, with incredible quickness, enter the yard, where I soon lost sight of him among the carriages.

CHAPTER III
DEATH AND LOVE TOGETHER MATED

WHEN the day drags, when a man is solitary, and in a fever of impatience and suspense; when the minute-hand of his watch travels as slowly as the hour-hand used to do, and the hour-hand has lost all appreciable motion; when he yawns, and beats the devil's tattoo,* and flattens his handsome nose against the window, and whistles tunes he hates, and, in short, does not know what to do with himself, it is deeply to be regretted that he cannot make a solemn dinner of three courses more than once in a day. The laws of matter, to which we are slaves, deny us that resource.

But in the times I speak of, supper was still a substantial meal, and its hour was approaching. This was consolatory. Three-quarters of an hour, however, still interposed. How was I to dispose of that interval?

I had two or three idle books, it is true, as travelling-companions; but there are many moods in which one cannot read. My novel lay with my rug and walking-stick on the sofa, and I did not care if the heroine and the hero were both drowned together in the water-barrel that I saw in the inn-yard under my window.

I took a turn or two up and down my room, and sighed, looked at myself in the glass, adjusted my great white 'choker', folded and tied after Brummel,* the immortal 'Beau', put on a buff waistcoat and my blue swallow-tailed coat with gilt buttons; I deluged my pocket hand-kerchief with eau-de-cologne (we had not then the variety of bouquets with which the genius of perfumery has since blessed us); I arranged my hair, on which I piqued myself, and which I loved to groom in those days. That dark-brown *chevelure*,* with a natural curl, is now repre-sented by a few dozen perfectly white hairs, and its place—a smooth, bald, pink head—knows it no more. But let us forget these mortifica-tions. It was then rich, thick, and dark-brown. I was making a very careful toilet. I took my unexceptionable hat from its case, and placed it lightly on my wise head, as nearly as memory and practice enabled me to do so, at that very slight inclination which the immortal person I have mentioned was wont to give to his. A pair of light French gloves and a rather club-like knotted walking-stick, such as just then came into vogue, for a year or two again in England, in the phraseology of Sir Walter Scott's romances, 'completed my equipment'.

All this attention to effect, preparatory to a mere lounge in the yard, or on the steps of the Belle Etoile, was a simple act of devotion to the wonderful eyes which I had that evening beheld for the first time, and never, never could forget! In plain terms, it was all done in the vague, very vague hope that those eyes might behold the unexceptionable get-up of a melancholy slave, and retain the image, not altogether with-out secret approbation.

As I completed my preparations the light failed me; the last level streak of sunlight disappeared, and a fading twilight only remained. I sighed in unison with the pensive hour, and threw open the window, intending to look out for a moment before going downstairs. I perceived instantly that the window underneath mine was also open, for I heard two voices in conversation, although I could not distinguish what they were saying.

The male voice was peculiar; it was, as I told you, reedy and nasal. I knew it, of course, instantly. The answering voice spoke in those sweet tones which I recognized only too easily. The dialogue was only for a minute; the repulsive male voice laughed, I fancied, with a kind of devilish satire, and retired from the window, so that I almost ceased to hear it.

The other voice remained nearer the window, but not so near as at first.

It was not an altercation; there was evidently nothing the least exciting in the colloquy. What would I not have given that it had been a quarrel—a violent one—and I the redresser of wrongs, and the defender of insulted beauty! Alas! so far as I could pronounce upon the character of the tones I heard, they might be as tranquil a pair as any in existence. In a moment more the lady began to sing an odd little *chanson*. I need not remind you how much farther the voice is heard *singing* than speaking. I could distinguish the words. The voice was of that exquisitely sweet kind which is called, I believe, a semi-contralto; it had something pathetic, and something, I fancied, a little mocking in its tones. I venture a clumsy, but adequate translation of the words:—

> 'Death and Love, together mated,
>   Watch and wait in ambuscade;
> At early morn, or else belated,
>   They meet and mark the man or maid.
>
> 'Earning sigh, or breath that freezes,
>   Numbs or maddens man or maid;
> Death or Love the victim seizes,
>   Breathing from their ambuscade.'

'Enough, madame!' said the old voice, with sudden severity. 'We do not desire, I believe, to amuse the grooms and hostlers in the yard with our music.'

The lady's voice laughed gaily.

'You desire to quarrel, madame!' And the old man, I presume, shut down the window. Down it went, at all events, with a rattle that might easily have broken the glass.

Of all thin partitions, glass is the most effectual excluder of sound. I heard no more, not even the subdued hum of the colloquy.

What a charming voice this Countess had! How it melted, swelled, and trembled! How it moved, and even agitated me! What a pity that a hoarse old jackdaw should have power to crow down such a Philomel!* 'Alas! what a life it is!' I moralized, wisely. 'That beautiful Countess, with the patience of an angel and the beauty of a Venus and the accomplishments of all the Muses, is a slave! She knows perfectly who occupies the apartments over hers; she heard me raise my window. One may conjecture pretty well for whom that music was intended—ay, old gentleman, and for whom you suspected it to be intended.'

In a very agreeable flutter I left my room, and descending the stairs, passed the Count's door very much at my leisure. There was just a chance that the beautiful songstress might emerge. I dropped my stick on the lobby near their door, and you may be sure it took me some little time to pick it up! Fortune, nevertheless, did not favour me. I could not stay on the lobby all night picking up my stick, so I went down to the hall.

I consulted the clock, and found that there remained but a quarter of an hour to the moment of supper.

Every one was roughing it now, every inn in confusion; people might do at such a juncture what they never did before. Was it just possible that, for once, the Count and Countess would take their chairs at the table-d'hôte?*

CHAPTER IV

MONSIEUR DROQVILLE

FULL of this exciting hope, I sauntered out, upon the steps of the Belle Etoile. It was now night, and a pleasant moonlight over everything. I had entered more into my romance since my arrival, and this poetic light heightened the sentiment. What a drama, if she turned out to be the Count's daughter, and in love with me! What a delightful—*tragedy*, if she turned out to be the Count's wife!

In this luxurious mood, I was accosted by a tall and very elegantly-made gentleman, who appeared to be about fifty. His air was courtly and graceful, and there was in his whole manner and appearance something so distinguished, that it was impossible not to suspect him of being a person of rank.

He had been standing upon the steps, looking out, like me, upon the moonlight effects that transformed, as it were, the objects and buildings in the little street. He accosted me, I say, with the politeness, at once easy and lofty, of a French nobleman of the old school. He asked me if I were not Mr Beckett? I assented; and he immediately introduced himself as the Marquis d'Harmonville (this information he gave me in a low tone), and asked leave to present me with a letter from Lord R——, who knew my father slightly, and had once done me, also, a trifling kindness.

This English peer, I may mention, stood very high in the political world, and was named as the most probable successor to the distinguished post of English minister at Paris.

I received it with a low bow, and read:

MY DEAR BECKETT,

I beg to introduce my very dear friend, the Marquis d'Harmonville, who will explain to you the nature of the services it may be in your power to render him and us.

He went on to speak of the Marquis as a man whose great wealth, whose intimate relations with the old families, and whose legitimate influence with the court rendered him the fittest possible person for those friendly offices which, at the desire of his own sovereign, and of our government, he has so obligingly undertaken.

It added a great deal to my perplexity, when I read, further—

By-the-bye, Walton was here yesterday, and told me that your seat is likely to be attacked; something, he says, is unquestionably going on at Domwell. You know there is an awkwardness in my meddling ever so cautiously. But I advise, if it is not very officious, your making Haxton look after it, and report immediately. I fear it is serious. I ought to have mentioned that, for reasons that you will see, when you have talked with him for five minutes, the Marquis—with the concurrence of all our friends—drops his title, for a few weeks, and is at present plain Monsieur Droqville.

I am this moment going to town, and can say no more.

Yours faithfully,

'R——'

I was utterly puzzled. I could scarcely boast of Lord ——'s acquaintance. I knew no one named Haxton, and, except my hatter, no one called Walton; and this peer wrote as if we were intimate friends! I looked at the back of the letter, and the mystery was solved. And now, to my consternation—for I was plain Richard Beckett—I read—

'To George Stanhope Beckett, Esq., M.P.'

I looked with consternation in the face of the Marquis.

'What apology can I offer to Monsieur the Mar—to Monsieur Droqville? It is true my name is Beckett—it is true I am known, though very slightly, to Lord R——; but the letter was not intended for me. My name is Richard Beckett—this is to Mr Stanhope Beckett, the member for Shillingsworth. What can I say, or do, in this unfortunate situation? I can only give you my honour as a gentleman, that, for me, the letter, which I now return, shall remain as unviolated a secret, as before I opened it. I am so shocked and grieved that such a mistake should have occurred!'

I dare say my honest vexation and good faith were pretty legibly written in my countenance; for the look of gloomy embarrassment which had for a moment settled on the face of the Marquis, brightened; he smiled, kindly, and extended his hand.

'I have not the least doubt that Monsieur Beckett will respect my little secret. As a mistake was destined to occur, I have reason to thank my good stars that it should have been with a gentleman of honour. Monsieur Beckett will permit me, I hope, to place his name among those of my friends?'

I thanked the Marquis very much for his kind expressions. He went on to say—

'If, monsieur, I can persuade you to visit me at Claironville, in Normandy, where I hope to see, on the 15th of August, a great many friends, whose acquaintance it might interest you to make, I shall be too happy.'

I thanked him, of course, very gratefully for his hospitality. He continued:

'I cannot, for the present, see my friends, for reasons which you may surmise, at my house in Paris. But monsieur will be so good as to let me know the hotel he means to stay at in Paris; and he will find that although the Marquis d'Harmonville is not in town, that Monsieur Droqville will not lose sight of him.'

With many acknowledgments I gave him the information he desired.

'And in the meantime,' he continued, 'if you think of any way in which Monsieur Droqville can be of use to you, our communication shall not be interrupted, and I shall so manage matters that you can easily let me know.'

I was very much flattered. The Marquis had, as we say, taken a fancy to me. Such likings at first sight often ripen into lasting friendships. To be sure it was just possible that the Marquis might think it prudent to keep the involuntary depository of a political secret, even so vague a one, in good humour.

Very graciously the Marquis took his leave, going up the stairs of the Belle Etoile.

I remained upon the steps, for a minute lost in speculation upon this new theme of interest. But the wonderful eyes, the thrilling voice, the exquisite figure of the beautiful lady who had taken possession of my imagination, quickly reasserted their influence. I was again gazing at the sympathetic moon, and descending the steps, I loitered along the pavements among strange objects, and houses that were antique and picturesque, in a dreamy state, thinking.

In a little while, I turned into the inn-yard again. There had come a lull. Instead of the noisy place it was, an hour or two before, the yard was perfectly still and empty, except for the carriages that stood here and there. Perhaps there was a servants' table-d'hôte just then. I was rather pleased to find solitude; and undisturbed I found out my lady-love's carriage, in the moonlight. I mused, I walked round it; I was as utterly foolish and maudlin as very young men, in my situation, usually are. The blinds were down, the doors, I suppose, locked. The brilliant moonlight revealed everything, and cast sharp, black shadows of wheel, and bar, and spring, on the pavement. I stood before the escutcheon painted on the door, which I had examined in the daylight. I wondered how often her eyes had rested on the same object. I pondered in a charming dream. A harsh, loud voice, over my shoulder, said suddenly,

'A red stork—good! The stork is a bird of prey; it is vigilant, greedy, and catches gudgeons. Red, too!—blood-red! Ha! ha! the symbol is appropriate.'

I had turned about, and beheld the palest face I ever saw. It was broad, ugly, and malignant. The figure was that of a French officer, in undress, and was six feet high. Across the nose and eyebrow there was a deep scar, which made the repulsive face grimmer.

The officer elevated his chin and his eyebrows, with a scoffing chuckle, and said,—'I have shot a stork, with a rifle bullet, when he thought himself safe in the clouds, for mere sport!' (He shrugged, and laughed malignantly.) 'See, monsieur; when a man like me—a man of energy, you understand, a man with all his wits about him, a man who has made the tour of Europe under canvas, and, *parbleu!* often without it—resolves to discover a secret, expose a crime, catch a thief, spit a robber on the point of his sword, it is odd if he does not succeed. Ha! ha! ha! Adieu, monsieur!'

He turned with an angry whisk on his heel, and swaggered with long strides out of the gate.

CHAPTER V

SUPPER AT THE BELLE ETOILE

THE French army were in a rather savage temper, just then. The English especially had but scant courtesy to expect at their hands. It was plain, however, that the cadaverous gentleman who had just apostrophized the heraldry of the Count's carriage, with such mysterious acrimony, had not intended any of his malevolence for me. He was stung by some old recollection, and had marched off, seething with fury.

I had received one of those unacknowledged shocks which startle us, when, fancying ourselves perfectly alone, we discover on a sudden, that our antics have been watched by a spectator, almost at our elbow. In this case, the effect was enhanced by the extreme repulsiveness of the face, and, I may add, its proximity, for, as I think, it almost touched mine. The enigmatical harangue of this person, so full of hatred and implied denunciation, was still in my ears. Here at all events was new matter for the industrious fancy of a lover to work upon.

It was time now to go to the table-d'hôte. Who could tell what lights the gossip of the supper-table might throw upon the subject that interested me so powerfully!

I stepped into the room, my eyes searching the little assembly, about thirty people, for the persons who specially interested me.

It was not easy to induce people so hurried and overworked as those of the Belle Etoile, just now to send meals up to one's private apartments, in the midst of this unparalleled confusion; and therefore, many people who did not like it, might find themselves reduced to the alternative of supping at the table-d'hôte, or starving,

The Count was not there, nor his beautiful companion; but the Marquis d'Harmonville, whom I hardly expected to see in so public a place, signed, with a significant smile, to a vacant chair beside himself. I secured it, and he seemed pleased, and almost immediately entered into conversation with me.

'This is, probably, your first visit to France?' he said.

I told him it was, and he said:

'You must not think me very curious and impertinent; but Paris is about the most dangerous capital a high-spirited and generous young gentleman could visit without a Mentor. If you have not an experienced friend as a companion during your visit——' He paused.

I told him I was not so provided, but that I had my wits about me; that I had seen a good deal of life in England, and that, I fancied, human nature was pretty much the same in all parts of the world. The Marquis shook his head, smiling.

'You will find very marked differences, notwithstanding,' he said. 'Peculiarities of intellect and peculiarities of character, undoubtedly, do pervade different nations; and this results, among the criminal classes, in a style of villainy no less peculiar. In Paris, the class who live by their wits, is three or four times as great as in London; and they live much better; some of them even splendidly. They are more ingenious than the London rogues; they have more animation, and invention, and the dramatic faculty, in which your countrymen are deficient, is everywhere. These invaluable attributes place them upon a totally different level. They can affect the manners and enjoy the luxuries of people of distinction. They live, many of them, by play.'

'So do many of our London rogues.'

'Yes, but in a totally different way. They are the *habituées* of certain gaming-tables, billiard-rooms, and other places, including your races, where high play goes on; and by superior knowledge of chances, by masking their play, by means of confederates, by means of bribery, and other artifices, varying with the subject of their imposture, they rob the unwary. But here it is more elaborately done, and with a really exquisite *finesse*. There are people whose manners, style, conversation, are unexceptionable, living in handsome houses in the best situations, with everything about them in the most refined taste, and exquisitely luxurious, who impose even upon the Parisian bourgeois, who believe them to be, in good faith, people of rank and fashion, because their habits are expensive and refined, and their houses are frequented by foreigners of distinction, and, to a degree, by foolish young Frenchmen of rank. At all these houses play goes on. The ostensible host and hostess seldom join in it; they provide it simply to plunder their guests, by means of their accomplices, and thus wealthy strangers are inveigled and robbed.'

'But I have heard of a young Englishman, a son of Lord Rooksbury, who broke two Parisian gaming-tables only last year.'

'I see,' he said, laughing, 'you are come here to do likewise. I, myself, at about your age, undertook the same spirited enterprise. I raised no less a sum than five hundred thousand francs to begin with; I expected to carry all before me by the simple expedient of going on doubling my stakes. I had heard of it, and I fancied that the sharpers, who kept the table, knew nothing of the matter. I found, however, that they not only knew all about it, but had provided against the possibility of any such experiments; and I was pulled up before I had well begun, by a rule which forbids the doubling of an original stake more than four times, consecutively.'

'And is that rule in force still?' I inquired, chap-fallen.

He laughed and shrugged, 'Of course it is, my young friend. People who live by an art, always understand it better than an amateur. I see you had formed the same plan, and no doubt came provided.'

I confessed I had prepared for conquest upon a still grander scale. I had arrived with a purse of thirty thousand pounds sterling.

'Any acquaintance of my very dear friend, Lord R——, interests me; and, besides my regard for him, I am charmed with you; so you will pardon all my, perhaps, too officious questions and advice.'

I thanked him most earnestly for his valuable counsel, and begged that he would have the goodness to give me all the advice in his power.

'Then if you take my advice,' said he, 'you will leave your money in the bank where it lies. Never risk a napoleon in a gaming-house. The night I went to break the bank, I lost between seven and eight thousand pounds sterling of your English money; and my next adventure, I had obtained an introduction to one of those elegant gaming-houses which affect to be the private mansions of persons of distinction, and was saved from ruin by a gentleman, whom, ever since, I have regarded with increasing respect and friendship. It oddly happens he is in this house at this moment. I recognized his servant, and made him a visit in his apartments here, and found him the same brave, kind, honourable man I always knew him. But that he is living so entirely out of the world, now, I should have made a point of introducing you. Fifteen years ago he would have been the man of all others to consult. The gentleman I speak of is the Conte de St Alyre. He represents a very old family. He is the very soul of honour, and the most sensible man in the world, except in one particular.'

'And that particular?' I hesitated. I was now deeply interested.

'Is that he has married a charming creature, at least five-and-forty years younger than himself, and is, of course, although I believe absolutely without cause, horribly jealous.'

'And the lady?'

'The Countess is, I believe, in every way worthy of so good a man,' he answered, a little drily.

'I think I heard her sing this evening.'

'Yes, I dare say; she is very accomplished.' After a few moments' silence he continued.

'I must not lose sight of you, for I should be sorry, when next you meet my friend Lord R——, that you had to tell him you had been pigeoned* in Paris. A rich Englishman as you are, with so large a sum at his Paris banker's, young, gay, generous, a thousand ghouls and harpies will be contending who shall be first to seize and devour you.'

At this moment I received something like a jerk from the elbow of the gentleman at my right. It was an accidental jog, as he turned in his seat.

'On the honour of a soldier, there is no man's flesh in this company heals so fast as mine.'

The tone in which this was spoken was harsh and stentorian, and almost made me bounce. I looked round and recognized the officer, whose large white face had half scared me in the inn-yard, wiping his mouth furiously, and then with a gulp of Maçon he went on—

'*No* one! It's not blood; it is ichor! it's miracle! Set aside stature, thew, bone, and muscle—set aside courage, and by all the angels of death, I'd fight a lion naked and dash his teeth down his jaws with my fist, and flog him to death with his own tail! Set aside, I say, all those attributes, which I am allowed to possess, and I am worth six men in any campaign, for that one quality of healing as I do—rip me up; punch me through, tear me to tatters with bomb-shells, and nature has me whole again, while your tailor would fine-draw an old coat. *Parbleu!* gentlemen, if you saw me naked, you would laugh? Look at my hand, a sabre-cut across the palm, to the bone, to save my head, taken up with three stitches, and five days after I was playing ball with an English general, a prisoner in Madrid, against the wall of the convent of the Santa Maria de la Castita! At Areola, by the great devil himself! that was an action. Every man there, gentlemen, swallowed as much smoke in five minutes as would smother you all, in this room! I received, at the same moment, two musket balls in the thighs, a grape shot through the calf of my leg, a lance through my left shoulder, a piece of a shrapnel in the left deltoid, a bayonet through the cartilage of my right ribs, a sabre-cut that carried away a pound of flesh from my chest, and the better part of a congreve rocket on my forehead. Pretty well, ha, ha! and all while you'd say *bah!* and in eight days and a half I was making a forced march, without shoes, and only one gaiter, the life and soul of my company, and as sound as a roach!'

'Bravo! Bravissimo! Per Bacco! un gallant uomo!'* exclaimed, in a martial ecstacy, a fat little Italian, who manufactured tooth-picks and wicker cradles on the island of Notre Dame; 'your exploits shall resound through Europe! and the history of those wars should be written in your blood!'

'Never mind! A trifle!' exclaimed the soldier. 'At Ligny, the other day, where we smashed the Prussians into ten hundred thousand milliards of atoms, a bit of a shell cut me across the leg and opened an artery. It was spouting as high as the chimney, and in half a minute I had lost enough to fill a pitcher. I must have expired in another minute, if I had not whipped off my sash like a flash of lightning, tied it round my leg above the wound, whipt a bayonet out of the back of a dead Prussian, and passing it under, made a tournequet of it with a couple of twists, and so stayed the hemorrhage, and saved my life. But, *sacré bleu!*

gentlemen, I lost so much blood, I have been as pale as the bottom of a plate ever since. No matter. A trifle. Blood well spent, gentlemen.' He applied himself now to his bottle of *vin ordinaire.**

The Marquis had closed his eyes, and looked resigned and disgusted, while all this was going on.

'Garçon,' said the officer, for the first time, speaking in a low tone over the back of his chair to the waiter; 'who came in that travelling carriage, dark yellow and black, that stands in the middle of the yard, with arms and supporters emblazoned on the door, and a red stork, as red as my facings?'

The waiter could not say.

The eye of the eccentric officer, who had suddenly grown grim and serious, and seemed to have abandoned the general conversation to other people, lighted, as it were, accidentally, on me.

'Pardon me, monsieur,' he said. 'Did I not see you examining the panel of that carriage at the same time that I did so, this evening? Can you tell me who arrived in it?'

'I rather think the Count and Countess de St Alyre.'

'And are they here, in the Belle Etoile?' he asked.

'They have got apartments upstairs,' I answered.

He started up, and half pushed his chair from the table. He quickly sat down again, and I could hear him *sacré*-ing and muttering to himself, and grinning and scowling. I could not tell whether he was alarmed or furious.

I turned to say a word or two to the Marquis, but he was gone. Several other people had dropped out also, and the supper party soon broke up.

Two or three substantial pieces of wood smouldered on the hearth, for the night had turned out chilly. I sat down by the fire in a great arm-chair, of carved oak, with a marvellously high back, that looked as old as the days of Henry IV.*

'Garçon,' said I, 'do you happen to know who that officer is?'

'That is Colonel Gaillarde, monsieur.'

'Has he been often here?'

'Once before, monsieur, for a week; it is a year since.'

'He is the palest man I ever saw.'

'That is true, monsieur; he has been taken often for a *revenant*.'

'Can you give me a bottle of really good Burgundy?'

'The best in France, monsieur.'

'Place it, and a glass by my side, on this table, if you please. I may sit here for half an hour?'

'Certainly, monsieur.'

I was very comfortable, the wine excellent, and my thoughts glowing and serene. 'Beautiful Countess! Beautiful Countess! shall we ever be better acquainted.'

CHAPTER VI

THE NAKED SWORD

A MAN who has been posting all day long, and changing the air he breathes every half hour, who is well pleased with himself, and has nothing on earth to trouble him, and who sits alone by a fire in a comfortable chair after having eaten a hearty supper, may be pardoned if he takes an accidental nap.

I had filled my fourth glass when I fell asleep. My head, I dare say, hung uncomfortably; and it is admitted, that a variety of French dishes is not the most favourable precursor to pleasant dreams.

I had a dream as I took mine ease in mine inn* on this occasion. I fancied myself in a huge cathedral, without light, except from four tapers that stood at the corners of a raised platform hung with black, on which lay, draped also in black, what seemed to me the dead body of the Countess de St Alyre. The place seemed empty, it was cold, and I could see only (in the halo of the candles) a little way round.

The little I saw bore the character of Gothic gloom, and helped my fancy to shape and furnish the black void that yawned all round me. I heard a sound like the slow tread of two persons walking up the flagged aisle. A faint echo told of the vastness of the place. An awful sense of expectation was upon me, and I was horribly frightened when the body that lay on the catafalque* said (without stirring), in a whisper that froze me, 'They come to place me in the grave alive; save me.'

I found that I could neither speak nor move. I was horribly frightened.

The two people who approached now emerged from the darkness. One, the Count de St Alyre, glided to the head of the figure and placed his long thin hands under it. The white-faced Colonel, with the scar across his face, and a look of infernal triumph, placed his hands under her feet, and they began to raise her.

With an indescribable effort I broke the spell that bound me, and started to my feet with a gasp.

I was wide awake, but the broad, wicked face of Colonel Gaillarde was staring, white as death, at me, from the other side of the hearth. 'Where is she?' I shuddered.

'That depends on who she is, monsieur,' replied the Colonel, curtly.

'Good heavens!' I gasped, looking about me.

The Colonel, who was eyeing me sarcastically, had had his demitasse of *café noir*, and now drank his tasse, diffusing a pleasant perfume of brandy.

'I fell asleep and was dreaming,' I said, lest any strong language, founded on the *rôle* he played in my dream, should have escaped me. I did not know for some moments where I was.

'You are the young gentleman who has the apartments over the Count and Countess de St Alyre?' he said, winking one eye, close in meditation, and glaring at me with the other.

'I believe so—yes,' I answered.

'Well, younker, take care you have not worse dreams than that some night,' he said, enigmatically, and wagged his head with a chuckle. 'Worse dreams,' he repeated.

'What does monsieur the Colonel mean?' I inquired.

'I am trying to find that out myself,' said the Colonel; 'and I think I shall. When *I* get the first inch of the thread fast between my finger and thumb, it goes hard; but I follow it up, bit by bit, little by little, tracing it this way and that, and up and down, and round about, until the whole clue is wound up on my thumb, and the end, and its secret, fast in my fingers. Ingenious! Crafty as five foxes! wide awake as a weazel! *Parbleu!* if I had descended to that occupation I should have made my fortune as a spy. Good wine here?' he glanced interrogatively at my bottle.

'Very good,' said I. 'Will Monsieur the Colonel try a glass?'

He took the largest he could find, and filled it, raised it with a bow, and drank it slowly. 'Ah! ah! Bah! That is not it,' he exclaimed, with some disgust, filling it again. 'You ought to have told *me* to order your Burgundy, and they would not have brought you that stuff.'

I got away from this man as soon as I civilly could, and, putting on my hat, I walked out with no other company than my sturdy walking stick. I visited the inn-yard, and looked up to the windows of the Countess's apartments. They were closed, however, and I had not even the unsubstantial consolation of contemplating the light in which that beautiful lady was at that moment writing, or reading, or sitting and thinking of—any one you please.

I bore this serious privation as well as I could, and took a little saunter through the town. I shan't bore you with moonlight effects, nor with the maunderings of a man who has fallen in love at first sight with a beautiful face. My ramble, it is enough to say, occupied about half-an-hour, and, returning by a slight *detour*, I found myself in a little square, with about two high gabled houses on each side, and a rude stone statue, worn by centuries of rain, on a pedestal in the centre of the pavement. Looking at this statue was a slight and rather tall man, whom I instantly recognized as the Marquis d'Harmonville: he knew me almost as quickly. He walked a step towards me, shrugged and laughed:

'You are surprised to find Monsieur Droqville staring at that old stone figure by moonlight. Anything to pass the time. You, I see, suffer from *ennui* as I do. These little provincial towns! Heavens! what an effort it is to live in them! If I could regret having formed in early life a friendship that does me honour, I think its condemning me to a sojourn in such a place would make me do so. You go on towards Paris, I suppose, in the morning?'

'I have ordered horses.'

'As for me I await a letter, or an arrival, either would emancipate me; but I can't say how soon either event will happen.'

'Can I be of any use in this matter?' I began.

'None, monsieur, I thank you a thousand times. No, this is a piece in which every *rôle* is already cast. I am but an amateur, and, induced, solely by friendship to take a part.'

So he talked on, for a time, as we walked slowly toward the Belle Etoile, and then came a silence, which I broke by asking him if he knew anything of Colonel Gaillarde.

'Oh! yes, to be sure. He is a little mad; he has had some bad injuries of the head. He used to plague the people in the War Office to death. He has always some delusion. They contrived some employment for him—not regimental, of course—but in this campaign Napoleon, who could spare nobody, placed him in command of a regiment. He was always a desperate fighter, and such men were more than ever needed.'

There is, or was, a second inn, in this town, called l'Ecu de France. At its door the Marquis stopped, bade me a mysterious good-night, and disappeared.

As I walked slowly toward my inn, I met, in the shadow of a row of poplars, the garçon who had brought me my Burgundy a little time ago. I was thinking of Colonel Gaillarde, and I stopped the little waiter as he passed me.

'You said, I think, that Colonel Gaillarde was at the Belle Etoile for a week at one time.'

'Yes, monsieur.'

'Is he perfectly in his right mind?'

The waiter stared. 'Perfectly, monsieur.'

'Has he been suspected at any time of being out of his mind?'

'Never, monsieur; he is a little noisy, but a very shrewd man.'

'What is a fellow to think?' I muttered, as I walked on.

I was soon within sight of the lights of the Belle Etoile. A carriage, with four horses, stood in the moonlight at the door, and a furious altercation was going on in the hall, in which the yell of Colonel Gaillarde out-topped all other sounds.

Most young men like, at least, to witness a row. But, intuitively, I felt that this would interest me in a very special manner. I had only fifty yards to run, when I found myself in the hall of the old inn. The principal actor in this strange drama was, indeed, the Colonel, who stood facing the old Count de St Alyre, who, in his travelling costume, with his black silk scarf covering the lower part of his face, confronted him; he had evidently been intercepted in an endeavour to reach his carriage. A little in the rear of the Count stood the Countess, also in travelling costume, with her thick black veil down, and holding in her delicate fingers a white rose. You can't conceive a more diabolical effigy of hate and fury than the Colonel; the knotted veins stood out on his forehead, his eyes were leaping from their sockets, he was grinding his teeth, and froth was on his lips. His sword was drawn, in his hand, and he accompanied his yelling denunciations with stamps upon the floor and flourishes of his weapon in the air.

The host of the Belle Etoile was talking to the Colonel in soothing terms utterly thrown away. Two waiters, pale with fear, stared uselessly from behind. The Colonel screamed, and thundered, and whirled his sword. 'I was not sure of your red birds of prey; I could not believe you would have the audacity to travel on high roads, and to stop at honest inns, and lie under the same roof with honest men. You! *you!* *both*—vampires, wolves, ghouls. Summon the gendarmes, I say. By St Peter and all the devils, if either of you try to get out of that door I'll take your heads off.'

For a moment I had stood aghast. Here was a situation! I walked up to the lady; she laid her hand wildly upon my arm. 'Oh! monsieur,' she whispered, in great agitation, 'that dreadful madman! What are we to do? He won't let us pass; he will kill my husband.'

'Fear nothing, madame,' I answered with romantic devotion, and stepping between the Count and Gaillarde, as he shrieked his invective, 'Hold your tongue, and clear the way, you ruffian, you bully, you coward!' I roared.

A faint cry escaped the lady, which more than repaid the risk I ran, as the sword of the frantic soldier, after a moment's astonished pause, flashed in the air to cut me down.

CHAPTER VII

THE WHITE ROSE

I was too quick for Colonel Gaillarde. As he raised his sword, reckless of all consequences but my condign punishment, and quite resolved to cleave me to the teeth, I struck him across the side of his head, with my heavy stick; and while he staggered back, I struck him another blow, nearly in the same place, that felled him to the floor, where he lay as if dead.

I did not care one of his own regimental buttons, whether he was dead or not; I was, at that moment, carried away by such a tumult of delightful and diabolical emotions!

I broke his sword under my foot, and flung the pieces across the street. The old Count de St Alyre skipped nimbly without looking to the right or left, or thanking anybody, over the floor, out of the door, down the steps, and into his carriage. Instantly I was at the side of the beautiful Countess, thus left to shift for herself; I offered her my arm, which she took, and I led her to her carriage. She entered, and I shut the door. All this without a word.

I was about to ask if there were any commands with which she would honour me—my hand was laid upon the lower edge of the window, which was open.

The lady's hand was laid upon mine timidly and excitedly. Her lips almost touched my cheek as she whispered hurriedly,

'I may never see you more, and, oh! that I could forget you. Go— farewell—for God's sake, go!'

I pressed her hand for a moment. She withdrew it, but tremblingly pressed into mine the rose which she had held in her fingers during the agitating scene she had just passed through.

All this took place while the Count was commanding, entreating, cursing his servants, tipsy, and out of the way during the crisis, my conscience afterwards insinuated, by my clever contrivance. They now mounted to their places with the agility of alarm. The postillions' whips cracked, the horses scrambled into a trot, and away rolled the carriage, with its precious freightage, along the quaint main street, in the moon-light, toward Paris.

I stood on the pavement, till it was quite lost to eye and ear in the distance.

With a deep sigh, I then turned, my white rose folded in my hand-kerchief—the little parting *gage*—the

'Favour secret, sweet, and precious';*

which no mortal eye but hers and mine had seen conveyed to me.

The care of the host of the Belle Etoile, and his assistants, had raised the wounded hero of a hundred fights partly against the wall, and propped him at each side with portmanteaus and pillows, and poured a glass of brandy, which was duly placed to his account, into his big mouth, where, for the first time, such a Godsend remained unswallowed.

A bald-headed little military surgeon of sixty, with spectacles, who had cut off eighty-seven legs and arms to his own share, after the battle of Eylau,* having retired with his sword and his saw, his laurels and his sticking-plaster to this, his native town, was called in, and rather thought the gallant Colonel's skull was fractured, at all events there was concussion of the seat of thought, and quite enough work for his remarkable self-healing powers, to occupy him for a fortnight.

I began to grow a little uneasy. A disagreeable surprise, if my excursion, in which I was to break banks and hearts, and, as you see, heads, should end upon the gallows or the guillotine. I was not clear, in those times of political oscillation, which was the established apparatus.

The Colonel was conveyed, snorting apoplectically, to his room.

I saw my host in the apartment in which we had supped. Wherever you employ a force of any sort, to carry a point of real importance, reject all nice calculations of economy. Better to be a thousand per cent over the mark, than the smallest fraction of a unit under it. I instinctively felt this.

I ordered a bottle of my landlord's very best wine; made him partake with me, in the proportion of two glasses to one; and then told him that he must not decline a trifling *souvenir* from a guest who had been so charmed with all he had seen of the renowned Belle Etoile. Thus saying, I placed five-and-thirty napoleons in his hand. At touch of which his countenance, by no means encouraging before, grew sunny, his manners thawed, and it was plain, as he dropped the coins hastily into his pocket, that benevolent relations had been established between us.

I immediately placed the Colonel's broken head upon the *tapis.** We both agreed that if I had not given him that rather smart tap of my walking-cane, he would have beheaded half the inmates of the Belle Etoile. There was not a waiter in the house who would not verify that statement on oath.

The reader may suppose that I had other motives, beside the desire to escape the tedious inquisition of the law, for desiring to recommence my journey to Paris with the least possible delay. Judge what was my horror then to learn, that for love or money, horses were nowhere to be had that night. The last pair in the town had been obtained from the Ecu de France, by a gentleman who dined and supped at the Belle Etoile, and was obliged to proceed to Paris that night.

Who was the gentleman? Had he actually gone? Could he possibly be induced to wait till morning?

The gentleman was now upstairs getting his things together, and his name was Monsieur Droqville.

I ran upstairs. I found my servant St Clair in my room. At sight of him for a moment, my thoughts were turned into a different channel.

'Well, St Clair, tell me this moment who the lady is?' I demanded.

'The lady is the daughter or wife, it matters not which, of the Count de St Alyre;—the old gentleman who was so near being sliced like a cucumber tonight, I am informed, by the sword of the general whom Monsieur, by a turn of fortune, has put to bed of an apoplexy.'

'Hold your tongue, fool! The man's beastly drunk—he's sulking— he could talk if he liked—who cares? Pack up my things. Which are Monsieur Droqville's apartments?'

He knew of course; he always knew everything.

Half an hour later Monsieur Droqville and I were travelling towards Paris, in my carriage, and with his horses. I ventured to ask the Marquis d'Harmonville, in a little while, whether the lady, who accompanied the Count, was certainly the Countess. 'Has he not a daughter?'

'Yes; I believe a very beautiful and charming young lady—I cannot say—it may have been she, his daughter by an earlier marriage. I saw only the Count himself to-day.'

The Marquis was growing a little sleepy and, in a little while, he actually fell asleep in his corner. I dozed and nodded; but the Marquis slept like a top. He awoke only for a minute or two at the next posting-house, where he had fortunately secured horses by sending on his man, he told me.

'You will excuse my being so dull a companion,' he said, 'but till to-night I have had but two hours' sleep, for more than sixty hours. I shall have a cup of coffee here; I have had my nap. Permit me to rec-ommend you to do likewise. Their coffee is really excellent.' He ordered two cups of *café noir*, and waited, with his head from the window. 'We will keep the cups,' he said, as he received them from the waiter, 'and the tray. Thank you.'

There was a little delay as he paid for these things; and then he took in the little tray, and handed me a cup of coffee.

I declined the tray; so he placed it on his own knees, to act as a mini-ature table.

'I can't endure being waited for and hurried,' he said, 'I like to sip my coffee at leisure.'

I agreed. It really *was* the very perfection of coffee.

'I, like Monsieur le Marquis, have slept very little for the last two or three nights; and find it difficult to keep awake. This coffee will do wonders for me; it refreshes one so.'

Before we had half done, the carriage was again in motion.

For a time our coffee made us chatty, and our conversation was animated.

The Marquis was extremely good-natured, as well as clever, and gave me a brilliant and amusing account of Parisian life, schemes, and dangers, all put so as to furnish me with practical warnings of the most valuable kind.

In spite of the amusing and curious stories which the Marquis related, with so much point and colour, I felt myself again becoming gradually drowsy and dreamy.

Perceiving this, no doubt, the Marquis good-naturedly suffered our conversation to subside into silence. The window next him was open. He threw his cup out of it; and did the same kind office for mine, and finally the little tray flew after, and I heard it clank on the road; a valuable waif, no doubt, for some early wayfarer in wooden shoes.

I leaned back in my corner; I had my beloved *souvenir*—my white rose—close to my heart, folded, now, in white paper. It inspired all manner of romantic dreams. I began to grow more and more sleepy. But actual slumber did not come. I was still viewing, with my half-closed eyes, from my corner, diagonally, the interior of the carriage.

I wished for sleep; but the barrier between waking and sleeping seemed absolutely insurmountable; and instead, I entered into a state of novel and indescribable indolence.

The Marquis lifted his despatch box from the floor, placed it on his knees, unlocked it, and took out what proved to be a lamp, which he hung with two hooks, attached to it, to the window opposite to him. He lighted it with a match, put on his spectacles, and taking out a bundle of letters, began to read them carefully.

We were making way very slowly. My impatience had hitherto employed four horses from stage to stage. We were in this emergency, only too happy to have secured two. But the difference in pace was depressing.

I grew tired of the monotony of seeing the spectacled Marquis reading, folding, and docketing, letter after letter. I wished to shut out the image which wearied me, but something prevented my being able to shut my eyes. I tried again and again; but, positively, I had lost the power of closing them.

I would have rubbed my eyes, but I could not stir my hand, my will no longer acted on my body—I found that I could not move one joint, or muscle, no more than I could, by an effort of my will, have turned the carriage about.

Up to this I had experienced no sense of horror. Whatever it was, simple night-mare was not the cause. I was awfully frightened! Was I in a fit?

It was horrible to see my good-natured companion pursue his occupation so serenely, when he might have dissipated my horrors by a single shake.

I made a stupendous exertion to call out but in vain; I repeated the effort again and again, with no result.

My companion now tied up his letters, and looked out of the window, humming an air from an opera. He drew back his head, and said, turning to me—

'Yes, I see the lights; we shall be there in two or three minutes.'

Ho looked more closely at me, and with a kind smile, and a little shrug, he said, 'Poor child! how fatigued he must have been—how profoundly he sleeps! when the carriage stops, he will waken.'

He then replaced his letters in the despatch-box, locked it, put his spectacles in his pocket, and again looked out of the window.

We had entered a little town. I suppose, it was past two o'clock by this time. The carriage drew up, I saw an inn-door open, and a light issuing from it.

'Here we are!' said my companion, turning gaily to me. But I did not awake.

'Yes, how tired he must have been!' he exclaimed, after he had waited for an answer.

My servant was at the carriage door, and opened it.

'Your master sleeps soundly, he is so fatigued! It would be cruel to disturb him. You and I will go in, while they change the horses, and take some refreshment, and choose something that Monsieur Beckett will like to take in the carriage, for when he awakes by-and-by he will, I am sure, be hungry.'

He trimmed his lamp, poured in some oil; and taking care not to disturb me, with another kind smile, and another word of caution to my servant, he got out, and I heard him talking to St Clair, as they entered the inn-door, and I was left in my corner, in the carriage, in the same state.

CHAPTER VIII

A THREE MINUTES' VISIT

I HAVE suffered extreme and protracted bodily pain, at different periods of my life, but anything like that misery, thank God, I never endured before or since. I earnestly hope it may not resemble any type of death, to which we are liable. I was, indeed, a spirit in prison; and unspeakable was my dumb and unmoving agony.

The power of thought remained clear and active. Dull terror filled my mind. How would this end? Was it actual death?

You will understand that my faculty of observing was unimpaired. I could hear and see anything as distinctly as ever I did in my life. It was simply that my will had, as it were, lost its hold of my body.

I told you that the Marquis d'Harmonville had not extinguished his carriage lamp on going into this village inn. I was listening intently, longing for his return, which might result, by some lucky accident, in awaking me from my catalepsy.

Without any sound of steps approaching, to announce an arrival, the carriage-door suddenly opened, and a total stranger got in silently, and shut the door.

The lamp gave about as strong a light as a wax-candle, so I could see the intruder perfectly. He was a young man, with a dark grey, loose surtout, made with a sort of hood, which was pulled over his head. I thought, as he moved, that I saw the gold-band of a military undress cap under it; and I certainly saw the lace and buttons of a uniform, on the cuffs of the coat that were visible under the wide sleeves of his outside wrapper.

This young man had thick moustaches, and an imperial,* and I observed that he had a red scar running upward from his lip across his cheek.

He entered, shut the door softly, and sat down beside me. It was all done in a moment; leaning toward me, and shading his eyes with his gloved hand, he examined my face closely, for a few seconds.

This man had come as noiselessly as a ghost; and everything he did was accomplished with the rapidity and decision, that indicated a well defined and prearranged plan. His designs were evidently sinister. I thought he was going to rob and, perhaps, murder me. I lay, nevertheless, like a corpse under his hands. He inserted his hand in my breast pocket, from which he took my precious white rose and all the letters it contained, among which was a paper of some consequence to me.

My letters he glanced at. They were plainly not what he wanted. My precious rose, too, he laid aside with them. It was evidently about the paper I have mentioned, that he was concerned; for the moment he opened it, he began with a pencil, in a small pocket-book, to make rapid notes of its contents.

This man seemed to glide through his work with a noiseless and cool celerity which argued, I thought, the training of the police-department.

He re-arranged the papers, possibly in the very order in which he had found them, replaced them in my breast-pocket, and was gone.

His visit, I think, did not quite last three minutes. Very soon after his disappearance, I heard the voice of the Marquis once more. He got in, and I saw him look at me, and smile, half envying me, I fancied, my sound repose. If he had but known all!

He resumed his reading and docketing, by the light of the little lamp which had just subserved the purposes of a spy.

We were now out of the town, pursuing our journey at the same moderate pace. We had left the scene of my police visit, as I should have termed it, now two leagues behind us, when I suddenly felt a strange throbbing in one ear, and a sensation as if air passed through it into my throat. It seemed as if a bubble of air, formed deep in my ear, swelled, and burst there. The indescribable tension of my brain seemed all at once to give way; there was an odd humming in my head, and a sort of vibration through every nerve of my body, such as I have experienced in a limb that has been, in popular phraseology, asleep. I uttered a cry and half rose from my seat, and then fell back trembling, and with a sense of mortal faintness.

The Marquis stared at me, took my hand, and earnestly asked if I was ill. I could answer only with a deep groan.

Gradually the process of restoration was completed; and I was able, though very faintly, to tell him how very ill I had been; and then, to describe the violation of my letters, during the time of his absence from the carriage.

'Good heaven!' he exclaimed, 'the miscreant did not get at my despatch-box?'

I satisfied him, so far as I had observed, on that point. He placed the box on the seat beside him, and opened and examined its contents very minutely.

'Yes, undisturbed; all safe, thank heaven!' he murmured. 'There are half-a-dozen letters here, that I would not have some people read, for a great deal.'

He now asked with a very kind anxiety all about the illness I complained of. When he had heard me, he said—

'A friend of mine once had an attack as like yours as possible. It was on board-ship, and followed a state of high excitement. He was a brave man like you; and was called on to exert both his strength and his courage suddenly. An hour or two after, fatigue overpowered him, and he appeared to fall into a sound sleep. He really sank into a state which he afterwards described so, that I think it must have been precisely the same affection as yours.'

'I am happy to think that my attack was not unique. Did he ever experience a return of it?'

'I knew him for years after, and never heard of any such thing. What strikes me is a parallel in the predisposing causes of each attack. Your unexpected, and gallant hand-to-hand encounter, at such desperate odds, with an experienced swordsman, like that insane colonel of dragoons, your fatigue, and, finally, your composing yourself, as my other friend did, to sleep.'

'I wish,' he resumed, 'one could make out who that *coquin** was, who examined your letters. It is not worth turning back, however, because we should learn nothing. Those people always manage so adroitly. I am satisfied, however, that he must have been an agent of the police. A rogue of any other kind would have robbed you.'

I talked very little, being ill and exhausted, but the Marquis talked on agreeably.

'We grow so intimate,' said he at last, 'that I must remind you that I am not, for the present, the Marquis d'Harmonville, but only Monsieur Droqville; nevertheless, when we get to Paris, although I cannot see you often, I may be of use. I shall ask you to name to me the hotel at which you mean to put up; because the Marquis being, as you are aware, on his travels, the Hotel d'Harmonville is, for the present, tenanted only by two or three old servants, who must not even see Monsieur Droqville. That gentleman will, nevertheless, contrive to get you access to the box of Monsieur le Marquis, at the Opera;* as well, possibly, as to other places more difficult; and so soon as the diplomatic office of the Marquis d'Harmonville is ended, and he at liberty to declare himself, he will not excuse his friend, Monsieur Beckett, from fulfilling his promise to visit him this autumn at the Château d'Harmonville.'

You may be sure I thanked the Marquis.

The nearer we got to Paris, the more I valued his protection. The countenance of a great man on the spot, just then, taking so kind an interest in the stranger whom he had, as it were, blundered upon, might make my visit ever so many degrees more delightful than I had anticipated.

Nothing could be more gracious than the manner and looks of the Marquis; and, as I still thanked him, the carriage suddenly stopped in front of the place where a relay of horses awaited us, and where, as it turned out, we were to part.

CHAPTER IX
GOSSIP AND COUNSEL

MY eventful journey was over, at last. I sat in my hotel window looking out upon brilliant Paris, which had, in a moment, recovered all its gaiety, and more than its accustomed bustle. Every one has read of the kind of excitement that followed the catastrophe of Napoleon, and the second restoration of the Bourbons. I need not, therefore, even if, at this distance, I could, recall and describe my experiences and impressions of the peculiar aspect of Paris, in those strange times. It was to be sure my first visit. But, often as I have seen it since, I don't think I ever saw that delightful capital in a state, pleasurably, so excited and exciting.

I had been two days in Paris, and had seen all sorts of sights, and experienced none of that rudeness and insolence of which others complained, from the exasperated officers of the defeated French army.

I must say this, also. My romance had taken complete possession of me; and the chance of seeing the object of my dream, gave a secret and delightful interest to my rambles and drives in the streets and environs, and my visits to the galleries and other sights of the metropolis.

I had neither seen nor heard of Count or Countess, nor had the Marquis d'Harmonville made any sign. I had quite recovered the strange indisposition under which I had suffered during my night journey.

It was now evening, and I was beginning to fear that my patrician acquaintance had quite forgotten me, when the waiter presented me the card of 'Monsieur Droqville'; and, with no small elation and hurry, I desired him to show the gentleman up.

In came the Marquis d'Harmonville, kind and gracious as ever.

'I am a night-bird at present,' said he, so soon as we had exchanged the little speeches which are usual. 'I keep in the shade, during the daytime, and even now I hardly ventured to come in a close carriage. The friends for whom I have undertaken a rather critical service, have so ordained it. They think all is lost, if I am known to be in Paris. First let me present you with these orders for my box. I am so vexed that I cannot command it oftener during the next fortnight; during my absence, I had directed my secretary to give it for any night to the first of my friends who might apply, and the result is, that I find next to nothing left at my disposal.'

I thanked him very much.

'And now, a word, in my office of Mentor. You have not come here, of course, without introductions?'

I produced half-a-dozen letters, the addresses of which he looked at.

'Don't mind these letters,' he said. 'I will introduce you. I will take you myself from house to house. One friend at your side is worth many letters. Make no intimacies, no acquaintances, until then. You young men like best to exhaust the public amusements of a great city, before embarrassing yourself with the engagements of society. Go to all these. It will occupy you, day and night, for at least three weeks. When this is over, I shall be at liberty, and will myself introduce you to the brilliant but comparatively quiet routine of society. Place yourself in my hands; and in Paris remember, when once in society, you are always there.'

I thanked him very much, and promised to follow his counsels implicitly.

He seemed pleased, and said—

'I shall now tell you some of the places you ought to go to. Take your map, and write letters or numbers upon the points I will indicate, and we will make out a little list. All the places that I shall mention to you are worth seeing.'

In this methodical way, and with a great deal of amusing and scandalous anecdote, he furnished me with a catalogue and a guide, which, to a seeker of novelty and pleasure, was invaluable.

'In a fortnight, perhaps in a week,' he said, 'I shall be at leisure to be of real use to you. In the meantime, be on your guard. You must not play; you will be robbed if you do. Remember, you are surrounded, here, by plausible swindlers and villains of all kinds, who subsist by devouring strangers. Trust no one, but those you know.'

I thanked him again, and promised to profit by his advice. But my heart was too full of the beautiful lady of the Belle Etoile, to allow our interview to close without an effort to learn something about her. I therefore asked for the Count and Countess de St Alyre, whom I had had the good fortune to extricate from an extremely unpleasant row in the hall of the inn.

Alas! he had not seen them since. He did not know where they were staying. They had a fine old house only a few leagues from Paris; but he thought it probable that they would remain, for a few days at least, in the city, as preparations would, no doubt, be necessary, after so long an absence, for their reception at home.

'How long have they been away?'

'About eight months, I think.'

'They are poor, I think you said?'

'What *you* would consider poor. But, monsieur, the Count has an income which affords them the comforts and even the elegancies of life, living as they do, in a very quiet and retired way, in this cheap country.'

'Then they are very happy?'

'One would say they *ought* to be happy.'

'And what prevents?'

'He is jealous.'

'But his wife—she gives him no cause?'

'I am afraid she does.'

'How, monsieur?'

'I always thought she was a little too—a *great deal* too——'

'Too *what*, monsieur?'

'Too handsome. But although she has remarkably fine eyes, exquisite features, and the most delicate complexion in the world, I believe that she is a woman of probity. You have never seen her?'

'There was a lady, muffled up in a cloak, with a very thick veil on, the other night, in the hall of the Belle Etoile, when I broke that fellow's head who was bullying the old count. But her veil was so thick I could not see a feature through it.' My answer was diplomatic, you observe. 'She may have been the Count's daughter. Do they quarrel?'

'Who, he and his wife?'

'Yes.'

'A little.'

'Oh! and what do they quarrel about?'

'It is a long story; about the lady's diamonds. They are valuable—they are worth, La Perelleuse says, about a million of francs. The Count wishes them sold and turned into revenue, which he offers to settle as she pleases. The Countess, whose they are, resists, and for a reason which, I rather think, she can't disclose to him.'

'And pray what is that?' I asked, my curiosity a good deal piqued.

'She is thinking, I conjecture, how well she will look in them when she marries her second husband.'

'Oh?—yes, to be sure. But the Count de St Alyre is a good man?'

'Admirable, and extremely intelligent.'

'I should wish so much to be presented to the Count: you tell me he's so——'

'So agreeably married. But they are living quite out of the world. He takes her now and then to the Opera, or to a public entertainment; but that is all.'

'And he must remember so much of the old *régime*, and so many of the scenes of the revolution!'

'Yes, the very man for a philosopher, like you! And he falls asleep after dinner; and his wife don't. But, seriously, he has retired from the gay and the great world, and has grown apathetic; and so has his wife; and nothing seems to interest her now, not even——her husband!'

The Marquis stood up, to take his leave.

'Don't risk your money,' said he. 'You will soon have an opportunity of laying out some of it to great advantage. Several collections of really good pictures, belonging to persons who have mixed themselves up in this Bonapartist restoration, must come within a few weeks to the hammer.* You can do wonders when these sales commence. There will be startling bargains! Reserve yourself for them. I shall let you know all about it. By-the-by,' he said, stopping short as he approached the door, 'I was so near forgetting. There is to be, next week, the very thing you would enjoy so much, because you see so little of it in England—— I mean a *bal masqué*,* conducted, it is said, with more than usual splendour. It takes place at Versailles—all the world will be there; there is such a rush for cards! But I think I may promise you one. Good-night! Adieu!'

CHAPTER X

THE BLACK VEIL

SPEAKING the language fluently and with unlimited money, there was nothing to prevent my enjoying all that was enjoyable in the French capital. You may easily suppose how two days were passed. At the end of that time, and at about the same hour, Monsieur Droqville called again.

Courtly, good-natured, gay, as usual, he told me that the masquerade ball was fixed for the next Wednesday, and that he had applied for a card for me.

How awfully unlucky. I was so afraid I should not be able to go.

He stared at me for a moment with a suspicious and menacing look which I did not understand, in silence, and then inquired, rather sharply,

'And will Monsieur Beckett be good enough to say, why not?'

I was a little surprised, but answered the simple truth: I had made an engagement for that evening with two or three English friends and did not see how I could.

'Just so! You English, wherever you are, always look out for your English boors, your beer and '*bifstek*';* and when you come here, instead of trying to learn something of the people you visit, and pretend to study, you are guzzling, and swearing, and smoking with one another, and no wiser or more polished at the end of your travels than if you had been all the time carousing in a booth at Greenwich.'*

He laughed sarcastically, and looked as if he could have poisoned me.

'There it is,' said he, throwing the card on the table. 'Take it or leave it, just as you please. I suppose I shall have my trouble for my pains; but it is not usual when a man such as I takes trouble, asks a favour, and secures a privilege for an acquaintance, to treat him so.'

This was astonishingly impertinent!

I was shocked, offended, penitent. I had possibly committed unwittingly a breach of good-breeding, according to French ideas, which almost justified the brusque severity of the marquis's undignified rebuke.

In a confusion, therefore, of many feelings, I hastened to make my apologies, and to propitiate the chance friend who had showed me so much disinterested kindness.

I told him that I would, at any cost, break through the engagement in which I had unluckily entangled myself; that I had spoken with too little reflection, and that I certainly had not thanked him at all in proportion to his kindness and to my real estimate of it.

'Pray say not a word more; my vexation was entirely on your account; and I expressed it, I am only too conscious, in terms a great deal too strong, which, I am sure, your good nature will pardon. Those who know me a little better are aware that I sometimes say a good deal more than I intend; and am always sorry when I do. Monsieur Beckett will forget that his old friend, Monsieur Droqville, has lost his temper in his cause, for a moment, and—we are as good friends as before.'

He smiled like the Monsieur Droqville of the Belle Etoile, and extended his hand, which I took very respectfully and cordially.

Our momentary quarrel had left us only better friends.

The Marquis then told me I had better secure a bed in some hotel at Versailles, as a rush would be made to take them; and advised my going down next morning for the purpose.

I ordered horses accordingly for eleven o'clock; and, after a little more conversation, the Marquis d'Harmonville bid me good-night, and ran down the stairs with his handkerchief to his mouth and nose, and, as

I saw from my window, jumped into his close carriage again and drove away.

Next day I was at Versailles.* As I approached the door of the Hotel de France, it was plain that I was not a moment too soon, if, indeed, I were not already too late.

A crowd of carriages were drawn up about the entrance, so that I had no chance of approaching except by dismounting and pushing my way among the horses. The hall was full of servants and gentlemen screaming to the proprietor, who, in a state of polite distraction, was assuring them, one and all, that there was not a room or a closet disengaged in his entire house.

I slipped out again, leaving the hall to those who were shouting, expostulating, wheedling, in the delusion that the host might, if he pleased, manage something for them. I jumped into my carriage and drove, at my horses' best pace, to the Hotel du Reservoir. The blockade about this door was as complete as the other. The result was the same. It was very provoking, but what was to be done? My postillion had, a little officiously, while I was in the hall talking with the hotel authorities, got his horses, bit by bit, as other carriages moved away, to the very steps of the inn door.

This arrangement was very convenient so far as getting in again was concerned. But, this accomplished, how were we to get on? There were carriages in front, and carriages behind, and no less than four rows of carriages, of all sorts, outside.

I had at this time remarkably long and clear sight, and if I had been impatient before, guess what my feelings were when I saw an open carriage pass along the narrow strip of roadway left open at the other side, a barouche in which I was certain I recognized the veiled Countess and her husband. This carriage had been brought to a walk by a cart which occupied the whole breadth of the narrow way, and was moving with the customary tardiness of such vehicles.

I should have done more wisely if I had jumped down on the *trottoir*, and run round the block of carriages in front of the barouche. But, unfortunately, I was more of a Murat than a Moltke,* and preferred a direct charge upon my object to relying on *tactique*. I dashed across the back seat of a carriage which was next mine, I don't know how; tumbled through a sort of gig, in which an old gentleman and a dog were dozing; stepped with an incoherent apology over the side of an open carriage, in which were four gentlemen engaged in a hot dispute; tripped at the far side in getting out, and fell flat across the backs of a pair of horses, who instantly began plunging and threw me head foremost in the dust.

To those who observed my reckless charge without being in the secret of my object I must have appeared demented. Fortunately, the interesting barouche had passed before the catastrophe, and covered as I was with dust, and my hat blocked, you may be sure I did not care to present myself before the object of my Quixotic devotion.

I stood for a while amid a storm of *sacre*-ing, tempered disagreeably with laughter; and in the midst of these, while endeavouring to beat the dust from my clothes with my handkerchief, I heard a voice with which I was acquainted call, 'Monsieur Beckett'.

I looked and saw the Marquis peeping from a carriage-window. It was a welcome sight. In a moment I was at his carriage side.

'You may as well leave Versailles,' he said; 'you have learned, no doubt, that there is not a bed to hire in either of the hotels; and I can add that there is not a room to let in the whole town. But I have managed something for you that will answer just as well. Tell your servant to follow us, and get in here and sit beside me.'

Fortunately an opening in the closely-packed carriages had just occurred, and mine was approaching.

I directed the servant to follow us; and the Marquis having said a word to his driver, we were immediately in motion.

'I will bring you to a comfortable place, the very existence of which is known to but few Parisians, where, knowing how things were here, I secured a room for you. It is only a mile away, an old comfortable inn, called Le Dragon Volant. It was fortunate for you that my tiresome business called me to this place so early.'

I think we had driven about a mile-and-a-half to the further side of the palace when we found ourselves upon a narrow old road, with the woods of Versailles on one side, and much older trees, of a size seldom seen in France, on the other.

We pulled up before an antique and solid inn, built of Caen stone, in a fashion richer and more florid than was ever usual in such houses, and which indicated that it was originally designed for the private mansion of some person of wealth, and probably, as the wall bore many carved shields and supporters, of distinction also. A kind of porch, less ancient than the rest, projected hospitably with a wide and florid arch, over which, cut in high relief in stone, and painted and gilded, was the sign of the inn. This was the Flying Dragon, with wings of brilliant red and gold, expanded, and its tail, pale green and gold, twisted and knotted into ever so many rings, and ending in a burnished point barbed like the dart of death.

'I shan't go in—but you will find it a comfortable place; at all events better than nothing. I would go in with you, but my incognito forbids.

You will, I dare say, be all the better pleased to learn that the inn is haunted—I should have been, in my young days, I know. But don't allude to that awful fact in hearing of your host, for I believe it is a sore subject. Adieu. If you want to enjoy yourself at the ball take my advice, and go in a domino.* I think I shall look in; and certainly, if I do, in the same costume. How shall we recognize one another? Let me see, something held in the fingers—a flower won't do, so many people will have flowers. Suppose you get a red cross a couple of inches long—you're an Englishman*—stitched or pinned on the breast of your domino, and I a white one? Yes, that will do very well; and whatever room you go into keep near the door till we meet. I shall look for you at all the doors I pass; and you, in the same way, for me; and we *must* find each other soon. So that is understood. I can't enjoy a thing of that kind with any but a young person; a man of my age requires the contagion of young spirits and the companionship of some one who enjoys everything spontaneously. Farewell; we meet to-night.'

By this time I was standing *on* the road; I shut the carriage-door; bid him good-bye; and away he drove.

CHAPTER XI

THE DRAGON VOLANT

I took one look about me.

The building was picturesque; the trees made it more so. The antique and sequestered character of the scene, contrasted strangely with the glare and bustle of the Parisian life, to which my eye and ear had become accustomed.

Then I examined the gorgeous old sign for a minute or two. Next I surveyed the exterior of the house more carefully. It was large and solid, and squared more with my ideas of an ancient English hostelrie, such as the Canterbury pilgrims* might have put up at, than a French house of entertainment. Except, indeed, for a round turret, that rose at the left flank of the house, and terminated in the extinguisher-shaped roof that suggests a French château.

I entered and announced myself as Monsieur Beckett, for whom a room had been taken. I was received with all the consideration due to an English milord, with, of course, an unfathomable purse.

My host conducted me to my apartment. It was a large room, a little sombre, panelled with dark wainscoting, and furnished in a stately and sombre style, long out of date. There was a wide hearth, and a heavy mantelpiece, carved with shields, in which I might, had I been curious enough, have discovered a correspondence with the heraldry on the outer walls. There was something interesting, melancholy, and even depressing in all this. I went to the stone-shafted window, and looked out upon a small park, with a thick wood, forming the background of a château, which presented a cluster of such conical-topped turrets as I have just now mentioned.

The wood and château were melancholy objects. They showed signs of neglect, and almost of decay; and the gloom of fallen grandeur, and a certain air of desertion hung oppressively over the scene.

I asked my host the name of the château.

'That, monsieur, is the Château de la Carque,'* he answered.

'It is a pity it is so neglected,' I observed. 'I should say, perhaps, a pity that its proprietor is not more wealthy?'

'Perhaps so, monsieur.'

'*Perhaps?*'—I repeated, and looked at him. 'Then I suppose he is not very popular.'

'Neither one thing nor the other, monsieur,' he answered; 'I meant only that we could not tell what use he might make of riches.'

'And who is he?' I inquired.

'The Count de St Alyre.'

'Oh! The Count! You are quite sure?' I asked, very eagerly.

It was now the innkeeper's turn to look at me.

'*Quite* sure, monsieur, the Count de St Alyre.'

'Do you see much of him in this part of the world?'

'Not a great deal, monsieur; he is often absent for a considerable time.'

'And is he poor?' I inquired.

'I pay rent to him for this house. It is not much; but I find he cannot wait long for it,' he replied, smiling satirically.

'From what I have heard, however, I should think he cannot be very poor?' I continued.

'They say, monsieur, he plays. I know not. He certainly is not rich. About seven months ago, a relation of his died in a distant place. His body was sent to the Count's house here, and by him buried in Père la Chaise,* as the poor gentleman had desired. The Count was in profound affliction; although he got a handsome legacy, they say, by that death. But money never seems to do him good for any time.'

'He is old, I believe?'

'Old? we call him the "Wandering Jew",* except, indeed, that he has not always the five *sous* in his pocket. Yet, monsieur, his courage does not fail him. He has taken a young and handsome wife.'

'And, she?' I urged—

'Is the Countess de St Alyre.'

'Yes; but I fancy we may say something more? She has attributes?'

'Three, monsieur, three, at least, most amiable.'

'Ah! And what are they?'

'Youth, beauty, and—diamonds.'

I laughed. The sly old gentleman was foiling my curiosity.

'I see, my friend,' said I, 'you are reluctant——'

'To quarrel with the Count,' he concluded.

'True. You see, monsieur, he could vex me, in two or three ways; so could I him. But, on the whole, it is better each to mind his business, and to maintain peaceful relations; you understand.'

It was, therefore, no use trying, at least for the present. Perhaps, he had nothing to relate. Should I think differently, by-and-by, I could try the effect of a few napoleons. Possibly he meant to extract them.

The host of the Dragon Volant was an elderly man, thin, bronzed, intelligent, and with an air of decision, perfectly military. I learned afterwards that he had served under Napoleon in his early Italian campaigns.

'One question, I think you may answer,' I said, 'without risking a quarrel. Is the Count at home?'

'He has many homes, I conjecture,' said the host, evasively. 'But—but I think I may say, monsieur, that he is, I believe, at present staying at the Château de la Carque.'

I looked out of the window, more interested than ever, across the undulating grounds to the château, with its gloomy background of foliage.

'I saw him to-day in his carriage, at Versailles,' I said.

'Very natural.'

'Then his carriage and horses and servants are at the château?'

'The carriage he puts up here, monsieur, and the servants are hired, for the occasion. There is but one who sleeps at the château. Such a life must be terrifying for Madame the Countess,' he replied.

'The old screw!' I thought. 'By this torture, he hopes to extract her diamonds. What a life! What fiends to contend with—jealousy and extortion!'

The knight having made this speech to himself, cast his eyes once more upon the enchanter's castle, and heaved a gentle sigh—a sigh of longing, of resolution, and of love.

What a fool I was! and yet, in the sight of angels, are we any wiser as we grow older? It seems to me, only, that our illusions change as we go on; but, still, we are madmen all the same.

'Well, St Clair,' said I, as my servant entered, and began to arrange my things. 'You have got a bed?'

'In the cock-loft, monsieur, among the spiders, and, *par ma foi!* the cats and the owls. But we agree very well. *Vive la bagatelle!*'

'I had no idea it was so full.'

'Chiefly the servants, monsieur, of those persons who were fortunate enough to get apartments at Versailles.'

'And what do you think of the Dragon Volant?'

'The Dragon Volant! monsieur; the old fiery dragon! The devil himself, if all is true! On the faith of a Christian, monsieur, they say that diabolical miracles have taken place in this house.'

'What do you mean? *Revenants?*'

'Not at all, sir; I wish it was no worse. *Revenants?* No! People who have *never* returned—who vanished, before the eyes of half-a-dozen men, all looking at them.'

'What do you mean, St Clair? Let us hear the story, or miracle, or whatever it is.'

'It is only this, monsieur, that an ex-master-of-the-horse of the late king, who lost his head—monsieur will have the goodness to recollect, in the revolution—being permitted by the Emperor to return to France, lived here in this hotel, for a month, and at the end of that time vanished, visibly, as I told you, before the faces of half-a-dozen credible witnesses! The other was a Russian nobleman, six feet high and upwards, who, standing in the centre of the room, downstairs, describing to seven gentlemen of unquestionable veracity, the last moments of Peter the Great,* and having a glass of *eau de vie* in his left hand, and his *tasse de café*, nearly finished, in his right, in like manner vanished. His boots were found on the floor where he had been standing; and the gentleman at his right, found, to his astonishment, his cup of coffee in his fingers, and the gentleman at his left, his glass of *eau de vie*——'

'Which he swallowed in his confusion,' I suggested.

'Which was preserved for three years among the curious articles of this house, and was broken by the *curé* while conversing with Mademoiselle Fidone in the housekeeper's room; but of the Russian nobleman himself, nothing more was ever seen or heard! *Parbleu!* when *we* go out of the Dragon Volant, I hope it may be by the door. I heard all this, monsieur, from the postillion who drove us.'

'Then it *must* be true!' said I, jocularly: but I was beginning to feel the gloom of the view, and of the chamber in which I stood; there had stolen over me, I know not how, a presentiment of evil; and my joke was with an effort, and my spirit flagged.

CHAPTER XII

THE MAGICIAN

No more brilliant spectacle than this masked ball could be imagined. Among other *salons* and galleries, thrown open, was the enormous perspective of the 'Grande Galérie des Glacés',* lighted up on that occasion with no less than four thousand wax candles, reflected and repeated by all the mirrors, so that the effect was almost dazzling. The grand suite of *salons* was thronged with masques, in every conceivable costume. There was not a single room deserted. Every place was animated with music, voices, brilliant colours, flashing jewels, the hilarity of extemporized comedy, and all the spirited incidents of a cleverly sustained masquerade. I had never seen before anything, in the least, comparable to this magnificent *fête*. I moved along, indolently, in my domino and mask, loitering, now and then, to enjoy a clever dialogue, a farcical song, or an amusing monologue, but, at the same time, keeping my eyes about me, lest my friend in the black domino, with the little white cross on his breast, should pass me by.

I had delayed and looked about me, specially, at every door I passed, as the Marquis and I had agreed; but he had not yet appeared.

While I was thus employed, in the very luxury of lazy amusement, I saw a gilded sedan chair, or, rather, a Chinese palanquin, exhibiting the fantastic exuberance of 'Celestial'* decoration, borne forward on gilded poles by four richly-dressed Chinese; one with a wand in his hand marched in front, and another behind; and a slight and solemn man, with a long black beard, a tall fez, such as a dervish is represented as wearing, walked close to its side. A strangely-embroidered robe fell over his shoulders, covered with hieroglyphic symbols; the embroidery was in black and gold, upon a variegated ground of brilliant colours. The robe was bound about his waist with a broad belt of gold, with cabalistic devices traced on it, in dark red and black; red stockings, and shoes embroidered with gold, and pointed and curved upward at the toes, in Oriental fashion, appeared below the skirt of the robe. The man's face was dark, fixed, and solemn, and his eyebrows black, and enormously heavy—he carried a singular-looking book under his arm, a wand of polished black wood in his other hand, and walked with his chin sunk on his breast, and his eyes fixed upon the floor. The man in front waved his wand right and left to clear the way for the advancing palanquin, the curtains of which were closed; and there was something so singular, strange, and solemn about the whole thing, that I felt at once interested.

I was very well pleased when I saw the bearers set down their burthen within a few yards of the spot on which I stood.

The bearers and the men with the gilded wands forthwith clapped their hands, and in silence danced round the palanquin a curious and half frantic dance, which was yet, as to figure and postures, perfectly methodical. This was soon accompanied by a clapping of hands and a ha-ha-ing, rhythmically delivered.

While the dance was going on a hand was lightly laid on my arm, and, looking round, a black domino with a white cross stood beside me.

'I am so glad I have found you,' said the Marquis; 'and at this moment. This is the best group in the rooms. *You* must speak to the wizard. About an hour ago I lighted upon them, in another *salon*, and consulted the oracle, by putting questions. I never was more amazed. Although his answers were a little disguised it was soon perfectly plain that he knew every detail about the business, which no one on earth had heard of but myself, and two or three other men, about the most cautious persons in France. I shall never forget that shock. I saw other people who consulted him, evidently as much surprised, and more frightened than I. I came with the Count St Alyre and the Countess.'

Ho nodded toward a thin figure, also in a domino. It was the Count.

'Come,' he said to me, 'I'll introduce you.'

I followed, you may suppose, readily enough.

The Marquis presented me, with a very prettily-turned allusion to my fortunate intervention in his favour at the Belle Etoile; and the Count overwhelmed me with polite speeches, and ended by saying, what pleased me better still—

'The Countess is near us, in the next *salon* but one, chatting with her old friend the Duchesse d'Argensaque; I shall go for her in a few minutes; and when I bring her here, she shall make your acquaintance; and thank you, also, for your assistance, rendered, with so much courage, when we were so very disagreeably interrupted.

'You must, positively, speak with the magician,' said the Marquis to the Count de St Alyre, 'you will be so much amused. *I* did so; and,

I assure you, I could not have anticipated such answers! I don't know what to believe.'

'Really! Then, by all means, let us try,' he replied.

We three approached, together, the side of the palanquin, at which the black-bearded magician stood.

A young man, in a Spanish dress, who, with a friend at his side, had just conferred with the conjuror, was saying, as he passed us by—

'Ingenious mystification! Who is that in the palanquin. He seems to know everybody!'

The Count, in his mask and domino, moved along, stiffly, with us, toward the palanquin. A clear circle was maintained by the Chinese attendants, and the spectators crowded round in a ring.

One of these men—he who with a gilded wand had preceded the procession—advanced, extending his empty hand, palm upward.

'Money?' inquired the Count.

'Gold,' replied the usher.

The Count placed a piece of money in his hand; and I and the Marquis were each called on in turn to do likewise as we entered the circle. We paid accordingly.

The conjuror stood beside the palanquin, its silk curtain in his hand; his chin sunk, with its long, jet-black beard, on his chest; the outer hand grasping the black wand, on which he leaned; his eyes were lowered, as before, to the ground; his face looked absolutely lifeless. Indeed, I never saw face or figure so move-less, except in death.

The first question the Count put, was—

'Am I married, or unmarried?'

The conjuror drew back the curtain quickly, and placed his ear toward a richly-dressed Chinese, who sat in the litter; withdrew his head, and closed the curtain again; and then answered—

'Yes.'

The same preliminary was observed each time, so that the man with the black wand presented himself, not as a prophet, but as a medium; and answered, as it seemed, in the words of a greater than himself.

Two or three questions followed, the answers to which seemed to amuse the Marquis very much; but the point of which I could not see, for I knew next to nothing of the Count's peculiarities and adventures.

'Does my wife love me?' asked he, playfully.

'As well as you deserve.'

'Whom do I love best in the world?'

'Self.'

'Oh! That I fancy is pretty much the case with every one. But, put-ting myself out of the question, do I love anything on earth better than my wife?'

'Her diamonds.'

'Oh!' said the Count.

The Marquis, I could see, laughed.

'Is it true,' said the Count, changing the conversation peremptorily, 'that there has been a battle in Naples?'

'No; in France.'

'Indeed,' said the Count, satirically, with a glance round. 'And may I inquire between what powers, and on what particular quarrel?'

'Between the Count and Countess de St Alyre, and about a docu-ment they subscribed on the 25th July, 1811.'

The Marquis afterwards told me that this was the date of their marriage settlement.

The Count stood stock-still for a minute or so; and one could fancy that they saw his face flushing through his mask.

Nobody, but we two, knew that the inquirer was the Count de St Alyre.

I thought he was puzzled to find a subject for his next question; and, perhaps, repented having entangled himself in such a colloquy. If so, he was relieved; for the Marquis, touching his arm, whispered—

'Look to your right, and see who is coming.'

I looked in the direction indicated by the Marquis, and I saw a gaunt figure stalking toward us. It was not a masque. The face was broad, scarred, and white. In a word, it was the ugly face of Colonel Gaillarde, who, in the costume of a corporal of the Imperial Guard, with his left arm so adjusted as to look like a stump, leaving the lower part of the coat-sleeve empty, and pinned up to the breast.* There were strips of very real sticking-plaster across his eyebrow and temple, where my stick had left its mark, to score, hereafter, among the more honourable scars of war.

CHAPTER XIII

THE ORACLE TELLS ME WONDERS

I forgot for a moment how impervious my mask and domino were to the hard stare of the old campaigner, and was preparing for an animated scuffle. It was only for a moment, of course; but the Count cautiously drew a little back as the gasconading* corporal, in blue uniform, white vest, and white gaiters—for my friend Gaillarde was as loud and swaggering in his assumed character as in his real one of a colonel of dragoons—drew near. He had already twice all but got himself turned out of doors for vaunting the exploits of Napoleon le Grand, in terrific mock-heroics, and had very nearly come to hand-grips with a Prussian hussar. In fact, he would have been involved in several sanguinary rows already, had not his discretion reminded him that the object of his coming there at all, namely, to arrange a meeting with an affluent widow, on whom he believed he had made a tender impression, would not have been promoted by his premature removal from the festive scene, of which he was an ornament, in charge of a couple of gendarmes.

'Money! Gold! Bah! What money can a wounded soldier like your humble servant have amassed, with but his sword-hand left, which, being necessarily occupied, places not a finger at his command with which to scrape together the spoils of a routed enemy?'

'No gold from him,' said the magician. 'His scars frank him.'*

'Bravo, monsieur le prophète! Bravissimo! Here I am. Shall I begin, mon conjureur, without further loss of time, to question you?'

Without waiting for an answer, he commenced, in Stentorian tones.

After half-a-dozen questions and answers, he asked—

'Whom do I pursue at present?'

'Two persons.'

'Ha! Two? Well, who are they?'

'An Englishman, whom, if you catch, he will kill you; and a French widow, whom if you find, she will spit in your face.'

'Monsieur le magicien calls a spade a spade, and knows that his cloth protects him. No matter! Why do I pursue them?'

'The widow has inflicted a wound on your heart, and the Englishman a wound on your head. They are each separately too strong for you; take care your pursuit does not unite them.'

'Bah! How could that be?'

'The Englishman protects ladies. He has got that fact into your head. The widow, if she sees, will marry him. It takes some time, she will reflect, to become a colonel, and the Englishman is unquestionably young.'

'I will cut his cock's-comb for him,' he ejaculated with an oath and a grin; and in a softer tone he asked, 'Where is she?'

'Near enough to be offended if you fail.'

'So she ought, by my faith. You are right, monsieur le prophète! A hundred thousand thanks! Farewell!' And staring about him, and stretching his lank neck as high as he could, he strode away with his scars, and white waistcoat and gaiters, and his bearskin shako.

I had been trying to see the person who sat in the palanquin. I had only once an opportunity of a tolerably steady peep. What I saw was singular. The oracle was dressed, as I have said, very richly, in the Chinese fashion. He was a figure altogether on a larger scale than the interpreter, who stood outside. The features seemed to me large and heavy, and the head was carried with a downward inclination! the eyes were closed, and the chin rested on the breast of his embroidered pelisse. The face seemed fixed, and the very image of apathy. Its character and *pose* seemed an exaggerated repetition of the immobility of the figure who communicated with the noisy outer world. This face looked blood-red; but that was caused, I concluded, by the light entering through the red silk curtains. All this struck me almost at a glance; I had not many seconds in which to make my observation. The ground was now clear, and the Marquis said, 'Go forward, my friend.'

I did so. When I reached the magician, as we called the man with the black wand, I glanced over my shoulder to see whether the Count was near.

No, he was some yards behind; and he and the Marquis, whose curiosity seemed to be, by this time, satisfied, were now conversing generally upon some subject of course quite different.

I was relieved, for the sage seemed to blurt out secrets in an unexpected way; and some of mine might not have amused the Count.

I thought for a moment. I wished to test the prophet. A Church-of-England man was a *rara avis** in Paris.

'What is my religion?' I asked.

'A beautiful heresy,' answered the oracle instantly.

'A heresy?—and pray how is it named?'

'Love.'

'Oh! Then I suppose I am a polytheist, and love a great many?'

'One.'

'But, seriously,' I asked, intending to turn the course of our colloquy a little out of an embarrassing channel, 'have I ever learned any words of devotion by heart?'

'Yes.'

'Can you repeat them?'

'Approach.'

I did, and lowered my ear.

The man with the black wand closed the curtains, and whispered, slowly and distinctly, these words, which, I need scarcely tell you, I instantly recognized:

I may never see you more; and, oh! that I could forget you! go— farewell—for God's sake, go!

I started as I heard them. They were, you know, the last words whispered to me by the Countess.

Good Heaven! How miraculous! Words heard, most assuredly, by no ear on earth but my own and the lady's who uttered them, till now!

I looked at the impassive face of the spokesman with the wand. There was no trace of meaning, or even of a consciousness that the words he had uttered could possibly interest me.

'What do I most long for?' I asked, scarcely knowing what I said.

'Paradise.'

'And what prevents my reaching it?'

'A black veil.'

Stronger and stronger! The answers seemed to me to indicate the minutest acquaintance with every detail of my little romance, of which not even the Marquis knew anything! And I, the questioner, masked and robed so that my own brother could not have known me!

'You said I loved some one. Am I loved in return?' I asked.

'Try.'

I was speaking lower than before, and stood near the dark man with the beard, to prevent the necessity of his speaking in a loud key.

'Does any one love me?' I repeated.

'Secretly,' was the answer.

'Much or little?' I inquired.

'Too well.'

'How long will that love last?'

'Till the rose casts its leaves.'

'The rose—another allusion!'

'Then—darkness!' I sighed. 'But till then I live in light.'

'The light of violet eyes.'

Love, if not a religion, as the oracle had just pronounced it, is, at least, a superstition. How it exalts the imagination! How it enervates the reason! How credulous it makes us!

All this which, in the case of another, I should have laughed at, most powerfully affected me in my own. It inflamed my ardour, and half crazed my brain, and even influenced my conduct.

The spokesman of this wonderful trick—if trick it were—now waved me backward with his wand, and as I withdrew, my eyes still fixed upon the group, by this time encircled with an aura of mystery in my fancy; backing toward the ring of spectators, I saw him raise his hand suddenly, with a gesture of command, as a signal to the usher who carried the golden wand in front.

The usher struck his wand on the ground, and, in a shrill voice, proclaimed: 'The great Confu* is silent for an hour.'

Instantly the bearers pulled down a sort of blind of bamboo, which descended with a sharp clatter, and secured it at the bottom; and then the man in the tall fez, with the black beard and wand, began a sort of dervish dance.* In this the men with the gold wands joined, and finally, in an outer ring, the bearers, the palanquin being the centre of the circles described by these solemn dancers, whose pace, little by little, quickened, whose gestures grew sudden, strange, frantic, as the motion became swifter and swifter, until at length the whirl became so rapid that the dancers seemed to fly by with the speed of a millwheel, and amid a general clapping of hands, and universal wonder, these strange performers mingled with the crowd, and the exhibition, for the time at least, ended.

The Marquis d'Harmonville was standing not far away, looking on the ground, as one could judge by his attitude and musing. I approached, and he said:

'The Count has just gone away to look for his wife. It is a pity she was not here to consult the prophet; it would have been amusing, I daresay, to see how the Count bore it. Suppose we follow him. I have asked him to introduce you.'

With a beating heart, I accompanied the Marquis d'Harmonville.

CHAPTER XIV

MADEMOISELLE DE LA VALLIÈRE

We wandered through the salons, the Marquis and I. It was no easy matter to find a friend in rooms so crowded.

'Stay here,' said the Marquis, I have thought of a way of finding him. Besides, his jealousy may have warned him that there is no particular advantage to be gained by presenting you to his wife, I had better go and reason with him; as you seem to wish an introduction so very much.'

This occurred in the room that is now called the 'Salon d'Apollon'.* The paintings remained in my memory, and my adventure of that evening was destined to occur there.

I sat down upon a sofa; and looked about me. Three or four persons beside myself were seated on this roomy piece of gilded furniture. They were chatting all very gaily; all—except the person who sat next me, and she was a lady. Hardly two feet interposed between us. The lady sat apparently in a reverie. Nothing could be more graceful. She wore the costume perpetuated in Collignan's full-length portrait of Mademoiselle de la Vallière.* It is as you know not only rich, but elegant. Her hair was powdered, but one could perceive that it was naturally a dark-brown. One pretty little foot appeared, and could anything be more exquisite than her hand?

It was extremely provoking that this lady wore her mask, and did not, as many did, hold it for a time in her hand.

I was convinced that she was pretty. Availing myself of the privilege of a masquerade, a microcosm in which it is impossible, except by voice and allusion, to distinguish friend from foe, I spoke—

'It is not easy, mademoiselle, to deceive me,' I began.

'So much the better for monsieur,' answered the mask, quietly.

'I mean,' I said, determined to tell my fib, 'that beauty is a gift more difficult to conceal than mademoiselle supposes.'

'Yet monsieur has succeeded very well,' she said in the same sweet and careless tones.

'I see the costume of this, the beautiful Mademoiselle de la Vallière, upon a form that surpasses her own; I raise my eyes, and I behold a mask, and yet I recognize the lady; beauty is like that precious stone in the "Arabian Nights" which emits, no matter how concealed, a light that betrays it.'

'I know the story,' said the young lady. 'The light betrayed it, not in the sun, but in darkness. Is there so little light in these rooms, monsieur, that a poor glowworm can show so brightly. I thought we were in a luminous atmosphere, wherever a certain countess moved?'

Here was an awkward speech! How was I to answer? This lady might be, as they say some ladies are, a lover of mischief, or an intimate of the Countess de St Alyre. Cautiously, therefore, I inquired,

'What countess?'

'If you know me, you must know that she is my dearest friend. Is she not beautiful?'

'How can I answer, there are so many countesses.'

'Every one who knows me, knows who my best beloved friend is. You don't know me?'

'That is cruel. I can scarcely believe I am mistaken.'

'With whom were you walking, just now?' she asked.

'A gentleman, a friend,' I answered.

'I saw him, of course, a friend but I think I know him, and should like to be certain. Is he not a certain marquis?'

Here was another question that was extremely awkward.

'There are so many people here, and one may walk, at one time, with one, and at another with a different one, that—'

'That an unscrupulous person has no difficulty in evading a simple question, like mine. Know then, once for all, that nothing disgusts a person of spirit so much as suspicion. You, monsieur, are a gentleman of discretion. I shall respect you accordingly.'

'Mademoiselle would despise me, were I to violate a confidence.'

'But you don't deceive me, You imitate your friend's diplomacy. I hate diplomacy. It means fraud and cowardice. Don't you think I know him. The gentleman with the cross of white ribbon on his breast. I know the Marquis d'Harmonville perfectly. You see to what good purpose your ingenuity has been expended.'

'To that conjecture I can answer neither yes nor no.'

'You need not. But what was your motive in mortifying a lady?'

'It is the last thing on earth I should do.'

'You affected to know me, and you don't; through caprice or list-lessness or curiosity you wished to converse, not with a lady, but with a costume. You admired, and you pretend to mistake me for another. But who is quite perfect? Is truth any longer to be found on earth?'

'Mademoiselle has formed a mistaken opinion of me.'

'And you also of me; you find me less foolish than you supposed. I know perfectly whom you intend amusing with compliments and melancholy declamation, and whom, with that amiable purpose, you have been seeking.'

'Tell me whom you mean,' I entreated.

'Upon one condition.'

'What is that?'

'That you will confess if I name the lady.'

'You describe my object unfairly,' I objected. 'I can't admit that I proposed speaking to any lady in the tone you describe.'

'Well, I shan't insist on that; only if I name the lady, you will promise to admit that I am right.'

'*Must* I promise?'

'Certainly not, there is no compulsion; but your promise is the only condition on which I will speak to you again.'

I hesitated for a moment; but how could she possibly tell? The Countess would scarcely have admitted this little romance to any one; and the masque in the La Vallière costume could not possibly know who the masked domino beside her was.

'I consent,' I said, 'I promise.'

'You must promise on the honour of a gentleman.'

'Well, I do; on the honour of a gentleman.'

'Then this lady is the Countess de St Alyre.' I was unspeakably surprised; I was disconcerted; but I remembered my promise, and said—

'The Countess de St Alyre *is*, unquestionably, the lady to whom I hoped for an introduction tonight; but I beg to assure you, also on the honour of a gentleman, that she has not the faintest imaginable suspicion that I was seeking such an honour, nor, in all probability, does she remember that such a person as I exists. I had the honour to render her and the Count a trifling service, too trifling, I fear, to have earned more than an hour's recollection.'

'The world is not so ungrateful as you suppose; or if it be, there are, nevertheless, a few hearts that redeem it. I can answer for the Countess de St Alyre, she never forgets a kindness. She does not show all she feels; for she is unhappy, and cannot.'

'Unhappy! I feared, indeed, that might be. But for all the rest that you are good enough to suppose, it is but a flattering dream.'

'I told you that I am the Countess's friend, and being so I must know something of her character; also, there are confidences between us, and I may know more than you think, of those trifling services of which you suppose the recollection is so transitory.'

I was becoming more and more interested. I was as wicked as other young men, and the heinousness of such a pursuit was as nothing, now that self-love and all the passions that mingle in such a romance, were roused. The image of the beautiful Countess had now again quite superseded the pretty counterpart of La Vallière, who was before me. I would have given a great deal to hear, in solemn earnest, that she did remember the champion, who, for her sake, had thrown himself before the sabre of an enraged dragoon, with only a cudgel in his hand, and conquered.

'You say the Countess is unhappy,' said I. 'What causes her unhappiness?'

'Many things. Her husband is old, jealous, and tyrannical. Is not that enough? Even when relieved from his society, she is lonely.'

'But you are her friend?' I suggested.

'And you think one friend enough?' she answered; 'she has one alone, to whom she can open her heart.'

'Is there room for another friend?'

'Try.'

'How can I find a way?'

'She will aid you.'

'How?'

She answered by a question, 'Have you secured rooms in either of the hotels of Versailles?'

'No, I could not. I am lodged in the Dragon Volant, which stands at the verge of the grounds of the Château de la Carque.'

'That is better still. I need not ask if you have courage for an adventure. I need not ask if you are a man of honour. A lady may trust herself to you, and fear nothing. There are few men to whom the interview, such as I shall arrange, could be granted with safety. You shall meet her at two o'clock this morning in the Parc of the Château de la Carque. What room do you occupy in the Dragon Volant?'

I was amazed at the audacity and decision of this girl. Was she, as we say in England, hoaxing me?

'I can describe that accurately,' said I. 'As I look from the rear of the house, in which my apartment is, I am at the extreme right, next the angle; and one pair of stairs up, from the hall.'

'Very well; you must have observed, if you looked into the park, two or three clumps of chestnut and lime-trees, growing so close together as to form a small grove. You must return to your hotel, change your dress, and, preserving a scrupulous secrecy, as to why or where you go, leave the Dragon Volant, and climb the park-wall, unseen; you will easily recognize the grove I have mentioned; there you will meet the Countess, who will grant you an audience of a few minutes, who will expect the most scrupulous reserve on your part, and who will explain to you, in a few words, a great deal which *I* could not so well tell you here.'

I cannot describe the feeling with which I heard these words. I was astounded. Doubt succeeded. I could not believe these agitating words.

'Mademoiselle will believe that if I only dared assure myself that so great a happiness and honour were really intended for me, my gratitude would be as lasting as my life. But how dare I believe that mademoiselle does not speak, rather from her own sympathy or goodness, than from a certainty that the Countess de St Alyre would concede so great an honour?'

'Monsieur believes either that I am not, as I pretend to be, in the secret which he hitherto supposed to be shared by no one but the Countess and himself, or else that I am cruelly mystifying him. That I am in her confidence, I swear by all that is dear in a whispered farewell. By the last companion of this flower!' and she took for a moment in her fingers the nodding head of a white rosebud that was nestled in her bouquet. 'By my own good star, and hers—or shall I call it our "*belle* etoile?" Have I said enough?'

'Enough?' I repeated, 'more than enough—a thousand thanks.'

'And being thus in her confidence, I am clearly her friend; and being a friend would it be friendly to use her dear name so; and all for sake of practising a vulgar trick upon you—a stranger?'

'Mademoiselle will forgive me. Remember how very precious is the hope of seeing, and speaking to the Countess. Is it wonderful, then, that I should falter in my belief? You have convinced me, however, and will forgive my hesitation.'

'You will be at the place I have described, then, at two o'clock?'

'Assuredly,' I answered.

'And monsieur, I know, will not fail, through fear. No, he need not assure me; his courage is already proved.'

'No danger, in such a case, will be unwelcome to me.'

'Had you not better go now, monsieur, and rejoin your friend?'

'I promised to wait here for my friend's return. The Count de St Alyre said that he intended to introduce me to the Countess.'

'And monsieur is so simple as to believe him?'

'Why should I not?'

'Because he is jealous and cunning. You will see. He will never introduce you to his wife. He will come here and say he cannot find her, and promise another time.'

'I think I see him approaching, with my friend. No—there is no lady with him.'

'I told you so. You will wait a long time for that happiness, if it is never to reach you except through his hands. In the meantime, you had better not let him see you so near me. He will suspect that we have been talking of his wife; and that will whet his jealousy and his vigilance.'

I thanked my unknown friend in the mask, and withdrawing a few steps, came, by a little 'circumbendibus',* upon the flank of the Count.

I smiled under my mask, as he assured me that the Duchesse de la Roqueme had changed her place, and taken the Countess with her, but he hoped, at some very early time, to have an opportunity of enabling her to make my acquaintance.

I avoided the Marquis d'Harmonville, who was following the Count. I was afraid he might propose accompanying me home, and had no wish to be forced to make an explanation.

I lost myself quickly, therefore, in the crowd, and moved, as rapidly as it would allow me, toward the Galérie des Glacés, which lay in the direction opposite to that in which I saw the Count and my friend the Marquis moving.

CHAPTER XVI

STRANGE STORY OF THE DRAGON VOLANT

THESE *fêtes* were earlier in those days, and in France, than our modern balls are in London. I consulted my watch. It was a little past twelve.

It was a still and sultry night; the magnificent suite of rooms, vast as some of them were, could not be kept at a temperature less than oppressive, especially to people with masks on. In some places the crowd was inconvenient, and the profusion of lights added to the heat. I removed my mask, therefore, as I saw some other people do, who were as careless of mystery as I. I had hardly done so, and began to breathe more comfortably, when I heard a friendly English voice call me by my name. It was Tom Whistlewick, of the —th Dragoons. He had unmasked, with a very flushed face, as I did. He was one of those Waterloo heroes, new from the mint of glory, whom, as a body, all the world, except France, revered; and the only thing I know against him, was a habit of allaying his thirst, which was excessive, at balls, *fêtes*, musical parties, and all gatherings, where it was to be had, with champagne; and, as he introduced me to his friend, Monsieur Carmaignac, I observed that he spoke a little thick. Monsieur Carmaignac was little, lean, and as straight as a ramrod. He was bald, took snuff, and wore spectacles; and, as I soon learned, held an official position.

Tom was facetious, sly, and rather difficult to understand, in his present pleasant mood. He was elevating his eyebrows and screwing his lips oddly, and fanning himself vaguely with his mask.

After some agreeable conversation, I was glad to observe that he preferred silence, and was satisfied with the *rôle* of listener, as I and Monsieur Carmaignac chatted; and he seated himself, with extraordinary caution and indecision, upon a bench, beside us, and seemed very soon to find a difficulty in keeping his eyes open.

'I heard you mention,' said the French gentleman, 'that you had engaged an apartment in the Dragon Volant, about half a league from this. When I was in a different police department, about four years ago, two very strange cases were connected with that house. One was of a wealthy *émigré*, permitted to return to France, by the Em—by Napoleon. He vanished. The other—equally strange—was the case of a Russian of rank and wealth. He disappeared just as mysteriously.'

'My servant,' I said, 'gave me a confused account of some occurrences, and, as well as I recollect, he described the same persons— I mean a returned French nobleman, and a Russian gentleman. But he made the whole story so marvellous—I mean in the supernatural sense—that, I confess, I did not believe a word of it.'

'No, there was nothing supernatural; but a great deal inexplicable,' said the French gentleman. 'Of course there may be theories; but the thing was never explained, nor, so far as I know, was a ray of light ever thrown upon it.'

'Pray let me hear the story,' I said. 'I think I have a claim, as it affects my quarters. You don't suspect the people of the house?'

'Oh! it has changed hands since then. But there seemed to be a fatality about a particular room.'

'Could you describe that room?'

'Certainly. It is a spacious, panelled, bed-room, up one pair of stairs, in the back of the house, and at the extreme right, as you look from its windows.'

'Ho! Really? Why, then, I have got the very room,' I said, beginning to be more interested—perhaps the least bit in the world, disagreeably. 'Did the people die, or were they actually spirited away?'

'No, they did not die—they disappeared very oddly. I'll tell you the particulars—I happen to know them exactly, because I made an official visit, on the first occasion, to the house, to collect evidence; and although I did not go down there, upon the second, the papers came before me, and I dictated the official letter despatched to the relations of the people who had disappeared: they had applied to the government to investigate the affair. We had letters from the same relations more than two years later, from which we learned that the missing men had never turned up.'

He took a pinch of snuff, and looked steadily at me.

'Never! I shall relate all that happened, so far as we could discover. The French noble, who was the Chevalier Château Blassemare, unlike most *émigrés*, had taken the matter in time, sold a large portion of his property before the revolution had proceeded so far as to render that next to impossible, and retired with a large sum. He brought with him about half a million of francs, the greater part of which he invested in the French funds; a much larger sum remained in Austrian land and securities. You will observe then that this gentleman was rich, and there was no allegation of his having lost money, or being, in any way, embarrassed. You see?'

I assented.

'This gentleman's habits were not expensive in proportion to his means. He had suitable lodgings in Paris; and for a time, society, the theatres, and other reasonable amusements, engrossed him. He did not play. He was a middle-aged man, affecting youth, with the vanities which are usual in such persons; but, for the rest, he was a gentle and polite person, who disturbed nobody—a person, you see, not likely to provoke an enmity.'

'Certainly not,' I agreed.

'Early in the summer of 1811, he got an order permitting him to copy a picture in one of these *salons*, and came down, here, to Versailles, for the purpose. His work was getting on slowly. After a time he left his hotel, here, and went, by way of change, to the Dragon Volant: there he took, by special choice, the bed-room which has fallen to you by chance. From this time, it appeared, he painted little; and seldom visited his apartments in Paris. One night he saw the host of the Dragon Volant, and told him that he was going into Paris, to remain for a day or two, on very particular business; that his servant would accompany him, but that he would retain his apartments at the Dragon Volant, and return in a few days. He left some clothes there, but packed a portmanteau, took his dressing-case, and the rest, and, with his servant behind his carriage, drove into Paris. You observe all this, monsieur?'

'Most attentively,' I answered.

'Well, monsieur, so soon as they were approaching his lodgings, he stopped the carriage on a sudden, told his servant that he had changed his mind; that he would sleep elsewhere that night, that he had very particular business in the north of France, not far from Rouen, that he would set out before daylight on his journey, and return in a fortnight. He called a fiacre,* took in his hand a leathern bag which, the servant said, was just large enough to hold a few shirts and a coat, but that it was enormously heavy, as he could testify, for he held it in his hand, while his master took out his purse to count thirty-six napoleons, for which the servant was to account, when he should return. He then sent him on, in the carriage; and he, with the bag I have mentioned, got into the fiacre. Up to that, you see, the narrative is quite clear.'

'Perfectly,' I agreed.

'Now comes the mystery,' said Monsieur Carmaignac. 'After that, the Count Château Blassemare was never more seen, so far as we can make out, by acquaintance or friend. We learned that the day before the Count's stockbroker had, by his direction, sold all his stock in the French funds, and handed him the cash it realized. The reason he gave him for this measure tallied with what he said to his servant. He told him that he was going to the north of France to settle some claims, and did not know exactly how much might be required. The bag, which had puzzled the servant by its weight, contained, no doubt, a large sum in gold. Will monsieur try my snuff?'

He politely tendered his open snuff-box, of which I partook, experimentally.

'A reward was offered,' he continued, 'when the inquiry was instituted, for any information tending to throw a light upon the mystery, which might be afforded by the driver of the fiacre "employed on the night of" (so-and-so), "at about the hour of half-past ten, by a gentleman, with a black-leather travelling-bag in his hand, who descended from a private carriage, and gave his servant some money, which he counted twice over". About a hundred-and-fifty drivers applied, but not one of them was the right man. We did, however, elicit a curious and unexpected piece of evidence in quite another quarter. What a racket that plaguey harlequin* makes with his sword!'

'Intolerable!' I chimed in.

The harlequin was soon gone, and he resumed.

'The evidence I speak of, came from a boy, about twelve years old, who knew the appearance of the Count perfectly, having been often employed by him as a messenger. He stated that about half-past twelve o'clock, on the same night—upon which you are to observe, there was a brilliant moon—he was sent, his mother having been suddenly taken ill, for the *sage femme** who lived within a stone's throw of the Dragon Volant. His father's house, from which he started, was a mile away, or more, from that inn, in order to reach which he had to pass round the park of the Château de la Carque, at the site most remote from the point to which he was going. It passes the old churchyard of St Aubin, which is separated from the road only by a very low fence, and two or three enormous old trees. The boy was a little nervous as he approached this ancient cemetery; and, under the bright moonlight, he saw a man whom he distinctly recognized as the Count, whom they designated by a soubriquet which means "the man of smiles". He was looking rueful enough now, and was seated on the side of a tombstone, on which he had laid a pistol, while he was ramming home the charge of another.

'The boy got cautiously by, on tiptoe, with his eyes all the time on the Count Château Blassemare, or the man he mistook for him; his dress was not what he usually wore, but the witness swore that he could not be mistaken as to his identity. He said his face looked grave and stern; but though he did not smile, it was the same face he knew so well. Nothing would make him swerve from that. If that were he, it was the last time he was seen. He has never been heard of since. Nothing could be heard of him in the neighbourhood of Rouen. There has been no evidence of his death; and there is no sign that he is living.'

'That certainly is a most singular case,' I replied; and was about to ask a question or two, when Tom Whistlewick who, without my observing it, had been taking a ramble, returned, a great deal more awake, and a great deal less tipsy.

'I say, Carmaignac, it is getting late, and I must go; I really must, for the reason I told you—and, Beckett, we must soon meet again.'

'I regret very much, monsieur, my not being able at present to relate to you the other case, that of another tenant of the very same room—a case more mysterious and sinister than the last—and which occurred in the autumn of the same year.'

'Will you both do a very good-natured thing, and come and dine with me, at the Dragon Volant, to-morrow?'

So, as we pursued our way along the Galérie des Glacés, I extracted their promise.

'By Jove!' said Whistlewick, when this was done; 'look at that pagoda, or sedan chair, or whatever it is, just where those fellows set it down, and not one of them near it! I can't imagine how they tell fortunes so devilish well. Jack Nuffles—I met him here to-night—says they are gipsies—where are they, I wonder? I'll go over and have a peep at the prophet.'

I saw him plucking at the blinds, which were constructed something on the principle of venetian blinds; the red curtains were inside; but they did not yield, and he could only peep under one that did not come quite down.

When he rejoined us, he related: 'I could scarcely see the old fellow, it's so dark. He is covered with gold and red, and has an embroidered hat on like a mandarin's; he's fast asleep; and, by Jove, he smells like a pole-cat! It's worth going over only to have it to say. Fiew! pooh! oh! It *is* a perfume. Faugh!'

Not caring to accept this tempting invitation, we got along slowly toward the door. I bid them good-night, reminding them of their promise. And so found my way at last to my carriage; and was soon rolling slowly toward the Dragon Volant, on the loneliest of roads, under old trees, and the soft moonlight.

What a number of things had happened within the last two hours! what a variety of strange and vivid pictures were crowded together in that brief space! What an adventure was before me!

The silent, moonlighted, solitary road, how it contrasted with the many-eddied whirl of pleasure from whose roar and music, lights, diamonds and colours, I had just extricated myself.

The sight of lonely Nature at such an hour, acts like a sudden sedative. The madness and guilt of my pursuit struck me with a momentary compunction and horror. I wished I had never entered the labyrinth which was leading me, I knew not whither. It was too late to think of that now; but the bitter was already stealing into my cup; and vague anticipations lay, for a few minutes, heavy on my heart. It would not have taken much to make me disclose my unmanly state of mind to my lively friend, Alfred Ogle, nor even to the milder ridicule of the agreeable Tom Whistlewick.

CHAPTER XVI

THE PARC OF THE CHÂTEAU DE LA CARQUE

THERE was no danger of the Dragon Volant's closing its doors on that occasion till three or four in the morning. There were quartered there many servants of great people, whose masters would not leave the hall till the last moment, and who could not return to their corners in the Dragon Volant, till their last services had been rendered.

I knew, therefore, I should have ample time for my mysterious excursion without exciting curiosity by being shut out.

And now we pulled up under the canopy of boughs, before the sign of the Dragon Volant, and the light that shone from its hall-door.

I dismissed my carriage, ran up the broad staircase, mask in hand, with my domino fluttering about me, and entered the large bedroom. The black wainscoting and stately furniture, with the dark curtains of the very tall bed, made the night there more sombre.

An oblique patch of moonlight was thrown upon the floor from the window to which I hastened. I looked out upon the landscape slumbering in those silvery beams. There stood the outline of the Château de la Carque, its chimneys, and many turrets with their extinguisher-shaped roofs black against the soft grey sky. There, also, more in the foreground, about midway between the window where I stood, and the château, but a little to the left, I traced the tufted masses of the grove which the lady in the mask had appointed as the trysting-place, where I and the beautiful Countess were to meet that night.

I took 'the bearings' of this gloomy bit of wood, whose foliage glimmered softly at top in the light of the moon.

You may guess with what a strange interest and swelling of the heart I gazed on the unknown scene of my coming adventure.

But time was flying, and the hour already near. I threw my robe upon a sofa; I groped out a pair of boots, which I substituted for those thin and heelless shoes, in those days called 'pumps', without which a gentleman could not attend an evening party. I put on my hat, and lastly, I took a pair of loaded pistols which I had been advised were satisfactory companions in the then unsettled state of French society: swarms of disbanded soldiers, some of them alleged to be desperate characters, being everywhere to be met with. These preparations made, I confess I took a looking-glass to the window to see how I looked in the moonlight; and being satisfied, I replaced it, and ran downstairs.

In the hall I called for my servant.

'St Clair,' said I; 'I mean to take a little moonlight ramble, only ten minutes or so. You must not go to bed until I return. If the night is very beautiful, I may possibly extend my ramble a little.'

So down the steps I lounged, looking first over my right, and then over my left shoulder, like a man uncertain which direction to take, and I sauntered up the road, gazing now at the moon, and now at the thin white clouds in the opposite direction, whistling, all the time, an air which I had picked up at one of the theatres.

When I had got a couple of hundred yards away from the Dragon Volant, my minstrelsy totally ceased; and I turned about, and glanced sharply down the road that looked as white as hoarfrost under the moon, and saw the gable of the old inn, and a window, partly concealed by the foliage, with a dusky light shining from it.

No sound of footstep was stirring; no sign of human figure in sight. I consulted my watch, which the light was sufficiently strong to enable me to do. It now wanted but eight minutes of the appointed hour. A thick mantle of ivy at this point covered the wall and rose in a clustering head at top.

It afforded me facilities for scaling the wall, and a partial screen for my operations, if any eye should chance to be looking that way. And now it was done. I was in the park of the Château de la Carque, as nefarious a poacher as ever trespassed on the grounds of unsuspicious lord!

Before me rose the appointed grove, which looked as black as a clump of gigantic hearse-plumes. It seemed to tower higher and higher at every step; and east a broader and blacker shadow toward my feet. On I marched, and was glad when I plunged into the shadow which concealed me. Now I was among the grand old lime and chestnut trees—my heart beat fast with expectation.

This grove opened, a little, near the middle; and in the space thus cleared, there stood with a surrounding flight of steps, a small Greek temple or shrine, with a statue in the centre. It was built of white marble with fluted Corinthian columns, and the crevices were tufted with grass; moss had shown itself on pedestal and cornice, and signs of long neglect and decay were apparent in its discoloured and weather-worn marble. A few feet in front of the steps a fountain, fed from the great ponds at the other side of the château, was making a constant tinkle and plashing in a wide marble basin, and the jet of water glimmered like a shower of diamonds in the broken moonlight. The very neglect and half ruinous state of all this made it only the prettier, as well as sadder. I was too intently watching for the arrival of the lady, in the direction of the château, to study these things; but the half-noted effect of them was romantic, and suggested somehow the grotto and the fountain, and the apparition of Egeria.*

As I watched a voice spoke to me, a little behind my left shoulder. I turned, almost with a start, and the masque, in the costume of Mademoiselle de la Vallière stood there.

'The Countess will be here presently,' she said. The lady stood upon the open space, and the moonlight fell unbroken upon her. Nothing could be more becoming; her figure looked more graceful and elegant than ever. 'In the meantime I shall tell you some peculiarities of her situation. She is unhappy; miserable in an ill-assorted marriage, with a jealous tyrant who now would constrain her to sell her diamonds, which are——'

'Worth thirty thousand pounds sterling. I heard all that from a friend. Can I aid the Countess in her unequal struggle? Say but how, and the greater the danger or the sacrifice, the happier will it make me. *Can* I aid her?'

'If you despise a danger—which, yet, is not a danger; if you despise, as she does, the tyrannical canons of the world; and, if you are chival-rous enough to devote yourself to a lady's cause, with no reward but her poor gratitude: if you can do these things you can aid her, and earn a foremost place, not in her gratitude only, but in her friendship.'

At those words the lady in the mask turned away, and seemed to weep.

I vowed myself the willing slave of the Countess. 'But,' I added, 'you told me she would soon be here.'

'That is, if nothing unforeseen should happen; but with the eye of the Count de St Alyre in the house, and open, it is seldom safe to stir.'

'Does she wish to see me?' I asked, with a tender hesitation.

'First, say have you really thought of *her*, more than once, since the adventure of the Belle Etoile.'

'She never leaves my thoughts; day and night her beautiful eyes haunt me; her sweet voice is always in my ear.'

'Mine is said to resemble hers,' said the mask.

'So it does,' I answered. 'But it is only a resemblance.'

'Oh! then mine is better?'

'Pardon me, mademoiselle, I did not say *that*. Yours is a sweet voice, but I fancy a little higher.'

'A little shriller, you would say,' answered the De la Vallière, I fancied a good deal vexed.

'No, not shriller: your voice is not shrill, it is beautifully sweet; but not so pathetically sweet as hers.'

'That is prejudice, monsieur; it is not true.'

I bowed; I could not contradict a lady.

'I see, monsieur, you laugh at me; you think me vain, because I claim in some points to be equal to the Countess de St Alyre. I challenge you to say, my hand, at least, is less beautiful than hers.' As she thus spoke she drew her glove off, and extended her hand, back upward, in the moonlight.

The lady seemed really nettled. It was undignified and irritating; for in this uninteresting competition the precious moments were flying, and my interview leading apparently to nothing.

'You will admit, then, that my hand is as beautiful as hers.'

'I cannot admit it, mademoiselle,' said I, with the honesty of irritation. 'I will not enter into comparisons, but the Countess de St Alyre is, in all respects, the most beautiful lady I ever beheld.'

The masque laughed coldly, and then, more and more softly, said, with a sigh, 'I will prove all I say.' And as she spoke she removed the mask: and the Countess de St Alyre, smiling, confused, bashful, more beautiful than ever, stood before me!

'Good heavens!' I exclaimed. 'How monstrously stupid I have been. And it was to Madame la Comtesse that I spoke for so long in the *salon*!' I gazed on her in silence. And with a low sweet laugh of good nature, she extended her hand. I took it, and carried it to my lips.

'No, you must not do that,' she said, quietly, 'we are not old enough friends yet. I find, although you were mistaken, that you do remember the Countess of the Belle Etoile, and that you are a champion true and fearless. Had you yielded to the claims just now pressed upon you by the rivalry of Mademoiselle de la Vallière, in her mask, the Countess de St Alyre should never have trusted or seen you more. I now am sure that you are true, as well as brave. You now know that I have not forgotten you; and, also, that if you would risk your life for me, I, too, would brave some danger, rather than lose my friend for ever. I have but a few moments more. Will you come here again to-morrow night, at a quarter past eleven? I will be here at that moment; you must exercise the most scrupulous care to prevent suspicion that you have come here, monsieur. *You owe that to me.*'

She spoke these last words with the most solemn entreaty.

I vowed again and again, that I would die rather than permit the least rashness to endanger the secret which made all the interest and value of my life.

She was looking, I thought, more and more beautiful every moment. My enthusiasm expanded in proportion.

'You must come to-morrow night by a different route,' she said; 'and if you come again, we can change it once more. At the other side of the Château there is a little churchyard, with a ruined chapel. The neighbours are afraid to pass it by night. The road is deserted there, and a stile opens a way into these grounds. Cross it and you can find a covert of thickets, to within fifty steps of this spot.'

I promised, of course, to observe her instructions implicitly.

'I have lived for more than a year in an agony of irresolution. I have decided at last. I have lived a melancholy life; a lonelier life than is passed in the cloister. I have had no one to confide in; no one to advise me; no one to save me from the horrors of my existence. I have found a brave and prompt friend at last. Shall I ever forget the heroic tableau of the hall of the Belle Etoile? Have you—have you really kept the rose I gave you, as we parted? Yes—you swear it. You need not; I trust you. Richard, how often have I in solitude repeated your name, learned from my servant. Richard, my hero! Oh! Richard! Oh, my king!* I love you.'

I would have folded her to my heart—thrown myself at her feet. But this beautiful and—shall I say it—inconsistent woman repelled me.*

'No, we must not waste our moments in extravagances. Understand my case. There is no such thing as indifference in the married state. Not to love one's husband,' she continued, 'is to hate him. The Count, ridiculous in all else, is formidable in his jealousy. In mercy, then, to me observe caution. Affect to all you speak to, the most complete ignorance of all the people in the Château de la Carque; and, if any one in your presence mentions the Count or Countess de St Alyre, be sure you say you never saw either. I shall have more to say to you to-morrow night. I have reasons that I cannot now explain, for all I do, and all I postpone. Farewell. Go! Leave me.'

She waved me back, peremptorily. I echoed her 'farewell', and obeyed.

This interview had not lasted, I think, more than ten minutes. I scaled the park-wall again, and reached the Dragon Volant before its doors were closed.

I lay awake in my bed, in a fever of elation. I saw, till the dawn broke, and chased the vision, the beautiful Countess de St Alyre, always in the dark, before me.

CHAPTER XVII

THE TENANT OF THE PALANQUIN

THE Marquis called on me next day. My late breakfast was still upon the table.

He had come, he said, to ask a favour. An accident had happened to his carriage in the crowd on leaving the ball, and he begged, if I were going into Paris, a seat in mine—I was going in, and was extremely glad of his company. He came with me to my hotel; we went up to my rooms. I was surprised to see a man seated in an easy chair, with his back toward us, reading a newspaper. He rose. It was the Count de St Alyre, his gold spectacles on his nose; his black wig, in oily curls, lying close to his narrow head, and showing, like carved ebony over a repulsive visage of boxwood. His black muffler had been pulled down. His right arm was in a sling. I don't know whether there was anything unusual in his countenance that day, or whether it was but the effect of prejudice arising from all I had heard in my mysterious interview in his park, but I thought his countenance was more strikingly forbidding than I had seen it before.

I was not callous enough in the ways of sin to meet this man, injured at least in intent, thus suddenly, without a momentary disturbance.

He smiled.

'I called, Monsieur Beckett, in the hope of finding you here,' he croaked, 'and I meditated, I fear, taking a very great liberty, but my friend the Marquis d'Harmonville, on whom I have perhaps some claim, will perhaps give me the assistance I require so much.'

'With great pleasure,' said the Marquis, 'but not till after six o'clock. I must go this moment to a meeting of three or four people, whom I cannot disappoint, and I know, perfectly, we cannot break up earlier.'

'What am I to do?' exclaimed the Count, 'an hour would have done it all. Was ever *contretemps** so unlucky!'

'I'll give you an hour, with pleasure,' said I.

'How very good of you, monsieur, I hardly dared to hope it. The business, for so gay and charming a man as Monsieur Beckett, is a little *funeste*. Pray read this note which reached me this morning.'

It certainly was not cheerful. It was a note stating that the body of his, the Count's cousin, Monsieur de St Amand, who had died at his house, the Château Clery, had been, in accordance with his written directions, sent for burial at Père La Chaise, and, with the permission of the Count de St Alyre, would reach his house (the Château de la Carque), at about ten o'clock on the night following, to be conveyed thence in a hearse, with any member of the family who might wish to attend the obsequies.

'I did not see the poor gentleman twice in my life,' said the Count, 'but this office, as he has no other kinsman, disagreeable as it is, I could scarcely decline, and so I want to attend at the office to have the book signed, and the order entered. But here is another misery. By ill luck, I have sprained my thumb, and can't sign my name for a week to come. However, one name answers as well as another. Yours as well as mine. And as you are so good as to come with me, all will go right.'

Away we drove. The Count gave me a memorandum of the Christian and surnames of the deceased, his age, the complaint he died of, and the usual particulars; also a note of the exact position in which a grave, the dimensions of which were described, of the ordinary simple kind, was to be dug, between two vaults belonging to the family of St Amand. The funeral, it was stated, would arrive at half-past one o'clock A.M. (the next night but one); and he handed me the money, with extra fees, for a burial by night. It was a good deal; and I asked him, as he entrusted the whole affair to me, in whose name I should take the receipt.

'Not in mine, my good friend. They wanted me to become an executor, which I, yesterday, wrote to decline; and I am informed that if the receipt were in my name it would constitute me an executor in the eye of the law, and fix me in that position. Take it, pray, if you have no objection, in your own name.'

This, accordingly, I did.

'You will see, by-and-by, why I am obliged to mention all these particulars.'

The Count, meanwhile, was leaning back in the carriage, with his black silk muffler up to his nose, and his hat shading his eyes, while he dozed in his corner; in which state I found him on my return.

Paris had lost its charm for me. I hurried through the little business I had to do, longed once more for my quiet room in the Dragon Volant, the melancholy woods of the Château de la Carque, and the tumultuous and thrilling influence of proximity to the object of my wild but wicked romance.

I was delayed some time by my stockbroker. I had a very large sum, as I told you, at my banker's, uninvested. I cared very little for a few days' interest—very little for the entire sum, compared with the image that occupied my thoughts, and beckoned me with a white arm, through the dark, toward the spreading lime-trees and chestnuts of the Château de la Carque. But I had fixed this day to meet him, and was relieved when he told me that I had better let it lie in my banker's hands for a few days longer, as the funds would certainly fall immediately. This accident, too, was not without its immediate bearing on my subsequent adventures.

When I reached the Dragon Volant, I found, in my sitting-room, a good deal to my chagrin, my two guests, whom I had quite forgotten. I inwardly cursed my own stupidity for having embarrassed myself with their agreeable society. It could not be helped now, however, and a word to the waiters put all things in train for dinner.

Tom Whistlewick was in great force; and he commenced almost immediately with a very odd story.

He told me that not only Versailles, but all Paris, was in a ferment, in consequence of a revolting, and all but sacrilegious, practical joke, played off on the night before.

The pagoda, as he persisted in calling the palanquin, had been left standing on the spot where we last saw it. Neither conjuror, nor usher, nor bearers had ever returned. When the ball closed, and the company at length retired, the servants who attended to put out the lights, and secure the doors, found it still there.

It was determined, however, to let it stand where it was until next morning, by which time, it was conjectured, its owners would send messengers to remove it.

None arrived. The servants were then ordered to take it away; and its extraordinary weight, for the first time, reminded them of its forgotten human occupant. Its door was forced; and, judge what was their disgust, when they discovered, not a living man, but a corpse! Three or four days must have passed since the death of the burly man in the Chinese tunic and painted cap. Some people thought it was a trick designed to insult the Allies, in whose honour the ball was got up. Others were of opinion that it was nothing worse than a daring and cynical jocularity which, shocking as it was, might yet be forgiven to the high spirits and irrepressible buffoonery of youth. Others, again, fewer in number, and mystically given, insisted that the corpse was *bona fide* necessary to the exhibition, and that the disclosures and allusions which had astonished so many people were distinctly due to necromancy.

'The matter, however, is now in the hands of the police,' observed Monsieur Carmaignac, 'and we are not the body they were, two or three months ago, if the offenders against propriety and public feeling are not traced, and convicted, unless, indeed, they have been a great deal more cunning than such fools generally are.'

I was thinking within myself how utterly inexplicable was my colloquy with the conjuror, so cavalierly dismissed by Monsieur Carmaignac as a 'fool'; and the more I thought the more marvellous it seemed.

'It certainly was an original joke, though not a very clean one,' said Whistlewick.

'Not even original,' said Carmaignac. 'Very nearly the same thing was done,* a hundred years ago or more, at a state ball in Paris; and the rascals who played the trick were never found out.

In this Monsieur Carmaignac, as I afterwards discovered, spoke truly; for, among my books of French anecdote and memoirs, the very incident is marked, by my own hand.

While we were thus talking the waiter told us that dinner was served; and we withdrew accordingly; my guests more than making amends for my comparative taciturnity.

CHAPTER XVIII

THE CHURCHYARD

OUR dinner was really good, so were the wines; better, perhaps, at this out-of-the-way inn, than at some of the more pretentious hotels in Paris. The moral effect of a really good dinner is immense—we all felt it. The serenity and good nature that follow are more solid and comfortable than the tumultuous benevolences of Bacchus.

My friends were happy, therefore, and very chatty; which latter relieved me of the trouble of talking, and prompted them to entertain me and one another incessantly with agreeable stories and conversation, of which, until suddenly a subject emerged, which interested me powerfully, I confess, so much were my thoughts engaged elsewhere, I heard next to nothing.

'Yes,' said Carmaignac, continuing a conversation which had escaped me, 'there was another case, beside that Russian nobleman, odder still. I remembered it this morning, but cannot recall the name. He was a tenant of the very same room. By-the-by, monsieur, might it not be as well,' he added, turning to me, with a laugh, half-joke whole earnest, as they say, 'if you were to get into another apartment, now that the house is no longer crowded? that is, if you mean to make any stay here.'

'A thousand thanks! no. I'm thinking of changing my hotel; and I can run into town so easily at night; and though I stay here, for this night, at least, I don't expect to vanish like those others. But you say there is another adventure, of the same kind, connected with the same room. Do let us hear it. But take some wine first.'

The story he told was curious.

'It happened,' said Carmaignac, 'as well as I recollect, before either of the other cases. A French gentleman—I wish I could remember his name—the son of a merchant, came to this inn (the Dragon Volant), and was put by the landlord into the same room of which we have been speaking, *your* apartment, monsieur. He was by no means young—past forty—and very far from good-looking. The people here said that he was the ugliest man, and the most good-natured, that ever lived. He played on the fiddle, sang, and wrote poetry. His habits were odd, and desultory. He would sometimes sit all day in his room writing, singing, and fiddling, and go out at night for a walk. An eccentric man! He was by no means a millionaire, but he had a *modicum bonum*,* you understand—a trifle more than half a million of francs. He consulted his stockbroker about investing this money in foreign stocks, and drew the entire sum from his banker. You now have the situation of affairs when the catastrophe occurred.'

'Pray fill your glass,' I said.

'Dutch courage, monsieur, to face the catastrophe!' said Whistlewick, filling his own.

'Now, that was the last that ever was heard of his money,' resumed Carmaignac. 'You shall hear about himself. The night after this financial operation, he was seized with a poetic frenzy; he sent for the then landlord of this house, and told him that he had long meditated an epic, and meant to commence that night, and that he was on no account to be disturbed until nine o'clock in the morning. He had two pairs of wax candles, a little cold supper on a side-table, his desk open, paper enough upon it to contain the entire Henriade,* and a proportionate store of pens and ink.

'Seated at this desk he was seen by the waiter who brought him a cup of coffee at nine o'clock, at which time the intruder said he was writing fast enough to set fire to the paper—that was his phrase: he did not look up, he appeared too much engrossed. But, when the waiter came back, half an hour afterwards, the door was locked; and the poet, from within, answered, that he must not be disturbed.

'Away went the *garçon*; and next morning at nine o'clock knocked at his door, and receiving no answer, looked through the key-hole; the lights were still burning, the window-shutters were closed as he had left them; he renewed his knocking, knocked louder, no answer came. He reported this continued and alarming silence to the inn-keeper, who, finding that his guest had not left his key in the lock, succeeded in finding another that opened it. The candles were just giving up the ghost in their sockets, but there was light enough to ascertain that the tenant of the room was gone! The bed had not been disturbed; the window-shutter was barred. He must have let himself out, and, locking the door on the outside, put the key in his pocket and so made his way out of the house. Here was, however, another difficulty, the Dragon Volant shut its doors and made all fast at twelve o'clock; after that hour no one could leave the house, except by obtaining the key and letting himself out, and of necessity leaving the door unsecured, or else by collusion and aid of some person in the house.

'Now it happened that, some time after the doors were secured, at half-past twelve, a servant who had not been apprised of his order to be left undisturbed, seeing a light shine through the key-hole, knocked at the door to inquire whether the poet wanted anything. He was very little obliged to his disturber, and dismissed him with a renewed charge that he was not to be interrupted again during the night. This incident established the fact that he was in the house after the doors had been locked and barred. The inn-keeper himself kept the keys, and swore that he found them hung on the wall above his head, in his bed, in their usual place, in the morning; and that nobody could have taken them away without awakening him. That was all we could discover. The Count de St Alyre, to whom this house belongs, was very active and very much chagrined. But nothing was discovered.'

'And nothing heard since of the epic poet?' I asked.

'Nothing—not the slightest clue—he never turned up again. I suppose he is dead; if he is not, he must have got into some devilish bad scrape, of which we have heard nothing, that compelled him to abscond with all the secrecy and expedition in his power. All that we know for certain is that, having occupied the room in which you sleep, he vanished, nobody ever knew how, and never was heard of since.'

'You have now mentioned three cases,' I said, 'and all from the same room?'

'Three. Yes, all equally unintelligible. When men are murdered, the great and immediate difficulty the assassins encounter is how to conceal the body. It is very hard to believe that three persons should have been consecutively murdered, in the same room, and their bodies so effectually disposed of that no trace of them was ever discovered.'

From this we passed to other topics, and the grave Monsieur Carmaignac amused us with a perfectly prodigious collection of scandalous anecdote, which his opportunities in the police department had enabled him to accumulate.

My guests happily had engagements in Paris, and left me at about ten.

I went up to my room, and looked out upon the grounds of the Château de la Carque. The moonlight was broken by clouds, and the view of the park in this desultory light, acquired a melancholy and fantastic character.

The strange anecdotes recounted of the room in which I stood, by Monsieur Carmaignac, returned vaguely upon my mind, drowning in sudden shadows the gaiety of the more frivolous stories with which he had followed them. I looked round me on the room that lay in ominous gloom, with an almost disagreeable sensation. I took my pistols now with an undefined apprehension that they might be really needed before my return tonight. This feeling, be it understood, in nowise chilled my ardour. Never had my enthusiasm mounted higher. My adventure absorbed and carried me away; but it added a strange and stern excitement to the expedition.

I loitered for a time in my room. I had ascertained the exact point at which the little churchyard lay. It was about a mile away; I did not wish to reach it earlier than necessary.

I stole quietly out, and sauntered along the road to my left, and thence entered a narrower track, still to my left, which, skirting the park wall, and describing a circuitous route, all the way, under grand old trees, passes the ancient cemetery. That cemetery is embowered in trees, and occupies little more than half an acre of ground, to the left of the road, interposing between it and the park of the Château de la Carque.

Here, at this haunted spot, I paused and listened. The place was utterly silent. A thick cloud had darkened the moon, so that I could distinguish little more than the outlines of near objects, and that vaguely enough; and sometimes, as it were, floating in black fog, the white surface of a tombstone emerged.

Among the forms that met my eye against the iron-grey of the horizon, were some of those shrubs or trees that grow like our junipers, some six feet high, in form like a miniature poplar, with the darker foliage of the yew. I do not know the name of the plant,* but I have often seen it in such funereal places.

Knowing that I was a little too early, I sat down upon the edge of a tombstone to wait, as, for aught I knew, the beautiful Countess might have wise reasons for not caring that I should enter the grounds of the château earlier than she had appointed. In the listless state induced by waiting, I sat there, with my eyes on the object straight before me, which chanced to be that faint black outline I have described. It was right before me, about half-a-dozen steps away.

The moon now began to escape from under the skirt of the cloud that had hid her face for so long; and, as the light gradually improved, the tree on which I had been lazily staring began to take a new shape. It was no longer a tree, but a man standing motionless. Brighter and brighter grew the moonlight, clearer and clearer the image became, and at last stood out perfectly distinctly. It was Colonel Gaillarde.

Luckily, he was not looking toward me. I could only see him in profile; but there was no mistaking the white moustache, the *farouche** visage, and the gaunt, six-foot stature. There he was, his shoulder toward me, listening and watching, plainly, for some signal or person expected, straight in front of him.

If he were, by chance, to turn his eyes in my direction, I knew that I must reckon upon an instantaneous renewal of the combat only commenced in the hall of the Belle Etoile. In any case, could malignant fortune have posted, at this place and hour, a more dangerous watcher? What ecstasy to him, by a single discovery, to hit me so hard, and blast the Countess de St Alyre, whom he seemed to hate.

He raised his arm; he whistled softly; I heard an answering whistle as low; and, to my relief, the Colonel advanced in the direction of this sound, widening the distance between us at every step; and immediately I heard talking, but in a low and cautious key.

I recognized, I thought, even so, the peculiar voice of Gaillarde.

I stole softly forward in the direction in which those sounds were audible. In doing so, I had, of course, to use the extremest caution.

I thought I saw a hat above a jagged piece of ruined wall, and then a second—yes, I saw two hats conversing; the voices came from under them. They moved off, not in the direction of the park, but of the road, and I lay along the grass, peeping over a grave, as a skirmisher might, observing the enemy. One after the other, the figures emerged full into view as they mounted the stile at the road-side. The Colonel, who was last, stood on the wall for awhile, looking about him, and then jumped down on the road. I heard their steps and talk as they moved away together, with their backs toward me, in the direction which led them farther and farther from the Dragon Volant.

I waited until these sounds were quite lost in distance before I entered the park. I followed the instructions I had received from the Countess de St Alyre, and made my way among brushwood and thickets to the point nearest the ruinous temple, and crossed the short intervening space of open ground rapidly.

I was now once more under the gigantic boughs of the old lime and chestnut trees; softly, and with a heart throbbing fast, I approached the little structure.

The moon was now shining steadily, pouring down its radiance on the soft foliage, and here and there mottling the verdure under my feet.

I reached the steps; I was among its worn marble shafts. She was not there, nor in the inner sanctuary, the arched windows of which were screened almost entirely by masses of ivy. The lady had not yet arrived.

CHAPTER XIX

THE KEY

I STOOD now upon the steps, watching and listening. In a minute or two I heard the crackle of withered sticks trodden upon, and, looking in the direction, I saw a figure approaching among the trees, wrapped in a mantle.

I advanced eagerly. It was the Countess. She did not speak, but gave me her hand, and I led her to the scene of our last interview. She repressed the ardour of my impassioned greeting with a gentle but peremptory firmness. She removed her hood, shook back her beautiful hair, and gazing on me with sad and glowing eyes, sighed deeply. Some awful thought seemed to weigh upon her.

'Richard, I must speak plainly. The crisis of my life has come. I am sure you would defend me. I think you pity me; perhaps you even love me.'

At these words I became eloquent, as young madmen in my plight do. She silenced me, however, with the same melancholy firmness.

'Listen, dear friend, and then say whether you can aid me. How madly I am trusting you; and yet my heart tells me how wisely! To meet you here as I do—what insanity it seems! How poorly you must think of me! But when you know all, you will judge me fairly. Without your aid I cannot accomplish my purpose. That purpose unaccomplished, I must die. I am chained to a man whom I despise—whom I abhor. I have resolved to fly. I have jewels, principally diamonds, for which I am offered thirty thousand pounds of your English money. They are my separate property by my marriage settlement; I will take them with me. You are a judge, no doubt, of jewels. I was counting mine when the hour came, and brought this in my hand to show you. Look.'

'It is magnificent!' I exclaimed, as a collar of diamonds twinkled and flashed in the moonlight, suspended from her pretty fingers. I thought, even at that tragic moment, that she prolonged the show, with a feminine delight in these brilliant toys.

'Yes,' she said; 'I shall part with them all. I will turn them into money, and break, for ever, the unnatural and wicked bonds that tied me, in the name of a sacrament, to a tyrant. A man young, handsome, generous, brave as you, can hardly be rich. Richard, you say you love me; you shall share all this with me. We will fly together to Switzerland; we will evade pursuit; my powerful friends will intervene and arrange a separation; and I shall, at length, be happy and reward my hero.'

You may suppose the style, florid and vehement, in which I poured forth my gratitude, vowed the devotion of my life, and placed myself absolutely at her disposal.

'To-morrow night,' she said, 'my husband will attend the remains of his cousin, Monsieur de St Amand, to Père la Chaise. The hearse, he says, will leave this at half-past nine. You must be here, where we stand, at nine o'clock.'

I promised punctual obedience.

'I will not meet you here; but you see a red light in the window of the tower at that angle of the château?'

I assented.

'I placed it there, that, tomorrow night, when it comes, you may recognize it. So soon as that rose-coloured light appears at that window, it will be a signal to you that the funeral has left the château, and that you may approach safely. Come, then, to that window; I will open it, and admit you. Five minutes after a travelling-carriage, with four horses, shall stand ready, in the *porte-cochère*.* I will place my diamonds in your hands; and so soon as we enter the carriage, our flight commences. We shall have at least five hours' start; and with energy, stratagem, and resource, I fear nothing. Are you ready to undertake all this for my sake?'

Again I vowed myself her slave.

'My only difficulty,' she said, 'is how we shall quickly enough convert my diamonds into money; I dare not remove them while my husband is in the house.'

Here was the opportunity I wished for. I now told her that I had in my banker's hands no less a sum than thirty thousand pounds, with which, in the shape of gold and notes, I should come furnished, and thus the risk and loss of disposing of her diamonds in too much haste would be avoided.

'Good heaven!' she exclaimed, with a kind of disappointment. 'You are rich, then? and I have lost the felicity of making my generous friend more happy. Be it so; since so it must be. Let us contribute, each, in equal shares, to our common fund. Bring you, your money; I, my jewels. There is a happiness to me even in mingling my resources with yours.'

On this there followed a romantic colloquy, all poetry and passion, such as I should, in vain, endeavour to reproduce.

Then came a very special instruction.

'I have come provided, too, with a key, the use of which I must explain.'

It was a double key—a long, slender stem, with a key at each end—one about the size which opens an ordinary room door; the other, as small, almost, as the key of a dressing-case.

'You cannot employ too much caution to-morrow night. An interruption would murder all my hopes. I have learned that you occupy the haunted room in the Dragon Volant. It is the very room I would have wished you in. I will tell you why—there is a story of a man who, having shut himself up in that room one night, disappeared before morning. The truth is, he wanted, I believe, to escape from creditors; and the host of the Dragon Volant, at that time, being a rogue, aided him in absconding. My husband investigated the matter, and discovered how his escape was made. It was by means of this key. Here is a memorandum and a plan describing how they are to be applied. I have taken them from the Count's escritoire. And now, once more I must leave to your ingenuity how to mystify the people of the Dragon Volant. Be sure you try the keys first, to see that the locks turn freely. I will have my jewels ready. You, whatever we divide, had better bring your money, because it may be many months before you can revisit Paris, or disclose our place of residence to any one; and our passports—arrange all that; in what names, and whither, you please. And now, dear Richard' (she leaned her arm fondly on my shoulder, and looked with ineffable passion in my eyes, with her other hand clasped in mine), 'my very life is in your hands; I have staked all on your fidelity.'

As she spoke the last word, she, on a sudden, grew deadly pale, and gasped, 'Good God! who is here?'

At the same moment she receded through the door in the marble screen, close to which she stood, and behind which was a roofless chamber, as small as the shrine, the window of which was darkened by a clustering mass of ivy so dense that hardly a gleam of light came through the leaves.

I stood upon the threshold which she had just crossed, looking in the direction in which she had thrown that one terrified glance. No wonder she was frightened. Quite close upon us, not twenty yards away, and approaching at a quick step, very distinctly lighted by the moon, Colonel Gaillarde and his companion were coming. The shadow of the cornice and a piece of wall were upon me. Unconscious of this, I was expecting the moment when, with one of his frantic yells, he should spring forward to assail me.

I made a step backward, drew one of my pistols from my pocket, and cocked it. It was obvious he had not seen me.

I stood, with my finger on the trigger, determined to shoot him dead if he should attempt to enter the place, where the Countess was. It would, no doubt, have been a murder; but, in my mind, I had no question or qualm about it. When once we engage in secret and guilty practices we are nearer other and greater crimes than we at all suspect.

'There's the statue,' said the Colonel, in his brief, discordant tones. 'That's the figure.'

'Alluded to in the stanzas?' inquired his companion.

'The very thing. We shall see more next time. Forward, monsieur; let us march.'

And, much to my relief, the gallant Colonel turned on his heel, and marched through the trees, with his back toward the château, striding over the grass, as I quickly saw, to the park wall, which they crossed, not far from the gables of the Dragon Volant.

I found the Countess trembling in no affected, but a very real terror. She would not hear of my accompanying her toward the château. But I told her that I would prevent the return of the mad Colonel; and upon that point, at least, that she need fear nothing. She quickly recovered, again bid me a fond and lingering good-night, and left me, gazing after her, with the key in my hand, and such a phantasmagoria* floating in my brain as amounted very nearly to madness.

Here was I, ready to brave all dangers, all right and reason, plunge into murder itself, on the first summons, and entangle myself in consequences inextricable and horrible (what cared I?) for a woman of whom I knew nothing, but that she was beautiful and reckless!

I have often thanked heaven for its mercy in conducting me through the labyrinths in which I had all but lost myself.

CHAPTER XX

A HIGH-CAULED CAP

I WAS now upon the road, within two or three hundred yards of the Dragon Volant. I had undertaken an adventure, with a vengeance! And by way of prelude, there, not improbably, awaited me, in my inn, another encounter, perhaps, this time, not so lucky, with the grotesque sabreur.

I was glad I had my pistols. I certainly was bound by no law to allow a ruffian to cut me down, unresisting.

Stooping boughs from the old park, gigantic poplars on the other side, and the moonlight over all, made the narrow road to the inn-door picturesque.

I could not think very clearly just now; events were succeeding one another so rapidly, and I, involved in the action of a drama so extravagant and guilty, hardly knew myself or believed my own story, as I slowly paced toward the still open door of the Flying Dragon.

No sign of the Colonel, visible or audible, was there. In the hall, I inquired. No gentleman had arrived at the inn for the last half hour. I looked into the public room. It was deserted. The clock struck twelve, and I heard the servant barring the great door. I took my candle. The lights in this rural hostelry were by this time out, and the house had the air of one that had settled to slumber for many hours. The cold moonlight streamed in at the window on the landing, as I ascended the broad staircase; and I paused for a moment to look over the wooded grounds to the turreted château, to me, so full of interest. I bethought me, however, that prying eyes might read a meaning in this midnight gazing, and possibly the Count himself might, in his jealous mood, surmise a signal in this unwonted light in the stair-window of the Dragon Volant.

On opening my room door, with a little start, I met an extremely old woman with the longest face I ever saw; she had what used to be termed, a high-cauled cap, on, the white border of which contrasted with her brown and yellow skin, and made her wrinkled face more ugly. She raised her curved shoulders, and looked up in my face, with eyes unnaturally black and bright.

'I have lighted a little wood, monsieur, because the night is chill.'

I thanked her, but she did not go. She stood with her candle in her tremulous fingers.

'Excuse an old woman, monsieur,' she said; 'but what on earth can a young English *milord*, with all Paris at his feet, find to amuse him in the Dragon Volant?'

Had I been at the age of fairy tales, and in daily intercourse with the delightful Countess d'Aulnois,* I should have seen in this withered apparition, the *genius loci*,* the malignant fairy, at the stamp of whose foot, the ill-fated tenants of this very room had, from time to time, vanished. I was past that, however; but the old woman's dark eyes were fixed on mine, with a steady meaning that plainly told me that my secret was known. I was embarrassed and alarmed; I never thought of asking her what business that was of hers.

'These old eyes saw you in the park of the château to-night.'

'*I!*' I began, with all the scornful surprise I could affect.

'It avails nothing, monsieur; I know why you stay here; and I tell you to begone. Leave this house to-morrow morning, and never come again.'

She lifted her disengaged hand, as she looked at me with intense horror in her eyes.

'There is nothing on earth—I don't know what you mean,' I answered; 'and why should you care about me?'

'I don't care about you, monsieur—I care about the honour of an ancient family, whom I served in their happier days, when to be noble, was to be honoured. But my words are thrown away, monsieur; you are insolent. I will keep my secret, and you, yours; that is all. You will soon find it hard enough to divulge it.'

The old woman went slowly from the room and shut the door, before I had made up my mind to say anything. I was standing where she had left me, nearly five minutes later. The jealousy of Monsieur the Count, I assumed, appears to this old creature about the most terrible thing in creation. Whatever contempt I might entertain for the dangers which this old lady so darkly intimated, it was by no means pleasant, you may suppose, that a secret so dangerous should be so much as suspected by a stranger, and that stranger a partisan of the Count de St Alyre.

Ought I not, at all risks, to apprise the Countess, who had trusted me so generously, or, as she said herself, so madly, of the fact that our secret was, at least, suspected by another? But was there not greater danger in attempting to communicate? What did the beldame mean by saying, 'Keep your secret, and I'll keep mine'?

I had a thousand distracting questions before me. My progress seemed like a journey through the Spessart,* where at every step some new goblin or monster starts from the ground or steps from behind a tree.

Peremptorily I dismissed these harassing and frightful doubts. I secured my door, sat myself down at my table, and with a candle at each side, placed before me the piece of vellum which contained the drawings and notes on which I was to rely for full instructions as to how to use the key.

When I had studied this for awhile, I made my investigation. The angle of the room at the right side of the window was cut off by an oblique turn in the wainscot. I examined this carefully, and, on pressure, a small bit of the frame of the woodwork slid aside, and disclosed a keyhole. On removing my finger, it shot back to its place again, with a spring. So far I had interpreted my instructions successfully. A similar search next the floor, and directly under this, was rewarded by a like discovery. The small end of the key fitted this, as it had the upper keyhole; and now, with two or three hard jerks at the key, a door in the panel opened, showing a strip of the bare wall, and a narrow, arched doorway, piercing the thickness of the wall; and within which I saw a screw-staircase of stone.

Candle in hand I stepped in. I do not know whether the quality of air long undisturbed is peculiar: to me it has always seemed so, and the damp smell of the old masonry hung in this atmosphere. My candle faintly lighted the bare stone wall that enclosed the stair, the foot of which I could not see. Down I went, and a few turns brought me to the stone floor. Here was another door, of the simple, old, oak kind, deep sunk in the thickness of the wall. The large end of the key fitted this. The lock was stiff; I set the candle down upon the stair, and applied both hands; it turned with difficulty, and as it revolved uttered a shriek that alarmed me for my secret.

For some minutes I did not move. In a little time, however, I took courage, and opened the door. The night-air floating in, puffed out the candle. There was a thicket of holly and underwood, as dense as a jungle, close about the door. I should have been in pitch-darkness, were it not that through the topmost leaves, there twinkled, here and there, a glimmer of moonshine.

Softly, lest any one should have opened his window, at the sound of the rusty bolt, I struggled through this, till I gained a view of the open grounds. Here I found that the brushwood spread a good way up the park, uniting with the wood that approached the little temple I have described.

A general could not have chosen a more effectually-covered approach from the Dragon Volant to the trysting-place where hitherto I had conferred with the idol of my lawless adoration.

Looking back upon the old inn, I discovered that the stair I descended, was enclosed in one of those slender turrets that decorate such buildings. It was placed at that angle which corresponded with the part of the panelling of my room indicated in the plan I had been studying.

Thoroughly satisfied with my experiment, I made my way back to the door, with some little difficulty, re-mounted to my room, locked my secret door again; kissed the mysterious key that her hand had pressed that night, and placed it under my pillow, upon which, very soon after, my giddy head was laid, not, for some time, to sleep soundly.

CHAPTER XXI

I SEE THREE MEN IN A MIRROR

I AWOKE very early next morning, and was too excited to sleep again. As soon as I could, without exciting remark, I saw my host. I told him that I was going into town that night, and thence to ——, where I had to see some people on business, and requested him to mention my being there to any friend who might call. That I expected to be back in about a week, and that in the meantime my servant, St Clair, would keep the key of my room, and look after my things.

Having prepared this mystification for my landlord, I drove into Paris, and there transacted the financial part of the affair. The problem was to reduce my balance, nearly thirty thousand pounds, to a shape in which it would be not only easily portable, but available, wherever I might go, without involving correspondence, or any other incident which would disclose my place of residence, for the time being. All these points were as nearly provided for as they could be. I need not trouble you about my arrangements for passports. It is enough to say that the point I selected for our flight was, in the spirit of romance, one of the most beautiful and sequestered nooks in Switzerland.

Luggage, I should start with none. The first considerable town we reached next morning, would supply an extemporized wardrobe. It was now two o'clock; *only* two! How on earth was I to dispose of the remainder of the day?

I had not yet seen the cathedral of Notre Dame; and thither I drove. I spent an hour or more there; and then to the Conciergerie, the Palais de Justice, and the beautiful Sainte Chapelle. Still there remained some time to get rid of, and I strolled into the narrow streets adjoining the cathedral. I recollect seeing, in one of them, an old house with a mural inscription stating that it had been the residence of Canon Fulbert, the uncle of Abelard's Eloise.* I don't know whether these curious old streets, in which I observed fragments of ancient gothic churches fitted up as warehouses, are still extant. I lighted, among other dingy and eccentric shops, upon one that seemed that of a broker of all sorts of old decorations, armour, china, furniture. I entered the shop; it was dark, dusty, and low. The proprietor was busy scouring a piece of inlaid armour, and allowed me to poke about his shop, and examine the curious things accumulated there, just as I pleased. Gradually I made my way to the farther end of it, where there was but one window with many panes, each with a bull's-eye in it, and in the dirtiest possible state. When I reached this window, I turned about, and in a recess, standing at right angles with the side wall of the shop, was a large mirror in an old-fashioned dingy frame. Reflected in this I saw, what in old houses I have heard termed an 'alcove', in which, among lumber, and various dusty articles hanging on the wall, there stood a table, at which three persons were seated, as it seemed to me, in earnest conversation. Two of these persons I instantly recognized, one was Colonel Gaillarde, the other was the Marquis d'Harmonville. The third, who was fiddling with a pen, was a lean, pale man, pitted with the smallpox, with lank black hair, and about as mean-looking a person as I had ever seen in my life. The Marquis looked up, and his glance was instantaneously followed by his two companions. For a moment I hesitated what to do. But it was plain that I was not recognized, as indeed I could hardly have been, the light from the window being behind me, and the portion of the shop immediately before me, being very dark indeed.

Perceiving this I had presence of mind to affect being entirely engrossed by the objects before me, and strolled slowly down the shop again. I paused for a moment to hear whether I was followed, and was relieved when I heard no step. You may be sure I did not waste more time in that shop, where I had just made a discovery so curious and so unexpected.

It was no business of mine to inquire what brought Colonel Gaillarde and the Marquis together, in so shabby, and even dirty, a place, or who the mean person, biting the feather end of his pen, might be. Such employments as the Marquis had accepted sometimes make strange bed-fellows.

I was glad to get away, and just as the sun set, I had reached the steps of the Dragon Volant, and dismissed the vehicle in which I arrived, carrying in my hand a strong box, of marvellously small dimensions considering all it contained, strapped in a leather cover, which disguised its real character.

When I got to my room, I summoned St Clair. I told him nearly the same story, I had already told my host. I gave him fifty pounds, with orders to expend whatever was necessary on himself, and in payment for my rooms till my return. I then eat a slight and hasty dinner. My eyes were often upon the solemn old clock over the chimney-piece, which was my sole accomplice in keeping tryste in this iniquitous venture. The sky favoured my design, and darkened all things with a sea of clouds.

The innkeeper met me in the hall, to ask whether I should want a vehicle to Paris? I was prepared for this question, and instantly answered that I meant to walk to Versailles, and take a carriage there. I called St Clair.

'Go,' said I, 'and drink a bottle of wine with your friends. I shall call you if I should want anything; in the meantime, here is the key of my room; I shall be writing some notes, so don't allow any one to disturb me, for at least half an hour. At the end of that time you will probably find that I have left this for Versailles; and should you not find me in the room, you may take that for granted; and you take charge of everything, and lock the door, you understand?'

St Clair took his leave, wishing me all happiness and no doubt promising himself some little amusement with my money. With my candle in my hand, I hastened upstairs. It wanted now but five minutes to the appointed time. I do not think there is anything of the coward in my nature; but I confess, as the crisis approached, I felt something of the suspense and awe of a soldier going into action. Would I have receded? Not for all this earth could offer.

I bolted my door, put on my great coat, and placed my pistols, one in each pocket. I now applied my key to the secret locks: drew the wainscot-door a little open, took my strong box under my arm, extinguished my candle, unbolted my door, listened at it for a few moments to be sure that no one was approaching, and then crossed the floor of my room swiftly, entered the secret door, and closed the spring lock after me. I was upon the screw-stair in total darkness, the key in my fingers. Thus far the undertaking was successful.

CHAPTER XXII

RAPTURE

DOWN the screw-stair I went in utter darkness; and having reached the stone floor, I discerned the door and groped out the keyhole. With more caution, and less noise than upon the night before, I opened the door, and stepped out into the thick brushwood. It was almost as dark in this jungle.

Having secured the door, I slowly pushed my way through the bushes, which soon became less dense. Then, with more ease, but still under thick cover, I pursued in the track of the wood, keeping near its edge.

At length, in the darkened air, about fifty yards away, the shafts of the marble temple rose like phantoms before me, seen through the trunks of the old trees. Everything favoured my enterprise. I had effectually mystified my servant and the people of the Dragon Volant, and so dark was the night, that even had I alarmed the suspicions of all the tenants of the inn, I might safely defy their united curiosity, though posted at every window of the house.

Through the trunks, over the roots of the old trees, I reached the appointed place of observation. I laid my treasure, in its leathern case, in the embrasure, and leaning my arms upon it, looked steadily in the direction of the château. The outline of the building was scarcely discernible, blending dimly, as it did, with the sky. No light in any window was visible. I was plainly to wait; but for how long?

Leaning on my box of treasure, gazing toward the massive shadow that represented the château, in the midst of my ardent and elated longings, there came upon me an odd thought, which you will think might well have struck me long before. It seemed on a sudden, as it came, that the darkness deepened, and a chill stole into the air, around me.

Suppose I were to disappear finally, like those other men whose stories I had listened to! Had I not been at all the pains that mortal could, to obliterate every trace of my real proceedings, and to mislead every one to whom I spoke as to the direction in which I had gone?

This icy, snake-like thought stole through my mind, and was gone.

It was with me the full-blooded season of youth, conscious strength, rashness, passion, pursuit, the adventure! Here were a pair of double-barrelled pistols, four lives in my hands? What could possibly happen? The Count—except for the sake of my dulcinea*—what was it to me whether the old coward whom I had seen, in an ague of terror before the brawling Colonel, interposed or not? I was assuming the worst that could happen. But with an ally so clever and courageous as my beautiful Countess, could any such misadventure befall? Bah! I laughed at all such fancies.

As I thus communed with myself, the signal light sprang up. The rose-coloured light, *couleur de rose*, emblem of sanguine hope, and the dawn of a happy day.

Clear, soft, and steady, glowed the light from the window. The stone shafts showed black against it. Murmuring words of passionate love as I gazed upon the signal, I grasped my strong box under my arm, and with rapid strides approached the Château de la Carque. No sign of light or life, no human voice, no tread of foot, no bark of dog, indicated a chance of interruption. A blind was down; and as I came close to the tall window, I found that half a dozen steps led up to it, and that a large lattice, answering for a door, lay open.

A shadow from within fell upon the blind; it was drawn aside, and as I ascended the steps, a soft voice murmured—'Richard, dearest Richard, come, oh! come; how I have longed for this moment!'

Never did she look so beautiful. My love rose to passionate enthusiasm. I only wished there were some real danger in the adventure worthy of such a creature. When the first tumultuous greeting was over, she made me sit beside her on a sofa. There we talked for a minute or two. She told me that the Count had gone, and was by that time more than a mile on his way, with the funeral, to Père la Chaise. Here were her diamonds. She exhibited, hastily, an open casket containing a profusion of the largest brilliants.

'What is this?' she asked.

'A box containing money to the amount of thirty thousand pounds,' I answered.

'What! all that money?' she exclaimed.

'Every *sous*.'

'Was it not unnecessary to bring so much, seeing all these,' she said, touching her diamonds. 'It would have been kind of you, to allow me to provide for both for a time, at least. It would have made me happier even than I am.'

'Dearest, generous angel!' Such was my extravagant declamation. 'You forget that it may be necessary, for a long time, to observe silence as to where we are, and impossible to communicate safely with any one.'

'You have then here this great sum—are you certain; have you counted it?'

'Yes, certainly; I received it to-day,' I answered, perhaps showing a little surprise in my face. 'I counted it, of course, on drawing it from my bankers.'

'It makes me feel a little nervous, travelling with so much money; but these jewels make as great a danger; *that* can add but little to it. Place them side by side; you shall take off your great coat when we are ready to go, and with it manage to conceal these boxes. I should not like the drivers to suspect that we were conveying such a treasure. I must ask you now to close the curtains of that window, and bar the shutters.'

I had hardly done this when a knock was heard at the room-door.

'I know who this is,' she said, in a whisper to me.

I saw that she was not alarmed. She went softly to the door, and a whispered conversation for a minute followed.

'My trusty maid, who is coming with us. She says we cannot safely go sooner than in ten minutes. She is bringing some coffee to the next room.'

She opened the door and looked in.

'I must tell her not to take too much luggage. She is so odd! Don't follow—stay where you are—it is better that she should not see you.'

She left the room with a gesture of caution.

A change had come over the manner of this beautiful woman. For the last few minutes a shadow had been stealing over her, an air of abstraction, a look bordering on suspicion. Why was she pale? Why had there come that dark look in her eyes? Why had her very voice become changed? Had anything gone suddenly wrong? Did some danger threaten?

This doubt, however, speedily quieted itself. If there had been anything of the kind, she would, of course, have told me. It was only natural that, as the crisis approached, she should become more and more nervous. She did not return quite so soon as I had expected. To a man in my situation absolute quietude is next to impossible. I moved restlessly about the room. It was a small one. There was a door at the other end. I opened it, rashly enough. I listened, it was perfectly silent. I was in an excited, eager state, and every faculty engrossed about what was coming, and in so far detached from the immediate present. I can't account, in any other way, for my having done so many foolish things that night, for I was, naturally, by no means deficient in cunning. About the most stupid of those was, that instead of immediately closing that door, which I never ought to have opened, I actually took a candle and walked into the room.

There I made, quite unexpectedly, a rather startling discovery.

CHAPTER XXIII

A CUP OF COFFEE

THE room was carpetless. On the floor were a quantity of shavings, and some score of bricks. Beyond these, on a narrow table, lay an object, which I could hardly believe I saw aright.

I approached and drew from it a sheet which had very slightly disguised its shape. There was no mistake about it. It was a coffin; and on the lid was a plate, with the inscription in French:

PIERRE DE LA ROCHE ST. AMAND.
ÂGÉE DE XXIII ANS.

I drew back with a double shock. So, then, the funeral after all had not yet left! Here lay the body. I had been deceived. This no doubt accounted for the embarrassment so manifest in the Countess's manner. She would have done more wisely had she told me the true state of the case.

I drew back from this melancholy room, and closed the door. Her distrust of me was the worst rashness she could have committed. There is nothing more dangerous than misapplied caution. In entire ignorance of the fact I had entered the room, and there I might have lighted upon some of the very persons it was our special anxiety that I should avoid.

These reflections were interrupted, almost as soon as begun, by the return of the Countess de St Alyre. I saw at a glance that she detected in my face some evidence of what had happened, for she threw a hasty look towards the door.

'Have you seen anything—anything to disturb you, dear Richard? Have you been out of this room?'

I answered promptly, 'Yes', and told her frankly what had happened.

'Well, I did not like to make you more uneasy than necessary. Besides, it is disgusting and horrible. The body *is* there; but the Count had departed a quarter of an hour before I lighted the coloured lamp, and prepared to receive you. The body did not arrive till eight or ten minutes after he had set out. He was afraid lest the people at Père la Chaise should suppose that the funeral was postponed. He knew that the remains of poor Pierre would certainly reach this to-night although an unexpected delay has occurred; and there are reasons why he wishes the funeral completed before to-morrow. The hearse with the body must leave this in ten minutes. So soon as it is gone, we shall be free to set out upon our wild and happy journey. The horses are to, the carriage in the *porte-cochère*. As for this *funeste* horror (she shuddered very prettily), let us think of it no more.'

She bolted the door of communication; and when she turned, it was with such a pretty penitence in her face and attitude, that I was ready to throw myself at her feet.

'It is the last time,' she said, in a sweet sad little pleading, 'I shall ever practise a deception on my brave and beautiful Richard—my hero? Am I forgiven?'

Here was another scene of passionate effusion, and lovers' raptures and declamations, but only murmured, lest the ears of listeners should be busy.

At length, on a sudden, she raised her hand, as if to prevent my stirring, her eyes fixed on me, and her ear toward the door of the room in which the coffin was placed, and remained breathless in that attitude for a few moments. Then, with a little nod towards me, she moved on tip-toe to the door, and listened, extending her hand backward as if to warn me against advancing; and, after a little time, she returned, still on tip-toe, and whispered to me, 'They are removing the coffin—come with me.'

I accompanied her into the room from which her maid, as she told me, had spoken to her. Coffee and some old china cups, which appeared to me quite beautiful, stood on a silver tray; and some liqueur glasses, with a flask, which turned out to be noyeau,* on a salver beside it.

'I shall attend you. I'm to be your servant here; I am to have my own way; I shall not think myself forgiven by my darling if he refuses to indulge me in anything.'

She filled a cup with coffee, and handed it to me with her left hand, her right arm she fondly passed over my shoulder, and with her fingers through my curls caressingly, she whispered, 'Take this; I shall take some just now.'

It was excellent; and when I had done she handed me the liqueur, which I also drank.

'Come back, dearest, to the next room,' she said. 'By this time those terrible people must have gone away, and we shall be safer there, for the present, than here.'

'You shall direct, and I obey; you shall command me not only now, but always, and in all things, my beautiful queen!' I murmured.

My heroics were unconsciously, I daresay, founded upon my ideal of the French school of love-making. I am, even now, ashamed as I recall the bombast to which I treated the Countess de St Alyre.

'There, you shall have another miniature glass—a fairy glass—of noyeau,' she said, gaily. In this volatile creature; the funereal gloom of the moment before, and the suspense of an adventure on which all her future was staked, disappeared in a moment. She ran and returned with another tiny glass, which, with an eloquent or tender little speech, I placed to my lips and sipped.

I kissed her hand, I kissed her lips, I gazed in her beautiful eyes, and kissed her again unresisting.

'You call me Richard, by what name am I to call my beautiful divinity?' I asked.

'You call me Eugenie, it is my name. Let us be quite real; that is, if you love as entirely as I do.'

'Eugenie!' I exclaimed, and broke into a new rapture upon the name.

It ended by my telling her how impatient I was to set out upon our journey; and, as I spoke, suddenly an odd sensation overcame me. It was not in the slightest degree like faintness. I can find no phrase to describe it, but a sudden constraint of the brain; it was as if the membrane in which it lies, if there be such a thing, contracted, and became inflexible.

'Dear Richard! what is the matter?' she exclaimed, with terror in her looks. 'Good heavens! are you ill? I conjure you, sit down; sit in this chair.' She almost forced me into one; I was in no condition to offer the least resistance. I recognized but too truly the sensations that supervened. I was lying back in the chair in which I sat without the power, by this time, of uttering a syllable, of closing my eyelids, of moving my eyes, of stirring a muscle. I had in a few seconds glided into precisely the state in which I had passed so many appalling hours when approaching Paris, in my night-drive with the Marquis d'Harmonville.

Great and loud was the lady's agony. She seemed to have lost all sense of fear. She called me by my name, shook me by the shoulder, raised my arm and let it fall, all the time imploring of me, in distracting sentences, to make the slightest sign of life, and vowing that if I did not, she would make away with herself.

These ejaculations, after a minute or two, suddenly subsided. The lady was perfectly silent and cool. In a very business-like way she took a candle and stood before me, pale indeed, very pale, but with an expression only of intense scrutiny with a dash of horror in it. She moved the candle before my eyes slowly, evidently watching the effect. She then set it down, and rang a hand-bell two or three times sharply. She placed the two cases (I mean hers containing the jewels) and my strong box, side by side on the table; and I saw her carefully lock the door that gave access to the room in which I had just now sipped my coffee.

CHAPTER XXIV

HOPE

SHE had scarcely set down my heavy box, which she seemed to have considerable difficulty in raising, on the table, when the door of the room in which I had seen the coffin, opened, and a sinister and unexpected apparition entered.

It was the Count de St Alyre, who had been, as I have told you, reported to me to be, for some considerable time, on his way to Père la

Chaise. He stood before me for a moment, with the frame of the doorway and a background of darkness enclosing him, like a portrait. His slight, mean, figure was draped in the deepest mourning. He had a pair of black gloves in his hand, and his hat with crape round it.

When he was not speaking his face showed signs of agitation; his mouth was puckering and working. He looked damnably wicked and frightened.

'Well, my dear Eugenie? Well, child—eh? Well, it all goes admirably?'

'Yes,' she answered, in a low hard tone. 'But you and Planard should not have left that door open.'

This she said sternly. 'He went in there and looked about wherever he liked; it was fortunate he did not move aside the lid of the coffin.'

'Planard should have seen to that,' said the Count, sharply. 'Ma foi! I can't be everywhere!' He advanced half-a-dozen quick short steps into the room toward me, and placed his glasses to his eyes.

'Monsieur Beckett,' he cried sharply, two or three times. 'Hi! don't you know me?'

He approached and peered more closely in my face; raised my hand and shook it, calling me again, then let it drop, and said—'It has set in admirably, my pretty *mignonne*.* When did it commence?'

The Countess came and stood beside him, and looked at me steadily for some seconds.

You can't conceive the effect of the silent gaze of those two pairs of evil eyes.

The lady glanced to where, I recollected, the mantel-piece stood, and upon it a clock, the regular click of which I sharply heard.

'Four—five—six minutes and a half,' she said slowly, in a cold hard way.

'Brava! Bravissima! my beautiful queen! my little Venus! my Joan of Arc! my heroine! my paragon of women!'

He was gloating on me with an odious curiosity, smiling, as he groped backward with his thin brown fingers to find the lady's hand; but she, not (I dare say) caring for his caresses, drew back a little.

'Come, ma chère, let us count these things. What is it? Pocket-book? Or—or—*what*?'

'It is *that*!' said the lady, pointing with a look of disgust to the box, which lay in its leather case on the table.

'Oh! Let us see—let us count—let us see,' he said, as he was unbuckling the straps with his tremulous fingers. 'We must count them—we must see to it. I have pencil and pocket-book—but—where's the key? See this cursed lock! My——! What is it? Where's the key?'

He was standing before the Countess, shuffling his feet, with his hands extended and all his fingers quivering.

'I have not got it; how could I? It is in his pocket, of course,' said the lady.

In another instant the fingers of the old miscreant were in my pockets: he plucked out everything they contained, and some keys among the rest.

I lay in precisely the state in which I had been during my drive with the Marquis to Paris. This wretch I knew was about to rob me. The whole drama, and the Countess's *rôle* in it, I could not yet comprehend. I could not be sure—so much more presence of mind and histrionic resource have women than fall to the lot of our clumsy sex—whether the return of the Count was not, in truth, a surprise to her; and this scrutiny of the contents of my strong box, an extempore undertaking of the Count's. But it was clearing more and more every moment; and I was destined, very soon, to comprehend minutely my appalling situation.

I had not the power of turning my eyes this way or that, the smallest fraction of a hair's breadth. But let any one, placed as I was at the end of a room, ascertain for himself by experiment how wide is the field of sight, without the slightest alteration in the line of vision, he will find that it takes in the entire breadth of a large room, and that up to a very short distance before him; and imperfectly, by a refraction, I believe, in the eye itself, to a point very near indeed. Next to nothing that passed in the room, therefore, was hidden from me.

The old man had by this time found the key. The leather case was open. The box, cramped round with iron, was next unlocked. He turned out its contents upon the table.

'Rouleaux of a hundred napoleons each. One, two, three. Yes, quick. Write down a thousand napoleons. One, two; yes, right. Another thousand, *write*!' And so, on and on till the gold was rapidly counted. Then came the notes.

'Ten thousand francs. *Write!* Ten thousand francs again: is it written? Another ten thousand francs: is it down? Smaller notes would have been better. They should have been smaller. These are horribly embarrassing. Bolt that door again; Planard would become unreasonable if he knew the amount. Why did you not tell him to get it in smaller notes? No matter now—go on—it can't be helped—*write*—another ten thousand francs—another—another.' And so on, till my treasure was counted out, before my face, while I saw and heard all that passed with the sharpest distinctness, and my mental perceptions were horribly vivid. But in all other respects I was dead.

He had replaced in the box every note and rouleau as he counted it, and now having ascertained the sum-total he locked it, replaced it, very methodically, in its cover, opened a buffet in the wainscoting, and, having placed the Countess's jewel-case and my strong box in it, he locked it; and immediately on completing these arrangements he began to complain, with fresh acrimony and maledictions of Planard's delay.

He unbolted the door, looked in the dark room beyond, and listened. He closed the door again, and returned. The old man was in a fever of suspense.

'I have kept ten thousand francs for Planard,' said the Count, touching his waistcoat pocket.

'Will that satisfy him?' asked the lady.

'Why—curse him!' screamed the Count. 'Has he no conscience? I'll swear to him it's half the entire thing.'

He and the lady again came and looked at me anxiously for awhile, in silence; and then the old Count began to grumble again about Planard, and to compare his watch with the clock. The lady seemed less impatient; she sat no longer looking at me but across the room, so that her profile was toward me—and strangely changed, dark and witch-like it looked. My last hope died as I beheld that jaded face from which the mask had dropped. I was certain that they intended to crown their robbery by murder. Why did they not despatch me at once? What object could there be in postponing the catastrophe which would expedite their own safety? I cannot recall, even to myself, adequately the horrors unutterable that I underwent. You must suppose a real night-mare— I mean a nightmare in which the objects and the danger are real, and the spell of corporal death appears to be protractable at the pleasure of the persons who preside at your unearthly torments. I could have no doubt as to the cause of the state in which I was.

In this agony, to which I could not give the slightest expression, I saw the door of the room where the coffin had been, open slowly, and the Marquis d'Harmonville entered the room.

CHAPTER XXV

DESPAIR

A MOMENT'S hope, hope violent and fluctuating, hope that was nearly torture, and then came a dialogue, and with it the terrors of despair.

'Thank heaven, Planard, you have come at last,' said the Count, taking him, with both hands, by the arm and clinging to it, and drawing him toward me. 'See, look at him. It has all gone sweetly, sweetly, sweetly up to this. Shall I hold the candle for you?'

My friend d'Harmonville, Planard, whatever he was, came to me, pulling off his gloves, which he popped into his pocket.

'The candle, a little this way,' he said, and stooping over me he looked earnestly in my face. He touched my forehead, drew his hand across it, and then looked in my eyes for a time.

'Well, doctor, what do you think?' whispered the Count.

'How much did you give him?' said the Marquis, thus suddenly stunted down to a doctor.

'Seventy drops,' said the lady.

'In the hot coffee?'

'Yes; sixty in a hot cup of coffee and ten in the liqueur.'

Her voice, low and hard, seemed to me to tremble a little. It takes a long course of guilt to subjugate nature completely, and prevent those exterior signs of agitation that outlive all good.

The doctor, however, was treating me as coolly as he might a subject which he was about to place on the dissecting-table for a lecture.

He looked into my eyes again for awhile, took my wrist, and applied his fingers to the pulse.

'That action suspended,' he said to himself.

Then again he placed something that, for the moment I saw it, looked like a piece of gold-beater's leaf, to my lips, holding his head so far that his own breathing could not affect it.

'Yes,' he said in soliloquy, very low.

Then he plucked my shirt-breast open, and applied the stethoscope,* shifted it from point to point, listened with his ear to its end, as if for a very far off sound, raised his head, and said, in like manner, softly to himself, 'All appreciable action of the lungs has subsided.'

Then turning from the sound, as I conjectured, he said,

'Seventy drops, allowing ten for waste, ought to hold him fast for six hours and a half—that is ample. The experiment I tried in the carriage was only thirty drops, and showed a highly sensitive brain. It would not do to kill him, you know. You are certain you did not exceed *seventy*?'

'Perfectly,' said the lady.

'If he were to die the evaporation would be arrested, and foreign matter, some of it poisonous, would be found in the stomach, don't you see? If you are doubtful, it would be well to use the stomach-pump.'

'Dearest Eugenie, be frank, be frank, do be frank,' urged the Count.

'I am *not* doubtful, I am *certain*,' she answered.

'How long ago, exactly? I told you to observe the time.'

'I did; the minute-hand was exactly there, under the point of that Cupid's foot.'

'It will last, then, probably for seven hours. He will recover then; the evaporation will be complete, and not one particle of the fluid will remain in the stomach.'

It was reassuring, at all events, to hear that there was no intention to murder me. No one who has not tried it knows the terror of the approach of death, when the mind is clear, the instincts of life unimpaired, and no excitement to disturb the appreciation of that entirely new horror.

The nature and purpose of this tenderness was very, very peculiar, and as yet I had not a suspicion of it.

'You leave France, I suppose?' said the ex-Marquis.

'Yes, certainly, to-morrow,' answered the Count.

'And where do you mean to go?'

'That I have not yet settled,' he answered quickly.

'You won't tell a friend, eh?'

'I can't till I know. This has turned out an unprofitable affair.'

'We shall settle that by-and-by.'

'It is time we should get him lying down, eh?' said the Count, indicating me with one finger.

'Yes, we must proceed rapidly now. Are his night-shirt and nightcap—you understand—here?'

'All ready,' said the Count.

'Now, madame,' said the doctor, turning to the lady, and making her, in spite of the emergency, a bow, 'it is time you should retire.'

The lady passed into the room, in which I had taken my cup of treacherous coffee, and I saw her no more.

The Count took a candle, and passed through the door at the further end of the room, returning with a roll of linen in his hand. He bolted first one door, then the other.

They now, in silence, proceeded to undress me rapidly. They were not many minutes in accomplishing this. What the doctor had termed my night-shirt, a long garment which reached below my feet, was now on, and a cap, that resembled a female nightcap more than anything I had ever seen upon a male head, was fitted upon mine, and tied under my chin.

And now, I thought, I shall be laid in a bed, to recover how I can, and, in the meantime, the conspirators will have escaped with their booty, and pursuit be in vain.

This was my best hope at the time; but it was soon clear that their plans were very different.

The Count and Planard now went, together, into the room that lay straight before me. I heard them talking low, and a sound of shuffling feet; then a long rumble; it suddenly stopped; it recommenced; it continued; side by side they came in at the door, their backs toward me. They were dragging something along the floor that made a continued boom and rumble, but they interposed between me and it, so that I could not see it until they had dragged it almost beside me; and then, merciful heaven! I saw it plainly enough. It was the coffin I had seen in the next room. It lay now flat on the floor, its edge against the chair in which I sat. Planard removed the lid. The coffin was empty.

CHAPTER XXVI

CATASTROPHE

'THOSE seem to be good horses, and we change on the way,' said Planard. 'You give the men a napoleon or two; we must do it within three hours and a quarter. Now, come; I'll lift him, upright, so as to place his feet in their proper berth, and you must keep them together, and draw the white shirt well down over them.'

In another moment I was placed, as he described, sustained in Planard's arms, standing at the foot of the coffin, and so lowered backward, gradually, till I lay my length in it. Then the man, whom he called Planard, stretched my arms by my sides, and carefully arranged the frills at my breast, and the folds of the shroud, and after that, taking his stand at the foot of the coffin, made a survey, which seemed to satisfy him.

The Count, who was very methodical, took my clothes, which had just been removed, folded them rapidly together and locked them up, as I afterwards heard, in one of the three presses which opened by doors in the panel.

I now understood their frightful plan. This coffin had been prepared for *me*; the funeral of St Amand was a sham to mislead inquiry; I had myself given the order at Père la Chaise, signed it, and paid the fees for the interment of the fictitious Pierre de St Amand, whose place I was to take, to lie in his coffin, with his name on the plate above my breast, and with a ton of clay packed down upon me; to waken from this catalepsy, after I had been for hours in the grave, there to perish by a death the most horrible that imagination can conceive.

If, hereafter, by any caprice of curiosity or suspicion, the coffin should be exhumed, and the body it enclosed examined, no chemistry could detect a trace of poison, nor the most cautious examination the slightest mark of violence.

I had myself been at the utmost pains to mystify inquiry, should my disappearance excite surmises, and had even written to my few correspondents in England to tell them that they were not to look for a letter from me for three weeks at least.

In the moment of my guilty elation death had caught me, and there was no escape. I tried to pray to God in my unearthly panic, but only thoughts of terror, judgment, and eternal anguish, crossed the distraction of my immediate doom.

I must not try to recall what is indeed indescribable—the multiform horrors of my own thoughts. I will relate, simply, what befell, every detail of which remains sharp in my memory as if cut in steel.

'The undertaker's men are in the hall,' said the Count.

'They must not come till this is fixed,' answered Planard. 'Be good enough to take hold of the lower part while I take this end.' I was not left long to conjecture what was coming, for in a few seconds more something slid across, a few inches above my face, and entirely excluded the light, and muffled sound, so that nothing that was not very distinct reached my ears henceforward; but very distinctly came the working of a turnscrew, and the crunching home of screws in succession. Than these vulgar sounds, no doom spoken in thunder could have been more tremendous.

The rest I must relate, not as it then reached my ears, which was too imperfectly and interruptedly to supply a connected narrative, but as it was afterwards told me by other people.

The coffin-lid being screwed down, the two gentlemen arranged the room, and adjusted the coffin so that it lay perfectly straight along the boards, the Count being specially anxious that there should be no appearance of hurry or disorder in the room, which might have suggested remark and conjecture.

When this was done, Doctor Planard said he would go to the hall to summon the men who were to carry the coffin out and place it in the hearse. The Count pulled on his black gloves, and held his white handkerchief in his hand, a very impressive chief-mourner. He stood a little behind the head of the coffin, awaiting the arrival of the persons who accompanied Planard, and whose fast steps he soon heard approaching.

Planard came first. He entered the room through the apartment in which the coffin had been originally placed. His manner was changed; there was something of a swagger in it.

'Monsieur le Comte,' he said, as he strode through the door, followed by half-a-dozen persons. 'I am sorry to have to announce to you a most unseasonable interruption. Here is Monsieur Carmaignac, a gentleman holding an office in the police department, who says that information to the effect that large quantities of smuggled English and other goods have been distributed in this neighbourhood, and that a portion of them is concealed in your house. I have ventured to assure him, of my own knowledge, that nothing can be more false than that information, and that you would be only too happy to throw open for his inspection, at a moment's notice, every room, closet, and cupboard in your house.'

'Most assuredly,' exclaimed the Count, with a stout voice, but a very white face. 'Thank you, my good friend, for having anticipated me. I will place my house and keys at his disposal, for the purpose of his scrutiny, so soon as he is good enough to inform me, of what specific contraband goods he comes in search.'

'The Count de St Alyre will pardon me,' answered Carmaignac, a little dryly. 'I am forbidden by my instructions to make that disclosure; and that I *am* instructed to make a general search, this warrant will sufficiently apprise Monsieur the Count.'

'Monsieur Carmaignac, may I hope,' interposed Planard, 'that you will permit the Count de St Alyre to attend the funeral of his kinsman, who lies here, as you see'—(he pointed to the plate upon the coffin)—'and to convey whom to Père la Chaise, a hearse waits at this moment at the door.'

'That, I regret to say, I cannot permit. My instructions are precise; but the delay, I trust, will be but trifling. Monsieur the Count will not suppose for a moment that I suspect him; but we have a duty to perform, and I must act as if I did. When I am ordered to search, I search; things are sometimes hid in such *bizarre* places. I can't say, for instance, what that coffin may contain.'

'The body of my kinsman, Monsieur Pierre de St Amand,' answered the Count, loftily.

'Oh! then you've seen him?'

'Seen him? Often, too often!' The Count was evidently a good deal moved.

'I mean the body?'

The Count stole a quick glance at Planard.

'N—no, monsieur—that is, I mean, only for a moment.' Another quick glance at Planard.

'But quite long enough, I fancy, to recognize him?' insinuated that gentleman.

'Of course—of course; instantly—perfectly. What! Pierre de St Amand? Not know him at a glance? No, no, poor fellow, I know him too well for that.'

'The things I am in search of,' said Monsieur Carmaignac, 'would fit in a narrow compass—servants are so ingenious sometimes. Let us raise the lid.'

'Pardon me, monsieur,' said the Count, peremptorily, advancing to the side of the coffin, and extending his arm across it. 'I cannot permit that indignity—that desecration.'

'There shall be none, sir,—simply the raising of the lid; you shall remain in the room. If it should prove as we all hope, you shall have the pleasure of one other look, really the last, upon your beloved kinsman.'

'But, sir, I can't.'

'But, monsieur, I must.'

'But, besides, the thing, the turnscrew, broke when the last screw was turned; and I give you my sacred honour, there is nothing but the body in this coffin.'

'Of course, monsieur the Count believes all that; but he does not know so well as I the legerdemain in use among servants, who are accustomed to smuggling. Here, Philippe, you must take off the lid of that coffin.'

The Count protested; but Philippe—a man with a bald head, and a smirched face, looking like a working blacksmith—placed on the floor a leather bag of tools, from which, having looked at the coffin, and picked with his nail at the screw-heads, he selected a turnscrew, and, with a few deft twirls at each of the screws, they stood up like little rows of mushrooms, and the lid was raised. I saw the light, of which I thought I had seen my last, once more; but the axis of vision remained fixed. As I was reduced to the cataleptic state in a position nearly perpendicular, and looking straight before me I continued looking straight before me, and thus my gaze was now fixed upon the ceiling. I saw the face of Carmaignac leaning over me with a curious frown. It seemed to me that there was no recognition in his eyes. Oh, heaven! that I could have uttered were it but one cry! I saw the dark, mean mask of the little Count suspiciously staring down at me from the other side; the face of the pseudo-marquis also peering at me, but not so full in the line of vision; there were other faces also.

'I see, I see,' said Carmaignac, withdrawing. 'Nothing of the kind there.'

'You will be good enough to direct your man to re-adjust the lid of the coffin, and to fix the screws,' said the Count, taking courage;

'and—and—really the funeral *must* proceed. It is not fair to the people who have but moderate fees for night-work, to keep them hour after hour beyond the time.'

'Count de St Alyre, you shall go in a very few minutes. I will direct, just now, all about the coffin.'

The Count looked toward the door, and there saw a gendarme; and two or three more grave and stalwart specimens of the same force were also in the room. The Count was very uncomfortably excited; it was growing insupportable.

'As this gentleman makes a difficulty about my attending the obsequies of my kinsman, I will ask you, Planard, to accompany the funeral in my stead.'

'In a few minutes,' answered the incorrigible Carmaignac. 'I must first trouble you for the key that opens that press.'

He pointed direct at the press, in which the clothes had just been locked up.

'I—I have no objection,' said the Count—'none, of course; only they have not been used for an age. I'll direct some one to look for the key.'

'If you have not got it about you, it is quite unnecessary. Philippe, try your skeleton-keys with that press. I want it opened. Whose clothes are these?' inquired Carmaignac when, the press having been opened, he took out the suit that had been placed there scarcely two minutes since.

'I can't say,' answered the Count. 'I know nothing of the contents of that press. A roguish servant, named Lablais, whom I dismissed about a year ago, had the key. I have not seen it open for ten years or more. The clothes are probably his.

'Here are visiting cards, see, and here a marked pocket-handkerchief— "R. B." upon it. He must have stolen them from a person named Beckett— R. Beckett. "Mr. Beckett, Berkley Square", the card says; and, my faith! here's a watch and a bunch of seals; one of them with the initials "R. B." upon it. That servant, Lablais, must have been a consummate rogue!'

'So he was; you are right, sir.'

'It strikes me that he possibly stole these clothes,' continued Carmaignac, 'from the man in the coffin, who, in that case, would be Monsieur Beckett, and not Monsieur de St Amand. For, wonderful to relate, monsieur, the watch is still going! That man in the coffin, I believe is not dead, but simply drugged. And for having robbed and intended to murder him, I arrest you, Nicolas de la Marque, Count de St Alyre.'

In another moment the old villain was a prisoner. I heard his discordant voice break quaveringly into sudden vehemence and volubility; now croaking—now shrieking, as he oscillated between protests, threats, and impious appeals to the God who will 'judge the secrets of men!' And thus lying and raving, he was removed from the room, and placed in the same coach with his beautiful and abandoned accomplice, already arrested; and, with two gendarmes sitting beside them, they were immediately driving at a rapid pace towards the Conciergerie.

There were now added to the general chorus, two voices, very different in quality; one was that of the gasconading Colonel Gailliarde, who had with difficulty been kept in the background up to this; the other was that of my jolly friend Whistlewick, who had come to identify me.

I shall tell you, just now, how this project against my property and life, so ingenious and monstrous, was exploded. I must first say a word about myself. I was placed in a hot bath, under the direction of Planard, as consummate a villain as any of the gang, but now thoroughly in the interests of the prosecution. Thence I was laid in a warm bed, the window of the room being open. These simple measures restored me in about three hours; I should otherwise, probably, have continued under the spell for nearly seven.

The practices of these nefarious conspirators had been carried on with consummate skill and secrecy. Their dupes were led, as I was, to be themselves auxiliary to the mystery which made their own destruction both safe and certain.

A search was, of course, instituted. Graves were opened in Père la Chaise. The bodies exhumed had lain there too long, and were too much decomposed to be recognized. One only was identified. The notice for the burial, in this particular case, had been signed, the order given, and the fees paid, by Gabriel Gaillarde, who was known to the official clerk, who had to transact with him this little funereal business. The very trick, that had been arranged for me, had been successfully practised in his case. The person for whom the grave had been ordered, was purely fictitious; and Gabriel Gaillarde himself filled the coffin, on the cover of which that false name was inscribed as well as upon a tombstone over the grave. Possibly, the same honour, under my pseudonym, may have been intended for me.

The identification was curious. This Gabriel Gaillarde had had a bad fall from a run-away horse, about five years before his mysterious disappearance. He had lost an eye and some teeth, in this accident, besides sustaining a fracture of the right leg, immediately above the ankle. He had kept the injuries to his face as profound a secret as he could. The result was, that the glass eye which had done duty for the one he had lost, remained in the socket, slightly displaced, of course, but recognizable by the 'artist' who had supplied it.

More pointedly recognizable were the teeth, peculiar in workmanship, which one of the ablest dentists in Paris had himself adapted to the chasms, the cast of which, owing to peculiarities in the accident, he happened to have preserved. This cast precisely fitted the gold plate found in the mouth of the skull. The mark, also, above the ankle, in the bone, where it had re-united, corresponded exactly with the place where the fracture had knit in the limb of Gabriel Gaillarde.

The Colonel, his younger brother, had been furious about the disappearance of Gabriel, and still more so about that of his money, which he had long regarded as his proper keepsake, whenever death should remove his brother from the vexations of living. He had suspected for a long time, for certain adroitly discovered reasons, that the Count de St Alyre and the beautiful lady, his companion, countess, or whatever else she was, had pigeoned him. To this suspicion were added some others of a still darker kind; but in their first shape, rather the exaggerated reflections of his fury, ready to believe anything, than well-defined conjectures.

At length an accident had placed the Colonel very nearly upon the right scent; a chance, possibly lucky for himself, had apprised the scoundrel Planard that the conspirators—himself among the number—were in danger. The result was that he made terms for himself, became an informer, and concerted with the police this visit made to the Château de la Carque, at the critical moment when every measure had been completed that was necessary to construct a perfect case against his guilty accomplices.

I need not describe the minute industry or forethought with which the police agents collected all the details necessary to support the case. They had brought an able physician, who, even had Planard failed, would have supplied the necessary medical evidence.

My trip to Paris, you will believe, had not turned out quite so agreeably as I had anticipated. I was the principal witness for the prosecution in this *cause célèbre*, with all the *agrémens** that attend that enviable position. Having had an escape, as my friend Whistlewick said, 'with a squeak' for my life, I innocently fancied that I should have been an object of considerable interest to Parisian society; but, a good deal to my mortification, I discovered that I was the object of a good-natured but contemptuous merriment. I was a *balourd*, a *benêt*, *un âne*,* and figured even in caricatures. I became a sort of public character, a dignity,

'Unto which I was not born,'

and from which I fled as soon as I conveniently could, without even paying my friend the Marquis d'Harmonville a visit at his hospitable château.

The Marquis escaped scot-free. His accomplice, the Count, was executed. The fair Eugenie, under extenuating circumstances—consisting, so far as I could discover of her good looks—got off for six years' imprisonment.

Colonel Gaillarde recovered some of his brother's money, out of the not very affluent estate of the Count and *soi-disant* Countess. This, and the execution of the Count, put him in high good-humour. So far from insisting on a hostile meeting,* he shook me very graciously by the hand, told me that he looked upon the wound on his head, inflicted by the knob of my stick, as having been received in an honourable, though irregular duel, in which he had no disadvantage or unfairness to complain of.

I think I have only two additional details to mention. The bricks discovered in the room with the coffin, had been packed in it, in straw, to supply the weight of a dead body, and to prevent the suspicions and contradictions that might have been excited by the arrival of an empty coffin at the château.

Secondly, the Countess's magnificent brilliants were examined by a lapidary, and pronounced to be worth about five pounds, to a tragedy-queen, who happened to be in want of a suite of paste.*

The Countess had figured some years before as one of the cleverest actresses on the minor-stage of Paris, where she had been picked up by the Count and used as his principal accomplice.

She it was who, admirably disguised, had rifled my papers in the carriage on my memorable night-journey to Paris. She also had figured as the interpreting magician at the *palanquin* at the ball at Versailles. So far as *I* was affected by that elaborate mystification it was intended to re-animate my interest, which, they feared, might flag in the beautiful Countess. It had its design and action upon other intended victims also: but of them there is, at present, no need to speak, The introduction of a real corpse—procured from a person who supplied the Parisian anatomists*—involved no real danger, while it heightened the mystery and kept the prophet alive in the gossip of the town and in the thoughts of the noodles with whom he had conferred.

I divided the remainder of the summer and the autumn, between Switzerland and Italy.

As the well-worn phrase goes, I was a sadder if not a wiser man.* A great deal of the horrible impression left upon my mind was due, of course, to the mere action of nerves and brain. But serious feelings of another and deeper kind remained. My after life was ultimately formed by the shock I had then received. Those impressions led me—but not till after many years—to happier though not less serious thoughts; and I have deep reason to be thankful to the all-merciful Ruler of events, for an early and terrible lesson in the ways of sin.

CARMILLA

CHAPTER I

AN EARLY FRIGHT

IN Styria,* we, though by no means magnificent people, inhabit a castle, or schloss. A small income, in that part of the world, goes a great way. Eight or nine hundred a year does wonders. Scantily enough ours would have answered among wealthy people at home. My father is English, and I bear an English name, although I never saw England. But here, in this lonely and primitive place, where everything is so marvellously cheap, I really don't see how ever so much more money would at all materially add to our comforts, or even luxuries.

My father was in the Austrian service,* and retired upon a pension and his patrimony, and purchased this feudal residence, and the small estate on which it stands, a bargain.

Nothing can be more picturesque or solitary. It stands on a slight eminence in a forest. The road, very old and narrow, passes in front of its drawbridge, never raised in my time, and its moat, stocked with perch, and sailed over by many swans, and floating on its surface white fleets of water-lilies.

Over all this the schloss shows its many-windowed front; its towers, and its Gothic chapel.

The forest opens in an irregular and very picturesque glade before its gate, and at the right a steep Gothic bridge carries the road over a stream that winds in deep shadow through the wood.

I have said that this is a very lonely place. Judge whether I say truth. Looking from the hall door towards the road, the forest in which our castle stands extends fifteen miles to the right, and twelve to the left. The nearest inhabited village is about seven of your English miles to the left. The nearest inhabited schloss of any historic associations, is that of old General Spielsdorf, nearly twenty miles away to the right.

I have said 'the nearest *inhabited* village', because there is, only three miles westward, that is to say in the direction of General Spielsdorf's schloss, a ruined village, with its quaint little church, now roofless, in the aisle of which are the mouldering tombs of the proud family of Karnstein,* now extinct, who once owned the equally desolate château which, in the thick of the forest, overlooks the silent ruins of the town.

Respecting the cause of the desertion of this striking and melancholy spot, there is a legend which I shall relate to you another time.

I must tell you now, how very small is the party who constitute the inhabitants of our castle. I don't include servants, or those dependents who occupy rooms in the buildings attached to the schloss. Listen, and wonder! My father, who is the kindest man on earth, but growing old; and I, at the date of my story, only nineteen. Eight years have passed since then. I and my father constituted the family at the schloss. My mother, a Styrian lady, died in my infancy, but I had a good-natured governess, who had been with me from, I might almost say, my infancy. I could not remember the time when her fat, benignant face was not a familiar picture in my memory. This was Madame Perrodon, a native of Berne, whose care and good nature in part supplied to me the loss of my mother, whom I do not even remember, so early I lost her. She made a third at our little dinner party. There was a fourth, Mademoiselle De Lafontaine, a lady such as you term, I believe, a 'finishing governess'. She spoke French and German, Madame Perrodon French and broken English, to which my father and I added English, which, partly to prevent its becoming a lost language among us, and partly from patriotic motives, we spoke every day. The consequence was a Babel,* at which strangers used to laugh, and which I shall make no attempt to reproduce in this narrative. And there were two or three young lady friends besides, pretty nearly of my own age, who were occasional visitors, for longer or shorter terms; and these visits I sometimes returned.

These were our regular social resources; but of course there were chance visits from 'neighbours' of only five or six leagues distance. My life was notwithstanding rather a solitary one, I can assure you.

My gouvernantes had just so much control over me as you might conjecture such sage persons would have in the case of a rather spoiled girl, whose only parent allowed her pretty nearly her own way in everything.

The first occurrence in my existence, which produced a terrible impression upon my mind, which, in fact, never has been effaced, was one of the very earliest incidents of my life which I can recollect. Some people will think it so trifling that it should not be recorded here. You will see, however, by-and-bye, why I mention it. The nursery, as it was called, though I had it all to myself, was a large room in the upper story of the castle, with a steep oak roof. I can't have been more than six years old, when one night I awoke, and looking round the room from my bed, failed to see the nursery-maid. Neither was my nurse there; and I thought myself alone. I was not frightened, for I was one of those happy children who are studiously kept in ignorance of ghost stories, of fairy tales, and of all such lore as makes us cover up our heads when the door creaks suddenly, or the flicker of an expiring candle makes the shadow of a bed-post dance upon the wall, nearer to our faces. I was vexed and insulted at finding myself, as I conceived, neglected, and I began to whimper, preparatory to a hearty bout of roaring; when to my surprise, I saw a solemn, but very pretty face looking at me from the side of the bed. It was that of a young lady who was kneeling, with her hands under the coverlet. I looked at her with a kind of pleased wonder, and ceased whimpering. She caressed me with her hands, and lay down beside me on the bed, and drew me towards her, smiling, I felt immediately delightfully soothed, and fell asleep again. I was wakened by a sensation as if two needles ran into my breast very deep at the same moment, and I cried loudly. The lady started back, with her eyes fixed on me, and then slipped down upon the floor, and, as I thought, hid herself under the bed.

I was now for the first time frightened, and I yelled with all my might and main. Nurse, nursery-maid, housekeeper, all came running in, and hearing my story, they made light of it, soothing me all they could meanwhile. But, child as I was, I could perceive that their faces were pale with an unwonted look of anxiety, and I saw them look under the bed, and about the room, and peep under tables and pluck open cupboards; and the housekeeper whispered to the nurse: 'Lay your hand along that hollow in the bed; someone *did* lie there, so sure as you did not; the place is still warm.'

I remember the nursery-maid petting me, and all three examining my chest, where I told them I felt the puncture, and pronouncing that there was no sign visible that any such thing had happened to me.

The housekeeper and the two other servants who were in charge of the nursery, remained sitting up all night; and from that time a servant always sat up in the nursery until I was about fourteen.

I was very nervous for a long time after this. A doctor was called in, he was pallid and elderly. How well I remember his long saturnine face, slightly pitted with small pox, and his chestnut wig. For a good while, every second day, he came and gave me medicine, which of course I hated.

The morning after I saw this apparition I was in a state of terror, and could not bear to be left alone, daylight though it was, for a moment.

I remember my father coming up and standing at the bedside, and talking cheerfully, and asking the nurse a number of questions, and laughing very heartily at one of the answers; and patting me on the shoulder, and kissing me, and telling me not to be frightened, that it was nothing but a dream and could not hurt me.

But I was not comforted, for I knew the visit of the strange woman was *not* a dream; and I was *awfully* frightened.

I was a little consoled by the nursery-maid's assuring me that it was she who had come and looked at me, and lain down beside me in the bed, and that I must have been half-dreaming not to have known her face. But this, though supported by the nurse, did not quite satisfy me.

I remember, in the course of that day, a venerable old man, in a black cassock,* coming into the room with the nurse and housekeeper, and talking a little to them, and very kindly to me; his face was very sweet and gentle, and he told me they were going to pray, and joined my hands together, and desired me to say, softly, while they were praying, 'Lord hear all good prayers for us, for Jesus' sake.' I think these were the very words, for I often repeated them to myself, and my nurse used for years to make me say them in my prayers.

I remember so well the thoughtful sweet face of that white-haired old man, in his black cassock, as he stood in that rude, lofty, brown room, with the clumsy furniture of a fashion three hundred years old, about him, and the scanty light entering its shadowy atmosphere through the small lattice. He kneeled, and the three women with him, and he prayed aloud with an earnest quavering voice for, what appeared to me, a long time.

I forget all my life preceding that event, and for some time after it is all obscure also, but the scenes I have just described stand out vivid as the isolated pictures of the phantasmagoria* surrounded by darkness.

CHAPTER II

A GUEST

I AM now going to tell you something so strange that it will require all your faith in my veracity to believe my story. It is not only true, nevertheless, but truth of which I have been an eye-witness.

It was a sweet summer evening, and my father asked me, as he sometimes did, to take a little ramble with him along that beautiful forest vista which I have mentioned as lying in front of the schloss.

'General Spielsdorf cannot come to us so soon as I had hoped,' said my father, as we pursued our walk.

He was to have paid us a visit of some weeks, and we had expected his arrival next day. He was to have brought with him a young lady, his niece and ward, Mademoiselle Rheinfeldt, whom I had never seen, but whom I had heard described as a very charming girl, and in whose society I had promised myself many happy days. I was more disappointed than a young lady living in a town, or a bustling neighbourhood can possibly imagine. This visit, and the new acquaintance it promised, had furnished my day dream for many weeks.

'And how soon does he come?' I asked.

'Not till autumn. Not for two months, I dare say,' he answered. 'And I am very glad now, dear, that you never knew Mademoiselle Rheinfeldt.'

'And why?' I asked, both mortified and curious.

'Because the poor young lady is dead,' he replied. 'I quite forgot I had not told you, but you were not in the room when I received the general's letter this evening.'

I was very much shocked. General Spielsdorf had mentioned in his first letter, six or seven weeks before, that she was not so well as he would wish her, but there was nothing to suggest the remotest suspicion of danger.

'Here is the general's letter,' he said, handing it to me. 'I am afraid he is in great affliction; the letter appears to me to have been written very nearly in distraction.'

We sat down on a rude bench, under a group of magnificent lime-trees. The sun was setting with all its melancholy splendour behind the sylvan horizon, and the stream that flows beside our home, and passes under the steep old bridge I have mentioned, wound through many a group of noble trees, almost at our feet, reflecting in its current the fading crimson of the sky. General Spielsdorf's letter was so extraordinary, so vehement, and in some places so self-contradictory, that I read it twice over—the second time aloud to my father—and was still unable to account for it, except by supposing that grief had unsettled his mind.

It said 'I have lost my darling daughter—for as such I loved her. During the last days of dear Bertha's illness I was not able to write to you. Before then I had no idea of her danger. I have lost her, and now learn *all*, too late. She died in the peace of innocence, and in the glorious hope of a blessed futurity. The fiend who betrayed our infatuated hospitality has done it all. I thought I was receiving into my house innocence, gaiety, a charming companion for my lost Bertha. Heavens! what a fool have I been! I thank God my child died without a suspicion of the cause of her sufferings. She is gone without so much as conjecturing the nature of her illness, and the accursed passion of the agent of all this misery. I devote my remaining days to tracking and extinguishing a monster. I am told I may hope to accomplish my righteous and merciful purpose. At present there is scarcely a gleam of light to guide me. I curse my conceited incredulity, my despicable affection of superiority, my blindness, my obstinacy—all—too late. I cannot write or talk collectedly now. I am distracted. So soon as I shall have a little recovered, I mean to devote myself for a time to enquiry, which may possibly lead me as far as Vienna. Some time in the autumn, two months hence, or earlier if I live, I will see you—that is, if you permit me; I will then tell you all that I scarce dare put upon paper now. Farewell. Pray for me, dear friend.'

In these terms ended this strange letter. Though I had never seen Bertha Rheinfeldt my eyes filled with tears at the sudden intelligence; I was startled, as well as profoundly disappointed.

The sun had now set, and it was twilight by the time I had returned the general's letter to my father.

It was a soft clear evening, and we loitered, speculating upon the possible meanings of the violent and incoherent sentences which I had just been reading. We had nearly a mile to walk before reaching the road that passes the schloss in front, and by that time the moon was shining brilliantly. At the drawbridge we met Madame Perrodon and Mademoiselle De Lafontaine, who had come out, without their bonnets, to enjoy the exquisite moonlight.

We heard their voices gabbling in animated dialogue as we approached. We joined them at the drawbridge, and turned about to admire with them the beautiful scene.

The glade through which we had just walked lay before us. At our left the narrow road wound away under clumps of lordly trees, and was lost to sight amid the thickening forest. At the right the same road crosses the steep and picturesque bridge, near which stands a ruined tower which once guarded that pass; and beyond the bridge an abrupt eminence rises, covered with trees, and showing in the shadows some grey ivy-clustered rocks.

Over the sward and low grounds a thin film of mist was stealing, like smoke, marking the distances with a transparent veil; and here and there we could see the river faintly flashing in the moonlight.

No softer, sweeter scene could be imagined. The news I had just heard made it melancholy; but nothing could disturb its character of profound serenity, and the enchanted glory and vagueness of the prospect.

My father, who enjoyed the picturesque, and I, stood looking in silence over the expanse beneath us. The two good governesses, standing a little way behind us, discoursed upon the scene, and were eloquent upon the moon.

Madame Perrodon was fat, middle-aged, and romantic, and talked and sighed poetically. Mademoiselle De Lafontaine—in right of her father, who was a German, assumed to be psychological, metaphysical, and something of a mystic—now declared that when the moon shone with a light so intense it was well known that it indicated a special spiritual activity. The effect of the full moon in such a state of brilliancy was manifold. It acted on dreams, it acted on lunacy, it acted on nervous people; it had marvellous physical influences connected with life. Mademoiselle related that her cousin, who was mate of a merchant ship, having taken a nap on deck on such a night, lying on his back, with his face full in the light of the moon, had wakened, after a dream of an old woman clawing him by the cheek, with his features horribly drawn to one side; and his countenance had never quite recovered its equilibrium.

'The moon, this night,' she said, 'is full of odylic and magnetic influence*—and see, when you look behind you at the front of the schloss, how all its windows flash and twinkle with that silvery splendour, as if unseen hands had lighted up the rooms to receive fairy guests.'

There are indolent states of the spirits in which, indisposed to talk ourselves, the talk of others is pleasant to our listless ears; and I gazed on, pleased with the tinkle of the ladies' conversation.

'I have got into one of my moping moods to-night,' said my father, after a silence, and quoting Shakespeare, whom, by way of keeping up our English, he used to read aloud, he said:

> '"In truth I know not why I am so sad:
> It wearies me; you say it wearies you;
> But how I got it—came by it."*

'I forget the rest. But I feel as if some great misfortune were hanging over us. I suppose the poor general's afflicted letter has had something to do with it.'

At this moment the unwonted sound of carriage wheels and many hoofs upon the road, arrested our attention.

They seemed to be approaching from the high ground overlooking the bridge, and very soon the equipage emerged from that point. Two horsemen first crossed the bridge, then came a carriage drawn by four horses, and two men rode behind.

It seemed to be the travelling carriage of a person of rank; and we were all immediately absorbed in watching that very unusual spectacle.

It became in a few moments greatly more interesting, for just as the carriage had passed the summit of the steep bridge, one of the leaders taking fright communicated his panic to the rest, and after a plunge or two the whole team broke into a wild gallop together, and dashing between the horsemen who rode in front, came thundering along the road towards us with the speed of a hurricane.

The excitement of the scene was made more painful by the clear, long-drawn screams of a female voice from the carriage window.

We all advanced in curiosity and horror; my father in silence, the rest with various ejaculations of terror.

Our suspense did not last long. Just before you reach the castle draw-bridge, on the route they were coming, there stands by the roadside a magnificent lime-tree, on the other stands an ancient stone cross, at sight of which the horses, now going at a pace that was perfectly frightful, swerved so as to bring the wheel over the projecting roots of the tree.

I knew what was coming. I covered my eyes, unable to see it out, and turned my head away; at the same moment I heard a cry from my lady-friends, who had gone on a little.

Curiosity opened my eyes, and I saw a scene of utter confusion. Two of the horses were on the ground, the carriage lay upon its side with two wheels in the air; the men were busy removing the traces,* and a lady, with a commanding air and figure, had got out, and stood with clasped hands, raising the handkerchief that was in them every now and then to her eyes. Through the carriage door was now lifted a young lady, who appeared to be lifeless. My dear old father was already beside the elder lady, with his hat in his hand, evidently tendering his aid and the resources of his schloss. The lady did not appear to hear him, or to have eyes for anything but the slender girl who was being placed against the slope of the bank.

I approached; the young lady was apparently stunned, but she was certainly not dead. My father, who piqued* himself on being some-thing of a physician, had just had his fingers to her wrist and assured the lady, who declared herself her mother, that her pulse, though faint and irregular, was undoubtedly still distinguishable. The lady clasped her hands and looked upward, as if in a momentary transport of grati-tude; but immediately she broke out again in that theatrical way which is, I believe, natural to some people.

She was what is called a fine looking woman for her time of life, and must have been handsome; she was tall, but not thin, and dressed in black velvet, and looked rather pale, but with a proud and commanding countenance, though now agitated strangely.

'Was ever being so born to calamity?' I heard her say, with clasped hands, as I came up. 'Here am I, on a journey of life and death, in prosecuting which to lose an hour is possibly to lose all. My child will not have recovered sufficiently to resume her route for who can say how long. I must leave her; I cannot, dare not, delay. How far on, sir, can you tell me, is the nearest village? I must leave her there; and shall not see my darling, or even hear of her, till my return, three months hence.'

I plucked my father by the coat, and whispered earnestly in his ear: 'Oh! papa, pray ask her to let her stay with us—it would be so delightful. Do, pray.'

'If madame will entrust her child to the care of my daughter, and of her good gouvernante, Madame Perrodon, and permit her to remain as our guest, under my charge, until her return, it will confer a distinction and an obligation upon us, and we shall treat her with all the care and devotion which so sacred a trust deserves.'

'I cannot do that, sir, it would be to task your kindness and chivalry too cruelly,' said the lady, distractedly.

'It would, on the contrary, be to confer on us a very great kindness at the moment when we most need it. My daughter has just been disappointed by a cruel misfortune, in a visit from which she had long anticipated a great deal of happiness. If you confide this young lady to our care it will be her best consolation. The nearest village on your route is distant, and affords no such inn as you could think of placing your daughter at; you cannot allow her to continue her journey for any considerable distance without danger. If, as you say, you cannot suspend your journey, you must part with her to-night, and nowhere could you do so with more honest assurances of care and tenderness than here.'

There was something in this lady's air and appearance so distinguished, and even imposing, and in her manner so engaging, as to impress one, quite apart from the dignity of her equipage, with a conviction that she was a person of consequence.

By this time the carriage was replaced in its upright position, and the horses, quite tractable, in the traces again.

The lady threw on her daughter a glance which I fancied was not quite so affectionate as one might have anticipated from the beginning of the scene; then she beckoned slightly to my father, and withdrew two or three steps with him out of hearing; and talked to him with a fixed and stern countenance, not at all like that with which she had hitherto spoken.

I was filled with wonder that my father did not seem to perceive the change, and also unspeakably curious to learn what it could be that she was speaking, almost in his ear, with so much earnestness and rapidity.

Two or three minutes at most I think she remained thus employed, then she turned, and a few steps brought her to where her daughter lay, supported by Madame Perrodon. She kneeled beside her for a moment and whispered, as Madame supposed, a little benediction in her ear; then hastily kissing her she stepped into her carriage, the door was closed, the footmen in stately liveries jumped up behind, the outriders spurred on, the postillions cracked their whips, the horses plunged and broke suddenly into a furious canter that threatened soon again to become a gallop, and the carriage whirled away, followed at the same rapid pace by the two horsemen in the rear.

CHAPTER III
WE COMPARE NOTES

WE followed the cortege* with our eyes until it was swiftly lost to sight in the misty wood; and the very sound of the hoofs and the wheels died away in the silent night air.

Nothing remained to assure us that the adventure had not been an illusion of a moment but the young lady, who just at that moment opened her eyes. I could not see, for her face was turned from me, but she raised her head, evidently looking about her, and I heard a very sweet voice ask complainingly, 'Where is mamma?'

Our good Madame Perrodon answered tenderly, and added some comfortable assurances.

I then heard her ask:

'Where am I? What is this place?' and after that she said, 'I don't see the carriage; and Matska,* where is she?'

Madame answered all her questions in so far as she understood them; and gradually the young lady remembered how the misadventure came about, and was glad to hear that no one in, or in attendance on, the carriage was hurt; and on learning that her mamma had left her here, till her return in about three months, she wept.

I was going to add my consolations to those of Madame Perrodon when Mademoiselle De Lafontaine placed her hand upon my arm, saying:

'Don't approach, one at a time is as much as she can at present converse with; a very little excitement would possibly overpower her now.'

As soon as she is comfortably in bed, I thought, I will run up to her room and see her.

My father in the meantime had sent a servant on horseback for the physician, who lived about two leagues away; and a bedroom was being prepared for the young lady's reception.

The stranger now rose, and leaning on Madame's arm, walked slowly over the drawbridge and into the castle gate.

In the hall servants waited to receive her, and she was conducted forthwith to her room.

The room we usually sat in as our drawing-room is long, having four windows, that looked over the moat and drawbridge, upon the forest scene I have just described.

It is furnished in old carved oak, with large carved cabinets, and the chairs are cushioned with crimson Utrecht velvet.* The walls are covered with tapestry, and surrounded with great gold frames, the figures being as large as life, in ancient and very curious costume, and the subjects represented are hunting, hawking, and generally festive. It is not too stately to be extremely comfortable; and here we had our tea, for with his usual patriotic leanings he insisted that the national beverage should make its appearance regularly with our coffee and chocolate.

We sat here this night, and with candles lighted, were talking over the adventure of the evening.

Madame Perrodon and Mademoiselle De Lafontaine were both of our party. The young stranger had hardly lain down in her bed when she sank into a deep sleep; and those ladies had left her in the care of a servant.

'How do you like our guest?' I asked, as soon as Madame entered. 'Tell me all about her?'

'I like her extremely,' answered Madame, 'she is, I almost think, the prettiest creature I ever saw; about your age, and so gentle and nice.'

'She is absolutely beautiful,' threw in Mademoiselle, who had peeped for a moment into the stranger's room.

'And such a sweet voice!' added Madame Perrodon.

'Did you remark a woman in the carriage, after it was set up again, who did not get out,' inquired Mademoiselle, 'but only looked from the window?'

'No, we had not seen her.'

Then she described a hideous black woman,* with a sort of coloured turban on her head, who was gazing all the time from the carriage window, nodding and grinning derisively towards the ladies, with gleaming eyes and large white eye-balls, and her teeth set as if in fury.

'Did you remark what an ill-looking pack of men the servants were?' asked Madame.

'Yes,' said my father, who had just come in, 'ugly, hang-dog looking fellows, as ever I beheld in my life. I hope they mayn't rob the poor lady in the forest. They are clever rogues, however; they got everything to rights in a minute.'

'I dare say they are worn out with too long travelling,' said Madame; 'Besides looking wicked, their faces were so strangely lean, and dark, and sullen. I am very curious, I own; but I dare say the young lady will tell us all about it to-morrow, if she is sufficiently recovered.'

'I don't think she will,' said my father, with a mysterious smile, and a little nod of his head, as if he knew more about it than he cared to tell us.

This made me all the more inquisitive as to what had passed between him and the lady in the black velvet, in the brief but earnest interview that had immediately preceded her departure.

We were scarcely alone, when I entreated him to tell me. He did not need much pressing.

'There is no particular reason why I should not tell you. She expressed a reluctance to trouble us with the care of her daughter, saying that she was in delicate health, and nervous, but not subject to any kind of seizure—she volunteered that—nor to any illusion; being, in fact, perfectly sane.'

'How very odd to say all that!' I interpolated. 'It was so unnecessary.'

'At all events it *was* said,' he laughed, 'and as you wish to know all that passed, which was indeed very little, I tell you. She then said, "I am making a long journey of *vital* importance—she emphasized the word—rapid and secret; I shall return for my child in three months; in the meantime, she will be silent as to who we are, whence we come, and whither we are travelling." That is all she said. She spoke very pure French. When she said the word "secret", she paused for a few seconds, looking sternly, her eyes fixed on mine. I fancy she makes a great point of that. You saw how quickly she was gone. I hope I have not done a very foolish thing, in taking charge of the young lady.'

For my part, I was delighted. I was longing to see and talk to her; and only waiting till the doctor should give me leave. You, who live in towns, can have no idea how great an event the introduction of a new friend is, in such a solitude as surrounded us.

The doctor did not arrive till nearly one o'clock; but I could no more have gone to my bed and slept, than I could have overtaken, on foot, the carriage in which the princess in black velvet had driven away.

When the physician came down to the drawing-room, it was to report very favourably upon his patient. She was now sitting up, her pulse quite regular, apparently perfectly well. She had sustained no injury, and the little shock to her nerves had passed away quite harmlessly. There could be no harm certainly in my seeing her, if we both wished it; and, with this permission, I sent, forthwith, to know whether she would allow me to visit her for a few minutes in her room.

The servant returned immediately to say that she desired nothing more.

You may be sure I was not long in availing myself of this permission.

Our visitor lay in one of the handsomest rooms in the schloss. It was, perhaps, a little stately. There was a sombre piece of tapestry opposite the foot of the bed, representing Cleopatra with the asps* to her bosom; and other solemn classic scenes were displayed, a little faded, upon the other walls. But there was gold carving, and rich and varied colour enough in the other decorations of the room, to more than redeem the gloom of the old tapestry.

There were candles at the bed side. She was sitting up; her slender pretty figure enveloped in the soft silk dressing gown, embroidered with flowers, and lined with thick quilted silk, which her mother had thrown over her feet as she lay upon the ground.

What was it that, as I reached the bed-side and had just begun my little greeting, struck me dumb in a moment, and made me recoil a step or two from before her? I will tell you.

I saw the very face which had visited me in my childhood at night, which remained so fixed in my memory, and on which I had for so many years so often ruminated with horror, when no one suspected of what I was thinking.

It was pretty, even beautiful; and when I first beheld it, wore the same melancholy expression.

But this almost instantly lighted into a strange fixed smile of recognition.

There was a silence of fully a minute, and then at length *she* spoke; *I* could not.

'How wonderful!' she exclaimed. 'Twelve years ago, I saw your face in a dream, and it has haunted me ever since.'

'Wonderful, indeed!' I repeated, overcoming with an effort the horror that had for a time suspended my utterances. 'Twelve years ago, in vision or reality, *I* certainly saw you. I could not forget your face. It has remained before my eyes ever since.'

Her smile had softened. Whatever I had fancied strange in it, was gone, and it and her dimpling cheeks were now delightfully pretty and intelligent.

I felt reassured, and continued more in the vein which hospitality indicated, to bid her welcome, and to tell her how much pleasure her accidental arrival had given us all, and especially what a happiness it was to me.

I took her hand as I spoke. I was a little shy, as lonely people are, but the situation made me eloquent, and even bold. She pressed my hand, she laid hers upon it, and her eyes glowed, as, looking hastily into mine, she smiled again, and blushed.

She answered my welcome very prettily. I sat down beside her, still wondering; and she said:

'I must tell you my vision about you; it is so very strange that you and I should have had, each of the other so vivid a dream, that each should have seen, I you and you me, looking as we do now, when of course we both were mere children. I was a child, about six years old, and I awoke from a confused and troubled dream, and found myself in a room, unlike my nursery, wainscoted clumsily in some dark wood, and with cupboards and bedsteads, and chairs, and benches placed about it. The beds were, I thought, all empty, and the room itself without anyone but myself in it; and I, after looking about me for some time, and admiring especially an iron candlestick, with two branches, which I should certainly know again, crept under one of the beds to reach the window; but as I got from under the bed, I heard someone crying; and looking up, while I was still upon my knees, I saw *you*—most assuredly you—as I see you now; a beautiful young lady, with golden hair and large blue eyes, and lips—your lips—you, as you are here. Your looks won me; I climbed on the bed and put my arms about you, and I think we both fell asleep. I was roused by a scream; you were sitting up screaming. I was frightened, and slipped down upon the ground, and, it seemed to me, lost consciousness for a moment; and when I came to myself, I was again in my nursery at home. Your face I have never forgotten since. I could not be misled by mere resemblance. You *are* the lady whom I then saw.'

It was now my turn to relate my corresponding vision, which I did, to the undisguised wonder of my new acquaintance.

'I don't know which should be most afraid of the other,' she said, again smiling—'If you were less pretty I think I should be very much afraid of you, but being as you are, and you and I both so young, I feel only that I have made your acquaintance twelve years ago, and have already a right to your intimacy; at all events it does seem as if we were destined, from our earliest childhood, to be friends. I wonder whether you feel as strangely drawn towards me as I do to you; I have never had a friend—shall I find one now?' She sighed, and her fine dark eyes gazed passionately on me.

Now the truth is, I felt rather unaccountably towards the beautiful stranger. I did feel, as she said, 'drawn towards her', but there was also something of repulsion. In this ambiguous feeling, however, the sense of attraction immensely prevailed. She interested and won me; she was so beautiful and so indescribably engaging.

I perceived now something of languor and exhaustion stealing over her, and hastened to bid her good night.

'The doctor thinks,' I added, 'that you ought to have a maid to sit up with you to-night; one of ours is waiting, and you will find her a very useful and quiet creature.'

'How kind of you, but I could not sleep, I never could with an attendant in the room. I shan't require any assistance—and, shall I confess my weakness, I am haunted with a terror of robbers. Our house was robbed once, and two servants murdered, so I always lock my door. It has become a habit—and you look so kind I know you will forgive me. I see there is a key in the lock.'

She held me close in her pretty arms for a moment and whispered in my ear, 'Good night, darling, it is very hard to part with you, but good night; to-morrow, but not early, I shall see you again.'

She sank back on the pillow with a sigh, and her fine eyes followed me with a fond and melancholy gaze, and she murmured again 'Good night, dear friend.'

Young people like, and even love, on impulse. I was flattered by the evident, though as yet undeserved, fondness she showed me. I liked the confidence with which she at once received me. She was determined that we should be very near friends.

Next day came and we met again. I was delighted with my companion; that is to say, in many respects.

Her looks lost nothing in daylight—she was certainly the most beautiful creature I had ever seen, and the unpleasant remembrance of the face presented in my early dream, had lost the effect of the first unexpected recognition.

She confessed that she had experienced a similar shock on seeing me, and precisely the same faint antipathy that had mingled with my admiration of her. We now laughed together over our momentary horrors.

CHAPTER IV

HER HABITS — A SAUNTER

I TOLD you that I was charmed with her in most particulars.

There were some that did not please me so well.

She was above the middle height of women. I shall begin by describing her. She was slender, and wonderfully graceful. Except that her movements were languid—*very* languid—indeed, there was nothing in her appearance to indicate an invalid. Her complexion was rich and brilliant; her features were small and beautifully formed; her eyes large, dark, and lustrous; her hair was quite wonderful, I never saw hair so magnificently thick and long when it was down about her shoulders; I have often placed my hands under it, and laughed with wonder at its weight. It was exquisitely fine and soft, and in colour a rich very dark brown, with something of gold. I loved to let it down, tumbling with its own weight, as, in her room, she lay back in her chair talking in her sweet low voice, I used to fold and braid it, and spread it out and play with it. Heavens! If I had but known all!

I said there were particulars which did not please me. I have told you that her confidence won me the first night I saw her; but I found that she exercised with respect to herself, her mother, her history, everything in fact connected with her life, plans, and people, an ever wakeful reserve. I dare say I was unreasonable, perhaps I was wrong; I dare say I ought to have respected the solemn injunction laid upon my father by the stately lady in black velvet. But curiosity is a restless and unscrupulous passion, and no one girl can endure, with patience, that hers should be baffled by another. What harm could it do anyone to tell me what I so ardently desired to know? Had she no trust in my good sense or honour? Why would she not believe me when I assured her, so solemnly, that I would not divulge one syllable of what she told me to any mortal breathing.

There was a coldness, it seemed to me, beyond her years, in her smiling melancholy persistent refusal to afford me the least ray of light.

I cannot say we quarrelled upon this point, for she would not quarrel upon any. It was, of course, very unfair of me to press her, very ill-bred, but I really could not help it; and I might just as well have let it alone.

What she did tell me amounted, in my unconscionable estimation to—nothing.

It was all summed up in three very vague disclosures:

First.—Her name was Carmilla.

Second.—Her family was very ancient and noble.

Third.—Her home lay in the direction of the west.

She would not tell me the name of her family, nor their armorial bearings, nor the name of their estate, nor even that of the country they lived in.

You are not to suppose that I worried her incessantly on these subjects. I watched opportunity, and rather insinuated than urged my inquiries. Once or twice, indeed, I did attack her more directly. But no matter what my tactics, utter failure was invariably the result. Reproaches and caresses were all lost upon her. But I must add this, that her evasion was conducted with so pretty a melancholy and deprecation, with so many, and even passionate declarations of her liking for me, and trust in my honour, and with so many promises that I should at last know all, that I could not find it in my heart long to be offended with her.

She used to place her pretty arms about my neck, draw me to her, and laying her cheek to mine, murmur with her lips near my ear, 'Dearest, your little heart is wounded; think me not cruel because I obey the irresistible law of my strength and weakness; if your dear heart is wounded, my wild heart bleeds with yours. In the rapture of my enormous humiliation I live in your warm life, and you shall die—die, sweetly die—into mine. I cannot help it; as I draw near to you, you, in your turn, will draw near to others, and learn the rapture of that cruelty, which yet is love; so, for a while, seek to know no more of me and mine, but trust me with all your loving spirit.'

And when she had spoken such a rhapsody, she would press me more closely in her trembling embrace, and her lips in soft kisses gently glow upon my cheek.

Her agitations and her language were unintelligible to me.

From these foolish embraces, which were not of very frequent occurrence, I must allow, I used to wish to extricate myself; but my energies seemed to fail me. Her murmured words sounded like a lullaby in my ear, and soothed my resistance into a trance, from which I only seemed to recover myself when she withdrew her arms.

In these mysterious moods I did not like her. I experienced a strange tumultuous excitement that was pleasurable, ever and anon, mingled with a vague sense of fear and disgust. I had no distinct thoughts about her while such scenes lasted, but I was conscious of a love growing into adoration, and also of abhorrence. This I know is paradox, but I can make no other attempt to explain the feeling.

I now write, after an interval of more than ten years, with a trembling hand, with a confused and horrible recollection of certain occurrences and situations, in the ordeal through which I was unconsciously passing; though with a vivid and very sharp remembrance of the main current of my story. But, I suspect, in all lives there are certain emotional scenes, those in which our passions have been most wildly and terribly roused, that are of all others the most vaguely and dimly remembered.

Sometimes after an hour of apathy, my strange and beautiful companion would take my hand and hold it with a fond pressure, renewed again and again; blushing softly, gazing in my face with languid and burning eyes, and breathing so fast that her dress rose and fell with the tumultuous respiration. It was like the ardour of a lover; it embarrassed me; it was hateful and yet overpowering; and with gloating eyes she drew me to her, and her hot lips travelled along my cheek in kisses; and she would whisper, almost in sobs, 'You are mine, you *shall* be mine, you and I are one for ever.' Then she has thrown herself back in her chair, with her small hands over her eyes, leaving me trembling.

'Are we related,' I used to ask; 'what can you mean by all this? I remind you perhaps of someone whom you love; but you must not, I hate it; I don't know you—I don't know myself when you look so and talk so.'

She used to sigh at my vehemence, then turn away and drop my hand.

Respecting these very extraordinary manifestations I strove in vain to form any satisfactory theory—I could not refer them to affectation or trick. It was unmistakably the momentary breaking out of suppressed instinct and emotion. Was she, notwithstanding her mother's volunteered denial, subject to brief visitations of insanity; or was there here a disguise and a romance? I had read in old story books of such things. What if a boyish lover had found his way into the house, and sought to prosecute his suit in masquerade, with the assistance of a clever old adventuress. But there were many things against this hypothesis, highly interesting as it was to my vanity.

I could boast of no little attentions such as masculine gallantry delights to offer. Between these passionate moments there were long intervals of commonplace, of gaiety, of brooding melancholy, during which, except that I detected her eyes so full of melancholy fire, following me, at times I might have been as nothing to her. Except in these brief periods of mysterious excitement her ways were girlish; and there was always a languor about her, quite incompatible with a masculine system in a state of health.

In some respects her habits were odd. Perhaps not so singular in the opinion of a town lady like you, as they appeared to us rustic people. She used to come down very late, generally not till one o'clock, she would then take a cup of chocolate, but eat nothing; we then went out for a walk, which was a mere saunter, and she seemed, almost immediately, exhausted, and either returned to the schloss or sat on one of the benches that were placed, here and there, among the trees. This was a bodily languor in which her mind did not sympathize. She was always an animated talker, and very intelligent.

She sometimes alluded for a moment to her own home, or mentioned an adventure or situation, or an early recollection, which indicated a people of strange manners, and described customs of which we knew nothing. I gathered from these chance hints that her native country was much more remote than I had at first fancied.

As we sat thus one afternoon under the trees a funeral passed us by. It was that of a pretty young girl, whom I had often seen, the daughter of one of the rangers of the forest. The poor man was walking behind the coffin of his darling; she was his only child, and he looked quite heartbroken. Peasants walking two-and-two came behind, they were singing a funeral hymn.

I rose to mark my respect as they passed, and joined in the hymn they were very sweetly singing.

My companion shook me a little roughly, and I turned surprised.

She said, brusquely, 'Don't you perceive how discordant that is?'

'I think it very sweet, on the contrary,' I answered, vexed at the interruption, and very uncomfortable, lest the people who composed the little procession should observe and resent what was passing.

I resumed, therefore, instantly, and was again interrupted. 'You pierce my ears,' said Carmilla, almost angrily, and stopping her ears with her tiny fingers. 'Besides, how can you tell that your religion and mine are the same; your forms wound me, and I hate funerals. What a fuss! Why *you* must die—*everyone* must die; and all are happier when they do. Come home.'

'My father has gone on with the clergyman to the churchyard. I thought you knew she was to be buried to day.'

'*She?* I don't trouble my head about peasants. I don't know who she is,' answered Carmilla, with a flash from her fine eyes.

'She is the poor girl who fancied she saw a ghost a fortnight ago, and has been dying ever since, till yesterday, when she expired.'

'Tell me nothing about ghosts. I shan't sleep to-night if you do.'

'I hope there is no plague or fever coming; all this looks very like it,' I continued. 'The swineherd's young wife died only a week ago, and she thought something seized her by the throat as she lay in her bed, and nearly strangled her. Papa says such horrible fancies do accompany some forms of fever. She was quite well the day before. She sank afterwards, and died before a week.'

'Well, *her* funeral is over, I hope, and *her* hymn sung; and our ears shan't be tortured with that discord and jargon. It has made me nervous. Sit down here, beside me; sit close; hold my hand; press it hard—hard—harder.'

We had moved a little back, and had come to another seat.

She sat down. Her face underwent a change that alarmed and even terrified me for a moment. It darkened, and became horribly livid; her teeth and hands were clenched, and she frowned and compressed her lips, while she stared down upon the ground at her feet, and trembled all over with a continued shudder as irrepressible as ague. All her energies seemed strained to suppress a fit, with which she was then breathlessly tugging; and at length a low convulsive cry of suffering broke from her, and gradually the hysteria subsided. 'There! That comes of strangling people with hymns!' she said at last. 'Hold me, hold me still. It is passing away.'

And so gradually it did; and perhaps to dissipate the sombre impression which the spectacle had left upon me, she became unusually animated and chatty; and so we got home.

This was the first time I had seen her exhibit any definable symptoms of that delicacy of health which her mother had spoken of. It was the first time, also, I had seen her exhibit anything like temper.

Both passed away like a summer cloud; and never but once afterwards did I witness on her part a momentary sign of anger. I will tell you how it happened.

She and I were looking out of one of the long drawing-room windows, when there entered the court-yard, over the drawbridge, a figure of a wanderer whom I knew very well. He used to visit the schloss generally twice a year.

It was the figure of a hunchback, with the sharp lean features that generally accompany deformity. He wore a pointed black beard, and he was smiling from ear to ear, showing his white fangs. He was dressed in buff, black, and scarlet, and crossed with more straps and belts than I could count, from which hung all manner of things. Behind, he carried a magic-lantern,* and two boxes, which I well knew, in one of which was a salamander, and in the other a mandrake.* These monsters used to make my father laugh. They were compounded of parts of monkeys, parrots, squirrels, fish, and hedgehogs, dried and stitched together with great neatness and startling effect. He had a fiddle, a box of conjuring apparatus, a pair of foils and masks attached to his belt, several other mysterious cases dangling about him, and a black staff with copper ferrules in his hand. His companion was a rough spare dog, that followed at his heels, but stopped short, suspiciously at the drawbridge, and in a little while began to howl dismally.

In the meantime, the mountebank, standing in the midst of the court-yard, raised his grotesque hat, and made us a very ceremonious bow, paying his compliments very volubly in execrable French, and German not much better. Then, disengaging his fiddle, he began to scrape a lively air, to which he sang with a merry discord, dancing with ludicrous airs and activity, that made me laugh, in spite of the dog's howling.

Then he advanced to the window with many smiles and salutations, and his hat in his left hand, his fiddle under his arm, and with a fluency that never took breath, he gabbled a long advertisement of all his accomplishments, and the resources of the various arts which he placed at our service, and the curiosities and entertainments which it was in his power, at our bidding, to display.

'Will your ladyships be pleased to buy an amulet against the oupire,* which is going like the wolf, I hear, through these woods,' he said, drop-ping his hat on the pavement. 'They are dying of it right and left, and here is a charm that never fails; only pinned to the pillow, and you may laugh in his face.'

These charms consisted of oblong slips of vellum, with cabalistic ciphers and diagrams upon them.

Carmilla instantly purchased one, and so did I.

He was looking up, and we were smiling down upon him, amused; at least, I can answer for myself. His piercing black eye, as he looked up in our faces, seemed to detect something that fixed for a moment his curiosity.

In an instant he unrolled a leather case, full of all manner of odd little steel instruments.

'See here, my lady,' he said, displaying it, and addressing me, 'I pro-fess, among other things less useful, the art of dentistry. Plague take the dog!' he interpolated. 'Silence, beast! He howls so that your ladyships can scarcely hear a word. Your noble friend, the young lady at your right, has the sharpest tooth,—long, thin, pointed, like an awl, like a needle; ha, ha! With my sharp and long sight, as I look up, I have seen it distinctly; now if it happens to hurt the young lady, and I think it must, here am I, here are my file, my punch, my nippers; I will make it round and blunt, if her ladyship pleases; no longer the tooth of a fish, but of a beautiful young lady as she is. Hey? Is the young lady dis-pleased? Have I been too bold? Have I offended her?'

The young lady, indeed, looked very angry as she drew back from the window.

'How dares that mountebank insult us so? Where is your father? I shall demand redress from him. My father would have had the wretch tied up to the pump, and flogged with a cart-whip, and burnt to the bones with the castle brand!'

She retired from the window a step or two, and sat down, and had hardly lost sight of the offender, when her wrath subsided as suddenly as it had risen, and she gradually recovered her usual tone, and seemed to forget the little hunchback and his follies.

My father was out of spirits that evening. On coming in he told us that there had been another case very similar to the two fatal ones which had lately occurred. The sister of a young peasant on his estate, only a mile away, was very ill, had been, as she described it, attacked very nearly in the same way, and was now slowly but steadily sinking.

'All this,' said my father, 'is strictly referable to natural causes. These poor people infect one another with their superstitions, and so repeat in imagination the images of terror that have infested their neighbours.'

'But that very circumstance frightens one horribly,' said Carmilla.

'How so?' inquired my father.

'I am so afraid of fancying I see such things; I think it would be as bad as reality.'

'We are in God's hands; nothing can happen without his permission, and all will end well for those who love him. He is our faithful creator; He has made us all, and will take care of us.'

'Creator! *Nature!*' said the young lady in answer to my gentle father. 'And this disease that invades the country is natural. Nature. All things proceed from Nature—don't they? All things in the heaven, in the earth, and under the earth, act and live as Nature ordains? I think so.'

'The doctor said he would come here to-day,' said my father, after a silence. 'I want to know what he thinks about it, and what he thinks we had better do.'

'Doctors never did me any good,' said Carmilla.

'Then you have been ill?' I asked.

'More ill than ever you were,' she answered.

'Long ago?'

'Yes, a long time. I suffered from this very illness; but I forget all but my pain and weakness, and they were not so bad as are suffered in other diseases.'

'You were very young then?'

'I dare say; let us talk no more of it. You would not wound a friend?' She looked languidly in my eyes, and passed her arm round my waist lovingly, and led me out of the room. My father was busy over some papers near the window.

'Why does your papa like to frighten us?' said the pretty girl, with a sigh and a little shudder.

'He doesn't, dear Carmilla, it is the very furthest thing from his mind.'

'Are you afraid, dearest?'

'I should be very much if I fancied there was any real danger of my being attacked as those poor people were.'

'You are afraid to die?'

'Yes, every one is.'

'But to die as lovers may—to die together, so that they may live together. Girls are caterpillars while they live in the world, to be finally butterflies when the summer comes; but in the meantime there are grubs and larvae, don't you see—each with their peculiar propensities, necessities, and structure. So says Monsieur Buffon, in his big book,* in the next room.'

Later in the day the doctor came, and was closeted with papa for some time. He was a skilful man, of sixty and upwards, he wore powder, and shaved his pale face as smooth as a pumpkin. He and papa emerged from the room together, and I heard papa laugh, and say as they came out:

'Well, I do wonder at a wise man like you. What do you say to hippo-griffs* and dragons?'

The doctor was smiling, and made answer, shaking his head—

'Nevertheless life and death are mysterious states, and we know little of the resources of either.'

And so they walked on, and I heard no more. I did not then know what the doctor had been broaching, but I think I guess it now.

CHAPTER V

A WONDERFUL LIKENESS

THIS evening there arrived from Gratz* the grave, dark-faced son of the picture cleaner, with a horse and cart laden with two large packing cases, having many pictures in each. It was a journey of ten leagues,* and whenever a messenger arrived at the schloss from our little capital of Gratz, we used to crowd about him in the hall, to hear the news.

This arrival created in our secluded quarters quite a sensation. The cases remained in the hall, and the messenger was taken charge of by the servants till he had eaten his supper. Then with assistants, and armed with hammer, ripping-chisel, and turnscrew, he met us in the hall, where we had assembled to witness the unpacking of the cases.

Carmilla sat looking listlessly on, while one after the other the old pictures, nearly all portraits, which had undergone the process of renovation, were brought to light. My mother was of an old Hungarian family, and most of these pictures, which were about to be restored to their places, had come to us through her.

My father had a list in his hand, from which he read, as the artist rummaged out the corresponding numbers. I don't know that the pictures were very good, but they were, undoubtedly, very old, and some of them very curious also. They had, for the most part, the merit of being now seen by me, I may say, for the first time; for the smoke and dust of time had all but obliterated them.

'There is a picture that I have not seen yet,' said my father. 'In one corner, at the top of it, is the name, as well as I could read, "Marcia* Karnstein", and the date "1698"; and I am curious to see how it has turned out.'

I remembered it; it was a small picture, about a foot and a half high, and nearly square, without a frame; but it was so blackened by age that I could not make it out.

The artist now produced it, with evident pride. It was quite beautiful; it was startling; it seemed to live. It was the effigy of Carmilla!

'Carmilla, dear, here is an absolute miracle. Here you are, living, smiling, ready to speak, in this picture. Isn't it beautiful, papa? And see, even the little mole on her throat.'

My father laughed, and said 'Certainly it is a wonderful likeness', but he looked away, and to my surprise seemed but little struck by it, and went on talking to the picture cleaner, who was also something of an artist, and discoursed with intelligence about the portraits or other works, which his art had just brought out into light and colour, while *I* was more and more lost in wonder the more I looked at the picture.

'Will you let me hang this picture in my room, papa?' I asked.

'Certainly, dear,' said he, smiling, 'I'm very glad you think it so like. It must be prettier even than I thought it, if it is.'

The young lady did not acknowledge this pretty speech, did not seem to hear it. She was leaning back in her seat, her fine eyes under their long lashes gazing on me in contemplation, and she smiled in a kind of rapture.

'And now you can read quite plainly the name that is written in the corner. It is not Marcia; it looks as if it was done in gold. The name is Mircalla, Countess Karnstein, and this is a little coronet over it, and underneath A.D. 1698. I am descended from the Karnsteins; that is, mamma was.'

'Ah!' said the lady, languidly, 'so am I, I think, a very long descent, very ancient. Are there any Karnsteins living now?'

'None who bear the name, I believe. The family were ruined, I believe, in some civil wars, long ago, but the ruins of the castle are only about three miles away.'

'How interesting!' she said, languidly. 'But see what beautiful moonlight!' She glanced through the hall-door, which stood a little open. 'Suppose you take a little ramble round the court, and look down at the road and river.'

'It is so like the night you came to us,' I said.

She sighed, smiling.

She rose, and each with her arm about the other's waist, we walked out upon the pavement.

In silence, slowly we walked down to the drawbridge, where the beautiful landscape opened before us.

'And so you were thinking of the night I came here?' she almost whispered. 'Are you glad I came?'

'Delighted, dear Carmilla,' I answered.

'And you asked for the picture you think like me, to hang in your room,' she murmured with a sigh, as she drew her arm closer about my waist, and let her pretty head sink upon my shoulder.

'How romantic you are, Carmilla,' I said. 'Whenever you tell me your story, it will be made up chiefly of some one great romance.'

She kissed me silently.

'I am sure, Carmilla, you have been in love; that there is, at this moment, an affair of the heart going on.'

'I have been in love with no one, and never shall,' she whispered, 'unless it should be with you.'

How beautiful she looked in the moonlight!

Shy and strange was the look with which she quickly hid her face in my neck and hair, with tumultuous sighs, that seemed almost to sob, and pressed in mine a hand that trembled.

Her soft cheek was glowing against mine. 'Darling, darling,' she murmured, 'I live in you; and you would die for me, I love you so.'

I started from her.

She was gazing on me with eyes from which all fire, all meaning had flown, and a face colourless and apathetic.

'Is there a chill in the air, dear?' she said drowsily. 'I almost shiver; have I been dreaming? Let us come in. Come; come; come in.'

'You look ill, Carmilla; a little faint. You must take some wine,' I said.

'Yes, I will. I'm better now. I shall be quite well in a few minutes. Yes, do give me a little wine,' answered Carmilla, as we approached the door. 'Let us look again for a minute; it is the last time, perhaps, I shall see the moonlight with you.'

'How do you feel now, dear Carmilla? Are you really better?' I asked.

I was beginning to take alarm, lest she should have been stricken with the strange epidemic that they said had invaded the country about us.

'Papa would be grieved beyond measure,' I added, 'if he thought you were ever so little ill, without immediately letting us know. We have a very skilful doctor near this, the physician who was with papa to-day.'

'I'm sure he is. I know how kind you all are; but, dear child, I am quite well again. There is nothing ever wrong with me, but a little weakness. People say I am languid; I am incapable of exertion; I can scarcely walk as far as a child of three years old; and every now and then the little strength I have falters, and I become as you have just seen me. But after all I am very easily set up again; in a moment I am perfectly myself. See how I have recovered.'

So, indeed, she had; and she and I talked a great deal, and very animated she was; and the remainder of that evening passed without any recurrence of what I called her infatuations. I mean her crazy talk and looks, which embarrassed, and even frightened me.

But there occurred that night an event which gave my thoughts quite a new turn, and seemed to startle even Carmilla's languid nature into momentary energy.

CHAPTER VI

A VERY STRANGE AGONY

WHEN we got into the drawing-room, and had sat down to our coffee and chocolate, although Carmilla did not take any, she seemed quite herself again, and Madame, and Mademoiselle De Lafontaine, joined us, and made a little card party, in the course of which papa came in for what he called his 'dish of tea'.

When the game was over he sat down beside Carmilla on the sofa, and asked her, a little anxiously, whether she had heard from her mother since her arrival.

She answered 'No'.

He then asked whether she knew where a letter would reach her at present.

'I cannot tell,' she answered ambiguously, 'but I have been thinking of leaving you; you have been already too hospitable and too kind to me. I have given you an infinity of trouble, and I should wish to take a carriage to-morrow, and post in pursuit of her; I know where I shall ultimately find her, although I dare not yet tell you.'

'But you must not dream of any such thing,' exclaimed my father, to my great relief. 'We can't afford to lose you so, and I won't consent to your leaving us, except under the care of your mother, who was so good as to consent to your remaining with us till she should herself return. I should be quite happy if I knew that you heard from her; but this evening the accounts of the progress of the mysterious disease that has invaded our neighbourhood, grow even more alarming; and my beautiful guest, I do feel the responsibility, unaided by advice from your mother, very much. But I shall do my best; and one thing is certain, that you must not think of leaving us without her distinct direction to that effect. We should suffer too much in parting from you to consent to it easily.'

'Thank you, sir, a thousand times for your hospitality,' she answered, smiling bashfully. 'You have all been too kind to me; I have seldom been so happy in all my life before, as in your beautiful château, under your care, and in the society of your dear daughter.'

So he gallantly, in his old-fashioned way, kissed her hand, smiling and pleased at her little speech.

I accompanied Carmilla as usual to her room, and sat and chatted with her while she was preparing for bed.

'Do you think,' I said at length, 'that you will ever confide fully in me?'

She turned round smiling, but made no answer, only continued to smile on me.

'You won't answer that?' I said. 'You can't answer pleasantly; perhaps I ought not to have asked you.'

'You were quite right to ask me that, or anything. You do not know how dear you are to me, or you could not think any confidence too great to look for. But I am under vows, no nun half so awfully, and I dare not tell my story yet, even to you. The time is very near when you shall know everything. You will think me cruel, very selfish, but love is always selfish; the more ardent the more selfish. How jealous I am you cannot know. You must come with me, loving me, to death; or else hate me and still come with me, and *hating* me through death and after. There is no such word as indifference in my apathetic nature.'

'Now, Carmilla, you are going to talk your wild nonsense again,' I said hastily.

'Not I, silly little fool as I am, and full of whims and fancies; for your sake I'll talk like a sage. Were you ever at a ball?'

'No; how you do run on. What is it like? How charming it must be.'

'I almost forget, it is years ago.'

I laughed.

'You are not so old. Your first ball can hardly be forgotten yet.'

'I remember everything about it—with an effort. I see it all, as divers see what is going on above them, through a medium, dense, rippling, but transparent. There occurred that night what has confused the picture, and made its colours faint. I was all but assassinated in my bed, wounded *here*,' she touched her breast, 'and never was the same since.'

'Were you near dying?'

'Yes, very—a cruel love—strange love, that would have taken my life. Love will have its sacrifices. No sacrifice without blood. Let us go to sleep now; I feel so lazy. How can I get up just now and lock my door?'

She was lying, with her tiny hands buried in her rich wavy hair, under her cheek, her little head upon the pillow, and her glittering eyes followed me wherever I moved, with a kind of shy smile that I could not decipher.

I bid her good-night, and crept from the room with an uncomfortable sensation.

I often wondered whether our pretty guest ever said her prayers. *I* certainly had never seen her upon her knees. In the morning she never came down until long after our family prayers were over, and at night she never left the drawing-room to attend our brief evening prayers in the hall.

If it had not been that it had casually come out in one of our careless talks that she had been baptized, I should have doubted her being a Christian. Religion was a subject on which I had never heard her speak a word. If I had known the world better, this particular neglect or antipathy would not have so much surprised me.

The precautions of nervous people are infectious, and persons of a like temperament are pretty sure, after a time, to imitate them. I had adopted Carmilla's habit of locking her bed-room door, having taken into my head all her whimsical alarms about midnight invaders and prowling assassins. I had also adopted her precaution of making a brief search through her room, to satisfy herself that no lurking assassin or robber was 'ensconced'.

These wise measures taken I got into my bed and fell asleep. A light was burning in my room. This was an old habit, of very early date, and which nothing could have tempted me to dispense with.

Thus fortified I might take my rest in peace. But dreams come through stone walls, light up dark rooms, or darken light ones, and their persons make their exits and their entrances as they please, and laugh at locksmiths.

I had a dream that night that was the beginning of a very strange agony.

I cannot call it a nightmare, for I was quite conscious of being asleep. But I was equally conscious of being in my room, and lying in bed, precisely as I actually was. I saw, or fancied I saw, the room and its furniture just as I had seen it last, except that it was very dark, and I saw something moving round the foot of the bed, which at first I could not accurately distinguish. But I soon saw that it was a sooty-black animal that resembled a monstrous cat. It appeared to me about four or five feet long, for it measured fully the length of the hearth-rug as it passed over it; and it continued toing and froing with the lithe sinister restlessness of a beast in a cage. I could not cry out, although as you may suppose, I was terrified. Its pace was growing faster, and the room rapidly darker and darker, and at length so dark that I could no longer see anything of it but its eyes. I felt it spring lightly on the bed. The two broad eyes approached my face, and suddenly I felt a stinging pain as if two large needles darted, an inch or two apart, deep into my breast. I waked with a scream. The room was lighted by the candle that burnt there all through the night, and I saw a female figure standing at the foot of the bed, a little at the right side. It was in a dark loose dress, and its hair was down and covered its shoulders. A block of stone could not have been more still. There was not the slightest stir of respiration. As I stared at it the figure appeared to have changed its place, and was now nearer the door; then, close to it, the door opened, and it passed out.

I was now relieved, and able to breathe and move. My first thought was that Carmilla had been playing me a trick, and that I had forgotten to secure my door. I hastened to it, and found it locked as usual on the inside. I was afraid to open it—I was horrified. I sprang into my bed and covered my head up in the bed-clothes, and lay there more dead than alive till morning.

CHAPTER VII

DESCENDING

It would be vain my attempting to tell you the horror with which, even now, I recall the occurrence of that night. It was no such transitory terror as a dream leaves behind it. It seemed to deepen by time, and communicated itself to the room and the very furniture that had encompassed the apparition.

I could not bear next day to be alone for a moment. I should have told papa, but for two opposite reasons. At one time I thought he would laugh at my story, and I could not bear its being treated as a jest; and at another I thought he might fancy that I had been attacked by the mysterious complaint which had invaded our neighbourhood. I had myself no misgivings of the kind, and as he had been rather an invalid for some time, I was afraid of alarming him.

I was comfortable enough with my good-natured companions, Madame Paradon, and the vivacious Mademoiselle de Lafontaine. They both perceived that I was out of spirits and nervous, and at length I told them what lay so heavy at my heart.

Mademoiselle laughed, but I fancied that Madame Paradon looked anxious.

'By-the-bye,' said Mademoiselle, laughing, 'the long lime-tree walk, behind Carmilla's bedroom-window, is haunted!'

'Nonsense!' exclaimed Madame, who probably thought the theme rather inopportune, 'and who tells that story, my dear?'

'Martin says that he came up twice, when the old yard-gate was being repaired, before sunrise, and twice saw the same female figure walking down the lime-tree avenue.'

'So he well might, as long as there are cows to milk in the river fields,' said Madame.

'I daresay; but Martin chooses to be frightened, and never did I see fool *more* frightened.'

'You must not say a word about it to Carmilla, because she can see down that walk from her room window,' I interposed, 'and she is, if possible, a greater coward than I.'

Carmilla came down rather later than usual that day.

'I was so frightened last night,' she said, so soon as we were together, 'and I am sure I should have seen something dreadful if it had not been for that charm I bought from the poor little hunchback whom I called such hard names. I had a dream of something black coming round my bed, and I awoke in a perfect horror, and I really thought, for some seconds, I saw a dark figure near the chimney-piece, but I felt under my pillow for my charm, and the moment my fingers touched it, the figure disappeared, and I felt quite certain, only that I had it by me, that something frightful would have made its appearance, and, perhaps, throttled me, as it did those poor people we heard of.'

'Well, listen to me,' I began, and recounted my adventure, at the recital of which she appeared horrified.

'And had you the charm near you?' she asked, earnestly.

'No, I had dropped it into a china vase in the drawing-room, but I shall certainly take it with me to-night, as you have so much faith in it.'

At this distance of time I cannot tell you, or even understand, how I overcame my horror so effectually as to lie alone in my room that night. I remember distinctly that I pinned the charm to my pillow. I fell asleep almost immediately, and slept even more soundly than usual all night.

Next night I passed as well. My sleep was delightfully deep and dreamless. But I wakened with a sense of lassitude and melancholy, which, however, did not exceed a degree that was almost luxurious.

'Well, I told you so,' said Carmilla, when I described my quiet sleep, 'I had such delightful sleep myself last night; I pinned the charm to the breast of my night-dress. It was too far away the night before. I am quite sure it was all fancy, except the dreams. I used to think that evil spirits made dreams, but our doctor told me it is no such thing. Only a fever passing by, or some other malady, as they often do, he said, knocks at the door, and not being able to get in, passes on, with that alarm.'

'And what do you think the charm is?' said I.

'It has been fumigated or immersed in some drug, and is an antidote against the malaria,' she answered.

'Then it acts only on the body?'

'Certainly; you don't suppose that evil spirits are frightened by bits of ribbon, or the perfumes of a druggist's shop? No, these complaints, wandering in the air, begin by trying the nerves, and so infect the brain, but before they can seize upon you, the antidote repels them. That I am sure is what the charm has done for us. It is nothing magical, it is simply natural.'

I should have been happier if I could have quite agreed with Carmilla, but I did my best, and the impression was a little losing its force.

For some nights I slept profoundly; but still every morning I felt the same lassitude, and a languor weighed upon me all day. I felt myself a changed girl. A strange melancholy was stealing over me, a melancholy that I would not have interrupted. Dim thoughts of death began to open, and an idea that I was slowly sinking took gentle, and, somehow, not unwelcome, possession of me. If it was sad, the tone of mind which this induced was also sweet. Whatever it might be, my soul acquiesced in it.

I would not admit that I was ill, I would not consent to tell my papa, or to have the doctor sent for.

Carmilla became more devoted to me than ever, and her strange paroxysms of languid adoration more frequent. She used to gloat on me with increasing ardour the more my strength and spirits waned. This always shocked me like a momentary glare of insanity.

Without knowing it, I was now in a pretty advanced stage of the strangest illness under which mortal ever suffered. There was an unaccountable fascination in its earlier symptoms that more than reconciled me to the incapacitating effect of that stage of the malady. This fascination increased for a time, until it reached a certain point, when gradually a sense of the horrible mingled itself with it, deepening, as you shall hear, until it discoloured and perverted the whole state of my life.

The first change I experienced was rather agreeable. It was very near the turning-point from which began the descent of Avernus.*

Certain vague and strange sensations visited me in my sleep. The prevailing one was of that pleasant, peculiar cold thrill which we feel in bathing, when we move against the current of a river. This was soon accompanied by dreams that seemed interminable, and were so vague that I could never recollect their scenery and persons, or any one connected portion of their action. But they left an awful impression, and a sense of exhaustion, as if I had passed through a long period of great mental exertion and danger. After all these dreams there remained on waking a remembrance of having been in a place very nearly dark, and of having spoken to people whom I could not see; and especially of one clear voice, of a female's, very deep, that spoke as if at a distance, slowly, and producing always the same sensation of indescribable solemnity and fear. Sometimes there came a sensation as if a hand was drawn softly along my cheek and neck. Sometimes it was as if warm lips kissed me, and longer and more lovingly as they reached my throat, but there the caress fixed itself. My heart beat faster, my breathing rose and fell rapidly and full drawn; a sobbing, that rose into a sense of strangulation, supervened, and turned into a dreadful convulsion, in which my senses left me and I became unconscious.

It was now three weeks since the commencement of this unaccountable state. My sufferings had, during the last week, told upon my appearance. I had grown pale, my eyes were dilated and darkened underneath, and the languor which I had long felt began to display itself in my countenance.

My father asked me often whether I was ill; but, with an obstinacy which now seems to me unaccountable, I persisted in assuring him that I was quite well.

In a sense this was true. I had no pain, I could complain of no bodily derangement. My complaint seemed to be one of the imagination, or the nerves, and, horrible as my sufferings were, I kept them, with a morbid reserve, very nearly to myself.

It could not be that terrible complaint which the peasants called the oupire, for I had now been suffering for three weeks, and they were seldom ill for much more than three days, when death put an end to their miseries.

Carmilla complained of dreams and feverish sensations, but by no means of so alarming a kind as mine. I say that mine were extremely alarming. Had I been capable of comprehending my condition, I would have invoked aid and advice on my knees. The narcotic of an unsuspected influence was acting upon me, and my perceptions were benumbed.

I am going to tell you now of a dream that led immediately to an odd discovery.

One night, instead of the voice I was accustomed to hear in the dark, I heard one, sweet and tender, and at the same time terrible, which said, 'Your mother warns you to beware of the assassin.' At the same time a light unexpectedly sprang up, and I saw Carmilla, standing, near the foot of my bed, in her white night-dress, bathed, from her chin to her feet, in one great stain of blood.

I wakened with a shriek, possessed with the one idea that Carmilla was being murdered. I remember springing from my bed, and my next recollection is that of standing on the lobby, crying for help.

Madame and Mademoiselle came scurrying out of their rooms in alarm; a lamp burned always on the lobby, and seeing me, they soon learned the cause of my terror.

I insisted on our knocking at Carmilla's door. Our knocking was unanswered. It soon became a pounding and an uproar. We shrieked her name, but all was vain.

We all grew frightened, for the door was locked. We hurried back, in panic, to my room. There we rang the bell long and furiously. If my father's room had been at that side of the house, we would have called him up at once to our aid. But, alas! he was quite out of hearing, and to reach him involved an excursion for which we none of us had courage.

Servants, however, soon came running up the stairs; I had got on my dressing-gown and slippers meanwhile, and my companions were already similarly furnished. Recognizing the voices of the servants on the lobby, we sallied out together; and having renewed, as fruitlessly, our summons at Carmilla's door, I ordered the men to force the lock. They did so, and we stood, holding our lights aloft, in the doorway, and so stared into the room.

We called her by name; but there was still no reply. We looked round the room. Everything was undisturbed. It was exactly in the state in which I had left it on bidding her good night. But Carmilla was gone.

CHAPTER VIII
SEARCH

AT sight of the room, perfectly undisturbed except for our violent entrance, we began to cool a little, and soon recovered our senses sufficiently to dismiss the men. It had struck Mademoiselle that possibly Carmilla had been wakened by the uproar at her door, and in her first panic had jumped from her bed, and hid herself in a press, or behind a curtain, from which she could not, of course, emerge until the major-domo* and his myrmidons* had withdrawn. We now recommenced our search, and began to call her by name again.

It was all to no purpose. Our perplexity and agitation increased. We examined the windows, but they were secured. I implored of Carmilla, if she had concealed herself, to play this cruel trick no longer—to come out, and to end our anxieties. It was all useless. I was by this time convinced that she was not in the room, nor in the dressing room, the door of which was still locked on this side. She could not have passed it. I was utterly puzzled. Had Carmilla discovered one of those secret passages which the old housekeeper said were known to exist in the schloss, although the tradition of their exact situation had been lost. A little time would, no doubt, explain all—utterly perplexed as, for the present, we were.

It was past four o'clock, and I preferred passing the remaining hours of darkness in Madame's room. Daylight brought no solution of the difficulty.

The whole household, with my father at its head, was in a state of agitation next morning. Every part of the château was searched. The grounds were explored. Not a trace of the missing lady could be discovered. The stream was about to be dragged; my father was in distraction;

what a tale to have to tell the poor girl's mother on her return. I, too, was almost beside myself, though my grief was quite of a different kind.

The morning was passed in alarm and excitement. It was now one o'clock, and still no tidings. I ran up to Carmilla's room, and found her standing at her dressing-table. I was astounded. I could not believe my eyes. She beckoned me to her with her pretty finger, in silence. Her face expressed extreme fear.

I ran to her in an ecstasy of joy; I kissed and embraced her again and again. I ran to the bell and rang it vehemently, to bring others to the spot, who might at once relieve my father's anxiety.

'Dear Carmilla, what has become of you all this time? We have been in agonies of anxiety about you,' I exclaimed. 'Where have you been? How did you come back?'

'Last night has been a night of wonders,' she said.

'For mercy's sake, explain all you can.'

'It was past two last night,' she said, 'when I went to sleep as usual in my bed, with my doors locked, that of the dressing-room, and that opening upon the gallery. My sleep was uninterrupted, and, so far as I know, dreamless; but I awoke just now on the sofa in the dressing-room there, and I found the door between the rooms open, and the other door forced. How could all this have happened without my being wakened? It must have been accompanied with a great deal of noise, and I am particularly easily wakened; and how could I have been carried out of my bed without my sleep having been interrupted, I whom the slightest stir startles?'

By this time, Madame, Mademoiselle, my father, and a number of the servants were in the room. Carmilla was, of course, overwhelmed with enquiries, congratulations, and welcomes. She had but one story to tell, and seemed the least able of all the party to suggest any way of accounting for what had happened.

My father took a turn up and down the room, thinking. I saw Carmilla's eye follow him for a moment with a sly, dark glance.

When my father had sent the servants away, Mademoiselle having gone in search of a little bottle of valerian and sal-volatile,* and there being no one now in the room with Carmilla, except my father, Madame, and myself, he came to her thoughtfully, took her hand very kindly, led her to the sofa, and sat down beside her.

'Will you forgive me, my dear, if I risk a conjecture, and ask a question?'

'Who can have a better right?' she said. 'Ask what you please, and I will tell you everything. But my story is simply one of bewilderment and darkness. I know absolutely nothing. Put any question you please. But you know, of course, the limitations mamma has placed me under?'

'Perfectly, my dear child. I need not approach the topics on which she desires our silence. Now, the marvel of last night consists in your having been removed from your bed and your room, without being wakened, and this removal's having occurred apparently while the windows were still secured, and the two doors locked upon the inside. I will tell you my theory, and first ask you a question.'

Carmilla was leaning on her hand dejectedly; Madame and I were listening breathlessly.

'Now, my question is this. Have you ever been suspected of walking in your sleep?'

'Never, since I was very young indeed.'

'But you did walk in your sleep when you were young?'

'Yes; I know I did. I have been told so often by my old nurse.'

My father smiled and nodded.

'Well, what has happened is this. You got up in your sleep, unlocked the door, not leaving the key, as usual, in the lock, but taking it out and locking it on the outside; you again took the key out, and carried it away with you to some one of the five-and-twenty rooms on this floor, or perhaps up-stairs or down-stairs. There are so many rooms and closets, so much heavy furniture, and such accumulations of lumber, that it would require a week to search this old house thoroughly. Do you see, now, what I mean?'

'I do, but not all,' she answered.

'And how, papa, do you account for her finding herself on the sofa in the dressing-room, which we had searched so carefully?'

'She came there after you had searched it, still in her sleep, and at last awoke spontaneously, and was as much surprised to find herself where she was as any one else. I wish all mysteries were as easily and innocently explained as yours, Carmilla,' he said, laughing. 'And so we may congratulate ourselves on the certainty that the most natural explanation of the occurrence is one that involves no drugging, no tampering with locks, no burglars, or poisoners, or witches—nothing that need alarm Carmilla, or any one else, for our safety.'

Carmilla was looking charmingly. Nothing could be more beautiful than her tints. Her beauty was, I think, enhanced by that graceful languor that was peculiar to her. I think my father was silently contrasting her looks with mine, for he said:

'I wish my poor Laura was looking more like herself'; and he sighed.

So our alarms were happily ended, and Carmilla restored to her friends.

CHAPTER IX

THE DOCTOR

As Carmilla would not hear of an attendant sleeping in her room, my father arranged that a servant should sleep outside her door, so that she could not attempt to make another such excursion without being arrested at her own door.

That night passed quietly; and next morning early, the doctor, whom my father had sent for without telling me a word about it, arrived to see me.

Madame accompanied me to the library; and there the grave little doctor, with white hair and spectacles, whom I mentioned before, was waiting to receive me.

I told him my story, and as I proceeded he grew graver and graver.

We were standing, he and I, in the recess of one of the windows, facing one another. When my statement was over, he leaned with his shoulders against the wall, and with his eyes fixed on me earnestly, with an interest in which was a dash of horror.

After a minute's reflection, he asked Madame if he could see my father.

He was sent for accordingly, and as he entered, smiling, he said, 'I dare say, doctor, you are going to tell me that I am an old fool for having brought you here; I hope I am.'

But his smile faded into shadow as the doctor, with a very grave face, beckoned him to him.

He and the doctor talked for some time in the same recess where I had just conferred with the physician. It seemed an earnest and argumentative conversation. The room is very large, and I and Madame stood together, burning with curiosity, at the further end. Not a word could we hear, however, for they spoke in a very low tone, and the deep recess of the window quite concealed the doctor from view, and very nearly my father, whose foot, arm, and shoulder only could we see; and the voices were, I suppose, all the less audible for the sort of closet which the thick wall and window formed.

After a time my father's face looked into the room; it was pale, thoughtful, and, I fancied, agitated.

'Laura, dear, come here for a moment. Madame, we shan't trouble you, the doctor says, at present.'

Accordingly I approached, for the first time a little alarmed; for, although I felt very weak, I did not feel ill; and strength, one always fancies, is a thing that may be picked up when we please.

My father held out his hand to me, as I drew near, but he was looking at the doctor, and he said:

'It certainly *is* very odd; I don't understand it quite. Laura, come here, dear; now attend to Doctor Spielsberg, and recollect yourself.'

'You mentioned a sensation like that of two needles piercing the skin, somewhere about your neck, on the night when you experienced your first horrible dream. Is there still any soreness?'

'None at all,' I answered.

'Can you indicate with your finger about the point at which you think this occurred?'

'Very little below my throat—*here*,' I answered.

I wore a morning dress, which covered the place I pointed to.

'Now you can satisfy yourself,' said the doctor. 'You won't mind your papa's lowering your dress a very little. It is necessary, to detect a symptom of the complaint under which you have been suffering.'

I acquiesced. It was only an inch or two below the edge of my collar.

'God bless me!—so it is,' exclaimed my father, growing pale.

'You see it now with your own eyes,' said the doctor, with a gloomy triumph.

'What is it?' I exclaimed, beginning to be frightened.

'Nothing, my dear young lady, but a small blue spot, about the size of the tip of your little finger; and now,' he continued, turning to papa, 'the question is what is best to be done?'

'Is there any danger?' I urged, in great trepidation.

'I trust not, my dear,' answered the doctor. 'I don't see why you should not recover. I don't see why you should not begin *immediately* to get better. That is the point at which the sense of strangulation begins?'

'Yes,' I answered.

'And—recollect as well as you can—the same point was a kind of centre of that thrill which you described just now, like the current of a cold stream running against you?'

'It may have been; I think it was.'

'Ay, you see?' he added, turning to my father. 'Shall I say a word to Madame?'

'Certainly,' said my father.

He called Madame to him, and said:

'I find my young friend here far from well. It won't be of any great consequence, I hope; but it will be necessary that some steps be taken, which I will explain by-and-bye; but in the meantime, Madame, you will be so good as not to let Miss Laura be alone for one moment. That is the only direction I need give for the present. It is indispensable.'

'We may rely upon your kindness, Madame, I know,' added my father.

Madame satisfied him eagerly.

'And you, dear Laura, I know you will observe the doctor's direction.'

'I shall have to ask your opinion upon another patient, whose symptoms slightly resemble those of my daughter, that have just been detailed to you—very much milder in degree, but I believe quite of the same sort. She is a young lady—our guest; but as you say you will be passing this way again this evening, you can't do better than take your supper here, and you can then see her. She does not come down till the afternoon.'

'I thank you,' said the doctor. 'I shall be with you, then, at about seven this evening.'

And then they repeated their directions to me and to Madame, and with this parting charge my father left us, and walked out with the doctor; and I saw them pacing together up and down between the road and the moat, on the grassy platform in front of the castle, evidently absorbed in earnest conversation.

The doctor did not return. I saw him mount his horse there, take his leave, and ride away eastward through the forest.

Nearly at the same time I saw the man arrive from Dranfeld* with the letters, and dismount and hand the bag to my father.

In the meantime, Madame and I were both busy, lost in conjecture as to the reasons of the singular and earnest direction which the doctor and my father had concurred in imposing. Madame, as she afterwards told me, was afraid the doctor apprehended a sudden seizure, and that, without prompt assistance, I might either lose my life in a fit, or at least be seriously hurt. This interpretation did not strike me; and I fancied, perhaps luckily for my nerves, that the arrangement was prescribed simply to secure a companion, who would prevent my taking too much exercise, or eating unripe fruit, or doing any of the fifty foolish things to which young people are supposed to be prone.

About half-an-hour after my father came in—he had a letter in his hand—and said:

'This letter has been delayed; it is from General Spielsdorf. He might have been here yesterday, he may not come till to-morrow, or he may be here to-day.' He put the open letter into my hand; but he did not look pleased, as he used when a guest, especially one so much loved as the General, was coming. On the contrary, he looked as if he wished him at the bottom of the Red Sea. There was plainly something on his mind which he did not choose to divulge.

'Papa, darling, will you tell me this?' said I, suddenly laying my hand on his arm, and looking, I am sure, imploringly in his face.

'Perhaps,' he answered, smoothing my hair caressingly over my eyes.

'Does the doctor think me very ill?'

'No, dear; he thinks, if right steps are taken, you will be quite well again, at least, on the high road to a complete recovery, in a day or two,' he answered, a little drily. 'I wish our good friend, the General, had chosen any other time; that is, I wish you had been perfectly well to receive him.'

'But do tell me, papa,' I insisted, '*what* does he think is the matter with me?'

'Nothing; you must not plague me with questions,' he answered, with more irritation than I ever remember him to have displayed before; and seeing that I looked wounded, I suppose, he kissed me, and added, 'You shall know all about it in a day or two; that is, all that *I* know. In the meantime you are not to trouble your head about it.'

He turned and left the room, but came back before I had done wondering and puzzling over the oddity of all this; it was merely to say that he was going to Karnstein, and had ordered the carriage to be ready at twelve, and that I and Madame should accompany him; he was going to see the priest who lived near those picturesque grounds, upon business, and as Carmilla had never seen them, she could follow, when she came down, with Mademoiselle, who would bring materials for what you call a pic-nic, which might be laid for us in the ruined castle.

At twelve o'clock, accordingly, I was ready, and not long after my father, Madame, and I set out upon our projected drive.

Passing the drawbridge we turn to the right, and follow the road over the steep gothic bridge, westward, to reach the deserted village and ruined castle of Karnstein. No sylvan drive can be fancied prettier. The ground breaks into gentle hills and hollows, all clothed with beautiful wood, totally destitute of the comparative formality which artificial planting and early culture and pruning impart.

The irregularities of the ground often lead the road out of its course, and cause it to wind beautifully round the sides of broken hollows and the steeper sides of the hills, among varieties of ground almost inexhaustible.

Turning one of these points, we suddenly encountered the old General, riding towards us, attended by a mounted servant. His portmanteaus were following in a hired waggon, such as we term a cart.

The General dismounted as we pulled up, and, after the usual greetings, was easily persuaded to accept the vacant seat in the carriage, and send his horse on with his servant to the schloss.

CHAPTER X

BEREAVED

IT was about ten months since we had last seen him; but that time had sufficed to make an alteration of years in his appearance. He had grown thinner; something of gloom and anxiety had taken the place of that cordial serenity which used to characterize his features. His dark blue eyes, always penetrating, now gleamed with a sterner light from under his shaggy grey eyebrows. It was not such a change as grief alone usually induces, and angrier passions seemed to have had their share in bringing it about.

We had not long resumed our drive, when the General began to talk, with his usual soldierly directness, of the bereavement, as he termed it, which he had sustained in the death of his beloved niece and ward; and he then broke out in a tone of intense bitterness and fury, inveighing against the 'hellish arts' to which she had fallen a victim, and expressing, with more exasperation than piety, his wonder that Heaven should tolerate so monstrous an indulgence of the lusts and malignity of hell.

My father, who saw at once that something very extraordinary had befallen, asked him, if not too painful to him, to detail the circumstances which he thought justified the strong terms in which he expressed himself.

'I should tell you all with pleasure,' said the General, 'but you would not believe me.'

'Why should I not?' he asked.

'Because,' he answered testily, 'you believe in nothing but what consists with your own prejudices and illusions. I remember when I was like you, but I have learned better.'

'Try me,' said my father; 'I am not such a dogmatist as you suppose. Besides which, I very well know that you generally require proof for what you believe, and am, therefore, very strongly pre-disposed to respect your conclusions.'

'You are right in supposing that I have not been led lightly into a belief in the marvellous—for what I have experienced *is* marvellous—and I have been forced by extraordinary evidence to credit that which ran counter, diametrically, to all my theories. I have been made the dupe of a preternatural conspiracy.'

Notwithstanding his professions of confidence in the General's penetration, I saw my father, at this point, glance at the General, with, as I thought, a marked suspicion of his sanity.

The General did not see it, luckily. He was looking gloomily and curiously into the glades and vistas of the woods that were opening before us.

'You are going to the Ruins of Karnstein?' he said. 'Yes, it is a lucky coincidence; do you know I was going to ask you to bring me there to inspect them. I have a special object in exploring. There is a ruined chapel, aint there, with a great many tombs of that extinct family?'

'So there are—highly interesting,' said my father. 'I hope you are thinking of claiming the title and estates?'

My father said this gaily, but the General did not recollect the laugh, or even the smile, which courtesy exacts for a friend's joke; on the contrary, he looked grave and even fierce, ruminating on a matter that stirred his anger and horror.

'Something very different,' he said, gruffly. 'I mean to unearth some of those fine people. I hope, by God's blessing, to accomplish a pious sacrilege here, which will relieve our earth of certain monsters, and enable honest people to sleep in their beds without being assailed by murderers. I have strange things to tell you, my dear friend, such as I myself would have scouted* as incredible a few months since.'

My father looked at him again, but this time not with a glance of suspicion—with an eye, rather, of keen intelligence and alarm.

'The house of Karnstein,' he said, 'has been long extinct: a hundred years at least. My dear wife was maternally descended from the Karnsteins. But the name and title have long ceased to exist. The castle is a ruin; the very village is deserted; it is fifty years since the smoke of a chimney was seen there; not a roof left.'

'Quite true. I have heard a great deal about that since I last saw you; a great deal that will astonish you. But I had better relate everything in the order in which it occurred,' said the General. 'You saw my dear ward—my child, I may call her. No creature could have been more beautiful, and only three months ago none more blooming.'

'Yes, poor thing! when I saw her last she certainly was quite lovely,' said my father. 'I was grieved and shocked more than I can tell you, my dear friend; I knew what a blow it was to you.'

He took the General's hand, and they exchanged a kind pressure. Tears gathered in the old soldier's eyes. He did not seek to conceal them. He said:

'We have been very old friends; I knew you would feel for me, childless as I am. She had become an object of very near interest to me, and repaid my care by an affection that cheered my home and made my life happy. That is all gone. The years that remain to me on earth may not be very long; but by God's mercy I hope to accomplish a service to mankind before I die, and to subserve the vengeance of Heaven upon the fiends who have murdered my poor child in the spring of her hopes and beauty!'

'You said, just now, that you intended relating everything as it occurred,' said my father. 'Pray do; I assure you that it is not mere curiosity that prompts me.'

By this time we had reached the point at which the Drunstall road, by which the General had come, diverges from the road which we were travelling to Karnstein.

'How far is it to the ruins?' enquired the General, looking anxiously forward.

'About half a league,' answered my father. 'Pray let us hear the story you were so good as to promise.'

CHAPTER XI

THE STORY

'WITH all my heart,' said the General, with an effort; and after a short pause in which to arrange his subject, he commenced one of the strangest narratives I had ever heard.

'My dear child was looking forward with great pleasure to the visit you had been so good as to arrange for her to your charming daughter.' Here he made me a gallant but melancholy bow. 'In the meantime we had an invitation to my old friend the Count Carlsfeld, whose schloss is about six leagues to the other side of Karnstein. It was to attend the series of fêtes which, you remember, were given by him in honour of his illustrious visitor, the Grand Duke Charles.'*

'Yes; and very splendid, I believe, they were,' said my father.

'Princely! But then his hospitalities are quite regal. He has Aladdin's lamp.* The night from which my sorrow dates was devoted to a magnificent masquerade. The grounds were thrown open, the trees hung with coloured lamps. There was such a display of fireworks as Paris itself has never witnessed. And such music—music, you know, is my weakness—such ravishing music! The finest instrumental band, perhaps, in the world, and the finest singers who could be collected from all the great operas in Europe. As you wandered through these fantastically illuminated grounds, the moon-lighted château throwing a rosy light from its long rows of windows, you would suddenly hear these ravishing voices stealing from the silence of some grove, or rising from boats upon the lake. I felt myself, as I looked and listened, carried back into the romance and poetry of my early youth.

'When the fireworks were ended, and the ball beginning, we returned to the noble suite of rooms that were thrown open to the dancers. A masked ball, you know, is a beautiful sight; but so brilliant a spectacle of the kind I never saw before.

'It was a very aristocratic assembly. I was myself almost the only "nobody" present.

'My dear child was looking quite beautiful. She wore no mask. Her excitement and delight added an unspeakable charm to her features, always lovely. I remarked a young lady, dressed magnificently, but wearing a mask, who appeared to me to be observing my ward with extraordinary interest. I had seen her, earlier in the evening, in the great hall, and again, for a few minutes, walking near us, on the terrace under the castle windows, similarly employed. A lady, also masked, richly and gravely dressed, and with a stately air, like a person of rank, accompanied her as a chaperon. Had the young lady not worn a mask, I could, of course, have been much more certain upon the question whether she was really watching my poor darling. I am now well assured that she was.

'We were now in one of the *salons*. My poor dear child had been dancing, and was resting a little in one of the chairs near the door; I was standing near. The two ladies I have mentioned had approached, and the younger took the chair next my ward; while her companion stood beside me, and for a little time addressed herself, in a low tone, to her charge.

'Availing herself of the privilege of her mask, she turned to me, and in the tone of an old friend, and calling me by my name, opened a conversation with me, which piqued my curiosity a good deal. She referred to many scenes where she had met me—at Court, and at distinguished houses. She alluded to little incidents which I had long ceased to think of, but which, I found, had only lain in abeyance in my memory, for they instantly started into life at her touch.

'I became more and more curious to ascertain who she was, every moment. She parried my attempts to discover very adroitly and pleasantly. The knowledge she showed of many passages in my life seemed to me all but unaccountable; and she appeared to take a not unnatural pleasure in foiling my curiosity, and in seeing me flounder, in my eager perplexity, from one conjecture to another.

'In the meantime the young lady, whom her mother called by the odd name of Millarca, when she once or twice addressed her, had, with the same ease and grace, got into conversation with my ward.

'She introduced herself by saying that her mother was a very old acquaintance of mine. She spoke of the agreeable audacity which a mask rendered practicable; she talked like a friend; she admired her dress, and insinuated very prettily her admiration of her beauty. She amused her with laughing criticisms upon the people who crowded the ball-room, and laughed at my poor child's fun. She was very witty and lively when she pleased, and after a time they had grown very good friends, and the young stranger lowered her mask, displaying a remarkably beautiful face. I had never seen it before, neither had my dear child. But though it was new to us, the features were so engaging, as well as lovely, that it was impossible not to feel the attraction powerfully. My poor girl did so. I never saw anyone more taken with another at first sight, unless, indeed, it was the stranger herself, who seemed quite to have lost her heart to her.

'In the meantime, availing myself of the licence of a masquerade, I put not a few questions to the elder lady.

'"You have puzzled me utterly," I said, laughing. "Is that not enough? won't you, now, consent to stand on equal terms, and do me the kindness to remove your mask?"

'"Can any request be more unreasonable?" she replied. "Ask a lady to yield an advantage! Beside, how do you know you should recognize me? Years make changes."

'"As you see," I said, with a bow, and, I suppose, a rather melancholy little laugh.

'"As philosophers tell us," she said; "and how do you know that a sight of my face would help you?"

'"I should take chance for that," I answered. "It is vain trying to make yourself out an old woman; your figure betrays you."

'"Years, nevertheless, have passed since I saw you, rather since you saw me, for that is what I am considering. Millarca, there, is my daughter; I cannot then be young, even in the opinion of people whom time has taught to be indulgent, and I may not like to be compared with what you remember me. You have no mask to remove. You can offer me nothing in exchange."

'"My petition is to your pity, to remove it."

'"And mine to yours, to let it stay where it is," she replied.

'"Well, then, at least you will tell me whether you are French or German; you speak both languages so perfectly."

'"I don't think I shall tell you that, General; you intend a surprise, and are meditating the particular point of attack."

' "At all events, you won't deny this," I said, "that being honoured by your permission to converse, I ought to know how to address you. Shall I say Madame la Comtesse?"

'She laughed, and she would, no doubt, have met me with another evasion—if, indeed, I can treat any occurrence in an interview every circumstance of which was pre-arranged, as I now believe, with the profoundest cunning, as liable to be modified by accident.

' "As to that," she began; but she was interrupted, almost as she opened her lips, by a gentleman, dressed in black, who looked particularly elegant and distinguished, with this drawback, that his face was the most deadly pale I ever saw, except in death. He was in no masquerade—in the plain evening dress of a gentleman; and he said, without a smile, but with a courtly and unusually low bow:—

' "Will Madame the Countess permit me to say a very few words which may interest her?"

'The lady turned quickly to him, and touched her lip in token of silence; she then said to me, "Keep my place for me, General; I shall return when I have said a few words."

'And with this injunction, playfully given, she walked a little aside with the gentleman in black, and talked for some minutes, apparently very earnestly. They then walked away slowly together in the crowd, and I lost them for some minutes.

'I spent the interval in cudgelling my brains for a conjecture as to the identity of the lady who seemed to remember me so kindly, and I was thinking of turning about and joining in the conversation between my pretty ward and the Countess's daughter, and trying whether, by the time she returned, I might not have a surprise in store for her, by having her name, title, château, and estates at my fingers' ends. But at this moment she returned, accompanied by the pale man in black, who said:

' "I shall return and inform Madame la Comtesse when her carriage is at the door."

'He withdrew with a bow.

CHAPTER XII

A PETITION

' "THEN we are to lose Madame the Countess, but I hope only for a few hours," I said, with a low bow.

' "It may be that only, or it may be a few weeks. It was very unlucky his speaking to me just now as he did. Do you now know me?"

'I assured her I did not.

' "You shall know me," she said, "but not at present. We are older and better friends than, perhaps, you suspect. I cannot yet declare myself. I shall in three weeks pass your beautiful schloss, about which I have been making enquiries. I shall then look in upon you for an hour or two, and renew a friendship which I never think of without a thousand pleasant recollections. This moment a piece of news has reached me like a thunderbolt. I must set out now, and travel by a devious route, nearly a hundred miles, with all the dispatch I can possibly make. My perplexities multiply. I am only deterred by the compulsory reserve I practise as to my name from making a very singular request of you. My poor child has not quite recovered her strength. Her horse fell with her, at a hunt which she had ridden out to witness, her nerves have not yet recovered the shock, and our physician says that she must on no account exert herself for some time to come. We came here, in consequence, by very easy stages—hardly six leagues a day. I must now travel day and night, on a mission of life and death—a mission the critical and momentous nature of which I shall be able to explain to you when we meet, as I hope we shall, in a few weeks, without the necessity of any concealment."

'She went on to make her petition, and it was in the tone of a person from whom such a request amounted to conferring, rather than seeking a favour. This was only in manner, and, as it seemed, quite unconsciously. Than the terms in which it was expressed, nothing could be more deprecatory. It was simply that I would consent to take charge of her daughter during her absence.

'This was, all things considered, a strange, not to say, an audacious request. She in some sort disarmed me, by stating and admitting everything that could be urged against it, and throwing herself entirely upon my chivalry. At the same moment, by a fatality that seems to have predetermined all that happened, my poor child came to my side, and, in an undertone, besought me to invite her new friend, Millarca, to pay us a visit. She had just been sounding her, and thought, if her mamma would allow her, she would like it extremely.

'At another time I should have told her to wait a little, until, at least, we knew who they were. But I had not a moment to think in. The two ladies assailed me together, and I must confess the refined and beautiful face of the young lady, about which there was something extremely engaging, as well as the elegance and fire of high birth, determined me;

and, quite overpowered, I submitted, and undertook, too easily, the care of the young lady, whom her mother called Millarca.

'The Countess beckoned to her daughter, who listened with grave attention while she told her, in general terms, how suddenly and per-emptorily she had been summoned, and also of the arrangement she had made for her under my care, adding that I was one of her earliest and most valued friends.

'I made, of course, such speeches as the case seemed to call for, and found myself, on reflection, in a position which I did not half like.

'The gentleman in black returned, and very ceremoniously con-ducted the lady from the room.

'The demeanour of this gentleman was such as to impress me with the conviction that the Countess was a lady of very much more import-ance than her modest title alone might have led me to assume.

'Her last charge to me was that no attempt was to be made to learn more about her than I might have already guessed, until her return. Our distinguished host, whose guest she was, knew her reasons. "But here," she said, "neither I nor my daughter could safely remain for more than a day. I removed my mask imprudently for a moment, about an hour ago, and, too late, I fancied you saw me. So I resolved to seek an opportunity of talking a little to you. Had I found that you *had* seen me, I should have thrown myself on your high sense of honour to keep my secret for some weeks. As it is, I am satisfied that you did not see me; but if you now *suspect*, or, on reflection, *should* suspect, who I am, I commit myself, in like manner, entirely to your honour. My daughter will observe the same secresy, and I well know that you will, from time to time, remind her, lest she should thoughtlessly disclose it."

'She whispered a few words to her daughter, kissed her hurriedly twice, and went away, accompanied by the pale gentleman in black, and disappeared in the crowd.'

'"In the next room," said Millarca, "there is a window that looks upon the hall-door. I should like to see the last of mamma, and to kiss my hand to her."

'We assented, of course, and accompanied her to the window. We looked out, and saw a handsome old-fashioned carriage, with a troop of couriers and footmen. We saw the slim figure of the pale gentleman in black, as he held a thick velvet cloak, and placed it about her shoulders and threw the hood over her head. She nodded to him, and just touched his hand with hers. He bowed low repeatedly as the door closed, and the carriage began to move.

'"She is gone," said Millarca, with a sigh.

' "She is gone," I repeated to myself, for the first time—in the hurried moments that had elapsed since my consent—reflecting upon the folly of my act.

' "She did not look up," said the young lady, plaintively.

' "The Countess had taken off her mask, perhaps, and did not care to show her face," I said; "and she could not know that you were in the window."

'She sighed, and looked in my face. She was so beautiful that I relented. I was sorry I had for a moment repented of my hospitality, and I determined to make her amends for the unavowed churlishness of my reception.

'The young lady, replacing her mask, joined my ward in persuading me to return to the grounds, where the concert was soon to be renewed. We did so, and walked up and down the terrace that lies under the castle windows. Millarca became very intimate with us, and amused us with lively descriptions and stories of most of the great people whom we saw upon the terrace. I liked her more and more every minute. Her gossip, without being ill-natured, was extremely diverting to me, who had been so long out of the great world. I thought what life she would give to our sometimes lonely evenings at home.

'This ball was not over until the morning sun had almost reached the horizon. It pleased the Grand Duke to dance till then, so loyal people could not go away, or think of bed.

'We had just got through a crowded saloon, when my ward asked me what had become of Millarca. I thought she had been by her side, and she fancied she was by mine. The fact was, we had lost her.

'All my efforts to find her were vain. I feared that she had mistaken, in the confusion of a momentary separation from us, other people for her new friends, and had, possibly, pursued and lost them in the extensive grounds which were thrown open to us.

'Now, in its full force, I recognized a new folly in my having undertaken the charge of a young lady without so much as knowing her name; and fettered as I was by promises, of the reasons for imposing which I knew nothing, I could not even point my inquiries by saying that the missing young lady was the daughter of the Countess who had taken her departure a few hours before.

'Morning broke. It was clear daylight before I gave up my search. It was not till near two o'clock next day that we heard anything of my missing charge.

'At about that time a servant knocked at my niece's door, to say that he had been earnestly requested by a young lady, who appeared to be in great distress, to make out where she could find the General Baron Spielsdorf and the young lady his daughter, in whose charge she had been left by her mother.

'There could be no doubt, notwithstanding the slight inaccuracy, that our young friend had turned up; and so she had. Would to heaven we had lost her!

'She told my poor child a story to account for her having failed to recover us for so long. Very late, she said, she had got to the house-keeper's bedroom in despair of finding us, and had then fallen into a deep sleep which, long as it was, had hardly sufficed to recruit her strength after the fatigues of the ball.

'That day Millarca came home with us. I was only too happy, after all, to have secured so charming a companion for my dear girl.

CHAPTER XIII

THE WOOD-MAN

'THERE soon, however, appeared some drawbacks. In the first place, Millarca complained of extreme languor—the weakness that remained after her late illness—and she never emerged from her room till the afternoon was pretty far advanced. In the next place, it was accidentally discovered, although she always locked her door on the inside, and never disturbed the key from its place till she admitted the maid to assist at her toilet, that she was undoubtedly sometimes absent from her room in the very early morning, and at various times later in the day, before she wished it to be understood that she was stirring. She was repeatedly seen from the windows of the schloss, in the first faint grey of the morning, walking through the trees, in an easterly direction, and looking like a person in a trance. This convinced me that she walked in her sleep. But this hypothesis did not solve the puzzle. How did she pass out from her room, leaving the door locked on the inside? How did she escape from the house without unbarring door or window?

'In the midst of my perplexities, an anxiety of a far more urgent kind presented itself.

'My dear child began to lose her looks and health, and that in a manner so mysterious, and even horrible, that I became thoroughly frightened.

'She was at first visited by appalling dreams; then, as she fancied, by a spectre, sometimes resembling Millarca, sometimes in the shape of a beast, indistinctly seen, walking round the foot of her bed, from side to side. Lastly came sensations. One, not unpleasant, but very peculiar, she said, resembled the flow of an icy stream against her breast. At a later time, she felt something like a pair of large needles pierce her, a little below the throat, with a very sharp pain. A few nights after, followed a gradual and convulsive sense of strangulation; then came unconsciousness.'

I could hear distinctly every word the kind old General was saying, because by this time we were driving upon the short grass that spreads on either side of the road as you approach the roofless village which had not shown the smoke of a chimney for more than half a century.

You may guess how strangely I felt as I heard my own symptoms so exactly described in those which had been experienced by the poor girl who, but for the catastrophe which followed, would have been at that moment a visitor at my father's château. You may suppose, also, how I felt as I heard him detail habits and mysterious peculiarities which were, in fact, those of our beautiful guest, Carmilla!

A vista opened in the forest; we were on a sudden under the chimneys and gables of the ruined village, and the towers and battlements of the dismantled castle, round which gigantic trees are grouped, overhung us from a slight eminence.

In a frightened dream I got down from the carriage, and in silence, for we had each abundant matter for thinking; we soon mounted the ascent, and were among the spacious chambers, winding stairs, and dark corridors of the castle.

'And this was once the palatial residence of the Karnsteins!' said the old General at length, as from a great window he looked out across the village, and saw the wide, undulating expanse of forest. 'It was a bad family, and here its blood-stained annals were written,' he continued. 'It is hard that they should, after death, continue to plague the human race with their atrocious lusts. That is the chapel of the Karnsteins, down there.'

He pointed down to the grey walls of the gothic building, partly visible through the foliage, a little way down the steep. 'And I hear the axe of a woodman,' he added, 'busy among the trees that surround it; he possibly may give us the information of which I am in search, and point out the grave of Mircalla, Countess of Karnstein. These rustics preserve the local traditions of great families, whose stories die out among the rich and titled so soon as the families themselves become extinct.'

'We have a portrait, at home, of Mircalla, the Countess Karnstein; should you like to see it?' asked my father.

'Time enough, dear friend,' replied the General. 'I believe that I have seen the original; and one motive which has led me to you earlier than I at first intended, was to explore the chapel which we are now approaching.'

'What! see the Countess Mircalla,' exclaimed my father; 'why, she has been dead more than a century!'

'Not so dead as you fancy, I am told,' answered the General.

'I confess, General, you puzzle me utterly,' replied my father, looking at him, I fancied, for a moment with a return of the suspicion I detected before. But although there was anger and detestation, at times, in the old General's manner, there was nothing flighty.

'There remains to me,' he said, as we passed under the heavy arch of the gothic church—for its dimensions would have justified its being so styled—'but one object which can interest me during the few years that remain to me on earth, and that is to wreak on her the vengeance which, I thank God, may still be accomplished by a mortal arm.'

'What vengeance can you mean?' asked my father, in increasing amazement.

'I mean, to decapitate the monster,' he answered, with a fierce flush, and a stamp that echoed mournfully through the hollow ruin, and his clenched hand was at the same moment raised, as if it grasped the handle of an axe, while he shook it ferociously in the air.

'What?' exclaimed my father, more than ever bewildered.

'To strike her head off.'

'Cut her head off!'

'Aye, with a hatchet, with a spade, or with anything that can cleave through her murderous throat. You shall hear,' he answered, trembling with rage. And hurrying forward he said:

'That beam will answer for a seat; your dear child is fatigued; let her be seated, and I will, in a few sentences, close my dreadful story.'

The squared block of wood, which lay on the grass grown pavement of the chapel, formed a bench on which I was very glad to seat myself, and in the meantime the General called to the woodman, who had been removing some boughs which leaned upon the old walls; and, axe in hand, the hardy old fellow stood before us.

He could not tell us anything of these monuments; but there was an old man, he said, a ranger of this forest, at present sojourning in the house of the priest, about two miles away, who could point out every monument of the old Karnstein family; and, for a trifle, he undertook to bring him back with him, if we would lend him one of our horses, in little more than half an hour.

'Have you been long employed about this forest?' asked my father of the old man.

'I have been a woodman here,' he answered in his *patois*, 'under the forester, all my days; so has my father before me, and so on, as many generations as I can count up. I could show you the very house, in the village here, in which my ancestors lived.'

'How came the village to be deserted?' asked the General.

'It was troubled by *revenants*,* Sir; several were tracked to their graves, there detected by the usual tests, and extinguished in the usual way, by decapitation, by the stake, and by burning; but not until many of the villagers were killed.

'But after all these proceedings according to law,' he continued—'so many graves opened, and so many vampires deprived of their horrible animation—the village was not relieved. But a Moravian nobleman, who happened to be travelling this way, heard how matters were, and being skilled—as many people are in his country—in such affairs, he offered to deliver the village from its tormentor. He did so thus: There being a bright moon that night, he ascended, shortly after sunset, the towers of the chapel here, from whence he could distinctly see the churchyard beneath him; you can see it from that window. From this point he watched until he saw the vampire come out of his grave, and place near it the linen clothes in which he had been folded, and then glide away towards the village to plague its inhabitants.

'The stranger, having seen all this, came down from the steeple, took the linen wrappings of the vampire, and carried them up to the top of the tower, which he again mounted. When the vampire returned from his prowlings and missed his clothes, he cried furiously to the Moravian, whom he saw at the summit of the tower, and who, in reply, beckoned him to ascend and take them. Whereupon the vampire, accepting his invitation, began to climb the steeple, and so soon as he had reached the battlements, the Moravian, with a stroke of his sword, clove his skull in twain, hurling him down to the churchyard, whither, descending by the winding stairs, the stranger followed and cut his head off, and next day delivered it and the body to the villagers, who duly impaled and burnt them.*

'This Moravian nobleman had authority from the then head of the family to remove the tomb of Mircalla, Countess Karnstein, which he did effectually, so that in a little while its site was quite forgotten.'

'Can you point out where it stood?' asked the General, eagerly.

The forester shook his head and smiled.

'Not a soul living could tell you that now,' he said; 'besides, they say her body was removed; but no one is sure of that either.'

Having thus spoken, as time pressed, he dropped his axe and departed, leaving us to hear the remainder of the General's strange story.

CHAPTER XIV
THE MEETING

'MY beloved child,' he resumed, 'was now growing rapidly worse. The physician who attended her had failed to produce the slightest impression upon her disease, for such I then supposed it to be. He saw my alarm, and suggested a consultation. I called in an abler physician, from Gratz. Several days elapsed before he arrived. He was a good and pious, as well as a learned man. Having seen my poor ward together, they withdrew to my library to confer and discuss. I, from the adjoining room, where I awaited their summons, heard these two gentlemen's voices raised in something sharper than a strictly philosophical discussion. I knocked at the door and entered. I found the old physician from Gratz maintaining his theory. His rival was combatting it with undisguised ridicule, accompanied with bursts of laughter. This unseemly manifestation subsided and the altercation ended on my entrance.

' "Sir," said my first physician, "my learned brother seems to think that you want a conjuror, and not a doctor."

' "Pardon me," said the old physician from Gratz, looking displeased, "I shall state my own view of the case in my own way another time. I grieve, Monsieur le General, that by my skill and science I can be of no use. Before I go I shall do myself the honour to suggest something to you."

'He seemed thoughtful, and sat down at a table and began to write. Profoundly disappointed, I made my bow, and as I turned to go the other doctor pointed over his shoulder to his companion who was writing, and then, with a shrug, significantly touched his forehead.

'This consultation, then, left me precisely where I was. I walked out into the grounds, all but distracted. The doctor from Gratz, in ten or fifteen minutes, overtook me. He apologized for having followed me, but said that he could not conscientiously take his leave without a few words more. He told me that he could not be mistaken; no natural disease exhibited the same symptoms; and that death was already very near. There remained, however, a day, or possibly two, of life. If the fatal seizure were at once arrested, with great care and skill her strength might possibly return. But all hung now upon the confines of the irrevocable. One more assault might extinguish the last spark of vitality which is, every moment, ready to die.

' "And what is the nature of the seizure you speak of?" I entreated.

' "I have stated all fully in this note, which I place in your hands upon the distinct condition that you send for the nearest clergyman, and open my letter in his presence, and on no account read it till he is with you; you would despise it else, and it is a matter of life and death. Should the priest fail you, then, indeed, you may read it."

'He asked me, before taking his leave finally, whether I would wish to see a man curiously learned upon the very subject, which, after I had read his letter, would probably interest me above all others, and he urged me earnestly to invite him to visit him there; and so took his leave.

'The ecclesiastic was absent, and I read the letter by myself. At another time, or in another case, it might have excited my ridicule. But into what quackeries will not people rush for a last chance, where all accustomed means have failed, and the life of a beloved object is at stake?

'Nothing, you will say, could be more absurd than the learned man's letter. It was monstrous enough to have consigned him to a madhouse. He said that the patient was suffering from the visits of a vampire! The punctures which she described as having occurred near the throat, were, he insisted, the insertion of those two long, thin, and sharp teeth which, it is well known, are peculiar to vampires; and there could be no doubt, he added, as to the well-defined presence of the small livid mark which all concurred in describing as that induced by the demon's lips, and every symptom described by the sufferer was in exact conformity with those recorded in every case of a similar visitation.

'Being myself wholly sceptical as to the existence of any such portent as the vampire, the supernatural theory of the good doctor furnished, in my opinion, but another instance of learning and intelligence oddly associated with some one hallucination. I was so miserable, however, that, rather than try nothing, I acted upon the instructions of the letter.

'I concealed myself in the dark dressing-room, that opened upon the poor patient's room, in which a candle was burning, and watched there till she was fast asleep. I stood at the door, peeping through the small crevice, my sword laid on the table beside me, as my directions prescribed, until, a little after one, I saw a large black object, very ill-defined, crawl, as it seemed to me, over the foot of the bed, and swiftly spread itself up to the poor girl's throat, where it swelled, in a moment, into a great, palpitating mass. For a few moments I had stood petrified. I now sprang forward, with my sword in my hand. The black creature suddenly contracted toward the foot of the bed, glided over it, and, standing on the floor about a yard below the foot of the bed, with a glare of skulking ferocity and horror fixed on me, I saw Millarca. Speculating I know not what, I struck at her instantly with my sword; but I saw her standing near the door, unscathed. Horrified, I pursued, and struck again. She was gone; and my sword flew to shivers against the door.

'I can't describe to you all that passed on that horrible night. The whole house was up and stirring. The spectre Millarca was gone. But her victim was sinking fast, and before the morning dawned, she died.'

The old General was agitated. We did not speak to him. My father walked to some little distance, and began reading the inscriptions on the tombstones; and thus occupied, he strolled into the door of a side-chapel to prosecute his researches. The General leaned against the wall, dried his eyes, and sighed heavily. I was relieved on hearing the voices of Carmilla and Madame, who were at that moment approaching. The voices died away.

In this solitude, having just listened to so strange a story, connected, as it was, with the great and titled dead, whose monuments were mouldering among the dust and ivy round us, and every incident of which bore so awfully upon my own mysterious case—in this haunted spot, darkened by the towering foliage that rose on every side, dense and high above its noiseless walls—a horror began to steal over me, and my heart sank as I thought that my friends were, after all, not about to enter and disturb this triste* and ominous scene.

The old General's eyes were fixed on the ground, as he leaned with his hand upon the basement of a shattered monument.

Under a narrow, arched doorway, surmounted by one of those demoniacal grotesques in which the cynical and ghastly fancy of old Gothic carving delights, I saw very gladly the beautiful face and figure of Carmilla enter the shadowy chapel.

I was just about to rise and speak, and nodded smiling, in answer to her peculiarly engaging smile; when with a cry, the old man by my side caught up the woodman's hatchet, and started forward. On seeing him a brutalized change came over her features. It was an instantaneous and horrible transformation, as she made a crouching step backwards. Before I could utter a scream, he struck at her with all his force, but she dived under his blow, and unscathed, caught him in her tiny grasp by the wrist. He struggled for a moment to release his arm, but his hand opened, the axe fell to the ground, and the girl was gone.

He staggered against the wall. His grey hair stood upon his head, and a moisture shone over his face, as if he were at the point of death.

The frightful scene had passed in a moment. The first thing I recollect after, is Madame standing before me, and impatiently repeating again and again, the question, 'Where is Mademoiselle Carmilla?'

I answered at length, 'I don't know—I can't tell—she went there', and I pointed to the door through which Madame had just entered; 'only a minute or two since'.

'But I have been standing there, in the passage, ever since Mademoiselle Carmilla entered; and she did not return.'

She then began to call 'Carmilla', through every door and passage and from the windows, but no answer came.

'She called herself Carmilla?' asked the General, still agitated.

'Carmilla, yes,' I answered.

'Aye,' he said; 'that is Millarca. That is the same person who long ago was called Mircalla, Countess Karnstein. Depart from this accursed ground, my poor child, as quickly as you can. Drive to the clergyman's house, and stay there till we come. Begone! May you never behold Carmilla more; you will not find her here.'

CHAPTER XV
ORDEAL AND EXECUTION

As he spoke one of the strangest looking men I ever beheld, entered the chapel at the door through which Carmilla had made her entrance and her exit. He was tall, narrow-chested, stooping, with high shoulders, and dressed in black. His face was brown and dried in with deep furrows; he wore an oddly-shaped hat with a broad leaf.* His hair, long and grizzled, hung on his shoulders. He wore a pair of gold spectacles, and walked slowly, with an odd shambling gait, with his face sometimes turned up to the sky, and sometimes bowed down toward the ground, seemed to wear a perpetual smile; his long thin arms were swinging, and his lank hands, in old black gloves ever so much too wide for them, waving and gesticulating in utter abstraction.

'The very man!' exclaimed the General, advancing with manifest delight. 'My dear Baron, how happy I am to see you, I had no hope of meeting you so soon.' He signed to my father, who had by this time returned, and leading the fantastic old gentleman, whom he called the Baron to meet him. He introduced him formally, and they at once entered into earnest conversation. The stranger took a roll of paper from his pocket, and spread it on the worn surface of a tomb that stood by. He had a pencil-case in his fingers, with which he traced imaginary lines from point to point on the paper, which from their often glancing from it, together, at certain points of the building, I concluded to be a plan of the chapel. He accompanied, what I may term, his lecture, with occasional readings from a dirty little book, whose yellow leaves were closely written over.

They sauntered together down the side aisle, opposite to the spot where I was standing, conversing as they went; then they begun measuring distances by paces, and finally they all stood together, facing a piece of the side-wall, which they began to examine with great minuteness; pulling off the ivy that clung over it, and rapping the plaster with the ends of their sticks, scraping here, and knocking there. At length they ascertained the existence of a broad marble tablet, with letters carved in relief upon it.

With the assistance of the woodman, who soon returned, a monumental inscription, and carved escutcheon, were disclosed. They proved to be those of the long lost monument of Mircalla, Countess Karnstein.

The old General, though not I fear given to the praying mood, raised his hands and eyes to heaven, in mute thanksgiving for some moments.

'To-morrow,' I heard him say; 'the commissioner will be here, and the Inquisition will be held according to law.'

Then turning to the old man with the gold spectacles, whom I have described, he shook him warmly by both hands and said:

'Baron, how can I thank you? How can we all thank you? You will have delivered this region from a plague that has scourged its inhabitants for more than a century. The horrible enemy, thank God, is at last tracked.'

My father led the stranger aside, and the General followed. I knew that he had led them out of hearing, that he might relate my case, and I saw them glance often quickly at me, as the discussion proceeded.

My father came to me, kissed me again and again, and leading me from the chapel, said:

'It is time to return, but before we go home, we must add to our party the good priest, who lives but a little way from this; and persuade him to accompany us to the schloss.'

In this quest we were successful: and I was glad, being unspeakably fatigued when we reached home. But my satisfaction was changed to dismay, on discovering that there were no tidings of Carmilla. Of the scene that had occurred in the ruined chapel, no explanation was offered to me, and it was clear that it was a secret which my father for the present determined to keep from me.

The sinister absence of Carmilla made the remembrance of the scene more horrible to me. The arrangements for that night were singular. Two servants, and Madame were to sit up in my room that night; and the ecclesiastic with my father kept watch in the adjoining dressing-room.

The priest had performed certain solemn rites that night, the purport of which I did not understand any more than I comprehended the reason of this extraordinary precaution taken for my safety during sleep.

I saw all clearly a few days later.

The disappearance of Carmilla was followed by the discontinuance of my nightly sufferings.

You have heard, no doubt, of the appalling superstition that prevails in upper and lower Styria, in Moravia, Silisia, in Turkish Servia, in Poland, even in Russia; the superstition, so we must call it, of the Vampire.

If human testimony, taken with every care and solemnity, judicially, before commissions innumerable, each consisting of many members, all chosen for integrity and intelligence, and constituting reports more voluminous perhaps than exist upon any one other class of cases, is worth anything, it is difficult to deny, or even to doubt the existence of such a phenomenon as the Vampire.

For my part I have heard no theory by which to explain what I myself have witnessed and experienced, other than that supplied by the ancient and well-attested belief of the country.

The next day the formal proceedings took place in the Chapel of Karnstein. The grave of the Countess Mircalla was opened; and the General and my father recognized each his perfidious and beautiful guest, in the face now disclosed to view. The features, though a hundred and fifty years had passed since her funeral, were tinted with the warmth of life. Her eyes were open; no cadaverous smell exhaled from the coffin. The two medical men, one officially present, the other on the part of the promoter of the enquiry, attested the marvellous fact, that there was a faint but appreciable respiration, and a corresponding action of the heart. The limbs were perfectly flexible, the flesh elastic; and the leaden coffin floated with blood, in which to a depth of seven inches, the body lay immersed.* Here then, were all the admitted signs and proofs of vampirism. The body, therefore, in accordance with the ancient practice, was raised, and a sharp stake driven through the heart of the vampire, who uttered a piercing shriek at the moment, in all respects such as might escape from a living person in the last agony.

Then the head was struck off, and a torrent of blood flowed from the severed neck. The body and head were next placed on a pile of wood, and reduced to ashes, which were thrown upon the river and borne away, and that territory has never since been plagued by the visits of a vampire.

My father has a copy of the report of the Imperial Commission, with the signatures of all who were present at these proceedings, attached in verification of the statement. It is from this official paper that I have summarized my account of this last shocking scene.

CHAPTER XVI

CONCLUSION

I WRITE all this you suppose with composure. But far from it; I cannot think of it without agitation. Nothing but your earnest desire so repeatedly expressed, could have induced me to sit down to a task that has unstrung my nerves for months to come, and reinduced a shadow of the unspeakable horror which years after my deliverance continued to make my days and nights dreadful, and solitude insupportably terrific.

Let me add a word or two about that quaint Baron Vordenburg,* to whose curious lore we were indebted for the discovery of the Countess Mircalla's grave.

He had taken up his abode in Gratz, where, living upon a mere pittance, which was all that remained to him of the once princely estates of his family, in Upper Styria, he devoted himself to the minute and laborious investigation of the marvellously authenticated tradition of Vampirism. He had at his finger's ends all the great and little works upon the subject. 'Magia Posthuma', 'Phlegon de Mirabilibus', 'Augustinus de curâ pro Mortuis', 'Philosophicae et Christianae Cogitationes de Vampiris', by John Christofer Herenberg;* and a thousand others, among which I remember only a few of those which he lent to my father. He had a voluminous digest of all the judicial cases, from which he had extracted a system of principles that appear to govern—some always, and others occasionally only—the condition of the vampire. I may mention, in passing, that the deadly pallor attributed to that sort of *revenants*, is a mere melodramatic fiction. They present, in the grave, and when they show themselves in human society, the appearance of healthy life. When disclosed to light in their coffins, they exhibit all the symptoms that are enumerated as those which proved the vampire-life of the long-dead Countess Karnstein. How they escape from their graves and return to them for certain hours every day, without displacing the clay or leaving any trace of disturbance in the state of the coffin or the cerements, has always been admitted to be utterly inexplicable. The amphibious existence of the vampire is sustained by daily renewed slumber in the grave. Its horrible lust for living blood supplies the vigour of its waking existence. The vampire is prone to be fascinated with an engrossing vehemence, resembling the passion of love, by particular persons. In pursuit of these it will exercise inexhaustible patience and stratagem, for access to a particular object may be obstructed in a hundred ways. It will never desist until it has satiated its passion, and drained the very life of its coveted victim. But it will, in these cases, husband and protract its murderous enjoyment with the refinement of an epicure, and heighten it by the gradual approaches of an artful courtship. In these cases it seems to yearn for something like sympathy and consent. In ordinary ones it goes direct to its object, overpowers with violence, and strangles and exhausts often at a single feast.

The vampire is, apparently, subject, in certain situations, to special conditions. In the particular instance of which I have given you a relation, Mircalla seemed to be limited to a name which, if not her real one, should at least reproduce, without the omission or addition of a single letter, those, as we say, anagrammatically, which compose it. *Carmilla* did this; so did *Millarca*.

My father related to the Baron Vordenburg, who remained with us for two or three weeks after the expulsion of Carmilla, the story about the Moravian nobleman and the vampire at Karnstein churchyard, and then he asked the Baron how he had discovered the exact position of the long-concealed tomb of the Countess Millarca? The Baron's grotesque features puckered up into a mysterious smile; he looked down, still smiling on his worn spectacle-case, and fumbled with it. Then looking up, he said:

'I have many journals, and other papers, written by that remarkable man; the most curious among them is one treating of the visit of which you speak, to Karnstein. The tradition, of course, discolours and distorts a little. He might have been termed a Moravian nobleman, for he had changed his abode to that territory, and was, beside, a noble. But he was, in truth, a native of Upper Styria. It is enough to say that in very early youth he had been a passionate and favoured lover of the beautiful Mircalla, Countess Karnstein. Her early death plunged him into inconsolable grief. It is the nature of vampires to increase and multiply, but according to an ascertained and ghostly law.

'Assume, at starting, a territory perfectly free from that pest. How does it begin, and how does it multiply itself? I will tell you. A person, more or less wicked, puts an end to himself. A suicide, under certain circumstances, becomes a vampire. That spectre visits living people in their slumbers; *they* die, and almost invariably, in the grave, develope into vampires. This happened in the case of the beautiful Mircalla, who was haunted by one of those demons. My ancestor, Vordenburg, whose title I still bear, soon discovered this, and in the course of the studies to which he devoted himself, learned a great deal more.

'Among other things, he concluded that suspicion of vampirism would probably fall, sooner or later, upon the dead Countess, who in life had been his idol. He conceived a horror, be she what she might, of her remains being profaned by the outrage of a posthumous execution. He has left a curious paper to prove that the vampire, on its expulsion from its amphibious existence, is projected into a far more horrible life; and he resolved to save his once beloved Mircalla from this. He adopted the stratagem of a journey here, a pretended removal of her remains, and a real obliteration of her monument. When age had stolen upon him, and from the vale of years he looked back on the scenes he was leaving, he considered, in a different spirit, what he had done, and a horror took possession of him. He made the tracings and notes which have guided me to the very spot, and drew up a confession of the deception that he had practised. If he had intended any further action in this matter, death prevented him; and the hand of remote descendant has, too late for many, directed the pursuit to the lair of the beast.'

We talked a little more, and among other things he said was this:

'One sign of the vampire is the power of the hand. The slender hand of Mircalla closed like a vice of steel on the General's wrist when he raised the hatchet to strike. But its power is not confined to its grasp; it leaves a numbness in the limb it seizes, which is slowly, if ever, recovered from.'

The following spring my father took me a tour through Italy. We remained away for more than a year. It was long before the terror of recent events subsided; and to this hour the image of Carmilla returns to memory with ambiguous alternations—sometimes the playful, languid, beautiful girl; sometimes the writhing fiend I saw in the ruined church; and often from a reverie I have started, fancying I heard the light step of Carmilla at the drawing-room door.

LAURA SILVER BELL

IN the five Northumbrian counties you will scarcely find so bleak, ugly, and yet, in a savage way, so picturesque a moor as Dardale Moss. The moor itself spreads north, south, east, and west, a great undulating sea of black peat and heath.

What we may term its shores are wooded wildly with birch, hazel, and dwarf-oak. No towering mountains surround it, but here and there you have a rocky knoll rising among the trees, and many a wooded promontory of the same pretty, because utterly wild, forest, running out into its dark level.

Habitations are thinly scattered in this barren territory, and a full mile away from the meanest was the stone cottage of Mother Carke.

Let not my southern reader who associates ideas of comfort with the term 'cottage' mistake. This thing is built of shingle, with low walls. Its thatch is hollow; the peat-smoke curls stingily from its stunted chimney. It is worthy of its savage surroundings.

The primitive neighbours remark that no rowan-tree grows near, nor holly, nor bracken, and no horse-shoe is nailed on the door.*

Not far from the birches and hazels that straggle about the rude wall of the little enclosure, on the contrary, they say, you may discover the broom and the rag-wort, in which witches mysteriously delight. But this is perhaps a scandal.

Mall Carke was for many a year the *sage femme** of this wild domain. She has renounced practice, however, for some years; and now, under the rose,* she dabbles, it is thought, in the black art, in which she has always been secretly skilled, tells fortunes, practises charms, and in popular esteem is little better than a witch.

Mother Carke has been away to the town of Willarden, to sell knit stockings, and is returning to her rude dwelling by Dardale Moss. To her right, as far away as the eye can reach, the moor stretches. The narrow track she has followed here tops a gentle upland, and at her left a sort of jungle of dwarf-oak and brushwood approaches its edge. The sun is sinking blood-red in the west. His disk has touched the broad black level of the moor, and his parting beams glare athwart the gaunt figure of the old beldame, as she strides homeward stick in hand, and bring into relief the folds of her mantle, which gleam like the draperies of a bronze image in the light of a fire. For a few moments this light floods the air—tree, gorse, rock, and bracken glare; and then it is out, and gray twilight over everything.

All is still and sombre. At this hour the simple traffic of the thinly-peopled country is over, and nothing can be more solitary.

From this jungle, nevertheless, through which the mists of evening are already creeping, she sees a gigantic man approaching her.

In that poor and primitive country robbery is a crime unknown. She, therefore, has no fears for her pound of tea, and pint of gin, and sixteen shillings in silver which she is bringing home in her pocket. But there is something that would have frighted another woman about this man.

He is gaunt, sombre, bony, dirty, and dressed in a black suit which a beggar would hardly care to pick out of the dust.

This ill-looking man nodded to her as he stepped on the road.

'I don't know you,' she said.

He nodded again.

'I never sid ye neyawheere,' she exclaimed sternly.

'Fine evening, Mother Carke,' he says, and holds his snuff-box toward her.

She widened the distance between them by a step or so, and said again sternly and pale,

'I hev nowt to say to thee, whoe'er thou beest.'

'You know Laura Silver Bell?'

'That's a byneyam;* the lass's neyam is Laura Lew,' she answered, looking straight before her.

'One name's as good as another for one that was never christened, mother.'

'How know ye that?' she asked grimly; for it is a received opinion in that part of the world that the fairies have power over those who have never been baptized.

The stranger turned on her a malignant smile.

'There is a young lord in love with her,' the stranger says, 'and I'm that lord. Have her at your house to-morrow night at eight o'clock, and you must stick cross pins through the candle, as you have done for many a one before, to bring her lover thither by ten, and her fortune's made. And take this for your trouble.'

He extended his long finger and thumb toward her, with a guinea temptingly displayed.

'I have nowt to do wi' thee. I nivver sid thee afoore. Git thee awa'! I earned nea goold o' thee, and I'll tak' nane. Awa' wi' thee, or I'll find ane that will mak' thee!'

The old woman had stopped, and was quivering in every limb as she thus spoke.

He looked very angry. Sulkily he turned away at her words, and strode slowly toward the wood from which he had come; and as he approached it, he seemed to her to grow taller and taller, and stalked into it as high as a tree.

'I conceited there would come something o't,' she said to herself. 'Farmer Lew must git it done nesht Sunda'. The a'ad awpy!'

Old Farmer Lew was one of that sect* who insist that baptism shall be but once administered, and not until the Christian candidate had attained to adult years. The girl had indeed for some time been of an age not only, according to this theory, to be baptized, but if need be to be married.

Her story was a sad little romance. A lady some seventeen years before had come down and paid Farmer Lew for two rooms in his house. She told him that her husband would follow her in a fortnight, and that he was in the mean time delayed by business in Liverpool.

In ten days after her arrival her baby was born, Mall Carke acting as *sage femme* on the occasion; and on the evening of that day the poor young mother died. No husband came; no wedding-ring, they said, was on her finger. About fifty pounds was found in her desk, which Farmer Lew, who was a kind old fellow and had lost his two children, put in bank for the little girl, and resolved to keep her until a rightful owner should step forward to claim her.

They found half-a-dozen love-letters signed 'Francis', and calling the dead woman 'Laura'.

So Farmer Lew called the little girl Laura; and her *sobriquet* of 'Silver Bell'* was derived from a tiny silver bell, once gilt, which was found among her poor mother's little treasures after her death, and which the child wore on a ribbon round her neck.

Thus, being very pretty and merry, she grew up as a North-country farmer's daughter; and the old man, as she needed more looking after, grew older and less able to take care of her; so she was, in fact, very nearly her own mistress, and did pretty much in all things as she liked.

Old Mall Carke, by some caprice for which no one could account, cherished an affection for the girl, who saw her often, and paid her many a small fee in exchange for secret indications of the future.

It was too late when Mother Carke reached her home to look for a visit from Laura Silver Bell that day.

About three o'clock next afternoon, Mother Carke was sitting knitting, with her glasses on, outside her door on the stone bench, when she saw the pretty girl mount lightly to the top of the stile at her left under the birch, against the silver stem of which she leaned her slender hand, and called,

'Mall, Mall! Mother Carke, are ye alane all by yersel'?'

'Ay, Laura lass, we can be clooas enoo, if ye want a word wi' me,' says the old woman, rising, with a mysterious nod, and beckoning her stiffly with her long fingers.

The girl was, assuredly, pretty enough for a 'lord' to fall in love with. Only look at her. A profusion of brown rippling hair, parted low in the middle of her forehead, almost touched her eyebrows, and made the pretty oval of her face, by the breadth of that rich line, more marked. What a pretty little nose! what scarlet lips, and large, dark, long-fringed eyes!

Her face is transparently tinged with those clear Murillo tints* which appear in deeper dyes on her wrists and the backs of her hands. These are the beautiful gipsy-tints with which the sun dyes young skins so richly.

The old woman eyes all this, and her pretty figure, so round and slender, and her shapely little feet, cased in the thick shoes that can't hide their comely proportions, as she stands on the top of the stile. But it is with a dark and saturnine aspect.

'Come, lass, what stand ye for atoppa t' wall, whar folk may chance to see thee? I hev a thing to tell thee, lass.'

She beckoned her again.

'An' I hev a thing to tell *thee*, Mall.'

'Come hidder,' said the old woman peremptorily.

'But ye munna gie me the creepin's' (make me tremble). 'I winna look again into the glass o' water, mind ye.'

The old woman smiled grimly, and changed her tone.

'Now, hunny, git tha down, and let ma see thy canny feyace,'* and she beckoned her again.

Laura Silver Bell did get down, and stepped lightly toward the door of the old woman's dwelling.

'Tak this,' said the girl, unfolding a piece of bacon from her apron, 'and I hev a silver sixpence to gie thee, when I'm gaen away heyam.'

They entered the dark kitchen of the cottage, and the old woman stood by the door, lest their conference should be lighted on by surprise.

'Afoore ye begin,' said Mother Carke (I soften her patois), 'I mun tell ye there's ill folk watchin' ye. What's auld Farmer Lew about, he doesna get t' sir' (the clergyman) 'to baptize thee? If he lets Sunda' next pass,

I'm afeared ye'll never be sprinkled nor signed wi' cross, while there's a sky aboon us.'

'Agoy!'* exclaims the girl, 'who's lookin' after me?'

'A big black fella, as high as the kipples,* came out o' the wood near Deadman's Grike,* just after the sun gaed down yester e'en; I knew weel what he was, for his feet ne'er touched the road while he made as if he walked beside me. And he wanted to gie me snuff first, and I wouldna hev that; and then he offered me a gowden guinea, but I was no sic awpy,* and to bring you here to-night, and cross the candle wi' pins, to call your lover in. And he said he's a great lord, and in luve wi' thee.'

'And you refused him?'

'Well for thee I did, lass,' says Mother Carke.

'Why, it's every word true!' cries the girl vehemently, starting to her feet, for she had seated herself on the great oak chest.

'True, lass? Come, say what ye mean,' demanded Mall Carke, with a dark and searching gaze.

'Last night I was coming heyam from the wake, wi' auld farmer Dykes and his wife and his daughter Nell, and when we came to the stile, I bid them good-night, and we parted.'

'And ye came by the path alone in the night-time, did ye?' exclaimed old Mall Carke sternly.

'I wasna afeared, I don't know why; the path heyam leads down by the wa'as o' auld Hawarth Castle.'*

'I knaa it weel, and a dowly path it is; ye'll keep indoors o' nights for a while, or ye'll rue it. What saw ye?'

'No freetin,* mother; nowt I was feared on.'

'Ye heard a voice callin' yer neyame?'

'I heard nowt that was dow, but the hullyhoo in the auld castle wa's,' answered the pretty girl. 'I heard nor sid nowt that's dow, but mickle that's conny* and gladsome. I heard singin' and laughin' a long way off, I consaited; and I stopped a bit to listen. Then I walked on a step or two, and there, sure enough, in the Pie-Mag field, under the castle wa's, not twenty steps away, I sid a grand company; silks and satins, and men wi' velvet coats, wi' gowd-lace striped over them, and ladies wi' necklaces that would dazzle ye, and fans as big as griddles; and powdered footmen, like what the shirra* hed behind his coach, only these was ten times as grand.'

'It was full moon last night,' said the old woman.

'Sa bright 'twould blind ye to look at it,' said the girl.

'Never an ill sight but the deaul finds a light,' quoth the old woman. 'There's a rinnin brook thar—you were at this side, and they at that; did they try to mak ye cross over?'

'Agoy! didn't they? Nowt but civility and kindness, though. But ye mun let me tell it my own way. They was talkin' and laughin', and eatin', and drinkin' out o' long glasses and goud cups, seated on the grass, and music was playin'; and I keekin' behind a bush at all the grand doin's; and up they gits to dance; and says a tall fella I didna see afoore, "Ye mun step across, and dance wi' a young lord that's faan in luv wi' thee, and that's mysel'"; and sure enow I keeked at him under my lashes, and a conny lad he is, to my teyaste, though he be dressed in black, wi' sword and sash, velvet twice as fine as they sells in the shop at Gouden Friars; and keekin' at me again fra the corners o' his een. And the same fella telt me he was mad in luv wi' me, and his fadder was there, and his sister, and they came all the way from Catstean Castle to see me that night; and that's t'other side o' Gouden Friars.'

'Come, lass, yer no mafflin;* tell me true. What was he like? Was his feyace grimed wi' sut? a tall fella wi' wide shouthers, and lukt like an ill-thing, wi' black clothes amaist in rags?'

'His feyace was long, but weel-faured, and darker nor a gipsy; and his clothes were black and grand, and made o' velvet, and he said he was the young lord himsel'; and he lukt like it.'

'That will be the same fella I sid at Deadman's Grike,' said Mall Carke, with an anxious frown.

'Hoot, mudder! how cud that be?' cried the lass, with a toss of her pretty head and a smile of scorn.

But the fortune-teller made no answer, and the girl went on with her story.

'When they began to dance,' continued Laura Silver Bell, 'he urged me again, but I wudna step o'er; 'twas partly pride, coz I wasna dressed fine enough, and partly contrairiness, or something, but gaa I wudna, not a fut. No but I more nor half wished it a' the time.'

'Weel for thee thou dudstna cross the brook.'

'Hoity-toity, why not?'

'Keep at heyame after nightfall, and don't ye be walking by yersel' by daylight or any light lang lone-some ways, till after ye're baptized,' said Mall Carke.

'I'm like to be married first.'

'Tak care *that* marriage won't hang i' the bell-ropes,'* said Mother Carke.

'Leave me alane for that. The young lord said he was maist daft wi' luv o' me. He wanted to gie me a conny ring wi' a beautiful stone in it. But, drat it, I was sic an awpy I wudna tak it, and he a young lord!'

'Lord, indeed! are ye daft or dreamin'? Those fine folk, what were they? I'll tell ye. Dobies* and fairies; and if ye don't du as yer bid, they'll tak ye, and ye'll never git out o' their hands again while grass grows,' said the old woman grimly.

'Od wite it!'* replies the girl impatiently, 'who's daft or dreamin' noo? I'd a bin dead wi' fear, if 'twas any such thing. It cudna be; all was sa luvesome, and bonny, and shaply.'

'Weel, and what do ye want o' me, lass?' asked the old woman sharply.

'I want to know—here's t' sixpence—what I sud du,' said the young lass. ''Twud be a pity to lose such a marrow,* hey?'

'Say yer prayers, lass; *I* can't help ye,' says the old woman darkly. 'If ye gaa wi' *the* people, ye'll never come back. Ye munna talk wi' them, nor eat wi' them, nor drink wi' them, nor tak a pin's-worth by way o' gift fra them—mark weel what I say—or ye're *lost*!'

The girl looked down, plainly much vexed.

The old woman stared at her with a mysterious frown steadily, for a few seconds.

'Tell me, lass, and tell me true, are ye in luve wi' that lad?'

'What for sud I?' said the girl with a careless toss of her head, and blushing up to her very temples.

'I see how it is,' said the old woman, with a groan, and repeated the words, sadly thinking; and walked out of the door a step or two, and looked jealously round. 'The lass is witched, the lass is witched!'

'Did ye see him since?' asked Mother Carke, returning.

The girl was still embarrassed; and now she spoke in a lower tone, and seemed subdued.

'I thought I sid him as I came here, walkin' beside me among the trees; but I consait it was only the trees themsels that lukt like rinnin' one behind another, as I walked on.'

'I can tell thee nowt, lass, but what I telt ye afoore,' answered the old woman peremptorily. 'Get ye heyame, and don't delay on the way; and say yer prayers as ye gaa; and let none but good thoughts come nigh ye; and put nayer foot autside the door-steyan again till ye gaa to be chris-tened; and get that done a Sunda' next.'

And with this charge, given with grizzly earnestness, she saw her over the stile, and stood upon it watching her retreat, until the trees quite hid her and her path from view.

The sky grew cloudy and thunderous, and the air darkened rapidly, as the girl, a little frightened by Mall Carke's view of the case, walked homeward by the lonely path among the trees.

A black cat, which had walked close by her—for these creatures sometimes take a ramble in search of their prey among the woods and thickets—crept from under the hollow of an oak, and was again with her. It seemed to her to grow bigger and bigger as the darkness deepened, and its green eyes glared as large as halfpennies in her affrighted vision as the thunder came booming along the heights from the Willarden-road.

She tried to drive it away; but it growled and hissed awfully, and set up its back as if it would spring at her, and finally it skipped up into a tree, where they grew thickest at each side of her path, and accompanied her, high over head, hopping from bough to bough as if meditating a pounce upon her shoulders. Her fancy being full of strange thoughts, she was frightened, and she fancied that it was haunting her steps, and destined to undergo some hideous transformation, the moment she ceased to guard her path with prayers.

She was frightened for a while after she got home. The dark looks of Mother Carke were always before her eyes, and a secret dread prevented her passing the threshold of her home again that night.

Next day it was different. She had got rid of the awe with which Mother Carke had inspired her. She could not get the tall dark-featured lord, in the black velvet dress, out of her head. He had 'taken her fancy'; she was growing to love him. She could think of nothing else.

Bessie Hennock, a neighbour's daughter, came to see her that day, and proposed a walk toward the ruins of Hawarth Castle, to gather 'blaebirries'. So off the two girls went together.

In the thicket, along the slopes near the ivied walls of Hawarth Castle, the companions began to fill their baskets. Hours passed. The sun was sinking near the west, and Laura Silver Bell had not come home.

Over the hatch of the farm-house door the maids leant ever and anon with outstretched necks, watching for a sign of the girl's return, and wondering, as the shadows lengthened, what had become of her.

At last, just as the rosy sunset gilding began to overspread the landscape, Bessie Hennock, weeping into her apron, made her appearance without her companion.

Her account of their adventures was curious.

I will relate the substance of it more connectedly than her agitation would allow her to give it, and without the disguise of the rude Northumbrian dialect.

The girl said, that, as they got along together among the brambles that grow beside the brook that bounds the Pie-Mag field, she on a sudden saw a very tall big-boned man, with an ill-favoured smirched face, and dressed in worn and rusty black, standing at the other side of the little stream. She was frightened; and while looking at this dirty, wicked, starved figure, Laura Silver Bell touched her, gazing at the same tall scarecrow, but with a countenance full of confusion and even rapture. She was peeping through the bush behind which she stood, and with a sigh she said:

'Is na that a conny lad? Agoy! See his bonny velvet clothes, his sword and sash; that's a lord, I can tell ye; and weel I know who he follows, who he luves, and who he'll wed.'

Bessie Hennock thought her companion daft.

'See how luvesome he luks!' whispered Laura.

Bessie looked again, and saw him gazing at her companion with a malignant smile, and at the same time he beckoned her to approach.

'Darrat ta!* gaa not near him! he'll wring thy neck!' gasped Bessie in great fear, as she saw Laura step forward, with a look of beautiful bash-fulness and joy.

She took the hand he stretched across the stream, more for love of the hand than any need of help, and in a moment was across and by his side, and his long arm about her waist.

'Fares te weel, Bessie, I'm gain my ways,' she called, leaning her head to his shoulder; 'and tell gud Fadder Lew I'm gain my ways to be happy, and may be, at lang last, I'll see him again.'

And with a farewell wave of her hand, she went away with her dismal partner; and Laura Silver Bell was never more seen at home, or among the 'coppies' and 'wickwoods', the bonny fields and bosky hollows, by Dardale Moss.

Bessie Hennock followed them for a time.

She crossed the brook, and though they seemed to move slowly enough, she was obliged to run to keep them in view; and she all the time cried to her continually, 'Come back, come back, bonnie Laurie!' until, getting over a bank, she was met by a white-faced old man, and so frightened was she, that she thought she fainted out-right. At all events, she did not come to herself until the birds were singing their vespers in the amber light of sunset, and the day was over.

No trace of the direction of the girl's flight was ever discovered. Weeks and months passed, and more than a year.

At the end of that time, one of Mall Carke's goats died, as she sus-pected, by the envious practices of a rival witch who lived at the far end of Dardale Moss.

All alone in her stone cabin the old woman had prepared her charm to ascertain the author of her misfortune.

The heart of the dead animal,* stuck all over with pins, was burnt in the fire; the windows, doors, and every other aperture of the house being first carefully stopped. After the heart, thus prepared with suitable incantations, is consumed in the fire, the first person who comes to the door or passes it by is the offending magician.

Mother Carke completed these lonely rites at dead of night. It was a dark night, with the glimmer of the stars only, and a melancholy night-wind was soughing through the scattered woods that spread around.

After a long and dead silence, there came a heavy thump at the door, and a deep voice called her by name.

She was startled, for she expected no man's voice; and peeping from the window, she saw, in the dim light, a coach and four horses, with gold-laced footmen, and coachman in wig and cocked hat, turned out as if for a state occasion.

She unbarred the door; and a tall gentleman, dressed in black, waiting at the threshold, entreated her, as the only *sage femme* within reach, to come in the coach and attend Lady Lairdale, who was about to give birth to a baby, promising her handsome payment.

Lady Lairdale! She had never heard of her.

'How far away is it?'

'Twelve miles on the old road to Golden Friars.'

Her avarice is roused,* and she steps into the coach. The footman claps-to the door; the glass jingles with the sound of a laugh. The tall dark-faced gentleman in black is seated opposite; they are driving at a furious pace; they have turned out of the road into a narrower one, dark with thicker and loftier forest than she was accustomed to. She grows anxious; for she knows every road and by-path in the country round, and she has never seen this one.

He encourages her. The moon has risen above the edge of the horizon, and she sees a noble old castle. Its summit of tower, watch-tower and battlement, glimmers faintly in the moonlight. This is their destination.

She feels on a sudden all but over-powered by sleep; but although she nods, she is quite conscious of the continued motion, which has become even rougher.

She makes an effort, and rouses herself. What has become of the coach, the castle, the servants? Nothing but the strange forest remains the same.

She is jolting along on a rude hurdle, seated on rushes, and a tall, big-boned man, in rags, sits in front, kicking with his heel the ill-favoured beast that pulls them along, every bone of which sticks out, and holding the halter which serves for reins. They stop at the door of a miserable building of loose stone, with a thatch so sunk and rotten, that the roof-tree and couples protrude in crooked corners, like the bones of the wretched horse, with enormous head and ears, that dragged them to the door.

The long gaunt man gets down, his sinister face grimed like his hands.

It was the same grimy giant who had accosted her on the lonely road near Deadman's Grike. But she feels that she 'must go through with it' now, and she follows him into the house.

Two rushlights were burning in the large and miserable room, and on a coarse ragged bed lay a woman groaning piteously.

'That's Lady Lairdale,' says the gaunt dark man, who then began to stride up and down the room, rolling his head, stamping furiously, and thumping one hand on the palm of the other, and talking and laughing in the corners, where there was no one visible to hear or to answer.

Old Mall Carke recognized in the faded half-starved creature who lay on the bed, as dark now and grimy as the man, and looking as if she had never in her life washed hands or face, the once blithe and pretty Laura Lew.

The hideous being who was her mate continued in the same odd fluctuations of fury, grief, and merriment; and whenever she uttered a groan, he parodied it with another, as Mother Carke thought, in saturnine derision.

At length he strode into another room, and banged the door after him.

In due time the poor woman's pains were over, and a daughter was born.

Such an imp! with long pointed ears, flat nose, and enormous restless eyes and mouth. It instantly began to yell and talk in some unknown language, at the noise of which the father looked into the room, and told the *sage femme* that she should not go unrewarded.

The sick woman seized the moment of his absence to say in the ear of Mall Carke:

'If ye had not been at ill work to-night, he could not hev fetched ye. Tak no more now than your rightful fee, or he'll keep ye here.'

At this moment he returned with a bag of gold and silver coins, which he emptied on the table, and told her to help herself.

She took four shillings, which was her primitive fee, neither more nor less; and all his urgency could not prevail with her to take a farthing more. He looked so terrible at her refusal, that she rushed out of the house.

He ran after her.

'You'll take your money with you,' he roared, snatching up the bag, still half full, and flung it after her.

It lighted on her shoulder; and partly from the blow, partly from terror, she fell to the ground; and when she came to herself, it was morning, and she was lying across her own door-stone.

It is said that she never more told fortune or practised spell. And though all that happened sixty years ago and more, Laura Silver Bell, wise folk think, is still living, and will so continue till the day of doom among the fairies.

EXPLANATORY NOTES

ABBREVIATIONS

DUM   *Dublin University Magazine*

Harris   *The History and Antiquities of the City of Dublin* by Walter Harris (Dublin, 1766)

KJB   King James Bible

Lewis   *A Topographical Dictionary of Ireland* by Samuel Lewis (London, 1837)

Mackay   *Extraordinary Popular Delusions and the Madness of Crowds* by Charles Mackay (London, 1856)

Madden   *The United Irishmen, Their Lives and Times* by Richard R. Madden (London, 1842)

MRJ   Prologue, *Ghost Stories and Tales of Mystery*, ed. M. R. James (London, 1923)

OED   *Oxford English Dictionary*

Peacock   *A Glossary of the Dialect of the Hundred of Lonsdale, North and South of the Sands, in the County of Lancaster* (etc.) by Robert Backhouse Peacock (London, 1869)

TLF   Thomas Le Fanu; usually in reference to the sale catalogue of the family library: *The Catalogue of the Library of the Very Rev. Thomas P. Le Fanu, L.L.D.* (n.p., 1845); it should be stressed, however, that many books mentioned throughout these Notes *are* listed in the catalogue, though not glossed as such; explicit reference to the catalogue is selective.

Tracy   Introduction, *In A Glass Darkly* (Oxford, 1993)

WLF   *Seventy Years of Irish Life* by William Le Fanu (London, 1893)

STRANGE EVENT IN THE LIFE OF SCHALKEN THE PAINTER

The original version of this story, which is reproduced here, appeared in the *DUM* in May 1839. Significantly revised, and retitled simply 'Schalken the Painter', it was included in Le Fanu's first collection of shorter fiction, *Ghost Stories and Tales of Mystery* (Dublin, 1851).

It has been suggested that one source for the story may have been the anonymous Dutch tale 'Jan Schalken's Three Wishes' (1820), though the connection would seem slight beyond the shared use of the name 'Schalken', and, perhaps, the earlier story's description of a mysterious stranger of whom 'little could be distinguished either of his face or figure, as he wore a large dark cloak, which he had contrived to pull over his head after the fashion of a cowl' (*Gothic Tales of Terror*, vol. 2, ed. Peter Haining (Baltimore, 1972), 317). Le Fanu's tale does, however, owe a clear debt to the 'demon lover' motif to be found in e.g. Thomas Percy's *Reliques of Ancient English Poetry* (1765) and

Gottfried August Bürger's *Lenore* (1773), though unlike the doomed women
in such earlier ballad-narratives, Rose Velderkaust has no prior relationship
with her unearthly lover. An interesting review of 'Italian Folk Lore', published in the *DUM* immediately after Le Fanu's sale of the magazine, connects
the tale with Irish writer Gerald Griffin's earlier, equally chilling story 'The
Brown Man' (*Tales of the Munster Festivals*, 1827), and both with a broader
vein of legend and folklore: 'This tale [the Neapolitan folk story 'Cannetella']
has many counterparts in the fictions of all nations. The prevailing idea, that
of a helpless wife in the power of a cruel and relentless master, of supernatural
powers—pervades the story of "Schalkin [*sic*] the Painter," the "Little Grey
Man," [*sic*] by Gerald Griffin, and many other weird tales of their kind' (*DUM*
(Feb. 1869), 188).

3 *the late Francis Purcell*: the stories posthumously collected as *The Purcell
   Papers* (London, 1880) are linked by the conceit of a wandering, story-
   collecting Catholic priest named Purcell (see Introduction); 'Schalken' is
   unique among the Purcell stories in its non-Irish setting.

   What had I to do with Schalken: the Dutch painter Godfried Schalcken
   (1643–1706) studied under both Samuel van Hoogstraten (1627–78) and
   Gerrit Dou (1613–75), themselves both pupils of Rembrandt van Rijn
   (1606–69). As a pupil of Dou ('Gerard Douw' in Le Fanu's story),
   Schalcken joined the ranks of the so-called *fijnschilders* ('fine-painters')
   centred in Leiden, genre painters specializing in the meticulously detailed
   scenes from everyday life which found favour with the commercial classes
   of seventeenth-century Holland. Possible sources of information for both
   Schalcken and Dou in Le Fanu's story include Michael Bryan's *Biographical and Critical Dictionary of Painters and Engravers* (1813–16) and
   John Smith's *Catalogue Raisonné of the Works of the Most Eminent Dutch,
   Flemish, and French Painters* (1829–37). Smith describes the typical
   Schalcken painting as 'represent[ing] fancy or familiar subjects, composed
   of two or three figures, and . . . more frequently illumed by the light of
   a candle or a lamp, than by that of day, as he had made the former his
   exclusive study, and had attained therein that degree of eminence, to
   which his pictures of daylight effects by no means entitle him' (*Biographical
   and Critical Dictionary*, vol. iv (London, 1833), 266).

   whose father had served King William . . . during the Irish campaigns: reference to the Williamite War between the forces of the Catholic James II and
   those of the Protestant William III, ending in final defeat for the Jacobite
   forces in Limerick, in 1691. The painting's provenance thus serves as the
   connecting link between Ireland and this tale of Golden Age Holland. Also
   of interest here, perhaps, is the fact that Godfried Schalcken painted
   William's portrait while resident in England in the 1690s; according to
   Horace Walpole, 'as the piece was to be by candle-light, he gave his majesty the candle to hold, till the tallow ran down upon his fingers'—damn-
   ing evidence, for Walpole, of the painter's 'ill-breeding' (*Anecdotes of
   Painting in England* (London, 1871), 297).

the distribution of light and shade: reference to chiaroscuro (literally 'light-dark'), a characteristic effect in the paintings of Rembrandt, as well as those of Dou and Schalcken; according to Michael Bryan, 'The chief merit of Schalcken consists in the neatness of his finishing, and the perfect intelligence of his chiaro-scuro' (*Dictionary of Painters and Engravers*, vol. v (London, 1905), 32).

a man equipped in the old fashion: in the 1851 version of 'Schalken', 'a man dressed in the old Flemish fashion'.

4 *unlicked*: crude, unpolished. Both 'unlick'd' and 'rugged' are mated by Shakespeare with 'bear' (rather than 'boor').

6 *a perspiring and pot-bellied St Anthony*: both the torments and temptations of Saint Anthony (or Antony) the Great (*c.* AD 251–356) have been depicted by generations of artists. In the context of this story, the presence of the demonic is obviously significant here, as is, perhaps, the association of Anthony with the theme of temptation—one fifteenth-century Sienese painting, for instance, showed him resisting (as Le Fanu's Douw cannot) the lure of a heap of gold. The young painter's depiction of the ascetic Anthony as 'pot-bellied' (and possibly drunk) indicates his lack of skill, and perhaps the worldliness of seventeenth-century Leiden.

inexpressibles: i.e. trousers (humorous euphemism).

7 *beaver*: even before the establishment of the Dutch Empire and the global networks of trade which sent Canadian beaver pelts across the Atlantic by the shipload, hats made from the under-fur of the animal had been associated with the Netherlands: Chaucer's Merchant wears 'a Flaundryssh bever hat'. Possibly there is a subtle intimation of spectrality here as well, by way of Shakespeare: Hamlet's ghostly father wears 'his beaver up' (meaning, here, a helmet's visor), disclosing his face.

Minheer Vanderhausen, of Rotterdam: 'Mynheer' (spelled 'Mynher' in the otherwise identical *Purcell Papers* text) is a respectful form of address, equivalent to 'Mr' or 'Sir', depending on context. Rotterdam in the 1660s (presumably when the tale is set) was a major merchant city and shipping port, as well as one of the bases of the Dutch East India Company (founded 1602). It may be worth noting as well that 'Mynheer Vander*deck*en' was the name given to the legendary undead mariner in numerous works of popular British fiction and drama during this period, e.g. Edward Fitzball's *The Flying Dutchman* (1826), Thomas Peckett Prest's *The Flying Dutchman; Or the Demon Ship* (1839), and Frederick Marryat's *The Phantom Ship* (1839).

8 *the Stadhouse*: Leiden's *Stadhuis* (Town Hall), whose Dutch Renaissance façade was designed in 1597 by master builder Lieven de Key (1560–1627).

a horologe: the word can refer to any timepiece; Le Fanu's description suggests one of the spherical watches, often of enamelled gold, which were about to be rendered obsolete by the horological innovations of former University of Leiden student Christiaan Huygens (1629–95).

9 *Jewish goldsmith*: this character is anachronistic as well as stereotypical; there were very few Jews in Leiden in the seventeenth century, and these were (a) chiefly Sephardic, not Ashkenazi (as the cry of 'Mein Gott!' would seem to imply), and (b) associated with the University.

10 *rix-dollars*: from *Rijcks-daalder* (very approximately, 'coin of the realm'), a unit equivalent to 2.5 Dutch guilders. For context, the average annual household income during the period was approximately 500 guilders; Dou's canvases, which were in extremely high demand, sold for as much as 1,000 guilders.

the church of St Lawrence: the medieval St Laurenskerk; there is today a painting of its interior by Dutch painter Antonie de Lorme (*c*.1610–73) in the National Gallery of Ireland, which faces Merrion Square.

14 *metallic medicines*: the pharmaceutical use of metals was particularly championed by Swiss physician and alchemist Paracelsus (Theophrastus von Hohenheim, *c*.1493–1541). It is tempting to pile horror upon horror here, to imagine Vanderhausen as not merely an ambulatory corpse but a syphilitic one (quicksilver, or mercury, being the preferred treatment for 'the French disease'). Mercury poisoning, however, causes a pink or red discoloration of skin (assuming pharmacological verisimilitude to be a consideration here); a 'bluish leaden hue' might be induced by the ingestion of toxic quantities of e.g. bismuth, silver, or lead. Or the description may indeed be only metaphorical, and Vanderhausen's 'livid[ity]' (as it is called in the tale's horrifying final tableau) is simply and literally that of a corpse.

15 *the wealth of the States*: i.e. the federated States of Holland.

Boom-quay: according to an early nineteenth-century English guidebook, 'The first part of Rotterdam, seen from the Maese, is the Boom Quay, or the Quay covered with Trees. This is the grandest as well as the most agreeable street in Rotterdam' (*The Traveller's Complete Guide through Belgium & Holland* (London, 1817), 229).

16 *a small party of men . . . standing in the centre of the road*: Le Fanu's tableau is perhaps meant to suggest the genre of group portraiture in Dutch art, e.g. Rembrandt's *The Night Watch* (1642).

19 *the dead and the living cannot be one*: cf. the epigraph Le Fanu added to the 1851 text, a modified quotation from Job 9:32–4: 'For he is not a man as I am that we should come together; neither is there any that might lay his hand upon us both. Let him, therefore, take his rod away from me, and let not his fear terrify me', a passage similarly concerning the incommensurability of two realms or orders of being (in the original context, human and divine).

polemic: i.e. polemicist, one given to disputation.

THE WATCHER

Of the five long tales contained in Le Fanu's 1872 collection *In a Glass Darkly*, four—'Green Tea', 'Mr Justice Harbottle' (originally titled 'The

Haunted House in Westminster'), 'The Room in the Dragon Volant', and 'Carmilla'— were written between 1869 and 1872. The outlier is the second story, 'The Familiar', which is a revised version of 'The Watcher' (first published in the *DUM* in November 1847, and subsequently appearing in the 1851 collection *Ghost Stories and Tales of Mystery*). An earlier generation of editors and critics was content to treat these two versions of the tale as identical except for the name, and the new prologue added to each story in *In a Glass Darkly* (other than 'Green Tea') to facilitate the conceit that they were all leaves taken from the case-book of the same 'metaphysical physician', e.g. the entry in Everett Bleiler's magisterial 1983 *Guide to Supernatural Fiction*: 'THE FAMILIAR. Alternate title for THE WATCHER, but set in terms of Dr Hesselius's practice' (p. 303). More recent scholarly editions of Le Fanu's shorter fiction, by contrast, have been far more careful in treating 'The Watcher' and 'The Familiar' as representing two distinct, and substantively different, versions or visions of the story that Jim Rockhill rightly calls 'a landmark in the development of the weird tale' (Introduction, *Schalken the Painter and Others* (Ashcroft, 2002), p. xxvi). Ash-Tree Press's three-volume edition of Le Fanu's supernatural fiction, edited by Rockhill, in fact includes both 'The Watcher' *and* 'The Familiar', while helpfully summarizing the salient differences between the two:

> Aside from the change in title, the author removed the epigraph, substituted a new frame introducing Dr Martin Hesselius, changed or removed the names of some of the characters, broke up all of the long paragraphs—sometimes into as many as five separate paragraphs—substituted the occasional word or phrase for ones more precise, and substantially reworked certain passages—such as the encounter with the man calling attention to Barton's apparent illness—in order to smooth the transitions between first-person and third-person narratives. (Introduction, *Mr Justice Harbottle and Others* (Ashcroft, 2005), p. xxix)

Similarly, existing critical editions of *In a Glass Darkly* provide notes throughout 'The Familiar' to indicate (for example) where its nomenclatural blanks and gaps ('Lady L——', 'Doctor R——', and so on) had, in 'The Watcher', been occupied by proper names.

Yet the case, it turns out, is even more complicated than this, since an examination of the story as originally published in the *DUM* shows that there are in fact not two, but *three* distinct variants of the story, and that the periodical version is in some respects *closer to* 'The Familiar' than either of these is to the 1851 (book) version of 'The Watcher'. Most conspicuously, the 1847 version and 'The Familiar' *both* elide surnames, and the same ones; only the 'middle' text supplies them. In other words, in reworking his narrative for *In a Glass Darkly*, Le Fanu did not 'remove' the names of his characters so much as he restored the story's original elisions (if this is not too headache-inducing a way to think about it). There is, moreover, no epigraph at all in the 1847 version, as well as at least one elision which is unique to it (see note to p. 32). It is this original version of the story which appears here.

23 [*Title*]: 'The Watcher' was followed in the pages of the *DUM* in January
   1848 by 'The Fatal Bride', a non-supernatural Gothic tale bearing the
   subtitle, 'Being a Second Contribution from the Reminiscences of
   a Bachelor'. For the 1851 revision of 'The Watcher', the original heading
   was replaced with an epigraph adapted from Job 7:14, 7:15, and 7:19: 'How
   long wilt thou not depart from me? Thou terrifiest me through visions: so
   that my soul chooseth strangling rather than my life.' Finally, for *In a Glass
   Darkly*, the following prologue was added to the tale now titled 'The
   Familiar' (it should be remembered the prologue to 'Green Tea' (see p. 96)
   comes first, introducing Hesselius and the book's premise):

   Out of about two hundred and thirty cases, more or less nearly akin to
   that I have entitled 'Green Tea', I select the following, which I call 'The
   Familiar'.

   To this MS., Doctor Hesselius, has, after his wont, attached some
   sheets of letter-paper, on which are written, in his hand nearly as compact as print, his own remarks upon the case. He says—

   'In point of conscience, no more unexceptionable narrator, than the
   venerable Irish Clergyman who has given me this paper, on Mr. Barton's
   case, could have been chosen. The statement is, however, medically
   imperfect. The report of an intelligent physician, who had marked its
   progress, and attended the patient, from its earlier stages to its close,
   would have supplied what is wanting to enable me to pronounce with
   confidence. I should have been acquainted with Mr Barton's probable
   hereditary predispositions; I should have known, possibly, by very early
   indications, something of a remoter origin of the disease than can now
   be ascertained.

   'In a rough way, we may reduce all similar cases to three distinct
   classes. They are founded on the primary distinction between the subjective and the objective. Of those whose senses are alleged to be subject
   to supernatural impressions—some are simply visionaries, and propa-
   gate the illusions of which they complain, from diseased brain or nerves.
   Others are, unquestionably, infested by, as we term them, spiritual agencies, exterior to themselves. Others, again, owe their sufferings to a mixed
   condition. The interior sense, it is true, is opened; but it has been and
   continues open by the action of disease. This form of disease may, in one
   sense, be compared to the loss of the scarf-skin, and a consequent exposure of surfaces for whose excessive sensitiveness, nature has provided
   a muffling. The loss of this covering is attended by an habitual impassi-
   bility, by influences against which we were intended to be guarded. But
   in the case of the brain, and the nerves immediately connected with its
   functions and its sensuous impressions, the cerebral circulation undergoes periodically that vibratory disturbance which, I believe, I have satisfactorily examined and demonstrated, in my MS. Essay, A. 17. This
   vibratory disturbance differs, as I there prove, essentially from the
   congestive disturbance, the phenomena of which are examined in A. 19.
   It is, when excessive, invariably accompanied by *illusions*.

'Had I seen Mr Barton, and examined him upon the points, in his case, which need elucidation, I should have without difficulty referred those phenomena to their proper disease. My diagnosis is now, necessarily, conjectural.'

Thus writes Doctor Hesselius; and adds a great deal which is of interest only to a scientific physician.

The Narrative of the Rev. Thomas Herbert, which furnishes all that is known of the case, will be found in the chapters that follow. (*In a Glass Darkly* (London, 1872), 55–7)

the American war: the American Revolution (1775–83).

24 *one of the then fashionable streets in the south side of the town*: probably in or near Le Fanu's own Merrion Square, south of the River Liffey and near Trinity College (Tracy, 323).

free-thinker: one who maintains independence of belief with respect to religious matters. Jonathan Swift wrote of 'the atheists, libertines, despisers of religion in general, that is to say, all those who usually pass under the name of freethinkers' (*Works of Swift*, vol. 2 (London, 1841), 210); by taking pains to establish that Barton is no libertine, Le Fanu seems to be already highlighting his unbelief.

the Dowager Lady L——: 'the Dowager Lady Rochdale' in *Ghost Stories and Tales of Mystery*; 'the Dowager Lady L——' in *In a Glass Darkly*.

reigning toast: a celebrated beauty.

25 *a handsome mansion at the north side of Dublin*: likely, as Robert Tracy suggests, in the new and fashionable Mountjoy Square, planned by Luke Gardiner, first Viscount Mountjoy, along with Gardiner Street, the probable site of Barton's eventful 'nocturnal walks'.

a line of streets which had as yet been merely laid out: in 1757, with the establishment of the Wide Streets Commission, a massive urban development project was launched, one which would radically reshape old Dublin.

the evidences of revelation: the phrase, also used later by the 'celebrated preacher' to whom Barton appeals for aid, suggests the 'natural theology' associated with, especially, William Paley (1743–1805): a type of inquiry which sought to deduce the existence of God through the use of reason and evidence, as opposed to revelation. Thomas Le Fanu's library contained Paley's *Natural Theology*, *View of the Evidences of Christianity*, *Clergyman's Companion in Visiting the Sick*, and *Horae Paulinae*, as well as works by several 'scriptural' geologists: Thomas Gisborne's *Testimony of Natural Theology to Christianity*, William Rhind's *Age of the Earth*, and George Fairholme's *General View of the Geology of Scripture* (see TLF 12, 24, 32).

'French principles': the phrase particularly calls to mind the great Anglo-Irish philosopher and statesman Edmund Burke (1729–97), who had fulminated against the influence of Jacobin political views and atheism upon English thought, particularly within his own Whig party. Thus Sir James Prior, in his 'Life of Burke' (in the Le Fanu family library):

'Mr. Pitt . . . leaned to [Burke's] views, urged that he was in order, that he was grateful to the right hon. gentleman for the manly struggle made against French principles . . . and that his zeal and eloquence in the cause entitled him to the warmest gratitude of all his fellow subjects' (*Memoir of the Life and Character of the Right Hon. Edmund Burke* (London, 1824), 382).

27 *the postman*: the 'Dublin Penny Post' had been established in 1773.

28 *the theatre . . . in Crow-street*: Crow Street Theatre was founded in 1758, in the face of strong opposition from Le Fanu's great-grandfather Thomas Sheridan, manager of the rival Smock Alley Theatre. Initially involved in the founding was the Irish actor and playwright Charles Macklin (1699?–1797); coincidentally or not, 'Macklin' is the surname Le Fanu later gave to the ineffectual clergyman (here unnamed) in the 1851 version of 'The Watcher'.

the college: Trinity College; the word 'college' is capitalized in the 1851 'Watcher', as is 'college park' in the next paragraph.

dead wall: i.e. blank, without windows or doors.

29 *the House of Commons*: the Parliamentary House in College Green was designed by Edward Lovett Pearce (1699–1733) and expanded by James Gandon (1743–1823); the domed House of Commons chamber was destroyed by fire in 1792.

a member: 'a Mr. Norcott, a member' in *Ghost Stories and Tales of Mystery*; 'a Member' in *In a Glass Darkly*.

30 *at the passage*: 'The Familiar' adds 'from College Green'.

a form: a bench.

chancery: i.e. involved in a lawsuit over property; Mr Boythorn, in Charles Dickens's *Bleak House* (1853), calls the Court of Chancery 'an infernal cauldron'. ('Chancery' is capitalized in later versions of the story.)

31 *Doctor R——*: 'Doctor Richards' in *Ghost Stories and Tales of Mystery*; 'Doctor R——' in *In a Glass Darkly*.

32 *lock-jaw*: tetanus; its horrifying symptoms had been depicted in anatomist Sir Charles Bell's 1809 painting *Opisthotonus*, of a naked Peninsular War soldier, his body contorted in agony.

foreign hospitals: at this point in the story, the place-name is elided; later it is given as Lisbon. In *Ghost Stories and Tales of Mystery* it is named (as Lisbon) both times; in *In a Glass Darkly* it has become Naples (also named twice).

33 *foremast-man*: the most likely meaning here is simply 'a common sailor'.

Freemasons: at this time, the Grand Lodge of Ireland would have met at Tailor's Hall, Back Lane (the Freemasons' Hall on Molesworth Street was not built until the 1860s) (*Encyclopaedia of Dublin* (Dublin, 1991), 213). This venerable brick guild hall is better remembered as the site of Wolfe Tone's 'Back Lane Parliament' (Catholic Committee) meeting in December 1792.

34 *twinkling oil lamps*: gas was not used to light Dublin streets until the 1820s.

35 *Dr——*: 'Doctor Macklin' in *Ghost Stories and Tales of Mystery*; 'Dr——' in *In a Glass Darkly*.

39 *The prince of the powers of the air*: Satan; from Ephesians 2:2. This particular characterization is surely significant in light of the avian form Barton's persecutor later inhabits.

'*resist the devil and he will flee from thee*': from James 4:7; the answer to Barton's subsequent question ('*how* resist him?') is also to be found in this verse—'Submit yourselves therefore to God'—but this is precisely, as we have already seen, what he cannot do.

41 *ague*: malaria or other strong fever.

whipped through the town, at the cart's-tail: a punishment delivering both public shame and physical pain; General Montague's vow is horribly ironic in light of Barton's treatment of his tormentor in life, as subsequently revealed.

42 *a rump and dozen*: proverbial stakes for a bet (a rump of beef and a dozen bottles of claret), originally an Irish expression. But this phrase can also refer to a flogging, and could in the early nineteenth century: an 1832 satirical cartoon titled 'A German governess; or, a rump and dozen' depicted the Queen whipping King William's bottom with a birch-rod (a tattooed anchor is conspicuously visible on one naked buttock of the 'Sailor King', an appropriate victim for a punishment particularly associated with naval discipline), www.britishmuseum.org/research/collection_online.

runs like a lamp-lighter: common expression; 'allusion to the rapidity with which the lamplighter ran on his rounds, or climbed the ladders formerly used to reach the street lamps' (*OED*).

peccavi: 'I have sinned' (Latin), an expression with painful pertinence, of course, to Barton's own case.

43 *Dover . . . Calais*: there is, perhaps, an echo of this episode in M. R. James's 'Casting the Runes', as Karswell is accompanied by his own demonic pursuer at the pier; but he is on the Dover side, taking passage to Calais.

44 *patois*: regional dialect.

personnel: personal appearance.

jockey: to outwit or outdo.

45 *Clontarf*: then still a village, and seaside resort, near Dublin.

46 *chain of associations*: here and elsewhere in the story, the language of associationist psychology, advocated by such English thinkers as David Hartley (1705–57) and Joseph Priestley (1733–1804), is on display.

54 *Plymouth*: port city in Devon; virtually a metonym for 'Royal Navy'.

those terrible and arbitrary severities: the brutality of naval discipline was legendary, and much criticized in, for instance, the nautical melodramas of Douglas Jerrold (1803–57). Of the particular 'sanguinary punishment' which Barton has administered with so little restraint, the English socialist, and former Royal Navy volunteer, Thomas Hodgskin wrote: 'Custom sanctions flogging in all cases when the captain thinks fit. . . . Captains are the sole judges of what is negligence, and the duty to be imposed has been interpreted by them as an obligation on all beneath them to do every thing in what ever manner they may think fit; and who can affix any other interpretation but captains? Any opposition to their will, any hesitation in obedience, and want of alacrity in fulfilling it, is punished by flogging' ('An Essay on Naval Discipline', 1813).

AN ACCOUNT OF SOME STRANGE DISTURBANCES IN AN OLD HOUSE IN AUNGIER-STREET

Published in the *DUM* in December 1853, this haunted-house tale did not appear in book form for seventy years, as one of M. R. James's 'discoveries' collected in *Madam Crowl's Ghost, and Other Tales of Mystery* (1923). While it is certainly connected with the 1872 story which originally appeared as 'The Haunted House in Westminster' (retitled 'Mr Judge Harbottle' for *In a Glass Darkly*), it is going too far to call this an earlier 'version' of the later tale, as has often been asserted. The Harbottle story is something more along the lines of a 'prequel', though the two narratives are far from smoothly continuous. Closer in several particulars to 'Aungier Street' (and almost certainly influenced by it) is Bram Stoker's 1891 story 'The Judge's House' (later collected in the posthumous *Dracula's Guest and Other Weird Stories*, 1914).

55 [*Title*]: Aungier Street, formerly St Stephen Street, was named after Sir Francis Aungier (1558–1632), Master of the Rolls, named 1st Baron Aungier of Longford in 1621 (and interestingly, given the story's subject matter, himself a justice of assize). It is not known whether Le Fanu had a particular house in mind when writing this story, but one intriguing candidate has recently emerged from years of obscurity and disrepair:

> Number 9/9a Aungier Street, which celebrates its 350th birthday this year, is considered the oldest, most intact domestic building in the city. It is one of the first buildings erected in the Aungier Estate, Dublin's first planned development, pre-dating the construction of Georgian Dublin. . . . The four-storey building is classified as of 'transitional typology', combining the timber framing techniques of medieval Ireland with mass masonry construction, making it a link between the medieval and Georgian cities. (*Irish Times*, 15 Aug. 2014)

'*mollia tempora fandi*': 'favourable occasions for speaking', cf. Virgil's *Aeneid*, book 4, lines 293–4.

a sacrifice to contagion: perhaps a reference to the Irish cholera epidemic of 1832–3 ('contagious' is a word the narrator is soon to apply to 'fear' as well).

56 *Chichester-House*: in College Green; meeting-place of the Parliament of Ireland between 1661 and 1727 (it was demolished the following year).

Sir Thomas Hacket, who was Lord Mayor of Dublin in James II's time: as Lord Mayor, Hacket would be condemned for his 'brutish and barbarous behavior . . . to the protestants [*sic*]' by Anglo-Irish historian Walter Harris (1686–1761) (Harris, 359).

Judge Horrocks: owing largely, no doubt, to its inclusion in the landmark volume *In a Glass Darkly*, 'Mr Justice Harbottle', with its English setting, has always been better known than 'Aungier-Street' (though not a few readers, M. R. James among them, have preferred the earlier—and Irish—story). It is unsurprising, then, that attempts to identify historical models for Le Fanu's conception of a monstrously cruel and lecherous judge have focused on figures from English history, two in particular: James II's 'hanging judge' George Jeffreys (1645–89), infamous for his conduct during the 'bloody assizes' following Monmouth's Rebellion (1685); and Sir John Willes (1685–1761), who appears as one of the grotesque figures depicted in the 1758 painting *The Bench* by William Hogarth (1697–1764). And very plausible candidates they are. Perhaps, however, Judge Horrocks— 'the hangin'est judge that ever was known in Ireland's ground', as the maid in 'Aungier-Street' calls him—was inspired, at least in part, by an Irish example: John 'Hanging Judge' Toler, Lord Norbury (1745–1831) (William Le Fanu was one of many who used the epithet, in his *Seventy Years of Irish Life*). During and after the insurrection of 1798, Toler, as attorney-general, prosecuted United Irishmen including, most famously, the brothers John and Henry Sheares. After their conviction Toler, fearful of a possible reprieve, pressed for a speedy execution; in the brief time before their hanging (and decapitation) outside Dublin's Newgate Prison the next day, it was Le Fanu's grandfather who comforted them: 'In the interval between conviction and execution, the Reverend Dr. Dobbin was unremitting in his attention to the prisoners. Both of them availed themselves of his pious services, and that good man invariably spoke of their demeanour as being such as befitted their awful situation' (Madden, vol. 2, 267–8).

A few years later Toland, now Chief Justice (and Lord Norbury), presided at the trial of Robert Emmet after his abortive revolt (it was to him that Emmet addressed the speech which would transform the failed revolutionary into a posthumous folk hero). And once again, the Revd Dr William Dobbin was present to succour the condemned man, while trying his best to save his immortal soul:

> The clergyman who attended him after sentence had been pronounced, vainly endeavoured to eradicate the erroneous opinions he had imbibed on the Continent—but all arguments were unavailing. While proceeding in a hackney-coach to the place of execution, the worthy divine made a last effort to remove his unbelief. Emmet listened to him for a short time patiently—then, turning to Dr. Dobbin he requested him to forebear: 'I appreciate your motives, and I thank you for your kindness; but you merely disturb the last moments of a dying man, unnecessarily. I am an infidel from conviction, and no reasoning can change my faith.' (Madden, vol. 3, 471)

Such family anecdotes concerning Toland's judicial victims (as, to a sympathetic eye, they would have seemed) must surely have made an impression on the young Le Fanu (the story of the Sheares brothers is also recalled by William Le Fanu (WLF, 18–21)).

57 *'sup full of horrors'*: see *Macbeth* 5.5.

58 *the hair . . . was white with age, while the eyebrows retained their original blackness*: the villainous Silas Ruthyn is described in similar terms: 'his eyebrows were still black, though his hair descended from his temples in long locks of the purest silver and fine as silk, nearly to his shoulders' (*Uncle Silas* (Oxford, 1981), 189).

'The cock he crew, away then flew': from 'The Old Woman of Berkeley' by Robert Southey (1774–1843), a Gothic poem about a witch whose reanimated corpse is claimed at last by the devil, and taken away to Hell. Matthew Lewis included the ballad in his 1801 collection *Tales of Wonder* (which also contained several of the 'Demon Lover'-themed pieces referenced in the headnote to 'Schalken the Painter').

phantasmagoria: popular form of eighteenth- and nineteenth-century horror theatre; see Introduction.

the invention of my poor stomach: cf. Ebenezer Scrooge in Charles Dickens's *A Christmas Carol* (1843): 'A slight disorder of the stomach makes them [the senses] cheats. You may be an undigested bit of beef, a blot of mustard, a crumb of cheese, a fragment of an underdone potato.'

59 *robing himself like Granuaile in one of my blankets*: reference to the so-called 'Pirate-queen of Connacht', Gráinne [Grace] O'Malley (1530–*c*.1603), given the name Granuaile in the abundant body of legend and folklore surrounding her and her exploits. The relevant story finds her charging naked out of bed to do battle: 'the very Day she was brought to bed of her first Child . . . a Turkish Corsair attacked her ships, and that they were Getting the Better of her Men she got up put the Quilt about her and a string about her neck took two Blunder Bushes in her hands came on Deck . . . fired the two Blunder Bushes at them and Destroyed the officers' (quoted in *The Shamrock*, vol. 15 (1877), 186).

60 *'Black spirits and white, | Blue spirits and grey'*: first line of one of the songs from Thomas Middleton's *The Witch* (*c*.1615) which he subsequently interpolated into *Macbeth* (4.1). The line actually reads, 'Red spirits and grey', but Nicholas Rowe (1674–1718) inexplicably turned them blue for his 1709 edition of Shakespeare. This is the version quoted by Matthew Lewis on the title-page of his *Tales of Wonder*, which Le Fanu seems to have kept near to hand while writing this story (see note to p. 58).

'kept my spirits up, by pouring spirits down': the likely source is a comic ballad by dramatist George Colman the Younger (1762–1836) variously titled 'Love and Brandy', 'Brandy O', and 'A Landlady of France'; as the last it appeared in the play *The Foundling of the Forest* by William Dimond (*c*.1784–1837). The landlady of the title is drinking with the 'bandy officer' she loves before he is 'order'd to the coast':

> She filled him out a bumper, just before he left the town,
> And another for herself, so neat and handy, oh!
> So they kept their spirits up, by pouring spirits down,
> For love is like the cholic, cur'd by brandy, oh!

See *Oliver's Comic Songs, A Selection of the Whimsical, Witty, Eccentric, Comical, Curious, Tragical, Odd, Droll, Humorous, Burlesque, and Laughable, Part I* (Edinburgh, 1805), 5.

'Anatomy': since Henry Gray's famous textbook would not be published for another half-decade, this may be John and Charles Bell's four-volume *Anatomy of the Human Body* (1804).

'Spectator': the essays contained in this famous periodical, founded in 1711 by Joseph Addison and Richard Steele, offered just the sort of cheerfully rational, 'healthy' reading that might indeed serve as a mental 'tonic' in such circumstances; similarly, in his classic tale 'The Haunted and the Haunters' (*Blackwood's*, 1859), Edward Bulwer-Lytton has his narrator bring a volume of Thomas Macaulay's *Essays* with him to the baleful house on Oxford Street, believing that 'there was so much of healthfulness in the style, and practical life in the subjects, that it would serve as an antidote against the influences of superstitious fancy'. It is possible that Le Fanu had in mind a particular number of the *Spectator*, in which a night of fireside ghost-story-telling (much like the one invoked at the beginning of this tale) is described, and condemned as a harmful influence upon the hearers: 'they talked so long, that the imaginations of the whole assembly were manifestly crazed, and, I am sure, will be the worse for it as long as they live' (*A Selection from the Papers of Addison* (London, 1827), 78).

62 *in true 'fancy' phrase*: i.e. boxing slang.

coute qui coute: properly *coûte que coûte*, 'at all costs' (French).

63 *Goliath*: Philistine giant, slain by the smaller David (1 Samuel).

Shakspeare says: slightly misquoted from *The Merchant of Venice* 4.1 (a rat is also mentioned in the relevant passage).

'chum': in Samuel Johnson's *Dictionary*, 'a chamber-fellow, a term used in the universities' (quoted in *OED*).

Digges'-street: shares a corner with Aungier Street at its southern end.

64 *plethoric*: swollen, fleshy, turgid; originally 'blood-filled' (the medical provenance of the word makes it particularly appropriate here).

Hebe: in Greek mythology, the cupbearer of the gods on Olympus.

delf: glazed earthenware, usually blue and white, made in Delft in the Netherlands.

65 *black cap*: in English law, worn by a judge when about to pronounce sentence of death.

66 *the then popular comic ditty*: there are three versions of 'Murphy Delany' in the Bodleian Libraries' collection of printed English ballad-sheets, dating

from *c*.1790 to *c*.1859 (none of the three has Le Fanu's 'door-nail'); the stanza which Tom Ludlow is ruminating on reads:

> Some folks passing by, pull'd him out of the river,
> And got a horse-doctor his sickness to mend,
> Who swore that poor Murph' was no longer a liver,
> But dead as a devil, and there was an end.
> Then they sent for the coroner's jury to try him:
> But Murph' not much liking this comical strife,
> Fell to twisting and turning the while they sat by him,
> And came, when he found it convenient, to life . . .

67 *the "Robin Hood" tavern*: there was an eighteenth-century tavern of that name in nearby Dame Street, associated with a Whiggish 'Robin Hood Society'.

69 *a mature girl of five-and-forty*: she is said to be 'two and fifty' on p. 56.

70 *Pether's churchyard*: demolished in 1983, St Peter's was a Church of Ireland (Protestant) parish church in Aungier Street. Sheridan Le Fanu married Susanna Bennett there on 18 December 1843.

72 *taythings*: tea-things (in dialect).

BORRHOMEO THE ASTROLOGER

Originally published in the *DUM* in Jan. 1862, this is one of two stories, along with the 1843 novella *Spalatro: From the Notes of Fra Giacomo* (which is, like 'Borrhomeo', a 'monkish tale' set in Italy), identified as Le Fanu's work by William McCormack in his 1980 biography.

73 [*Title*]: the aristocratic House of Borromeo (without Le Fanu's added 'h') played a central role in both Milanese politics and Catholic history during the Renaissance. The two relevant figures here are the most famous members of the family, Charles Borromeo (1538–84) and, especially, his cousin Federico (1564–1631), both Cardinals and Archbishops of Milan see next note.

the famous plague of Milan: this devastating outbreak of bubonic plague in 1629–31 had been famously described in the novel *I Promessi Sposi* and its pendant, *Storia della Colonna Infame*, by Alessandro Manzoni (1785–1873). From these texts, published together in English in 1845, Le Fanu might have derived not only the general idea of a story set in Milan during the plague but also the name Borromeo (Federico is a character in the novel, and Charles's sainted relics appear as well) and the theme of the *untori* (anointers) believed to be deliberately spreading the infection (as well as the related theme of the hideous punishments meted out to those believed to be guilty). There is another text, however, that also has numerous striking affinities with Le Fanu's story, namely Charles Mackay's *Extraordinary Popular Delusions and the Madness of Crowds* (1841), which contains sections on astrology and alchemy as well as the Milan plague.

Mackay, who seems independently to have used Mazzoni's primary source text on the plague—Italian historian Giuseppe Ripamonti's Latin work *De peste Mediolani quae fuit anno 1630* (1640)—penned a sensational account which tracks closely with 'Borrhomeo' in many particulars, from the description of the comet and its interpretation by astrologers, to the idea of Satanic agency:

At the time of the plague in Milan, in 1630, of which so affecting a description has been left us by Ripamonte [sic], in his interesting work, *De Peste Mediolani*, the people, in their distress, listened with avidity to the predictions of astrologers and other impostors. It is singular enough that the plague was foretold a year before it broke out. A large comet appearing in 1628, the opinions of astrologers were divided with regard to it. Some insisted that it was a forerunner of a bloody war; others maintained that it predicted a great famine; but the greater number, founding their judgment upon its pale colour, thought it portended a pestilence. The fulfilment of their prediction brought them into great repute while the plague was raging. . . . One singular prediction almost drove the unhappy people mad. An ancient couplet, preserved for ages by tradition, foretold, that in the year 1630 the devil would poison all Milan. Early one morning in April . . . the passengers were surprised to see that all the doors in the principal streets of the city were marked with a curious daub, or spot, as if a sponge, filled with the purulent matter of the plague-sores, had been pressed against them . . . the greater number were convinced that the powers of hell had conspired against them, and that the infection was spread by supernatural agencies. . . . The Devil himself had been seen. He had taken a house in Milan, in which he prepared his poisonous unguents, and furnished them to his emissaries for distribution.

It is difficult, too, to put down to mere coincidence the similarities between Borrhomeo's visit to the 'Red Hat' and the following account of a man compelled to accompany a mysterious stranger, in whose presence he becomes invisible, to an infernal cabal:

Onward they went, with the rapidity of the wind, the stranger speaking no word, until they stopped before a door in the high-street of Milan. There was a crowd of people in the street, but, to his great surprise, no one seemed to notice. . . . From this he concluded that they were invisible. The house at which they stopped appeared to be a shop, but the interior was like a vast half-ruined palace. . . . In one of [the rooms], surrounded by huge pillars of marble, a senate of ghosts was assembled, debating on the progress of the plague . . . the stranger led him into another large chamber, filled with gold and precious stones, all of which he offered him if he would kneel down and worship him, and consent to smear the doors and houses of Milan with a pestiferous salve which he held out to him. He now knew him to be the Devil . . . (Mackay, vol. 1, 225–8)

virus: term denoting, at that time, any infectious agent; the origins of virology proper date from the very end of the nineteenth century.

74 *astrology . . . alchymy*: considered kindred 'sciences'.

the grand arcanum: the great secret, i.e. of the 'elixir vitae, or the philosopher's stone', often used interchangeably; the ultimate goal of the alchemists.

projection: in alchemy, '[t]he throwing or casting of an ingredient into a crucible; *esp.* the casting of powdered philosopher's stone on to molten metal to effect its transmutation into gold or silver' (*OED*).

He collects the powder . . . it was a failure: one of several distracting shifts of grammatical tense within the story.

75 *an angel of wisdom, in power and immortality like a god*: recalls part of Hamlet's famously ambivalent description of man: 'In action how like an angel, In apprehension how like a god' (3.2). Interestingly, the subsequent line, 'And yet to me, what is this quintessence of dust?', contains the alchemical term 'quintessence', while also perhaps suggesting to Le Fanu the 'dust' which Borrhomeo's melancholy tempter has just used to describe, counterintuitively if not paradoxically, the philosopher's stone itself.

76 *to commute*: i.e. to effect the change into gold.

78 *Per Baccho*: 'by Bacchus', the god of wine.

'Geber, perhaps, or Alfarabi': Muslim alchemist Abū Mūsā Jābir ibn Ḥayyān (*c.* AD 721–815) and philosopher Abū Naṣr al-Fārābī (*c.* AD 870–950). The two figures are discussed consecutively by Charles Mackay (also as 'Geber' and 'Alfarabi'); the latter, he writes, 'refused to rest until he had discovered the great object of his life—the art of preserving it for centuries, and of making gold as much as he needed', while Geber 'affirmed, that the secret of the philosopher's stone had been more than once discovered; but that the ancient and wise men who had hit upon it would never, by word or writing, communicate it to men, because of their unworthiness and incredulity' (Mackay, vol. 1, 97–8). Both descriptions resonate with aspects of Le Fanu's tale.

79 *a thin round film of human skin*: William McCormack suggests that Honoré de Balzac's novel *Le Peau de chagrin* (1831) 'engages uncannily with ['Borrhomeo']; both revolve round the infernal powers of a magical piece of skin which endows its possessor wonderfully—but at a price' (*Dissolute Characters*, 10).

80 *a cup of Falernian*: a celebrated wine.

fascinorous: properly 'facinorious' or 'facinorous', wicked.

Stygian: of the infernal river Styx; i.e. hellish, from Hell.

83 *in no wise decayed, but fresh and sound*: perhaps Le Fanu was thinking of the chemically preserved dead in the crypt of St Michan's, where his maternal grandfather had been prebendary, and where the Sheares brothers (who had, like Borrhomeo, also been hanged) lay 'fresh as on the day that they were laid' to rest, as one *DUM* writer put it, adding in a note that 'The vaults of St. Michan's Church, Dublin, possess the property of keeping the dead for ages fresh as on the day of their internment' ('Lives of the Lord Chancellors of Ireland' (Oct. 1871), 28).

Get thee hence, Satan: from Matthew 4:10 (KJB); spoken by Jesus to the devil, who has just tempted him with dominion over 'all the kingdoms of the world, and the glory of them'.

WICKED CAPTAIN WALSHAWE, OF WAULING

The last of Le Fanu's short stories to appear in the *DUM* (April 1864), this tale, which moves from Ireland to England, may be taken as emblematically marking a shift towards English settings, one which had already begun in his novels (at the insistence of his publisher, Richard Bentley) with the sensational *Wylder's Hand* (1863–4).

87 *this strange brown robe . . . a wax candle*: Irish folk traditions; cf. William Carleton's 'The Funeral, and Party Fight', *Traits and Stories of the Irish Peasantry*, vol. 2 (Dublin, 1830). In 1895, folklorist Fanny Dickerson Bergen recorded the following oral tradition: 'All Roman Catholics who have been enrolled in a certain order, called the Order of the Blessed Virgin, have the right to be buried in a garment called a "habit." These garments of brown cloth are usually made by nuns, have been blessed by a priest, and may be purchased at a convent by members of the above-mentioned order. Elderly or infirm persons often have the habit laid away ready for use if death come suddenly . . .' ('Burial Customs and Beliefs of the Irish Peasantry', *The Journal of American Folk-Lore*, vol. 8, no. 28).

press: particularly in Irish and Scottish English, 'A large (usually shelved) cupboard, esp. one placed in a recess in the wall, for holding linen, clothes, books, etc., or food, plates, dishes, and other kitchen items' (*OED*).

the 'Flash Songster': this particular title suggests more than one salacious songbook published in the early *nineteenth* century, e.g. *The Rambler's Flash Songster* and *The Flashsongster and Cockchafer, A Choice Selection of Flash, Frisky and Funny Songs*; I am grateful to Dr Jennifer Skipp for suggesting some eighteenth-century compendiums of 'erotic, lewd, or innuendo-filled poems, toasts, jokes, songs, and limericks' which might have been in the rakehelly Walshawe's possession at this time: *The Frisky Songster. Being a Select Choice of such Songs as are Distinguished for their Jollity, High Taste and Humour. And above Two Hundred Toasts and Sentiments of the Most Delicious Order* (London: Sold by the Booksellers in Town and Country, 1776), and *The Merry Companion: or, Universal Songster* (London: Printed for Mess. Hazard, Ward and Chandler, 1739).

88 *edax rerum*: 'tempus, edax rerum': 'time, devourer of things'; from Ovid's *Metamorphoses*, book 15.

Mr Holloway: Thomas Holloway (1800–83), the Victorian era's pre-eminent vendor of patent medicines; according to a typical advertisement of the 1860s, Holloway's Ointment was 'marvellous[ly]' effective on 'bad legs, bad breasts, sores, wounds, and ulcers', at least when 'briskly and perseveringly rubbed upon the parts affected' (when used in conjunction with 'Holloway's admirable Pills', recovery was, apparently, all but

assured). The author of an 1866 *DUM* article discussing alchemy seemed
more troubled by the nostrum's unglamourousness than its inefficacy: 'The
notions associated with that panacea [the Philosopher's Stone] were certainly more calculated to strike the imagination than the ideas connected
with Holloway's Pills. Compounds of flour and sawdust are infinitely more
prosaic than the divine powder of the wise. . . . If there must be quackery
in the world, it ought to be as attractive as possible' ('Paracelsus and the
Revival of Science in the Sixteenth Century', July 1866, 7).

88 *'class-leader'*: spiritual leader of a 'class', or subdivision, of a Methodist society.

89 *Ananias and Sapphira*: in Acts 5, husband and wife struck dead after holding back a portion of the money they were supposed to donate to the
Apostles, and lying about it.

90 *whose founder . . . has sanctioned ghosts*: John Wesley (1703–91), who is supposed to have grown up in a poltergeist-haunted rectory, traced a slippery
slope whereby disbelief in ghosts led dangerously to unbelief, full stop:

> It is true likewise, that the English in general, and indeed most of the men
> of learning in Europe, have given up all accounts of witches and appar-
> itions, as mere old wives' fables. I am sorry for it; and I willingly take this
> opportunity of entering my solemn protest against this violent compli-
> ment, which so many that believe the Bible pay to those who do not believe
> it . . . these are at the bottom of the outcry which has been raised . . . in
> direct opposition not only to the Bible, but to the suffrage of the wisest and
> best of men, in all ages and nations. They well know, (whether Christians,
> know it or not,) that the giving up witchcraft is, in effect, giving up the
> Bible; and they know, on the other hand, that if but one account of the
> intercourse of men with separate spirits be admitted, their whole castle in
> the air (Deism Atheism, Materialism) falls to the ground.

See *The Journal of the Rev. John Wesley, A. M.* (Devon, 1822), 610.

91 *the legs of a satyr*: i.e. the legs of a goat; these minor deities from classical
mythology were associated with debauchery and lust.

in articulo: 'in articulo mortis', 'at the point of death'.

92 *St Paul's shipwrecked companions*: reference to Acts 27, in which the ship
carrying Paul to trial in Rome is wrecked near Malta: 'Then fearing lest we
should have fallen upon rocks, they cast four anchors out of the stern, and
wished for the day' (KJB).

93 *Lilliputian*: refers to the tiny inhabitants of Lilliput in Jonathan Swift's
Gulliver's Travels (1726).

95 *stanch*: well-constructed.

GREEN TEA

First appeared as serial in *All the Year Round* (Oct.–Nov. 1869), then included
as the first story in *In a Glass Darkly* (it is the only story in the collection originally, and as it were organically, featuring Dr Hesselius). 'Green Tea' has

proved both one of Le Fanu's most celebrated stories and one of its most crit-
ically investigated ('Carmilla' being its only rival in both respects). At the same
time, the story also testifies to the importance to Le Fanu of the *Dublin
University Magazine*'s writerly 'ecology', the influence of the work of such col-
leagues as James Clarence Mangan and Henry Ferris upon his fiction. In 1841
Ferris, anagrammatizing his name into 'Irys Herfner', recorded or invented
a pair of anecdotes which must have lodged themselves firmly in the young Le
Fanu's mind, for they contain much, *en germe*, of the premise of the story he
was to write over a quarter of a century later:

> The writer knew an English clergyman who saw, as he lay in bed, his cur-
> tains drawn, and two grim heads thrust in, their eyes glaring goblinly upon
> him. But he was aware that it was merely 'bile in his stomach', which was
> very satisfactory to know. There is an English physician at a town on the
> Continent, who cannot drink green tea, or even mixed, without seeing in
> the course of the evening, a certain tall woman, sallow, clothed in black,
> open the door, walk in (no matter who or how many may be present), and sit
> down on the nearest vacant chair, looking at him. But he believes that this
> woman (and not merely his power of seeing her) is 'just the effect of green
> tea on the nerves'. He does not suspect that the sallow woman is there,
> evening by evening, though he drink the weakest Bohea; and that the green
> does but open in him the mystic eye of the soul, and make him aware who is
> sitting in the nearest—to common eyes vacant—chair, looking at him.
> Better for him, perhaps, not to suspect it. ('German Ghosts and Ghost
> Seers', in *A Night with Mephistopheles: Selected Works of Henry Ferris*
> (Horam, 1997), 155)

Another possible influence is Samuel Warren's *Diary of a Late Physician*, originally serialized in *Blackwood's Magazine* 1832–7 (see William Hughes, 'The
Origins and Implications of J. S. Le Fanu's "Green Tea"', *Irish Studies Review*,
13.1 (Feb. 2005), 45–54).
    The story has been analysed in light of Freudian psychology, Darwinian
evolutionary theory, and the Swedenborgian theology in which it is steeped—
and such analyses have produced compelling readings of this complex and
ambiguous text. Just possibly, however, there may also be some significance in
the fact that in 1868, the year before 'Green Tea' was published, a new monkey
house was opened at the Dublin Zoo. If so, Le Fanu would not be the only
Dublin journalist for whom an afternoon spent staring at monkeys (who no
doubt stared back) set in motion a train of deeper speculations (this contemporary
article is from the *Irish Times*):

> A party of my fellow creatures staring . . . at the antics of the caged monkeys
> in the Zoological Gardens is, to me, a pitiful and a painful spectacle; it is
> enough to persuade a man of the truth of Darwinism. Mr Gladstone, who,
> not long ago, deplored the fact that his special duties gave him no leisure to
> read Darwin and Wallace . . . might perhaps now find time to spend an hour

in front of the monkey-house in the Zoological Gardens. He would, I am
sure, come away a strong believer in the fashionable doctrine.

Quoted in Catherine De Courcy, *Dublin Zoo: An Illustrated History* (Cork,
2009), 58–9; see also Introduction, p. xix.

96 *A Case Reported . . . Preface*: in *In a Glass Darkly*, this section is headed
'Prologue'.

Martin Hesselius: there was a Swedish family of this name; three Hesselius
brothers, Gustavus, Andreas, and Samuel, all first cousins to Emmanuel
Swedenborg, travelled to America in the 1710s, Gustavus remaining to
become an artist of note.

97 *high-church*: flavour of Anglicanism more inclining to such 'Catholic'
elements within the church as ritual, tradition, and the authority of
priests.

the funds: government securities.

98 *Kenlis*: there is none in England; Le Fanu has imported it from Ireland (it
is another name for Kells): 'This place, formerly called Kenlis, is of remote
antiquity, and appears to have acquired, at a very early period, a considerable degree of importance' (Lewis, vol. 2, 36).

99 *the resurrection 'in power'*: a reference to the Second Coming of Christ; see
note to p. 168 in 'The Haunted Baronet'.

103 *Turkey*: Turkish (or Persian).

Swedenborg's Arcana Caelestia, in the original Latin: the Swedish scientist
and mystic Emmanuel Swedenborg (1688–1772) first published his
Arcana Cœlestia (as it is more usually spelled), or 'Heavenly Mysteries', in
eight volumes between 1749 and 1756. Volume 2 was translated into
English in 1750, under Swedenborg's own direction; the entire work was
translated by 1806 (approximately the time of the story's setting).

'There are with every man at least two evil spirits': an idea captured in such
interlinked passages of the *Arcana* as 5849, 5976, and 5977 (the work,
which feels somewhat like a hypertext *avant la lettre*, adapts naturally to
the digital age):

> The two spirits who are linked to a person provide a communication
> with hell, while the two angels provide a communication with heaven. . . .
> But I realize few believe that any spirit is present with them, or indeed
> that spirits exist at all. . . . [One] reason for that lack of belief is that they
> do not see spirits with their eyes; for they say, 'If I could see them
> I would believe in them; what I can see exists, but whether what I cannot
> see exists I do not know'. Yet they do know or are capable of knowing
> that the human eye is so deficient and limited that it cannot see even the
> more observable details of the natural creation, as is made evident from
> optical devices which make such details visible. So how is the eye going
> to be able to see things that exist within an even purer creation where
> spirits and angels are? . . . The reason for two [spirits] is that there are

two kinds of spirits in hell and two kinds of angels in heaven, who correspond to the two mental powers in a person of will and understanding. The first kind of spirits are called simply spirits, and they act on the thoughts in a person's understanding; the second kind are called genii, and these act on the desires in a person's will . . . those called genii instill evils; they act on a person's affections and cravings, scenting in an instant what is the object of the person's desire. If the desire is good they bend it with very great skill into what is evil, and they experience the delight of their life when they can make a person perceive good as evil, and evil as good. They have been allowed to act on my own desires . . . and I must confess that unless the Lord had employed angels to protect me, those genii would have turned my desires into cravings for evil, which they would have carried out so secretly and silently that I would have known scarcely anything about it. . . . The genii are in hells deep down behind the back, out of spirits' sight; and when anyone looks down there they look like shadows flitting around. (http://e-swedenborg.com/writings; John Elliot, trans.)

105 *Dr Harley*: probably a reference to London's Harley Street, associated with physicians and their practices; he is thus an apt representative of—one might say an allegorical figure for—'official' medicine, in all its unimaginative materialism.

106 *hippish*: in low spirits (from 'hyp'-ochondria).

109 *a portrait of Schalken's*: see note to p. 3.

   nemesis: avenging goddess of Greek mythology.

   tea, or coffee, or tobacco: all staples of imperial trade (see Nicholas Allen, 'Sheridan Le Fanu and the Spectral Empire', in *The Ghost Story from the Middle Ages to the 20th Century: A Ghostly Genre*, ed. Helen Conrad-O'Briain and Julie Anne Stevens (Dublin, 2010), 114).

110 *City*: City of London, the historic centre of London, long associated with finance.

   omnibus: horse-buses were not, in fact, yet in operation in England.

111 *a small black monkey*: it has been noted that there is no monkey mentioned in the *Arcana*; 'monkey' and 'ape' are not, however, differentiated in Latin, and there are several 'simiae' in Swedenborg, including in his 1758 *Spiritual Diary*; the Trinity-educated classicist Le Fanu might have read the entry 'De simiae facie' in *Diarii Spiritualis, Pars Secunda*, published in London in 1843, and later translated thus:

> CONCERNING THE FACE OF A MONKEY. There appeared to me the face of a monkey, and it was said that those are of such a quality who apply to themselves what belongs to others, in order to deceive them. In the other life spirits can impersonate anyone, and present not only the idea of the man, but also images or representatives of his speech and other things, as also whatever anyone may be inclined to favor.—1748, December 11. (*The Spiritual Diary of Emmanuel Swedenborg, or A Brief Record of His Supernatural Experience*, vol. 2, trans. George Bush (Boston, 1872))

112 *scaunce*: oblique ('skance' in *In a Glass Darkly*).

"spectral illusions": these are discussed at length, for instance, in the first of
Walter Scott's *Letters on Demonology and Witchcraft* (which, like David
Brewster's *Letters on Natural Magic*, TLF possessed). One anecdote in
particular which might well have had an influence on Le Fanu concerns
a gentleman visited by an (initially) animal apparition; as he confesses to
his physician (who proves no more helpful in the end than Hesselius):

> 'My visions', he said, 'commenced two or three years since, when
> I found myself from time to time embarrassed by the presence of
> a large cat, which came and disappeared I could not exactly tell how, till
> the truth was finally forced upon me, and I was compelled to regard it
> as no domestic household cat, but as a bubble of the elements, which
> had no existence save in my deranged visual organs or depraved
> imagination . . . within the course of a few months, it gave place to, or
> was succeeded by, a spectre of a more important sort, or which at least
> had a more imposing appearance. This was no other than the appar-
> ition of a gentleman-usher. . . . After a few months the phantom of the
> gentleman-usher was seen no more, but was succeeded by one horrible
> to the sight and distressing to the imagination, being no other than the
> image of death itself—the apparition of a skeleton. Alone or in com-
> pany', said the unfortunate invalid, 'the presence of this last phantom
> never quits me. I in vain tell myself a hundred times over that it is no
> reality, but merely an image summoned up by the morbid acuteness of
> my own excited imagination and deranged organs of sight. But what
> avail such reflections, while the emblem at once and presage of mortal-
> ity is before my eyes. . . . Science, philosophy, even religion, has no cure
> for such a disorder; and I feel too surely that I shall die the victim to so
> melancholy a disease, although I have no belief whatever in the reality
> of the phantom which it places before me' . . . [the physician] resorted
> to other means of investigation and cure, but with equally indifferent
> success. The patient sunk into deeper and deeper dejection, and died
> in the same distress of mind in which he had spent the latter months of
> his life . . .

See Walter Scott, *Letters on Demonology and Witchcraft* (Ware, 2001),
24–6.

116 *power to dissipate thought*: an inversion of the tea's properties: 'it cleared
and intensified the power of thought so'.

the optic nerves: Sir David Brewster, responding to Scott's *Letters*, has
a good deal to say on the subject in his *Letters on Natural Magic*, as well as
yet more on 'spectral illusions' (including another spectral cat).

117 *the "paries"*: i.e. partition.

118 *Dee*: the River Dee, part of the boundary between England and Wales.

122 *a certain good old French surgeon*: Ambroise Paré (1510–90): 'I dressed him,
and God healed him', Stephen Paget, *Ambroise Paré and His Times,
1510–1590* (New York and London, 1897), 31.

MADAM CROWL'S GHOST

Another of Le Fanu's stories published by Dickens in *All the Year Round* (31 Dec. 1870), this dialect tale was subsequently interpolated into the non-supernatural novella 'A Strange Adventure in the Life of Miss Laura Mildmay' for the three-volume collection *Chronicles of Golden Friars* (London, 1871). ('Miss Laura Mildmay' had itself been serialized, without the story, in *Cassell's Magazine*, Oct.–Nov. 1869; for *Chronicles of Golden Friars* a brief introduction, not reproduced here, was added to the tale to integrate it into the novella.) M. R. James, for one, thought highly of 'Madam Crowl's Ghost', not only making it the title story of his collection of Le Fanu's fiction but placing it first, noting, 'Ghost stories and tales of mystery are what this volume contains, and, in order to lure the reader on, I have placed the most striking and sensational of them at the beginning of it.'

Le Fanu's invented Northumbrian village of Golden Friars, in Wordsworth's Lake District, is the setting for the three novellas comprising the *Chronicles* ('The Bird of Passage', 'Miss Laura Mildmay', and 'The Haunted Baronet'), as well as the stories 'The Dead Sexton' (1871) and 'Laura Silver Bell' (1872). It seems plausible that Le Fanu's conception of this imaginary locale was inflected, perhaps even prompted, by the appearance in 1869 of a book published by the London Philological Society, entitled *A Glossary of the Dialect of the Hundred of Lonsdale, North and South of the Sands, in the County of Lancaster, Together with an Essay on Some Leading Characteristics of the Dialects Spoken in the Six Northern Counties of England (Ancient Northumbria)*, by Robert Backhouse Peacock (London, 1869). If nothing else, this linguistic guide is likely to have been at Le Fanu's elbow as he wrote the dialect which plays such a significant role in bringing his hallucinatory Northern English setting to life. For the three Northumberland stories included in this volume—'Madam Crowl's Ghost', 'The Haunted Baronet', and 'Laura Silver Bell'—dialect words and phrases will be largely glossed by reference to this text (as 'Peacock').

125 *Lexhoe*: while Golden Friars itself is presumably in Cumbria, in the north-west of England (the villages of Hawkshead and Ambleside have been suggested as analogues), the name 'Lexhoe' points interestingly eastward, to North Yorkshire—specifically to Sexhow (sometimes spelled 'Saxhoe'), a North Riding town which possesses not only its own dragon (the 'Worm of Sexhow') but a local legend involving an old woman's ghost ('Old Nannie'). This folktale does not otherwise much resemble Le Fanu's story, but he would seem to have taken at least the name 'Lexhoe' from William Henderson's retelling of it in his 1866 volume, *Folk Lore of the Northern Counties of England and the Borders*, in which it is used in place of Sexhow/Saxhoe (where, according to Jennifer Westwood and Jacqueline Simpson, the 'Old Nannie' story is invariably set; see *The Penguin Book of Ghosts* (London, 2008)). In John Marius Wilson's *Imperial Gazetteer of England and Wales* (1870–2), Sexhow is described as 'a township, with a r. station, in Rugby-in-Cleveland parish, N. R. Yorkshire; on the North Yorkshire and Cleveland railway, 5 miles S W by W of Stokesley. Acres, 501. Real

property, £593. Pop., 42. Houses, 5' (*A Vision of Britain through Time*, University of Portsmouth).

125 *dowly*: 'Applied to a person it signifies *melancholy*; to a place, *lonely*' (Peacock, 26).

126 *proas*: 'talk, conversation of a gossiping order' (Peacock, 65).

sackless: 'dejected, spiritless, helpless' (Peacock, 69).

127 *spired*: to 'spire' is 'to shoot up luxuriantly' (Peacock, 79).

wad na du a' that lids: '"Don't du a that *lids*" = Don't do in that manner, etc.' (Peacock, 51).

yak: oak (Peacock, 95).

aupy: as a noun, 'a childish or silly person' (Peacock, 4).

Jack the Giant Killer or Goody Twoshoes: the first is a sanguinary English fairytale which first appeared in print in early eighteenth-century chap-books; the great Victorian illustrator Richard Doyle produced an iconic version of the story in 1842 (*The Marvellous History of Jack the Giant-Killer*); *The History of Little Goody Two-Shoes* (1755), possibly written by Oliver Goldsmith, is a pioneering work of children's literature now remembered mostly, if somewhat unjustly, as a byword for irritatingly egregious do-goodery. Mrs Wyvern's remark, which of course refers to Madam Crowl's 'aupy' state of mind, might also be considered particularly grotesque in light of her being a child-murderer.

128 *torflin'*: to 'torfle' is 'to decline in health, to die' (Peacock, 87).

sizzup: 'a hard blow' (Peacock, 74).

kinkin': 'to be affected with a convulsive stoppage of breath, through immoderate laughing or crying' (Peacock, 47).

129 *frump*: 'to be rude to, to rebuke' (Peacock, 33).

the pictures in the old Aesop's Fables: there were numerous English versions of the animal fables of Aesop, the (perhaps legendary) Greek storyteller, beginning with William Caxton's *Subtyl Historyes and Fables of Esope* (1484); the copy at Applewale may be novelist Samuel Richardson's 1739 edition, the first prepared specifically with children in mind: *Aesop's fables: with instructive morals and reflections . . . containing two hundred and forty fables, with a cut engraved on copper to each fable*.

130 *i' noo*: soon.

by Jen: 'By St John' (Peacock, 14).

131 *ogglin'*: 'Oggle, *v.i.* to stare' (Peacock, 60).

132 *whiteheft*: 'flattery, cunning' (Peacock, 93).

flittin': 'flight, removal' (Peacock, 32).

rabblin' . . . skirlin' . . . scrafflin': rabble, 'to talk rapidly or confusedly'; skirl, 'to scream, to shriek'; scraffle, 'scramble' (Peacock 66, 75, 71).

133 *pymag*: magpie (Peacock, 65).

tike: dog.

fuffin low: fuff, 'a puff of wind'; low, 'a flame' (Peacock 33, 52).

134 *'Sart'*: certainly (Peacock, 70).

a bo or a freet: respectively, 'hobgoblin' and 'a spectre, an apparition, a frightful object' (Peacock, 10, 33).

135 *kist*: 'a chest' (Peacock, 48).

consayt: in Peacock, 'consait'; 'to think or suppose, to imagine, to suspect' (20).

pick: pitch (Peacock, 63).

flayin': 'a spectre, an apparition' (Peacock, 31).

136 *bayans*: in Peacock, 'beyans'; bones (8).

at-efter: 'after, afterwards' (Peacock, 4).

THE HAUNTED BARONET

Serialized in *Belgravia* in five parts (July–Nov. 1870), this long tale, which Everett Bleiler called 'One of the half-dozen best Victorian supernatural novels', was republished, with 'A Strange Adventure in the Life of Miss Laura Mildmay' and 'The Bird of Passage', in *Chronicles of Golden Friars* (1871).

137 *'as from the stroke of the enchanter's wand'*: from Canto IV of Lord Byron's *Childe Harold's Pilgrimage*: 'I stood in Venice, on the Bridge of Sighs; | A palace and a prison on each hand: | I saw from out the wave her structures rise | As from the stroke of the enchanter's wand'.

138 *nout at dow*: worthless.

139 *hangment*: the devil.

lang deod: long dead.

short-waisted: quick-tempered.

shouther: push (shoulder).

teathy: peevish.

140 *kye*: cattle.

141 *blud-stean*: blood-stone; 'Blud-steyan . . . a green semi-transparent pebble, with red spots in it like blood spots' (Peacock, 9).

bootlese bene: 'unavailing prayer' (Peacock, 10). William Wordsworth's poem 'The Force of Prayer' begins, 'What is good for a bootless bene? | With these dark words begins my Tale, | And their meaning is, whence can comfort spring | When prayer is of no avail?'

142 *blea*: 'livid, of a pale bluish colour' (Peacock, 9).

dobby: apparition, ghost.

mafflin . . . lang gaumless gawky: i.e. a great big simpleton.

sib: kin, related.

144 *sincducing and catre-acing*: backgammon terminology (continued throughout their game): 'Cinq. Deuce, to play two Men from the 5 placed in your Adversary's Tables, for a Gammon, or for a Hit'; 'Quatre Ace, to play

a Man from the 5 placed in your Adversary's Tables for the Quatre, and for the Ace, to play a Man down upon the Cinq' (Edmond Hoyle, *A Short Treatise on the Game of Back-Gammon* (Dublin, 1744)).

144 *Guy Fawkes*: i.e. a straw-stuffed dummy.

145 '*And an old fellow they call the Doctor, that helps him*': William Le Fanu collects a number of similar 'doctor' jokes in *Seventy Years of Irish Life*.

146 *As the candles burn blue . . . the Evil One*: see e.g. Daniel Defoe's *History of the Devil* (listed in the TLF): 'the Devil not have a cloven foot! . . . he could not be a devil without it, any more than he could come into the room and the candles not burn blue, or go out and not leave a smell of brimstone behind him' (*Novels and Miscellaneous Works of Daniel De Foe*, vol. 3 (London, 1875), 481).

147 *sentenced by drum-head*: as in a drumhead court-martial, held in the field; i.e. hasty.

149 *like Haworth*: see note to p. 444.

150 *endure this contumelious life*: i.e. he is treated abusively; cf. *Hamlet* 3.1.

snuggery: 'A cosy or comfortable room, esp. one of small size, into which a person retires for seclusion or quiet' (*OED*).

151 *Killiecrankie*: refers to battle in the 1689 Jacobite rising; John Graham of Claverhouse, 1st Viscount Dundee (1648–89), was, like Sir Guy, fatally shot there.

Whole Duty of Man . . . Pilgrim's Progress: Anglican devotional work (treated with humorous irreverence by Richard Brinsley Sheridan in *The Rivals*), and Christian allegorical narrative by John Bunyan.

Ladies Bountiful: Lady Bountiful is a character in Irish dramatist George Farquhar's Restoration comedy *The Beaux' Stratagem* (1707); the term is more often used to mean 'charitable women of means', but here the reference is to Farquhar's character's practice of herbal medicine.

154 *saque*: loose gown.

funeste: portending death.

mob-cap: bonnet; see note to p. 258.

155 *Be always as merry . . . a sorrowful man*: Mrs Julaper is a veritable storehouse of old English proverbs; perhaps an unnamed companion to the other seventeenth-century works on her shelf is John Ray's *A Compleat Collection of English Proverbs* or a similar volume, in which this and subsequent sayings might be found.

black-ox-trodden: careworn (Peacock, 9).

161 *resemblance to . . . Charles II*: J. M. Barrie would similarly make his Captain James Hook resemble 'the Merry Monarch', in his less merry aspect.

Sidney Smith: Sydney Smith (1771–1845), clergyman and author associated with the founding of the *Edinburgh Review* ('Many run after felicity like an absent-minded man hunting for his hat, while all the time it is on his head or in his hand').

a German conjurer: two figures Le Fanu might have had in mind are Gustavus Katterfelto, who made astrological predictions (and died in North Yorkshire in 1799), and Peter Breslaw, whose book *Last Legacy; or The Magical Companion* includes such chapters as 'Palmistry Displayed, or the Art of Telling Fortunes by Lines in the Hands' and 'The Art of Fortune-Telling by Cards', in which he observes, 'This method of telling fortunes is innocent, and much better than for a young woman to tell her secrets to a fortune-teller, who can inform her no better, if she pays a shilling for the intelligence' (London, 1784), 104.

166 *'before the speedy gleams the darkness swallowed'*: from the Gothic poem 'Tam o'Shanter', by Robert Burns (1759–96).

  wide-leafed: broad-brimmed.

167 *As the man of God . . . Jeroboam*: see 1 Kings 13:1–6.

168 *he will but go in weakness to return in power*: reminiscent of language used in discussing the Second Coming of Christ.

  threaped . . . tazzle . . . taggelt . . . waaly: respectively, 'contradict[ed]', 'a wicked, drunken person', 'an idle, dirty, disreputable person', 'oppressed with woe' (Peacock, 29, 84, 84, 90).

174 *scug*: 'a sheltered place' (Peacock, 71).

  It's nobbut a prass wi' himsel': perhaps 'only a quarrel [i.e. 'press', fight] with himself'.

  something white come out o' t'water . . . like a hand: recalls the mythic figure of the Lady of the Lake, from Arthurian legend; in Tennyson's version of the myth, *Idylls of the King*, Arthur recalls how he received Excalibur: 'for thou rememberest how | In those old days, one summer noon, an arm | Rose up from out the bosom of the lake, | Clothed in white samite, mystic, wonderful, | Holding the sword'.

175 *all my eye*: nonsense.

176 *good-humoured mock-heroics*: the recently-quoted 'Tam o'Shanter', by Robert Burns, would fit the bill.

182 *beeswing*: 'second crust, consisting of shining filmy scales of tartar, formed in port and some other wines after long keeping; so called from its appearance' (*OED*); here its presence (or rather absence) distinguishes Sir Bale's (cheaper) sherry from his port.

183 *I wish there was no post here*: the mail-coach has already appeared in the novella, though in reality, the first did not run until 1784 (on the Bristol–Bath–London road), conflicting slightly with the dating of the story.

  the faculty: i.e. the entire medical profession, imagined as a collective entity.

184 *scaur*: cliff or hill-ridge.

186 *Antaeus*: in Greek mythology, opponent of Herakles ('opponent' is also the meaning of his name).

190 *Dr Faustus*: the archetypal figure of the man who makes a deal with the devil, dramatized, most famously, by Christopher Marlowe in *The Tragical*

History of the Life and Death of Doctor Faustus (1604) and Johann Wolfgang von Goethe in *Faust* (1808). 'The Haunted Baronet' is one of several versions or variations on the Faust legend written by Le Fanu, along with 'The Fortunes of Sir Robert Ardagh', 'Sir Dominick's Bargain', 'The Dead Sexton', and 'Schalken the Painter'; the legend seemed to have functioned for him as 'a dramatic memento mori' (Ivan Melada, *Sheridan Le Fanu* (Boston, 1987), 112).

191 *Egyptians*: i.e. gypsies (Romani), once thought to have come from Egypt.

Marston Moor: 1644 battle in the First English Civil War.

193 *ascendency*: an interesting choice of word, given that a reversal in power relations such as that which Le Fanu dramatizes here was a real anxiety among members of the Protestant Ascendancy class in nineteenth-century Ireland.

194 *'grand mufti'*: 'In this game one of the company sits in a chair, and is called the Mufti, or the Grand Mufti. He makes whatever grimace or motion he pleases. . . . When he says, "Thus says the Grand Mufti", everyone must make just such a motion as he does; but when he says, "So says the Grand Mufti", every one must keep still. A forfeit for a mistake is exacted' (*The Sociable, Or, One Thousand and One Home Amusements* (Philadelphia, 1858), 204).

199 *an old Druidic altar-stone*: the druids were a priestly class in pre-Roman Celtic cultures; a description of a putative example in Ireland can be found in Samuel Carter Hall's *Ireland: Its Scenery, Character and History* (1842), a work in the preparation of which Hall wrote that Joseph and William Le Fanu 'aided us largely': 'A "druid's altar" stands on a rocky eminence near Dunmore. . . . The altar consists of fourteen perpendicular stones, forming a perfect circle of thirty-six yards in circumference, on the outside. Across the centre, forming the diameter, are two horizontal stones parallel to each other, each two yards wide and seven long. They are covered by five flat flags, forming a covered passage about two feet high, closed at one end... One stone of the roof is raised on one side . . . so as to resemble a cromliac or sacrificial flag, "from which the blood of the victim flowed off"' (vol. 2 (Boston, 1911), 206–7).

200 *the 'cunning man'*: fortune-teller, wizard; in Shakespeare's *Henry VI, Part 2* the Duke of Suffolk says, 'A cunning man did calculate my birth | And told me that by water I should die'; in the event, he dies 'by [a] *Walter*', but Sir Bale has had similar premonitions about the lake.

201 *in a wax*: angry.

huffed: taken offence.

202 *frumped*: snubbed, insulted.

203 MYSTAGOGUS: mystagogue (*mystagogus* is the Latin, from the Greek μυσταγωγός), one who initiates another into mysteries or teaches mystical doctrines.

204 *the Colonies*: the story is set shortly before the American Revolution.

his share of the curse . . . bitter crust: see Genesis 3:14–19.

209 *Queen Anne's reign*: from 1702 to 1714.

219 *dis iratis*: 'angry gods'.

220 *phantasmagoria*: see note to p. 58.

225 *that which befell Robinson Crusoe*: refers to the episode in Daniel Defoe's 1719 novel in which the stranded Crusoe is startled by the return of his own parrot: 'judge you, if you can, that read my story, what a surprise I must be in, when I was awaked out of my sleep by a voice, calling me by my name several times, "Robin, Robin, Robin Crusoe; poor Robin Crusoe! Where are you, Robin Crusoe? Where are you? Where have you been?"... [I] was at first dreadfully frightened, and started up in the utmost consternation; but no sooner were my eyes open, but I saw my Poll sitting on the top of the hedge; and immediately knew that it was he that spoke to me' (London, 1855), 97.

227 *very faint, with something undulatory in it*: there is perhaps a suggestion here of such pre- or proto-telephonic devices as Édouard-Léon Scott's 1857 phonautograph.

228 *the worm and fire of remorse*: see Isaiah 66:24 and Matthew 25:41.

229 *George the First or Second*: this would span the period 1714–60.

231 *the waters at Bath*: fashionable spa town.

235 *struck her repeater*: repeating clock or watch, needing to be pressed to chime the hour and, sometimes, minute; an expensive luxury item, useful in the dark of a midnight coach-ride. Perhaps this is one of the 'minute repeaters' manufactured and sold by John Ellicott, clockmaker to George III until 1772.

238 *the odd sharp lights in which Schalken delighted*: see note to p. 3.

245 *a little quinine*: anachronistic; cinchona bark was used to treat malaria well before this time, but quinine was not isolated from the bark, or given its name, until 1820.

247 *armorial bearings*: in light of the prominence of the figure of the hand throughout the novella, it may be worth noting that King James I 'graunt[ed] for him, his heirs, and successours, that the baronets and their descendants, shall and may beare, either in a canton in their coate of armes, or in an inscutchion, at their election, the armes of Ulster, that is in a field argent, a hand geules, or a bloudy hand' (Walter Scott, ed., *A Collection of Scarce and Valuable Tracts*, vol. 2 (London, 1809), 260).

ailles de pigeon: i.e. he is wearing the familiar eighteenth-century wig with stiff curls above the ears (literally 'pigeon-winged').

THE HAUNTED HOUSE IN WESTMINSTER

As 'Mr Justice Harbottle', one of Le Fanu's best-known stories. Published in Mary Elizabeth Braddon's *Belgravia* magazine in January 1872, it was included the same year, with minor revisions, in *In a Glass Darkly*, the primary differences being the change of title, a division into nine chapters, and the addition of a series prologue:

> On this case Doctor Hesselius has inscribed nothing more than the words, 'Harman's Report', and a simple reference to his own extraordinary Essay on 'The Interior Sense, and the Conditions of the Opening thereof'.
>
> The reference is to Vol. I, Section 317, Note Z\ᵃ. The note to which reference is thus made, simply says: 'There are two accounts of the remarkable case of the Honourable Mr. Justice Harbottle, one furnished to me by Mrs. Trimmer, of Tunbridge Wells (June, 1805); the other at a much later date, by Anthony Harman, Esq. I much prefer the former; in the first place, because it is minute and detailed, and written, it seems to me, with more caution and knowledge; and in the next, because the letters from Dr. Hedstone, which are embodied in it, furnish matter of the highest value to a right apprehension of the nature of the case. It was one of the best declared cases of an opening of the interior sense, which I have met with. It was affected too, by the phenomenon, which occurs so frequently as to indicate a law of these eccentric conditions; that is to say, it exhibited what I may term, the contagious character of this sort of intrusion of the spirit-world upon the proper domain of matter. So soon as the spirit-action has established itself in the case of one patient, its developed energy begins to radiate, more or less effectually, upon others. The interior vision of the child was opened; as was, also, that of its mother, Mrs. Pyneweck; and both the interior vision and hearing of the scullery-maid, were opened on the same occasion. After-appearances are the result of the law explained in Vol. II., Section 17 to 49. The common centre of association, simultaneously recalled, unites, or *re*unites, as the case may be, for a period measured, as we see, in Section 37. The *maximum* will extend to days, the *minimum* is little more than a second. We see the operation of this principle perfectly displayed, in certain cases of lunacy, of epilepsy, of catalepsy, and of mania, of a peculiar and painful character, though unattended by incapacity of business'.
>
> The memorandum of the case of Judge Harbottle, which was written by Mrs. Trimmer, of Tunbridge Wells, which Doctor Hesselius thought the better of the two, I have been unable to discover among his papers. I found in his escritoire a note to the effect that he had lent the Report of Judge Harbottle's case, written by Mrs. Trimmer, to Dr. F. Heyne. To that learned and able gentleman accordingly I wrote, and received from him, in his reply, which was full of alarms and regrets, on account of the uncertain safety of that 'valuable MS.', a line written long since by Dr. Hesselius, which completely exonerated him, inasmuch as it acknowledged the safe return of the papers. The narrative of Mr. Harman is therefore, the only one available for this collection. The late Dr. Hesselius, in another passage of the note that I have cited, says, 'As to the facts (non-medical) of the case, the narrative of Mr. Harman exactly tallies with that furnished by Mrs. Trimmer'. The strictly scientific view of the case would scarcely interest the popular reader; and, possibly, for the purposes of this selection, I should, even had I both

papers to choose between, have preferred that of Mr. Harman, which is given, in full, in the following pages. (*In a Glass Darkly*, 119–21)

249 *annuity . . . on the quarter-day*: the English quarter days, associated with religious holidays, fall on 25 March, 24 June, 29 September, and 25 December; an annuity is a yearly allowance or pension.

Westminster: area of London; home of Westminster Abbey, Parliament, and, until the nineteenth century, the Law Courts.

a closet: i.e. a smaller adjoining room.

Hogarth: the great English painter and engraver William Hogarth (1697–1764), referenced both explicitly and implicitly at several points in the story. In particular, Le Fanu very likely had the painting *The Bench* in mind for his conception of Harbottle (see note to p. 56), the later-referenced Southwark Fair was the subject of a famous 1733 painting by Hogarth, the story's grotesque hangman is likened to his counterpart in the penultimate engraving in Hogarth's 1747 series, *Industry and Idleness*, and the discussion of 'a marriage *à-la-mode*' invokes the artist's 1743–5 series of paintings with that title. (TLF lists both 'Hogarth's Works, illustrated by Prose Descriptions, no plates, wants title' and 'Hogarth's Works, 3 vols. in 1, *plates*, cloth'.)

scurvy: disease caused by lack of vitamin C; in 1753, the Scottish doctor James Lind published his *Treatise of the Scurvy*, urging the prescription of 'genuine spruce beer, with lemon and orange juice' (Edinburgh, 1753), 247.

250 *perukes*: wigs.

no consideration the world could offer: compare with Tom Ludlow's declaration in 'Some Strange Disturbances . . . in Aungier-Street' (p. 64).

the Court of Common Pleas: common law court; John Willes served for twenty-four years as the Chief Justice of the Common Pleas in England; John Toland was Chief Justice of the Common Pleas for Ireland for twenty-seven (see note to p. 56).

'winter's tales': i.e. a fantastic tale, fit for telling at the fireside.

improvement, with its preliminary demolitions: refers to slum clearance schemes in the middle decades of the nineteenth century. (The 'Devil's Acre', as Dickens called it, was a particularly notorious—and, with its scenes of poverty, beggary, crime, and vice, Hogarthian—slum area in Westminster.)

251 *a Turkey Merchant in the reign of King James I*: the Turkey Company, an overseas trading company chartered in 1581, was merged into the Levant Company the following decade.

chairs: sedan-chairs; a kind of litter carried by porters or 'chairmen', in use from the seventeenth century to the early nineteenth century.

Judge Harbottle: Sir John Willes and George Jeffreys are the most likely candidates for historical figures that Le Fanu might have drawn upon for his conception of Harbottle, though the Irish 'Hanging Judge' John Toler (also known as 'Nero' Norbury) is another possibility (see note to p. 56). Historian Thomas Babington Macaulay wrote at length of Jeffrey's demeanour on the bench and his predilection for after-hours 'debauchery', as well as the common people's desire, after his fall, for a revenge in kind:

> [H]e became the most consummate bully ever known in his profession. . . . The glare of his eyes had a fascination for the unhappy victim on whom they were fixed; yet his brow and eye were said to be less terrible than the savage lines of his mouth. His yell of fury, as was said by one who had often heard it, sounded like the thunder of the judgment day. . . . His evenings were ordinarily given to revelry. . . . He often came to the judgment-seat, having kept the court waiting long, and yet having but half slept off his debauch, his cheeks on fire, his eyes staring like those of a maniac.
>
> Hanging [the people thought] would be too mild a death for him: a grave under the gibbet too respectable a resting-place: he ought to be whipped to death at the cart's tail: he ought to be tortured like an Indian: he ought to be devoured alive. . . . They exhorted him to hang himself in his garters, and to cut his throat with his razor.

See Macaulay, *Critical and Miscellaneous Essays and Poems*, vol. 6 (New York, 1865), 124–9. (It might be mentioned that Norbury was similarly noted, in his younger days, for his love of carousing.)

253 *roquelaure . . . cocked-hat*: articles of eighteenth-century dress; knee-length cloak and tricorn hat.

Circean enchantment: the sorceress Circe, in Homer's *Odyssey*, could transform men into beasts and monsters (in the case of Odysseus' men, swine).

254 *such stimulating expletives . . . indulge in nowadays*: reflects the change in social mores between Harbottle's time and Le Fanu's.

255 *a Jacobite plot*: the Jacobites (i.e. followers of James) were partisans of the Stuart royal family, whom they sought to restore to the throne in several failed plots and revolts; as an 'honest Whig', Hugh Peters would presumably be a supporter of the Hanoverian succession. This is also the set-up for Harbottle's subsequent 'three kings' joke.

256 *guinea*: gold coin, worth £1 1s.

'hunkers': haunches.

ran like a lamplighter: see note to p. 42.

257 *the Old Bailey to . . . the hangman's lash*: i.e. to trial, prison, punishment, and execution.

'affidavit man': professional perjurer.

pharisaical: like the Pharisees as depicted in the New Testament, 'Strict in matters of doctrine and ritual observance but lacking in charity or inner devotion' (*OED*).

Withershins: the word, also spelled 'Widdershins', means counter-clockwise.

258 *Foolish pity | Ruins a city*: approximation of a proverb used by Puritan pastor John Robinson in the discussion 'Of Rewards, And Punishments By Men' in his *Observations Divine and Morall*: 'There is then a mercifull crueltie, when men save, by severitie, the persons themselves that are *punished*, and others also; the *punishment* reaching to one, or a few: and the fear and warning to many. There is, on the other side, a cruell mercy, when men by spareing spoyl both the persons offending and others, who by their *impunity* take boldnes to offend. This *foolish pitty spoyls the cittie*, if the magistrate use it: so doth the fond love of parents the family' (*Observations* (n.p., 1625), 271). In his influential *Exposition of the Old and New Testament*, Matthew Henry (1662–1714) invokes the saying in connection with Ahab's encounter, in the first Book of Kings, with Elijah (which is also Harbottle's Christian name).

mob-cap . . . saque: a mob-cap is a bonnet of the type made fashionable by actress Fanny Abington (see note to p. 264); a sacque or 'sack' is a loose gown.

Rhadamanthus: Hadean judge in Greek mythology; a stern or severe judge.

259 *in furore*: in a rage.

Mother Carey's chickens: a sailors' name for storm petrels.

crown solicitor: assists in the government's criminal prosecution.

Judge Harbottle went circuit: i.e. made a periodic tour to preside over the judicial sessions ('assizes') held throughout the counties of England.

260 *Morning Advertiser*: more likely to have been the printer Henry Woodfall's *Public Advertiser*, which would publish the famous 'Junius' letters in 1769–72, or even, perhaps, the *Morning Chronicle and Daily Advertiser*, founded in 1770; the *Morning Advertiser*, still in existence, was not founded until the 1790s.

261 *He had*: corrected, as in other editions, from 'has' (as in both *Belgravia* and the first edition of *In a Glass Darkly*).

262 *tipstaff*: court officer, so named for the 'tipped' (metal-capped) staff he carried.

scrivinary: writing by a clerk.

263 *true bill*: preliminary to an indictment.

'Sblood: oath ('God's blood!').

264 *piggins*: used variously to mean bowls, pails, or other types of container.

enjoying: happy, cheerful.

Drury-lane: to the extent that Le Fanu's dating of the story is to be trusted, this incarnation of the Theatre Royal, founded in 1674, had just begun its period of highly successful management under actor David Garrick (1717–79); his successor would be Richard Brinsley Sheridan. The most performed play that season was *Romeo and Juliet*; others included Philip Massinger's *A New Way to Pay Old Debts* and Colley Cibber's *She Would and She Would Not*.

264 *Lincoln's-inn*: one of the four Inns of Court associated with the legal profession.

Counsellor Thavies: Thavies was the name of an Inn of Chancery, where the poet John Donne (1572–1631) studied law.

Mrs Abington: Frances or 'Fanny' Abington (1737–1815) did not in fact take the stage until 1755, first appearing at Drury Lane (while still 'Miss Barton') the following year, in Congreve's *The Double Dealer*. Sir Joshua Reynolds (1723–92) painted her several times, depicting her in a suggestive pose in *Mrs. Abington as Miss Prue in 'Love for Love' by William Congreve*, and in a loose floral gown in *Mrs. Abington as 'the Comic Muse'*; ignoring, again, strict chronological considerations, Harbottle appears to have created a domestic impersonation of Fanny Abington in his housekeeper-paramour, with her Abington-cap and 'saque of flowered silk'.

265 *Bow-street officers*: this pioneering police force was not founded until the following year (by novelist and magistrate Henry Fielding).

check-string: pulled to stop the coach.

died in an hospital: in 'Mr Justice Harbottle', 'died in prison of the jail-fever' (typhus).

266 *cere-clothes*: waxed shrouds, to wrap corpses.

'*Idle Apprentice*': see note to p. 249.

brutum fulmen: empty threat.

porte-cochère: carriage entrance.

267 *Themis*: Greek goddess of justice.

in limine: at the outset.

enhanced awfully in power: in 'Mr Justice Harbottle', 'enhanced awfully'.

269 *gyves*: fetters, especially for the legs.

a marriage à-la-mode: see note to p. 249; the phrase 'à la mode' was also used in several dramatic titles, such as Charles Macklin's *Love à la Mode*, performed in Drury Lane; there is also a record of a *Marriage à la Mode, or Conjugal Douceurs*, performed in Ireland and featuring Mrs Abington.

the vapours: i.e. depressed.

Buxton: spa town in Derbyshire.

what stuff dreams are: cf. *Tempest* 4.1; one of several Shakespearean echoes in the story.

270 *maggot*: fantastic idea.

Odsbud! odsheart!: oaths ('God's blood', 'God's heart').

271 *blue devils*: depression.

Aesculapius: Greek god of medicine.

272 *Southwark fair*: annual fair depicted by Hogarth (see note to p. 249), whose attractions included waxworks, as did Bartholomew Fair and other charter

fairs (see Thomas Frost, *Old Showmen and the Old London Fairs* (London, 1874)).

273 *posset*: 'drink made from hot milk curdled with ale, wine, or other liquor, flavoured with sugar, herbs, spices, etc., and often drunk for medicinal purposes' (*OED*).

scullery-maid: kitchen servant, responsible for scouring and 'scalding' dishes (cleaning them with boiling water); see e.g. William Ellis's *The Country Housewife's Family Companion* (1750).

vally: value.

274 *Looking in . . . ghastly vision*: the corresponding portion of 'Mr Justice Harbottle' reads as follows:

> Looking in, she very dimly beheld a monstrous figure, over a furnace, beating with a mighty hammer the rings and rivets of a chain.
>
> The strokes, swift and heavy as they looked, sounded hollow and distant. The man stopped, and pointed to something on the floor, that, through the smoky haze, looked, she thought, like a dead body. She remarked no more; but the servants in the room close by, startled from their sleep by a hideous scream, found her in a swoon on the flags, close to the door, where she had just witnessed this ghastly vision. (*In a Glass Darkly*, 171)

275 *atrabilious*: refers, once more, to depression.

'the rich man died, and was buried': from Jesus' 'Lazarus and Dives' parable (Luke 16:22); his final destination is Hell.

THE ROOM IN THE DRAGON VOLANT

First appeared as a five-part serial in *London Society: An Illustrated Magazine of Light and Amusing Literature for the Hours of Relaxation* (Feb.–June 1872); in the three volumes of *In a Glass Darkly*, it occupied the entire second volume (chapters 1–23), with its conclusion sharing the third with 'Carmilla'. The prologue added for the Bentley edition reads:

> The curious case which I am about to place before you, is referred to, very pointedly, and more than once, in the extraordinary Essay upon the Drugs of the Dark and the Middle Ages, from the pen of Doctor Hesselius.
>
> This Essay he entitles 'Mortis Imago' [Latin: 'picture of death'], and he, therein, discusses the *Vinum letiferum*, the *Beatifica*, the *Somnus Angelorum*, the *Hypnus Sagarum*, the *Aqua Thessalliæ*, and about twenty other infusions and distillations, well known to the sages of eight hundred years ago, and two of which are still, he alleges, known to the fraternity of thieves, and, among them, as police-office inquiries sometimes disclose to this day, in practical use.
>
> The Essay, *Mortis Imago*, will occupy as nearly as I can, at present, calculate, two volumes, the ninth and tenth, of the collected papers of Dr. Martin Hesselius.

This Essay, I may remark in conclusion, is very curiously enriched by citations, in great abundance, from mediæval verse and prose romance, some of the most valuable of which, strange to say, are Egyptian.

I have selected this particular statement from among many cases equally striking, but hardly, I think, so effective as mere narratives, in this irregular form of publication, it is simply as a story that I present it. (*In a Glass Darkly*, 173–4)

276 *the eventful year, 1815*: Napoleon Bonaparte, Emperor of France, had been defeated in 1814, and exiled to the Mediterranean island of Elba. The Bourbon dynasty had been restored. Then, in late February 1815, Bonaparte had escaped and returned to power for the 'Hundred Days' (actually 111). A final defeat, at the Battle of Waterloo (18 June 1815), led to a second Restoration of the Bourbons, and a second exile for Bonaparte (to the remote South Atlantic island of St Helena).

leaders: lead horses.

tournure: contour.

Bruxelles lace: costly, high-quality lace from Brussels.

277 *'field or'*: golden background.

honest Dobbin's manly devotion: refers to William Dobbin, the rather pathetically devoted admirer of Amelia Sedley in William Makepeace Thackeray's *Vanity Fair* (1847–8); perhaps Le Fanu reread the novel, set at the end of the Napoleonic Wars and in their aftermath, in preparation for writing his novella. Dobbin is also the maiden name of Le Fanu's mother.

282 *petit souper*: little supper.

devil's tattoo: irritated tapping of fingers.

283 *Brummel*: George Bryan 'Beau' Brummell (1778–1840), iconic Regency-era dandy.

chevelure: head of hair.

284 *such a Philomel*: Philomela, mythological Athenian princess, raped by Tereus and changed into a nightingale; Beckett thus refers to her singing voice while also intimating, or fantasizing, that she is unwillingly or unhappily married to her husband. Venus is the Roman name for Aphrodite, the Greek goddess of love; the Muses are Greek goddesses of the arts and sciences.

285 *table-d'hôte*: shared dinner table; the idea is that the supposed Count and Countess are unlikely to eat with *hoi polloi*.

291 *pigeoned*: gulled, tricked, cheated.

292 *un gallant uomo*: a gallant man, in a fittingly macaronic mix of French and Italian (the Italian should be 'un uomo galante').

293 *vin ordinaire*: the ordinary (and cheaper) table wine.

Henry IV: King of France, reigned 1589–1610.

294 *I took mine ease in mine inn*: from *Henry IV, Part 1*, 3.3; the words are
Falstaff's: 'Shall I not take mine ease in mine inn, but I shall have my
pocket picked?' Beckett, too, will have his pocket picked (literally as well
as figuratively); meanwhile, Colonel Gaillarde, who may have inherited
some of his braggadocio from Shakespeare's 'sweet creature of bombast', is about to call Beckett 'younker' (youngster), a word Falstaff has
used in the preceding sentence.

catafalque: platform, usually in a church, to bear a coffin.

299 *'Favour secret, sweet, and precious'*: from the poem 'Tam o'Shanter' by
Robert Burns (1759–96).

Eylau: extremely bloody 1807 battle in the East Prussian town of
Preussisch Eylau (now part of Kaliningrad).

tapis: the French expression, 'sur le tapis', means literally 'on the table-
cloth'; i.e. to put a topic on the table for discussion.

303 *imperial*: a small beard or tuft of hair under the lower lip as popularized by
Napoleon III.

305 *coquin*: rascal, rogue.

the Opera: this would then have been at the Théâtre National in the Rue de
Richelieu (renamed Rue de la Loi during the Revolution), built in 1793 by
the successful actress and director Marguerite Brunet.

309 *to the hammer*: 'The French Revolution and subsequent wars had a dramatic
impact on the art market at the end of the 18th century and the beginning of
the 19th. The sale from 1792 onwards of the collection of Louis Philippe
Joseph, Duc d'Orléans . . . occurred just when rich English collectors were
beginning to take an informed interest in Old Masters. . . . The Peace of
Amiens (1801–2) encouraged further dealing, and in 1815 much Napoleonic
loot was retrieved or sold' (*Oxford Art Online*).

bal masqué: masked ball.

310 *'bifstek'*: (properly 'bifsteck'), steak.

Greenwich: i.e. Greenwich Fair, of which Dickens wrote: 'In our earlier
days, we were a constant frequenter of Greenwich Fair, for years. . . . We
cannot conscientiously deny the charge of having once made the passage
in a spring-van, accompanied by thirteen gentlemen, fourteen ladies, an
unlimited number of children, and a barrel of beer; and we have a vague
recollection of having, in later days, found ourself the eighth outside, on
the top of a hackney-coach, at something past four o'clock in the morning, with a rather confused idea of our own name, or place of residence'
(*Sketches by Boz*, vol. 1 (London, 1864), 150). It is, indeed, not too difficult to picture Beckett, with such companions as Tom Whistlewick,
'carousing' there.

311 *Versailles*: originally the site of a royal hunting lodge, transformed into
a palace by Louis XIV; primary residence of French monarchs until the
Revolution.

311 *more of a Murat than a Moltke*: Joachim-Napoléon Murat (1767–1815), daring cavalry commander (with a Beau Brummell-like *chevelure*), and Helmuth von Moltke (1800–91), Prussian field marshal and celebrated tactician.

313 *domino*: half-mask.

you're an Englishman: and therefore it is fitting that he should wear St George's Cross, the flag of England.

ancient English hostelry . . . the Canterbury pilgrims: recalls Harry Bailly's Tabard Inn in Chaucer's *Canterbury Tales*.

314 *Château de la Carque*: 'carque' means 'burden' or 'labour' in Old French; 'karke' in Anglo-Norman (the midwife in 'Laura Silver Bell' is appropriately named 'Carke').

Père la Chaise: the Cimetière du Père-Lachaise had been established by Napoleon in 1804, only eleven years earlier.

315 *the 'Wandering Jew'*: legendary figure, condemned to wander the earth until Judgement Day for insulting Christ; in the seventeenth-century French ballad 'Complainte du Juif-Errant' he says, 'J'ai cinq sous dans ma bourse' ('I have five pennies in my purse').

316 *Peter the Great*: the Russian tsar died in 1725; supposedly, he began to write a will on his deathbed, but expired after managing to write only 'leave all to . . .'.

317 *'Grande Galerie des Glaces'*: the great Hall of Mirrors in Versailles (one of many mentions of 'glasses' and 'mirrors' in this and the other stories of *In a Glass Darkly*).

'Celestial': i.e. Chinese, in reference to the 'Celestial Empire'.

320 this ungrammatical sentence was not corrected by Le Fanu for *In a Glass Darkly*; perhaps 'with' should read 'had'.

321 *gasconading*: swaggering, boastful.

'His scars frank him': i.e. entitle him, as British MPs were entitled to free use of the postal service by 'franking' letters.

322 *rara avis*: a rarity (literally 'rare bird').

324 *Confu*: no doubt from 'Confucius' (Chinese philosopher K'ung Fû-tsze, 551–479 BC).

dervish dance: dervishes were Islamic mendicants, known for dancing or 'whirling'.

'Salon d'Apollon': 'Apollo's room', once the throne room at Versailles.

325 *Collignan's full-length portrait of Madame de le Vallière*: Louis XIV's mistress Louise de La Vallière (1644–1710) was often painted, but the artist is fictitious, though the name may have been suggested by the contemporary engraver (not painter) François Collignon.

329 *'circumbendibus'*: i.e. in a roundabout way.

332 *fiacre*: carriage akin to hackney-coach.

333 *harlequin*: stock pantomime character. An 1866 article connecting the figure with the more familiar 'Punch' character noted, 'Harlequin's wand is the flat flexible sword with which the Vice belaboured all opponents, to make the groundlings laugh, who always relished such antics' ('At a Pantomime', *St James Magazine*, vol. 3, 198).

  sage femme: wise woman, usually a midwife, like Moll Carke in 'Laura Silver Bell'.

337 *Egeria*: nymph in Roman mythology; a possible (and appropriately 'romantic') reference would be to the poem 'Egeria's Grotto' by Letitia Elizabeth Landon (1802–38), though this did not appear until 1826, in the *New Monthly Magazine*.

339 *Oh! Richard! Oh, my king!*: from Grétry's celebrated 1784 opera *Richard Coeur-de-lion*, associated in after-years with royalist causes.

  repelled me: that is, she pushes him off (rather than his finding her suddenly repulsive).

340 *contretemps*: bad luck, bad timing.

343 *the same thing was done*: this 'Masquerade Incident' is related in an 1866 collection of anecdotes:

> At Christmas, 1834, a ball was given at a house at St. Petersburg, and candles were placed in the windows of the house, as a well-understood signal that masks might enter without special invitation. . . . At length a party entered dressed as Chinese, and bearing on a palanquin a person whom they called their chief. . . . They set him down very respectfully in the middle of the room, and commenced dancing what they called their national dance around him. . . . After awhile they began gradually to disappear unnoticed. . . . At last they were all gone, but their chief still remained sitting motionless in dignified silence in his palanquin in the middle of the room. The ball began to thin, and the attention of those who remained was wholly drawn to the silent figure of the Chinese mask. . . . He still took no notice of all that was passing around him, and the master of the house at length, with his own hand, took off the mask, and discovered to the horrified by-standers the face of a corpse . . .

  See John Timbs, *English Eccentrics and Eccentricities* (London, 1877), 402–3.

344 *modicum bonum*: i.e. a good but not excessive income (literally 'a good little').

  Henriade: epic poem by Voltaire, celebrating Henry IV of France.

346 *I do not know the name of the plant*: for its associations with death, *Cupressus sempervirens* (the Italian or funereal cypress) would seem a good candidate, though a cedar such as *Thuja occidentalis*, introduced to France in the sixteenth century, would be a better fit, strictly dendrologically speaking.

347 *farouche*: here the meaning would seem to be 'wild' or 'ferocious'.

349 *porte-cochère*: carriage entrance.

351 *a phantasmagoria*: see note to p. 58.

353 *Countess d'Aulnois*: Marie-Catherine Le Jumel de Barneville, Baroness d'Aulnoy (*c.*1650–1705), pioneering writer of literary fairy tales.

genius loci: the spirit of the place.

Spessart: mountainous Bavarian woodland and inspiration for fantastic tales (and childhood home of the Brothers Grimm).

355 *Canon Fulbert . . . Abelard's Eloise*: Peter Abélard (1079–1142) and Héloïse (1090?–1164) were secret lovers whose tragic story took on mythic status over the centuries to come. Beckett's state of mind may cause him to pay particular attention to this cautionary example (Abélard was castrated by Héloïse's uncle Fulbert).

358 *dulcinea*: peasant girl transformed in imagination to a lady of high estate in Cervantes's novel *Don Quixote*. Beckett is, of course, the profoundly deluded Quixote (he has already written, in Chapter X, of his 'Quixotic devotion').

362 *noyeau*: also 'noyau', 'liqueur made of brandy or spirit of wine flavoured with the kernels of stone fruits, almonds, citrus peel, and (sometimes) spices' (*OED*).

364 *mignonne*: i.e. 'pretty one'.

367 *stethoscope*: this would not be invented for over another decade.

375 *agrémens*: agreeable circumstances (ironic).

a balourd, a benêt, un âne: an oaf, a dullard, an ass.

376 *a hostile meeting*: a duel.

the Countess's magnificent brilliants . . . a suite of paste: i.e. the diamonds are fake, but suitable for an actress to wear onstage.

a person who supplied the Parisian anatomists: presumably a body-snatcher or 'resurrection man'.

a sadder if not a wiser man: recalls the case of the wedding-guest in Coleridge's narrative poem *The Rime of the Ancient Mariner* after hearing the mariner's harrowing tale:

> He went like one that hath been stunned,
> And is of sense forlorn:
> A sadder and a wiser man,
> He rose the morrow morn.

CARMILLA

Published in *The Dark Blue* in four instalments (Dec. 1871, Jan. 1872, Feb. 1872, Mar. 1872), then included, with added 'Hesselian' prologue, as the final story in *In a Glass Darkly*. This landmark vampire tale, considered by many to be the finest in the genre, would prove the most enduring work to appear in the short-lived (1871–3) magazine edited by Oxonian John Christian Freund (the periodical's title invokes the colour of his alma mater) (John Sutherland, *Stanford Companion to Victorian Fiction* (Stanford, 1989), 170). Le Fanu's primary source for vampire lore was a work titled *Traité sur les Apparitions des*

Esprits, et sur les Vampires, ou les Revenans de Hongrie, de Moravie, &c., written in the mid-eighteenth century by the French Benedictine monk Augustin Calmet and translated into English in 1850 by Henry Christmas (as *The Phantom World*). With respect to fiction, the best-known vampires before 'Carmilla' were male: Lord Ruthven ('The Vampyre; a Tale' by John Polidori, 1819) and Sir Francis Varney (*Varney the Vampyre; or, the Feast of Blood* by James Malcolm Rymer or Thomas Peckett Prest, 1845–7). There had, however, been earlier examples of female vampires, or vampire-like figures, in narratives ranging from some which Le Fanu almost certainly knew to others which he almost certainly did not: Samuel Taylor Coleridge's unfinished poem 'Christabel' (1816); E. T. A. Hoffmann's 'Vampirismus' (1821); Théophile Gautier's 'La Morte amoureuse' (often translated as 'Clarimonde', 1836); and Alexis Tolstoy's *Oupyr* (1841). (The penny dreadful allegedly written by Elizabeth Caroline Grey, 'The Skeleton Count, or The Vampire Mistress', is, alas, most likely a hoax.) One possible literary influence is Paul Féval's novel *La Vampire*, which features a female vampire whose prolonged life is stolen (along with scalp and hair) from a succession of young women; it first appeared in 1856 in a volume entitled *Les Drames de la Mort* and was republished in 1865 (Féval and his work were the subject of an uncredited essay that had appeared in the *DUM* during Le Fanu's editorial tenure, 'Paul Feval, a Breton Man of Letters', Jan. 1864). Another, real-life, inspiration was probably the Hungarian Countess Elizabeth Báthory (1560–1614), who was reputed to have bathed in the blood of hundreds of young women to keep herself young; Le Fanu might have read the lurid story of Báthory and her victims in, for instance, John Paget's *Hungary and Transylvania; with Remarks on their Condition, Social, Political and Economical* (1839, 1850) or Sabine Baring-Gould's *Book of Were-Wolves* (1865).

The prologue added to the story for *In a Glass Darkly* reads:

Upon a paper attached to the Narrative which follows, Doctor Hesselius has written a rather elaborate note, which he accompanies with a reference to his Essay on the strange subject which the MS. illuminates.

This mysterious subject he treats, in that Essay, with his usual learning and acumen, and with remarkable directness and condensation. It will form but one volume of the series of that extraordinary man's collected papers.

As I publish the case, in this volume, simply to interest the 'laity', I shall forestall the intelligent lady, who relates it, in nothing; and, after due consideration, I have determined, therefore, to abstain from presenting any *précis* of the learned Doctor's reasoning, or extract from his statement on a subject which he describes as 'involving, not improbably, some of the profoundest arcana of our dual existence, and its intermediates'.

I was anxious, on discovering this paper, to re-open the correspondence commenced by Doctor Hesselius, so many years before, with a person so clever and careful as his informant seems to have been. Much to my regret, however, I found that she had died in the interval.

She, probably, could have added little to the Narrative which she communicates in the following pages, with, so far as I can pronounce, such a conscientious particularity. (*In a Glass Darkly*, 358)

378 *Styria*: the Duchy of Styria in south-eastern Austria, today broken up into an Austrian state and a region in Slovenia.

Austrian service: presumably military service under a commander of the army of the Austrian Empire during the Napoleonic Wars.

Karnstein: perhaps meant to suggest 'cairn-stone'; there is also the state (then Duchy) of Kärnten (or Carinthia), which borders Styria.

379 *Babel*: mix of languages, after the Bible story (Genesis 11:1–9).

381 *cassock*: clerical tunic.

phantasmagoria: see note to p. 58.

384 *odylic and magnetic influence*: the odic or odylic force was supposed to be a vital force, allied to magnetism, posited by Karl Ludwig von Reichenbach in the 1840s. Perhaps Le Fanu has named Laura's 'metaphysically' inclined governess after celebrity mesmerist Charles Lafontaine (1803–92), who came to England in 1841.

"In truth I know not . . . came by it": slightly misquoted from *The Merchant of Venice* 1.1.

385 *the traces*: part of the harness.

piqued: congratulated.

387 *cortege*: procession of attendants (more properly *cortège*, as it appears in *In a Glass Darkly*).

Matska: diminutive in a Slavic language (Tracy).

388 *Utrecht velvet*: thick furniture plush, associated with Utrecht, Holland.

a hideous black woman: cf. 'The Child that Went with the Fairies': 'The upper sides of the carriage were chiefly of glass, so that the children could see another woman inside, whom they did not like so well. This was a black woman, with a wonderfully long neck . . . and on her head was a sort of turban of silk striped with all the colours of the rainbow' (*All the Year Round* (5 Feb. 1870), 231).

390 *Cleopatra with the asps*: a reference to the Egyptian ruler's baroque suicide by snakebite (obviously suggestive of Carmilla's own feeding methods), a scene immortalized in Plutarch's Life of Mark Antony in *Parallel Lives* and (closely following this account) Shakespeare's *Antony and Cleopatra* (1607).

397 *magic-lantern*: as Sir David Brewster pointed out, 'the magic lantern, containing in a small compass its lamp, its lenses, and its sliding figures, was peculiarly fitted for the itinerant conjurer, who had neither the means of providing a less portable and more expensive apparatus, nor the power of transporting and erecting it' (*Letters on Natural Magic* (London, 1834), 76).

salamander . . . mandrake: in prosaic reality, an amphibian and a plant (*Mandragora officinarum*), respectively, but both have potent folkloric associations, often with monstrosity, hybridity, and/or morphological ambiguity (the early fourteenth-century Hereford Map, for instance, depicts a winged, dragon-like 'Salamandra' alongside a grotesquely humanoid

'Mandragora'); Le Fanu's mountebank has stitched together a pair of composite figures. Carmilla is herself a monster condemned to an 'amphibious existence', as Baron Vordenburg later tells us.

398 *oupire*: Slavic form of 'vampire'. Augustin Calmet wrote in 1751 (the English translation is mid-Victorian):

> The *revenans* of Hungary, or vampires, which form the principal object of this dissertation, are men who have been dead a considerable time, sometimes more, sometimes less; who leave their tombs, and come and disturb the living, sucking their blood, appearing to them, making a noise at their doors and in their houses, and lastly, often causing their death. They are named vampires, or oupires, which signifies, they say, in Sclavonic, a leech. The only way to be delivered from their haunting, is to disinter them, cut off their head, impale them, burn them, or pierce their heart. (*The Phantom World: or, the Philosophy of Spirits, Apparitions &c.*, vol. 2 (London, 1850), 5–6)

Similarly, in Alexis Tolstoy's 1841 novella *Oupyr* (*The Vampire*), one encounters this bit of etymology: 'Oupyrs . . . are what you would call vampires, though only the Lord knows why, since the real Russian name is oupyrs— I can assure you of that. They're pure Slavic in origin, though you find them throughout Europe and even Asia. It's spurious to use the latinized version coined by the Hungarian monks who distorted our "oupyrs" into "vampires". Vampires . . . vampires. . . . As if we should call our ghosts *fantômes*, like the French' (Alexis Tolstoy, *Vampires*, trans. Fedor Nikanov (New York, 1969), 10). It is interesting, then, that Paul Féval should premise that the difference hinges upon not language but gender; in *La Vampire*, the 'oupire', also called 'succubus' and occasionally 'ghoul', is simply the female of the species: 'la femelle du vampire est l'oupire ou succube, appelé aussi goule au Moyen Age' (Paul Féval, *Les Drames de la Mort* (Verviers, 1969), 368).

400 *Monsieur Buffon, in his big book*: a volume, or an abridgement, of the monumental and influential *Histoire naturelle, générale et particulière* (1749–88) by Georges-Louis Leclerc, Comte de Buffon; Buffon's discussion of how and why 'La chenille devient papillon' ('the caterpillar becomes a butterfly') centres upon the problematics of reproduction, as does Baron Vordenburg's discussion of vampire 'multiplication' in the final chapter of the story (*Oeuvres complètes de Buffon*, vol. 4 (Paris, 1818), 608).

hippogriffs: mythical animal, half-horse and half-eagle.

Gratz: Graz, capital of Styria.

ten leagues: about 30 miles (50 kilometres).

401 *Marcia*: a possible connection to Féval, whose female vampire is named 'Marcian'.

409 *the descent of Avernus*: i.e. into Hell; see Virgil's *Aeneid*, book 6, lines 124–9.

411 *major-domo*: 'the head servant of a wealthy household in a foreign country' (*OED*).

411 *myrmidons*: devoted followers (originally Achilles' warriors, in Homer's *Iliad*).

412 *valerian and sal-volatile*: restoratives of, respectively, vegetable and mineral origin.

416 *Dranfeld*: possibly derived from Old English 'drone' (i.e. bee) and 'field' (it is one variant of the Derbyshire town of Dronfield).

419 *scouted*: rejected, dismissed.

420 *Grand Duke Charles*: if reference to a real historical figure is intended, this may be one of several consecutive Grand Dukes of Saxe-Weimar-Eisenach; Karl August (Charles Augustus) reigned until 1828, his son Karl Friedrich (Charles Frederick) until 1853, and *his* son Karl Alexander (Charles Alexander) until 1901. The world of the story feels unmoored at times from considerations of strict historical setting, but Charles Frederick would seem to be the best candidate. Certainly the musical component of Count Carlsfeld's 'series of fêtes' would be appropriate, as Weimar was a major musical and operatic centre during his reign. Another possibility might be *Arch*duke Charles of Austria (1771–1847).

Aladdin's lamp: from the story in the *Arabian Nights*; i.e. the power to make things magically appear, or else simply the possession of fantastic wealth.

430 *revenants*: cf. Calmet's 'revenans', literally 'the returned'.

who duly impaled and burnt them: the story, like many details to follow, is derived from Calmet's *Traité*.

433 *triste*: sad, melancholy.

434 *leaf*: brim.

436 *blood, in which . . . the body lay immersed*: on the possible influence of Elizabeth Báthory on Le Fanu's conception of Carmilla, see headnote.

437 *Baron Vordenburg*: possibly derived from the place-name 'Vordernberg', discussed in the travel book *Schloss Hainfeld; Or, A Winter in Lower Styria* by Basil Hall (London, 1836).

'Magia Posthuma' . . . Herenberg: these are all texts cited by Calmet (Tracy).

LAURA SILVER BELL

This story exploring the dark side of fairy lore appeared in the *Belgravia Annual* (Dec. 1872), two years after the similarly-themed 'The Child that Went with the Fairies' (*All the Year Round*, 5 Feb. 1870). Unlike the earlier tale, however, which M. R. James included in his 1923 collection, 'Laura Silver Bell' had to wait over a century for republication in book form, in E. F. Bleiler's second volume of Le Fanu's short fiction, *Ghost Stories and Mysteries* (Dover, 1975). While set in Northumberland, the story's roots lie ultimately in Le Fanu's interest in the Irish folklore to which he had been exposed as a boy in County Limerick. Peter Bell has connected Le Fanu's 'reawakened interest in the superstitions of his youth' towards the end of his career—he also published 'Stories of Lough Guir' and 'The White Cat of Drumgunniol' at this time—with a more general awakening of interest in the subject, as evidenced by the appearance in 1869–70 of illustrator Richard Doyle's *In Fairyland: A Series of Pictures from the Elf World* (' "The Child that Went with the Fairies": The Folk Tale and The Ghost Story', *Reflections In a Glass Darkly*, 419). A quarter of a century later, Arthur Machen would more fully exploit the horrific potential of the 'Good People' in a series of tales set in Wales.

440 *no rowan-tree grows near . . . no horse-shoe is nailed on the door*: all supposed to afford protection from witches; in other words, Mother Carke is herself one. Compare with the description, in 'The Child that Went with the Fairies', of Moll Ryan's similarly deteriorated cabin, though it is the 'Good People' she particularly fears: 'But whatever other dangers threatened, there was one well provided against. . . . Round the cabin stood half a dozen mountain ashes, as the rowans, inimical to witches, are there called. On the worn planks of the door were nailed two horse-shoes. . . . Here certainly were defences and bulwarks against that unearthly and evil power . . .'

sage femme: midwife.

under the rose: 'sub rosa'; secretly.

441 *byneyam*: byname; sobriquet or nickname; listed by Peacock (with the spelling 'by-neyam') as in common Northumberland use.

442 *one of that sect*: presumably Baptist; there has been a Baptist presence at the probable location of Le Fanu's Golden Friars since 1678, when it 'pleased God, by his special grace, to call a people, and raise them up for himself, in measure out of the world, and put them into his holy fear and service, in and about Torver'—a hamlet long associated with farming— 'and afterwards known as the church at Hawksheadhill, in Furness-fells, Lancashire' (David Douglas, *History of the Baptist Churches in the North of England, from 1648 to 1845* (London, 1846), 100). The Hawkshead Hill Baptist Church, in Ambleside, is still active today.

her sobriquet of 'Silver Bell': 'Silver Bell' is also the name of the losing horse backed by Sir Bale in Chapter XVIII of 'The Haunted Baronet'.

443 *Murillo tints*: Spanish Baroque painter Bartolomé Esteban Murillo (1617–82), known for his rich colouring; also relevant here is his fondness for depicting gypsies and (romanticized) beggar children.

canny feyace: pretty face.

444 *'Agoy!'*: 'a petty oath' (Peacock, 2).

kipples: rafters.

Grike: 'crevice, chink, or rut' (Peacock, 37).

sic aupy: such a fool.

Hawarth Castle: no doubt meant to suggest Haworth, of Brontë sisters fame, with its surrounding moorland.

No freetin: nothing frightening (Peacock, 33).

conny: pretty (Peacock, 20).

shirra: sheriff.

445 *mafflin*: simpleton.

  hang i' the bell-ropes: be postponed.

446 *Dobies*: or 'dobbies'; ghosts (Peacock, 25).

  'Od wite it!': 'an imprecation = God punish it' (Peacock, 94).

  marrow: a companion (Peacock, 54).

448 *Darrat ta!*: 'a sort of veiled oath, the same as "Od rot"' (Peacock, 23).

449 *The heart of the dead animal*: in his *Witchcraft in Old and New England*
  (1929), George Lyman Kittredge listed a number of counter-charms
  against the actions of a witch involving the burning of an animal's heart
  stuck with pins.

  Her avarice is roused: in this story, as in 'Borrhomeo the Astrologer',
  Le Fanu is less than scrupulous about maintaining a strict consistency of
  tense.

American Literature

British and Irish Literature

Children's Literature

Classics and Ancient Literature

Colonial Literature

Eastern Literature

European Literature

Gothic Literature

History

Medieval Literature

Oxford English Drama

Philosophy

Poetry

Politics

Religion

The Oxford Shakespeare

A complete list of Oxford World's Classics, including Authors in Context, Oxford English Drama, and the Oxford Shakespeare, is available in the UK from the Marketing Services Department, Oxford University Press, Great Clarendon Street, Oxford OX2 6DP, or visit the website at www.oup.com/uk/worldsclassics.

In the USA, visit www.oup.com/us/owc for a complete title list.

Oxford World's Classics are available from all good bookshops. In case of difficulty, customers in the UK should contact Oxford University Press Bookshop, 116 High Street, Oxford OX1 4BR.

CHARLES DICKENS	The Old Curiosity Shop
	Our Mutual Friend
	The Pickwick Papers
GEORGE DU MAURIER	Trilby
MARIA EDGEWORTH	Castle Rackrent
GEORGE ELIOT	Daniel Deronda
	The Lifted Veil and Brother Jacob
	Middlemarch
	The Mill on the Floss
	Silas Marner
EDWARD FITZGERALD	The Rubáiyát of Omar Khayyám
ELIZABETH GASKELL	Cranford
	The Life of Charlotte Brontë
	Mary Barton
	North and South
	Wives and Daughters
GEORGE GISSING	New Grub Street
	The Nether World
	The Odd Women
EDMUND GOSSE	Father and Son
THOMAS HARDY	Far from the Madding Crowd
	Jude the Obscure
	The Mayor of Casterbridge
	The Return of the Native
	Tess of the d'Urbervilles
	The Woodlanders
JAMES HOGG	The Private Memoirs and Confessions of a Justified Sinner
JOHN KEATS	The Major Works
	Selected Letters
CHARLES MATURIN	Melmoth the Wanderer
HENRY MAYHEW	London Labour and the London Poor

ÉMILE ZOLA · · · **L'Assommoir**
The Belly of Paris
La Bête humaine
The Conquest of Plassans
The Fortune of the Rougons
Germinal
The Kill
The Ladies' Paradise
The Masterpiece
Money
Nana
Pot Luck
Thérèse Raquin